THE VALKYRIE SERIES
THE FIRST FLEET

LOOK SHARPE!

ILL WIND

DEAD RECKONING

KAREN PERKINS

Published in Great Britain by LionheART Publishing House

ISBN: 978-1-912842-03-2

LionheART Publishing House
Harrogate
UK

www.lionheartgalleries.co.uk
www.facebook.com/lionheartpublishing
lionheartpublishinghouse@gmail.com

Caribbean, 17th Century, United States, Pirates, Sea Stories, Women Pirates, Adventure, Historical fiction, Colonial history, Caribbean history, African American history, Sailing

Cover Design by Cecelia Morgan

Author's Note

Throughout the Valkyrie Series, I have used the historical and phonetic spellings of place names, and where possible taken these from Edmund Halley's map of 1699.

For Mum and Dad,
who taught me to right a capsize, sheet in,
and sail my new course.

Contents

Look Sharpe!

PART ONE
1678

Chapter 1

I stared at the coffin, the only one not shrouded in dust and cobwebs. *So that's it—I'm alone. Well, apart from Uncle Richard.* I fingered the letter in my pocket; but he was an ocean away, on the same continent as Elizabeth and our child. She had never returned; I didn't even know if she'd had a girl or boy. Hellfire, for all I knew she'd perished on the passage out.

"I heard from Uncle Richard today, Father," I said to the coffin and drew out the letter. "He sends his greetings from Jamaica, although as always he is a little late." I managed a half smile at the weak joke. It was one of Father's frustrations that both my mother and her brother were perpetually tardy, but it was a joke of affection. My mother was ever late now, of course, having passed in childbirth twenty years before. Father had missed her terribly. I still did.

I pulled the candle closer and held the letter to the meagre light.

My Dear Nephew Henry,

It bereaves me to hear of your father's illness, Charlotte thought so highly of him, as I do myself. I beg of you to be good enough to pass on my regards and prayers for swift progress in his recovery.

Life in the Indies suits me well, as I am sure it would yourself should you ever desire to escape England's green shores. Jamaica is a lively island, filled with diverse characters, although regrettably there is a vast shortage of ladies. Some of the four-legged and marine life are just as diverse as the fellows, simply amazing to behold. The color and noise of the place is too wondrous to describe and my door is always open to you, my boy.

Windhaven is successful beyond my most desirous dreams. My sugar cane stretches for leagues in every direction and needs a small army to tend it. The Great House is magnificent, even in comparison to Rowleston Hall, and I am certain you would soon feel at home here.

The only disadvantages are the malodorous airs and the greed of the merchants. They charge abominable rates to ship my sugar, rum and molasses. The situation is so dire, I am considering a venture into shipping myself. Surely funding my own vessel will save me quite a pretty penny.

I must now take my leave, a ship is departing for England's bonny coast within the hour and I must hurry to press this missive into the captain's hand.

Your Loving Uncle —
Richard Tarpington

"I'm going to go, Father," I said, relieved to tell him of my decision, even though he could no longer hear or advise me. "The death duties, added to the other debts, have crippled the estate. I've had to sell off fifty acres to pay everything. Barker can manage the rents and tenancies, keep everything ticking over until I come back. Three years, that's all, Father. Long enough to make my fortune in sugar. White gold they call it. I'll come home in time, buy the land back, and restore Rowleston Hall to its former glory, you see if I don't. Anyway." I pulled myself together, realizing I was asking for approval from a coffin. "I'll make you proud, Father," I added into the silence.

I blew out the candle, then walked toward the square of light and out into fresh air. I pushed the door of the mausoleum closed, locked it, then took out my hip flask and drank a deep draught of brandy.

Unhitching my horse, Maximillian, I swung up onto his back and turned his head away from Rowleston Hall. I turned in the saddle to take one last look at the only home I'd ever known, then pointed Max's nose toward Bristol, the docks, and the New World.

Chapter 2

I sat down at the table and raised my tankard in greeting to the three men I was joining.

I'd been in Bristol a fortnight; my ship, *Pride of the Orient*, was more than a week overdue and nobody had any news of her. I could well be waiting on a ship that rested on the sea bottom, but I had nothing better to do but stay and hope.

I threw the dice. Three. I groaned. I'd lost most of my money. I had nothing left with which to buy my own stake in sugar, and was a little short for my passage out. I had to win tonight. I could ill afford any more aces and deuces.

Like father, like son, I thought. Neither of us could ever resist the dice, cards or anything that resembled competition; or drew bets for that matter. My father's losing streak had killed him. Mine was about to kill my dreams. I threw again. Four. I kept my face impassive. I had to turn this around. I had to.

I raised my tankard again as another man sat down to the dice, threw and nicked.

I'd had enough and stood to leave. The latest addition to the table joined me outside.

"Jonesy." The man stuck his hand out as he introduced himself. I shook.

"Lord Henry Rowleston."

"Ah, that explains it."

"Explains what?" I withdrew my hand, not liking his comment.

"Why they were fleecing you in there."

"Fleecing me?"

"Aye, did you not realize them dice were weighted? You had no chance. You don't go into a tavern like that one with your fancy clothes and wig, calling yourself Lord Summat Or Other, not if you want to keep your coin and that fine cloth on your back."

"What do you mean?"

"I mean, this is sailortown, mate. The people here live tough lives. They're worked like dogs and paid little, they see a gentleman like yourself in their lair, they're gonna take whatever advantage is in their power."

"They were *cheating*?"

"Blimey, that's took you long enough, you're not exactly sharp are you? Aye, 'course they were bleedin' cheating—this ain't one of your poncey gentlemen's clubs here you know."

I stopped walking. "Why are you telling me this? You took a fair bit of my coin yourself tonight if I remember rightly."

"Aye, well. You needed a lesson. I were once a little like you and I'd have ended up in t' gutter with the rats if some kind soul hadn't taken me to one side and explained the way o' things. I'm just passing the good deed on."

"Well, I'm grateful to you, Jonesy. Although passing it on a bit earlier would have been more helpful."

"Aye, well. Men don't like to be told, not when they have a purse full of coin and a plan to win more."

I shrugged, but realized he was right. Dressed in dirty breeches and shirt, grime under every fingernail, I wouldn't have given him the time of day a week ago.

"Come on, let's have an ale, you look like you could do with a bit of fortification."

Chapter 3

"No. No, no, no, no, no," Jonesy said when I opened the door of my boarding house to him the next evening.

"What's amiss? You said to dress in breeches and shirt."

"Old breeches and shirt."

"These are old."

"Not old enough. Not tatty enough. Not dirty enough. Where's yer room?"

Silently, I led the way.

"Right, breeches first."

I looked at him in confusion.

"Breeches. Off."

"What?" I stared at him. Was he really trying to help me, or was my humiliation at the dice not enough, was he trying to compound it?

He sighed. "What do you see when you look at me?"

I shrugged, embarrassed.

"No, tell me what you see, I won't be offended."

"All right. I see a ruffian, a scoundrel, a scallywag."

He drew himself up to his full height, plucked my wig from its stand and put it on his head, then spoke with a very different accent. "So you would be surprised to know my real name is Fotheringay, and I'm as much lord as you are?"

I gaped at him.

"Hard times, Rowleston, hard times. My family lost everything to bloody Cromwell in the wars. I've had to turn my hand to many a distasteful task since and have learned how to prevent myself from becoming prey. You remind me of myself a few years ago." He removed the wig. I couldn't move for shock. "Now get them bleedin' breeches off," he added in his low-born accent. I hurried to obey.

* * *

After we had stomped the muck of the floor and our boots into my clothes and rubbed ash into my hair, Jonesy appraised me once more.

"Aye, that's better, but you can't go round introducing yourself as Henry Rowleston, with or without the Lord." He stood, his hand raised to his chin in thought.

"Sharpe," I said, thinking back to a comment he'd made the night before. "Henry Sharpe."

He laughed and clapped me on the shoulder.

"Aye, Sharpe's the name all right. Let's hope it'll soon be thy nature too."

"Different tavern, different luck," Jonesy said as we entered. I paused and surveyed the room, but nobody had stopped what they were doing to look in the normal manner occasioned by my entrance into one of these places.

"Seems like it," I said, nonplussed at my new anonymity, although I did draw a glance or two as I strode to the bar.

"Sharpe," Jonesy said with a warning look, and I hunched my shoulders a little, kept my voice low when I asked for ale, and dropped a few aitches. Jonesy nodded his approval and we dragged our feet over to one of the noisier tables where the dice were rolling.

Three hours later, pockets full, we stepped back outside and congratulated each other.

"The game's a bit different when all's fair and square," said Jonesy.

"Ain't that the truth!" I clapped him on the back. "I owe you, Jonesy, I can't thank you enough."

"I told you, passing the kindness on. I've done nothing for you that wasn't once done for me."

"Still." I held out my hand and he shook it. "I won't forget."

He nodded, then his eyes widened. I spun on my heel and drew my knife. One of the men we'd rolled with stopped in his tracks.

“What can we do for you, sir?” I was Lord Rowleston, Earl of Shirehampton again, just for a moment.

He started in surprise at my accent, glanced at my blade, shook his head and melted back into the shadows.

“Aye, you’re a sharp one all right,” Jonesy said. I laughed and we staggered back to the boarding house.

Chapter 4

As had become my habit, my first duty after breaking my fast was to take a stroll to the docks and inquire after *Pride of the Orient*.

The wharves had been built where the River Avon met the Frome and, looking out over the water, all I could see were hulls and spars. I stared for a moment, as I always did, marveling at the skill involved in bringing these ships to rest amongst so many without wrecking.

"Watch it!"

I stumbled backwards as a runaway cask careered toward my legs, just managing to avoid it.

"Begging your pardon, watch out!" a young boy cried as he chased it down on its path to the next unsuspecting pedestrian.

I shook my head at the chaos and continued my trek to the coffee house to meet with the Merchant Venturers.

"Lord Rowleston."

I turned at the shout and greeted my accoster. "Jonesy, good morning to you." We shook hands. "What are you doing here?"

"Ah, just watching the shipping and dreaming of faraway lands." He gave an embarrassed laugh, then continued, "No Henry Sharpe today?"

I grinned. "No. Some things, at least, are better done as an earl." I indicated the harbor with a jerk of my head. "My ship has come in, I'm on my way to the Venturer's Rest to speak to the owner, pay my passage, and claim the best berth for the voyage."

Jonesy nodded, but said nothing. I realized I would miss the man; he had been a good friend to me in the short time we had known each other. "Why don't you join me?"

He shrugged. "Got nothing better to do today, I suppose."

We wended our way past stacks of casks waiting to be loaded; crowds of people, also waiting to be loaded I presumed; and tangles of hemp and canvas.

"I'll wait out here," Jonesy said when we reached the coffee house. "I'm not dressed proper for this type of company."

I hesitated, then nodded. "I won't be long."

Business transacted, I blinked as I stepped outside. The sky was overcast, but still seemed hellishly bright after the gloom of the interior of the coffee house.

"All done?"

I nodded at Jonesy. "It will take them five days to unload. Then they'll swab it out, erect the cabins and load supplies. We leave on Wednesday next."

"A little over a week." He looked despondent, then confused and the corners of my lips tugged upwards. "Hang on. We?"

Now my lips stretched wide. "Yes, we, you're coming with me."

"What? But . . ."

"Those faraway lands you were dreaming of? We'll be standing on their shores in about seven weeks from now."

"But . . ."

I raised my eyebrows in question. "But what? What's keeping you here? You're alone, earning a living at the dice table. There's a whole new world out there, let's see what it will give us."

I could see him getting ready to "but" me again, then his brow smoothed, his eyes sparkled, and his shoulders straightened.

"Aye," he said. "All right, mate, you've a deal. But I'll pay you back the cost of the passage."

"No you won't, yer daft bugger," I said, slipping into Sharpe's vernacular. "If you 'adn't taken me under your wing when you did, I'd be penniless now. I only 'ave the money for the passage 'cause of your intervention. I still don't 'ave enough to buy into my uncle's sugar plantation, but no matter, our fortunes 'ave changed, we'll manage it somehow."

Jonesy laughed. "The New World. The Caribbees, here we come!" He grabbed me in a bear hug and spun me round, both of us giggling like girls now. People gave us a wide berth and strange looks as they passed us: the gentleman and the ruffian. I didn't care. I'd be traveling after all and in the company of a friend.

Chapter 5

I shrugged off my frockcoat and stared around in horror at the tiny gloomy space I would have to call home for the coming six weeks. I hung my coat on a nail then stretched out both arms. My fingertips brushed each "wall"—in reality a flimsy partition of wood—as I swayed with the floor.

"Jonesy?"

"Aye?" The answer floated, clearly audible from next door, over the six-inch gap at the top of the wall.

"What in hellfire is that canvas thing?"

"Judging by the lack of a cot, I can only assume it's a bed, Sharpe."

"A bed? But how the hell do you stay in it? How the hell do you get in it in the first place?"

"Hmm."

There was a pause and I tugged at the loop of cloth suspended from the deckhead. A grunt and a crash made me jump.

"Not like that!" Jonesy laughed.

Alarmed, I rushed next door. "Are you well?"

"A little bruised, but well enough." Jonesy extended his hand. I took it and pulled him off the deck. He stood before the bed, hands on hips, then said, "Maybe if I roll?"

He clambered in sideways, rolling over as he did so. "Got it!"

Laughter escaped my throat despite my despair at our sleeping arrangements. "How will you sleep like that?"

"I'll have you know it's very comfortable," he said, voice muffled.

"Can you turn over?"

"I'm not sure I want to risk it."

I laughed again. "A crown says you'll tumble."

"A crown you say?" He lifted his head and arms and wriggled. At least no longer face down, he still looked extremely uncomfortable twisted on his side.

"All the way if you want the crown."

He grumbled, but resumed wriggling.

"Aha," he exclaimed, then, "No!" as the material swayed and tipped him to the deck.

I held my hand out to him again, this time with palm open to claim my winnings, then spun round at a loud guffaw at my back.

"Out of the way, gentlemen, I'll show you how it's done," said the man, one of the crew by the look of his weathered face and muscled arms, still laughing at Jonesy's antics.

I raised my eyebrows at him and he stopped laughing.

"Tom Little," he introduced himself.

"How d'you do, Little?" Jonesy called from the floor and I helped him up. "I'm Jonesy, and this here's my good friend, Lord Rowleston, Sharpe to his friends." I nodded at the sailor. "By all means, show us how to get in these infernal things," he continued.

I stepped aside and Little squeezed into the tiny space.

He reached up and found a handhold in the beams above, then jumped up, swung himself across, lay back in the hammock, and sighed in satisfaction. "Nothin' to it, sirs."

"See, Jonesy? Easy!" I mocked as Little jumped back down. "My thanks, Little, you've saved our bruises and further embarrassment."

"Any time, sirs."

Jonesy held out his hand and something shiny passed between them.

"That better not have been my crown, Jonesy."

"For no bruises and embarrassment? 'Tis cheap at the price."

"That was my winnings!"

"Winnings you say?" Little butted in. "Do you gentlemen enjoy the roll of the dice, by chance?"

Jonesy and I glanced at each other.

"We have been known to occupy ourselves with the dice on occasion," I said, hesitant, or at least hoping to appear that way.

"Well, if either of you are at a loose end during the passage, there's usually a game to be found on the lower deck, near the bow. Tell 'em Little sent ya."

"Our thanks, Little," Jonesy said and shook his hand. I smiled and nodded at him, but spotted a smirk as he turned to leave. I watched him head to another "cabin" that had just emitted a loud thump and a curse, then turned back to Jonesy who was rubbing his hands in glee.

"We need to take care," I said, and told him about the expression I'd seen on Little's face. "They'll try to fleece us."

"O'course they will. We're traveling in style, they think we're rich and simple just like that night we met."

I frowned.

"But we know their game, we'll suck 'em in, take their money and spit 'em out again!"

"Care, Jonesy. There's nowhere to go and very few places to hide. Don't forget we're aboard a ship, their ship. Play them too hard and we could end up overboard."

He slapped me on the back. "Ah, Sharpe, ever the cautious one. Let go, live a little, take a few risks."

"What the hell do you call this?" I waved my arms to indicate the ship. "This is the biggest gamble of my life! I'm leaving behind everything I know, with no idea as to what's ahead, and you call me cautious?"

"Aye, you've a point there. Come on, let's go up on deck, get a last glimpse of Bristol."

I nodded, then stumbled as the ship jolted beneath my feet.

"Don't fret, it's the anchor coming free of the bottom," Little called out from somewhere to our right.

"Come on, Sharpe, hurry," Jonesy said, leading the way back up to daylight.

Chapter 6

I breathed deeply, and wondered just how foul the air would get in our sleeping quarters.

"Come on, Sharpe, mate, out of the way."

I moved from the hatch to give Jonesy some room and apologized. A team of sailors worked at the bow pushing a capstan round to haul the anchor aboard, and I glanced up in unease at the still-furled sails.

I turned to look at Bristol; the wharf a heaving mass of people, warehouses, and traveling and boarding houses crammed in higgledy-piggledy behind it. The River Avon was full of ships in various stages of preparation: being unloaded, loaded and made ready for sail; the water itself full of all manner of flotsam and jetsam. I wrinkled my nose in disgust at the smell and sight of sewage floating past.

The sailors at the bow cheered as the anchor broke free of the water and the ship moved sideways, the bow slowly swinging round.

"*Helm to windward.*"

"*Stand by to fend off.*"

"Why aren't the sails being used?" I grabbed Little's arm in panic as he passed.

He laughed, enjoying my fear. "Wind ain't steady, it swirls around like a doxy's skirts here. Even worse in t' gorge. Tide's stronger and will take us out."

"But, but, how can the captain steer without the sails?"

"Can't, not by much." He grinned, then took pity on me.

"Then why doesn't he have a boat out to guide us through?"

"Don't fear, sir, we've a pilot aboard, he does this every tide, and it's a strong tide, too fast for the boats. Sails are next to useless till we hit the Severn."

He pulled away from my grasp as I winced at his use of the word hit.

After a few more shouted commands and a number of jarring bumps against other ships, we were in the main channel and racing seaward.

"Ladies and gentlemen," the captain (at least I presumed he was captain) called, and I wondered if he ever spoke in a normal tone of voice.

"Welcome aboard *Pride of the Orient.* I hope you find her comfortable." There were a few mutterings at this. "I realize the accommodations are not what you are used to, but they are the finest any oceangoing vessel out of Bristol can boast."

"'Tis a feeble boast, man, my slaves can tell of better!"

I craned my neck, as did Jonesy and everyone else to see who had spoken, but he perchance regretted his comment and fell silent.

The captain frowned and did not respond to the insult.

"The passage will take a little under six weeks given fair winds, please feel free to walk the decks but mind my crew. Your lives are in their hands for the coming voyage and I advise you keep that in mind in your dealings with them."

A few more mutterings. My heart sank; this was not shaping up to be a pleasant voyage, I had already taken a dislike to a number of the dozen gentleman and even one or two of the ladies who stood complaining on the deck.

"We'll be out of the shelter of the gorge soon, and when the wind picks up it'll be coming from larboard." He pointed to his left. "If you feel ill, I recommend the starboard rail." He pointed to his right, then turned his back on his passengers to confer with one of the sailors.

"Not much of a welcome aboard, was it?" Jonesy remarked to the man standing next to us.

"Hmpf," he grunted and turned away.

Jonesy shrugged his shoulders. "Friendly ship," he said, and I laughed.

"Hopefully people will be a bit friendlier once they're settled in and have got over their nerves."

"Nerves? What do they have to be nervous about? It's a fine ship with, you heard the captain: 'accommodation of the highest standard'."

"Are you serious? Crossing an ocean to a new land in a ship this size and no one to help us if we find trouble? Hellfire, I'm not bloody nervous, I'm downright scared and so should you be." I stopped when I realized Jonesy was laughing at me.

"Just playing with you, Sharpe, trying to ease the tension."

I frowned and pressed my lips together. My belly was fluttering with fear at what may lie ahead; both at sea and after our arrival at Jamaica, assuming we made it. I was not in the mood for jokes and as I gazed at the lulling waves my mind drifted back in time. *Heavens, it must be ten years since, and yet seems like yesterday—a part of me I'll never forget and will always regret.*

"Henry."

I turned at the shout, searching the crowd for her. A pale arm waved above the sea of hats and bonnets. Elizabeth. I pushed through the throng. I'd found her.

She stepped into my arms and I held her close, aware of the faint swell of her belly against mine, then buried my face into her mass of curls. I'd been distraught when she had disappeared and had interrogated the other maids and servants to finally find the truth. My father, the Earl of Shirehampton, on discovering our affair and Elizabeth's condition, had arranged passage to the New World. He would not countenance the thought of the next Lord Rowleston being the father of a kitchen maid's bastard at seventeen years of age.

"I thought I'd never see you again."

"I couldn't let you go without saying farewell."

She pulled away from me, a look of horror and despair marring her delicate features. "Farewell? You're . . . you're not coming with me?"

I took hold of her hands." I can't, you know that. My father, the estate . . ."

She pulled her hands away. "What about me? What about our child? You told me you loved me, that you'd never forsake me."

I hung my head in shame. "I do love you, Elizabeth, I do. But I have a duty to my father and family name. When he's gone, then

I'll be free. I'll come and find you. Keep our child safe and I'll find you."

She stared at me, her large beautiful eyes full of pain. She did not believe me.

I fished in my pocket and pulled out a necklace. A large amethyst teardrop hung from a fine chain. I opened the clasp and held it up to her. She did not move. I fastened it around her neck. She did not take her eyes from mine.

"It was my mother's." My fingers brushed the stone now resting on her chest. "The love we share is impossible, but that does not mean it is not true. I love you, Elizabeth, but I have to let you go."

Still she did not speak.

"You're embarking on a new life, in a new land. You can be anybody you want to be there, in America."

A tear fell and caressed her cheek." I want to be with you. I want to be your wife."

"You know that can't happen. Not here. An earl—even a courtesy earl—and a maid cannot marry in England and have any kind of meaningful life. We would be ridiculed and shunned, our child would have no prospects."

Elizabeth hung her head, tears dripping freely now. I pressed a fold of banknotes into her hand, then gripped her shoulders, and planted a kiss on her crown.

"I'll never forget you, Elizabeth. Never."

She nodded, picked up her valise, turned and was soon lost to me.

My senses were overcome by the hustle and bustle of the docks, but I stayed where I stood, my feet rooted to the dirty cobbles.

The mob of humanity thinned as the pilgrims and émigrés boarded the great ship anchored in the River Avon, and which would take them a world away.

* * *

"*Standby at the braces.*"

I jumped at the captain's shout and wondered what was happening. Crew men ran to positions by the tangle of rope that stretched from mast to hull and I glanced ahead with trepidation. The high cliffs sheltering the river were diminishing to nothing and the water was a wholly different color only a cable's length ahead.

As sails unfurled, another shout rang out. "*Haul to leeward.*"

Sailors released some ropes and hauled on others as the wind hit. *Pride of the Orient* lurched over a couple of waves, then settled into a new rhythm.

I joined the rush to the starboard rail, the churning in my belly suddenly too violent to ignore. I swallowed a couple of times, but knew what was coming and emptied the contents of my stomach into the Severn. My wig was whipped off my head and I grabbed for it, knocking Jonesy's arm. He released his hold and I watched my hair drift alongside for a moment, then it was in our wake and gone. I punched Jonesy's upper arm in frustration.

"What the hell, Sharpe?"

"What do you mean? I thought the wind had taken it, not you, what were you doing?"

"Trying to save the cleanliness of your curls, mate."

"Nice job," I replied through gritted teeth, "they're well and truly washed now."

"Aye, well, I guess that's it for Lord Rowleston, ain't it, Sharpe?"

I didn't answer, but hung my head over the side again. I'd worry about the wig later.

Chapter 7

Three days later, I lay in my hammock and wondered if I should try to exit it. With Little's guidance I had managed to get in, but had not yet attempted the reverse procedure.

I sniffed and groaned. The stench down here was unbelievable; the buckets that served as pisspot, shittenpot and of course vomitpot were nearly full. Jonesy had reckoned, on one of his brief visits, that near a score of my fellow passengers were similarly affected.

I grabbed the side of the hammock and shifted my weight. I reached the deck a little earlier and harder than I had intended, but I had made it without upsetting the bucket. Good enough; I'd have plenty of time to practice my technique.

I clambered to my feet and staggered, regained my balance, then fell against the walls. A little foul-smelling liquid slopped out of the bucket and I realized that had been happening for some time.

I picked the bucket up by its rope handle and held it away from my body as I made my unsteady way to the steep stairs and quickly worked out that balance was easiest to attain with feet planted wide apart with each step.

A rather awkward, one-handed climb—complete with a little more spillage—later and I was in fresh air. I lifted my face to the breeze and breathed deeply. Heaven. A slight, fresh aroma of salt tingled my nose and taste buds.

"*Sharpe.*"

I turned at Jonesy's shout and headed toward him. "No! Other rail," he called and pointed to the other side of the ship.

"Some daft bugger emptied his bucket to windward," he said when he joined me. "Emptied t' bucket into the wind and covered his face and chest, and those of his wife, with the contents!" He laughed, but I grimaced. They would have little chance of being clean again until we made land. Water was a precious commodity aboard ship and there had already been numerous arguments about the amount rationed to drink, even by those who had been suffering from seasickness. There would be no water for washing until the next rainstorm.

"Good to see you on your feet again, mate." Jonesy slapped me on the back.

I groaned. "Have a care, Jonesy, everything's still a little . . . unsettled."

"Oh, sorry." He stepped back a pace and I grinned.

"Maybe you need something to take your mind off your belly?" Jonesy added. "That Little and his mates play a mean game of dice."

"Maybe later. For now I need fresh air, water and something solid to put in my belly."

"Oh, aye, o'course. Sorry, mate, things 'ave been a bit quiet with you laid up."

I nodded. "Where's the kitchen?"

"Galley, mate, galley. We're at sea now."

I stared around me in surprise. I had been so preoccupied with my stomach I had taken no notice of my surroundings. I turned in a slow circle, amazed.

"There's, there's nothing there," I told Jonesy.

"Nope, just sea and sky," Jonesy replied, indicating the horizon. "Just sea and sky to look at for six weeks."

I smiled. I quite liked the sound of that.

Chapter 8

"That's not our dice!"

"It damn well is," Jonesy shouted back.

"*No*," Abbots insisted. "Look, it's bigger than the other."

"Are you calling me a blackguard?" Jonesy jumped to his feet as he shouted, and cracked his skull against the deckhead.

I drew my knife and stabbed it into the wooden barrel top between Little's fingers.

"Make one more move toward his or my own coin and you'll lose a finger," I warned.

Little withdrew his hand and Jonesy sat down.

"You were trying to steal from me?"

Little shrugged. "You've cleared me out, we'll be sighting Jamaica soon. I've a woman there who likes silver."

The group of men huddled around the barrel burst into guffaws. I stared at them, then glanced at Jonesy. This hadn't been one man spotting an opportunity to help himself, but two: Abbots had caused the distraction. I wouldn't have been surprised if all of them had been in on it. We gathered our coin.

"Well, I'd like to say it's been a pleasure, gentlemen, but this game is turning a little sour. It's time for us to go up on deck for a little . . . fresh air." Jonesy said, and we stood, stooping to avoid the wood above our heads. We had spent most of the past six weeks down in this dank hole; sweating and stinking, huddled around a barrel doubling as gaming table. Things had been genial up to now; I guessed we were nearing the end of our voyage and the crew wanted back the coin we had won from them as well as that we had carried aboard.

"Not so fast," said Whitey, the largest and burliest man of the group. "Little here has made his apologies."

I cocked an eyebrow at this.

"I heard no apology," I said, "only excuses."

"Well, that's as may be," Whitey continued, "but apologetic he be, ain't that right, Little?"

Little nodded a vigorous assent.

"We've all been mates for the past month or so, there's no reason to fall out now."

"No reason?" Jonesy asked, incredulous. "No reason? We've given you ample opportunity to win our coin, you lack the skills to do so and attempted to steal it from us instead!"

"Law of the sea, mate," Little muttered, and the rest of the sailors laughed.

"Aye, on a pirate ship, perhaps," I said, wincing at the "aye"; a month and a half in the company of Jonesy and the sailors had proved decidedly unhealthy for my linguistic capability.

The sailors laughed, the tension broken.

"*Land oh. All hands on deck.*"

The shout carried down through the decks to our ears and the men stood, shoveled what coin they had left into their pockets and, with a sarcastic tug of the forelock by Little and a wink from Abbots, they rushed topside.

I looked at Jonesy, more than a little bewildered. I had been prepared for a fight and suddenly had no adversaries.

Jonesy shrugged. "We're here," he said. "Let's go have a gander."

Chapter 9

I wiped my face and blinked more sweat from my eyes, then waved my hand to disperse the cloud of flies for a moment. The sun was fierce and far hotter than anything I'd experienced before.

I shielded my eyes with the flat of my hand and peered at Port Royal, Jamaica.

It was Bristol in the making. Huge warehouses, filled with God only knew what treasures; brick-built mansions, three or four, some *five* stories high above the sand; and I even spotted the spire of what could only be a cathedral rising above it all. The wharf was piled high with goods: huge casks, filled with sugar I presumed; piles of animal skins tied with twine and stinking in the sun, even at this distance; enormous tree trunks which I guessed was the logwood that provided the deep red, purplish color so enamored by the ladies of England. And everywhere was hustle and bustle. Small boats filled so high with goods that their gunwales only barely cleared the water were being rowed out to the ships. Empty versions of the same proved the profitability of their trade. So this was "the richest and wickedest city in the world".

Over to the left, a large, empty space was filled with lengths of rope and I realized the Jamaicans had established their own ropewalk. Huge wheels spun and twisted the tremendous lines of hemp, and I was amazed that so much had been achieved and established in little more than twenty years.

Our trunks were lowered into one of the small rowing boats and I glanced at Jonesy. "Are you coming, mate?" I asked with a concerned smile. He stood stock still, staring at the town built on white sand and turquoise water. He looked terrified; a state of being I had not witnessed in him before.

"What's wrong?"

He shook himself out of his reverie and turned to me. "It's just so . . . different."

I laughed. "What did you expect? This is the New World, I hope to God it's different to the old one!"

Jonesy managed a smile. "I know, I just didn't expect it to be *this* different." He swatted a hand at the reformed swarm of flies hovering about our heads and hitched his shirt away from his skin. I grimaced and did the same with mine. There had been no opportunity to wash our clothing in fresh water for almost a month and everything was stiff with salt. It was bad enough when first donning a seawater-washed shirt, but half an hour in the oven of the holds playing dice and it was sodden, itchy and extremely uncomfortable. Ten minutes in the baking heat above deck was enough to sweat, dry and sweat it through again; our attire was hardly recognizable as sartorial.

"Come on, stop worrying. This may be Jamaica, but it's still English, man, they're waiting for us in the boat."

Little, on his best behavior when, as now, he was in view of his captain and first mate, tugged his forelock after casting our little boat off from the mothership, and I gave him a friendly wave that in actuality was the complete opposite.

I didn't personally know the sailors at the oars, and relaxed as we moved away from *Pride of the Orient*, Little and his shifty mates.

I clambered up onto the wharf, closely followed by Jonesy, and looked about me.

"There." I pointed to an inn with a depiction of horses displayed on its frontage. "We need to hire horses and get directions to Windhaven."

Jonesy nodded and we dragged our trunks to the waiting establishment. After a couple of very welcome jugs of ale in the relatively cool interior, and with my pockets considerably lightened, a cart containing our trunks stood at the ready with the ostler's young son at the reins. Two horses, saddled and bridled, shifted their hooves behind it. We crossed to them, unhitched them and mounted.

"Lead the way, lad," I called, and our little caravan moved off into the island's interior and the unknown.

I prayed for a friendly welcome; it had been many years since I'd set eyes on my mother's brother. I'd been a child when he'd last made one of his rare visits home. I'd been fascinated by his stories; he had been part of Cromwell's expedition, the first official sailing to the New World, and Mother had often warned Uncle Richard as his tales of cannibals, boucaniers and fierce savages grew too lurid for my young ears.

Admittedly, deep down I was grateful to her. I remember I had always suffered nightmares after a day spent in the company of my uncle, but had always hankered after this faraway place of which he had been so enamored.

I glanced into the lush green forest on either side of the track. Strange noises emanated all around, and I jumped at a particularly loud cawing and a flash of bright color, then sighed in relief; not a savage, but a tropical bird.

I caught Jonesy's eye and he chuckled. I frowned. *How has he recovered his equanimity so quickly? Our surrounds are now far stranger than at the docks.*

"Windhaven," our guide called and guided the cart between two great stone pillars. I glanced at the name etched onto the stone and felt a shiver of excitement; how often I'd dreamed of this moment.

I looked ahead, eager for a glance at the house, but could see naught but tall plants swaying in the gentle breeze: sugarcane. I itched to stop and taste some, but, with a glare at the cart pulling ahead, I decided to wait.

"You there! Out of my way. Goddamn you!"

Startled, I broke into a trot to catch up to the cart and was shocked to see the young lad still berating men on the track; men who were many years his senior.

"What's the problem?" I asked.

"Nothin' to fret about, sir," the young lad replied. "Just a bunch of lazy negras in the road."

"Since when do you speak to or about your elders with such

disrespect?" I demanded, and the boy jumped in surprise.

"Elders? They're slaves. Animals. Don't waste your respect on them, they're nothing."

I stared at him, then turned in my saddle to look back at the men we had now passed.

Thin and wiry, with skin glistening in the sunlight, the man in front met my eyes and I shuddered at the dull despair I saw there.

"Welcome to the New World," Jonesy muttered beside me, and I glanced at him, my excitement at finally reaching Windhaven having dissipated.

We passed through a bend in the track and at last I had my first glimpse of the house. I was disappointed; I had expected something grander. Uncle Richard had boasted it was fit to rival Rowleston Hall. *He must have had a different property in mind*, I mused, staring at the squat, single-story wooden building. It had an air of neglect about it: greenery growing wild, paint peeling, even a shutter hanging off at a window.

A man came out of the front door and stood on the veranda, hands on hips, watching us approach.

"Richard Tarpington," I called. "Where is he?"

"Who's asking?"

"Lord Henry Rowleston-Sharpe," I said, combining my two personas. "His nephew." I was annoyed, *Does no one on this island possess any manners?*

The man visibly started, then approached, his frown smoothing out into a welcome smile.

"Harry Stanton," he said, "at your service, My Lord. I'm afraid you've had a wasted journey. Mr. Tarpington is not here and isn't expected for some time."

"Why? Where is he?"

"Wherever the wind has blown him." I frowned at the man and he added, "Aboard the *Edelweiss*. He puts into Port Royal regularly. If the ship's there he'll be somewhere about."

Chapter 10

"You knew, didn't you? You and your father."

The boy shrugged. "Not for us to say."

"You didn't want to talk yourself out of the hire, more like," Jonesy added.

"We just hire the horses to them that asks, and drive the carts to where we's told."

"Leave it, Jonesy," I interrupted. "I would still have come out here to see for myself."

He glowered at me and I shrugged. I couldn't see the point of getting irate over something that couldn't be changed.

Jonesy huffed and said not another word until we were back with the ostler, who raised an eyebrow yet failed to look surprised.

I glanced at Jonesy to stay his grumbling, and dismounted.

"No luck, I'm afraid. Do you know if Richard Tarpington's ship, the *Edelweiss*, is here?"

"The *Edelweiss*, is it?" The man perked up and glanced at his son, then jerked his head seaward. "Aye, she's the one at anchor over yonder, that one off to the left with the three masts."

Jonesy humpfed and the man glanced at him warily.

"For all I knew, your man was at Windhaven. His ship's in, isn't it?"

"Of course, don't mind my friend here. Can you kindly direct us to the best boarding house on the seafront?"

"That would be Mrs. Sue's, hundred yards down that way."

"Where you goin', boy?" Jonesy demanded. "Them trunks won't take themselves."

The ostler glanced at Jonesy, then myself, and nodded at his son, who sat himself back down with a grimace of protest.

"My thanks." I shook his hand, remounted my horse and followed the boy to Mrs. Sue's.

* * *

"Tarpington? Never heard of him," Mrs. Sue responded when I inquired of my uncle. I nodded and looked around the room Jonesy and I had taken. Two cots, a washstand, and our trunks took up most of the space. Basic to say the least, although it felt like luxury after six weeks on *Pride of the Orient,* even though it was as hot as an oven. I threw the window wide and drew in a lungful of fresh air; if dockside air could ever be called fresh.

"You'd best take care with the window, especially at night," Mrs. Sue remarked. I turned an inquiring eyebrow to her. "Flies," she said. "Little fighting ones—makes sleeping a bugger. You'll be right when you've got used to the heat. Anyway, I'll leave you to it, got bread in t' oven."

She bustled out of the room and Jonesy and I looked at each other.

"You know the best thing for this heat?"

"Ale," I replied, and we laughed.

"Shall we inspect the local taverns?"

"Aye, let's do that."

We chuckled again, I shut the window and we made our way outside.

"*Sharpe. Jonesy.*"

I peered through the clouds of tobacco smoke from myriad clay pipes to see who had called our names.

"Little," Jonesy said. "Why's he being so friendly?"

"Let's find out," I replied, and led the way through the crowd of carousing sailors. Even a man like Little could pass for a friend in a room full of strangers.

He stood in a crowd watching half a dozen men at the dice "table"—another upturned barrel. Everyone held their breath as the next man rolled, then roared their approval at the double six and his shout of, "*Nick.*"

"Fancy joining them, Sharpe?" Little asked.

"Not if you or your mates are in any way involved," I retorted.

The men around me, including Little, laughed, and a few amused glances were sent my way from the men seated at the game.

"Well, you've some sense in your head, at least, boy," said the older man, his voice sounding as grizzled as his face looked. He threw, and the audience groaned.

Little shrugged. "'Twasn't me who done the cheating."

I'd had enough. I was not going to let my name be maligned any further.

I pulled my dagger and held the tip to his throat. Silence fell on the men and game around us, and people backed away to give us space.

"Lord Rowleston-Sharpe," I said slowly, dragging my name out for effect, "does not cheat. Nor do his friends. I thank you to keep that in mind and would be grateful if you would educate your mouth to that effect. You have maligned my own character as well as that of my friend. You tried to steal from us. One further misplaced step and my blade will not stop at your throat. Do you understand me?"

He started to nod, thought better of it, and said, "Aye. Beg your pardon, Lord Rowleston."

I grunted acceptance of his apology and withdrew my knife. Little backed away, and the game restarted.

"Lord Rowleston-Sharpe?" the grizzled player asked.

"Yes," I said warily. No one could know the name, not an amalgamation of my true moniker and my pseudonym.

"Henry?"

Comprehension dawned. "Uncle Richard?"

"Well I never. Look at you all grown up. Landlord, more ale, make it your best and keep it coming! My prodigal nephew has arrived!"

The crowd cheered, whether for us or the ale I wasn't sure.

"Less of the Uncle Richard, boy. Tarr or Captain is the only way I want these men to think of me, understand?" he instructed quietly under the noise.

I nodded dumbly, shocked by the menace in his voice as he whispered this aside. I glanced up at him and, although the eyes were a color and shape I remembered from boyhood, their expression was cold and hard, and could not have been more different from my childhood recollections. What had happened to Uncle Richard to turn him into Captain Tarr?

Chapter 11

I blinked my eyes open with a groan, then a yell as I swayed violently on my attempt to sit up. The Brazilian bed, or hammock as the sailors aboard *Pride of the Orient* had called it, tipped me unceremoniously on the floor; no, *deck*, I realized.

"*Hellfire and damnation.*"

"Good morning to you, Henry."

"Wha—?"

"Welcome aboard the *Edelweiss*."

"The what?" Images from the night before flickered through my mind. "Uncle Richard?"

Richard Tarpington strode into view. Face weatherworn from years under the tropical sun, untidy whiskers, brown eyes the color of good, fertile English soil and the same brown of my mother's eyes, the only thing I remembered of her. His dress was tatty: breeches, shirt and hat. He was barefoot.

Jonesy would be impressed, I thought, then said aloud, "My mate, Jonesy, where is he?"

A sound akin to the grunt of a hungry pig sounded behind me. I turned in time to see a hand flopping back into another Brazilian bed.

I realized I was still sprawled in a heap on the floor—deck—and made to get up, only to bang my head on the wood, which had lurched beneath me. At least, I think it had lurched; or was I still addled?

Uncle Richard laughed and offered me a hand. "It's a bit choppy today, but you'll soon get your sea legs."

Sea legs? Choppy? Understanding dawned. "Are we sailing?"

My uncle guffawed so loudly, Jonesy's head popped up out of the folds of canvas to see what was going on.

"Do you not remember putting out to sea, lad?"

I shook my head, then quickly stopped the movement and put a hand to my pounding temple. "No," I said, as substitute for the gesture.

My uncle laughed again.

"Do you by chance have water, Uncle Richard?"

"Aye, and plenty of it." He passed me a beaker and I drank greedily, immediately feeling slightly better. "So, Lord Henry Rowleston-Sharpe. That's quite a mouthful."

I made as if to nod, remembered my affliction in time and spoke instead. "Aye." I winced, I was really going to have to take more care over my speech or I'd end up talking like Jonesy and the sailors.

"I take it from the 'Lord' that your father has passed?"

"Yes, three months ago now. I did write . . ."

Uncle Richard shook his head. "Never reached me. It's a bit difficult to collect letters when at sea most of the time. My commiserations to you, lad, he was a good man." This time I did nod; blast the pain in my skull. "So, where did the Sharpe come from?"

I told him the story about Jonesy and the games of dice in Bristol.

He nodded and remarked, "Sounds like you've got a good mate there, one with an intelligent head on his shoulders." Another porcine grunt emitted from the occupied Brazilian bed.

"Where are we headed, Uncle Richard?" The repercussions of the fact we were sailing had just hit me.

"Wherever the wind takes us, lad." He laughed at the horrified expression I'd been unable to keep from my face. "Sayba, lad, the island of Sayba, with the blessing of a wind fair and fresh. And I told you last night, boy, I want none of that Uncle Richard malarkey. It'll win you no favors with the crew to keep reminding them you're family. You'll call me Tarr or Captain when aboard the *Edelweiss*."

"Why Tarr?"

"Tarpington's a bit of a mouthful, like Rowleston. And it reminds the crew I'm a cut above them. Tarr makes me one of the men, they have more respect for me as Tarr than Tarpington." He chuckled at my amazement. "The majority may be Englishmen, but this ain't England, lad, her fine and fertile lands are far away. In the Caribbees it's every man for himself. It's deeds that earn respect out here, not names. I'd advise you to drop the Rowleston, too, stick to Sharpe, Henry."

"Aye," Jonesy grunted from his canvas pit.

The implication of this struck me. "So we're staying aboard, then?"

Uncle Richard—Tarr—chuckled again and shook his head. "You've no head for rum have you, lad? You and your mate there," he nodded toward Jonesy, "signed me articles last night. Both of ye's part of a privateer crew now. Mrs. Sue were none too happy though, to lose her lodgers so soon."

"Privateer? Mrs. Sue?"

"Aye." He pointed to the side of the room; no, cabin. I kept forgetting we were at sea and the rolling of the floor—deck—was real and not down to my addled state. I squinted and made out the shape of our trunks. I crossed to the only unoccupied chair in the cabin and sat down, my mind a blank, unable to process the events of the morning so far.

"What's a privateer?" I asked eventually. "Is that like a pirate?"

"No, it blasted well isn't!" Tarr roared. "Pirates are scum of the seas, robbing and killing with no impunity. Privateers are licensed and perform a vital service to our merry monarch, King Charles."

Jonesy mumbled something and Tarr narrowed his eyes. Thank the Lord he hadn't heard what was mumbled: By robbing and killing *with* impunity.

"*Edelweiss* is commissioned by Henry Morgan himself, the acting governor of Jamaica, and the best privateer Jamaica has ever seen. England may be at peace with the Netherlands, France and Spain, but that won't always be the case. Morgan's put us in league with a couple of Dutchman in Sayba, but France and Spain's ships are fair game, as long as we either sink or commandeer the ships and leave no survivors to give account."

"Dead men tell no tales," I said dully, having heard the phrase in a Bristol tavern.

"Aye, that's it, no bugger can tell a tale from under the sea, can they, lad? The plunder's shared out between the crew and any seaworthy ships taken to Sayba."

"What happens to them there?"

“Refitted, crewed and sailed to Africa. We need strong, healthy men to harvest the sugar.”

I thought back to my brief visit to Windhaven and the man the ostler’s boy had insulted in such an offhand manner.

“Slaves? You trade in slaves?”

“Not us, boy, we trade in ships. It’s not for us to say how they’re used. Those Dutchmen are nasty characters, though. Jan, the elder, is bad enough, but watch out for his son, lad. There’s something not right about Eric van Ecken. I’ve never seen the eyes of a living man look so dead.”

A crash made me jump, and Tarr spun round—Jonesy had fallen out of his bed.

“Get him sorted, lad, then I’ll reintroduce you to the crew. And no more ‘Uncle Richard’, understand?”

I nodded and got up to see to Jonesy. *What the hell had we gotten ourselves into?*

Chapter 12

"*Cheval. Here.*"

One of the men dropped the line he was coiling and scampered over to Uncle Richard—I still found it difficult to think of him as Captain Tarr—giving me and Jonesy the once-over; one of the most calculating looks I'd ever seen.

I glanced over at Jonesy, who raised an eyebrow in reply. I didn't like where this was headed.

"Cheval, I have a couple of new deckhands for you to train up. Meet my nephew, Henry Sharpe, and his good mate, Jonesy."

Cheval smiled at us, but I spotted a fleeting glimpse of something else in his eyes before his mouth stretched. *Wariness? Distrust?*

"Welcome aboard," he said, his voice accented with France.

"Cheval will show you the ropes, you'll master the deck before you head into the tops or onto the quarterdeck."

The Frenchman visibly recoiled at the mention of the quarterdeck but I ignored him and smiled at my uncle.

"Don't let me down, boys. It's serious work, Cheval here will show you how to stay safe." He paused, clearly waiting for Cheval's affirmation—which did not come. "Won't you, Cheval?"

"Oui, Capitaine."

"Sharpe here is precious to me." He grasped my shoulder. "If anything happens to him, it'll be your neck I string up."

I glanced between the two men, realizing the first impression Jonesy and I had formed of the Frenchman was shared by my uncle. I narrowed my eyes in confusion. *Why would he put us under the care of a man he does not trust? Is this a test? And if so, whom is he testing, Cheval—or me?*

"You'll need to shed those coats and boots—footing's bad enough in bare feet, never mind leather. Gather by the foremast in two minutes, then I'll show you 'ow to swab the decks." Cheval grinned, turned his back, and sauntered forward.

I raised my eyebrows in question at my uncle. I was a lord for Christ's sake! This Frenchman was having me do the work of a scullery maid!

Uncle Richard shrugged. "No rank aboard ship, lad, unless captain. Everyone starts at the bottom—you'll find your places naturally. I wouldn't keep Cheval waiting, he has a cruel streak."

Jonesy pulled my arm and I let him lead me to the hatch to stow our outer clothing. I glanced back once at Uncle— no. *Captain* Tarr. It was already easier to think that way.

Jonesy nudged me. "Listen," he whispered and glanced toward a gaggle of men at the rail. I stopped pushing the bible-sized block of sandstone over the deck and sat back on my heels, my back popping as I stretched.

I looked over and realized Cheval was holding court over half a dozen men. Even had I been unable to understand French, it would have been clear by the amused smirks and frequent glances thrown our way that Jonesy and I were the subject of their amused conversation.

I caught the odd word as the Frenchman's voice rose. Babysitting, neveu—nephew, inutile—useless.

I made to stand and Jonesy grabbed my arm and shook his head. "Your uncle has done us a service by introducing you as Henry Sharpe rather than Lord Rowleston. We have a card up our sleeve, no sense in telling him we speak French—knowledge gleaned may come in useful later."

I nodded, my teeth gritted, and bent back to my task while keeping both ears primed.

"*Sail oh.*"

I jumped at the shout from overhead.

"Where away?" came Tarr's answering bellow.

"A league off to starboard."

I watched my uncle jump into the ladder of rope leading up the mast—the ratlins—glass to his eye. After a moment he leaped back down, shouting.

"*All hands, clear the decks. Prize to leeward.*"

"You 'eard 'im, clear that away and get yourselves some weapons."

I gaped at Cheval, who laughed. "Welcome to battle. Don't worry, the first one's the worst—assuming you survive it!"

Jonesy took hold of my arm once again and we looked at each other. Neither of us had any words.

"*Go.* Dump that water overboard and put the bibles away. Arms and blades are being brought up. Step to or you'll be left with the duds."

He walked away, still cackling, and Jonesy and I swung into action. Whatever happened now would depend on the gods—and my uncle.

Chapter 13

Standing at the starboard rail, the ship was clear to see. Two masts and a hull low in the water.

"A nice bonus there, lads."

"Little!" I greeted him in surprise. "What are you doing here?"

He shrugged. "Dunno. Seemed a good idea last night when I signed the articles." He looked off to the other ship. "Not so sure now, though."

Neither I nor Jonesy had a reply and we watched the ship draw closer in silence.

"Follow my lead, boy, I'll see you right."

I started at my uncle's hand on my shoulder and could barely hear his words over the cacophony of the crew shouting, "*Kill! Death! Blood!*" in accompaniment to a percussion of weapons striking the rail.

I nodded, my mouth dry.

"Don't mind this," he indicated the bloodlust around us, "it's theatre. If *you're* feeling awed, imagine what that crew are feeling, seeing us bear down on them like this, knowing there's no escape."

"No escape?" Jonesy asked.

"None." Tarr indicated the flag now flying at the top of the mainmast. "Blood red. It tells everyone at sea there'll be no quarter given if they resist.

"And do they? Resist?"

"Not for long, boy. Look at those men—they have cannon aboard. They aren't firing. Just as well, she'd make a good prize to accompany us to Sayba, and she's no good to us underwater. But we board as if they'll fight to the death." Tarr grinned and I recoiled at this caricature of the uncle I'd known and admired as a boy. "Here." He passed us both a long, wide silk ribbon. "Tie each end to a pistol and drape it round your neck. It's easy to bring your guns to bear and your ball won't fall out, even if it's not properly wadded. Probably." He stooped to pick up something else. "You'll need one of these, too." He handed me a grappling hook knotted onto a line. "Throw hard and throw high. Get that secure in their rigging, then swing—just like when you were a boy, eh Henry?"

Still unable to speak in my fear, I could only take the small iron boat anchor and rope. The rope swing I'd used as a boy had been about merriment. This was about battle. Death. Nothing like my boyhood games.

Tarr—I was thinking of him that way most of the time now—clapped me on the shoulder, almost hard enough to threaten an undignified tumble over the rail as our bow cannon exploded with a warning shot. Only Jonesy's steadying hand saved me.

"Keep your wits about you, boy." He raised his voice to include Jonesy and Little. "Your eyes peeled, your weapons handy and your fear in check. You're privateers now, lads—buccaneers. The seas are rich for a man brave enough to help himself."

I nodded, my mouth still arid and lacking coherent speech.

"Steady, men, on my mark.

"*Tops—covering fire if you please.*"

I jumped as muskets fired above, then again as Tarr roared. "*Go.* Throw them high, throw them sweet, we'll be rich men come dusk!"

Screams caterwauled in accompaniment to a multitude of three-pronged iron spikes clanging against each other, then spars.

I'd thrown my own with the others, barely realizing it, and joined my new crewmates in jumping and swinging. I wondered if their screams were for effect or contained as much terror as mine did.

I pulled my blade as soon as I landed, despite falling to my knees, and just managed to parry a blade swinging for my neck. I headbutted the man in the groin, then scrambled to my feet, glancing around to see if anyone had witnessed my ungentlemanly conduct. Cheval grinned at me. *Why did it have to be him?*

My heart jumped when I spotted a man with his eye on Tarr and bringing his pistol to bear.

"*Capitaine.*" Cheval shouted the warning and we both took aim—Cheval belatedly due to his call. My ball felled the man before Cheval even got his shot off.

He swung round and stared at me in amazement. "That was a hard shot! But I'd have got 'im myself, you know."

I smiled at his attempt to negate his praise, and looked around for another target. There were none. The crew were overwhelmed and under-armed. We had the ship.

"My thanks, Henry." My uncle shook my hand. "I didn't realize you're such a crack shot, you'll be in the rigging next time with a barrel full of muskets."

" 'Twas an easier shot than it looked, Un— Captain," I hastily corrected myself. I glanced over at Cheval, who had flushed bright red in rage. I smiled at him, amused that he hated the thought of another earning praise from his captain. I flicked my eyes lower, to his hand which still held his gun, now pointed at me.

"Do you intend to use that?"

"*Cheval,*" Tarr reprimanded.

The Frenchman's jaw worked furiously—he looked like he was chewing the words he did not quite dare utter. Then he lowered the gun. I laughed as the ball fell from it, unable to help myself in the relief of the fight being over. My mirth proved infectious as the men nearby realized what had happened and joined in. I could almost see Cheval's fury turn to hate and my laughter died in my throat. I had made an enemy this day, and something told me he was not a man to let go of a grudge lightly.

"*Sharpe.*"

I turned at Jonesy's shout, then burst into laughter once more.

"To replace the one you lost overboard at Bristol," he said as he presented me with a perfectly curled periwig.

PART TWO
June 1683

Chapter 14

"Captain?" Blake, Tarr's quartermaster and second in command, prompted, and Tarr tore his eyes away from his intense inspection of one of the ships in Eckerstad's harbor.

"*Down helm. Let go anchor,*" he boomed. A man at the bow struck a pin and three and a half tuns of iron smacked the surface then plunged to the depths.

"*Main topsail aback.*

"*Loose all sail.*"

Amidst the frantic activity of the crew stowing sail and line, Tarr beckoned both myself and Blake to come closer.

"That twinmaster," Tarr almost whispered to Blake. "Isn't she the one we took two months ago off Saint Lucia?"

Blake gave the vessel a close examination of his own. "Aye, Captain, you're right, she is, but she don't look to have been refitted as a slaver."

"No, she's been fitted for speed, look at the rake of those masts."

Blake nodded. They were leaning back at an angle rather than standing straight upright like the other vessels in the harbor, making the ship faster, but harder to work.

"There's not many sacrifice ease for speed," Tarr added. "Them that do are usually privateers, pirates or men-of-war."

"So which is that one then?" I asked.

"Good question. I'm guessing we'll find out soon enough. Keep your eyes and ears peeled today, lad. I don't like the look of this at all."

Tarr, Blake and I dismounted in front of the most ostentatious buildings I had seen since my arrival in the West Indies. It was huge. Built of brick—*where do they get that out here?* I wondered—it had two stories and towers topped with Dutch whatnots at either end of the house. I had thought Rowleston Hall impressive, but this was arrogance beyond belief.

"*Henry.*"

My uncle's voice knocked me out of my reverie and I blinked at him.

"Give Wilbert the horse."

I realized an African man dressed in indigo and gold livery was standing by me, patiently waiting for me to put the reins in his outstretched hand.

"My apologies," I said, and smiled as I passed my horse over to him. He didn't look up, but kept his eyes turned down then led the three horses away, all without saying a word.

"Come on, lads, time to enter the lions' den. Keep your eyes open and your mouths shut. The elder van Ecken is sound enough, but his son scares the bejesus out of me."

I looked at him in surprise, then at Blake, who nodded silently. I faced the house again, nervous now about meeting the Dutchmen.

The door opened and another African man stepped aside to allow us entry. My eyes widened at the opulence of the entrance hall. Open to the roof—*all that space, wasted*—a staircase fit for any of King Charles's palaces rose before us, then widened to serve both corridors of the upper floor.

"You're expected in the drawing room," the liveried man said.

"Right you are, Hendrik, or is it Hans? I can never tell you two apart. Open the door then!"

The man didn't react, but took our frockcoats and opened one of the two doors leading off the entrance hall.

I flicked a smile at him as I passed, but again, no reaction. *The rules of etiquette are different in the New World*, I mused, remembering the ostler's boy on my arrival. *I don't like it, good manners cost nothing*.

Inside, four men sat on sofas, glasses already nearly empty.

"About time, Tarr," a middle-aged, rather rotund man remarked, and all four stood.

"Sir Henry. This is a surprise," Tarr exclaimed.

"Aye, well, I've been too long in England and neglected my business interests. Who's this?" He flicked his cane in my direction.

"My apologies. May I present my nephew, Lord Rowleston the Earl of Shirehampton, Sir Henry Sharpe. Henry, this is the revered Sir Henry Morgan, Deputy Governor of Jamaica."

Even I'd heard of Henry Morgan: Admiral, Buccaneer, Scourge of the Spanish. He'd been sent to England in disgrace after his attack on Panama; only to be feted by all of London society and King Charles himself, knighted and made deputy governor of Jamaica. He had then turned against his fellow buccaneers, and was responsible for the hanging of scores of former colleagues. A ruthless bastard, currently engaged in a bitter war with the new governor, Thomas Lynch, Morgan was not a man on whom to turn your back.

I bowed. "I'm very pleased to meet you, Sir Henry. Your reputation precedes you, this is truly an honor."

"Hmm. Another Sir Henry, hey? Can the Caribbees bear two of us, do you think?" He turned to include all the men in the room in the joke, then faced me again. "You have a big name to live up to, boy, let's hope you prove yourself. Blake." He nodded a greeting to Tarr's quartermaster, preventing me from making any reply.

"Sharpe," Tarr said, careful not to use my Christian name again in front of Morgan. "May I present Mijnheer Jan van Ecken and his son, Erik."

"Pleased to meet you." I shook their hands. With no title, they did not merit a bow and I was slightly flustered that neither offered one to me.

"And this, if I'm not very much mistaken, is Edward Hornigold."

I nodded a greeting to the man who stood behind Morgan, and he narrowed his eyes at me.

"Aye, the two of ye sailed together, did ye not?" Morgan asked. "All three of ye were with me at Panama. Ah, those were the days." He knocked the rest of his drink back; rum by the color of it. "Right, enough chitchat. Now that you're finally here, let's eat."

He led the way through another door and I noticed the set jaws of both van Eckens. They had barely uttered a word, and clearly did not enjoy being treated as guests—and lesser guests at that—in their own home.

Chapter 15

I was surprised to see Henry Morgan take the seat at the head of the table and Ecken Senior seemed resigned to the foot, but his son Erik looked, to my eye, to be amused at this usurping of his father's position at his own dining table.

I took my seat between my uncle and Blake.

"What's he doing here?" Blake whispered across me to Tarr.

"Hornigold? Nothing good, that's for sure," he replied. And to me he added, "We sailed with him at Panama in '71. It was a nightmare: a jungle road to Hell that Morgan led us down. Hundreds of men died by starvation and Spanish lead, and the rest of us only survived by eating the leather of our belts and boots. And then there were barely any spoils to be had."

I gaped at him as he shuddered; the story he had told in his letters had included no mention that he'd partaken in the destruction of that city.

"Aye, lad, it weren't pretty," Tarr continued in a murmur. "When we finally reached Panama City, them that still lived, anyroad . . ." He paused. "I'm ashamed to say we were all gripped by a murderous madness. Too many people died too many torturous deaths. Aye, some of them at my own hands," he added in response to my unspoken question.

I looked down at the table, unable to meet my uncle's eyes. I didn't know how to react; he wasn't the man I'd always thought him to be. *Had* all *his letters been lies?*

"Me and Blakey here, regret the things we did that day even if they were Spaniards, and it were mainly for nothing. We found no gold to speak of. But Hornigold? Hornigold's an evil bastard. He enjoyed the slaughter, danced in the blood of them townsfolk, and worse. I got him off my crew, first opportunity that presented itself. But Morgan's always had a soft spot for him."

"Aye, that's right, Tarr, and you'd do best to remember it."

All three of us—Tarr, Blake and myself—looked up, startled,

into the grinning face of Ed Hornigold. He'd heard every word. He raised his glass in a toast, and I shook my head at the folly of using such a delicate vessel to drink from.

"To Sir Henry Morgan, Admiral of the Fleet, Deputy Governor of Jamaica, and Knight of the Realm!"

"Henry Morgan," the rest of us muttered and drank. I noticed the van Eckens staring at Hornigold in open dislike. I don't think he even realized he had insulted the Dutchmen by proposing the first toast. Or maybe he just didn't care.

The serving girl flinched at Morgan's pat on her behind as she took his plate, then grimaced at whatever Hornigold did to her backside. She moved to the younger van Ecken, Erik, who put a protective arm around the girl's hips and glared at his two guests.

"Gentlemen, shall we to the drawing room retire?" Jan van Ecken stood and asked. It was the first thing he'd said apart from dinner table chitchat, and I began to realize just how much tension there was in this room. Not only between Tarr, Blake and Hornigold, but between the van Eckens and Morgan as well. They did not enjoy having any one of us at their table.

"Aye, well meant, if not well said, van Ecken." Morgan lumbered to his feet and van Ecken flushed at the criticism of his English. "It's time we got down to business." He led the way out of the dining room, and I watched the van Eckens' reactions: tight smiles and gritted teeth. I glanced at Tarr and he nodded as we got up and followed them from the room.

Settled in comfortable seats, delicate glasses of rum in hand, we waited whilst Morgan guffawed something at the girl, his head again out of sight behind her. Jan van Ecken gripped his son's arm so tightly that Erik shook him off.

"Klara, put the jug on the table and leave us. We can help ourselves."

She bobbed a little curtsy and did not bother to hide the relief in her eyes. She almost ran in her escape from the room.

"Sir Henry, maybe you could us enlighten to your plans?" Jan suggested, his speech heavily accented and forestalling any further comment from Erik. "Why is Captain Hornigold here?"

Morgan glared at him; clearly he liked to do things his own way and at his own pace. I felt a sneaking admiration for the Dutchman—the only one who had dared question the legendary buccaneer.

"Hmpf, well," Morgan began. "As I gather ye've not yet heard, that obdurate bugger, Lynch, has finally got his wish and succeeded in removing me from the Assembly." Shocked silence fell on the room. *Is he no longer deputy governor then?* No one dared ask for clarification. "I have more time on my hands and I've decided to expand our little . . . venture. Oh, you're doing well enough, Tarr." He held up his hands to forestall my uncle's protest. "But you know well enough two ships working in consort have more success than two ships working alone."

"I take it Captain Hornigold here has the command of that twinmaster?"

"Aye, the *Freyja*," Hornigold said. "A little beauty she is too —"

"I know her well, Ed," Tarr butted in. "I was the one who took her in the first place."

Hornigold said nothing.

"If ye've quite finished," Morgan said, his voice booming. "The pair o' ye will sail together, Tarr in command."

Tarr didn't react, and Hornigold looked sullen. Morgan took a long draught of rum and belched.

"The bloody Spaniards have it too easy these days. I want their ships. I want them running scared of the waters around Jamaica, if not the entire Caribbees. The West Indies are English, not bloody Spanish, and the sooner the stubborn buggers realize it, the better."

I'd heard rumors of Morgan's hatred for Spain, but had thought them exaggerated. Now I was not so sure. Apparently the Spaniards thought him some kind of devil, as they had Sir Francis Drake a century before.

"Surely England's not at war with Spain again," Erik exclaimed. Morgan turned on him, his face red.

"England may not be, but I bloody well am! And always will be as long as I've wind in my sails. Do you understand?"

Erik stared at him, jaw clenched, and said nothing.

"Bring the vessels to Sayba, those large enough for slavers, anyroad. The others can go to the bottom. We only need a small number of men to work a slaver; take volunteers, the rest can sail their ships to the seabed. There must be no survivors to tell tales, understand?"

"Aye." Tarr, Blake and Hornigold nodded. I didn't move, I couldn't believe the callousness of the man.

"You too, Sir Henry, do you understand?"

I nodded, as much at the spite in which he'd said my name as in agreement to his terms. I smiled to myself. Having been trumped by Sir Thomas Lynch, he now had the further indignity of sharing his title with the nephew of one of his lieutenants.

Tarr nudged me and I realized my smile had grown and was showing on my face.

"Captain," he said. Morgan raised an eyebrow and my uncle quickly amended his title. "Sir Henry, what of the crews? How many men does *Freyja* have?"

"Thirty, hale and hearty," Hornigold answered for Morgan, with a self-satisfied smirk. Whether at the number of men under his command, or the rhyme he had made was known only to him.

"She'll need more to fight well. Sharpe here will join you." I started and looked at Tarr in surprise. "You'll take Jonesy and Little as well. Any ideas, Blake?"

"Cheval."

"Oh yes, Cheval. We'll find you a half dozen more in addition."

My heart sank. Of all the men to sail with, I had to endure the company of the sycophantic Frenchman as well as the "evil little bastard". So much for my new life running a sugar plantation.

"Excellent." Morgan downed another glass of rum and slammed it onto the table with a loud crack. Shards of glass fountained over his hand to the table and floor.

"*Damn it*," Morgan shouted. "Damn fool bloody things! He wiped blood from the back of his hand. "It's been a long time since anyone's bloodied me, van Ecken, the last one lost his guts and danced around them."

The van Eckens blanched.

"Luckily for ye, knights of the realm don't indulge in such activities, but that won't stop me if it happens again. Ye'll serve me with a tankard on my next visit."

The elder van Ecken opened his mouth, but Morgan waved him to silence. "We'll take our leave. Hornigold, where's my coat?"

Erik stuck his head through the dining room door and shouted for Hendrick, who soon appeared with a selection of gaily colored frockcoats, and Tarr took the opportunity to whisper in my ear.

"Keep an eye on him, Henry. I need someone I can trust on that boat. You're my eyes and ears."

I was handed my coat before I could respond.

Chapter 16

I, along with every other man aboard *Freyja* and, no doubt, *Edelweiss*, held my breath as we glided past the huge fort of San Felipe de Todo Fierro. Phil's Iron Fort as Tarr insisted on calling it.

We had waited for a moonless night and a gentle breeze. The sails, after being coated with the blackest of tar, were set and would not be adjusted until we were past the fort; we could not afford any creaking lines or flapping canvas. There was no noise and little to see in the dark of night. Soon, the glimmers of lantern light that marked the fort were at our stern, then in our wake. Another five minutes and a bend in the river, and the fort was gone. As one, the men on *Freyja's* deck heaved a sigh of relief to have made it past the huge rectangular structure, laden with iron, but we had bigger challenges ahead.

Porto Belo was guarded by two more forts—two! Santiago de la Gloria—Santiago's Glory—and San Jerónimo. Together they bristled with over a score of guns and boasted over a hundred men to fire them.

"I hope your uncle knows what he's doing," Jonesy whispered.

"So do I," I replied.

"Don't fret, boys," Little stepped in, "Tarr and Blake were here with Morgan back in '68. They know the town and its defenses well."

"A lot can change in fifteen years," Jonesy said.

"Four or five years ago, everything was the same, just not as heavily guarded," Little said.

"How do you know?" I asked.

"Coxton raided it in '78, La Sonda the year after. Apparently the captain knows them both well." Little nodded toward Hornigold.

"Why not as heavily guarded?" I asked. "If they've been raided so often why haven't they employed more guards?"

"They have, but there are only so many men—the extra men all sail with the treasure fleet itself. With any luck we'll have our pick of the treasures before the fleet gets here."

The treasure fleet—near a score of galleons packed to the gunwales with gold, silver and jewels –sailed for Spain most years in March and September. Porto Belo was one of the stops of the Armada de Tierra Firme to load up; mainly with silver from the enormous mine that was Potosi—a mountain literally of silver—but also with gold and jewels from Peru. They would spend over a month here loading up before journeying on to Cartagena and other treasure-rich ports, then Havana to meet up with the second fleet; the Fleet of New Spain, before embarking for Old Spain.

"Lights ahead," an urgent whisper was thrust back along the deck to Hornigold.

"Helm a lee," he responded, putting as much urgency into his hoarse whisper as possible. "Put her head to wind and bring the canoe alongside. Sharpshooters, get your muskets."

With a sigh, Jonesy, Little and I bent to pick up our loads. Muskets, ball, powder and plenty of match. I checked my pockets for my steel and flint, then passed the bundles down to the men stowing them.

When everything was safely aboard, the three of us, plus half a dozen more, clambered into the long canoe and cast off.

Tarr's canoe, similarly filled, came alongside and we paddled eastward. We needed to sneak up to Santiago's Glory's beach, and trek up the hill to our positions. It was going to be a long night.

Chapter 17

The sky had lightened enough for us all to see each other, and it wouldn't be long before the sun broke the horizon.

We had reached the hill without incident and were near the top when Cheval whispered, "Down!"

I immediately fell to my belly, as did the others. "There's a sentry up there, they must 'ave posted him after Morgan used these 'ills last time." Cheval sounded worried.

I lifted my head, then rose to my knees to have a proper look. A single-story stone building perched on top of the hill. A man's head appeared above the castellations of its roof. I waited a while, but could not see anyone else. I fumbled to untie one of the muskets from my bundle, loaded it, and crept a little further up the slope.

"What are you doing? You'll never 'it 'im at this range!" Cheval hissed. I ignored him, took aim and fired. The man fell and my crewmates cheered.

I met Cheval's eyes. He looked furious. I raised my eyebrows at him but he stayed silent.

"Come on, let's go, Tarr will have taken that shot as the signal, we need to get into position quickly."

Cheval said, "Wait . . ." but everyone ignored him and twenty men stormed up the final incline. Jonesy and I were the first to reach the stone building and we ran inside. Nobody there, just a table, chair and cot. Basic accommodations for one.

Back outside, Cheval was arguing again; this time over shooting positions. He wanted the prime spot on the roof.

"You can't shoot for shit, Cheval," Little said.

Cheval made to protest, but was stayed by everybody else's agreement. "Sharpe and Jonesy take the roof, you're the two most likely to hit anything," he said instead. "The rest of you, spread out." His voice rose to a shout as he pointed out to sea.

I squinted and spotted sail approaching through the early morning mist.

"They'll be in range soon. We have to be ready." He grabbed his muskets and lay on the slope above Santiago, as did the rest of the men.

I ran up the outside steps to the roof of the hut, closely followed by Jonesy and one of the boys, Billy Mac, who would reload for us. Dropping the muskets, I grabbed the dead soldier's shoulders, and Jonesy his feet, then we heaved him over the wall.

Turning back to seaward, I saw the boy had already untied both bundles of muskets and he handed a loaded one to me, then another to Jonesy. The two of us found our positions, standing and bracing on one of the crenelations, and stared down at the view.

The sun broke free and the first rays danced over turquoise water, lush green slopes, and enormous stone forts bristling with ironwork.

San Jerónimo was across the harbor mouth. A copy of Phil's Iron Fort, its longest side presented to the harbor with near a dozen great guns aimed at the water, and our vessels. It was well out of range of our muskets; Tarr and Hornigold would have to work hard to best it. But Santiago's Glory, nestled on another hill below, was ours to suppress.

It was enormous, with a pitched roof in the middle of its quad, housing who knew how many men. I counted seven guns and scores of men rushing to them. My shot had raised the alarm.

I waited, as did the rest of us. Billy loaded the last muskets and I nodded my thanks at him. *Edelweiss* and *Freyja* glided closer. The mist was burning off quickly, and surely the Spaniards would spot their dull sails soon. Even as I thought the words, one of Jerónimo's great guns exploded, and both ships immediately retaliated, deadly iron ball flying back and forth.

The fort below us exploded into action. Men, still half-dressed, at the laborious task of preparing their first volley. I focused on the officer bellowing orders and waving his arms. The musket was heavy in my hands and I used the weight rather than fighting it to find the right balance. I shifted my feet a little. That was better.

I aimed carefully for his gut. The guns were far from accurate, and aiming there would give me the best chance of hitting the man. I took a deep breath, let it out. Breathed in again, then out. A third breath, then a squeeze of the trigger as I exhaled. I blinked, my calm shattered by the noise of the musket firing, then grinned in satisfaction at the sight of my quarry dropping, his head a bloody mess. I handed the empty gun to Billy and picked up another full one. My crewmates opened fire and panic reigned Santiago; Spanish soldiers dived for cover, leaving their canon unattended.

I squeezed the trigger and another man fell. Exchanged guns. Fired. On and on until the only soldiers still in view on Santiago's battlements were either dead or dying. Tarr and the others would have no problems from this shore.

Chapter 18

The battle across the harbor mouth was in full force. Fountains of water sprayed when balls missed the attacking ships, but enough hit their targets to make life difficult for Tarr and Hornigold.

I fell to the floor in a tangle of limbs with Jonesy and Billy. Deafened, I pushed myself to my feet and peeped over the battlements of our miniature tower. San Jerónimo was a smoking ruin. The shore party, putting off under the bellow of cannon, had successfully landed and infiltrated the huge building whilst its men had been preoccupied with the two ships. They'd only had one objective—to find the armory and blow up the powder magazine within it. By the looks of things it had been well-stocked.

The Edelweissers and Freyjamen had their longboats halfway back to the ships. Next, it was the turn of Santiago's Glory to be demolished.

A great gun fired from below us. "What's that?" Jonesy cried. "Where is it?"

"I can't see! It must be lower down, out of sight of this place. *Come on.* Bring the guns, Billy!"

We raced down the steps and re-joined our crewmates.

"The gun's positioned so we can't see it from here, Jonesy and I will go and see if we can silence it." I pointed down the hill. We would have to skirt the castle and come up on its flank.

"*No.* You stay 'ere, keep these guns silenced, I'll go with Little."

I couldn't argue, Cheval was my quartermaster. I glanced at Jonesy and he met my eye; we both knew his motivation, and it wasn't to save the two ships still under fire. He wanted glory; and to prevent us from obtaining any more.

A gun from the ramparts fired, and I ran up the steps again. Tarr and the others didn't have time for me to argue with Cheval.

I fired, again hitting my mark; the guns placed in the battlements were silent once more, their remaining men fleeing back to safety. Cheval and half a dozen others ran downhill and were soon out of sight. I could only hope Cheval's bravery matched his cunning. *Edelweiss* and *Freyja* bombarded the castle walls, and I saw ball still issuing from the castle and winced as one hit the water close enough for the spray to soak the men on deck. They were too close! If the ships went down we were all dead.

A cheer behind me startled me; my hearing was returning. I turned to glare at Billy, then looked to where he was pointing. A stream of men was running across the hillside, away from the fort, chased by Cheval and his group. They were fleeing! They'd abandoned their castle.

"*They're running*." Billy was dancing a jig now." Yellow-bellied, lily-livered scum!"

I glanced at Jonesy and smiled in relief. We knew it had been a possibility; they'd run when Morgan had attacked and, by the looks of things, there were even fewer men stationed here today than there had been then.

"It seems the men of New Spain are not of the same determined breed as their brethren of Old," Jonesy smirked.

The longboats landed to no resistance and privateers stormed the castle. Grappling hooks attached to long lines provided easy access to men who had been swarming rigging most of their lives.

"Come on, we done here," I said to Jonesy and Billy. We re-gathered the muskets, all reloaded now, thanks to Billy's nimble fingers, and headed back down to join the others.

By the time we reached the longboats, there was a steady stream of men returning and clutching prizes: pistols; a Spanish rapier; a tortoiseshell box; a decorative frockcoat. Cheval and his group were with them; they hadn't bothered with the chase for long.

We clambered in and pushed off.

Mighty shoulders, developed through years of hauling hemp and canon, powered the boats through the choppy water and we were back aboard our motherships in moments.

Hornigold grasped Cheval's hand. "Well done, mate. That was some shooting up there, you cleared them out faster than rats leaving a sinking prize!"

Cheval grinned in pleasure, but the men glanced uneasily at each other, then at Jonesy and me. I stayed quiet, knowing the men knew who had the sharp eyes and steady trigger fingers. The captain could be voted out; the crew were the important ones on this ship.

"*Full sail,*" Hornigold shouted. "*Porto Belo ahoy.*"

The crew cheered and the topmen swarmed to the topyards, forty feet above the deck. Swathes of canvas fell and were hauled in until they bellied with wind. Speed was important now, not stealth.

We held our breath—and our great guns at the ready—as we approached the town.

Chapter 19

The mist had cleared, but sulfurous gun smoke hung over the sheltered harbor, wisping against the sails. Our speed slowed as we approached, the high land sheltering our lower courses from the wind and they flapped as the topsail did its best to drive us forward.

I was on the maintop with Jonesy, a dozen muskets tied loosely to the mast to prevent them falling, my wig jammed tightly to my head. Our sharpshooting duties had not yet resumed though; for the moment we were simply lookouts.

Jerónimo was still ablaze; its smoke our companion on our slow drift toward Porto Belo. I glanced at Jonesy, his eyes were red raw and streaming and I blinked and wiped my own to peer through the shifting, stinking tendrils.

A shape became more distinct as we neared. I squinted; large and rectangular, it could only be one thing.

"*Gun battery off our larboard bow,*" I cried loudly enough for the men on deck to hear.

"Ready your guns," Hornigold ordered in response.

I glanced over at *Edelweiss*, just behind and to larboard. As the wind had lightened, the larger, heavier ship had slowed and the light, maneuverable *Freyja* had crept ahead to lead the way.

I jumped as the sound of a cannon reverberated around the harbor and the hills surrounding it. The battery may be small, but it was armed and manned.

Edelweiss swung slowly to starboard, presenting her broadside to the stone rampart, and *Freyja* followed suit.

We both flung broadside after broadside at them; upwards of twenty ball every three minutes from the two vessels.

Their return fire was sporadic and I realized they only had men for three or four guns. I thought back; those Spaniards hadn't fled Santiago's Glory, they'd retreated here. And Cheval had let them run!

I glanced down at the deck and spotted him at Hornigold's right hand, strutting around the quarterdeck with his captain, relaying orders to the gunners. I was tempted to pick up one of the muskets and shoot him myself. Jonesy stayed my hand before I even realized I'd reached out for a weapon.

"Not worth it, Sharpe mate, you'd only end up hanged or worse."

I glanced up at him in surprise. He raised his eyebrows and I realized my thoughts had been clear on my face. I'd have to take more care over that.

Freyja rolled under the force of another broadside and we both grabbed the mast and each other to steady ourselves. The maintop was a four-by-four-foot wooden platform at the height of the mainyard; thirty feet above deck, and precarious at the best of times, never mind in the midst of a gun battle.

"If he'd chased down those Spaniards, or let us go after them, those guns would be silent," I told Jonesy angrily.

"You don't know that; men from the town itself could be manning them."

"The fat, rich merchants? Has the sun addled your wits? They wouldn't have the strength to bring one of those guns to bear."

Jonesy shrugged and I sighed in exasperation. He was right. It didn't matter who was loading and setting a match to them, we could do nothing about it now bar fight back.

"We're drifting closer, let's see if we can pick some of these buggers off," Jonesy said, handing me a loaded musket.

I steadied myself against the mast, swayed with *Freyja's* motion over the waves, and paid attention to the rhythm of the gunners below. *Freyja's* reaction to their powder going off was more than enough to disturb my aim.

A broadside exploded and Freyja heeled to starboard. I pressed against the mast, waiting for her to level out and settle. I kept my eye trained on my mark, a man in red and white standing behind the closest cannon wedged into the small castellation. I squeezed my trigger, but missed. The range was still too great. Then he fell as another musket fired and Jonesy cheered. "*Hah*. I beat you to a shot, mate! What's wrong, your hands atremble?"

I turned to face him, his hands aloft holding the musket like a trophy. “Lucky sh—” I broke off as another broadside fired below us.

Jonesy’s face turned from elation to terror. He dropped the musket, arms waving to find some purchase. I grabbed the mast with one hand and lunged, but was too late. My grasping fingers found only air.

Jonesy’s scream was cut off by a thump and I stared down at his broken body on the deck below. Hornigold and Cheval rushed to him and bent over him, then straightened and looked up at me. He was dead.

I squinted. *Is Cheval grinning?*

I rubbed my eyes of smoke, but he had turned away and I could no longer see his face.

I glanced up at a cheer from *Edelweiss* and noticed her jibs in tatters and her bowsprit missing, then I turned my gaze to the gun battery and saw the reason for their elation. It had crumbled. Porto Belo and her treasures were defenseless.

Chapter 20

The guns silenced and a hush filled the air along with more gun smoke. I slowly made my way down the ratlins, terrified of what I'd find on deck.

A circle of men had formed around Jonesy and I pushed my way through as Hornigold shouted for the boats to be launched. I knelt in a vacated space and lifted Jonesy's head, then dropped it in recoil at the grinding, squelching noise my action had produced. He would not draw breath again.

"*Sharpe*," a voice shouted loudly enough to raise me from my contemplation of my friend's visage. "To the boats. Quick, man!"

"Oh leave 'im, Capitaine, 'e's no use to man nor beast shedding tears over 'is mate. Leave 'im to keep ship," Cheval called. "Look at 'im, you'd think 'im a spinster who'd lost 'er last chance at an 'usband!" He laughed and a couple of his cronies joined in, then the deck cleared and I was alone with Jonesy.

"I'm so sorry, my friend, so sorry," I whispered, stroking his hair away from his face. "You joined me to find new life, only to find death."

I stayed, kneeling in his blood for some time, then rose and made my way below decks. I pulled at the securing lines of his Brazilian bed and the canvas fell to the deck. I gathered it up and made my way to the closest sail locker for needle and twine, then hefted my load back up the ladder to the topdeck.

I laid the canvas out alongside Jonesy and carefully, painstakingly, shifted his body across until he lay on his bed, careful to straighten his legs, his arms, his neck. Next, I placed a 6lb ball at his feet for ballast then sewed the edges of his shroud together, enclosing him in canvas; up to his knees, thighs, belly.

"*Damn and blast,*" I exclaimed, the sound of my own voice startling me as I jabbed the thick needle into the pad of my thumb. Blood, mixed with tears I'd been unaware of, dripped onto the canvas and I continued to sew.

I tugged the canvas hard to wrap it around his shoulders, the two edges only just meeting, and secured it tightly. Now only his face was visible: pale, with bloodstains creeping across his skin. I stared at him a minute; two; five; then folded the bloody canvas over and finished my task. My hands, arms and knees were soaked in blood; both mine and his. I knotted the twine for the final time, cut it and whispered a final prayer over his corpse. "Sleep well, my friend, sleep well."

Chapter 21

An explosion from the shore dragged my attention away from my shrouded mate and I made my way forward. I squinted toward the town and held my breath against the stink of the exposed mud a couple of hundred yards ahead. Hours had passed whilst I'd knelt over Jonesy and the tide was going out quickly; my shipmates would have to hurry or we'd be stranded here until the next tide's flood.

I glanced across at *Edelweiss*; with her deeper draught she was anchored further out, but I didn't know how far the tide ebbed here. I was pleased to see they had rigged up a replacement bowsprit—no doubt a spare mainyard—she'd be able to make sail at least.

Another gunshot echoed from the town and I turned my attention landward again. At least half the seafront warehouses were ablaze. I could see no Spaniards, only privateers firing into the air, dragging chests, clutching leather bags full of booty, and whooping and hollering as they brought Hell to Porto Belo in their quest for gold.

I loaded one of the 2lb rail guns and fired to catch the attention of the sailors. Gold, Spanish brandy, and no doubt Spanish women had taken their minds and hearts far from any shipboard concerns. They needed reminding. We had no idea if any of the Spanish soldiers had gone for reinforcements; we could not tarry and be caught here till the next tide with no means of escape.

After a second shot from the rail gun, I saw the men drift toward the boats and I stood unmoved—no pity, no horror, no delight—and waited for the boats to return. I turned my attention back to Jonesy. Soon the decks would be heaving with gold-rich, besotted privateers. This would be my last chance to pay quiet respects to my fallen friend.

I got back to my feet as the first boat arrived at the ship. Hornigold was first aboard, followed by a young woman. *No, still a girl*, I thought.

"The customs house was empty. *Goddammit*. That's Tarr for you—always bloody tardy. But there were plenty of spoils if you knew where to look, and I've found a beauty!" He dragged the girl closer to him and she cringed away, although kept her composure I noted, impressed. Young with long, dark, curly hair, piercing eyes and a defiant cast to the set of her jaw, she reminded me a little of Erik van Ecken's new wife, Gabriella, but I pushed those thoughts out of mind. I could not, would not, think of her. I had met her two months before, just after meeting Morgan. *Freyja* had been dispatched to Massachusetts Bay to bring her to Sayba and her marriage. She'd had a spirit I'd admired on that passage, and had managed to hold onto it despite her wedding. I doubted it would last much longer.

"Oui, plenty of gold too," Cheval chimed in. "The treasure fleet may 'ave sailed, but they spent a lot of coin 'ere first!" He held up a heavy pouch, bulging no doubt with silver rather than the gold he claimed.

"Ah. What do we have here?" He crossed to Jonesy's body. "So you've been paying respects to the dead while we've been at work making profit? Where's the sense in that? You fool, 'e's gone, 'e can't 'elp you now." He kicked Jonesy and I leapt at him, but was stilled by screams. The girl. She was staring at the bloody shroud, then at me, still screaming. I looked down at myself. I was covered in blood and saw myself as she no doubt did: a murderous devil, my attire reflecting the color of the flag at our masthead.

I held out my hand in a placating gesture, but Hornigold shook her and threw her to the deck. "Blast thee, girl! Avast that infernal noise."

She stopped and Hornigold grinned in relief. He clearly hadn't seen the fire in her eyes, the hate that burned there as she regarded him.

I pulled myself up to my full height, squared my shoulders, and glared at my captain, thankful that I wore my wig for any battle or foray ashore. It reminded me of my old life, the man I had been—Lord Rowleston, the Earl of Shirehampton—and brought me the authority my title and position bestowed, even aboard a privateer vessel.

His gaze flickered under my stare and I knew that was my cue. "What are you doing with her?"

"Whatever I like and it's none of your damn concern, Sharpe!"

I raised my eyebrows and paused before I spoke. "Anything that occurs aboard this boat is Tarr's concern, and as his agent and nephew, it is therefore mine. No women aboard *Edelweiss* or *Freyja*, it's in the articles you signed, as you know well."

"*Bah*. Hellfire on the articles, she's a spoil of war. Anyway, she won't be aboard long, just time enough for us all to enjoy her, then she's shark food!"

A handful of men cheered at this and I stared at them, noting who had given their approval to this course of action. Cheval, of course, Prince, Savage and half a dozen others. I glared at them each in turn and they quietened.

"We are under license from King Charles, we do nothing to dishonor his name, nor will I allow you to sully the reputation of my uncle!"

"Well, we're under Morgan's license, anyroad." Hornigold laughed and I narrowed my eyes at him, but I let the comment pass. I glanced down at the girl, she was my concern now; if I did not save her, I would truly become the devil she thought I was.

"Put her ashore, Hornigold."

"No. Who the blazes do you think you are to give me, the *captain*, orders?"

"Lord Rowleston-Sharpe, nephew of your commander. I take my orders from him, not you," I sneered. "And you'd do well to take heed."

Hornigold opened his mouth, but nothing came out. The deck was shrouded in silence as the Freyjamen waited to see who would win this battle of wills. Even the girl was silent, glancing between myself and Hornigold from her position on the deck.

Freyja lurched slightly and a shout rose up, "*Captain*. The tide! If we don't go now we'll be stuck in this infernal, stinking mud."

"*Slip the anchor,*" Hornigold shouted, but not before I saw a flash of relief pass over his eyes. "Set the jibs and topsail, get us away from this hellhole!"

Men ran to do his bidding, Little giving me a nod as he passed, blade drawn to cut the anchor line. More ran to mast and sheet to set sail, while others pushed us out to sea on the next wave with long boathooks. Sinking into the mud with every thrust, they were of little more use than none, but we needed every inch to escape.

I glanced over to *Edelweiss*, worried about her larger hull, but she was already free of her anchor and setting sail. I furrowed my brow, wondering why she was towing the one ship we hadn't sunk in this harbor, then transferred my attention back to Hornigold.

He turned back to me in triumph. "No one's going ashore now, Sharpe, you can show her to my cabin to wait until I'm ready for her."

"No."

He stared at me, but I could sense he was intimidated. I had not forgotten that flash of relief when we'd been interrupted earlier, and knew he was terrified of Uncle Richard, however much bravado he showed in his presence. He could not punish me in the way he would any other member of his crew; Tarr would have him keelhauled, and he knew it. Tarr had been very clear that I was aboard as his agent, to ensure obedience to the commander of our little fleet. The only recourse Hornigold had was to challenge me to a duel, but he knew well, as did every other man aboard, that he was no match for my skill with blade or pistol.

He glanced around. Every man was busy, no one had heard my refusal except himself and Cheval. I stared at the Frenchman; he would feel my ire soon. I would not let his kick to Jonesy go unpunished, but for now I had to protect the living.

"She stays with me and we will take the second cabin."

Hornigold smirked and the girl stared at me in disgust.

"No man, including myself, will touch you unless you permit it," I told her. She stared at me a moment, then nodded. I turned my attention back to Hornigold. "Any man touches her, I will gut him, do you understand?"

He moved his head; barely perceptible, but it was a nod nonetheless.

"But that's *my* cabin," Cheval whined.

"Not anymore, Quartermaster, we have a guest," Hornigold said without looking at him.

I nodded to the captain and held my hand out to the girl. She hesitated, then took it and allowed me to help her to her feet. I offered her my arm, which she also took, then I led her aft to the hatch and the cabins below.

"Get that lump of meat off my decks."

My step faltered at Hornigold's command, but I didn't stop. I had already spoken the appropriate words over Jonesy, paid my respects, and said my goodbyes.

"What's your name, girl?" I asked as a distant part of me registered the splash of Jonesy's journey to his final resting place.

"Magdalena."

Chapter 22

I ushered Magdalena into the cabin and told her to make herself comfortable.

"What do wi' me?" She stood tall, chin jutting out, fire in her eyes, despite her broken English.

"Calm yourself, no harm will come to you whilst you are under my protection."

"What will . . . *protection*," she spat the word at me, "cost? What price?"

I shook my head with a rueful smile. "Did you not hear me out on deck?" I nodded toward the cabin door. "No man aboard this vessel, including myself, will touch you without your permission. Allow it," I amended at her blank look.

"You think I'll give *you* allow?" She was bolder now it was only the two of us and I smiled in appreciation of her strong spirit.

"I haven't asked for it," I said mildly.

Her mouth opened, then closed as she found no rejoinder.

"Sit down, we have a long voyage ahead, you may as well make yourself comfortable."

"I prefer stand," she said, then staggered as *Freyja* picked up speed and heeled. We were leaving the harbor for the less sheltered River Chagres. "Where going?"

"Sayba," I replied, "in the Northern Antilles."

"And what there?"

I sighed and sat on the cot. "I don't yet know. My uncle captains the other ship you saw, I will transfer us both there at the first opportunity so Captain Hornigold cannot cause us harm. Then I'll find a way to get you home."

"I don't want," she said, finally sitting on the chair by the chart table. "No Porto Belo."

I raised my eyebrows. "Why ever not?"

She sighed. "Is long story."

"As I said, long voyage ahead."

She looked at me a moment, then her shoulders slumped. She was badly in need of a friend, and had just come to the realization herself. My heart went out to her, this lost soul, and in that instant she reminded me of myself before Jonesy had found me and rescued me from my folly. My vision clouded as I thought of him. His salvation of me had led to his own death, and I vowed I would honor his memory any way I could; by living well myself, and making sure this slip of a girl came to no harm.

"Your story?" I prompted, anxious to drag myself away from thoughts of Jonesy.

She stared at her hands, then looked up at me. "I waited Leo. I thought your sail his, then saw two and heard guns. I knew. No Leo."

"Who's Leo?"

"Friend. I know him long time, we survive Panama."

"Morgan's attack?"

She nodded. "His papá y mamá dead. Mi familia bring him Porto Belo. We hate. The stink, the way town go mad with treasure fever then dies, ever year. I die ever year too."

I nodded, I could imagine all the hustle and excitement, then . . . nothing.

"When Leo old, he work for mi papá, sailing. His next sail, he captain, and I be wife, stuck in hellhole, bebés hanging off skirts, dying ever year. No. No live that. So when piratas come—"

"Privateers," I corrected.

"—I no run."

"Do you realize what would have happened to you had I not been aboard?"

She shrugged. "I no think. I just . . . run. I want escape, Aventura. You both."

"Come here," I said, and led her to the gallery of windows. I threw them open and we stood in the fresh air on the small railed ledge over the sea.

"There. That's what we have to offer." I pointed at the remains of Santiago's Glory and San Jerónimo. "Destruction and death. That's what these men offer. Yes, there may be adventure, but who will it turn you into?"

Chapter 23

When I walked back out onto deck, dusk was already falling and I recognized the shape of the headland ahead. San Felipe de Todo Fierro was not far away.

"Leave your fancy woman be, Sharpe," Cheval snapped, and I glared at him. He ignored my stare. "You're needed in the tops, Little's already there. Look sharp, Sharpe." He laughed at his own joke and I headed for the main ratlins to begin my climb. Cheval could wait; for now.

The mainsail flogged loudly and I flinched. It was strange to climb past the tarred sails, they were all but invisible in the gloom; ghostly wraiths of sail. Last time, they had brought us safely past the heavily defended fort unseen, but these men would know of our attack on Porto Belo; they would not be dozing at their guns tonight.

I greeted Little as I swung myself onto the maintop platform and picked up a musket.

"All loaded?" I inquired.

"Aye, ready and willing," came the reply.

I said no more and settled down to await the first shooting opportunity.

I could only make out Tarr's ship ahead by the eerie white glow of her wake and remembered the ship he had towed out of Porto Belo harbor.

"You'll see," Little said with a chuckle when I mentioned it. "He's a wily old bastard, your uncle, don't do anything without good reason, him."

I pursed my lips and decided it was a compliment, then shifted position to get as comfortable as possible.

With no lights showing, blackened sails, and the crew below working in near silence, there was scarce anything to see or hear. It felt as if Little and I were floating along on one of the Moorish magic carpets I'd heard tell of in stories. Forty feet above the sea;

blackness above and darkness below. Then a spark flared ahead and burst into flame.

"What the blazes?" I exclaimed, jumping to my feet and grabbing the mast to peer closely at the phenomenon.

"Hah. Wily old bastard, told you," Little said. "Get your gun ready. With any luck, their night sight will be killed by the fireship and it'll draw all their ball, but you never know."

I realized the fireball was the ship Uncle Richard had towed and as it drifted downriver on the tide, it was being pulled closer and closer to the fort.

I squinted and just made out the *Edelweiss* as she bore away toward the shore opposite the fort, and felt *Freyja* cant as she changed course to follow.

Cannon fired from the fort and a cheer below was quickly hushed by Hornigold. The ruse had worked, they were firing on the decoy.

I joined Little in mumbling a small, although slightly blasphemous, prayer and kept my eyes on the fort. Little breathed a sigh of relief. "All clear, we're past."

A shout off our larboard bow caught my attention and I peered into the night. *Is Edelweiss in trouble?*

"Little! What's happening?"

He stopped laughing and squinted toward our sister ship. "Oh bugger, she's aground." He dropped his musket, grabbed hold of the backstay and slid down the fifty-foot stretch of hemp to the deck below. I winced; the skin on his hands must be thicker than leather.

I heard him talk to Hornigold, then our course adjusted back to the middle of the river. "What? No!"

I took a deep breath, then jumped and caught hold of the backstay as I'd seen Little do, and screamed in pain all the way down to the deck, my hands burning from the rope. I let go a little too early, unable to grip it any longer and fell in a heap, much to Hornigold's amusement.

"What are you doing? We've got to help them."

"Ahh, he's only touched bottom, he'll get the boats out, haul himself off and be out of the Chagres in no time."

"You don't know that. His jib is jury-rigged. Go back, *Freyja* can haul him free."

"We're in the dammed river, Sharpe. There's no room to tack or wear round. Tarr knows it even if you don't, blasted land-crab that you are. *Edelweiss* is on her own, just as *Freyja* would be had it been the other way round. Now get back up that blasted mast and stay there, we're sailing blind, I need my sharpest eyes in the tops, and unfortunately that means you."

Chapter 24

"You're no use to sailor nor ship," Prince said as he joined me on the maintop. "You're supposed to be keeping a lookout ahead not astern. Captain's sent me to relieve you. That woman's whipping up a storm in t' cabin, you've to set her to rights."

"*Edelweiss* is free of the shore," I told him. "But she must be damaged, she's slow."

"Tarr'll be right. He'll bring ship and crew home safe, don't fret."

I glanced at him with a smile, then remembered the rest of his message. "What's Magdalena doing?"

"Dunno, mate, but it don't sound good. Best get in there before Captain or Quartermaster beat you to it."

"Aye, ta, mate." My elocution was definitely heading south, and at rapid speed. I glanced at the backstay and grimaced, then noticed Cheval was not on deck. I leaped for the stay and slid, my hands red raw. I jumped through the hatch to the deck below, tucking my poor hands under my armpits, but it didn't help.

Making my way aft, I found Little lounging on a barrel before the cabin door. "Little," I said, wary, "what are you doing?"

"Oh, Sharpe, thank the Christ, I didn't know what to do." He thumped the wooden wall and shouted. I looked at him in puzzlement, then opened the door.

Cheval had hold of Magdalena's wrist. It looked like she'd just slapped him. He turned. "Little! I told you to make sure no one—" He broke off when he saw me.

"My apologies, Quartermaster, I tried, but he overpowered me," Little said, holding his jaw. Now I understood why he had hit the wall. He glanced at me and dipped his head, urging me toward Cheval and Magdalena.

"Let go of her."

Cheval sneered. "Make me."

Magdalena suddenly thrust her knee upwards, catching Cheval

between the legs, and wrenched her arm free.

I stared at her in surprise as Cheval grunted and doubled over in pain. Behind me, Little stifled a laugh and Cheval glared at me. "I'll teach you to laugh at me, Sharpe, I'll teach you!"

He pushed past us and made his way out of the cabin. Little met my eye, looking worried. I held up my hand to forestall his apology.

"No need to fret, Little. He's already gunning for me, there's little sense in both of us having him for an enemy." I tilted my head toward the door and he nodded, then made his way out. I turned back to Magdalena.

"Did he hurt you?"

"No, I didn't allow."

I wanted to reprimand her, I'd had enough problems with Cheval and Hornigold before having this woman aboard under my protection, I didn't need her making things worse, but I couldn't help the twitch of my lips.

Her own twitched in response and I burst out laughing so hard I was bent almost double and had to prop myself up on my knees. All the emotion of the past few days flooded out of me as tears streamed down my face: the tension of the raid, the men I had killed, Jonesy's death, Uncle Richard aground, and my public disagreements with Cheval and Hornigold.

Eventually my guffaws died down and I wiped my eyes. Magdalena's merriment had subsided long before my own and she was looking at me strangely.

"My apologies, señorita, it has been an eventful two days."

"Aventura?"

"Aye, you could say that." I looked up at her and the smile on her face, and my heart plummeted. This was only the start.

PART THREE
February 1684

Chapter 25

Tarr and *Edelweiss* had caught up with us at Sayba, and I had never been so relieved to see somebody in my life. He was all I had; my only family and my closest friend. Little and Prince had proved to be worthwhile acquaintances, but I wouldn't call either of them a true friend, neither of them could rival Jonesy. And then there was Magdalena. Ah, Magdalena, what to say of her? Headstrong, beautiful, infuriating, strong-willed, beautiful, beautiful, beautiful. I spent almost every minute I was not on watch, with her; I had kept her safe aboard *Freyja*, yet she never let me touch her apart from the odd, supplicating kiss of her hand.

Tarr had been furious and had wanted to leave her ashore in Sayba. She may have been good company for Gabriella van Ecken, but I could not imagine her presence in that house bringing anything other than hardship for both women. Besides, I was becoming enamored of her. I could not be in Gabriella's life or make things right for her, but I could for Magdalena.

After a few months, Magdalena remaining at my side, Tarr had relented, and I transferred to *Edelweiss* with my prize, leaving the powder keg of jealousy and resentment that *Freyja* had become.

As soon as I'd vacated Hornigold's decks, he'd disappeared. He'd been off our larboard quarter at dusk, and was nowhere to be seen come dawn. Tarr was furious.

"*Sail oh.*" My eyes had spotted the prize to the west: a three-master with beautiful lines and a hull low in the water, laden with cargo.

Tarr held his glass to his eye and beckoned me to join him on deck. I grabbed the backstay and slid down; my palms now as tough as old leather.

"She's a beauty," my uncle said. "I reckon it's time to trade up, we could do with more room aboard now the crew numbers over a hundred, and it'll put that bugger Hornigold in his place when he shows his face again. "*All hands on deck*," he added at a roar, taking me by surprise. "Ready the guns, prepare for battle!"

Edelweiss's decks heaved with purpose as cannon were readied, powder and shot brought up, and a preparatory round of rum downed. Little and I carried *Edelweiss's* collection of muskets topside, loaded them and stacked them butt down in a couple of barrels which we then swayed to the tops. I followed the guns to the maintop and helped Little secure them to the mast. I also had large pouches of powder, ball and wadding in case we needed to reload.

I glanced down and watched my crewmates clear everything bar weapon and line from the decks, then cursed. Magdalena, dressed in a pair of my breeches and shirt appeared on deck.

"That bleedin' woman!" Little spluttered. "What in the name of Hell does she think she's doing?"

I sighed, noticed Tarr make his way over to her, and slid down to the deck for the second time in less than an hour.

"—bloody skirt on my deck in battle!" Tarr's face was cochineal red as he roared at Magdalena. She looked down at herself then back up at Tarr.

"I see no skirt, Capitán, only willing hands and sharp eye."

I landed beside them, grabbed Magdalena and pulled her off to the main hatch before Tarr could retaliate. He looked to be ready to use his fists; or a blade.

"What the blazes do you think you're doing? You're barely tolerated at the best of times aboard this ship, did you really think you'd be welcomed in a battle?"

"*No*. That's lie!"

"Is it?"

"Sí. I most welcome from crew."

I laughed. "Only the ones who want to explore beneath your skirts."

She thrust her hands on her hips and pushed her face up toward mine. "*Mierda.* That's all bloody men think, sí? What under skirt. And I know all *you* blasted well think."

I held up my hands in defense, shocked at her command of the vulgarities of the English language. "Watch your mouth, señorita, I've never laid a hand on you, *or* tried to lift your skirts!"

"No, but you want, why else you keep me?"

I opened my mouth, but no words were ready. Magdalena raised her eyebrows in a smirk. "Play your game, or your . . . dice, right, and you may get."

I reddened with embarrassment. "Have you no shame?"

"Shame? Me? No. But steady hands and sharp eyes. I no leave Porto Belo to be hide and lock in cabin."

I raised my own eyebrows. "You did not choose to leave Porto Belo, señorita, you were taken."

"Sí?"

I looked away from her frank gaze, unsure what to believe. After eight months of her stubborn, wilful, *infuriating* company, I still did not know what to believe of her. My breath grew heavy as I regarded her, and her look turned triumphant.

"Go to the cabin. When the fight begins, no one will have a mind as to your whereabouts. But stay on this ship and I want no complaints if you're hurt."

She smiled, rose up to her toes, caressed my cheek with her hand, and planted a small kiss on my lips, then turned and clambered through the hatch and out of sight.

I sighed and raised my fingers to my lips. I would have to keep a close eye on the decks this day to ensure she was not injured. I smiled, then winked at Tarr when I caught him watching me. He made a show of shaking his head, but did not hide his mocking smile well enough.

My heart feeling lighter, even as it beat harder, I climbed back up to my perch.

Chapter 26

I took a musket out of the barrel and made myself comfortable. Little and I would not be needed until we were within a cable's length of the other ship, and I took the time to study her.

Three-masted, with a hull nearly twice the length of *Edelweiss*, she had the high, narrow stern that marked her as Spanish. Even to my eye, fairly experienced now (I had finally left the 'land-crab' epitaph behind me) but still not as knowledgeable as the men who had spent their entire lives at sea; she looked handy. She didn't wallow as many of the larger ships did, but danced from wave to wave as she curved peaks either side of her bow.

Her colors were hauled to her main-masthead and my heart lurched; for a moment I had thought she flew a cross of St George, but no, the red cross was on the diagonal and jagged: the Cross of Burgundy. I smiled at my correct assumption of her nationality.

I glanced above my head. We flew no colors as of yet. I knew from any number of engagements that Tarr would wait until the last second to frustrate his prey. Unsure whether friend or foe, the prize captain would likely be paying more attention to us than the set of his sails, allowing us to catch up in half the time. But this one seemed canny; he set his topgallant, one of the few I'd seen, and I smiled in further appreciation of the ship ahead. Not many had the balance and the skill to fly three sails from a single mast, and I understood why Tarr wanted her.

I braced myself against the maintop as *Edelweiss* changed course from north to west to follow our prey.

She would be hard to catch, running downwind with all that sail, but we were dead astern. If we could just get closer, and she did look to be heavily laden which would work against her in this race for the lives of all aboard, we could steal the very wind from out her sails and claim our prize.

Then, a crash, and I caught my balance.

"She's jettisoning her cargo," Little said, and I glanced up at our newly unfurled blood-red flag—La Jolie Rouge—that shouted our intentions across the sea: Your blood will be spilled. Ask no quarter, none will be granted.

The three-master hardened up and Tarr followed, both decks a heaving mass of men hauling brace and sheet to bring the sails to their new set. We were stealing her wind; she was trying to shake us, but it would take a magician—or a devil—to shake Tarr off her wake.

More barrels littered the waves ahead. I was concerned over their contents until I realized they floated; they were unlikely to be enough to hole our bow on collision.

At a shouted command from below, Little and I readied ourselves for the battle. Our bow cannon fired—a warning shot, well over their bow—a nice illustration that they were well within our range.

I glanced down, but could not see Magdalena. *Good, at the very least she's heeded my words.* Although I doubted she would remain in safety.

The crew had left sheets and braces to gather at the larboard rail, slamming their blades against the wood and chanting their promises of death and blood. I shivered; even viewed from this ship it was a terrifying spectacle and sound. Each man dripped arms. Pistols draped around necks, knives in hand and sheathed in sashes, plus all manner of deadly instruments found on deck: spikes, clubs and slings.

I glanced back over to the other deck. They were ready to fight, and for a moment I felt sorry for them. They were sailors not warriors, they stood not a chance.

I shifted my gaze to the deck below me and gritted my teeth. There she was, standing just below the hatch. Difficult to see from on deck, but clear to my eyes and Little's. Magdalena.

Chapter 27

The doomed ship fired on us, so close her ball could not miss, and our starboard side exploded into vicious splinters. I winced, seeing blood, but none of my crewmates fell; their wounds not serious enough to keep them from the fight and spoils.

I glanced aft at Magdalena, but she had ducked below out of danger.

"*Sharpe.*"

I muttered an apology to Little, already on his third musket; took aim, lost myself in the sway of the ships and fired, felling one of the gunners.

Edelweiss lurched to larboard as her starboard guns fired simultaneously, and both Little and I cursed. I dropped my recently fired musket as I grabbed for a handhold and Little's shot flew wild.

As the smoke cleared, our men cheered and boarded the stricken ship in a relentless wave of destruction and death. The partridge shot from our cannon had decimated the crew, and the remainder were outnumbered by at least three to one.

Our muskets emptied, Little and I made our own way to the prize deck, swinging and sliding through the rigging of both ships. I fired a pistol to fell one man waiting for us on deck then, as I landed, an enemy sailor raised his blade to swipe and I stared at him, eyes wide with terror. I did not have time to draw my own cutlass.

A musket ball hit his temple and bounced off, but the impact had been enough to distract him; I drew my blade and sliced his throat. I looked over to *Edelweiss* and saw Magdalena load her sling with another ball and launch it. She glanced over at me and I grinned. Thank God she had joined the fight; she had saved my life.

I pulled my attention back to this deck, now slick with blood. The fight was nearly won, but I spotted one man before me knock

Peters to the deck, blood gushing into a puddle around him. The man then raised his pistol and my heart leapt to my throat; he had Uncle Richard in his sights. I jumped at him, my fist connecting with his temple, and he fell overboard. I looked across at Magdalena in triumph, only to recoil from the look of horror on her face.

Chapter 28

I turned my attention back to the melee on deck. I didn't have time to worry about Magdalena at the moment.

A shot came from above and I looked up, then cursed. One of the sharpshooters was still up there, loading another musket.

I took my second pistol—I had two draped around my neck on a silk sash—took careful aim and fired, just as he lifted his eyes from his gun and spotted me. He jerked to the side in panic, then toppled off the maintop platform. His musket clattered harmlessly to the deck, but his quick reflexes had saved the man himself. He'd caught hold of one of the footropes at the top of the mainsail—the ropes on which the topmen stood when handing the sails.

He swung from one to the next until he reached the outside edge, then with a final swing he let go and plummeted into the waves, feet first.

I shook my head in disbelief, I would much prefer death or maiming by steel and lead than by shark and water.

A blur on the edge of my vision shocked me back to my current situation. I had been so busy contemplating the death of the Spanish sharpshooter, I had nearly invited my own.

I brought my hand, still clutching my pistol, up quickly to block a blow from a blade, then parried with my own cutlass and fought off the Spanish sailor. I was well-practiced with a blade by now, and dealt with him quickly. I looked around for my next opponent, then paused, puzzled. The few men who were left standing were voluntarily jumping from the rails. I knew our flag promised no quarter, but in my experience, men still begged for it rather than leap to the terrors of the deep.

I broke into a run to have a look over the side and cursed. There was a boat, into which half a dozen men were scrambling. I grabbed my pistols to reload them, aimed and shot. Aimed and shot again, but to no avail; they were now too far away, even for my marksmanship.

"Sharpe, well done, my boy." Tarr clapped me on the back and I turned to him with a smile. "That bastard nearly had me," he added.

"He won't be causing any more trouble now, Captain."

"Hah, only for the sharks, lad, eh?"

"Hope so, Captain," I said, pointing at the boat.

"Damn and blast it! No survivors. No Spanish bastards left to go bleating to their king with tales!"

"Not a lot we can do about it now, Captain," I said. "They're out of range of small arms."

Tarr glanced at the cold cannon shackled in place. "No ball or powder—they didn't prepare the starboard guns, and *Edelweiss* can't shoot for fear of sinking the prize." He shook his head and looked over the two ships. "We can't give chase, *Edelweiss* is taking on water and we've a lot of work to do to clear all our gear and stow it aboard this one. Then we've to get the prize shipshape again after the fight."

"What about *Edelweiss*?

Tarr shrugged. "You're standing on her decks. Sea'll reclaim the old one, welcome to your new home, boy."

"You're naming her *Edelweiss*, too?"

"Aye, sailors know to fear that name, makes no sense to lose it, boy." He clapped me on the back again and I grimaced. I hated it when he called me boy.

He made to move away, then hesitated. "I saw that woman on deck."

"Aye."

"She's a good shot with a sling."

"Aye, she is that," I said, proud of Magdalena's skill, even though it had naught to do with me. "She saved my life."

Tarr nodded. "That's good, boy, but I don't want to see her on deck in a fight again. It's bad luck."

I opened my mouth to protest, but shut it again at his glare. He pointed to the longboat, now hidden intermittently by the swell. "There's the proof of it, boy."

"But—"

"I don't want to hear it. Your life wouldn't have been at risk if you hadn't been distracted by her. And they wouldn't have got away neither. She's bad luck."

I gritted my teeth in frustration, but knew my uncle well enough to know further argument would be futile.

"Right, you mangy curs, welcome aboard the *Edelweiss*. Get them bodies off our new decks and overboard, and start swaying our cargo across. The old tub's going down, I want everything shiny or useful salved. Get to it!"

The men cheered, their blood still up from the battle, and ran to do my uncle's bidding.

I went in search of Magdalena.

Chapter 29

I quietly closed the cabin door behind me. Magdalena had the gallery of windows flung wide and stood with her back to me, staring out to sea. I took a deep breath, not knowing what to say. *How will she react to the brutality she's witnessed today?* I remembered the look of hatred on her face the last time I'd glimpsed her on deck. She had saved my life, but taken another in doing so. *Does she blame me for making her a killer?*

I walked up to her and put my hands on her shoulders. "Magdalena—"

She whirled round before I could utter another word, her nails scraping my cheek, and I stepped back in shock, putting one hand to my face and holding the other out to fend her off.

"Blast you, woman! What the blazes do you think you're doing?"

"You killed him, you *bastard*. You killed him."

"What? Who?" I asked, bewildered as much by the words as the English profanity from this Spanish señorita. In the past eight months she had exhibited only a basic grasp of English, now she seemed fluent in all aspects of the language.

"*Leo*. My fiancée, you killed him."

I regarded her in incomprehension. *What madness is this*? She raised her arm to strike again and I grasped her wrist, pulled her close so she had no room to kick, and grabbed hold of her other wrist. "What are you talking about?"

"Leo! Remember I told you about him? He sailed for my father. He must be the captain of his own ship now. He was the man you knocked overboard."

"The one who had a pistol aimed at my uncle?"

She nodded, tears flowing so freely she could no longer talk. She sagged in my grasp and I gently lifted her and carried her to the cot against the starboard bulkhead.

She lifted her hands to her face and sobbed. "You killed Leo."

The words came out between sobs, unconnected yet creating a terrible truth.

I sat and wrapped my arms around her and held her close. "I'm sorry, Magdalena, I had no idea who he was. He was just a man trying to kill my uncle. I acted to save my uncle's life, just as you acted to save mine."

"That's not true though, is it? *You* attacked that ship, Leo's ship. He'd be alive if you and your blasted uncle hadn't coveted his ship and my papá's cargo!"

"This is what you wanted, Magdalena. Excitement and adventure, remember?"

She glared at me, but I was saved from the ferocity of her reply by Little, who burst through the cabin door.

"Whatcha doing in here? The ship's going down. Get your gear stowed and over to the new 'un, quick sharp!"

He rushed off without waiting for a reply and left the cabin door swinging. It was only then I realized the urgency of the shouts outside and the frenetic activity as stores and belongings were hauled topside. I rushed to my feet and had a quick look out over the stern; we were definitely low in the water and the deck beneath my feet listed.

I hurried back to Magdalena and pulled her to her feet, then pulled out a couple of seachests. "Hurry, put everything in these." We had both accumulated myriad possessions over the months: clothing, gold, trinkets and the like. "We've no time for tears now, we need to get off this ship."

Still sniffing, Magdalena did as she was told; her instinct for her wellbeing was greater than her grief, and I dragged both chests to the hatch ready to be swayed topside. I kept a tight grip of Magdalena's waist and ignored the odd smirk. Although we shared a cabin, my presence there was as guard rather than lover; not that anyone aboard believed that.

I pushed her up the ladder and led the way to the starboard rail. Planks had been braced to bridge the gap between the two vessels and we crossed over to our new home.

The new *Edelweiss* was much larger than the old, and the cabins were on the top deck. I smiled; the airs would be far less noxious than those below.

I opened one of the doors to find my uncle standing in the center of a cabin filled with seachests, charts, weapons and all manner of detritus.

He grunted. "There you are. Get that infernal woman," he stared at Magdalena behind me as he spoke, "stowed in yonder cabin. And keep her out of the way whilst we sort the ships out." He pushed past me, glared at Magdalena again, and strode down the deck, shouting orders as we went.

"What's got his goat?" Magdalena asked. I stared at her and she met my gaze, her face void of expression.

I led the way to the second cabin and ushered her in, grasped her arms, walked her to the cot and pushed her down to a sitting position, then stood in front of her, hands on my hips as I regarded her. She raised her eyebrows in question.

"What's got his *goat*?" I asked.

"Yes, why is he so unfriendly all of a sudden? Even more than usual, I mean."

I ignored her question. "Magdalena, you are Spanish. In all the time I've known you, since you first came aboard, your English has been basic, to say the least. And now you're using expressions such as 'got his goat'. What is happening here?"

She shrugged and said nothing.

"No, that won't wash anymore. You clearly have a far better command of English than you have led me to believe."

She shrugged again. "Yes, my English is good. But I am alone here—a woman aboard a ship, unwanted by most. Well, unwanted in the way I want to be wanted. Unfortunately I am only wanted in the way I do not want to be wanted."

I stared at her, trying to decipher all the 'wanteds' and still trying to assimilate the fact that this woman, with whom I had lived in close quarters for months and had only conversed in broken English in all that time, was now uttering tongue twisters that, after a little consideration, I realized made perfect sense.

She continued, and I suspected she was amused by my confoundment.

"These men are hunters. *You* are a hunter. You all regard me as prey."

I found my voice. "I do *not* regard you as prey."

"Yes you do. You regard me as *their* prey."

I opened my mouth, then shut it again. Now she was beating me in debate.

"I know what it is to hunt, I hunted the jungle around Panama City as a child with my slingshot. I know prey has to use every advantage at its disposal to outwit a hunter. Understanding the crew's words when they think me ignorant is one of my advantages."

I nodded in understanding, I had done similar when I first joined the ship.

"Please do not destroy my advantage, Henry."

I shook my head. "Your secret is safe with me. But how did you learn?"

"Leo." Her voice hitched with repressed sobs, but she took a deep breath and continued. "His mamá was English. She insisted on teaching him her language and he paid more attention if I was there. She would bribe me with treats—fruits, sweetmeats and the like—so that I would join him rather than taunting him by gaming outside the window." She smiled at the memory. Though silent tears dripped down her face, I did not think she was aware of them. I sat on the cot beside her and rubbed her back.

"Then it became our secret language. Nobody else in Panama could speak it and we drove the other children wild by talking in English. They never found our favorite berry patches, or den. All our secret places were safe."

"And now you're hiding your English to be safe."

She shrugged and smiled. "Excitement and adventure." Her face fell. "And now Leo's dead. I always thought he would be there, you know, when I went home. I always thought we would meet again."

"I'm so sorry, Magdalena. If I had known . . ." I tailed off in the knowledge that I would still have killed him to save the life of my uncle. She rested her head on my shoulder and I put my arm around her properly and lifted my free arm so I completely encircled her in my embrace. I held her tight, her tears soaking my shirt.

She jerked away and I started to apologize, but she interrupted. “You didn’t answer my question.”

“What question?”

“The captain, what’s got his goat?”

I smiled again at the coarse English phrase spoken in Magdalena’s breathy Spanish accent, then frowned as I considered my answer.

He has . . . superstitions. He believes women bring bad fortune to a ship.”

She grimaced, but I ignored it; she would have to get used to that attitude, and I was surprised she hadn’t already done so, what with listening to the crew’s unguarded conversations. “We are not officially at war with Spain at present, we should leave no survivors to tell of our attacks, but today a boat got away. He blames you for being aboard.”

“A boat got away?”

I nodded.

“So Leo, he may still live?”

I looked into her eyes and thought about my answer, whether to give her hope or dash it, then decided on the gentlemanly thing to do and nodded. “Aye, he may still live.”

Chapter 30

"You lie." She spat the words.

I rubbed my face with my hands then shrugged. "You know as well as I do he was injured when he went into the water. The boat got away much later—he would have drowned by then. I'm sorry."

She broke into sobs again, then slapped my face, hard.

"Don't lie to me, *don't* lie to me. It's bad enough you killed him, don't lie about it too!"

I grabbed her arms, yet again restraining her, my patience exhausted. I opened my mouth to berate her. This was a privateer ship. We attacked Spanish interests, and anyone else we fancied, if we thought we could get away with it. But instead of words, my head bent and I pressed my lips to hers. She tried to push me away, then her attempts grew feeble, her lips parted and she returned my kiss.

When we finally broke for air, I started to speak, but she placed her finger to my lips, hushing me. It was just as well, I had no idea what I wanted to say.

I bent my head again and sought out her mouth, her tongue with my own. The kiss was gentle at first, then grew urgent once again. The emotion we had both experienced this day: the battle; the grief; the guilt; it all merged into one. We shared each other's senses and everything melted into a want, a need for each other.

I pulled the shirt she still wore from her breeches, and hauled it over her head—barely breaking the kiss until the material caught her chin and lifted her lips away from mine. I quickly discarded my own shirt and my hands explored her bare skin, caressing her back, shoulders, arms, then moving to her sides. My hands at her waist slid upwards until I was caressing the sides of her breasts. Her breath hitched, then I felt her own hands exploring my shoulders, my arms, my chest.

I broke off and looked into her eyes, a question, did she want this? For answer she stretched her neck until we were once again lip to lip.

I cupped her breasts with my hands, her skin delightfully soft under my rope-worn leathery palms and I groaned. I could not remember the last time I had felt something so smooth and soft.

My thumbs circled her nipples and I gasped as they hardened under my touch. I realized I was losing control. It was too much. I had desired her for too long.

I fumbled at the ties to her breeches and she brushed my clumsy fingers away and deftly untied her knots, then mine.

I pulled her to stand, our lips not parting, and we stepped out of the remainder of our clothes, teeth clashing as we stumbled, the motion of the ship and the heavy beating of our hearts not aiding our balance.

In the back of my mind I realized we had set sail; the old ship had sunk or would soon, and we were on our way. I felt a pang of guilt at shirking the mountain of hard work that was no doubt waiting to be undertaken, then gently laid Magdalena on the cot.

I curled next to her in the narrow space and she shifted to face me, both of us lying on our sides, but it was not my face she was looking at. I grew harder under her direct gaze and ran my hand down her side, over the swell of her hips, then down.

As I explored her, she tensed and I paused, then she relaxed and parted her knees slightly. We both groaned, then I lifted myself up.

"Lie on your back." My voice was hoarse, cracking with need. I could not wait any longer.

I used my knee to nudge her thighs apart. Again she tensed before relaxing and I told myself to be gentle; this was no sailortown doxy, she was not used to this.

I positioned myself and looked into her eyes. One final question, although I doubt if I would have been able to stop had the answer been no. Very carefully, very gently, I pushed. Magdalena's eyes widened—in pain or surprise I did not know—then she closed them.

"Are you well?" I asked.

"Sí."

I carried on. *Gently, gently,* I told myself, but could not heed my own words. Soon, far too soon, I slumped on top of her. After a moment, she pushed me and I rolled to her side, taking my weight from her. She smiled at me, and I stroked her face.

"It will be better next time," I whispered.

"Better?"

"Aye, much better."

Chapter 31

"*Sail oh*," I roared down from my customary place on the maintop. "Two sail—looks like a fight!"

I squinted to make sure I was right in my identification of one of the ships. "*Freyja*!"

Below me, Tarr grabbed his glass and jumped into the ratlins to get a better view. I could hear his curse from my position forty feet above his head.

Two minutes later, Little swung onto my platform. "Cap'n wants you on the quarterdeck, Mr. Sharpe, sir."

I grinned at him, loving the fact that this man who had tried to cheat me now held me in such high regard to necessitate both a mister and a sir.

"Right you are, Little," I said, and slid down the backstay to join my uncle, hardly feeling the burn now.

"That damned Hornigold," Tarr fumed.

"What's wrong?" I was puzzled, Hornigold wasn't doing anything out of order to my mind. We both attacked any ship that caught our fancy. He held a Letter of Marque after all, giving him license to attack almost any ship at sea, so long as it wasn't English.

"*What's wrong*? That's a van Ecken ship! We took her a year ago! Van Ecken will kill us if he hears of this."

The elder van Ecken had died at sea not eight months ago. It was widely held to have been an accident, although I knew better. And I suspected everyone else did too. Erik van Ecken was even worse than his father, having not an ounce of compassion in his soul. I thought briefly of his wife, Gabriella, then pushed her out of my head. I could not bear to think of her married to that evil scum, but I could do nothing about it—yet.

"Maybe he hasn't recognized the ship?"

"Bollocks. This close to Sayba, flying Dutch colors? The ship could be no one else's. What's that bastard up to? *All hands, clear the decks*."

I winced as his words became a bellow.

"Ready the bow cannon. Make your course north-north-west," he shouted to the helmsman at the whipstaff below deck.

Our bow nosed to larboard, the sails were adjusted, and we headed directly toward the ongoing battle, the wind with us.

It took Hornigold longer than it should have to notice us, but when he did he fired a warning shot.

"Raise the colors," Tarr yelled. "And shoot back at that mangy cur!"

Our bow cannon boomed, its ball falling short of the warring ships. I realized that Hornigold hadn't recognized us in our new vessel, but surely flying a bloody flag on course for Sayba he would work out who we were? I glanced at Tarr and decided to keep my mouth shut. I had never seen him look so angry. In this mood, one push and he was likely to sink *Freyja* just for the hell of it.

"What's going on?" a feminine voice behind us asked.

"Get back to your cabin, out of the way, woman. We don't need your ill fortune on deck now."

I glared at Tarr, then turned to Magdalena and nodded toward her, indicating with my eyes for her to go back inside. Thank heaven she understood.

Freyja did nothing, and I could just imagine the confusion aboard her decks. Then she fired another broadside at the Dutch ship and I sighed in relief.

We drew closer and Tarr ordered the helmsman to bear up to starboard until our larboard side faced the battle.

"*Ready the guns.*"

"Er, which ship are we aiming for, Cap'n?" Gun Master Prince asked.

"I don't bloody care, just fire at them! That Dutch ship cannot be allowed to sail on, and if Hornigold is sunk as well, it's his own blasted fault."

"Aye, aye, Cap'n."

Within seconds, the gunports below us were opened and two stories of muzzles hauled out and aimed at the warring ships.

"*Fire.*"

The cacophony of a dozen cannon going off deafened me and, when the smoke cleared, I reckoned both ships had been hit.

"*Reload.*"

Freyja ceased fire on the Dutch ship and bore off to circle away.

"Get us broadside onto that prize. On my mark . . ."

We were sailing at a right angle to the two ships, just passing the prize's bows.

"Steady . . . steady . . . *Now*. Hard to larboard!"

Edelweiss swung around and men hauled on sheet and brace to keep the wind in our sails and the ship powering toward our prey.

"Make ready on the guns . . . *Fire*."

Again, a dozen great guns fired. This time, when the sulfurous airs had cleared, the prize was already low in the water.

"She's going down, make chase on *Freyja*. Make your course due west."

Chapter 32

"*Ready guns.*"

The crew stared at their captain.

"What are you waiting for? Jump to it, you lazy curs!"

"Uh . . . Captain."

Tarr turned and glared at me.

"They've fought alongside those men." No reaction, I tried again. "Your argument is with Hornigold, not the crew."

Tarr clenched his fists, released and clenched again, his knuckles white.

"We'll only fire if he fires on us," he said eventually. "Now, ready those guns, damn you."

The crew jumped to their tasks, hauling in cannon, sponging, reloading and finally heaving them back to their firing positions.

Freyja swung round and Tarr followed suit until both ships were sailing toward each other. I held my breath. On our current course, *Freyja* would pass by fifty yards to starboard. In a few moments we would be in range.

Tarr stood in the middle of the quarterdeck, legs apart, arms akimbo. I glanced at him; with his bright-red frockcoat, his hat, and the bloody flag above, surely Hornigold would recognize us. He came on, his own board bristling with gun muzzles.

"Gunner Prince, fire warning shot."

The decks were deathly silent, the crew exchanging glances and raised eyebrows. Not one man began the battle chant. Not one man brought his personal arms to bear.

The bow cannon boomed and *Freyja's* outer jib split. I held my breath.

I glanced at my uncle and the hard expression set on his face and for a fleeting moment felt pity for Hornigold and the Freyjamen.

"He's struck his colors!"

A cheer—more of reprieve than celebration—rang out and I

sighed as I watched Hornigold's bloody flag sink to the deck. His guns were drawn in and the relief on *Edelweiss's* deck was palpable.

I risked another glance at Tarr. He looked disappointed.

"Bring us alongside. Sharpe, Little, Prince, Dupont, Fitzroy, Grosvenor, Fortescue, prepare to board. Blake, you keep these guns trained on that slimy bastard—I don't trust him an inch."

Hornigold, perspiring through his shirt, awaited us on the quarterdeck, flanked by Cheval and Neville, his crew milling about and trying to appear unperturbed by the showdown between the captains.

I stepped up smartly from the longboat to ship and stood beside my uncle, hands at my belt, loaded pistols slung around my neck. I had to hurry to keep up with him as he strode aft to confront Hornigold.

"What by the gods of Hades did you think you were doing? That was van Ecken's ship!"

Hornigold shrugged. "She was heavily laden."

"What does that matter? Is your head that addled? Nobody crosses van Ecken and lives—he's a madman!"

"There were no survivors, if you hadn't joined us nobody would have known."

"No, just every damned sailor on this deck—each of whom only need a couple of pints of rum to loosen their tongues!"

Hornigold surveyed the deck then brought his eyes back up to meet Tarr's. "My men are loyal to me."

"Then they are fools!"

I glanced around at the angry faces of insulted men and inwardly winced. My eyes met those of Cheval and I squared my shoulders under his mocking gaze.

"I should flay you alive and string you up to the mainyards for the seabirds to feast. You're a bumbling fool and you've put every life on this deck at risk for your greed."

Tarr's face matched his frockcoat, his eyes bulged and spittle flew with each word. I had never seen a man so angry.

The men surrounding us shifted at Tarr's words, exchanging uneasy glances. Hornigold looked round at them and not one met his eye.

"You were instructed by van Ecken to sail with me—under *my* command. You've mutinied. You know what that means—keelhauling."

Hornigold crumbled. He knew as well as every other man aboard that no one survived being dragged under the ship aft to stern. Flesh ripped open by barnacles was an easy meal for the ever-present sharks; it was a blessing to drown. But he wasn't giving up yet.

"No. Morgan appointed me, Captain. I answer only to him."

"Aye," his men chorused, finally in support of their captain.

I thought Tarr would burst; his whole body clenched in his efforts to retain control. But Hornigold was right. Tarr sailed for van Ecken; Hornigold sailed for Henry Morgan. And no man in his right mind crossed Morgan, even if he was in his dotage.

"Very well. But *Freyja was* put under my command. Welcome your new quartermaster, my nephew, Sharpe."

"What?" Hornigold was startled.

"*Non*," Cheval protested, then quietened at a glare from Tarr. I kept my own lips sealed.

"I will also be changing your crew—half your men will sail aboard *Edelweiss* and I'll replace them with my own men. I'll leave it to you and Sharpe as to who stays."

Hornigold opened his mouth, but no words emerged. He cast his eyes to the deck, deflated of all protest. He knew he was getting off lightly. He may be under Morgan's protection; but Morgan wasn't here.

I glared at Tarr. Yes, I had received a promotion, but I did not want to sail with Hornigold. And what of Magdalena? My eyes narrowed as I realized he had neatly maneuvered his bad luck charm off his own decks.

Chapter 33

"Bear off, Cheval, we're supposed to be running with the wind."

He scowled at me and adjusted the tiller until the wind was due astern. I smiled. Hornigold was in his cabin making up the log. I had command of *Freyja*; and of Cheval.

I curled my arm around Magdalena's waist, knowing it would inflame Cheval further, then stroked her cheek, wishing we could retire immediately to our cabin, but knowing that was impossible while I had the quarterdeck. All thoughts of Cheval had fled my head.

I watched Magdalena retreat, skirts swishing, a sound and sight wholly incongruous to a privateer deck.

My grin turned to a grimace as I caught the sight of the boom heading toward my head. I dived to the deck to avoid being knocked overboard, but was not quick enough.

The sound of Magdalena's scream accompanied the burst of blackness and stars that thrust through my skull.

"Henry, *Henry*. Can you hear me?"

I tried to open my eyes, but they seemed glued together.

A cool dampness swept across them, my forehead, and my face. I tried again, but could only see blurred shapes.

I shut my eyes and squeezed them tight, then tried to re-open them. Blurry images confronted me. A brown haze—*the deckhead? Am I below decks? How did I get here?*

Then a pale orb floating before the brown.

I tried to concentrate, to focus. *What's that? Where am I? What happened?*

"Henry?"

I blinked, painfully, and the orb took on the features of a face. I continued to blink until I could recognize it.

"Magdalena?"

She threw herself on me, her words indistinguishable through her tears.

"What happened? What's wrong with my eyes?"

Another voice, a man's voice. "We caught a bad windshift. Cheval could do nothing. You were in the wrong place at the wrong time, the boom caught you in the face."

The memories came back to me: the quarterdeck; Magdalena's kiss; Cheval's smirk. Then the wooden spar swinging toward me; diving to the deck to avoid it. It seemed I had not been successful.

I put my hand to my face, but it was caught by a pale, dainty one.

"Henry, don't," Magdalena said, pulling my hand away.

"Why, what is it?"

No answer.

"What's wrong with my face?" I bellowed.

Magdalena sobbed.

After a moment, I heard Little's voice. "Quartermaster. Sharpe. Henry." My heart iced as he fought to find the correct moniker.

"Just tell me."

"You caught the boom full in your face. Thank God you were not knocked overboard."

"*Tell me,*" I shouted in frustration.

"Your nose—is broken. Maybe your cheekbone too. And your eye . . ."

I waited; he did not continue. I shook Magdalena's grip away and put my hand to my face. Over my right eye, I could see it. Indistinct and blurred, but I could see it. I moved my fingers across to the other side of my face. I could still see, but only my thumb and the tips of my fingers. I moved it back to my right, my left, right, left, right, left . . .

"Henry, I'm sorry." Magdalena's voice. "Your left eye is lost. I'm so sorry." She collapsed into sobs, draping herself across my chest. I made no move to comfort her.

My eye? My left eye? Gone? I shuddered. *I'm a sharpshooter and lookout, how can I do either now?*

I stared up at the deckhead with my one eye, the beams slowly—ever so slowly—taking shape before me. *How will I survive now? How will I survive aboard ship, in the Caribbees, with only one eye?*

Chapter 34

I winced at the glare of bright light in my remaining eye.

"Shut the blasted door!" I roared.

A swish of skirts announced my visitor. *Why would she not leave me be?*

She crossed to the stern gallery and tugged hard on the coverings I'd nailed to the wood.

"Damn and blast it, woman! Leave me be."

"Goddammit, Henry, you're not blind. You've lost an eye, yes, but only the one. Yet you sit in the dark and won't have candle or lantern lit. Enough."

I rose, grabbed the window coverings, and tore them from her grasp. I began the laborious task of hooking them on the nails by feel, the Caribbee sun so harsh on my eye it was squinted almost closed.

"You've sat in the dark a sennight. If you don't let light to your eye you'll lose the sight in that one too and spend the rest of your life in gloom."

I found another nail with my fingers, forced the cloth onto it and made no reply. I worked in silence and turned to her—just as a lantern flared into life.

"*Magdalena.* Devil's bones, woman, douse that light!"

She stood before the lantern, which at least dimmed its flare, but I would not be able to reach it without assaulting her. As I considered my options, she held something out to me. I stared. Well, half-stared.

"Cheval is out on those decks, prancing and swaggering. He loves that you've shut yourself away, he's calling you the sequestered quartermaster. You've become a joke." She proffered the object once more. "Take it, put it on."

I reached my hand and brushed my fingers against it. It was soft; velvet.

"It's an eyepatch. I took a scrap from the inside cuff of your frockcoat so they'll match. I think you'll look quite distinguished."

"Distinguished? Bah. I'll look like a blind cripple!"

"Oh, Madre de Dios. For the love of God, you're aboard a pirate ship! There's barely a man on that deck who isn't missing some part of his anatomy—and not one of them can carry off a patch or a hook or a pegleg the way you can. Now put it on!"

"Privateer."

"What?"

"Privateer ship, not pirate."

"Put. It. On."

Her words were issued through gritted teeth and I meekly took the scrap of material from her, the image of Cheval enjoying my plight finally calming me.

I fumbled with the ties, finding it difficult to guide my fingers until Magdalena took it from me and tied it around my head. Then she lifted my wig into place, made a small adjustment, and nodded.

"Do you want to see?"

I didn't have to be able to focus on her to know the words had been issued with an eyebrow raised in challenge.

For answer, I turned back to the window and tore down the curtains I had struggled to replace, blinked in the glare a few times and wiped tears from my cheeks. I stared at the moisture on my hand. My lost eye was still crying.

When I was ready, I turned and took the looking glass Magdalena held out to me. I stared for a while, trying to make sense of the image before me, then the lines and shapes became clear, the fuzziness lifted and I stared into my new face. I looked up at Magdalena and kissed her. "It'll do until I can fashion a leather one," I said, paused, then asked, "Prancing and swaggering?"

"Prancing and swaggering," she confirmed with a small smile.

"I'd best do something about that."

I crossed to the door, opened it and stepped into the Caribbean sun.

Chapter 35

The quarterdeck hushed as I strode onto it, the crews pausing in their tasks to stare. I resisted the urge to put my hand to my face and adjust the velvet eyepatch, and straightened my back instead.

"Captain." I greeted Hornigold with a nod. He dipped his own head in acknowledgement but uttered not a word.

I heard a rustle behind me and knew Magdalena was at my back, and I was grateful she was letting me take the lead in front of the men after her forceful ejection of me from the cabin.

I continued forward, my eye fixed on Cheval. He had not noticed my reappearance, nor the anxious glances his audience shot my way as the Frenchman doubled up, clutching his face—no doubt re-enacting my "accident" for the benefit of his fellows.

He fell to the deck in parody then silenced on noticing me. I drew my cutlass and directed it toward his throat.

"On your feet, Cheval. You and I have a score to reckon. I demand restitution."

He scrabbled upright, clumsy but quick, and glanced about him, but his mates had melted back at the glimpse of steel.

The Frenchman raised his hands as if to ward me off and I gestured for him to raise them further—his left hand was far too close to the hilt of his own cutlass for my liking.

"It was accident," he whined. "*Accident.*"

I grimaced at the deterioration of his English, something that always marked his play-acting portrayal of a victim.

"That was no accident, Cheval, and you know it as well as I. I intend to make reparation for the injury you have occasioned."

"Reparation? What is *reparation*? I no understand."

"You understand all too well, you scurvy French dog. Reparation—recompense—vengeance—making good a loss. You cost me an eye, I will take both of yours as my price!"

I made to lunge forward, the tip of my blade mere inches from his face and was halted by Hornigold's shout of, "*Sharpe.*"

I took my time to turn to him, instead smirking at Cheval backing away from me, his blade now drawn.

"Captain," I acknowledged.

"You know the law, Sharpe, you signed the articles. Any grievances to be settled ashore, not aboard. I'm not having the two of you cutting up my decks and rigging while you chase each other round like rats in a barrel."

I forced my jaw to relax, then nodded.

"Very well. A duel, with pistols, ashore. Make for land, Captain, this vessel will not sail smoothly until this is settled."

"Ah. What good will you be in a duel? You've only the one eye, you'll not be able to see me, never mind shoot me!"

I advanced toward him, my blade still threatening. "Even blindfolded I can shoot better than you, dog." I spat in his face. "Nothing's wrong with *my* aim, how's yours?"

Silence.

Slowly, I sheathed my blade, nodded to Hornigold—although I did not miss the expression of alarm on his face—proffered my arm to Magdalena and sauntered back to the cabin.

"Can you really shoot better blindfolded than he can?"

"I'll have to by the time we go ashore, Magdalena, I'll have to. Fetch me as many pistols as you can find, I have to sharpen my skills before I truly find my aim like this."

Her face paled and I squeezed her arm. "That French weasel will *not* get the better of Henry Sharpe. I promise you that."

Chapter 36

"*Land oh.*"

"Henry." Magdalena shook me awake. "Henry, it's time."

I grunted and rolled over, hoping she would think me still asleep. I stared at the planks of the bulkhead, my eye focusing on the knots in the wood, and considered the day ahead.

I had spent the past three days in the cabin, throwing empty casks and other jetsam off the stern for target practice. My aim was not true. I was not the man I had once been. I had very little chance of hitting Cheval with lead ball, but even less at beating him by sword. I would not win this duel. Not with only half my sight.

"Henry," Magdalena called again, pulling me over to my back.

"Calm yourself, Magdalena, I'm awake."

She looked at me for a moment and my heart missed a beat at the fear I saw in her eyes. "Are you ready?"

I pulled my face into a smile. "As ready as I'll ever be." I tried to immerse my words in confidence, but immediately realized I had fooled neither her nor myself.

"You can do this, Henry. You will win, you have to." She bent to kiss me and I savored the feel of her lips, the taste of her tongue. This may be the last time I would hold her in my arms.

I grew aware of wetness on my face and could not tell if the tear was hers or mine. I pulled away from her embrace and climbed out of the cot, my back to her. "This is not goodbye, stop that sniveling. I need all my wits about me this morn."

I heard the breath catch in a sob in her throat, but refused to turn or offer her comfort. I pulled on my breeches and tied them around my waist, then pulled a clean shirt over my head.

I turned to pick up my frockcoat and paused. I thrust my arms into the proffered sleeves and allowed Magdalena to arrange it over my shoulders and fuss with my collar.

I spun round and pulled her harshly into my arms, burying my face in her hair. This time there was no doubt as to the proprietor of the tears on my cheek. I pulled away and caressed her jaw. "Magdalena . . ."

"Hush. Tell me once it's all over."

"But—"

She pressed fingers to my lips and shook her head with a small smile. "I love you, Henry."

"And I you." I drew her close again, then gathered my wits and let go.

She passed me my eyepatch and wig and I arranged each perfectly before taking a deep breath and letting it whoosh out of me.

My eye drew back to Magdalena and I opened my mouth to speak but could find no words. She nodded in understanding then motioned toward the door. "It's time."

I raised my hand and clasped hers briefly, then turned and walked out to the deck.

Hornigold's face was almost comical in the speed it fell when he saw me.

I raised my eyebrows at him. "You seem surprised to see me on deck, Captain. Did you expect me to renege?"

He recovered his senses. "No one would blame you if you did, Sharpe. No one in his right mind would challenge another to a duel with your particular—misfortune—still so fresh. You would not lose face if you backed out."

"I have lost enough of my face to that cove. This duel goes ahead. Where are the boats?"

"Ashore. They'll pull back to *Freyja* shortly."

I nodded and walked to the rail to have a look at the sand. I wondered if it was about to become my grave. It looked like any other in this godforsaken sea. Two of *Freyja's* three boats were pushing out through the surf. One of them would be my hearse.

I grew aware of Magdalena standing beside me but she said nothing. Her presence so close was all I needed.

The first boat bumped against the hull and I finally turned to her. "You stay aboard *Freyja*."

"*No*. Henry, I want to be with you!"

"I cannot be distracted and I will not have you witness my death. You stay aboard *Freyja*."

Her mouth opened, closed, opened again before she snapped it shut, gritted her teeth and nodded. I gave her a curt nod in return then made my way to the gate in the rail and climbed down to the boat. Little nodded at me in greeting, but no man spoke and we headed out through the waves to the beach in silence.

I turned, once, to catch Magdalena's eye, raised my arm in a wave, then focused my attention ahead.

Chapter 37

I waded through the surf, the chatter on the beach diminishing as I approached the huddle of men. A number of them nodded to me or grasped my arm in a show of support. Others looked away.

I took a deep breath; even the air felt tense. As one, the crew drifted up the beach and formed two lines about twenty yards apart. I took my place at one end of the space left between them and waited for Cheval. No doubt he had a big entrance planned. I squared my shoulders and lifted my chin high. No matter what occurred here today, I would meet my death with courage and pride. I could do nothing about the pounding of my heart, so concentrated on my breathing; keeping it measured and deep. I would not show Cheval or any member of this crew an ounce of fear.

My nerves turned to irritation as the men grew restless. Coin changed hands and their whispers grew loud enough for me to realize that they were not wagering on my death, but on Cheval's absence.

I cleared my throat, praying my nerves would not tell in my voice. "Put me down for a sovereign, Little, Cheval's liver is too yellow for this."

"Aye, aye, Quartermaster Sharpe, that I'll do with pleasure."

The men roared with laughter and their formerly rigid line began to blur and disperse.

I turned to glance at Hornigold. He stood arms akimbo, staring at me, a smirk on his face, and I knew Cheval had gone. I remembered there had only been two boats ferrying the last of the crew ashore; Hornigold had given the third to Cheval. I staggered as my legs trembled and a strong arm checked my stumble.

"It appears this is your day after all, Sharpe," Little whispered in my ear before clouting my shoulder. I could only nod in response. Cheval had run.

* * *

"What the Devil's going on here?"

I turned in surprise at Tarr's voice and spotted *Edelweiss* at anchor near *Freyja*.

"And what the Devil's happened to your eye, boy?"

I glanced at Hornigold, who had turned pale, his black bushy eyebrows even more out of place against milky skin.

Tarr rushed at him, fist flying, and knocked him to the sand. What in Hell have you done to my nephew, Hornigold? I'll have your neck for this."

He swung his fist and Hornigold's nose spurted blood.

"Captain," I called. "It was *Cheval*."

Tarr spat onto Hornigold's bloody face, "Cheval? Nothing that man does is without the approval of this dog." He pulled his arm back again, only for Blake to catch it. "Captain! Tarr," he urged, "let him be, he's the wrong man."

Tarr's physique visibly shrunk and he allowed Blake and Little to pull him away. Hornigold scrambled to his feet, wiping his face with his sleeve.

"'Twas an accident, Tarr, an unlucky windshift on a dead run."

"Hmpf," Tarr grunted, all he needed to convey his disbelief, and Hornigold cast his eyes to the sand in supplication.

"Sharpe, get to my boat, we'll ferry you to *Freyja* to collect your belongings then transfer back to *Edelweiss*."

I nodded and hurried to the water's edge with half a dozen men in tow while Tarr turned back to Hornigold.

"If you cross me again or sail off on your own, I will scour the Carib Sea, sink that blasted tub, and hang you from the yardarm for mutiny."

Hornigold remained staring at the sand and did not react; the calm menace in Tarr's voice having far more impact than his normal rant.

"The rest of you remember that—if your *captain*," he spat the word, "sails off course once more, he will have signed all your death warrants."

The men muttered amongst themselves, but none spoke up.

Tarr leaned into Hornigold again. "Take note of my words, Ed, and heed my orders. If you don't, you had better pray your crew has some sense and throws you overboard before I kill every last man."

Hornigold nodded.

"What was that, man? Speak up!"

"Aye, aye, Captain."

Tarr pressed his lips together, met every eye on the beach, then turned and walked to join me in the boat. I wondered if he realized he had just redeployed Magdalena to his decks.

August 1685
Chapter 38

"*Ready the guns.*"

I hurried out of the cabin, Magdalena right behind me, and cast my eyes to larboard then starboard. A Spanish merchantman, fully laden by the looks of her, was down to leeward, hastily erecting boarding nets, whilst *Freyja* was readying her own guns just off our stern. Hornigold had given us no problems since the debacle on the beach a year ago, and had proved himself a worthy consort—at least for the moment.

"What the—"

I took a deep breath at Tarr's exclamation. I had tried to talk Magdalena out of this, but she could be too damn willful for her own good, never mind mine.

"Get the *hell* out of those clothes, woman."

"I will not sit by in the cabin through another fight, wondering if their next ball will be coming through my wall." She stamped her foot to accentuate her words, but Tarr's color only rose higher.

"You shouldn't even be on this ship, woman! You will *not* be a part of my fight."

"She's an excellent shot, Captain," I ventured, driven to protect Magdalena from my uncle's scorn. "She can join Little in the tops, I'm not much good up there now."

"The *tops*? A woman in my rigging? Are you out of your mind, man?" He inflicted the full force of his glare onto Magdalena, thrusting a pointed finger at her with every word. "Get back into that cabin and into a gown!" He turned to me. "And you, Sharpe, get up to that maintop. You're a damn sight better shot than you think you are—and you're getting better with every battle." Back to Magdalena. "Are you still here? Get back to that cabin." He thrust his arm out so suddenly Magdalena flinched. "Or I'll heave you overboard myself for your mutiny. See how you get on fighting the sharks."

Magdalena turned and fled. I moved to go after her, but Tarr grabbed my arm. “Oh no you don’t, boy. Get aloft!”

Seething at the “boy”, I nonetheless hurried over to the ratlins to begin my climb. I had seen Magdalena pause at the cabin door; seen the glare of hate; and knew there would be trouble ahead.

Chapter 39

"I can't stay aboard this blasted ship," Magdalena shouted when I joined her in the cabin after another prize had been successfully taken.

"That uncle of yours hates me. He demeans me at every turn and would prefer I never left this cabin."

I took hold of her shoulders in an attempt to calm her down.

"Hush, Magdalena, calm yourself."

"Calm myself? How can I be calm? I'm naught but a prisoner on this ship! This is not the adventure I had in mind."

I had grown exasperated with her and her arguments. We'd had this discussion many times since we had re-joined *Edelweiss*.

"This is a privateer ship—you know well that women are not made welcome aboard, most of the crew share Tarr's superstition. These men put their very lives in danger every day we're at sea. If not for Tarr and myself, you'd have been used and thrown overboard or worse for bringing bad fortune to these decks."

"What bad fortune? What is it I've caused?" Tears of frustration poured down her cheeks.

"I know well you have done nothing, but every accident, every injury, every problem is laid at your feet. The men need someone to blame for anything that goes wrong."

"And that someone is me?"

"Aye, I'm afraid it is. The safest place for you is in here, out of sight and mind. Many women have met far worse fates on the deck of a ship than sailing in luxury."

"Sailing in luxury? You jest, surely? Bare floors, bare walls, a cot for a bed, and a great gun for company! This is hardly luxury, Henry."

"So what do you suggest? If you don't like it, stay ashore next time we make land—maybe you'll find the adventure you seek there."

"But where would we go? What would we do?"

"We? I made no mention of we. Look at me, Magdalena." I spread my arms wide, displaying my bloodied shirt and torn breeches. "I'm a sailor now. A one-eyed privateer. Shore holds no sanctuary for me now. My place is here, aboard ship. You are welcome to keep my company, but do not forget, you are here of your own volition."

"That's not true." She stamped her foot in her rage. "Hornigold brought me aboard—I did not make my own way here."

"We both know the falsity of that, Magdalena. You said yourself you were looking for adventure, and you thought you could find it here. Well, this is as adventurous as it gets for a woman in the Caribbees—a woman who is not a doxy, at least."

She slapped my face and I put a palm to my stinging cheek, then sighed and sat on the bunk, my head in my hands.

"I have kept you safe from the first day you stepped on *Freyja's* deck. Do you have any idea of what would have befallen you had I not been present?"

She cast her eyes to the floor.

"The only way I can keep you safe is in this cabin away from Tarr and the rest of them."

She sighed and joined me on the cot. "I should never have left Porto Belo."

"No, nor betrayed your fiancé."

She buried her face in her hands. "What have I done? Oh Mother Mary, what have I done?"

I put my arm around her and pulled her close as she sobbed and sighed, tears threatening my own eye. I could think of no solution to this predicament.

September 1685
Chapter 40

"*Sail oh*. Triple-master. Looks a beauty," Little called from the tops.

"Where away?" Blake bellowed from the quarterdeck.

"A deuce of leagues ahead."

"Colors?"

"None."

"Clear the decks. Ready the guns."

"Blake?" Tarr had joined his quartermaster on deck.

"Triple-master ahead, Captain."

"Merchant?"

"Don't know, she's flying no colors."

Tarr frowned. "Well, we'd better see what she's about then, Blake. But show caution, I want to know what we're up against."

"Aye, aye, Captain."

Everyone on deck held their breath as the ship drew closer. The wind blew amidships to each vessel and this was a test of nerve. We still had no idea who or what the other vessel was, but if we could get close enough before hardening up and taking the wind advantage, she would be ours. Trouble was, we could not make our move too soon; she would be at maximum range of our guns, still bow on and a hard target to hit. Also, a change of course too precipitant would mean presenting a larger target of our own larboard to her and make our stern and steering vulnerable should she be heavily armed.

"Dammit!" Tarr and Blake cursed together as the other ship headed up to take the weather gage, and finally showed her colors—a square of black silk. Pirates or fellow privateers. Whoever they were, we had a fight on our hands.

"Bear off, fire when ready," Tarr bellowed as the ship fired all her starboard cannon at us.

I ducked as small ball flew above. *What's going on? Why are they firing partridge shot at our rigging? Surely there could be no advantage in taking our ship as opposed to our plunder. Do they really think we would ask for quarter?*

"What are you still doing on the quarterdeck, Sharpe? Get aloft."

I nodded to Blake and rushed to the ratlins to begin my swarm. I glanced at the cabin door and breathed a sigh of relief. Magdalena had stayed put. This promised to be a close fight; for once I was glad of Tarr's edict that she stayed off deck—however fierce the tantrum later.

I emptied my last musket and had no choice but to reload—there was no room for Billy and his nimble fingers up here with two of us braced on the maintop. I grabbed hold of the mast as *Edelweiss* rocked with the force of another direct hit and shared a glance with Little. Both ships were taking a lot of damage.

"Harden up. *Harden up,* damn you!"

Our course did not change and I glanced astern at the helmsman shrugging his shoulders and shaking his head.

I squinted my eye and spotted a longboat just aft; they must have jammed the rudder.

As I watched, the longboat drew closer again and one of her men stood and hallooed at our stern. My brow furrowed. *Why's he trying to attract attention?* Then my heart plummeted. *Magdalena.*

I dropped the musket I was loading and leaped for the backstay, ignoring Little's shout of "*Sharpe*!"

I landed hard and ran for the cabin, wrenching the door open just in time to see Magdalena's skirts as she jumped from the ledge to the waters below.

"Magdalena! No!" I screamed and rushed to the rail.

She surfaced, spitting water and flailing to stay afloat. Already, *Edelweiss* was leaving her behind; even if I jumped myself, I would not reach her in time and would no doubt drown myself. I screamed, "*Man overboard,*" but no one could hear me over the guns.

Shots rang out above me and I shouted at them to hold their fire, then called Magdalena's name again as she was caught in the disturbed water of our wake and pulled under once more.

A man jumped from our stern and I looked at him, then the transom in surprise. Yes, chocks had been driven in between the rudder and hull. I couldn't think about that, though, and strained my eye to find Magdalena. I called her name again—she was weakening, her saturated gown heavy. The man reached her, and I thanked the Lord he was a swimmer; probably why he'd been chosen to sabotage our rudder.

"Hold your blasted fire, damn you!" I shouted as shots continued to rain down, but no one paid heed and I could only stare aghast as Magdalena was hit time and again. She convulsed and the water around her turned pink. She was gone.

I screamed insults at my crewmates, then shouted again as Uncle Richard fell, his body hitting the rail as he went, nearly taking me with him.

I had no voice left. No words. No nothing. Everybody who meant something to me was dead. My mother and father, Jonesy, Magdalena, now Tarr. I was on my own.

I glared at the longboat, trying to make out the features of the men inside. They were hauling Magdalena in, but it was clear she was gone. The man I had noticed standing in the boat earlier looked furious, berating the other men, and suddenly I knew who he was. Leo Santiago; Magdalena's childhood sweetheart; the man she had run from to look for adventure.

He lived after all and his attempt at rescuing her had resulted in her death. I swore I would avenge her.

Chapter 41

I raced back onto deck. I needed my muskets.

Chaos reigned; Blake screamed orders, but with Tarr newly dead, not many appeared to realize Blake was now their captain.

I climbed to the tops quickly, where Little passed me a loaded musket. He gave me a small nod, but didn't speak. I was grateful, what was there to say? I had just witnessed the murders of my uncle and my lover.

I focused astern to see Blake bodily hauling a man to the rail before forcing him over. *What's he thinking?* The stern was taking a heavy pounding from Santiago's ship and I realized the fate of the unfortunate sailor when Blake forced another to follow. As brutal as it seemed, I realized Blake was doing the only thing he could to save the ship and crew. Without steerage, we were all dead.

I turned my attention to the longboat and fired. Short. They were too far away. Still without a word, Little and I reloaded our cache of muskets. *Edelweiss* was badly damaged. That ship would not just sail away now. This was a fight to the death.

I dropped the last musket I was loading as a cannon fired and *Edelweiss* shuddered. The gun clattered to the deck and I saw men scattered on the poop deck; far too many remained still. The stern was in pieces—now mere splinters and shards of wood.

Blake stood and stared around him, looking lost.

"We've lost the rudder," I told Little.

"Aye. And that damned ship's wearing round to finish the job."

I glanced up and saw he was right. It took time for a triple-master to turn, even with the wind, but she had no reason to hurry; we weren't going anywhere.

"She's disengaging. Look, she's hardening up again!"

"*What?*" I shared Little's confusion and scanned the horizon. "*Freyja*! It's Hornigold!" I bellowed the news to the deck below, and the remaining crew all but slumped to the deck in relief.

Little and I clasped hands, our mouths stretched wide. For the first time, I was overjoyed to see that scoundrel.

Chapter 42

"So what do you have to say for yourselves?"

Bellies full, the relaxed and somber mood from the dining room broken, Blake, Prince, Hornigold and myself all shifted in our chairs and glanced around the room. No one looked at Erik van Ecken.

"Tarr is dead. He was the only competent one of the lot of you and you allowed him to be killed."

"He was a good captain. A good captain is always to be found in the thick of the fight."

"Shut up, Hornigold. I do not know why you are here. You were Morgan's man, now irrelevant."

"Aye, it's true Morgan has swallowed the anchor . . ." Blake started.

"Swallowed the anchor? What does that mean? Speak English for God's sake!"

Blake took a breath, then tried again. "Morgan is no longer a man of power or influence—in Jamaica or London."

"Exactly. He is nothing, an old man living out his days in comfort and boredom," van Ecken interrupted. "So why is his man here?"

Blake glanced at Hornigold, who was only containing himself with great difficulty.

"Hornigold has proved himself. *Edelweiss* and *Freyja* work well together. If not for Hornigold, *Edelweiss* would have been lost and most if not all of her crew with her."

Van Ecken grunted. "I have been hearing rumors. Rumors that a certain twinmaster flying a red flag has attacked a number of my ships."

"Sailortown is full of rumor, Mijnheer van Ecken," Hornigold replied. "Gossip is a sailor's vice, especially when coupled with rum and the dice." He stared at van Ecken and I could barely believe the audacity of the man. He had no shame when it came to gainsaying.

"Hmpf. Very well, but if I find out there is any truth to the rumor, you will spend your last days in my cage."

Hornigold paled. He had seemingly succeeded in his ploy, but we all knew van Ecken would not hesitate to carry out his threat. We had seen many a man locked in that tiny cage over the years. Unable to move or defend himself as he thirsted and starved to death; his sight taken by birds who did not have the patience to wait for his death before helping themselves to the delicacy; his skin erupting in sores under the unrelenting sun; and tormented by flies.

The silence stretched out until van Ecken felt he had made his point.

"How many men *were* lost?"

"Twenty seven," Blake answered. "Twenty seven, all good men and true."

"And how do you plan to replace them?"

"We will reorganize both Edelweissers and Freyjamen to crew both ships as effectively as possible, then force new topmen and gunners from prizes."

"And how will you control Hornigold?"

Blake glanced nervously at his fellow captain, whose face had flushed bright red at van Ecken's manner. "Hornigold will not cause any problems. He is loyal to me and will sail with Sharpe as his quartermaster."

"*What*? Now wait a minute, Blake . . ."

I glanced at van Ecken; he appeared amused at Hornigold's outburst.

Blake turned to me and raised his eyes to stare at my face. "You are Tarr's nephew, Sharpe, your presence aboard Edelweiss is disruptive. You sail with Hornigold."

I nodded, resigned. I had expected this. Blake did not command the respect Tarr had enjoyed on the deck of *Edelweiss*. Captains were elected by their crews and many of the crew had passed comment that *I* should have succeeded my uncle as captain. Blake knew he had to get rid of me before I garnered enough support to challenge him and take his position.

I was relieved he had chosen this recourse and not sent me

overboard during a quiet dog watch.

"Ahh, poor Sharpe, lost his place, his uncle and his whore. Welcome aboard the *Freyja*. And you'll have to be *elected* quartermaster."

Blake quietened Hornigold with, "He will be."

"What do you mean? What's happened to Magdalena?"

The men fell silent and I gasped. *How long had Gabriella been in the room?* I stood and walked over to her. She and Magdalena had met on a number of occasions and, although not natural friends, they had got on well. Probably because each was the only woman the other encountered on a regular basis. Apart from the slaves of course.

"I'm so sorry, Mevrouw van Ecken. I'm afraid she was killed on our last voyage."

"No," she whispered and I caught her as her legs gave way beneath her. "No."

"Get your damned filthy hands off my wife, Sharpe. I've warned you before."

I glanced at van Ecken, sure my contempt for him was clear on my face. He made no move toward his wife and I risked a quick look at Gabriella, pleased to see her small nod before I let her go. She made her unsteady way to a spare seat and van Ecken shouted for Klara, her slave, to tend her.

I retook my own seat, glancing between husband and wife, hardly daring to think about the reality of her life as this man's wife. My gaze lingered a moment on her chest and the amethyst that rested there before van Ecken again claimed my attention.

"You hold far too much interest in my wife than is healthy, Sharpe. You'll bed Klara tonight—that should take your mind off her, eh?" He slapped the African woman's behind, hard.

"You are all guests tonight," he continued. "I'll find bed partners for you all. I have more plans to impart to you, but they'll wait for the morn—and clear heads." He was joined in his laughter by Hornigold and Prince. Blake did not appear amused.

I risked a glance at the women. Gabriella looked horrified, and was in danger of losing her battle with tears. She would not look at me. Klara's gaze was steady: haughty and resigned. I gave her a small smile to reassure her. She did not yet know it, but she would be safer tonight than, no doubt, any other night she had spent in this house. I had already lost everyone I cared about, I would not inflict any suffering on this woman. Her world was cruel enough.

My gaze flickered back to Gabriella, and I realized I did still have someone I cared about.

I shuddered anew at the thought of her married to the beast that was Erik van Ecken, and I resolved to do anything I could to improve her lot in life. And if I could take my reckoning on Leo Santiago as well, so much the better.

* * * * *

Ill Wind

Part 1
31st May 1683

Chapter 1

"What do you think he wants, Mam?"

"I don't know, Gabriella." Mam frowned at me. "Just hear him out and don't react. You know how he hates it when you answer back."

"But he's never summoned us to work before!" Father was the chief customs officer in charge of all shipping in and out of Massachusetts Bay, and was very proud of his position—nobody could trade in the colony without his consent. He usually forbade us from bothering him at the docks, although that was no hardship—the sheltered water there stank with all the waste thrown overboard from anchored ships, and turned my stomach, although it would be worse in a couple of hours when the sun warmed and rotted the putrid filth.

"Very well," I agreed.

We looked at each other, worried, and Mam reached up to tuck a wayward curl behind my ear, then gave me a nervous smile.

"Elizabeth!" Father called. I smiled back at Mam; everybody but Father called her Ellie.

"About time. I want you to meet Mijnheer van Ecken." He presented the tall, distinguished-looking gentleman standing by his side. Father hadn't looked at me yet, but this stranger hadn't taken his eyes off me since our arrival. I looked back at him. He didn't smile; neither did I.

"And this—" Father said with a flourish, "is my beloved daughter, Gabriella."

I jerked my eyes away from the stranger and stared at Father in shock. He'd never described me as beloved before, never mind introduced me as such. I glanced at Mam; her normally rosy cheeks had turned pale. I tried to swallow, but my mouth was dry. *What's happening here?*

"She'll do." The stranger, Mr. van Ecken, spoke for the first time, and my eyes darted back to him. He still didn't smile.

"John?" Mam asked, warily.

"Great news, Elizabeth, I've procured for our beloved daughter—" that word again "—a most suitable match. Mijnheer van Ecken here is one of the West Indies' most successful merchants, and his son, Erik, is looking for a bride."

Mam gasped and turned paler still. I just stood there. Had Father said bride?

"You must remember my mentioning Mijnheer van Ecken," Father continued, oblivious to our reactions. "He's one of my best customers." He laughed, slapping Mr. van Ecken on the shoulder. The man attempted a smile, but it failed.

"He has done us a great service by selecting Gabriella as his son's bride, and this is the start of a very lucrative partnership between our families."

I looked at him and cringed at the delight on his face. I knew I should say something, but nothing came to mind. *Bride? West Indies? Married?* But I was to marry Peter! We'd been talking about it for ages, Father knew that. My breath hitched in my throat and I pressed my hand to my chest, trying to stop the panting—all of a sudden I found it hard to catch any air. He couldn't do this. He would *not*.

"John, no—" Mam tried.

"Elizabeth!" Father reprimanded, and Mam said nothing more, just stared at the ground. We both knew he didn't like to be contradicted, especially in public. Our arguments would have to wait until we were in private, and I shuddered at the thought of the scene to come.

"Mijnheer van Ecken has been more than generous and Gabriella will want for nothing in her new home in Sayba. She should be pleased."

New home? Sayba? Where on earth is Sayba? I looked at Mam, stepping back in my panic, but she stared at the ground, too used to doing Father's bidding.

"Stay where you are, Gabriella, it's all agreed, so calm yourself and do as you're told. You're flushed, you know that makes you ugly—all those freckles! You will marry Erik van Ecken and be a good wife to him—be ready to sail on the tide."

That's three hours away. I looked at his eyes. Dark and wrinkled from working outdoors, there was no emotion there. He'd sold me to a stranger, was packing me off to God knew where, and he felt nothing.

"John!" Mam exclaimed, her shock overriding her fear. "You can't, it's too soon, she's only fourteen!"

"Elizabeth!" Father thundered, his square jaw set, and I knew it was only the stranger's presence that stayed his fist. "I've made my decision." He glared at her, and her shoulders slumped in resignation. I gritted my teeth in frustration. *Why can't she stand up to him? Why can't she stand up for me?*

Tears rolled down my face—of anger, frustration, despair. I wondered when they would stop.

Chapter 2

Mam had been incapable of words since Father had silenced her at the docks. I looked at her in frustration; she was my mam, she should be standing up for me, not breaking down like this and allowing Father to do what he wanted with me.

I'd packed my few belongings myself, breaking off frequently to comfort her, but had finally finished.

"What's going to happen to me?" I whispered.

She shook her head. "Just do as your husband instructs and make the best life you can—it's all you can do."

"Maybe I should run away."

"Oh, Gabriella, where would you go? What would you do? A worse life awaits you if you flee. You have to do as your father instructs!" She opened her arms and I fell into her embrace. She stroked my hair and I knew I'd have a devil of a job to tame my wild, dark curls back into some sort of order. I shrugged. *What do I care about that, now?*

A knock at the door jolted us apart. I opened it to one of Father's wharfmen.

"It's time," he said.

I nodded at him. He sounded upset as well. He came in, picked up my small chest, and we followed him. Mam was still crying. My own tears had dried. I couldn't believe I had to leave her and all I knew, to live with a stranger as his wife. I still didn't know what that would entail.

We walked through the Massachusetts Bay Colony in silence. I wanted to run, but heeded Mam's warning. There was nothing outside the colony, just wilderness with all its dangers—unless I ran to the sea, and I could see no way of doing that.

Past the meeting house, the small wooden cottages of our neighbors, fields full of crops, woodlots and pasture. My heart leapt when I saw Peter. We'd known each other since we were babes and were best friends, but Mam's hand on my arm stayed me and I could only stare until I'd left him behind.

"Gabriella." Mam stopped and grabbed my arm. Words failed her again and, sobbing, she stretched her arms behind her neck and unfastened her necklace. I'd never known her take it off before.

"Your father gave me this—your true father," she said, "the earl." Mam had been a housemaid he'd taken a fancy to, then shipped off to the New World when she—or rather her belly—had become too much trouble. She'd met John Berryngton on the passage out.

She fastened the necklace around my neck and I looked down at the purple teardrop of amethyst, then held it up to the light. My own tears started to fall again and Mam hugged me.

"Get a move on! The tide won't wait for you!" We sprang apart at Father's words and Mam kissed me, then we continued our walk toward the docks—toward my future. I watched Father stride ahead and felt a glimmer of hope. My future could only be an improvement on my past.

He was there, my soon-to-be father-in-law; looking at his pocket watch, clearly impatient. He stooped slightly and wore a gray curled periwig over a face full of angles—nose, cheekbones, jaw. His clothes were of good quality, although of a cut that was unfamiliar, just like his accent—Dutch I assumed from his name, but nobody had bothered to confirm it.

"About time," he snapped. "The tide's about to turn, we need to on it be."

"Yes, yes, she's ready," Father said. "Take her chest to that longboat," he added to the wharfman. I watched him obey, though he avoided my eyes as he took everything I could call my own away from my home. I knew I'd have to follow. I turned to Mam and hugged her. I had no words, and joined her in sobs.

"Gabriella!" Father pulled me away. "It's time to go. Don't embarrass me, the van Eckens are important merchants. Don't forget you're representing this family! Now go."

"No!" I tried to wrench myself free of him. "I won't and you can't—" His slap made me stumble before I'd finished my protest and I huddled on the ground, shocked. I raised my hand to my stinging cheek, but he grabbed my arm again and hauled me to my feet, then pushed me toward the boat.

"Goodbye, Gabriella," Mam managed through her sobs. "Keep well and safe."

I ignored her. Even now she wouldn't fight for me. I turned at Mr. van Ecken's hand on my other arm, and allowed him to lead me to the boat. *What else can I do?*

I looked out at the bay and the ships anchored there. *Which one will take me away?* I turned. "Mam!" I cried, and almost fell when Mr. van Ecken pulled me into the boat.

By the time we'd left the wharf, I'd calmed. Mam and Father were still visible on the quayside, but they were small now—far away. I was sure Mam was still crying, and shuddered. Father hated tears; Mam would not have a pleasant afternoon, or evening.

I watched Father grab her arm and pull her away, dragging her back to the house like a naughty child. I sighed and twisted on my seat to look ahead.

I looked up at the bulk of the ship we'd approached. I'd never been aboard one before but had spent hours watching them arrive and leave Massachusetts Bay, dreaming I was sailing away in one of them. My wish was about to come true. I'd just never imagined these circumstances. *What will become of me?*

The boat bumped alongside the larger vessel and a rope was thrown down to us. I stood up.

"Not yet, stay where you are, I'll tell you when to stand," Mr. van Ecken snapped. I sat back down. I had no fight left in me.

"Now, come here and on this sit," he said a few moments later. I looked at him in surprise at his strange English, but supposed I'd get used to it.

A wooden plank, held by rope at either end, had been lowered to us. I looked at the basic seat, then at the hull, and pointed at the battens nailed onto the side like a ladder. "I'd rather use those," I said.

"You'll do as you're told! Your father told me you obedient were, though I have not much evidence of that seen. Be warned—I do not tolerate disrespect."

I looked at him in dislike, but I didn't want to go back to Father, whatever that might mean for my future. I sat on the wooden seat and allowed myself to be hauled up the side.

A thin bald man with the most startling black eyebrows I'd ever seen offered me a hand to step onto the deck.

"Greetings, Mistress Berryngton," he said, kissing my hand. "Welcome aboard *Freyja*, I'm Captain Edward Hornigold."

"Enough of that, Hornigold, get this tub moving, I don't time to waste have."

Captain Hornigold nodded and smiled at me before walking away, shouting. His men scurried around the decks.

"This way," van Ecken barked at me, and I followed him to a hole in the deck and below. I clambered down the ladder and kept following him—I think toward the back of the boat. I was nervous, my belly twisting. *What does he expect of me? Am I really to marry his son, or was that a ruse?*

Light flooded over us when he opened a door, and he stood aside for me. I walked into a cabin—a bank of windows in the back wall provided the light. There was a bunk, table and chair, my chest, and an African woman.

"This is Klara. She's yours to do with as you will. Here." He gave me a small silver-handled whip. "You might need this to remind her of that, though." He turned and left. I looked at the woman in shock, but she kept her eyes on the floor.

"Hello," I said tentatively. No reaction. A shudder made me step to one side as the floor moved beneath my feet, and I braced myself against the wall. We were off.

Chapter 3

I looked at the whip in my hand. It was heavy; heavy enough for the foot-long handle to have been forged from solid silver. It was decorated with images of horses, but this was no horsewhip. It had three leather lashes, each about three feet long and knotted at the ends. The last few inches were darker than the rest, and I realized they were stained with blood. I threw it onto the table and looked back at Klara. Her eyes darted to the floor. She'd been studying me as I'd studied the whip. I stepped closer to her and tried again, "Hello Klara, I'm Gabriella."

She raised her eyes to mine, but said nothing, and I stepped back again under the force of her glare.

"Um, could you help me unpack, please?"

Again she said nothing, but turned to my chest and started pulling out the few gowns I possessed.

I lay awake on the small cot whilst Klara lay on a mat on the floor. I couldn't possibly sleep. On the one hand, I *was* sailing away from Father, *and* his stinking harbor, but I was also leaving Mam and Peter behind and had no idea what I was sailing toward—my future was blank in my mind. I wondered if I'd ever see Mam again. I missed her already, missed Peter, and missed having a friendly face smiling at me. I was terrified of the woman who lay on the floor, knowing she hated me.

I turned onto my side to study her in the gloom. I couldn't see her well but pictured her slim yet full body; wild black curls escaping from her headscarf; full mouth and nose. I'd heard about the dark-skinned people from Africa, but had never seen one before today. The way people talked, I'd thought they were ugly and dull-witted, little more than beasts, but this woman was beautiful. Intelligence shone out of her eyes in the way she glanced at me, full of appraisal and cunning when she thought I wasn't looking. I caught a flicker of movement as those eyes opened and I rolled over; for some reason ashamed to have been caught watching her. I vowed never to underestimate her.

I was startled by a knock at the door.

"Just a moment," I called, flustered. *Who could be asking for entry to my cabin at this time of night?*

Klara rose and lit a lantern, and I pulled on my robe. She waited for my nod, then unlocked and opened the door. A young sailor stood there, probably in his early twenties—maybe a couple of years older than Klara. He was very handsome—or would have been had he been cleaner. I could smell him from across the cabin.

"I beg your pardon, Mistress Berryngton," he said with a French accent. "I am Cheval, *Freyja's* quartermaster. The captain sends 'is apologies, but 'e would like to see your slave in 'is cabin."

"Very well," I said, confused. *What does the captain want with Klara?* But it was none of my business.

Klara shot a hate-filled glare at me, then followed the sailor out of my cabin to the one next door. I sat back on the cot in relief once the door had closed behind them, glad to finally have a bit of time to myself. I realized I couldn't remember my selected husband's name, and tears began to roll once again. "Oh Mam," I whispered to the empty room. "What's going to happen to me?"

My sobs quietened, and I realized I could hear more cries. It must be Klara—as far as I knew, we were the only women aboard the ship. A man cried out as well, though in pleasure, and I finally understood why Klara had been summoned. And I had given my consent. I raised my hands to my mouth in shock; no wonder she hated me. Now I'd proved myself deserving of her contempt.

I covered my ears as the screams and grunts rose in volume and my sobs restarted. I wasn't sure whether I cried for Klara or myself. Presumably Mr. van Ecken condoned this. *What will my life be like as his daughter-in-law?*

I didn't sleep that night, and lay alone in the dark until dawn slowly lightened the cabin. The door opened and Klara entered.

"Are you all right?" I asked.

She nodded, but didn't speak and limped to her sleeping mat.

"Your eye!" I exclaimed. It was bruised and half-closed. She gave me her hate look again, but now I didn't blame her. She lay down and curled into a ball with her back to me.

"I'm sorry," I whispered. "I didn't know." Nothing. Once again, no reaction. I stared at the ceiling. *Will my husband do that to me?*

Chapter 4

I was thrown against the cabin wall hard enough to wake me, and lay on the cot for a few moments trying to work out where I was and what was happening.

Oh yes: aboard a ship; sold into marriage to a stranger; shut inside a cabin with a woman who hates me.

Everything moved far more than it had yesterday and the ship was rocking violently from side to side, which is what had woken me so rudely. There was more noise, too: the sea as we crashed through it; thumping from overhead; as well as the creaking of wood and cracking of sail. I was thrown against the wall again and grabbed the edge of the cot, then looked up. *Where's Klara?*

I pulled myself to sit on the edge of the bed. She wasn't in the cabin. Fresh salty wind, a relief after the stinking air of the harbor, blew my curls over my face and I realized the door to the ledge outside was open and Klara was leaning over the rail. I jumped up and staggered toward her, bracing my hands against the ceiling to stop myself falling.

I reached the balcony door and clung to the frame. The sea had changed from a beautiful calm blue to a forbidding dark gray, and I shivered.

"Klara!" I called.

She looked up at me, then leaned over the rail again and retched. I sighed in relief; she was seasick, not trying to jump, although I didn't understand why she was ill now. The fresh air had quietened my own stomach.

"Are you well? Can I help you?"

She shook her head. "Leave me," she said.

I hesitated. They were the first words she'd spoken to me, but I didn't want to leave her alone in such misery.

She retched again. "Leave me!" she repeated, more insistently.

I went back into the cabin. She'd been humiliated enough in the day I'd known her: once when van Ecken had given me the whip, and again by Captain Hornigold. I would not humiliate her further.

I crossed to the jug and bowl on the table and poured out a small amount of water to wash myself. I noticed the table had a wooden rim built into it to prevent the china falling, but I'd poured out too much and water sloshed everywhere. I washed my face as best I could considering I needed one hand to hold on, then turned to find something to wear.

Klara had laid out an emerald-green gown, which went well with my dark hair and pale complexion. I stripped my nightgown off and pulled a clean shift over my head. It wasn't easy with one hand and a moving floor. I picked up my stays and looked in the glass, wondering how I would tie them, when they were taken from me.

Klara wrapped the garment around my middle and I adjusted it so the wooden supports were as close to comfortable as possible. She pulled on the strings and I gasped in pain. She loosened them slightly and I thanked her; she nodded. Progress. We finished my dressing in silence and I sat down. I noticed the whip had gone from the table and didn't care—I hoped she'd thrown it overboard.

A loud explosion startled both of us, and we looked at each other in horror. We could see nothing but sea behind, were we being attacked?

"I'm going to find out what's happening," I said to her with a bravery I didn't feel.

"No!" She bowed her head, then added, quieter. "You'd be better off staying here, out of their way."

"I need to know what's happening, and if Mr. van Ecken or the crew don't have the courtesy to inform us, I'll have to go and ask them." I couldn't stay blind in the cabin; I had to know.

I stumbled to the door, unlocked it, and went out. What had yesterday been a dark, quiet deck was now filled with light and men. Holes in the side had been opened, and I now saw the deck was full of guns; each with its muzzle pointing out through one of the gunports. I didn't like this, but I couldn't slink back to the cabin and Klara after my show of bravado.

There were posts at intervals supporting the ceiling, and I made my way from one to the next; managing not to fall until I reached the ladder van Ecken had led me down yesterday. I climbed up, kicking my petticoats out of the way to find every foothold.

Up on deck, wind whipped at my face and body, and I stumbled to the empty rail to hold on. The rail on the other side was full of men shouting and making an awful noise, and I saw another, bigger, ship a few yards away.

Musket fire sounded above me and I looked up. Men were in the rigging and crowded small platforms up there, firing at the ship, and a blood-red flag streamed above them.

I gasped, I knew what that meant—pirates! Father had put me aboard a ship of pirates!

I screamed when my arm was grabbed, and van Ecken shoved his face in mine. "What are you doing? Get back to your cabin; this is no place for my son's wife!"

"But, but, but . . ." was all I managed. It didn't seem worthwhile to point out that I hadn't met his son, never mind married him.

He pulled me roughly back to the hatch in the deck.

"But, what's happening?" I managed.

"Business," he said. "Just business." He stood over me as I scrambled back down the ladder and followed me to the cabin.

"These men were hired by your King Charles as privateers. Now the wars are over, what are they supposed to do? You can't blame them for continuing a trade in which they excelled, and I'll that ship and her cargo have for a very good price—business."

He pulled open the door and shoved me inside. "Now stay there until I give you leave to go on deck!"

His words were accompanied by a tremendous boom. I fell as the ship lurched over and the gundeck and cabin filled with acrid, stinking smoke. He slammed the door. I crawled to the cot and pulled myself onto it, tears streaming down my face yet again.

Klara sat in the far corner, as far away from the door and rest of the ship as possible, clutching her knees, terrified.

"Pirates," I told her. "They're pirates."

She nodded, put her head on her knees, and hugged herself.

Chapter 5

Things quietened maybe half an hour after I'd found out the truth about my hosts, but that half hour had been the most terrifying of my life.

We'd sat and listened to gunshots and screams; fallen when our ship bumped into the other; coughed when the cabin flooded with gunsmoke; and stayed together silent and unmoving when the other hull cut out most of our light. We could do nothing but pray for it to be over.

Now that it was, I didn't know what to say or do. I went to the privy ledge outside, but didn't use it as I'd be in full view of the other ship now sailing along to one side and just behind us.

A knock at the door startled me, and I came back into the cabin as Klara opened it. Three men stood there. Two held plates of meat and beakers of rum punch—our dinner—and Klara took the plates from them. The third I hadn't met before. He was clean-shaven and dressed differently to the others—oh, he had on shirt and breeches, as did the rest of the crew, but he also wore leather boots, a frockcoat and sported a neat curled periwig. He looked almost respectable, although the way his eyes flicked over my bodice was anything but.

"Good evening, Mistress Berryngton." He bowed. "I'm Henry Sharpe."

"Good evening," I replied. "Where's the other one, Cheval?"

He looked a little taken aback, but recovered without any loss of manners. "He's taken the helm of our prize, sailing alongside." My jaw clenched at the casual way he talked about the other ship. "Mijnheer van Ecken is also aboard and has charged me with your care. If you need anything, please don't hesitate to ask."

I nodded, his manners shaming me into remembering my own. "Thank you, Mr. Sharpe," I managed. "Um, there is one thing." I paused, embarrassed, but had to ask. "Is it possible to have a chamber pot? I cannot use the privy ledge with that ship so close."

He smiled but didn't laugh. "Of course, I will see to it for you. Forgive me, I should have thought about that."

I smiled, still embarrassed, and the pirates took their leave. I crossed to the table where Klara had arranged the food, and sighed. Every meal so far had been the same: meat, meat and more meat; although this time we had a treat—an onion. Raw and whole, but still, something other than meat. I supposed the sailors ate like this every day. I picked mine up and bit into it, enjoying the sharp taste flooding my mouth.

"What meat is it this time?" I asked Klara.

She took a bite and smiled. "Goat," she replied.

"Goat?" I asked. I hadn't eaten goat before. "What's it like?"

"Try it," she urged. "It's delicious, watch out for the bones though, their cook is no butcher." She pulled a sliver of bone from her mouth to demonstrate.

I sat and picked up my knife, stabbing a slice of meat. Dark-yellow fat was already congealing on the plate and my stomach turned, but I was hungry. I put the meat in my mouth and chewed. Klara was right, it was full of flavor, and I stabbed another piece.

I sat back, replete, my plate empty, and watched Klara clear the table. She'd definitely grown a little friendlier after the events of the day, but not much.

I took a sip of rum punch and someone knocked on the door again: Henry Sharpe holding a bucket, which Klara took without a word, then handed him the plates. He passed them to another man behind him then cleared his throat. "Ah, my apologies once more, Mistress Berryngton, but the Captain, ah, would like to see Klara immediately."

I heard Klara's gasp and my shoulders stiffened.

"My own apologies, Mr. Sharpe, but I require Klara's services myself this evening. I regret I am unable to comply with Captain Hornigold's request." My voice sounded firm enough, but inside I felt liquid.

He gave a small smile and nodded. "Very well." He left.

I let my breath out in a sigh—I hadn't realized I'd been holding it—then slumped against the wall and looked at Klara, who was staring back at me.

"Can you pass me that bucket, please?" I'd been holding it in all day, and really needed to relieve myself, especially after that.

"Th . . . thank you," Klara stuttered as she passed it to me.

"If I'd known last night—" I couldn't continue, but she understood, nodded, and turned her back as I used the bucket. When I'd finished, she took it and threw the contents over the rail of the privy ledge.

Another knock at the door; this one heavy and insistent. Klara and I looked at each other, then I shook my head and opened the door myself. The captain stood there, his face red with anger, and I couldn't take my eyes off his black bushy eyebrows. He looked at me, then over my shoulder at Klara, then back to me. I noticed Sharpe standing behind him.

"What's the meaning of this?" he asked, his voice loud.

"I beg your pardon?" I asked, pretending confusion.

"I have requested Klara's company this evening."

"I beg your pardon," I said again, "but I require Klara's services myself this evening."

"Why?"

I stepped back, for some reason I hadn't expected to be challenged. I thought quickly and held onto the door; my legs felt weak and I wasn't completely sure they could hold me up on their own. "I need her to prepare my bath."

"Bath?" This is a working ship, not a traveling inn," the captain said, his voice full of scorn.

"I am aware of that, Captain, but I'm on my way to meet my future husband and I'd like to bathe." I knew I had to stay calm, but it was an effort.

"I could cut down one of the hogsheads for her," Sharpe said from behind Hornigold. "That may work as a bathtub." Hornigold turned and glared at him, and I was interested to see him take a breath to calm himself. Sharpe was unaffected by his anger.

"You sort it then," Hornigold snapped. "And get one of the deckhands to fetch warm water from the galley." He turned back to me, calm now. "It's all organized, my crew will arrange your bath, Klara is not needed."

"I'm not having any of your filthy crew in my cabin!" I retorted.

"They can leave the buckets of water outside the door, and Klara will take it from there. I'll also need her to help with my dressing. I cannot possibly spare her at all tonight." I looked him in the eye and refused to blink or let my gaze drift up to those eyebrows. I noticed Sharpe wink at me from behind him and felt myself blush, but I didn't back down.

"Klara is *my* slave, and is here to attend to *me*," I continued. "I am sure my fiancé will be very interested to hear *all* the details of my journey."

Hornigold clenched his fists and made a noise like a growl, then spun round and strode away. Sharpe smiled at me and followed. I closed the door in relief, then sighed. I was shaking and felt faint, but was cheered by the flicker of a smile from Klara. *Why couldn't I have stood up to Father like that? Why did Mam not resist Father like that?*

My return smile dissolved into giggles that I couldn't stop, and Klara soon joined in. I'd been terrified defying the captain—a pirate—like that and had expected a blow. Who'd have guessed a villain would stay his fist where Father would not? Eventually, my relieved hysteria subsided, and I sat on the cot to wait for the bathtub and water. I had to focus on the future and not the past if I was to survive this.

"This worked tonight, but we need to find more reasons why I can't spare you," I said.

Klara looked up, then smiled and crossed to the cot. She knelt down and reached underneath it, then pulled out a chest I hadn't realized was there. I moved out of her way as she opened the lid and looked inside at lace, ribbons and a parcel of white silk.

She lifted out the silk, and said, "We have to make your wedding gown. It could be a lengthy task."

I stared at the material, feeling numb as it finally sank in that I was to marry into this life, and Mam would not be there to guide me.

Chapter 6

Mr. van Ecken summoned me, and I left Klara packing my chest and joined him and Captain Hornigold on the deck at the back of the ship above the cabin. I looked shoreward. There it was—Sayba. We'd entered a small bay, bathed in sunshine, around which a town huddled.

"Eckerstad," Mr. van Ecken said with pride. Klara had been tight-lipped about my fiancé, Erik, but she had told me about the town. Eckerstad had been founded by the man beside me—Jan van Ecken—and he was also Governor. It was the only town on the island, and Jan and Erik lived in the largest estate—my new family was the most important in Sayba.

Captain Hornigold shouted, "Let go anchor!" and a man on the foredeck swung a large mallet. The anchor, which had been suspended on a wooden frame to the side of the bow, dropped with a tremendous splash. The ship slowed and swung round until the anchor warp jerked tight and we were held in place.

"Ready the longboat!"

It was time to go and van Ecken led me to the side of the ship and that carrying seat suspended from the spars above. I didn't protest this time but sat in silence, drenched with sweat in the heat, as I was lowered to the small boat already loaded with our chests. Van Ecken then Klara followed and we were rowed ashore.

A short, heavy, red-faced man with a basic open carriage was waiting for us. *My fiancé?*

"Rensink," van Ecken gruffly greeted. "Where's my son?"

Not Erik then. I sighed in relief.

"He sends his apologies for not meeting you in person, there was an important matter that needed his attention."

"Hmpf!" Mr. van Ecken did not seem pleased. "May I present Mistress Berryngton? This is Rensink, Brisingamen's overseer," he introduced. "Erik should be here his wife to greet," he continued.

I stayed silent—I'd already learned it was the best tactic where Jan van Ecken was concerned.

We climbed aboard the carriage; van Ecken sitting up front with Rensink, who took the reins of the single horse. Klara and I sat behind and the chests were lifted up into the bed of the cart. We left with no farewells to the sailors who'd brought us here.

We were soon surrounded by jungle and I gazed about me at every shade of green imaginable and every description of bloom: red spikes, soft yellows, blues, pinks and more. The air was flooded with scent and filled with noise, and the heat made me feel faint—it could not have been more different from Massachusetts Bay.

After half an hour the trees thinned out and we drove through sugarcane fields. I noticed something to one side, and peered closer, then faced Klara to ask about it. Her head was turned and she refused to look or answer. I turned back, fascinated, until the shape of it started to make sense. A cage—just large enough to hold a man—and suspended from one of the larger trees. We drew level and I gasped when I saw the base was littered with bones.

"The slaves may have the strength of beasts, but they also have the minds of beasts." Van Ecken had turned in his seat to address me. "They need sometimes reminding who their masters are."

I stared at him in shock, unable to find any words, and he turned to face forward again.

"Here we are—Brisingamen," he said a few moments later and with obvious pride. I craned my neck to see past him and Rensink to catch my first glimpse of my new home.

It was very large: two stories painted gold, with a steep roof and a short, squat tower at either end. A broad veranda ran the length of the front and overlooked a large lawn. It made Father's cottage in Massachusetts Bay look like a shack. I smiled, although I couldn't quite shake the image of that cage from my mind.

Chapter 7

I followed Mr. van Ecken through the largest of the seven arches framing the veranda into a large entrance hall in the center of the house. Dominated by a grand staircase straight ahead and with the walls painted white so as not to clash with the black-and-white tiled floor, it was an ostentatious display of the van Eckens' wealth. I could see only two doors, one to the left, the other to my right, and I jumped when two men dressed in indigo livery with gold braiding appeared out of the shadows behind the staircase.

"Hans, Hendrik, get the chests from the carriage," van Ecken ordered. They both nodded once and gave us a wide berth as they walked outside. I smiled as they passed me, but neither met my eyes.

I glanced at Klara, but she also kept her eyes to the floor.

"In here," van Ecken said, marching to the left-hand door and opening it. I walked through into a large, airy drawing room. Decorated in gold-flock wallpaper, it had three large settees and a number of small carved tables.

A large oil painting of a formidable-looking woman dressed in black dominated the walls, and she looked across the room toward the veranda and outside. I crossed to the veranda doors and looked out at the large expanse of garden in front of the house, and wondered what there would be to do here.

Raised voices disturbed my thoughts, but I couldn't understand what was being said. I watched two men leave the house; they looked quite similar in that they both had broad shoulders and bowed legs; just like the sailors on the ship. They also wore the same clothes—linen shirts and short, baggy breeches, but these two had added all sorts of finery to the basic outfit. Good quality leather boots on their feet, colorful sashes around their waists, and the brightest, most heavily decorated frockcoats I'd ever seen. One was in cochineal red with lace at the cuffs and collar, braiding around every hem and seam, embroidery in between, plus large brass buttons.

The other wore bright yellow over an emerald green sash with similar fripperies. They had clashing silk scarves over their heads, and large-brimmed hats on top. I'd never set eyes on such gaudy gentlemen in my life, and I giggled to myself, imagining the reactions if they walked into the puritan Massachusetts Bay Colony dressed like that.

Hans and Hendrik appeared leading a couple of horses for them, but I turned as the door to the room opened and didn't see them leave.

Mr. van Ecken entered ahead of a younger man. *Erik?* They didn't acknowledge me at first, but continued arguing in a language I didn't understand. I looked from one to the other as they quarreled, wondering what they were saying and feeling very uncomfortable.

The younger man—presumably my husband-to-be—looked presentable enough. About my height, he wore a tightly curled periwig—the yellow of which clashed with his dark, exaggerated mustaches. He'd dressed with care, his clothes of obvious quality. *Although the gold buckles on his shoes are overdoing it a bit.* I looked back at his face—his lips were thin and eyes cold. There was very little expression on that face, and I shuddered a little. He didn't look like a man who smiled very often.

"This is her," the elder van Ecken finally said in English. "Gabriella Berryngton."

I stepped forward. "Pleased to meet you."

He looked me up and down, then said something else to his father that I couldn't understand. It did not sound complimentary. He stepped toward me, bowed stiffly and took my hand to kiss.

"Welcome," he said, coldly. "I'm Erik van Ecken. The wedding is planned for next month so you have time to prepare. There'll be five extra for dinner—tell Belinda and organize the menu. I have work to do." He left the room.

I looked at the father. "Belinda?" I asked.

"You haven't met Belinda yet?" He sounded angry. "What is that bloody girl thinking?" He marched to the door and shouted for Klara. I flinched. When did he think Klara had had chance to introduce me to anyone? Why hadn't he made any introductions himself? He hadn't even introduced his son—I'd been forced to guess that was who he was.

I realized then what Erik had said. *The wedding's arranged for next month. Did they make the arrangements before finding a bride?*

My thoughts were interrupted by Klara's entrance. I noticed she gave Jan a wide berth.

"About time, girl! Your mistress hasn't been introduced to Belinda yet—see to it! She has a dinner party to plan, apparently our nautical friends are joining us." He marched out and Klara and I looked at each other in amazement.

"He doesn't seem to like these 'nautical friends'," I remarked.

"With good reason," muttered Klara. "I'll fetch Belinda," she continued before I could ask what she meant.

Chapter 8

I lay my head against the edge of the bathtub and sighed. Klara looked up from her unpacking and giggled. "You've had a bath nearly every day that I've known you. I'm surprised you don't wash away!"

"I know." I laughed with her. "I hated them at home, barely had one a month, but it was the only way I could think of to keep you out of Hornigold's cabin—there's only so much sewing I can do in a day. They must have thought me mad!" Klara stopped smiling and put her head down. "And it's so hot here, I'm going to need one every day just to cool down," I carried on, trying to rescue the mood.

Klara looked up at me again. "Thank you," she said. "He'd have carried on taking me every night if you hadn't stopped him."

"I'm sorry about that first night, I didn't understand—" I tailed off again, not knowing what to say. Klara stayed silent. I hoped I hadn't spoilt the tentative friendship growing between us.

She shut the lid of my chest, which had been placed at the foot of the ornate four-poster bed. There hadn't been much to do; I'd found a full wardrobe of gowns through a door off my room—all of them of much better quality than even my best. Mine would stay in the chest.

I looked around the room. The bed itself was draped with fine muslin curtains and smothered in velvets and brocades. The walls were also richly decorated in a deep red and hung with tapestries—even the floor was adorned with rugs—and the furniture was solid and elaborately carved. My chest looked completely out of place.

"Would you cover that with something please, Klara?"

She smiled and threw a length of burgundy brocade over it. I thanked her and thought back over the events of the day.

"Belinda seems very nice," I said, and Klara smiled and nodded.

"I don't know what I'd do without her," she said. "She arrived a couple of years ago from England with her husband, John." I leaned back with my eyes closed to listen to her story. "They'd signed up for five years servitude, but John died within weeks—of the jungle fever."

"Oh no!" I sat up, shocked at the misfortune of the large, friendly woman I'd met earlier—the only person so far who'd welcomed me on sight.

"Yes, it was the same fever that took Mevrouw van Ecken—that's her in that picture over the fireplace in the drawing room. Horrible woman she was."

I nodded, remembering the painting, and I realized there was a fireplace in this room too. *Why do we need fireplaces on an island this hot?*

"Anyway, Mijnheer Jan told her she'd have to work John's passage off as well as her own—I don't think she'll ever get away from this place."

"The poor woman," I exclaimed. "But she's so cheerful."

"Yes, she keeps saying she has nowhere else to go, and at least she's needed here."

I didn't know what to say so changed the subject. "What about these 'nautical friends' that are coming tonight—do you think Hornigold will be one of them?"

"Sure to be. And his quartermaster, Cheval, do you remember him? There'll be Captain Tarr and *his* quartermaster as well, Blake. And probably Sharpe, too, though he's not too bad."

I stared at her in horror. On my first night in my new home, I had to dine not only with my overbearing future father-in-law and my downright rude fiancé, but near half-a-dozen pirates—one of whom at least already hated me. "How am I going to do this?" I whispered. "I can't think of anything worse."

"Oh, there'll be worse all right, believe me, there'll be worse." She spoke quietly and I looked up at her, not sure I'd heard her properly.

"We'll make sure you're dressed perfectly, so Mijnheer Erik can't find fault—I know what he likes and what he doesn't. Stay as quiet as you can at the table—don't give them reason to notice you—that would be my advice."

I nodded, unable to find words, then stood so Klara could dress me.

"Ow! What are you doing?" She'd put the stays around my middle and was pulling the strings extremely tight behind my back. The belt with the supporting wooden bars was cutting into my flesh.

"That's how he likes it, as tight as possible. It's just for the evening, you'll hardly see him during the day."

I bit my tongue and trusted her to prepare me for the ordeal ahead.

Chapter 9

I made my way downstairs and entered the drawing room through an elaborately carved door. The room was empty.

I sat down, but was too nervous about the evening ahead and uncomfortable in my new gown with the tight stays. I stood again, and wandered over to the picture of Erik's mother. She was dressed in black with a high white lace collar and stared out at the room in disapproval. *Had that been her usual expression? It must have been if she was painted that way.* Her brow was furrowed, her nose hooked and her lips almost non-existent, but that could just have been the effects of her bad humor. I peered closer at the frame: *Adelheid*—a beautiful name for an ugly woman.

I turned quickly as the door opened to men's voices. Jan, Erik and the two gaudies from earlier came in first. My heart sank as I recognized Captain Hornigold behind them, Cheval was also here—and Mr. Sharpe. Was I really to dine alone with these seven men? It would have been unheard of in Massachusetts Bay. I straightened my shoulders and held my head high—I would not show these men my unease.

"Good evening," I said.

"Goedenavond," Jan van Ecken replied, which I assumed was good evening in Dutch. Erik only grunted.

"Captain Hornigold, Cheval and Sharpe you already know." Jan waved an arm in their direction. Hornigold and Cheval smirked, but Mr. Sharpe offered me a small bow.

"And may I Captain Tarr and Quartermaster Blake present?" The Gaudies approached me. Tarr was the one in red, Blake wore the yellow. They both bowed, kissed my hand, and murmured greetings. I concentrated my entire will on not cringing away from them.

I looked at Erik; he hadn't yet greeted me properly. He'd donned a dark green frockcoat for the evening and carried a silver-tipped cane. He looked very distinguished and I offered him a small smile. Jan barked something at him in Dutch and he walked over to me and took my hand.

"You look lovely," he said.

I dropped my eyes and blushed. Angry at the reddening in my cheeks, which I knew made my freckles even more obvious, I whispered my thanks. We were saved from any more awkwardness by the entrance of the two liveried men from earlier carrying trays of drinks. Wine for myself and the van Eckens; what smelled like rum for the sailors.

We sat with our drinks, Erik next to me on one of the sofas, and struggled to find conversation until the dining room doors were opened—our cue to walk through to the table.

Erik showed me to a chair next to his at one end of the table, his father sat at the far end, and the sailors arranged themselves in the remaining seats. I was relieved to find Mr. Sharpe sitting at my left, although was not looking forward to a meal sitting opposite Captain Hornigold.

Jan said grace and Klara, Hans and Hendrik brought in the food. Soup to start, then the stewed goat I'd agreed with Belinda earlier. I looked up at Klara as she placed a plate in front of Erik and froze. His hand was on her thigh, and she had not reacted.

I gasped in shock and was aware of Hornigold smirking across from me. Klara wouldn't look at me and Erik didn't seem to have realized anything was amiss until Jan spoke sharply in Dutch, and he snatched his hand away.

I stared at my plate, mortified, with no idea of what to do or say, but knowing from years of living with Father not to make a scene, especially in front of company.

"So, are you enjoying being on dry land again?" Sharpe asked, his voice light and breaking the tension. I turned to him gratefully, and told him how beautiful the island and house was. I carried on talking—most of it nonsensical and my voice shrill, but he feigned interest. Soon, the rest of the party struck up conversations and the incident was over. I smiled my gratitude at Sharpe and started to eat, desperate for the evening to be over.

* * *

The meal passed in a blur. Erik hardly spoke to me, and the pirates were loud, coarse and thought nothing of swearing at the table. Only Sharpe paid me any attention, and I was aware of drinking more glasses of wine than was prudent.

I concentrated on using the knife and fork, and wondered if we would be using them every night. At home, the forks were only used when we had company, the rest of the time we used our fingers. I was amused to see Hornigold and Cheval struggle with the dainty instruments, and giggled to myself as I saw their food dropping from the tines so often that they were reduced to watching the others to see how the forks were properly used.

I excused myself as soon as I was able, leaving the men in the drawing room and escaping to my room. I pulled the cloth covering my old chest away. I didn't fit in here, but I wouldn't hide, nor would I hide my belongings.

Klara entered a few minutes later and I glared at her, the wine emboldening me.

"You said something earlier, that you know what Erik likes."

She said nothing, just looked at me, her face expressionless.

"Exactly what is your relationship with my fiancé?" I asked as mildly as I could.

"Relationship?" She laughed. "The only *relationship* is that of master and slave. I was born into slavery, and given to Erik on his sixteenth birthday. I was twelve, and he could do with me what he wished. If I didn't please him, I was beaten." She looked at the floor, tears in her eyes. I felt ashamed.

"He still does whatever he wants with me," she continued. "I dare not refuse him. His beatings have got worse since he started using that cane, and his father hates me—he would welcome any opportunity to lock me inside that cage we passed on the way here and leave me to starve or thirst to death." She looked at me again, tears running down her cheeks.

I remembered Hornigold on the boat, and how meekly Klara

had gone to him that first night when she'd been summoned, and felt sick. *Is that all she knows of men? Is that all there* is *to know? Do I really have to marry a man such as that?*

I stood and passed her a lace kerchief to dry her eyes. I wanted to hug her, but something held me back. She dried her eyes and pocketed the kerchief.

"Would you like those stays loosening now, Miss Gabriella?"

"My goodness, yes! I could hardly eat, they're so tight!" I was relieved to move off the subject. I needed time to think about it all, my head was awhirl.

Klara's fingers started the laborious task of untying the various layers of my gown and I put my hand to my head.

"Are you well, Miss Gabriella?"

"Dizzy," I gasped. In fact I felt as if I was going to faint.

"It's because of the stays—lean forward and put your head between your knees, I'll fetch you some water."

I did as I was told, and did start to feel better. I straightened when Klara returned with a glass of water and sipped gratefully.

"Better?"

"Yes, thank you."

My head had stopped spinning and I started to relax. I wanted to ask her why Jan hated her, and why he hadn't sold her in that case, but couldn't find a tactful way of phrasing my questions. They'd have to wait for another day.

I sighed in relief as the stays were finally removed and I massaged the tender skin of my stomach, which felt bruised. Klara took a pot of something from the dresser.

"Belinda makes this—it's wonderfully soothing for damaged flesh.

I scooped out a handful and rubbed it into my belly, and Klara did the same for my back. I stared at the wall in silence.

Chapter 10

I was woken by Klara. I blinked at her for a few seconds and looked around the room; the events of yesterday, and especially the revelations of last night rushing back to me. I sat up in bed and she put a breakfast tray on my lap. I managed to mumble a thank you—a poor response considering she'd had to carry it from the cookhouse and up two flights of stairs to my room in the small turret on the right-hand side of the house. I suddenly realized somebody would have had to carry all that water the same distance for my bath the night before. I wouldn't be able to soak so often.

I sipped the lemongrass tea. A bit cold, but it tasted well—very refreshing and perfect for breakfast. The tray was laden with strange fruits, toast and preserves. I spread a thin slice of toast with the preserve, in the hope it may still be warm. It wasn't, but the jam was delicious.

"Oh, what's this?" I exclaimed.

Klara smiled. "Mammee apple. It grows wild on the island, and Belinda makes the preserve."

"It's delicious!"

I cheered up a little. I may be marrying into a family of brutes who consorted with pirates, but I was away from Father and the food was exquisite. At home, it had been bland and boring—usually porridge or stewed rabbit.

In the Caribbees I'd already found goat and mammee apple, what else was waiting for me to discover? I looked at the fruit as I ate, enjoying the tang of the preserve, but wanting to finish it so I could try the next new flavor.

Klara busied herself about the room, pouring water into the basin, then taking and laying out another set of clothing for me to wear.

"Where does Erik sleep?" I asked her, suddenly thinking about my married life. *Will I have to leave this room or will he join me here?*

"In the room below," she answered. "And Mijnheer Jan has a room on the same floor but at the other end of the house. There are two guest rooms between them, and another in the far tower."

It was the most talkative she'd been so far, and I realized she was relieved at my friendly tone after last night's disclosures.

"And where do you sleep?"

In one of the huts beyond the trees, unless I'm . . . I'm . . . required at the house." She dropped her eyes and I pressed my lips together in disapproval. Then I realized I wasn't being fair; Klara had no choice, she wasn't to blame for the arrangements.

"Well, I'm sure you'll be spared those duties once Erik is married," I said. She glanced at me quickly and turned so I couldn't read her expression.

"Would you like the blue or the green gown this morning?"

"The blue, I think," I said, watching her pile stays, petticoats and mantua onto the bed, and wondering what she wasn't saying. I sighed and rose to dress.

"Don't pull the stays so tight, Klara! I'm still sore from wearing them like that last night!"

"But Mijnheer Erik, he likes stays to be tight, Miss Gabriella. He always says he should be able to put both hands around a woman's waist and his fingers meet."

"I don't care what *Mijnheer Erik—*" I sneered the name "—says about ladies' waists. He is not my husband yet, and he does not decide how I dress. Loosen it, Klara, it's too tight!"

She said nothing, but obediently loosened the ties.

Downstairs, there was no one about. I wandered into the drawing room, but there was nothing to do in there. I decided to explore my new home and crossed the hall to the other carved door—a nautical scene to complement the others.

I gasped at the large room full of books I'd stumbled upon. I loved to read, but at home we'd only had bibles and prayer books; this library was a dream come true. I wandered about the shelves, looking at spines, and was dismayed to find only Dutch titles. Of course, why would the van Eckens have an English library?

Disappointed, I crossed to the other door in the room and opened it.

"What the Devil do you think you're doing? Get out of this room! At once!"

"Oh!" I gasped at my welcome from my future husband. Jan was also there, but didn't speak. "I'm sorry," I stuttered, backed out, and shut the door. I ran out of the library and out of that house, across the lawns and down the road. I'd never felt so humiliated and unwanted, not even at my father's house.

I tried to keep my eyes averted from the hanging cage, but found it impossible. Despite my intention to give it as wide a berth as I could as I passed, my feet took me closer. I glanced inside and gasped. Two human skulls lay in a litter of picked-clean bones. I shuddered, had a living man been locked inside with the bones of a dead?

I ran past a field of sugarcane, turning left up a smaller road that I hadn't spotted when I arrived, wondering what could be up there, yet dreading the answer.

The road opened up into a large space, surrounded by thatched buildings. None of them had walls, and none seemed to be in use at the moment. I turned in a circle and looked around me, then squinted. There was movement in the distance. I studied it for a moment and realized it was men working the field.

"What are you doing here?"

I whirled round and saw a scruffy man with a young boy—still a child, yet laden down with hoes and picks. I recognized Rensink—the man who had driven the cart on my arrival. He carried only a whip.

I squared my shoulders. "I'm looking around my estate. What's it to you?"

He looked me up and down, then smiled. I felt very uncomfortable. "Ah yes, the little English miss." I scowled. He approached me, hand outstretched, took mine and shook it. "I didn't expect you to be running around the mill."

I nodded, unwilling to explain myself. "What are all these buildings?"

He looked around and pointed each out. "Toolshed, mill, boiling house, cooling house, curing house. All that's needed to turn that cane into sugar. You'd best not come here once we start the harvest—too dangerous. Now if you'll excuse me, we have a lot of cane to weed and more jungle to clear, and those clumsy oafs keep blunting the hoes and snapping the picks." He stared at me until I turned and walked away. I looked back when I heard a cry and a clatter of metal. The boy had dropped his load; I'd turned just in time to see the man hit him.

"Stop! Do not hit that boy!"

Rensink laughed at me and hit the boy again, then turned his back and they walked away.

I stared after them in frustration, then walked back to the house, but didn't feel like going in yet. I crossed the lawns to a small path I could see leading into the trees. I would find out where that went.

I soon came out of the trees and halted at the sight before me. I stood on a cliff top and looked out on leagues of sparkling turquoise water. It was the most beautiful sight I'd ever seen. I looked behind me at the trees—why on earth had they screened this view from the house?

Cheered, I started to walk along the cliff top and squealed in delight when I spotted a small beach below me. There was a path too; steep and not often walked, but it *was* a path, and I scrambled down it.

On the sand, I removed my stockings and shoes, and reveled in the feel of warm sand between my toes. It was so *fine*. I walked closer to the water's edge, lifted my skirts and paddled—the water was *warm*. I squealed again when a larger wave splashed me, and made my way back to the warm sand to let the sun dry my feet and gown. Life would be far from perfect here, but there were definite compensations.

* * *

I shivered and looked at the sky. Clouds were moving in to obscure the sun. Reluctantly, I donned my footwear and started the climb up the cliff. I was getting hungry anyway, it must be near lunchtime.

I slipped once or twice, but was able to steady myself with my hands and didn't have too much difficulty. At the top, I looked down at my gown and grimaced. White salt spots around the hem showed where the sea had caught me, and there was a small tear in the left sleeve. I'd have to sneak up to my room to change and hope Klara could fix it. Next time I came here, I would wear one of the gowns I'd brought with me.

The path was hard to follow through the undergrowth and trees, but when I emerged I saw my sense of direction wasn't too far out. I was at one corner of the lawn rather than the center that I'd aimed for, but that was better; I could hug the trees and not cross the empty space in full view.

Suddenly, I was drenched. The clouds had burst in a rainstorm the likes of which I'd never seen before, and I ran toward the house, all thoughts of concealment washed away.

I clattered onto the veranda, shaking my dripping arms and gasped. The van Eckens stood on the covered terrace, watching me.

Erik looked me up and down in disgust, turned and went inside without a word.

"Those gowns are expensive, child, you need to better care take," Jan van Ecken said and followed his son. "Get changed quickly, luncheon ready is."

I followed them: embarrassed, ashamed and furious. There had not been a single inquiry about my health after such a soaking—the concern had only been for my gown.

Klara followed me upstairs and I shivered as we got rid of the ruined clothes. I dried my hair as best I could and dressed quickly in the green gown.

Klara looked in amazement at the gown I'd discarded and I shrugged. "Do you think it can be fixed?"

She smiled at me, "I'll do my best, Miss Gabriella." I thought she was going to say something else, but she must have changed her mind.

"Are you laughing?" I asked, smiling myself.

"Not at all, Miss Gabriella." She tied the new stays loosely.

Downstairs again, I walked through the drawing room into the dining room and sat before a full plate of food. Jan and Erik hadn't waited for me, and were already eating. We sat in silence until the peppermint tea was served. I'd barely tasted my meal, and wondered what delicious new treat I'd been too anxious to enjoy.

"My son wishes to apologize for the way he earlier to you spoke," Jan said, breaking the awkward silence. "Our study is out of bounds, we should have told you that, before you in barged."

I nodded in acknowledgement, not sure if I was receiving an apology or a reprimand.

"The drawing room is for your private use unless we guests have. You are free for the library to use, although we'd prefer you to bring books to the drawing room to read rather than in there remain."

I nodded again.

"There is a collection of books in English near the veranda doors."

Now I looked at him in interest, but he'd finished and the two men rose from the table. Erik hadn't spoken a word.

I followed them from the room and into the library. They both ignored me and went straight into the study and shut the door. I crossed to the shelves Jan had mentioned and ran my hand over the spines.

Books in English! There must be a hundred of them. I chose one about Norse mythology and opened the door to the veranda. I could hear raised voices coming from the study, but didn't care. They could shout at each other as much as they liked.

I sat in a comfortable chair at the table in front of the drawing room and began to read, soon losing myself in tales of ancient gods, Valkyries and Nordic heroes.

Chapter 11

At the dinner table again, I stared at my plate. Jan and Erik were arguing in Dutch once more. Truth be told, it was less awkward than sitting in silence, but only marginally, and I'd had enough.

"Do you have any idea how rude you're being?" I said. They stopped talking and stared at me in surprise.

"You've brought me to this house and expect me to marry into this family, yet you rarely speak to me. Now, at the dinner table, you're speaking a language I don't understand. I can't follow the conversation. I can't join in. I am not included in any way." I was near tears with the frustration of my brief stay. Jan looked shocked, Erik angry, but I couldn't hold back the words.

"I was subjected to the company of pirates at my first dinner here, and have never heard such language or seen such table manners before. I have not been shown around the house or estate, and was spoken to in the worst manner imaginable when I explored on my own!"

I stopped, breathing heavily, surprised at myself. I'd never have dared to speak to Father this way, and I could barely believe I'd found the courage to speak to the van Eckens like this. I only knew I couldn't live the rest of my life the way I'd lived the last few days.

After a moment, Jan spoke. "You are quite right, my child, we have been neglecting you. There has not for two years a woman in this house been, and we have forgotten how to behave."

I smiled at him, relieved he'd taken my outburst so well. Erik still frowned at me.

"We were those very pirates you mentioned discussing."

Erik looked at his father sharply, but Jan waved a hand at him and he said nothing.

"You see, we a dilemma have, and it's taking over everything, even your wedding, my child, and we only apologize can."

"A dilemma—about those pirates?" I asked.

"Well, yes, but it's not really your concern."

"Oh, why stop now, Vader? Why not tell her it all? You want her to make a van Ecken, don't you?" I noticed his English was better than his father's.

Jan looked at his son, then turned back to me.

"Excuse my son's manners, he finds this wedding very sudden, as I'm sure you do, but this family a new generation needs." He glared at Erik again, then turned back to me.

"It's right that you should our family history know—your sons will one day need to know it.

"The van Eckens have been directors of the Dutch West Indies Company since the start, and I and my wife in 1650 came to the Caribbees. It was clear to me there would myriad opportunities in the New World be, and I wanted advantage of them to take.

"Originally based in Sint Eustatius, I moved in 1655 to Sayba once the war was over, founded the town Eckerstad, and this house built. All went well for many years—our businesses grew and the island flourished. Erik was born and we could not have happier been."

I glanced at Erik as he took a long drink of wine. He kept his eyes on his plate and said nothing.

"Five years later, Thomas Morgan—Henry Morgan's uncle, have you of him heard?"

I nodded, who hadn't heard of Henry Morgan, the flamboyant buccaneer turned knight? Even in Massachusetts Bay, he was famous.

"Well, Thomas Morgan was from the same cloth cut, and he Sayba attacked. We were merchants, not warriors, and did not a chance have. We were into servitude taken whilst strangers in our beautiful home lived."

I gasped, it sounded horrible.

"Adelheid—my wife—Erik and I were taken to Henry Morgan to serve. He had Elizabeth just married and was a sugar plantation in Jamaica establishing. It wasn't long before I running it for him was."

I nodded, not knowing what to say and having to concentrate to understand his English.

"After a couple of years, I had a good business in his name built up, and then England and the Netherlands signed the Treaty of Breda and the second war between our nations over was.

"I implored Morgan to allow my family and me to Sayba return. He had first-hand my talents as a businessman seen, and I was able to convince him that I on his sugar plantation wasted was. I could make him more money if I were able to my own empire build with him as a partner. He would a percentage of the profits take—a large percentage, I may add," he glanced at his son, "and he agreed."

"He would have been a fool not to, and Henry Morgan is no fool," Erik said.

"Quite. He did a little more than expected though, and provided me with a ship and, er, crew as well as helping me the sugar plantation here set up. Tarr was a young man then, and would goods and prize ships me bring which I would from them purchase."

"At very low prices," Erik butted in.

"Yes, at lower prices than the norm." Jan nodded slowly. "And we would the goods on sell and fit the ships out as Africa slavers."

"Our profits soared," Erik added.

"Yes, and a large part of our profit was loaded into Tarr's hold, Jamaica bound," Jan snapped. "But for all my complaints," his voice softened, "our lives had monumentally improved. I was my own master again, we freely in our own home lived, and ran the island more or less as we before had." He paused. "We were happy for many years, until in '81 Adelheid died."

"I'm sorry," I murmured, fascinated by the story and not knowing what else to say.

"Jungle fever. Couldn't be helped. We manage as best we can without her, but Brisingamen has long enough without a mistress been." He smiled at me and I smiled back.

"But now, Governor Lynch has suspended Morgan, he is out of favor, and my father wants to break the arrangement that has served us well for many years," Erik said.

Jan looked at him in annoyance. "Henry Morgan has for nearly twenty years a millstone around my neck been. His influence and power is weak. This is our opportunity to free of him be!"

"Henry Morgan's resourceful, Vader, you know that as well as I. He may be today weak, but he will tomorrow strong again be. Tarr and Hornigold's efforts more than make up for the percentage he takes, and the island safe is." Erik's English had deteriorated with his anger. "The whole of the Caribbees know of them and they know Sayba under Tarr's protection is. No one will dare to attack our island whilst they interests here have. Keeping them close will prevent history repeating itself, and I'm surprised you can't see that!"

"With last year's profits we can our own protectors hire, preferably Dutch—Sayba would still be safe!"

Erik shook his head. "You would start another war, Vader. Neither Morgan nor Tarr would easily give up on this arrangement, it's far too profitable for them. If we set ships against them, we would lose more to sinkings than we to the Englanders give. The arrangement works, Vader. Tarr and the others are good men, and by now they are near as loyal to us as they are to Morgan. You would be a fool to now change things."

I gasped as Jan's face turned bright red at his son's insult. He glanced at me, then controlled himself with visible effort. I was gratified to see Erik look concerned—he knew he'd gone too far.

Klara and the two men brought the next course, roasted suckling pig, and we ate in silence.

Jan placed his cutlery on his plate and looked at me. "So, are you excited about your wedding, child?"

I smiled nervously. *Is he serious?*

"You only have three weeks left to wait, then you will husband and wife be!"

Erik scowled and I stared at them both. *Three weeks!* I kept my gaze on my future husband, wondering if I might shame him into a smile, but he didn't look at me. Jan spoke to him in Dutch.

"Mr. van Ecken! I thought we'd agreed to speak English at the table," I said, not sure where I'd found the courage to speak to him in this manner again. He bowed his head.

"Quite right, child, but you can't keep calling me Mr. van Ecken. Call me Schoonvader—it means father-in-law, and will soon true enough be. And don't mind my son's bad manners. He sees the necessity of the marriage, and is only with nerves suffering. All will be well once the nuptials over are." He glanced at Erik, who nodded, once.

"You must some thought to your wardrobe give, child. I understand you and that slave," he glanced at Erik again, "did some good work on the journey on your wedding gown. It needs to finished be. If you need fabric for more gowns, please let me know—we have warehouses full of the stuff, but please take better care than you this morning did."

I stared at my empty plate and mumbled an apology.

"Very well, then. I think we're here finished. You may to the drawing room retire, Gabriella. Erik and I will to the library go to continue our discussions."

Later that night, I lay in bed, my head swimming with all that I'd seen and heard that day. I was much happier, and only wished that Erik and his father would reach some agreement soon. I was still wary of my future husband, but hoped he would prove to be friendlier once this current disagreement was at an end.

I caught my breath at a sound and listened hard. It came again from below. I realized I'd heard something similar—aboard Hornigold's ship on the first night. I stared at the canopy over the bed—angry, jealous and ashamed. *If he thinks so little of me that he would bed my slave in my hearing, why on earth had he agreed to marry me?*

Part 2
30th June 1683

Chapter 12

I took a deep breath and held the looking glass up to my face. Eyes darkened with kohl, lips reddened with cochineal, face powdered with chalk, and cheeks rouged with cerise. My shining dark hair was set off well by my veil and hung in perfect curls just past my shoulders.

My gown of white silk left my shoulders bare, its sleeves were tied with more silk and fell to my elbows. The bodice was ruffled and the mantua, hanging in perfect drapes to enhance the length of my body, was embroidered with red and yellow flowers, and drawn back over my hips to show off matching petticoats. I twisted slightly to look at my back. The sash at my hips was tied into a perfect bustle and the dress trailed behind. I had never looked so well and smiled at myself. It was the last day of June—my wedding day.

"You look beautiful, Miss Gabriella," Klara said and smiled. I smiled back, but my smile faltered with nerves for the day and life ahead of me. An image of Peter floated in my mind, but I pushed it away. I could not think of him—ever again.

"It's time," she added.

I sighed and nodded, pulled on my matching gloves and picked up my fan. I was ready and couldn't put this off any longer.

The past three weeks had been awful. Jan and Erik had rowed constantly behind library and study door. Presumably it was still about Morgan and his pirates, but I couldn't be sure. I could only hope they weren't arguing about me. At least Jan tried to be polite and remember his manners, but Erik barely spoke to me. It was clear this marriage was Jan's idea and Erik a reluctant participant. At least we only saw each other at mealtimes and most of the days were my own.

That didn't mean much; there was only so much time I could spend sitting on a beach, reading or working at my embroidery, and my only friend was a slave who was regularly bedded by my almost-husband, whether she wanted to be or not. Looking at her now, and the genuine smile on her face, I thought I believed her when she said she did not.

I shuddered, thinking of the man I was to marry. *What kind of man would behave as he does?* I didn't want to marry him, but knew I would. I had no choice. My father had sold me to the van Eckens. I was at their mercy and had no power of my own. If somehow I found a way to leave and went home, Father would be furious. I had no doubt he would send me straight back, if not worse—I suspected he may even be capable of murder if defied so publicly.

I couldn't escape anyway. I was trapped on an island—surrounded by water. I didn't have a boat or know how to sail one. Every visiting ship worked for or with Jan and Erik, and there was nowhere else to go but jungle—full of strange sounds in the dark. I wouldn't survive a week in the Caribbean wilds—the thought of that terrified me more than the thought of life as Mevrouw van Ecken.

"Ready?" Klara's prompt shook me out of my thoughts. I nodded and moved to the door. Klara gathered and lifted my train, and we struggled down the stairs. My embroidered white silk shoes were higher than I was used to, and the excessive amount of silk I wore made the narrow, steep staircase difficult to negotiate. I breathed a sigh of relief when we reached the landing without mishap, and we walked to the top of the main staircase in silence.

This staircase had been built to make an impression on everyone who entered the house and would be much easier to descend. I straightened my shoulders and lifted my chin, determined at least to get through the day with dignity. Joy wasn't an option.

Erik was nowhere to be seen; only Jan waited for me in the large, grand hall.

"Why the hell are you that dress wearing? That one's for tomorrow!"

I looked at him in confusion. This was my wedding dress and this my wedding day.

"We arrange today the legal affairs. We only the marriage celebrate once it has consummated been—tomorrow! Well, it's now too late to change. You'll just have to it wear. Don't damage or wrinkle it—it needs tomorrow to be perfect!"

I nodded, near tears. I'd assumed the wedding customs would be those I knew, and realized now that assumption had been foolish. Nothing about these men was what I knew: not their manners, habits or language.

Jan walked ahead to the carriage. I heard him mutter, "*Vrouen*," under his breath and cringed. By now, I knew what that meant: *women*. My slow, awkward climb into the carriage only increased his impatience, and he left Klara and Hendrik to find a way to fold my dress with a minimum of wrinkles.

Eventually we were ready and started the drive to Eckerstad.

"Is that why Mam and Father aren't here yet? Are they coming tomorrow for the celebrations?" I asked. I needed to know; they hadn't been mentioned, but I hoped with all my heart that I'd see Mam again.

Jan looked at me and sighed. "They're not coming, child. Your father is too busy and he would not permit your mother unaccompanied to travel."

"Oh," I said, stung. I blinked back tears and stared, unseeing, at the trees and scenery we passed, and clasped Mam's amethyst in my hand. How could I have been so stupid as to think they'd come?

Chapter 13

"Where's the church?"

"There is no church, child. It costs time and money to a church build. And what for? We can talk to God in the comfort of our own homes. I'm not for a minister paying to tell everyone what to think. I'll myself do that!" Jan laughed.

I tried to smile. I'd enjoyed the informal prayer time on Sundays that seemed to be the only way the van Eckens celebrated their religion. They'd been a relief after the solemn day-long worship at home, but I'd expected something more for my wedding.

In Massachusetts, life, and even celebration, was taken so seriously, a wedding was a simple statement sworn by bride and groom, at home, before a magistrate. I'd been envious of the stories I'd heard of other cultures and their big wedding services and subsequent parties, and had hoped for something like that now. But there was no one else here.

I took Hendrik's hand so he could help me down from the carriage and offered a nervous smile to Klara, who jumped down from the seat behind me and organized the dress, preventing any part of the train touching the dirt of the square. I squinted at her; her eyes looked wet, but she turned her head away and I said nothing.

We climbed the steps to the largest brick building in Eckerstad, my arm on Jan's, Klara following, and entered the town hall. I took a deep breath and tried to calm my nerves.

Jan led me to a door on the right and opened it. He stopped, standing still a moment to look at Erik sitting behind a large, ornate desk. He said something unfriendly in Dutch and Erik rose, then walked around the desk and stood before it. Father and son stared at each other a moment, then Erik looked at me. His eyes softened and he smiled. I smiled back. *Maybe this won't be too bad, after all.*

We walked toward my almost-husband, and Jan dropped my arm to move behind the desk and take his seat. Klara arranged my dress, gave me a discreet pat on the arm, and retreated to the back of the room. I looked at Erik, then at Jan in expectation. I was ready.

Jan cleared his throat and spoke—in Dutch. My face fell. Not only was my Mam missing from my wedding, but so was my language.

Erik spoke. I couldn't understand a word.

Jan told me to say, "Ja'. I did.

Fifteen minutes later, Erik walked me back out of the room and to the square. As we walked into the bright sunshine, a loud cheer greeted us. I blinked. The square was full of people wishing us well. I smiled and offered a small wave before I was ushered into the carriage.

Jan and Erik shook a few hands and exchanged brief words with people, but I wasn't introduced. I supposed it was obvious who I was, but I'd have liked to know who was who.

With no other option I waited as patiently as I could until they both climbed into the carriage and we started for home. I stiffened with the realization that I'd thought of Brisingamen as home for the first time.

Jan had insisted I change out of the gown before dinner, and that Klara ensure not one speck of dirt or wrinkle remained on it by morning.

I smiled at her once we were alone in the safety of my room.

"Which gown would you like to wear to dinner, Mevrouw van Ecken?" she asked and I shuddered.

"The pale-gold silk, I think, Klara. And please keep calling me Miss Gabriella—I may be married to a Dutchman, but I'm not ready for Mevrouw yet." I laughed and she smiled at me.

I sat down heavily as the realization sank in. I was no longer Gabriella Berryngton, I *was* Mevrouw Gabriella van Ecken. I thought of Peter again, then forced his image from my mind. It was useless to think of him, I'd never see him again.

I stayed in my room as long as I could, but when I heard a door slam downstairs, I knew I couldn't put it off any longer. I rose, took a deep breath, and made my way downstairs.

The evening meal was awkward and silent. I was nervous about the night ahead. Erik barely looked at me, never mind spoke, and Jan soon gave up his attempts at conversation. It was still over far too quickly, and as we rose from the table, I thought I'd throw up what little I had managed to eat.

The men went to their study, as usual, and I stayed in the drawing room and tried to read, but could not concentrate. I had no idea what to expect from the marriage bed except grunts and screams. I was unclear about what caused them, though. My departure from Massachusetts Bay had been so sudden, and Mam so upset, we'd not spoken about my marital duties—we hadn't expected my marriage to Peter for many years. I only had advice to do as my husband instructed, and the memory of guilty gossip from my friends, and I was terrified.

I rang for Hendrik and asked him for another glass of wine "to steady my nerves", as Father used to say.

Chapter 14

I put down my empty wine goblet and book, and stood. I couldn't put it off any longer. My head spun and I grimaced. I'd drunk too much wine. It was time to go to bed.

I went upstairs carefully. I'd heard no voices when I passed the library door, but knew the heavy door hadn't been opened whilst I had sat alone in the drawing room. They were still in there: my husband and father-in-law. I giggled. *My husband.* Then hushed. *Husband. I have a husband.* I carried on upstairs.

I sat at my dresser and pulled the round enameled brush through my hair until Klara entered. She offered me a smile, but I was too nervous. I had no idea what Erik would expect of me. I wanted to ask Klara, but knew I wouldn't. I was the mistress of the house and she my slave; I couldn't ask her how to bed my husband.

She untied and unlaced until she'd removed all the pieces of my gown. She poured out some water and I washed my face, under my arms and—after a suggestive glance from Klara—between my legs.

I dressed again in my night shift—it hung to my knees, had pink ribbon decorating the neck line and sleeves, plus embroidery on the chest. Klara held up the looking glass and I stared. My face was turning brown from the sun and my freckles had doubled, at least. I looked like a child, not a married woman.

"Thank you, Klara," I said, my voice betraying my nerves and fear. She looked as if she wanted to say something, but thought better of it, put the glass away and, with a final, concerned look in my direction, left the room.

I climbed into bed, smoothed the covers over myself and lay with my head propped on a bolster. I waited.

* * *

The door banged open and I woke with a start. The room was dark, but my husband held a lantern which he placed on my dresser. I could see him outlined by the light as he undressed. When he pushed his breeches down, I looked away, embarrassed, but curiosity got the better of me and I turned my eyes back to him.

I'd never seen a man without breeches before, although knew what they had down there. As a child, I and my friends had giggled at the boys when we splashed in the sea—naked so as not to spoil our clothes. Father would have flogged us had he known. None of those boys had anything like this, though. They'd been small and floppy, I'd never expected anything so . . . aggressive, and I shrank back against the bed. I didn't want him coming anywhere near me with that thing.

He pulled the muslin tester to one side and climbed onto the bed, flung the covers back and knelt over me. I felt deeply embarrassed when he pushed my shift up, exposing me and staring in the dim light. I tried to cover myself, but he batted my hands away.

He leaned over me, bracing his weight on his hands, and looked at my eyes for the first time. I screwed my nose up at the smell of sour rum, but forced myself to stare back and tried to tell him through my look to be gentle. I couldn't read anything in his eyes, and was sure he hadn't understood.

I screamed as a pain tore through me from between my legs. Erik smiled and pushed into me harder. I bit my lip to keep my screams in. He'd enjoyed the first one, I wouldn't give him any more.

He kept pushing, over and over, until finally he groaned and moved off me. I stared at his back and was relieved when he immediately started to snore.

Is that it? As his wife, do I really have to let him do that to me whenever he wants?

I turned over onto my side, hugged my knees to my belly and let the tears come. I moved one hand to my mouth to quieten my sobs when they threatened to burst out of me. I didn't want to wake him.

Chapter 15

I woke alone in the morning. The memories of the day and night before came back to me, and I couldn't stop the tears.

I turned away when Klara entered, but by the pause in her step I realized she knew I was crying and didn't know what to do about it. She put the armful of linen she carried onto the chest and left the room again.

By the time she came back, I had myself under control, my face dry. "Good morning, Klara," I said, my voice steady.

"Morning, Miss Gabriella. Are you well?" I nodded and flung the covers back, then stood. I gasped when I saw the sheets. He'd made me bleed! He must have known, but he hadn't cared!

"Don't worry, Miss Gabriella, it's normal the first time."

I looked at Klara as she threw the covers back down to hide the red stains. "I'll take care of it." She nodded toward the pile of linen she'd brought to my room. I swallowed and nodded.

"Thank you," I tried to say, but it came out as a whisper.

I crossed to the bowl of water she prepared and winced as I pulled my shift over my head. My body hurt. I washed carefully, then dressed in the pale-blue gown Klara had laid out whilst I was washing.

"Where's the wedding gown? Am I not wearing that today?" I asked.

"Later, this afternoon," Klara replied. "You'll need to change after lunch, before the guests arrive, but this morning is your own."

I let out a sigh of relief. After the surprises of yesterday, I didn't know what to expect from today, but at least I had a few hours as Gabriella before I had to play the part of Mevrouw van Ecken again.

* * *

At the breakfast table, Jan was all smiles and full of congratulations, and I knew I was blushing as I carefully sat down.

"Good morning," I said to my husband, refusing to allow him to ignore me.

"Morgen," he muttered, then lifted his eyes and smiled at me. I dropped my own eyes, unable to hold his gaze with that expression on his face. There was no warmth or emotion in that smile—it was a simple stretching of his lips.

I stared at my plate and picked at the fruit, my appetite gone.

"Eat up, child. With any luck, you'll be eating for two soon, you need to build up your strength," Jan said.

I froze. I couldn't imagine bearing them a child. I couldn't imagine having Erik as the father of my child. I started at a discreet touch from Klara and glanced at her. She smiled. I wondered what she was trying to tell me.

Eventually, breakfast over, I could escape. I needed to get away from the house and everything van Ecken, and headed through the trees to the cliff top, then my beach. I didn't move until the position of the sun told me it was noon.

Lunch was just as awkward as breakfast, but the fresh air had made me hungry and I wolfed down the spiced chicken. I'd barely finished when Erik sent me upstairs to change. I climbed the stairs slowly. I wasn't looking forward to spending the afternoon and evening in the company of Jan, Erik and their friends.

Chapter 16

Klara had the white dress looking perfect again, and I congratulated her as she entered my room. She nodded at my words and held out a cup of steaming liquid.

"I saw your face, Miss Gabriella, when Mijnheer Jan talked about children."

I looked at her, remembering the way she'd smiled and touched my shoulder. "I cannot bring a baby into this house, Klara. I won't let those two men raise my child, but what can I do?"

"Drink this," she said, and I took the cup. "It's a tea made from plants that grow nearby. I and some of the other women drink it every morning. None of us have had a child since."

I smiled at her, hardly daring to believe it. "You're sure? I won't have his baby if I keep drinking this?"

"I'm sure," Klara said. I drank it, and grimaced—it was bitter.

"You'll get used to the taste," Klara said, smiling.

"Or you could add sugar," I said, laughing with the relief I felt.

"Or I could add sugar," Klara repeated, smiling. "Turn around."

I did, and she untied the discreet ribbons holding my mantua in place, then removed it. Petticoats and stays followed, and I quickly washed then dressed in my wedding gown.

There was a knock at the door and we glanced at each other.

"Just a moment," I called, but the door was flung open despite my words.

"You need to hurry up," Erik said. "You've wasted the morning, you were nowhere to be seen when you should have been making preparations. Now our guests are arriving and you are still nowhere to be seen. This is not behavior I expect from my wife and the mistress of Brisingamen." He accented his words with a regular thumping of his cane on the floor and I noticed Klara flinch every time he brought it down.

"Oh, I thought everything was already done," I replied. "I didn't know I was needed—if you'd told me, I'd have stayed at the house." I noticed Klara's fingers stilled on the ties of my bodice at my words.

Erik just looked at me.

"Pull those stays tighter, Klara," he said, without taking his eyes from me. I stared back at him. I wouldn't give him the satisfaction of protesting and gritted my teeth as the wooden slats were drawn into my flesh.

Klara draped the mantua around me and secured it, and I checked my hair and face in the mirror. I was ready.

Erik turned and strode out of the room and I followed. I glanced at Klara as I left and she gave my hand a little squeeze, then I was on my own. I followed my husband down the first flight of creaking stairs, my stays digging into me on every step, but I was aware of Erik standing at the bottom watching me and I wouldn't give him the pleasure of a whimper or complaint. I glanced at the door nearest my stairs—Erik's room. I knew now we'd keep separate rooms and he would visit me at his own convenience. I wasn't welcome in his room—not that I could ever imagine myself wanting to visit him. I realized that I was effectively trapped. I wouldn't be able to descend these wooden stairs without alerting anyone in that room of my movements.

"Hurry up, wife, our guests are waiting!" Erik tapped my back in impatience with his cane and I glared at him, then swept past him toward the main staircase. He caught up with me at the top and grabbed my arm, linking it with his own. I knew it wasn't for my benefit, but for that of the crowd of people gathered in the hall and cheering.

I stretched my lips in a smile and stared at all the faces. I'd wished for a large party for my wedding day, and here it was. I knew nobody. Not one person was there for me. My eyes continued to sweep the room as we descended the stairs, and my smile became genuine when I recognized someone—Mr. Sharpe, standing with the Gaudies, Hornigold and Cheval. There was only one friendly face in this crowd of people, and he was a pirate. My smile faded.

Chapter 17

Erik led me around the room on his arm as he greeted our guests and introduced me. At least, I think that's what he was doing—he spoke only in Dutch, but when he said my name, he and the others looked at me and bowed. I gave a smile and small curtsey back. If he told me their names, I was unable to pick them out from the stream of Dutch.

I couldn't understand anyone here, so I watched them instead, trying to spot clues to the conversation in the way they held their bodies, crossed their arms or touched my husband. Also in the way they spoke—I couldn't understand the words, but I could still hear the fear, the dislike, the flattery, and I found it fascinating. I realized I'd been doing exactly this since I'd arrived to try and understand the van Eckens when they didn't have the manners to speak English in front of me.

There were few women here, and all those present were on the arm of a husband—we seemed as much a rarity in the Caribbees as the Massachusetts Bay Colony—and I smiled at every woman I met, hoping to find a friend. The only smiles I received back were of pity or embarrassment, and I began to despair. Was *anybody* here happy for us or wishing us well for the future?

I looked around me for Klara—at least she'd have a genuine smile for me, but she was surrounded by the sailors.

Eventually we, or rather Erik, had greeted each guest and we re-joined Jan. Both van Eckens ignored me and, aware of everyone in the room staring at me and their lack of manners, I was grateful when Mr. Sharpe approached.

"You look beautiful, Mrs. van Ecken," he said, and his eyes dropped to admire my dress.

"Thank you, Mr. Sharpe," I replied and stared hard. His eyes had not yet risen from my cleavage.

"Mr. Sharpe?" I said, and his eyes darted up to mine. His suddenly pale face flushed.

"Oh, I do beg your pardon, Mrs. van Ecken." His gaze dropped then rose again. "Forgive me, but your amethyst—it's such a beautiful stone." His hand moved toward it and I grabbed the pendant myself, cupping the stone in my hand to protect it from the pirate. His hand dropped.

"Where did you get it?"

I frowned at his rudeness, but decided to answer—up to now, he'd behaved well toward me and—after Klara—was the closest thing I had to a friend in the Caribbees.

"My mother gave it to me when I left Massachusetts to get married—it had been given to her by my true father."

"Your true father?"

Yes. Some English earl who persuaded her he loved her, then put her aboard a ship to the New World rather than face the consequences of his courtship. He gave her the stone as a keepsake." I wrinkled my nose in disgust.

"You don't think well of him."

"Of course not! At best he's a coward, at worst a devil. He lied to her, made her love him, used her, then shipped her off."

"What happened to her?"

"A man on the ship took pity on her and married her. But he turned out to be another devil—just of a different ilk." I looked at him, my eyes narrowed. He was asking a lot of questions. I realized my hand had dropped from the necklace as I had been talking, and he was staring at it again.

"Sharpe! Stop bothering my wife!"

My heart sank, Erik had noticed our conversation. Sharpe struggled to tear his eyes away from my chest, and Erik thumped the floor with his cane in anger, silencing the room.

"Captain Tarr!" Tarr was already crossing the room to join us. "Your nephew is drunk and making a nuisance of himself, kindly remove him from the presence of my wife. And teach him some manners!"

Tarr nodded once. "I beg your pardon, Mijnheer van Ecken, he is not feeling himself." He took one of Sharpe's arms and indicated to Blake to take the other. They half-pulled Sharpe out of the hall and into the Caribbean afternoon sunshine.

"Do not ever let me see you encouraging that man again," Erik hissed. "You are my wife and you will behave accordingly!"

He turned and left me standing alone in a sea of people. I looked around the room, embarrassed, self-conscious and confused.

I spotted Hornigold and Cheval in one corner, unable to conceal their amusement at the turn of events; Cheval even raised his glass to me. Jan stared, disapproval etched onto his features, and nobody else met my eye. Gazes darted away wherever I looked.

"Be careful, Miss Gabriella," Klara spoke softly at my shoulder. "It seems you have an admirer. Mijnheer Erik won't like that—be very careful around him."

I looked at her and nodded at the concern I saw in her eyes, then took another glass of wine from the tray she held.

Chapter 18

The rest of the wedding celebrations passed in a blur of strange faces and not-understood language. I didn't feel much different as a married woman than I had as a girl—apart from Erik's nocturnal visits, and those I could do without.

The household woke later on a Sunday and had a relaxed breakfast, then the three of us gathered in the library for prayers. As soon as I could escape, I found Klara and told her to come with me.

"But where are we going, Miss Gabriella?"

"You'll see, Klara, I want to show you something."

"But I have much work to do," she protested.

"The work can wait—you toil too hard as it is, I want us to have some fun today!" I grabbed her arm and pulled her through the trees to the cliff top.

"Isn't it beautiful?" I asked Klara. She nodded.

"Wouldn't it be wonderful if we could sail away one day, just go?"

"Go where?"

"Anywhere we wanted," I said.

"It'll get better, Miss Gabriella, just give it time, you've only been married a week."

I looked at Klara and gave her a small smile. I didn't believe her, but appreciated her trying to cheer me. We stared out to sea a little longer, dreaming of the impossible, then I urged her along the cliff path to the beach.

Once on the sand, I kicked off my shoes, lifted my petticoats, and ran to the water, splashing in the shallows. "Come on, Klara!" I laughed, urging her to follow me. She shook her head, but with a smile, and followed me to the water's edge. She took off her shoes and jumped back as a small wave covered her toes.

I laughed at her. You act like you've never seen the sea before!"

She shrugged. "Not this close."

"But how?" I was flabbergasted. "This is such a small island, and we live so close."

She shrugged again. "I don't have time. I work at the house every day, and when there is some time on a Sunday, I have much to do at my hut."

I gasped. "Oh, Klara, I didn't think. When you said you had a lot to do, I thought you meant at the house. Is Sunday your day off?"

She laughed. "I don't have days off, but there's usually a little time to clean my hut, wash my clothes . . ." she tailed off, staring at the sand.

"I'm sorry, I didn't realize. Go if you want to," I said, embarrassed at my selfishness, my assumption that she'd be happy to come to the beach with me.

"Soon," she said. She looked up at me with a smile. "I quite like this, the work can wait just a little while."

I laughed and kicked water at her. She squealed and ran back to dry sand. I followed and sat next to her, laughing.

"Mama! Mama!"

Startled, I looked round at the voice and saw a small boy scrambling down the cliff path. I squinted and realized I'd seen him before, at the sugar mill.

"Who's that?"

"My son," Klara replied, without looking at me. She got up and went to meet the boy.

He was small, maybe four or five years old, and was much lighter skinned than Klara—not much darker than myself now that I'd spent a month or so in the Caribbean sun.

They spoke for a while, then the boy ran off, looking round at me before he started to climb.

Klara re-joined me on the sand. "He and Wilbert were worried, they couldn't find me at the house."

"Wilbert?" I asked.

"He's one of the field slaves—he was there at the wedding celebration."

I remembered the dozen or so men dressed in the same livery Hans and Hendrik usually wore, and carrying trays of drinks and food.

"I didn't know you had a son," I said, shocked at how little I knew about this woman who was my main companion. "What's his name?"

She glanced at me, then looked back out to sea. "Jan."

"I beg your pardon?" She had spoken quietly and I thought I'd misheard.

She looked me in the eye. "Jan," she repeated, louder this time.

I stared at her, the implication of the name hitting me. I felt sick. "Jan," I repeated. "Oh, Klara." The revulsion I'd felt at first was swept aside by pity.

Klara looked out to sea again. "You know I was given to Mijnheer Erik for his sixteenth birthday—put into a pretty dress with a ribbon tied in my hair." She snorted with something like laughter. "My mama was so proud that I'd be working in the big house, and when I didn't come home at night, she thought I had a nice room of my own. She wouldn't listen to anyone who told her different."

"Not even when you told her?"

"I couldn't tell her what was happening, what Mijnheer Erik wanted from me every night. Her heart was already weak, all I could do for her was give her the fantasy."

"But, but, you said you were twelve?"

She nodded. "It didn't matter to Mijnheer Erik—I was just a slave girl to do with as he wished—my age didn't matter."

"And you had a son."

"Yes, I had a son—I didn't know about the tea then. Mijnheer Erik left me alone when my belly started to grow—and his father ignored me. In fact, I think he was pleased—they would have a free slave!"

I turned away, unable to look at the expression on her face. "But why did you call him Jan? You were forced! Surely calling him Jan celebrated his father?"

She laughed; a desperate sound with no humor in it. "I was young. I thought by calling him Jan they would recognize him as blood—show him favor, maybe even free him."

"They didn't," I guessed.

She made the laughing noise again. "No, they didn't. They put him to work as soon as he turned four. He's been weeding and picking up sugarcane after the harvest for two years already. Wilbert does his best to keep an eye on him, but he comes home covered in injuries.

I thought back to the boy I'd seen. I could hardly believe he was six years old—he certainly didn't look strong enough to do a day's work.

"He's stronger than he looks," Klara said. "He needs to be."

I looked at her in sympathy.

"Mijnheer Jan hates him; hates that I named him for him. If it weren't for Mijnheer Erik, I'm sure he'd have killed us both a long time ago."

"What? Why?"

"If you name someone for a Dutchman, you give the child a piece of their soul."

"What?" I didn't understand.

"Mijnheer Jan believes that by naming my son Jan, I have stolen part of his soul and given it to the boy." She looked at me. "He wants it back."

I felt cold and shivered. I remembered the way my father-in-law had been with Klara on the ship, and the way he'd spoken to her since.

"And Erik is protecting you?" I asked.

She nodded. "For the moment, at least. But now you're here, I don't know what to expect. I had hoped they'd both mellow with a new mistress of the house, but—" She paused and stared at the waves.

"At least he gave me to you when you came. Mijnheer Jan can't dispose of us if we're not his. But if Mijnheer Erik grows tired of us—" she paused again and I noticed tears running down her face. She turned to me.

"If you have a child, he *will* tire of Jan, and my son will die."

"Oh, Klara." I thought of the little boy who had scrambled down the cliff path to his mama, and tears ran from my own eyes. I didn't want Erik's child, not at the moment, anyway. But what if that changed? I may want a child one day, but if Klara was telling the truth—and I did believe her—then the birth of my child could mean the death of hers.

Chapter 19

I'd been going to the beach every day. It was the place where I found it easiest to think, and a place I was never disturbed. I had been cool toward Klara since her confession, though knew I wasn't being fair. She was a slave and had been given from one man to another, used and violated, then vilified for the consequences. She'd been even younger than I was now when it had started. I shuddered, my heart going out to her and the poor, frightened child she'd been.

I reached the cliff top and stopped, shading my eyes from the sun. Yes, I knew I'd seen something—a ship, its sails glinting in the harsh sun. As I watched, some of the sails were taken in—she must be coming to the island.

I walked along the cliff, watching the ship draw closer to shore. *Surely she must tack soon?* If she carried on much further, she wouldn't be able to clear the headland between here and Eckerstad. But she kept coming.

The beach was below me, but I didn't climb down. I sat instead and watched the ship sail closer to the rocks, my heart in my mouth. She was going to wreck.

I knew I should run and get help—those men would soon need it—but my legs were jelly. I couldn't stand, I could only watch. Closer and closer. I wanted to close my eyes, but needed to see.

I gasped—she was through! She kept coming and jarred as she ran aground. I stood, my legs strong again, to get a better view. Her remaining sails were dropped and an impossible number of men ran about her decks and climbed down to the beach.

As the crowd on deck thinned, I recognized bright flashes of color—the Gaudies. Captain Tarr and Quartermaster Blake were here.

I stared for a moment at the invasion of my special place, then turned and walked slowly back to Brisingamen. Belinda would need to know there may be extra mouths to feed this evening.

* * *

I went through my usual routine: deep breath, shoulders back, head up, then opened the door—and stopped in surprise.

The drawing room was full of people. The Gaudies were here, as expected, but also *Freyja's* men—Hornigold, Cheval and Sharpe—and there was a woman with them, too. I stared at her, wondering who she was. She was beautiful: long, dark hair tumbled down her back, pale skin—despite the sun—contrasted with her dark eyes, but she didn't smile.

Hornigold stepped back for a moment, and she came fully into my view. Her gown was simple and of quality, though she must have been wearing it for a number of days and it was starting to look tatty. I wondered what had brought her to this house, in this company, and we gazed at each other: two lost souls.

Hendrik opened the dining room door. I wouldn't have chance to speak to her yet—maybe at the table.

But no, she was seated as far away as possible from me on the opposite side and at Jan's left hand. Sharpe took the seat next to her, and I was surprised to feel a pang of regret. Of everyone at this table, he was the one man whose conversation and company I enjoyed.

Cheval took the seat to my left, and smiled at me. I offered a polite smile back. With his square jaw and pale-blue eyes, he was a good-looking man, but I always felt uncomfortable in his presence. His eyes were cold, and his face portrayed little expression, whatever his topic of conversation—which was usually himself. I never knew what he was thinking, but couldn't shake the impression that it was often contrary to what he was saying. I picked up my knife to spread butter on bread.

"Mevrouw van Ecken." I looked up at Sharpe. "Forgive me, I was unable to introduce my companion to you beforehand." I smiled at him and the woman. "This is Magdalena Ortega. Magdalena, I'm honored to introduce Gabriella van Ecken."

We smiled and nodded to each other. Erik grunted and I looked at him, wary of his mood.

"My apologies, Mijnheer van Ecken, Magdalena was . . . an

unexpected guest. I didn't feel able to leave her aboard ship with the crew."

I noticed Hornigold glare at him and realized there was something more going on here.

"She should not be with you at all!" Erik finally said. "What were you thinking, attacking Porto Belo?"

"It's a rich port," said Captain Tarr. "Our holds are full, and you will do very well out of the raid."

"It was reckless! Porto Belo is Spanish territory. Neither of our countries are at war with Spain at present, and you have stolen one of their women." He gestured to Magdalena and I dropped my knife with a clatter. "You could have started another war with your actions!"

I stared at Sharpe, shocked. *He kidnapped this woman!* The regard I had for him was shattered. Cheval sniggered beside me and I glanced at him. He was enjoying this.

Hornigold waved his hand. "There won't be a war over a single raid and one woman," he said, dismissive.

Erik flushed red, and I flinched before his fist connected with the table. "You don't seem to realize just how precarious your position is, any of you." He glared round the table. "Morgan is suspended and Governor Lynch wants him gone—preferably hanged. And Lynch won't stop with Morgan—he wants total power over Jamaica, he'd see every one of Morgan's men in chains and shipped off to London for trial as pirates. He can't touch me or Vader, but all of *you* are in his sights." He stared at Tarr, who dropped his eyes. Nobody looked at Erik now except Jan.

"My son is quite correct," he said. "Morgan is finished, and you do not have many friends in these waters at the moment. You took an unnecessary risk and have given Lynch all he needs to arrest you."

"What do you propose?" asked Tarr, his jaw set as he stared at Erik.

"You keep well away from Jamaica, and from New Spain. Their ships are fair game, but leave no witnesses. Bring the ships and their cargoes here. Any coin you find is your own."

"Now wait a minute." Tarr banged his own fist on the table. "There are valuable cargoes out there, we won't just hand them over! Not many ships carry coin enough to be worth the risks, not when the haul is to be shared with near two hundred men!"

Erik stood and leaned forward, bracing himself with both hands on the table. I pushed my chair back a little.

"You *will* hand them over. In return, you will have safe haven on this island—out of Lynch's grasp. If he attacks here he risks his own war, and London has already suffered enough at the hands of Amsterdam. If he attacks a Dutch island now, it will be him in chains in a cargo hold bound for London, and he knows it. Sayba is your best chance. You work for us now, and we will keep you free."

Tarr and the other pirates glared at him, but said nothing. Erik sat back down and beckoned to Klara, who placed a plate of meat before him, then served everyone else.

We ate in silence.

Chapter 20

The three of us sat in the drawing room, still not speaking, and I picked up the cushion cover I was embroidering for something to do. The pirates had escaped as soon as the meal was over, and I couldn't help but worry about Magdalena. I jumped and exclaimed out loud—I'd pricked my thumb with my needle. The van Eckens glared at me, but didn't ask after my welfare. I sucked my thumb and examined my work for blood. Clean.

She'd seemed wary of Hornigold, and I couldn't blame her, but Sharpe was also attentive and, truth be told, his attentions had at least appeared welcome. I sighed, even if she was in trouble, there was a not a thing I could do to help her.

I pricked my thumb again and put my work away in exasperation. If I carried on, I'd only ruin what I'd already completed.

Klara brought more drinks. I took another glass of wine, then she carried brandy over to Jan and Erik. I gasped to see Erik blatantly fondle Klara's bottom when he took his glass.

Jan leapt to his feet, furious, and shouted in Dutch. He swept his arm across, connected with Klara's face, and she fell.

"Klara!" I rushed to her. She was conscious, but already her eye was closing and that side of her face seemed to be swelling.

Erik also jumped to his feet, and the two men stood a fraction of an inch apart, both bright red, spitting their words in rage.

Klara and I cowered on the floor, wondering what they were saying. I remembered what she'd said about Jan and how he hated her—if I had any doubt of that before, I had none now.

We both flinched as Jan struck again. Erik didn't fall, though. Nor did he raise his hand to his jaw. He stood and stared at his father, then turned and left the room.

Jan glanced at the two of us still huddled on the floor, but said nothing. He was clearly embarrassed. He walked past us, careful not to get too close, and stood in front of his dead wife's portrait.

He spoke to it in Dutch, then left the room.

"Are you all right?" I asked Klara.

She nodded and stood. "I'm scared, Miss Gabriella—he really is going to kill me, he hates me so much."

I didn't know what to say. I thought she was right. I'd never seen anyone so angry or full of vitriol. We looked at each other a moment longer, then Klara moved to collect the shards of the glass scattered over the floor.

I looked up at the picture of Adelheid, and started to pity her. *How long will it be before that sour expression lives permanently on my own face?* I turned back to Klara.

"We'll find a way to keep you and Jan safe, Klara. I promise. We'll find a way."

She looked at me and smiled; I think in pity. She didn't look reassured.

Part 3
7th October 1683

Chapter 21

"Help, help, the molasses!"

We all looked up at the scrawny, filthy boy who had run into the dining room. It took me a moment to recognize him as Klara's boy—he was covered in a thick sticky brown substance.

"What's the meaning of this?" Jan thundered, slamming his open hand against the table top. "Get that out of here!"

Klara had run to her son as soon as he entered the room and placed herself between him and Jan van Ecken, who stood and glared at the boy.

"The molasses! Flood! The molasses!"

Jan strode over to the boy, pushed Klara out of the way and struck him. The younger Jan fell to the floor, sobbing in terror.

"Talk sense, boy, what's happened to the molasses?"

"Tank broke! Molasses everywhere!"

Jan took in a sharp breath and kicked the boy. Klara and I screamed, but the six-year-old only managed a grunt.

Jan Senior looked at Klara cradling her son, and drew his leg back for another kick.

"Vader!" Erik warned, and stepped in front of his father, a restraining hand on his chest. Things had calmed down since their fight, but I held my breath, wondering what was going to happen now.

Jan glared at his son a moment, then nodded. I sighed in relief. Erik knelt down by little Jan and said, "Now, boy, tell us what happened."

I looked at him in surprise at the tender note in his voice and glanced at Klara, but all her attention was on her son.

"What happened, Jan? Tell Mama what happened."

The child sobbed and curled tighter in Klara's arms, she bent her head to his murmur, then looked up. "One of the molasses' tanks has burst. It's flooded the road, just as the men were walking back. They need help!"

"But those tanks were full," Erik said. "They were to be shipped next week." He looked at his father. "We've lost a fortune!"

"Those men could be losing their lives," I snapped at them. "Come on!"

They rushed out of the room, followed by Hans and Hendrik, who had heard the commotion from the cookhouse.

"Come on, Klara, maybe we can help, too."

"Wilbert?"

Jan looked at her.

"Jan, is Wilbert safe?"

"I don't know, Mama. They were all covered, I couldn't see who was who."

"Come on, Klara, we'll go and see—go and help Wilbert."

She nodded and got to her feet. She was in shock, and I grabbed her arm and pulled to get her moving faster.

"Are you well, Jan, can you walk?" I asked him. He winced as he got to his feet and coughed, but nodded. I smiled at him, impressed by his bravery, and hated the van Eckens a little more for the way they treated this child.

We left the room and followed Jan's sticky footprints back out of the house and down the road to the sugar mill.

Chapter 22

Klara and I reached the junction and stopped in shock. A thick river of brown syrup blocked the way. Brisingamen was cut off—no carriage would get through that. Even the air seemed impassable—sickly sweet and cloying; it seemed to stick in my throat as I breathed.

We could hear shouts from up the mill road and looked at each other in dread. Klara was clinging onto Jan, holding him close, and was almost as filthy as he was. I looked at him and shuddered—if he'd been in the way of that river of treacle . . .

Klara moved to the bank and climbed up into the field of sugarcane stumps, dragging Jan after her, and I followed. We cut through to the mill road and stopped. The road was lower than the surrounding fields and had acted as a channel. It was now full of molasses. Molasses-covered men moved at the edges, trying to haul out those caught in the middle.

I jumped when Klara screamed a name: 'Wilbert!"

One of the molasses-covered men turned and rushed over to us, grabbing Jan and holding him tight, then Klara. The three of them hung onto each other and sobbed. Klara was soon only recognizable by her hair.

I looked back at the molasses river, wondering what to do. I couldn't see Erik and Jan anywhere—I doubted they were any of the treacle-covered rescuers I could see. I went closer to the edge. Sticky brown shapes heaved in the mess and showed life. Unmoving humps showed where life had been lost—there were many; too many.

Hans and Hendrik and half a dozen unrecognizable men were in a line, dragging a heaving shape out of the morass into the safety of the sugarcane, and I hurried over as the victim reached higher ground.

I tore a length of cloth from my petticoat and used it to wipe the dense syrup from the man's nose and mouth. I realized the orifices were completely clogged and the man hadn't been able to breathe for some time. I sat back on my heels in despair, then screamed as something struck my chest and I fell to the side, winded.

"What the hell are you doing? Don't touch those filthy animals!" Erik raised his cane to strike again and I cowered in the field, waiting for the blow.

"*Zoon*, Son," Jan cautioned, and Erik lowered his cane then turned and stalked up the hill back to the collection of buildings at the top of the lane.

Jan offered me a hand and helped me up, but said nothing. He escorted me to Erik's side, standing with Rensink, and we looked down at the mess.

"Aren't you going to help them? Somebody may still be alive," I ventured, stunned at my treatment, but even more appalled at the sight before my eyes. As far as I could tell, Jan and Erik had done nothing to help the rescue effort. I coughed in the sweet air.

"What happened?" Erik demanded of Rensink.

"One of the hoops of the full tank snapped," Rensink said. "The men were on their way home and molasses just . . . engulfed them. They didn't have a chance. I was still up here, reprimanding the boy, or I would have drowned too."

"Reprimanding the boy?" Jan asked. "Why, what did he do? Was this his fault?"

"No, no," Rensink said. "I caught him chewing on some cane—gave him a hiding, but he saved my life."

Jan looked disappointed. I realized Rensink was in shock. I breathed a sigh of relief. Little Jan's sweet tooth had saved him from a horrific fate.

"Get those men organized, Rensink, the ones that are left. Anyone still in there is dead now. I want the molasses collected and re-boiled. We'll have lost a fortune from this, but we'll rescue what we can. It'll make an inferior rum, but at least we'll get more sugar, and it can't be helped. And don't use those tanks anymore—if I remember rightly, they came from Hornigold. It wouldn't surprise me if they were riddled with shipworm!"

I stared at him in disbelief, horrified at their indifference to the deaths of so many men in their care.

Chapter 23

Everything stank of sweetness. Everything was sticky—the very air seemed to be composed of sugar. It had been three days since the accident, and most of the molasses had been shoveled up and put on to boil—the muck of the ground skimmed off as it rose to the surface. The road to Eckerstad was open—although lined with molasses. Six men had lost their lives.

Klara coughed as she brushed my hair; we were all coughing, but the men who'd been caught up in the flood were the worst afflicted.

"How's Jan?" I asked her.

She shook her head. "Not good. He's still struggling to breathe, and the coughing's so violent, I keep thinking it will shake his little body apart."

"Remember what the doctor said—it's just our lungs clearing the residue. We'll all stop coughing soon."

"Mmm," she said. The doctor had only seen Jan, Erik and myself. I'd begged the van Eckens to allow the doctor to see everybody else, especially the children, but they'd refused to spend money on the health of slaves—there were plenty more available if need be. I was hoping the diagnosis he'd given us held true for the others, but I was concerned for little Jan.

"The men are being buried this morning," Klara changed the subject. "At the cemetery on the other side of our village."

I nodded. Jan and Erik hadn't mentioned it to me and were unlikely to attend. Klara knew I'd want to pay my respects to the men who had died, despite my husband and father-in-law's indifference.

After an awkward, silent breakfast, I slipped out of the house and took the northern path away from Eckerstad into the jungle. The sugarcane hadn't reached this side of the estate yet—another thing Jan and Erik argued about: Jan wanted to keep the sugar plantation small and concentrate on shipping; Erik wanted to expand both.

I passed Rensink's house—a modest two-story building—and continued to the slave village. A collection of huts housed the women and families—I knew Klara shared one of them with Wilbert and Jan—and there was also a long, low building where the single men slept.

The village was empty and I paused. I walked up to the men's hut, opened the door and peered inside. The room was lined with wooden platforms and, as my eyes got used to the dim light, I saw a manacle and chain at the foot of each bed. There was no privacy, no comfort, no nothing. I imagined the life these men led—breaking their backs in the fields or sugar mill by day, sleeping like this by night. My fear and dislike of the van Eckens hardened and I realized I'd started to despise them.

I left the men's hut and continued to the cemetery. It was already far too large for such a community, and my tears dripped throughout the service. Rensink led the mourning—another insult—and in Dutch.

Nobody understood what was being said for their lost colleagues, friends, husbands. English-speaking slaves fetched a higher price than Dutch, and by keeping their language private, the van Eckens could talk freely without anybody knowing their business. This funeral meant nothing, and nobody participated bar standing as expected with bowed heads.

"We'll give them a proper send-off later," Klara told me, "in our own way." I nodded. "It would be better if you stayed away, though." I nodded again. I understood that as a van Ecken I wouldn't be welcome.

Chapter 24

I got ready for dinner quickly so that Klara could go to the funeral proper, then went downstairs. Captain Hornigold was sitting with the van Eckens in the drawing room, and I stopped in surprise on seeing him. His company was the last thing I needed, especially as he was on his own and hadn't brought Mr. Sharpe.

I said little at the table, still shocked after the accident. Hornigold was surprised at the extent of our coughing, and I could see he was uncomfortable until Erik explained and he realized the house hadn't been struck down by fever.

The fact that we were all afflicted, however, didn't stop my father-in-law berating Hans and Hendrik for their own difficulty in breathing. I smiled at them, aware they were missing the funeral for their fallen friends. Hendrik tried to return my smile, but broke down in a coughing fit worse than anything I'd heard so far.

"For God's sake, shut up!" Jan shouted. Hendrik did his best, but clamping his mouth shut against the coughs made them worse, and I jumped to my feet as he collapsed. I pulled his hand away from his mouth and was horrified to see a black treacly substance covering his palm.

"Right, that's it, I've enough of this had!" Jan exclaimed. "Cough, cough, cough! And now look, that rug ruined is!" There was a small spot of coughed-up molasses on it.

"Hornigold, your arrival proves propitious to be. The sugar is waiting to be transported to Cornelius's rum distillery in Sint Eustatius, you can load up *Freyja*, and us as well take. We need to get away from this foul air—the sea air will do us all good and our lungs clear. By the time we return, the slaves will either recovered or died have."

I looked at him in renewed shock at his callousness.

"We can't leave now, Vader, it's our busiest time. We need to oversee the rest of the sugar manufacture and the clearing of more jungle for the next field. We *can't* leave."

"Rensink can that handle, I want us to spend a month or two away from here. This stench and the constant hacking is driving me mad. It will good business be to Onkle Cornelius personally see. It's been too long since we've him a visit paid, I'm sure he thinks he can advantage take. If we deliver the sugar personally, we can a harder bargain drive."

"But Captain Aalbers and *Adelheid* will be putting in soon to take the sugar," Erik protested.

"That's his bad luck. He can *Adelheid* refit for slaves and to Africa head. It will more profits bring, anyway. Gabriella, get that slave of yours to pack, we're in the morning leaving."

"I want Klara and her son to join us," I said. I knew better than to use little Jan's name.

"No," Jan said. "They stay here."

"You told me she was mine to do with as I wished, when I first boarded *Freyja*," I said, my whole body tense with fear at standing up to him, but I knew it could be little Jan's only chance. "I can't manage without her now, not with the way Erik likes me to dress."

I glanced at my husband, gambling that he'd take my side. He had shown small moments of tenderness toward the boy, and still enjoyed Klara's company at times. Plus his relationship with his father was fraught at best. I held my breath.

"I think it's a good idea. My wife needs her slave, and the boy will be useful as well. Klara can't look after the three of us by herself. If you insist on us making this trip, Klara and the boy will join us."

Jan glared at his son, and I let out my held breath– very quietly.

Nothing was said for some time as father and son stared at each other.

"Very well," said Jan, eventually. "Your whore and her bastard son with us come."

I stared after him in shock as he strode out of the room. Erik continued eating and ignored us. I couldn't bear to look at him and watched Hans bundle Hendrik out of the room.

Chapter 25

"Welcome aboard," Sharpe said to me, taking my hand and kissing it. I smiled at him in greeting. He stood a little apart from Hornigold and Cheval, who were greeting my husband and his father. Klara and Jan boarded behind us, and Sharpe nodded to them in greeting. The other men ignored them.

Sharpe led us below, and I made for the cabin I'd used on my first passage.

"No, Magdalena and I have that one. Hornigold has vacated the captain's cabin for the use of you and your husband." He indicated some structures on the deck that hadn't been there last time. "We've erected temporary cabins for him and Mr. van Ecken Senior, although we'll have to take them down again if we get into a fight." He laughed and opened the door to the captain's cabin.

I smiled at him and entered, followed by Klara and Jan, then looked around. I smiled again. It was bigger than the other, and I was relieved. I'd been dreading sharing such a small space with Erik. Whilst the coming days would still not be pleasant, at least there was a little more space to help me endure the journey.

The meal had been awkward and mainly silent; even our coughs had reduced. I hadn't been able to chat with Sharpe or speak to Magdalena, and had no desire to talk to anyone else at the table. Erik was still angry about leaving Brisingamen, and Hornigold and Cheval appeared to be sulking—they must have had other plans than sailing to Sint Eustatius with the van Eckens and a hold full of sugar. The only one in any good humor was Jan, but even he had tired of the atmosphere and lapsed into silence by the time Klara put the main course before us—roasted goat.

The men left us to go on deck and Klara served both myself and Magdalena with wine, then took a tray of brandy and glasses to the men. Magdalena and I were alone.

I looked at her, suddenly nervous. She was a few years older than I, maybe twenty two or twenty three. Her hair curled down her back—way past her shoulders. Her skin was pale and freckle- and blemish-free, and I put my hand to my own freckled face in shame. Her green eyes glittered in the lantern-light over a long straight nose and full mouth. I had no idea how to ask her if she'd been kidnapped or needed help; I couldn't imagine this woman needing anything I could offer. Then she smiled, and her whole demeanor changed. I smiled back and sipped my wine.

"How are you enjoying married life?" she asked in English.

I grimaced. "It's not what I'd hoped," I answered truthfully.

She smiled, though looked sad. "No, I expect it rarely is," she said. We sat in silence for a while.

"I should be married now too," she said, breaking the silence. She stood, walked to the windows and stared out into the night. "To my childhood friend."

I looked at her in expectation, but she did not explain. "What happened?" I asked at last.

Her shoulders tightened, but she didn't turn back to me; she seemed to be talking to the empty sea. "I loved him, I really did; it's just that . . . he was all I knew."

"What do you mean?"

She didn't answer for a moment, then, "Porto Belo and Panama were all I knew, and I wanted to know more. My fiancé did—he sailed the world trading goods for my father—I hoped to join him on his voyages once we were married, but I knew he wouldn't allow it. He was too traditional, too protective. I would have had a life alone, waiting for him to return, not knowing when or even if he would come back." Now she turned, looked at me, then approached and sat down.

"I wanted adventure," she smiled, "but got a little more than I bargained for."

I looked at her in confusion.

"Leo was overdue from a voyage to Spain, and I was keeping an eye out for his sail. We were to be married once he'd arrived home, and I was both looking forward to seeing him and dreading it. At first, I thought the sail was his, but realized it wasn't when it was joined by a second. I didn't give them another thought until the first cannonball was fired—they were pirates!"

I drew my breath in sharply, even though I already knew who it had been. I was surprised she was opening up to me and wanted to encourage her. I guessed she was as lonely as I was.

"The ships in the harbor sank as they were holed, then the buildings started to fall."

"Did you have no defenses?" I asked, genuinely horrified as I pictured the scene.

"Not then—the treasure fleet calls at Porto Belo twice a year to load up silver from the mines inland and take it to Spain. Before their arrival, and during their stay, the town is heavily fortified, but once they've sailed, there's nothing left to guard. The men either return inland or sail with the fleet, and the town's reduced to an ordinary merchant town again. The forts are barely manned."

I nodded, trying to imagine it: one day busy, rich and important; the next abandoned, ignored and under fire.

"Once the buildings had been destroyed, the pirates came ashore to loot and take whatever they could find. Hornigold found me." She stared at me, but showed no expression.

"Hornigold?" I was surprised. "I thought Sharpe . . ."

She shook her head. "Sharpe was horrified. He's a good man, you know." She looked at me again, eyebrows raised. I offered her a small smile. Admittedly, I thought him the best of a bad lot, but he was still a pirate—I couldn't go as far as agreeing that he was a good man.

"He's Captain Tarr's nephew," Magdalena continued. "And Hornigold is terrified of Tarr. Sharpe makes the most of it. He 'confiscated' me." She laughed. "Hornigold was furious! But he gave me up."

"Had he— Did he . . ." I didn't know how to ask and stopped. She shook her head.

"He didn't hurt me—Sharpe didn't give him the chance, thank the Lord." She looked up, crossed herself, and muttered a short prayer.

"So now you're with Sharpe." I said, surprised at the tone of my voice. I couldn't decide whether it was disapproval or anger.

Magdalena stared at me, cool now. "Yes, now I am with Sharpe."

"Do you miss your fiancé?"

She gave no answer, but her face showed so much pain that she had no need to.

"That's why Hornigold is in such a bad mood," I finally said, embarrassed by the lull in the conversation.

"Yes, he's jealous."

I raised my eyes and looked at her. We sat staring at each other a moment, then she continued, "That's why we came to Sayba. We were hoping to rendezvous with Captain Tarr. His ship is bigger, and Henry wants to get me away from Hornigold—he does not trust him."

Henry. I'd forgotten his first name. I nodded at her.

"But now we have to endure another passage with Hornigold and his sycophantic crony, Cheval."

I smiled at her description.

"At least you seem to be comfortable," I said, nodding at the cabin next door.

"Oh, yes." She smirked. "We're definitely comfortable." She relaxed her smile. "And it's certainly an adventure."

Chapter 26

Magdalena had left some time ago, and I was almost ready for bed. I sat while Klara brushed my hair, and thought about the woman I'd spent the evening with. I liked her, I thought, though I felt sorry for her family left behind in Porto Belo. They sounded wonderful. *How could she have left them like that to go in search of adventure?* I knew she hadn't left entirely by choice, but it was clear that she'd hoped to join the pirates, and had stayed rather than run from them. *And what of her fiancé, Leo? What became of him?*

I sighed and stood, then crossed to the bed. Whatever her motivations, I was sure she regretted them now. She hadn't bargained on Hornigold; and whilst she seemed happy enough with Sharpe, there had definitely been a wistful note to her voice when she spoke of her childhood sweetheart.

I got under the cover, whispered goodnight to Klara—she would spend the night on a mat on the floor with little Jan—and tried to sleep. I had no idea if Erik would join me, or whether he also had one of the small temporary cabins that had been erected on the gundeck. I prayed I had seen the last of him for the night.

I woke to a cold draught—the bed clothes had been thrown off. Moonlight bathed the cabin and I could see Erik standing over me, swaying with the motion of the ship and removing his clothes. I hoped it was a dream, but knew it was not. My heart sank.

Naked, he climbed in next to me—there wasn't much room, and I was pressed up between him and the cabin wall. Tears started to fall.

He lifted his thumb and wiped my cheek, smiling. I looked at him in surprise at his tenderness, then realized he was enjoying my tears, my fear. I resolved not to give him any more. His hand dropped from my face and pushed my nightshift up. I didn't protest, nor help. He did not care.

He straddled me and I bit my lip to hold in my gasp of pain at his entry. I looked up at him in the moonlight, keeping my face calm and my eyes dry. He looked away. I closed my eyes for a moment at my small triumph, but realized his thrusts had grown more urgent. Then I understood what he was looking at, and opened my eyes again to make sure. Yes, he was staring at Klara, while he was . . . while he was . . . on top of me. I looked at his face, but couldn't read his expression. I didn't recognize it, I'd never seen it on his face.

Then I realized I *had* seen it before—on Hornigold's face when he'd asked for Klara on my passage to Sayba. And on Cheval's face, too. It was desire. I looked at her, huddled on the floor, her back to us, arms around her son to protect him, and felt the tears threaten again.

I turned my face to the wall and stared, refusing to give life to my tears. I felt utterly humiliated. I didn't want to be here, aboard this ship, married to this man, here in this bed.

My mind drifted, and I imagined my little beach, the sand warm, the waves gentle. I imagined walking to the water's edge and sitting on the wet sand, my toes digging into it.

A wave cooled my feet, then pulled at them and the sand around them. I dug my toes in again; again the sand was washed away. It wasn't enough. Suddenly I wanted to be in the water, have it wash me away, rather than the sand. I removed my clothing—it took only an instant—and waded into the sea.

The waves were larger now, crashing into me, jolting my body, over and over and over, one after the other. But I kept going; I would not go back. The rhythmic motion soothed me and I lay in the water, letting it caress and comfort me. I felt bruised and battered, but it didn't matter, the water took the pain away. The sea eased my distress and rocked me as a mother would a babe.

The waves calmed, but still I floated, drifting, drifting, knowing I could return whenever I wanted.

Chapter 27

I stared around me. Nothing. No land; just sea. I closed my eyes, smiled and lifted my face to the sun. But for the noises of the ship and its men, I could be completely alone. I opened my eyes and turned away from the aft rail and the emptiness, back to the ship.

About half the crew were on deck, working the sails or doing other sailor things, and I watched the men up the masts in amazement—they moved so fast, yet so surely they should have been born squirrels.

My eyes searched for my husband—it had become my habit to know his whereabouts so that I could avoid him. There he was, near the mainmast with Sharpe, his father close by at the rail.

I saw a small shape running along deck and grinned—Jan. He never walked when he could run; he was always so full of life and excitement, and was worse aboard ship—he loved it, even following the crew up the knotted ladders of rope that led up the masts. I don't think Klara knew about that though.

A coughing fit hit him mid-stride and he stumbled, crashing into Jan Senior and knocking him back against the rail of the ship. I cried out, my hands to my mouth, shocked. This was just the excuse Jan had been looking for to rid himself of his namesake.

He shouted and grabbed the child, hauling him back to his feet and toward the rail, still shouting—I couldn't tell whether in English or Dutch—but his intention was obvious: he was going to throw Jan overboard.

Jan's screams froze me to the wooden planking, but they made Erik move. He joined the pair, shouting himself, and grabbed hold of the boy, preventing his father from lifting him any further.

Jan Senior let go and the child fell, then scurried to the mainhatch, his face awash with tears. He jumped below decks and was gone, presumably to find his mother.

Erik and his father were still arguing at the rail, and it looked to be as bad as any argument I'd witnessed so far. Jan prodded his son's chest once, twice, three times, and Erik swatted his hand away. Jan's voice rose even further, his face bright red. Erik's temper rose to match, and he prodded his father in return. Jan didn't hesitate, and swung his fist. Erik took a couple of steps back, but this time he was not going to submit. He had witnesses, and witnesses who were much more important to him than Klara and myself.

He stepped forward and threw his own fist, snapping Jan's head back. Jan tried to step back to regain his balance, but had nowhere to go—he was already against the rail.

His body angled further back until his feet lifted and he tipped over. I hardly heard the splash. I stood rooted to the spot in shock.

I jumped at a hand on my arm: Sharpe. I hadn't noticed him join me at the stern; all my attention had been on the van Eckens. I looked him in the eye and he slowly shook his head. I knew he'd seen what I had seen: as Jan fell, he had held his arms out to his son, who had made no move to catch him.

I looked back at Erik, now leaning over the rail shouting, "*Vader, Vader!*" and shivered. He had just killed his own father.

"Man overboard!" Sharpe shouted beside me. "Heave-to! Man overboard!"

The ship turned, and the sails shook, then roared. Men pulled one of the towed boats alongside and set off to look for Jan.

An hour later, they returned. Nothing.

"The weight of his frockcoat will have pulled him under," Sharpe said to me. "He wouldn't have had a chance—he's gone."

I nodded, but said nothing, just stared at my husband who was still playing the part of distraught son. Nobody had approached him—even Hornigold watched from a safe distance. *Do they all know it had been no accident?*

I made my way to the mainhatch, wanting to get away from the maindeck and the sight of my husband. I dreaded him seeing me and demanding I play the part of the mourning daughter-in-law. I had to find Klara first, and tell her that she and her son were safe.

Chapter 28

I stared into the mirror and smiled at Klara as she dressed my hair. I had never seen her so relaxed; her eyes sparkled and an easy smile sat on her face. I remembered how surly she'd been when we first met—it was good to see such a change in her.

We'd arrived back at Brisingamen yesterday and I'd barely seen Erik. He'd spent the rest of the journey to Sint Eustatius locked in his father's small cabin—all I'd heard of him was the occasional call for more rum.

When we anchored in Oranjestad Bay he appeared: eyes dull, skin pale, but clean and shaven; and went ashore to greet his uncle. I'd been left aboard the ship. Apparently he'd told his uncle of his brother's death, claimed we didn't have the proper mourning attire, and I would remain secluded until we could put back out to sea.

The sugar was unloaded, Erik finalized the details of the sale, and *Freyja* loaded up with fresh food and water. We set sail again in less than a week. I hadn't been allowed out of the cabin, but was not upset to have avoided meeting more van Eckens.

The return journey had been uneventful—Erik had remained in his father's cabin and I'd spent the majority of the passage with Magdalena and occasionally Sharpe. I'd enjoyed their company, despite the difference in ages.

After our arrival home the day before, Erik had sequestered himself in the study and I'd eaten alone. I was enjoying the new routine, but tonight the usual Freyjamen were dining with us and we would have Erik's company. I hoped Sharpe would bring Magdalena.

I was surprised when Erik took Jan's seat at the head of the table, although was not sure why—he was the head of the household now, after all. It just seemed disrespectful—too soon.

I was directed to Erik's old seat at the foot of the table and was pleased. I may have to sit facing him, but he was a long way away and I would not have to talk to him.

Hornigold and Cheval sat to my left, Sharpe and Magdalena to my right. I focused my attention on them.

The starter course passed without incident—soup flavored with pumpkin and peppers. Then Hendrik brought in the main—spiced and roasted boar—and the level of noise in the room rose from a respectful and mournful quiet to excited anticipation. Klara poured more drinks and I sipped my wine, feeling suddenly anxious.

Cheval leaned closer to me as the meat was carved. "I know it's a terrible time, but you look very good in black, Madame, you should wear it more often." I blinked and stared at him in surprise, then glanced at Erik. He looked angry.

"Thank you, Cheval," I said and took another sip of wine, then glanced at Sharpe on my other side and widened my eyes in disbelief. He smirked and Cheval thumped his glass down hard enough to break the stem.

"Ah, pardon, pardon!" he exclaimed with a nervous look at Erik. He waved the apology away with a grimace and Klara cleared up the mess, then brought and filled another glass. The table lapsed into uncomfortable silence and it was a relief when everyone had been served and we could eat.

I glanced at Sharpe again and grimaced. He smiled back.

"So, Hornigold, now my father has gone we have a little more freedom."

I looked at him in shock.

"You are aware he and I did not always see eye to eye, especially where your role in our business was concerned. You will find I am more . . . accommodating to your ideas."

The table silenced.

"Erik, please, we're still in mourning," I protested without thinking. I jumped when he immediately slammed his fist onto the table top.

"I was not talking to you, wife! Be good enough to keep your silence until I do."

I glanced at Magdalena and Sharpe in embarrassment, but their eyes stayed on their plates.

"Look at me when I'm talking!" He thumped the table again and I looked at him.

"There will be many changes around here now that I'm master of Brisingamen and governor of Sayba." He glared around the table, and it was clear that he really meant now that he was master of us. My embarrassment turned to fear.

"Hornigold, you will stay here until Captain Tarr arrives, then the three of us will discuss my plans." Hornigold nodded once. "Until then, I wish to reward you for your concern and actions when Vader died. I was pleased with how quickly you reacted to put a boat off to look for him, and how efficient you were at Sint Eustatius."

He glanced around the room and his eyes rested on Klara. She froze.

"Take my wife's slave for the night; she will reward you for me." He laughed.

"Erik, no!" I shouted, horror-stricken.

He stood and thumped the table again. I shrank back in my chair.

"Yes! She is mine to do with as I will—as are you. You will never disagree with me in public again!" Another thump. "Do you understand?"

I glared at him. His threat was obvious.

"Do you understand?" he repeated, his voice low. Sharpe touched my wrist in warning and I nodded.

"Get your hand off my wife, Sharpe. I've been watching you and you're far too friendly. Keep your distance—you already have one whore, let that be enough for you!"

I gasped, and Sharpe stared at Erik, withdrew his hand and nodded. Magdalena's face reflected pure fury, but she wisely kept her silence.

"Klara, you will entertain Captain Hornigold tonight. Take the blue room and do not disappoint him—I do not want to hear any complaints tomorrow."

I risked a glance at her—tears ran down her face. I looked back at Erik; he was smiling. He raised his glass as if for a toast, but said nothing. He looked at each of us in turn, then drank.

Chapter 29

I dressed for bed alone, Klara was already with Hornigold and I shuddered. *Why is Erik doing this to her?* I'd always thought he felt tenderly toward her; it was Jan who had hated her. *Is he trying to make it up to his father? Some kind of twisted apology for letting him die?*

I shuddered again and climbed under the bed sheet. I glanced at the door in trepidation. I hardly dared hope he would leave me alone, but prayed for it anyway.

Tonight, the prayers didn't work—his step was loud on the stairs to my room. He stumbled through the door and I watched his progress in the gloom. He was drunk—he'd thrown glass after glass of wine down his throat after pronouncing Klara's sentence, then called for brandy.

He used the pisspot, threw his clothing to the floor and muddled his way through the thin tester curtains. He grinned at me, enjoying my fear.

"You're mine, wife, and so is that whore. I can and will do with both of you as I wish. Do not anger me, or I will give you to worse than Hornigold." I stared at him, too revolted to react. I believed him.

He straddled me and pushed up my shift. As usual, I neither helped nor hindered. He was right: I was his, and completely powerless.

He tried to push inside me and I bit my lip in anticipation of pain, but there was none. I looked at him in surprise—there was nothing there.

His eyes met mine and he slapped me. "Teef—bitch," he said. He hit me again, and now I could start to feel something down there. He grabbed a fistful of my hair and yanked my head back. I cried out in pain and was aware my throat was exposed and vulnerable. He recognized my fear and grew bigger.

He bent his mouth to my throat and I bit my lip, terrified at what he would do. He kissed my skin, gently, and laughed at my cry of surprise. I'd expected a bite and he knew it. He was playing with me.

Tears ran down my face and I stifled a sob. I tried to push him away, but my efforts had no effect.

"Stop it," he said, pulling my hair again, and I did, scared he would snap my neck.

I remembered that night aboard *Freyja* with him and shut my eyes. I could not take my body away from this, but my mind didn't have to stay.

I pictured my beach. It was gloomy, with storm clouds overhead and rain poured down.

Something smashed into my face. "Open your eyes!" I saw my husband's face, red with anger, but I didn't react. I stared past him, at the canopy, and returned to the beach.

My nightgown was already saturated from the rain and I ran straight into the sea, the surf battering me. I was knocked down, the wave spinning the world about me, but I found my feet and pressed on. The next wave hit me and I staggered back and lost my footing, but this time managed to stay on the surface. I swam forward, deeper and deeper, the storm surge buffeting my body.

Lightning lit the sea around me and I realized I could no longer see the shore. I didn't care. I was safe out here in the waves. I was not safe on land.

I rode the next wave, and the next, then a particularly large one broke early—it felt like stone hitting me, not water. I spluttered my way back to the surface and looked for the next one. It wasn't there.

The waves rocked me now, rather than threatened. The sun was coming out, the sea calming. The storm was abating.

I rolled onto my back and floated on the surface, allowing the sea to rock me to sleep. I knew I wouldn't drown, not now. I was alone here. I was safe. I had survived.

Chapter 30

I woke on sand. I blinked my eyes open slowly—the sunlight hurt them and they felt wrong. I looked around and smiled, relieved. I was on my beach. I'd been washed up on my beach. I was safe. I sat up and cried out in pain. My whole body hurt. It had been quite a storm and the waves had taken their toll on me.

I blinked my eyes open. Weak dawn light showed me the familiar white canopy over my bed. I clenched my fist and lifted it to within my sightline. It held fabric, not sand. I frowned in confusion, then remembered the night before. I was not on my beach; that had been a dream. I was in my bed—my marital bed.

I gathered my courage and turned my head to the side. Erik wasn't there; he was gone. I breathed a sigh of relief which ended in a sob. He wasn't here to enjoy my distress so I surrendered to it, scarcely able to breathe through the violence of my tears.

When they were finally spent, I jumped and cried out in surprise. Klara stood there with a breakfast tray. We stared at each other, taking in the other's bruises, shamefully aware of our own.

"I didn't think you would want to go to the dining room this morning," she said and placed the tray on the bed.

I shook my head, or tried to, relieved and thankful, but not yet trusting myself to speak.

I pushed myself up to a sitting position—very carefully—and winced as I leant back against the headboard. Klara glanced at me in concern, but I ignored her and looked at the tray.

Fruit—pawpaw and carambola—both ripe, both easy to eat. Bread (untoasted) and preserves: the usual jar of mammee apple that I enjoyed, and another, larger jar, that I did not recognize.

I picked up the cup and sipped tea. It was definitely more palatable with three teaspoons of sugar. I put the cup down and ate some pawpaw. Perfect—soft enough that I didn't have to chew; tasty enough to stimulate my appetite; its juice mild enough not to sting the cut on my lip.

I lifted the lid of the strange jar and looked at Klara. I recognized the smell; it was full of the salve we used to ease the bruises left by my stays. Tears started to fall again, and Klara sat on the bed and put her arm around my shoulders. I leaned against her.

"We're going to need a lot of this stuff," I said through my tears.

"I know. I've told Belinda, she has an army of slaves out in the jungle picking what she needs whenever they have a chance." She squeezed my shoulder, but neither of us managed to laugh.

I pulled myself together and sat up. I looked at her.

"What are we going to do?"

She shrugged. "I don't know. He may just be mourning his father. He may return to being the Erik he was before Mijnheer Jan died."

"Klara, the Erik he was before Jan died, killed his father! This *is* Erik. This is the *real* Erik. God knows what he's capable of without Jan here to temper him."

Tears rolled down her face and she sobbed. "What are we going to do? What are we going to do?"

I held her. "I don't know, Klara, I don't know."

I stared at the wall. We were trapped here, with a monster. We had to find a way out—if we didn't find a way, and find it soon, he would kill us both long before our times. I thought back to my beach—pictured the sand and the waves. I had to find a way to the sea. We'd be safe there. Life had changed again; this time I would find a way to escape my fate.

* * * * *

DEAD RECKONING

Prologue

LEO
28th January 1671
Panama City

Papá was dead. He'd been deployed with General González to stop Henry Morgan and his buccaneers from approaching and attacking Panama City. He'd failed, and two thousand bloodthirsty Englanders had arrived. We did not have enough soldiers left to stop them.

I stood in the fringes of the jungle, hidden by the trees, and watched a horde of half-starved filthy pirates swarm into my city, intent on destroying everything they could see, until my neighbors' screams and the smell of their burning homes made it impossible for me to do nothing.

"I've got to go back," I told my friend, Magdalena, then coughed from the smoke. "Mamá's alone in the house and Papá's gone. I'm the head of the family now, I've got to go and get her." I was trying hard to stay calm and not panic Magdalena.

"Let me come with you, Leo, please. Don't leave me on my own," Magdalena cried.

"*No*, go back to the camp and stand guard. We have food and water; someone needs to stay with it. Make sure no one finds it. You'll be fine, I'll be back soon, I promise."

Two years younger than me at ten, Magdalena nodded solemnly, and I knew she wouldn't let anyone near our stores. She was a deadly shot with her sling, able to fell a fast-moving lizard with a stone flung from the leather straps. She'd never fired a missile at a man before, but I didn't think she would hesitate.

"I won't be long," I reassured her, and crept out of the undergrowth. Barefoot and wearing only breeches and a filthy shirt, I could easily pass as a ship's boy. The blue eyes that normally made me stand out would help me blend in with the marauders.

I went as quickly as I could to the house where I knew Mamá waited, too stubborn to flee into the jungle and too frightened of the sea to run to the coast. I was too late; the buccaneers had already found her. I wanted to run, afraid of what I might see, but peered through the window anyway. I gasped in shock. Three men surrounded Mamá and threatened her with blade and pistol, demanding gold.

"I don't have any," Mamá cried in English. "I don't have any gold!"

"Blake, Hornigold, search the house," the older one ordered. The other two emptied and tipped over the furniture, destroying everything we owned.

"Look at the house," Mamá gasped. "My husband's a soldier, we're not rich, we don't have gold."

"Captain Tarr." The youngest one, Hornigold, came back into the room with a plateful of cold beef. The captain grabbed it and stuffed meat into his mouth until it was so full he could hardly chew.

"Nothing." The other one, Blake, came back in and his face lit up at the sight of the food. "There's nothing here at all." He crossed the room and grabbed a handful of beef, cramming it into his mouth as his captain had done.

I looked back at Mamá, forgotten in the corner, and wondered how I could get her out past these men. She saw me and tried to tell me to run. Tarr heard her "Vamos" and turned to her. I wish I had run, but I couldn't. My legs wouldn't work. I couldn't turn my head. I couldn't shut my eyes. I felt as if my body were not my own; a part of me—the important part—broke.

"Hold her," Tarr ordered and his men each grabbed one of Mamá's arms, pinning her to the floor, despite her kicking legs. I still couldn't look away, even when her eyes met mine through the window and I saw how terrified she was. My own terror exploded inside me, shredding my soul, when I saw that look on her face.

Mamá kicked harder and writhed on the floor to free her arms. She couldn't do it. Tarr watched her and laughed as he untied his breeches and let them fall. He fell to his knees, forcing Mamá's apart. She kept kicking, but her blows did no damage.

"Lie still, you dirty Spanish whore," Tarr growled and he thrust into her.

Mamá screamed, her noise covering my own cries. My heart burst into flame, the fire consuming my whole body, but I could do nothing to stop them. I was an unarmed boy. I could only watch, and hate—hate them, and hate myself for my inaction. My mind wouldn't work properly, all I could think was, *she's not Spanish, you ignorant bastard, she's English, your countrywoman. It's Papá who's Spanish.*

I kept watching. Tarr cried out and moved away from Mamá. I heaved a sigh of relief. It was over.

No, it was not. Tarr took Blake's place, holding Mamá down, but her struggles were growing weaker. Blake's breeches fell and he moved between Mamá's legs. If anything, he was even more enthusiastic than Tarr and cried out with every thrust. Mamá's screams reduced to sobs. It was all she was capable of now. She did not look at me again.

When Blake changed places with Hornigold, I noticed the floor around Mamá's legs was red with blood. It did not put Hornigold off. Between them they had torn her apart like animals with a piece of meat.

I felt cold inside. The fire had gone out. I still couldn't tear my eyes away. I noticed every detail about the men. Every detail of Mamá's shame. I would repay it all. I would make them suffer for this.

When Hornigold finished, the other two let go of Mamá and they laughed down at her. Mamá curled into a ball. I could only imagine how much pain she must have been in to prevent her covering herself properly or moving away.

I put my hands to my face to cover my eyes, then looked at them in surprise. They were wet. I was crying and hadn't realized. I looked through the window again just as Tarr grabbed Mamá by the hair.

"Finish it," he commanded, then hawked and spat down at her huddled form on the floor.

"Yeah, finish her, finish her." Hornigold was almost dancing with laughter.

Blake stepped forward, dagger drawn, and slashed it across Mamá's throat. I cried out despite myself and stared at the three faces turned toward me, carving their features into my memory. I swore that I would avenge this. If it took the rest of my life, I would kill those three men. Then I ran; back to the jungle and Magdalena.

Chapter 1

GABRIELLA
31st March 1686
Brisingamen, Sayba

I stretched my hand out to the door, then stopped. I did not want to go in there. I did not want to face the evening that lay behind that carved piece of wood.

"Klara." I could hear Erik's Dutch accent even through the timber. "What's keeping my wife? Leave that there and fetch her. She's neglecting our guests and I won't have it!"

I took a deep breath and reached for the door again, forced the handle down, and stepped into the dining room.

"Finally! What kept you?" Erik said in greeting. "You have the right idea, gentlemen," he addressed the room. "A life at sea—no women to contend with." He laughed. "Sit down, Gabriella."

I walked the length of the room to the empty chair at the foot of the table and tried to ignore the laughter of the dozen men seated at Erik's pleasure. His buccaneers—the men who brought my husband, and his father before him, the riches to build and furnish this house. Pirates, even if they preferred to avoid that title, instead calling themselves privateers, buccaneers or Brethren of the Coast.

I had lived on the island of Sayba, in the northern Caribbees, with Erik van Ecken for three years. Surrounded by jungle and sugarcane, Brisingamen was a beautiful house: built of brick, it had four stories at its highest and was painted gold. The long lower floor had a decorative and comfortable veranda with a series of seven arches, and the center of the next was topped directly by a steep roof to the width of the middle three arches. Either side of the middle section were two third and fourth floors with shuttered windows and topped by gables built in the Dutch taste of carved pediments with curves and swirls added to the basic flat triangle. Most women would be envious, but they didn't know Erik.

I took my seat and glanced up at Klara as she spread a napkin on my lap and filled my glass. We both knew well how these evenings ended. At least I'd only have my husband to contend with; she had no idea which of the loud, coarse, stinking men at this table Erik would decide to reward with her favors. Blake, Hornigold and Sharpe were the main contenders, but my husband had a warped sense of humor and all the men here were hopeful.

"Look at me when I'm talking to you!" Erik slammed his fist onto the table, silencing the room. I looked up at him in alarm; he was drunk early. That did not bode well. "Three years, and you still haven't learned to look at me when I talk to you! Do you have this trouble with your crews, Blake? No, 'course you don't. Maybe I should send her to sea and let you whip some obedience into her."

His favorite subject was our marriage and my failings.

"God bless my dear father, he had a good head for ships and business, none at all for women. Saddling me with this useless barren English whore." He looked around the table to make sure he had everyone's attention. "He went to the Massachusetts Bay Colony to sort out the customs official there who was getting greedy, and came back with his daughter for my wife. Her own family didn't want her, which should have been Vader's first clue. She can't run the house properly and lets the slaves get away with anything, especially this one." He slapped Klara's backside as she placed a joint of beef on the table. "I'm sure she thinks they're friends. My wife needs to learn her place. It's a pity the cage is full, although it would be a shame to waste her like that."

I looked up sharply. The cage was barely big enough to hold a grown man, and once Erik put someone in it, they did not come out alive. The local wildlife wasn't fussy about its food being dead before it dined, and any victim was left there until his bones were picked clean.

"Ahh, thought that would get your attention. I know everything that happens on this island, you forgot that when you let that . . . that filthy swine touch you, didn't you, Gabriella?"

"What are you talking about?"

"What am I talking about? What am I talking about? I saw you! You let him touch you!"

Then I realized and my heart plummeted. I looked at Klara; she'd frozen in place.

"What? Do you mean Wilbert? I tripped, he saved my fall! What have you done to him?" Wilbert was one of Erik's slaves.

"You know exactly what I've done to him. I'm not having one of those animals touch my wife! How did he look, Blake?"

The men would have passed the cage on the approach to the house.

"Like he's remembered who's the captain here." Blake laughed.

"Erik, please." I knew begging wouldn't sway him, but I had to try. "Please let him out, he only tried to help me, he doesn't deserve this."

Erik slammed his fist into the table again. "*I* decide who deserves what, and don't you forget it, Gabriella. Maybe this'll teach you not to be so friendly. Now eat your dinner!"

I looked at my plate. I knew more words would anger him further, but I could feel Klara's eyes on me. I knew she loved Wilbert. I couldn't look at her. I could do nothing for him. I couldn't even try. I'd only make things worse. I picked up my knife and fork and cut a small piece of meat. I hoped it would choke me.

"So, Blake, have you dealt with our Spanish problem yet?" Erik changed the subject and I risked a look at Klara now that I no longer had my husband's attention. Her face showed no expression and she did not return my glance.

"He's not been seen since the fight with Hornigold. He's hiding somewhere, but we'll find him. We have a lot of friends in these waters, we'll find him."

"You'd better. I lost a good man in Tarr; you need to prove to me you can fill his boots, Blake. I have to say I have my doubts.

"And you can stop sniggering, Hornigold. I have no idea why Blake has so much confidence in you, if I had my way you'd be

Freyja's cook, not her captain. In fact, *you* can concentrate on finding the Spaniard, you can prove yourself and leave Blake to carry on our business interests—I need more ships, and I need them quickly. My slave sheds are full to bursting, I need to transport them to the Caribbee slave marts before too many die on me. Bringing them across from Africa isn't cheap, you know!"

Hornigold flushed. "I nearly had him! It wasn't my fault!" He glared at Erik, but dropped his eyes and quietened almost immediately. No one else spoke and Erik glowered around the table, his point made.

"Come on, what's wrong with you all? Eat!

"Klara? The wine's running low, fill the jugs. Get on with it."

Chapter 2

I escaped upstairs as soon as the meal was finished and I was no longer required. Lying in bed, I heard the voices below grow louder and more raucous as Erik and his pirates continued to drink. A cheer announced Klara's entry into the room with more jugs and bottles. I couldn't bear to think what she had to endure, but I could do nothing for her. I thought again of Wilbert, hanging in his tiny suspended cage, waiting to die, and clenched my fists. I was at the mercy of my husband and could do nothing for the people he tortured. I had to do something. I had to. But for the moment I could only pray. Pray that Erik passed out downstairs and I'd be spared more humiliation tonight.

If there was a God out there, he wasn't listening. Eventually, I heard Erik's tread on the stairs, and Klara's screams from elsewhere in the house. The door slammed open and Erik staggered in. He was only a vague shape beyond the thin tester curtains that kept the insects from the bed, but it was a shape I knew too well. I tried to keep my breathing even—I knew not to show him my fear.

He bent down and pulled the pisspot from under the bed, then filled the room with the stench of himself. He could not stand up straight, and his water hit porcelain, rug, bedding—he didn't notice. Then he was done and pulled the rest of his clothes off.

Despite my best efforts, my breathing had become faster and shallower. I wanted to run, somewhere, anywhere, but had nowhere to go. The house was surrounded by jungle, and everybody on the island was either in business with my husband or terrified of him. I had to stay with Erik. I flinched when I heard another scream from Klara, and Erik laughed.

He fell onto the bed, got tangled in the curtains, then found his way through. I was too scared to laugh at his buffoonery. He pulled the cover down, shoved up the nightgown I'd put on to cover myself despite the heat, and climbed on top of me.

Nothing. He was soft. He'd drunk too much. I couldn't help the sigh of relief that shot through my body and immediately cursed myself. He'd heard me, and my head slammed to the right with the force of his slap. Then left. Then a punch to the mouth, all accompanied by insults and hate. It was working for him. I wasn't going to be spared tonight, after all. He grabbed my gown at the neck and lifted me up until I was half sitting, then he closed his fist and punched harder. I tried to scramble away, but his weight pinned me to the bed. My kicks were ineffectual, and he batted my fists away with laughter. He grabbed my throat and he was ready.

I lay on the bed, hugged my knees to my chest, and waited for daylight, Erik snoring beside me. I had long ago learned to cry silently, and the bolster was soaked with my tears. I had to do something. I had to. Klara's screams had stopped about the same time as my own. We had to get away from here or he'd kill us both. And we had to get Wilbert out of that cage as well. Somehow.

Chapter 3

Erik left the room not long after dawn without looking at me. I wondered if he'd even notice if he killed me one of these nights. Probably not. I looked at the door as it opened, my heart in my mouth, even though I knew it wouldn't be Erik. Klara came in, eyes to the floor, and I looked away. It was always the same the day after a dinner party; the two of us too ashamed to look at each other.

She put her load of fresh bedding on the chest and bent to see to the pisspot. I sat up and swung my legs over the side of the bed, unable to prevent my cry of pain. Klara was there in a moment and we clung to each other, sobbing.

"How bad is it?" I asked.

She looked at me, then brought me a glass and I stared at my reflection. Long, dark, wavy hair; pale skin with those freckles over my nose that I hated; blue eyes. My right eye had blackened and my lip was split; I stretched my neck and could see the marks of my husband's hand there. I could cover those with silk. The damage to my face would be harder to disguise; I'd have to wear the Spanish mantilla again and hide behind a fan. I looked at Klara more closely; bruises did not show up as starkly on her skin, but they were still there, and I noticed she favored her right arm.

"Hornigold," she whispered.

She wouldn't tell me what he had done, but she didn't need to; I could guess well enough.

"Sit still and close your eye," she said. I saw she had a bowl of the salve that Belinda made in such large quantities. It had a strange, sickly smell, but soothed the bruises. She applied more to my neck. I took it from her and rubbed some over my arms and legs and attempted to stand. My legs felt sore and weak, but they held. He hadn't done me serious harm. I looked at Klara as she glanced away, and sighed.

"Have they gone?"

"Yes, just after dawn."

I nodded. With any luck the pirates would be setting sail and Erik would stay in Eckerstad, the island's main port a few leagues down the coast. I doubted it was out of shame, but he tended to stay away after nights like the last one. What he did and who with, I didn't know, and didn't particularly care. We had some time alone with only his overseer, Rensink, to contend with. He'd been with Erik and his family for most of his life and could be just as brutal, but at least he let us be.

"Have you seen Wilbert?"

Klara nodded and started crying again. I walked her to the bed, sat her down, and held her.

"We have to get away, Klara."

"I can't leave Wilbert or Jan." Jan was her son.

"I know. Erik won't be back tonight. We'll deal with Rensink, free Wilbert and the four of us will go."

"Deal with Rensink?" Klara sounded incredulous. "How? And where would we go?"

I paused. I'd been thinking about it all night, and it had seemed plausible before dawn; now I wasn't so sure.

"Rensink likes his rum, and Belinda has given me a tincture to help me sleep before now. If we combine the two, he'll be senseless by sundown." I smiled. "Then we find the keys and set Wilbert free." It sounded simple when I said it quickly. "Is Jan chained with the rest of the men at night?"

"Yes, but he's so thin he can slip the shackles."

"Good. We'll have to find our way to Eckerstad and hope nobody sees us, then we'll board a ship and just go." I had another thought. "Oh, we might find that easier if we're dressed as men."

"Board what ship? Most of the ships here are pirates or slavers; I don't know which is worse."

"As long as we avoid Blake and Hornigold, we'll manage. We have to take the risk. Even if we stowaway on a slaver, we can stay hidden long enough to sneak off when they dock at one of the other islands. You never know, we may be able to free the slaves and take Erik's ship for ourselves!" I laughed, although I knew it wasn't funny.

"What about the others here? We can't just leave them. Think what Erik will do to them if he comes back and you're gone. He'll kill them, never mind that they're shackled and unable to do anything to stop us."

I looked at her. We both knew that a large group would be caught. Four of us would find it hard enough to stay hidden. But she was right; I couldn't leave those men and women to Erik's mercy.

"We'll loose their shackles and let them find their own way."

"And what will your husband do when he recaptures them?"

I looked at the floor. "We'll have given them the choice. They can stay if they want, or hide in the jungle—there's plenty out there."

"Belinda?" Klara asked.

I looked up at her again. Belinda was Erik's housekeeper and was a large, friendly woman who liked her comfort. I couldn't see her in the jungle or at sea. She had signed on for five years with her husband, John, as an indentured servant and had been here long before I'd arrived. John died soon after their arrival in the tropics and Erik had forced her to work his passage off as well as her own, but I didn't think she really minded. Where else would she go now that John was dead? What else would she do? She got her board and food, and she had come to some sort of understanding with Erik so that he didn't torment her as he did his other Brisingameners.

"Belinda will have to take her chances. If she knows nothing, she can't be held accountable. Maybe we should put something in her rum too?"

"She'll never forgive us for not saying goodbye."

"Yes she will."

"Only if we make it."

We stared at each other's battered faces again. If we didn't make it, we'd die; we had no choice but to try.

Chapter 4

"We're making good progress with the clearing, Mevrouw van Ecken, although work has slowed down a bit without Wilbert." Rensink was beginning to slur his words.

"Shouldn't you let him out of the cage if the work's suffering? I'm sure Erik would agree clearing the jungle for more sugarcane is more important than punishing one man." My spirits soared at the possibility of freeing Wilbert legitimately. "We're already busy watering and weeding the existing fields, I'm certain I heard my husband saying the new field should have been cleared by now, surely we need all the workers we've got?"

I looked up and smiled at Klara who was pouring Rensink more adulterated rum, but she gave me such a look of pity my heart sank again.

"He has . . . has . . . warehouses full of them." Rensink confirmed Klara's expectations. "He'll no doubt be bringing more slaves back with him to get the . . . the . . . work done."

I nodded. Of course he would. Rensink put his hand to his head.

"Excuse me, Mevrouw . . . Mevrouw . . . I'm not feeling well." He tried to get to his feet and stumbled.

"Oh, Mijnheer Rensink, I hope you're not sickening for something, the jungle fever is relentless. Of course I excuse you, you must go and lie down."

"I can't, Mevrouw van Ecken. I must deal with the slaves for the night."

"I can do that for you, you really don't look well at all. You must lie down and leave everything to me."

"Dank u Mevrouw Ecken, I . . . I think I will." He gave me his keys, grabbed hold of the rail and made his unsteady way toward his hut. I looked at Klara and heaved a sigh of relief. I'd been worried he'd demand she help him to bed, but he was too fuddled to think of it.

"Belinda?" I asked.

"Dead to the world," Klara replied. "She'll know nothing until morning and have a most undeserved head, but it can't be helped."

"Does Jan know what to do?"

"Yes, he'll wait till the moon's over the house, then go through Mijnheer Erik's study window and back out to bring us the keys. He's a good boy, he won't let us down."

I nodded. At nine years old, Jan was expected to do the work of a man, yet he was always full of energy and laughter. Klara was right to be so proud of him. I looked at the bunch of keys on the table. I had no idea if the key to the cage was on there. We had to make sure we could free Wilbert, which meant Jan still had to take that risk.

"You might as well sit down, Klara, there's no one else here to see you. We have to wait to be sure Rensink is too deeply asleep to stir, and hope Erik stays away."

We looked at each other. I did not expect Erik back that night, but he enjoyed doing the unexpected purely to catch people out, and I could never be sure of his movements. We could only hope. If he stayed away, we had a chance. If he came home, we'd die.

"I'll clear this rum away first."

I settled back on the chair and tried to relax. So far everything was going well. Erik was still absent. Rensink and Belinda were asleep and wouldn't wake before morning. I stared out at the jungle and the road to Eckerstad. Dark and overgrown, I wasn't looking forward to that walk, but it was the best way. We couldn't ride; if we met anyone on the way we wouldn't be able to hide the horses, and Klara wasn't confident enough in the saddle to survive a chase. On foot, we could dive into the undergrowth until they passed, or even walk through the jungle; we'd have a much better chance of escaping undiscovered.

I started as Klara came back out onto the veranda wearing hat, shirt and breeches. I'd almost failed to recognize her. I smiled, *This might work*. She carried the same for me, along with a bottle of wine and two fresh glasses. I took a glass of wine, fiddled with my favorite necklace—a large teardrop of amethyst that Mam had given to me—and stared at the clothing. *Are we really going to do this? We can still call it off with no harm done, it isn't too late. Rensink will assume jungle fever or a bad bottle of rum. Belinda may be a little harder to placate, but she'll protect us. If I get changed and Erik arrives, he'll know. Once I put on a man's clothing, I'm committed to escape and all the perils that entails. Stay or go?*

I downed the wine, picked up the clothing and went inside to change. There really was no other choice.

Chapter 5

GABRIELLA

"Jan, no! Gabriella!"

I gasped in fear at the panic in Klara's voice. Erik? Had he come home?

"Gabriella, hurry, it's Jan!"

I rushed back outside, tucking my shirt into my breeches, and saw Jan disappear into the treeline.

"What's he doing? I thought you said he knew what to do?"

"He does, he's trying to be a hero and rescue Wilbert himself. Oh, the stupid boy!"

"We have to go after him, come on!" I rushed down the veranda and ran after the child, cursing. There was danger enough in following the plan without this, and chances were that the key we needed was on Rensink's bunch anyway. We should have known better than to involve Jan; he was too eager to please.

"Klara!" I shouted. She was still on the veranda, frozen in place with her hands to her mouth. I ran back and grabbed her. "Come on! We have to go *now*!" I grabbed the knapsack she'd prepared with food and weapons, and dragged her after her son, then stopped at the sound of gunshots and stared at the trees.

"No." Klara spoke quietly and sank to her knees. "No."

I stared at her. Her son or lover was dead, maybe both, and we hadn't left the plantation yet.

"Klara, come on, we have to go," I urged, tugging on her arm to drag her back to her feet.

"Wilbert."

I turned to see Wilbert stumble out of the trees, followed by one of Erik's pirates: Sharpe. He raised a pistol in his left hand, took aim and fired. Wilbert and Klara screamed at the same instant, and Wilbert fell to the ground. Sharpe stared at us for a moment, turned and walked back toward the trees. I watched him go in disbelief, unable to comprehend that the man hadn't stopped us.

"Klara! Klara! Quick, we have to go now! Stand up!" I pulled at her again as I spoke, and she got to her feet. I hugged her quickly. "He's letting us go, but if *he's* here, Erik won't be far behind. If we don't go now, we'll die too. Come on." I picked the knapsack back up and led her to the trees, although to a different path than the one Sharpe had taken. We'd have to follow the cliff tops to Eckerstad. We'd be more exposed, but hopefully would miss anyone approaching the house. I had no desire to get lost in the jungle, so it was the only feasible option we had left.

"Mistress Gabriella?"

"Hans." I turned to the man who'd approached from the direction of the slave huts. "Jan and Wilbert are dead. Rensink's asleep, but Erik will be on his way home. Let everyone know: if anyone wants to make a run for it, this is the night to do it, but they have to hurry!" He looked at me as if I were mad, than saw Wilbert's body, nodded, and rushed back the way he'd come.

"Klara, can you walk?" She nodded, took one look back, then ran toward the cliffs and the jungle.

In daylight it was beautiful here: a riot of every shade of green contrasting with the profuse red trumpet flowers of bromeliads and rich with fruit: naseberry, passion, mango, pawpaw and, my favorite, mammee apple; plus the intoxicating perfumes of a myriad of flowers: oleander, hibiscus, begonia. Now the riot of color was dark, the trees guardians of the night. Their foliage protected the land with thorns and spikes, and hid all sorts of creatures I'd rather not think about. It was noisy too—nearly as discordant as during the day, but different sounds, frightening sounds: the scream of a tropicbird, a sudden dashing run of a large lizard away from the noise of our passage, and the ever-present cacophony of tree frogs and crickets. It seemed another world without the sun.

"What was that?"

We'd been walking about an hour and had at least another two to go. This was the sixth time Klara had heard a pursuit.

"I didn't hear anything."

"There it is again."

"It's an animal."

"But what if it isn't?"

I looked at her. She was right. We couldn't afford to lose our caution. I looked around for the best place to hide.

"In here." The thickest undergrowth I could see was just ahead, and we forced our way through banana fronds and bromeliad spikes. I settled down and tried to get comfortable. I didn't know how long it would take for Klara to be ready to start moving again, but I knew I'd have to wait for her. It was a tight fit, and I couldn't be sure we'd be out of sight if she was right this time.

I caught my breath. Klara *was* right. I could hear it too now; it wasn't an animal, it was the sound of men slashing at the undergrowth, accompanied by orbs of light—lanterns.

"They must have come this way. They're not on the road; they've not taken any horses and won't have risked the jungle. She must have come this way." I shivered at the sound of Erik's voice. "Find her. I'll reward well the man who returns my wife to me—no one defies me like this!"

I wondered what Erik would do if he found me; or what he would do if he did not, and to whom he would do it; but I couldn't think like that. What about the slaves? Did he realize they'd gone too? Were they safe? Or did he think we were all together?

Closer. I could see him now through the greenery, still wearing his expensive frockcoat, slashing indiscriminately at the flora with his cane. I shuddered, I couldn't help myself; I was used to being on the receiving end of that cane. Klara clamped her hand on my arm so tightly I almost cried out. Someone had come to a stop just in front of us. *Can he see us? Hear us? Who is it?* I felt a kick on the sole of my boot, knocking my foot further into the tangle of green, out of sight of the men. I grabbed hold of Klara and we clutched each other. Her eyes were wide and terrified. I knew my own looked the same.

"Nothing here!" Sharpe shouted. I gasped. *That's twice he's helped us, but why?* If Erik realized what he was doing, he'd kill him without hesitation. I looked at Klara and squeezed her hand. It didn't matter why, the fact was we had an ally and he'd already probably saved our lives.

"They're here somewhere!" Erik shouted back. "They can't have got much further, keep going!"

They were gone; we were safe. Klara's hand was still painful on my already bruised arm, and I slowly pried her fingers loose. I clamped my hand on her mouth as she sobbed in terror.

"Shh, shh," I comforted her, and did my best to get my arm around her and rock her to silence. "They might still hear us. Just a little while longer, Klara, just a little while longer till we're safe."

"Jan!" she sobbed. "I left him there alone."

"I know, Klara, I know. You couldn't do anything else. Try not to think of him or Wilbert, not till we're safe. We have to get away or it's all been for nothing!"

"I don't care anymore! I don't care if he kills us, they're both gone!"

"You know as well as I do he won't just kill us, he'll make us suffer first. Both Wilbert and Jan want you to be free; they died trying to make that happen, Klara. Shh, shh." I rocked her again despite the discomfort. I could no longer hear Erik or the others.

"Can you carry on? If we go quietly and slowly we should be safe, they're ahead of us."

"What if they ambush us?"

"Erik would never believe he's missed us, he won't ambush us, he'll press on ahead to Eckerstad. Anyway, Sharpe's with them and helping us, he'll find a way to warn us if we get too close. Are you ready? Let's go." I didn't know if what I'd said was true, and had no idea of Sharpe's motives, but I had to get her moving again.

I went first, easing myself out of the vegetation and back onto the path. I held my hand out to help Klara.

"We should be safe now until we get to Eckerstad." I wished I felt sure of my words.

Chapter 6

GABRIELLA

We'd been in the jungle all night, and I was exhausted. Yet I was in better shape than Klara. She kept stumbling, and I was worried she'd lost too much tonight and wouldn't be able to see this through. I couldn't let that happen. I couldn't do this alone.

We'd sneaked past the gun on the cliff and the coconut palms Erik was so proud of without incident—if there'd been any men with the great gun then they had been focused out to sea, not on jungle. At least we had a little light now: the trees were thinning and letting the dawn through. We were close to Eckerstad and would soon be in more danger than we had been in all night. If Erik had decided to stage an ambush or even a simple lookout, it would be coming up. And despite what I had said to Klara, we could not rely on Sharpe. Even if there was no one lying in wait, we would soon be in the open, dressed in men's clothing, amongst people who knew me. The chances of being discovered were high.

"Aaargh!"

I stopped dead at Klara's cry. *What now?* The path was not quite wide enough to stand two abreast, but I got as close as I could.

"What is it?"

She pointed, and I squinted at the path ahead. A snake, three feet long and darkly colored with red on its belly—a Sayban racer. Was it poisonous? Erik had told me it was, but he loved to exaggerate the dangers of the jungle that surrounded Brisingamen. I did not know how deadly it really was, nor how aggressive, but we could not risk it striking and biting one of us; there would be no help for us if it did have poison in its fangs. We would have to go around it. I sighed and looked into the darkness of the thick undergrowth. The path had been hard enough to walk, I did not relish the prospect of leaving it. I was aware of the increased noise as the birds and tree frogs greeted the dawn. At least their cacophony would drown out any sounds we made.

"Follow me," I said, drew my knife and started to clear a way through, thankful that I would not have to do this for long. We would be back on the path after a few feet. I was so tired, I hardly cared any more if we were discovered. I wanted to get out of this jungle; I never wanted to see another tree or vine again.

The sun had risen over the horizon by the time we were finally free of green, and we had a clear view of our next challenge. Eckerstad was not a large town, but it was sizable enough and centered on the wharf. There were a handful of estates and plantations further inland—none as large as Brisingamen—but most of the houses here were lived in by Erik's men: merchants and their workers and families. The municipal buildings, where Erik had his offices as governor, lined the cobbled square, but the largest properties hugged the waterfront itself. I knew they warehoused the people Erik stole and sold off all around the Caribbees. There was also a sizable sailortown full of inns, bawdy houses and gambling dens.

The harbor itself was full of small supply vessels and three seagoing ships. I recognized one as Hornigold's ship, *Freyja*, and my heart sank. Of course I knew Sharpe's presence meant that not all the pirates had sailed, but I had still hoped. I did not recognize the other two, but they both flew the red, white and blue colors of the Netherlands, so I knew they were Erik's. Were they slavers or did they carry cacao, molasses or rum? I had no way of knowing until we were aboard, by which time it would be too late.

Which one should we pick anyway? The smaller would probably be easier to board, but the larger would be easier to hide on; although it would have a bigger crew and likely a more competent captain. Or a more brutal one. I did not know. I did not know what to do for the best.

* * *

I looked at Klara and tucked her hair back under her hat, then she did the same for me.

"Are you ready?"

She looked as tired as I felt, but smiled and nodded. I hugged her, nearly moved to tears by her shaky smile after the night's events. We were still on the cliff top, but the ground started to slope down to the town now and we had a choice.

"Can you swim if we make our way down to the beach?" I asked.

Klara stared at the stretch of water between the beach below and the harbor. We were both good swimmers—I had taught Klara myself at the small secluded beach below Brisingamen—but it was a long way and we were both shattered. She looked at me, stricken, and whispered, "No, I'm sorry Gabriella, I don't think I can."

I nodded, secretly relieved. I did not think I had the strength left either.

"Then we have to brazen it out and walk into town. If we keep our heads down, don't look anybody in the eye and keep to the shadows, we might get away with it. We'll look for a rowing boat or something."

"How are we going to get aboard one of those ships from a rowing boat?"

I did not answer. I did not know. One thing at a time. We had to get down to the wharf. Then I would think of something.

Chapter 7

GABRIELLA

"Thank you, Klara," I gasped as I stumbled again and grabbed hold of her. When I'd ventured into Eckerstad in the past, I'd been with my husband, and we'd stuck to the large, rich streets. I'd never visited sailortown before, and was struggling to negotiate the narrow, dirty alleyways littered with loose cobblestones and piled high with casks of God alone knew what. We both had handkerchiefs tied around our mouths and noses—ostensibly to reduce the stench of rotten meat, piss and vomit, but they were essential to hide our faces.

We tiptoed around a rum-soaked sailor lying face down in the filth, and kept going. I guessed we were almost parallel with the wharf now, but we had to stick to these back alleys as long as possible. Once we ventured onto the waterfront we'd have nowhere to hide, and I'd still not worked out how to get aboard a ship.

"You! Stop there!"

Both of us froze, glanced at each other, then ran. I couldn't see anybody, but the shout had come from behind us. Klara pulled me into a small, dank, stinking alley, then another and another. I lost my sense of where the water lay, but for the moment my only concern was to escape detection. We crouched behind a pile of empty rotting casks and strakes, and tried to control our breathing. I glanced into Klara's wide staring eyes, and knew I looked just as frightened.

"They must be here somewhere," I heard Erik shout. He sounded furious—as angry as I'd ever heard him. I shuddered and grabbed Klara's hand for reassurance. His voice faded. He'd gone the wrong way.

"We have to move, or those ships may sail," I whispered after half an hour of silence. "We have to risk it."

Klara nodded. "Just be careful, we're so close."

I took a deep breath and stood up, my cramped muscles complaining, my dagger in my right hand.

"It's fine, there's no one here, come on, we have to do this."

We stayed close to the walls, and slowly made our way back out of the labyrinth. I grabbed Klara's arm; the shadows ahead had moved. *Erik? Or Sharpe?*

Two men stepped out in front of us, flintlocks draped around their necks and cutlasses drawn. I looked at the dagger in my hand and realized we didn't have a chance—even if we'd had any experience of fighting with blades. They came closer. I glanced at Klara; she'd come to the same conclusion.

I could see their features now in the early morning light and didn't recognize them, but that didn't mean anything—I only knew a few of Hornigold's crew. But these men were definitely sailors—it was obvious from their broad shoulders and rolling walk. Closer. I could see the grins on their faces now. They thought they had us. But did they know who we were? We wore hats, kerchiefs over our faces, loose shirts, breeches and boots. I had a sudden flash of hope. They *didn't* know who we were!

"Follow my lead," I whispered to Klara. "We can still get out of this!"

I let them get closer, but I wasn't scared any more—I had a plan. I needed them close, but not quite close enough to be able to touch or cut us. A little closer.

"Now!"

I grabbed my shirt and pulled it up. Klara, bless her, did the same just a fraction of a second later. I'd been right; they hadn't known who we were, they'd assumed us men.

"Run!"

We'd gone before they recovered their wits, and instead of pursuit, all I heard was laughter.

* * *

Our own, slightly hysterical, laughter died away as we burst into the open space of the waterfront. We waited and watched from the shadows for a while. It was busy on the water, and I realized two of the ships were getting ready to sail. We didn't have much time.

I looked up the wharf. There were a lot of small craft lading up and rowing or sailing out to the ships with last minute stores. I ran toward one of the larger wherries, knowing Klara would be right behind me, and grabbed a sack of grain, staggering under its weight. I got it onto my shoulder, somehow, and walked onto the boat. Just in time.

"Cast off."

I breathed a sigh of relief and sat down with Klara, heads bowed so the crew wouldn't realize they didn't know us.

"You—there's no time to sit, I don't care how much rum you squandered last night. Cast off I said!"

I looked up sharply; the captain was talking to *me*. I jumped up and moved to the bow and the rope that still tethered us to the wharf, but stopped when I realized who was standing in front of me. One of the men from the alley! He grinned at me, bent, untied the rope from the iron ring and threw it toward me, then doffed his hat, turned and left, still with that mocking smile on his face. I glanced at Klara, then coiled the rope as best I could and rejoined her as the breeze caught the newly hoisted sail and we headed out into the harbor. I watched Eckerstad fall behind, wondering where Erik was. *How many of the men I took for wharfmen are actually his, looking for us?* No matter, we were on the water. I turned and looked ahead.

Oh no. Oh no. We were heading directly for Hornigold's ship. *No!* After everything we'd done, we were going to be delivered right to my husband's men. I looked at Klara in despair. We'd have to jump overboard and swim. I stared at the filthy water, full of the debris of sailors at anchor: rotting food and worse—much worse. There was nothing for it; we couldn't board Hornigold's ship. I looked toward the other ships; the larger was closest to us.

Despite our tiredness, we could make it. They were still loading supplies and had netting slung over their bulwarks, we could get aboard. I steeled myself for the jump.

"Ready about!"

What? We were turning—tacking. Oh, thank God, we were sailing toward the large ship. No swimming. I was ready to cry in relief. I couldn't take much more of this.

"How are we going to get aboard? How can we hide, Gabriella? What are we going to do now?"

I took a deep breath and willed my eyes to stay dry. I didn't quite trust myself to speak, but I had a hold of myself again. I smiled at Klara in what I hoped was reassurance. It was the only answer to her questions I could manage.

"Up you go, lads, we'll haul the stuff up, then you help the crew stow it, they're a bit shorthanded."

We bumped against the side of the ship, and I caught hold of the cargo net and started to climb.

"Get a move on, we haven't got all day."

I tried to speed up, but it was difficult. It was hard to get a foothold on the thin rope, and I scraped my knuckles every time I moved my hands up the hull. I looked down, Klara wasn't doing much better, but we were nearly there. Luckily, most of the crew's attention was taken up by the cargo being hoisted aboard, and the only notice I received when I finally clambered onto deck was a shout to carry the sacks to the mainhatch. I helped Klara over the rail, we grabbed a sack each and staggered in the direction the man had pointed. We left our loads with the ones already piled high and slipped down the open hatch. I glanced around before I stepped onto the ladder, but everyone was busy; not only bringing the stores aboard, but hoisting yards and sails. Nobody had eyes for anything except what they were doing.

Below decks was dark, and stank worse than the alleyways earlier, but we were nearly safe. We paused at the bottom of the ladder to give our eyes a chance to see, and to make sense of the noises. There was the expected sound of water against the hull, the creak of wood and rope—even down here—but a low groaning underlay it all. I heard Klara's sharp intake of breath and realized: we were aboard a slaver. The smell should have given it away. My eyes slowly got used to the gloom and I saw we were in a large hold, full to bursting with people, all in various states of distress.

"The men will be further forward," Klara whispered, and I realized I could only see women. There were basic bunks against each bulkhead—shelves really—with two women shackled together on each. The people in the lower bunks had no room to sit up. More women were shackled in pairs in the center of the hold, and I started to walk through them, careful of where I put my feet, trying to find deck space. Even at anchor, the floor didn't stay still, and it wasn't an easy undertaking: I trod on more than one limb and fell twice. But we had to find somewhere to hide. There *had* to be a gap we could squeeze into. There *had* to be some space for us.

There—bare planking by the large shittenpot. We sat down on the filthy deck, and I wondered how long it would be before I vomited. The air was heavy with the smell of fear and so many unwashed human bodies as well as the pot, and the journey hadn't begun yet. I felt Klara's arms around me as she shook—in exhaustion, fear or misery, I didn't know. I looked around me. What would these women do if they knew I was married to the man who had stolen them?

Then a new sound; a rhythmic tramping, and the ship lurched. The anchor was being hauled up. There was no going back now.

Chapter 8

LEO
12th July 1683
Two Leagues North of Porto Belo

I swung into the ratlins and started my climb up the knotted ladder of rope to the tops, my body moving with the rhythm of the ship as she rolled through the small swell. At last, after six months away, we were nearly home. It was a perfect Caribbean day—bright sun, with a gentle breeze to take the burn off the heat and push us onward.

After the destruction of Panama City, Magdalena's parents had found us and given me a home. We'd moved to Porto Belo where Luis now concentrated his business affairs, and he'd welcomed me into his family. I really would be part of the family soon—Magdalena and I were to be married on my return, and I would also be a full partner in the family business—trading cacao, indigo and coffee between New Spain and Old. My next voyage would be as Ship's Master.

I would soon have everything I wanted—my childhood friend as my bride, a ship of my own and, in time, a family.

I reached the maintop—a square wooden platform forty feet above the deck—and leaned back against the mast with the wind on my cheek and sun on my face. I squinted ahead, trying to be the first to spot land. Nothing, just blue and sun as far as I could see in every direction. I usually loved the isolation of a ship at sea, but now it felt lonely. I'd had enough of the men with whom I shared this floating island; enough of the vast empty space surrounding us; I wanted people again. People and bustle and smells other than unwashed sailor, salt and tar. I wanted to hear women's laughter, costermongers shouting their wares, and heated discussions that didn't concern wood, canvas or hemp.

But I knew it wouldn't be long before I again craved the sounds of life at sea—waves lapping against wood, tarred lines creaking through blocks, and wind whistling through taut rigging. Not to mention the chanting of men working together, heaving on rope, and sailing this wondrous beast across the known world and beyond.

There! Cloud on the horizon!

"Land oh!" I cried, loud enough to be heard on deck below. I smiled at the rush of men to ratlin and foredeck to see for themselves. It was just a grayish smudge at the moment, but five years at sea told me it was what I was looking for, and it would soon take on the shape and color of the Spanish Main. Home. Magdalena.

I still hadn't seen another ship, and didn't like it. Something was wrong. Porto Belo was a busy port on the northern coast of Panama—there should be ships both putting in and putting off out to sea. *Where are they?* I told myself there was nothing to worry about; there'd be a simple explanation. But I think I knew.

I climbed down and sent up the boy, Alonso, as lookout, then went aft to the quarterdeck and Capitán Valdez.

"It's too quiet," I said, "where's all the shipping?"

He nodded, he'd realized the absence too. "Get the guns ready," he said, "but do it quietly; I don't want to worry the men unnecessarily."

"Sí, Capitán," I replied, and went forward to speak to Lopez and Rafael.

We were a merchantman and not heavily armed, but these waters were infested with pirates of every nationality, and we'd had to defend ourselves before. We all knew it was a part of life at sea, but none of us relished the prospect of a meeting with any one of them.

Lopez and Rafael went below to start shifting cargo. We had four cannon, but they were stowed to make room for goods—we were loaded with brandy, cloth and other home comforts from Spain. We'd have to bring some of it topside to make space to rig the guns and give them room enough to fire. Above deck we had two smaller rail guns, and while they were always in position, their powder and ball were below. I wouldn't start bringing that up, in full view, until we had a better idea of what lay ahead.

I went aft again to the captain.

"Smoke," he said, nodding his head forward.

I looked and realized he was right—it wasn't cloud hanging over Porto Belo, but smoke. It had been sacked—again. It was likely that pirates were nearby.

"Ready the guns," he shouted, and everybody stopped what they were doing and looked aft at us, then forward toward Porto Belo. They were professionals though, and the starboard watch immediately went below to the magazine to bring up muskets, pistols and ammunition. The rest of the men coiled down sheets and braces to keep all the rope out of the way, and packed bolts of cloth that had once been cargo against the bulwarks to try and afford some protection against splinters if we were caught in a fight.

Porto Belo was one of the Spanish Main's treasure ports, loading up the bi-annual treasure fleet with silver from the mountain at Potosi, and had been raided again and again over the years, primarily by Englander and Frank. In times of war, the raiders were privateers, in times of peace they were pirates—or buccaneers as the Englanders styled themselves. In reality they were the same men, committing the same deeds, just with or without a letter of marque as license from their King; it didn't seem to matter to them either way. And now they'd done it again, even though Spain and England had signed a peace treaty thirteen years before. I wondered if they'd missed the silver fleet—it should have sailed over a month ago to avoid the Carib hurricane season, but things rarely went to plan in the New World.

I raised my telescope—the one thing I had in memory of Papá—and looked at the harbor. The pirates were long gone. A lot of ships were sinking, but some were already on the bottom, only their topmasts visible above the waves. We'd have to take care on our approach to anchor, and I glanced up at Alonso on the maintop. It was only his second voyage and I hoped his eyes and wits were up to it.

I looked back at the waterfront. It had taken a pounding—most of the warehouses had been shattered by cannonball, including the one belonging to Luis. Panic gripped me and I found it hard to breathe. *Please don't let me have lost them too. Please don't let me have lost Magdalena.*

I glanced up at the sails—*where's the wind? I need more wind!* I needed to know, but there was nothing I could do to get ashore any quicker.

"Let go anchor!"

Finally. I made sure I was in the first longboat with Capitán Valdez—even though as first mate my duty should have been aboard the ship. But it was Luis' ship, and, for the first time, I used my family connection to get my own way. I had to know.

The pull ashore was intolerable; the water littered with debris of every description, including human. It already had the stench of a graveyard in the hot sun. I could hardly bear to think about what I would find ashore.

At long last, I stepped onto terra firma and tied the boat off, then straightened up and looked about me. The brick buildings were all in a state of collapse and fire had ravaged the wooden. There was nothing left.

"Leo!"

I started at the shout and turned.

"Luis!"

I hurried toward him. *They're alive!*

"Gracias a Dios! Thank God you're well!"

"Sí, I and Marisol were inland, we missed the raid."

"And Magdalena?"

He looked at me, but said nothing.

"Luis, what of Magdalena? Is she well? Where is she?"

He shook his head. "Leo, I'm sorry, she's gone. They took her."

"Then we have to go after her!"

"Leo, no. You know what the buccaneers do to the women they take. She's dead or soon will be. There's nothing we can do. She's gone." He was in tears.

I clenched my teeth and fists equally hard, but he was right. They'd take their pleasure and toss her overboard; we could do nothing for her.

"Who?" I asked.

"Tarr. It was the Englander, Tarr."

Tarr, Blake and Hornigold. Again. The same men who had killed Mamá. I'd been unable to do anything to stop them then. I could do nothing for Magdalena now.

Chapter 9

LEO
5th March 1684
Four Leagues West of Dominico

"Sail oh! To East'ard! No colors!"

I looked up at the shout from the tops, grabbed my telescope, and jumped into the ratlins to see for myself. We were heading north past the islands of Martinico and Dominico and it was probably nothing—these waters were full of merchant ships—but I also knew that made them ideal hunting grounds for pirates.

I trained my glass to the east and could see topsails—a twinmaster, fully canvassed, still with no flag flying. That in itself meant very little, most ships only flew their colors when they met another at sea or were approaching landfall. Merchantmen of the same nationality would take the opportunity to meet with their countrymen and swap news. Merchantmen of differing nationalities would keep well clear of each other for fear of attack.

"Break out the Cross of Burgundy," I said, and our Spanish colors unfurled at the main-masthead and snapped in the stiff breeze. I watched the other ship. Nothing. It was etiquette to reply with one's own colors. I didn't like this. I studied her again and realized she was carrying a little too much sail for the conditions. Whoever was on her quarterdeck was driving her hard and still showing no colors.

"Bear off!" I shouted, and jumped back down to the deck.

"Set the topgallant!"

Every instinct screamed at me that the vessel was trouble. I *could not* lose my ship on my first voyage as captain. I needed speed and for that I needed canvas. Setting the highest sail on the mainmast would put the rig under a lot of strain in this wind, but I was sure she could take it. We could well be in a race for our lives.

Pinta slowly turned westward, downwind—our fastest point of sailing—and men swarmed up the mainmast whilst others trimmed the rest of the sails on my three-masted command. We were bigger, with a longer waterline, and we had a good chance of outrunning the smaller vessel, as long as the masts stood firm with the extra canvas. But I was painfully aware that *Pinta* was built to carry cargo, and if that *was* a pirate ship astern, she would be fitted and rigged for speed.

I squeezed my eyes shut for a moment to rid them of salt, then looked aft at the vessel behind. There was no doubt now that she was chasing us; she had adjusted her own course and was dead astern. She was still too far behind to affect our wind, but she was gaining and there was little I could do about it. I still hoped she was friendly, but realized there was little chance, and my worst fears were confirmed when she finally showed her colors. A plain red flag. La Jolie Rouge. Pirates—and the worst kind. Those that flew black offered quarter and would spare the lives of a crew that surrendered to them. Those that flew red offered none. They'd force the strongest and fittest men to join their own crew, and would likely torture and kill everyone else just for the sport of it.

We were in big trouble.

"Harden up!"

Pinta turned and the crew ran to sheets and braces to haul the sails around. I watched the pirates. They copied my maneuver, staying between us and the wind. I kept watching. Damn it, she was faster.

"Bear off!"

We turned back downwind.

"Lighten ship! Cargo overboard!"

My crew ran to obey. We would make no money from this voyage, but we were beyond profit now—we had to do everything we could just to escape with our lives, and a lighter ship was a faster ship.

Barrels of cacao and coffee littered our wake, but the pirates were relentless and crashed through both wave and cask. They were gaining.

I watched the topsails—the most powerful sails on the ship—and cursed as their canvas rippled. The pirates were close enough to steal our wind. If we kept this course, they'd be on us in minutes.

"Harden up!"

"Haul braces!"

It was our only chance, even though I already knew it wouldn't work.

"Ready the guns!"

We had no choice but to fight. I looked at my decks and my crew of thirty men; then looked aft again. That vessel might be smaller, but there'd likely be over a hundred men crammed onto her decks and many more guns. I looked up at her masthead again and the bloody flag that flew there. There could be no surrender. It was time to start praying in earnest.

Chapter 10

I ducked, as did everyone else on my decks. It had been a warning shot; the ball hit the water ahead of us. That meant they wanted the ship; they weren't going to sink us. That was something. If I was right.

The roar of the cannon died away, and I became aware of another noise, just as terrifying: a slamming of a hundred steel blades against the wooden rail of a ship, accompanied by the chanting of a hundred men.

"Kill! Kill! Kill! Blood! Blood! Blood! Die! Die! Die!"

They were almost alongside. My belly knotted in fear and I felt sick. Every weapon aboard was in the hands of my suddenly insignificant crew. We each had a pistol and a cutlass. Some of us had a dagger too. My two best shots, Mendez and the Portuguese Juaquim, had half a dozen muskets each up on the main- and foretops.

The pirates outnumbered us by more than three to one. They each had two, and in some cases four, pistols draped around their necks on wide silk ribbons. They had blades in hand, and more were stuck into the red, black or blue sashes wrapped around their waists. They had boarding axes and marlin spikes, chains, clubs and grappling hooks.

We had no chance.

I looked up at the bloody flag.

We had to fight.

"Now!"

Both my larboard cannon, loaded with cannonball, fired into the pirate ship—we had one chance to sink them. At this range we couldn't miss—and did not.

They answered with their own cannon, and I realized they had loaded partridge shot. They didn't care if they lost their ship; I'd been right, they weren't trying to sink *Pinta*, they wanted to take and keep her. The small lead balls and bits of metal they fired were designed to kill men, not send our ship to the bottom. At least *Pinta* was bigger than their own vessel; maybe they would keep most of my men on as crew.

They wouldn't want me, though. That captain wouldn't want another on his crew to challenge him. Killing me would be the first thing he'd do to dominate my men.

Should I surrender, despite the flag? Hope he'll want my men? Maybe save some lives?

I looked around the decks and at the strained faces. Would they surrender if I asked them to?

"We fight, Captain."

I looked at Frazer, my Scottish first mate, who had spoken. One look at his face, and I knew he was right. We would fight.

The pirates' chant stopped and was replaced with a blood-curdling scream and volley of pistol shot, which sent my men crashing to the decks to avoid being hit. Grappling hooks flew through the air into *Pinta's* rigging, and men flew on the attached lines. My crew scrambled back to their feet to meet them.

Musket shot rang out from both tops and men fell. Mendez screamed all the way to the deck. Juan, my second mate, was hit as he stood at my side. Blood spurted over my face. He was dead before he could complete his cry of pain.

Pinta's decks were full of men overwhelming her wooden boards. After the first volley of shots, it was too hard to distinguish pirate from Spaniard, and all I could hear was the clash of metal blade on metal blade; the thump of cutlass against flesh; screams of triumph, fear and pain.

I ducked and slashed my swordarm upwards to fend off the blade heading toward my head. I staggered backwards and thrust the dagger in my left hand forward into the man's stomach. He fell.

I turned to meet the next challenge and gasped. My hesitation was nearly fatal, but I recovered my wits enough to fight off the man trying to kill me. He fell.

I spun back to look for the face I had recognized in the melee. Yes, it *was* him. Captain Richard Tarr. He was here, on my decks! This was my chance. I raised my still unfired pistol.

I never saw the man who hit me. One moment I had Tarr in my sights, the next I hit the rail and was falling overboard.

I surfaced, coughing brine, and watched my stricken ship, my crew, and my chance at revenge sail and fight on without me.

Chapter 11

LEO
7th March 1684
Somewhere West of Dominico

I was in the sea for days, clinging to one of the casks that had recently been my cargo, and more than once thought that was it. If I didn't die of the sun and lack of water, I'd be eaten alive by the beasts living in my new home. I saw countless dark triangular fins heading toward me, as straight and true and *fast* as any ball that had been fired at *Pinta* but, when they reached me, instead of teeth, there was an overwhelming blackness, and I'd jerk awake once again, almost crying with relief until I realized that only part of my nightmare was a dream.

Eventually, I felt sand under my feet instead of water, but still didn't trust my senses. Even though I'd seen the island intermittently over the last day or so, I hadn't believed my eyes, and had thought it part of another nightmare; slipping in and out of the early morning mist in front of my eyes, one minute there, then gone. Tantalizing me, giving hope just to strip it away again.

I knew I'd been lucky to have drifted onto the beach; if I'd had more faith in myself and believed in what was right in front of me, I could have got here much faster, but I didn't care. I was out of my watery grave.

I lay on the beach, too tired to move, overpoweringly thirsty, and realized I could hear another sound over the heartbeat of the waves—a splashing, not a pulsing, *a river? Fresh water?*

I slowly got to my feet, the wind cold on my body, and walked; legs and arms feeling as heavy as cannonball. Soon my legs were shaking with the effort. It was ridiculous; I was a grown man, a strong man of the sea, and I was staggering along the beach like a babe, lurching from one step to another. *Just how long have I been adrift?*

Eventually, I reached the line of trees and shade, but instead of getting easier away from the relentless sun, the going got worse. The undergrowth seemed to cling to my bare feet, trying to hold me back, and I sat down, my back against a palm tree, and rested. It was just as well; sitting there in silence I realized the sound I was following was echoing off the cliffs I could just about make out through the canopy of green. I'd been about to head off in the wrong direction.

Once more full of doubt, I dallied with myself, thinking again that I was imagining things; there was no water. I'd reached land, surrounded by the water with which I'd chosen to share my life, and it had killed me. Frustrated and despairing, I banged my head against the bole of the palm behind me, the pain reminding me I was still alive, and it was up to me to make sure I stayed that way.

I went to push myself upright again and saw plants off to my side—ananás. Three of them nestled, cocooned and protected inside a shield of spiky leaves—and I realized I was going to live.

Desperately, I fumbled for my sheath knife with swollen fingers and cut into the ripe fruit. The cloying, sickly sweetness took my breath away, although it didn't manage to eradicate the taste of brine. Halfway through the second fruit I started retching, throwing away the only food I had eaten in . . . I don't know how long. Once the heaving was over, I cut open another fruit. This time I just sucked the juice and managed to keep it down.

With renewed hope, I set off again to find the river.

The sound I'd heard was from a waterfall, and the pool beneath looked big enough to swim in. After only just escaping from swimming to my death such a short time ago, I desperately wanted to be immersed in water again. *Heaven—no salt!* I drank as much as I swam, and finished up sitting under the waterfall, being sluiced with fresh clean water. It washed the old me away; washed the old memories away, but it couldn't wash away the image of Tarr's face on my decks. I renewed my oath of vengeance. I'd tried living well and honestly, and he'd killed that life—again. It was time to fight back. To take what I wanted. To do things differently.

Chapter 12

LEO
14th March 1684
Unknown Island West of Dominico

By my reckoning, I'd been alone a week and hadn't seen any sail. Not a single one. I looked at the unlit fire I'd built on the beach, and fingered the flint that had survived my swim tied to my breeches. I was ready, but if there was no sail, this beacon was useless. *Will I spend the rest of my life here?*

I looked around. It wasn't so bad really. I had plenty of fresh water and fruit. There were birds, fish and turtle in abundance. I could survive here. But I needed people, and I needed to settle my debt with Tarr and his men. I needed to get off this island.

I stared out to sea again, and swept the horizon with my glass. Nothing. If I was going to get back out into the world, it would be up to me. I'd have to build a boat.

I turned and studied the treeline. The only blade I had was my three-inch sheath knife; I had to get this right first time. So, I had a choice to make: *do I start felling the palm trees near the shore to make a raft; or one of the sturdier cedar trees further inland and hollow out a canoe?*

Both options would be hard work, but which would take longer? And which would be most likely to keep me afloat once I headed back out into the waves?

I thought the cedar might be best—it was what the Carib Indians used, after all. It would be sturdier and more seaworthy than a raft, but it would take a lot of hewing to cut down and hollow out, and how would I get it to the beach?

I sat on the sand and lay back in the sun. I'd think on it. There was no point in starting the work until I'd formed a plan. I had only the one blade and it was small. I couldn't waste it.

I closed my eyes. *Raft or canoe? Raft or canoe? Cedar or palms? How many palm trees will I need to cut down anyway?*

"Leo?"

I grunted and turned over on the sand.

"Leo! Captain!"

I sat up quickly and blinked. This was cruel, to dream so vividly about Frazer and the others.

"Leo? Are you well?"

Frazer reached out and grabbed my arm. I flinched. Dreams couldn't do that, could they?

"Frazer? Is that really you?" My voice was hoarse from disuse.

"Aye, Captain." He laughed—a rarity. "It's me. Juaquim's here too, and Alonso, Lopez and Rafael."

He grabbed my arm and hauled me to my feet. I stared at the men, then staggered to the waterline and the pinnace that was hauled up on the sands. *A boat!*

I turned back to Frazer.

"How?" I asked, unable to form a more coherent welcome.

Tarr's men had overpowered the crew quickly, and Frazer had followed my lead and jumped overboard; albeit with the forethought to cast off the pinnace's line (the pinnace was the larger of the two boats we towed). He hung onto the line, hauled himself aboard, and picked up the others from the water. The six of us were the only survivors.

I'd known Frazer since I was little more than a boy; Luis had put him in charge of my welfare when I first went to sea. It had taken some time—he was a surly, bad-tempered bastard—but we'd become close friends over the years, and I'd learned to trust him with my life.

He'd insisted on following the current westwards to look for me, and they'd spent the past week visiting every cay in the vicinity. It appeared my washing up on the island had been more inevitability than luck after all—I'd drifted past two or three others.

* * *

"There's something else, Leo," Frazer said after we'd eaten a feast of turtle. I looked up in expectation. *I've lost my ship and most of my crew, what else can there be?*

"Juaquim?" He looked at the topman, who nodded and quickly finished his mouthful of meat.

"Sim, yes, Mr. Frazer. Well, as you know, I was in the tops and had a good view of the pirate deck," he began.

"Yes, yes, I know," I said, impatient.

"Well, I saw her."

"Who?"

"Magdalena."

I stared at him.

"What do you mean you saw Magdalena? You can't have, she's dead."

"No, she isn't. It was Tarr's ship that took her, wasn't it? Well, she's still aboard. She looked well."

I jumped to my feet, grabbed him by the neck of his shirt, and hauled his face close to mine.

"Are you certain? Are you absolutely certain it was Magdalena?"

"Sim. Yes. I've sailed for her family most of my life, I'd know her anywhere. It was Magdalena, for sure."

I let go of him and staggered backwards. *She's alive? All this time I'd thought her dead, and she's alive? What have I done? What has she lived through? And I abandoned her to her fate. Madre de Dios! Mother of God!*

I looked at the men sat around the large fire.

"We have to get her back," I said. "We have to go after Tarr."

They stared at me.

"You know that means sailing as pirates?" Frazer asked. "We need a ship and a lot of guns, plus the men to fire them. We need to learn to fight at sea and fight well. It will take time."

"Sí, pirates," I said. "Will you help me? However long it takes?"

"Aye, Leo, we'll help you. We've nothing to lose and scores of our own to settle with that bastard and his crew."

I looked at him and shook his hand, then did the same with the other men, and I realized they'd already decided to do this before they'd found me.

I grinned. "Pirates," I said again, and laughed. I had a future, and Magdalena would be in it.

Chapter 13

LEO
26th September 1685
Three Leagues Southeast of the Island of Sayba

"Don't fire on their stern, Frazer. If Magdalena's aboard, that's where she'll be, in one of the aft cabins."

My quartermaster nodded. Our normal tactic in a fight at sea were to pound the other vessel's stern to disable the rudder and prevent them from maneuvering. Once they were unable to steer, they were at the mercy of our guns. I was asking my closest friend and crew to attack one of the most feared ships in the Carib Sea, and to do it the hard way, with little chance of success. But this wasn't a fight for gain or prestige. We fought by different rules today.

"We'll aim for the rigging; disable them that way," said Jean-Claude, my master gunner.

"Broadsides," I reminded them. "I want Tarr's whole crew kept busy."

"Aye, Captain, we know." Frazer sounded impatient. "Be off with you, they're drawing close."

I looked to the northeast at Tarr's ship, *Pinta*—although she now bore boards proclaiming her to be *Edelweiss*—and swung myself over the rail. Since Frazer and the others had found me on my island, we'd taken successively larger boats, honing our fighting skills as we did so. A year after I'd lost *Pinta* to Tarr, we took our first proper ship. One hundred feet long, with a burthen of 245 tuns and twenty three cannon, most of her crew chose to join us (I didn't force anyone to my crew, and no one would have lost their lives had they chosen differently). I renamed her *Sound of Freedom* for the noise of her bow wave against her wooden hull as she cut through the Carib Sea. She'd be Magdalena's freedom.

After a year and a half at sea as a pirate, I was ready to take on Tarr.

* * *

I looked at the three men with me in the pinnace. After my earlier experience at the hands of Tarr, we filled the small vessel with food, water and gold as a precaution against losing *Freedom*, put her off and kept her out of the way of every fight. Today we were still a rescue boat, but the mast remained unstepped, and the four of us waited in *Freedom's* lee for the battle to begin in earnest before we sailed into the thick of it.

Sheltered by *Freedom's* bulk, I couldn't see *Pinta—Edelweiss—* but I knew she was drawing close, because *Freedom* had hardened up. Steering closer to the direction the wind was coming from would give an advantage to the ship that got her timing exactly right. Both ships wanted this weather gage—to be closer to the wind gave them more options and more freedom in maneuvering as well as controlling the other vessel's wind. But to make the move too soon meant exposing the vulnerable stern and rudder to the other ship's cannon. Tarr didn't know that *Freedom* would not fire on his afterquarters.

"Get ready," I said to King and Phillippe on the oars. "We'll go as soon as Jean-Claude fires his first broadside."

Almost as soon as I'd spoken, all the starboard cannon fired and *Freedom* rolled toward us; almost on top of us, then righted herself.

"Cast off, Alonso."

Alonso released the line that tethered our bow to *Freedom,* and Phillippe pushed us off with his oar.

Tarr answered *Freedom's* broadside with one of his own, just as we rowed around *Freedom's* bow. The two ships were almost level, with *Freedom* slightly upwind. Frazer had beaten Tarr to the weather gage. My smile of satisfaction didn't quite make it to my face. We were exposed with open water between the two ships, and we had to cross it quickly. The water was choppy and confused by cannonball, and hard work to row through. If just one of Tarr's gunners spotted us it would only take one well-aimed ball to sink us.

"Pull! Pull!" I instructed, urging my men to row harder. At least we didn't have far to go—less than a hundred yards.

* * *

Alonso leapt from the boat to climb *Edelweiss's* stern with mallet rather than cutlass tucked into the black sash wound around his waist, and the boat fell behind. He drove wooden wedges between rudder and hull, preventing Tarr from steering, and disabling the ship.

I looked up at the gallery of windows twenty five feet above my head. I'd have a much longer and more difficult climb to make, and couldn't be sure I'd find Magdalena at the end of it. But the cabins were the most likely place for her to be in a fight. *Even Magdalena wouldn't be on deck, surely?*

I urged King and Phillippe to get close-to again, and hung a coil of rope around my neck and one shoulder in readiness. It was hard work for the two on the oars to regain the ship, and I had no choice but to wait before I could follow Alonso onto the hull.

"Captain!"

I checked myself at Alonso's shout and looked up. Magdalena. Her familiar face surrounded by a mass of dark curls had appeared through one of the windows.

"Stay there, Magdalena, I'm coming up!" I shouted. I felt a pang of guilt for leaving her to fend for herself at Tarr's mercy for so long. But she hadn't changed, not even after two years aboard a pirate ship, and I watched in frustration as she clambered over the rail. She was going to jump.

"Magdalena, no! Wait! It's too high!"

She took no notice and leaped into the water, her skirts billowing around her.

"Magdalena!" I screamed.

She hit the water. I held my breath. *There*! There she was, clawing her way back to the surface.

"Pull!" I shouted at my men. "Hurry!" I had to get to her. I had to grab her; hold her; pull her aboard to safety.

I looked up at a cry from the ship. The helmsman had noticed a problem with his steerage, leaned over to check his rudder and seen us. *Mierda! It's too soon!* I looked back to Magdalena to urge her to swim harder, but couldn't find her. *There*! Her head broke the surface again. She was caught in the eddy created by the jammed rudder, and her saturated gown was pulling her down.

"Magdalena!" I shouted as she was dragged under again. Alonso dived after her.

I looked up at the sound of pistol fire—the rail was lined with men, all shooting at the two in the water and my boat, and I recognized both Tarr and Blake amongst them. I searched the other faces as I fired back, looking to see if I recognized anyone from *Pinta's* crew before Tarr had taken the ship from me. I did not. There was no one I knew.

"Magdalena!" I looked up at a face leaning over the rail she'd jumped from. A long, curly wig and an eyepatch. *Who's he? Why's he not shooting at us? What is Magdalena to him?*

I looked back to the water. Magdalena's struggles were getting weaker, but Alonso had reached her. The ship had moved further ahead, and the swimmers were in calmer water. Alonso started to drag Magdalena toward the boat and the gap between us closed.

"Get back to your oar!" I shouted at King. He'd dropped it to fire back at the men on the ship, unwilling to keep his back to a volley of pistol fire. He dropped his spent pistol and grabbed the oar again. I picked up another pistol from the pile in the bottom of the boat, fired it and leaned over the side. Magdalena and Alonso were close now, but lead balls fountained the water around us.

"No!" I screamed as Magdalena's body jerked from an impact, then another. The water around her reddened.

I grabbed another pistol, and fired at the men who had killed her, then grimaced as Tarr silently toppled overboard. But I couldn't get any satisfaction from his death. It wasn't enough. Not now.

I grabbed hold of Magdalena again and hauled her still body aboard. I knew we had to get out of there and quickly, but I wouldn't leave her for the sharks. Alonso climbed in, and we started the pull back to *Freedom*.

Chapter 14

We didn't have far to go; the two ships had almost sailed past each other and Frazer and my crew did their best to keep the *Edelweiss* gunners busy, but lead rained around my small, vulnerable pinnace. I sheltered Magdalena's body as best I could while I reloaded my pistols. I knew it made no sense, but I refused to let her be hurt again. I'd already failed her too much. A scream made me look up. Alonso pushed King out of his way—and on top of Magdalena.

"Mierda!"

"He's dead, Capitán, and we will be too if we don't get into *Freedom's* lee quickly," Alonso snapped in Spanish. He took King's oar and matched Phillippe's stroke.

I nodded and fired again at *Edelweiss's* stern and the men gathered there. One unfortunate tar had started the climb down to free the rudder, and I aimed carefully. The longer *Edelweiss* was dead in the water, the better.

Yes! The man fell and another started to descend—Blake was obviously just as brutal a master as Tarr had been. I aimed again. Missed. I tried again, but realized they were out of range. I reloaded and kept firing anyway. Tarr might have fallen, but Blake still lived.

Alonso and Phillippe cheered as *Freedom's* stern chaser put a two-pound ball through the other ship's stern, shattering the rudder and scattering the men there. *Edelweiss* was ours—crippled with no way of maneuvering. *Pinta* was mine again.

"Pull," I shouted, and realized *Freedom* had loosed her sails and slowed—we'd soon be back aboard.

"She's likely going down, Leo," Frazer said as I stepped onto my decks. He didn't ask after Magdalena. He had no need to; he'd seen what had occurred.

"Wear round and let's finish her," I ordered. "I want that ship and her crew of cut-throats on the bottom!"

He shouted the orders and *Freedom* started the laborious turn that would take us back into cannon range of the damaged pirate ship.

"*Sail oh,*" Juaquim shouted from the masthead.

"Mierda!" *Now what?* We were still only halfway through our turn, *Freedom* had taken damage, our supply of cannonball was running low, and my gunners were exhausted. I needed no more complications.

I jumped up into the ratlins, telescope in hand, to have a look at the new arrival for myself. She was headed straight for the two ships and I realized who she was as soon as I recognized her for a twinmaster. *Freyja*—Hornigold.

"Mierda! Shit!" I swore in both Spanish and English.

I climbed back down to the quarterdeck and Frazer.

"We're too badly damaged to take them both on, Captain."

I knew Frazer was serious when he addressed me as Captain rather than Leo. I nodded, reluctant. If I carried on I had a good chance of sinking the crippled *Edelweiss,* and sending her entire murderous crew to the bottom. But *Freedom* had so many problems of her own that she'd be no match for the smaller, fast, maneuverable and fully-armed *Freyja.* I'd already lost two people in the pinnace, including Magdalena, and another had died aboard *Freedom* from the splinters sprayed around the gundeck from one of Tarr's hits. I looked at my decks and the men for whom I was responsible. I'd lost enough for one day, I wouldn't send any more to their deaths in a fight we were unlikely to win.

"Bear off," I said, and Frazer repeated my order at full shout. I slammed my fist into the bulkhead aft of the quarterdeck and swore, loudly, then went into my cabin. I could not let my men see me lose control.

Chapter 15

LEO
29th September 1685
La Isla Magdalena

We buried King and Hitchens at sea, but Magdalena didn't belong there. I'd brought her to the island where I'd been washed ashore from *Pinta*. She could sleep here, and she'd never be forgotten on La Isla Magdalena.

I stared into the flames. The sorrow of the past three days had been superseded by the revelry of the rum punch, and my men were now celebrating life. I counseled myself to let them; the work on *Freedom* was nearly done, and we were safe here. I knew I had to let them work off the tension of the fight and our losses, but their laughter set my teeth on edge.

"Here, Leo." Frazer handed me a chunk of pork from the spit. "Eat."

I took it, only now aware of the smell of roasting pig. I bit into the warm flesh, suddenly ravenous, and realized I hadn't eaten all day. I tried to smile at Frazer in thanks, and refilled our rumpots.

"To Magdalena," I toasted.

"Magdalena," he repeated, and we drank. I stared into the fire again.

"What now?" Frazer asked.

I looked at him in surprise, what did he think was next?

"Blake and Hornigold," I said.

"Why? Magdalena's dead, we can't achieve anything and will only lose more men. We'd do better going after gold."

"They have to pay."

Frazer nodded, but said no more. I felt myself angering.

"They'll be coming for us now in retribution for Tarr. I want to be hunter, not prey." My voice was growing louder despite my efforts to keep calm. He nodded again and I took a deep breath. "If they saved *Edelweiss*, Blake'll be ashore somewhere making repairs; likely at Sayba if he could make it, and that's too well defended to attack with only one ship." I tried to keep my temper under control. "We'll go after Hornigold and *Freyja* first, save Blake for last. Losing first Tarr then Hornigold will– Mierda!"

Cheval, my second mate, stumbled into me. My meat and rum went flying and I got a face full of sand. I leapt to my feet, cutlass drawn.

"Have a care, Second!" I snarled.

"Pardon, Capitaine, pardon." He laughed, and the sight of his grinning face—not a face I was particularly fond of—was too much.

"Not good enough," I shouted, and held my cutlass up in challenge.

He backed off, waving his hands.

"Non, non, Capitaine, it was an accident, no 'arm intended."

I didn't believe him. He'd been nothing but trouble since he'd come aboard, and I was sure he'd done this on purpose to challenge me. I wanted to kill him.

"You kicked sand in my face, Second." I drew my blade.

He stopped laughing and drew his cutlass. He was all business now, and we slowly circled each other, ringed by my Freedom Fighters.

I lunged, my rage making me reckless, but he danced out of my way. I realized I'd lose this fight if I didn't get a hold of myself. I backed off a few paces and took a deep breath. I needed to stay calm and concentrate on his eyes and his sword arm. I stepped to my left again and he followed, his eyes never leaving my face.

I'd learned the skills of a swordsman as a young man, but they had no bearing here. This wasn't a duel between gentlemen for honor. This was about killing, and Cheval had learned his skills aboard buccaneer ships. I'd seen him in action and knew his style was brutal and effective. He lunged at me, his blade hacking at my throat. I dodged and knocked the steel away. He didn't pause, and immediately thrust the tip of his blade toward my chest. I jumped backwards and fell, then kicked out to bring him down to the beach. I leaped to my feet and held my blade to his throat, ready to finish it.

"Captain, he's not worth it," Frazer's calm voice interrupted. I looked at him, then at the silent circle of faces around me. "Save it for Blake and Hornigold."

"Oui, Blake and 'Ornigold," Cheval said. "You know I used to sail with them, I know their tactics—you need me."

I looked at him, then again at my men. I nicked the flesh at the base of his throat—first blood—and tucked the cutlass back into my sash. I recognized the real danger of the situation. If I killed a member of my own crew, even Cheval, for something so trivial, I'd lose my captaincy. Many pirate captains, including the late Captain Tarr, kept command through fear and killing anyone who stepped out of line. I wouldn't follow his example, and had promised the crew as much when I first took command. Cheval knew it.

"You make a good point there, Second. Fill the rumpots, Frazer, the night's still young!"

The watching crew relaxed and emptied what was left in their beakers ready for a refill. I bent down to Cheval, offering him a hand up.

"And Second? You need to be more careful, do you understand me?"

Cheval's smile faltered and he nodded. I saw a different look in his eyes, though, and knew I'd have to watch my back. This had been no accident—he'd chosen his moment with care. He wanted my ship.

I withdrew my hand and left him where he was—lying prostrate on the sand.

Chapter 16

LEO
17th March 1686
Six Leagues West-Northwest of Sayba

I watched the large red square of silk unfurl through my telescope. Another bloody flag. Like his dead master, Tarr, Captain Edward Hornigold offered no quarter. He would only stop killing when we were all dead or sworn to his own crew, and my ship his prize. I slammed the telescope shut hard enough to sting my hands, took a deep breath, and checked the sails. *Sound of Freedom* was bigger than Hornigold's twin-masted boat, *Freyja*, and I had most of my canvas flying. Above the sails, I flew the red-and-white Cross of Burgundy and would not show my true colors until the fight had begun. Hornigold had of course seen *Freedom* when I'd killed Tarr, but that had been six months ago and at a distance. I was hoping he wouldn't recognize me until it was too late. My best chance was to take him by surprise.

I'd searched for Hornigold ever since we'd left La Isla Magdalena, but with only rough charts and no way of finding longitude, it had been a frustrating hunt. El infierno, *latitude* was hard enough to find on the moving deck of a ship, and if I did place us on the right line of parallel, the actual position of even the best navigator could easily be twenty leagues out. A poor navigator could be anywhere. It was difficult enough to work out where *we* were, never mind another ship, especially a ship more used to being the hunter than the prey. But there he was, finally, almost in range of my guns, and rage flashed through me. I was so close to avenging my family. At last, he was right there; but I had to calm down. Hornigold was an English buccaneer and had been fighting and killing at sea for at least twenty years. I'd only sailed as a pirate for two, but that was long enough to know that rage would not win me this fight.

Calmer now, I looked aft at the *Magdalena*. A small single-masted sloop, we'd taken her a couple of months ago, and she sailed under Frazer's command in convoy with *Freedom*. She chased us with black flag flying, and I hoped this would convince Hornigold that *Freedom* was a helpless merchantman fleeing from a pirate attack; a rich prize ripe for the taking. The *Magdalena* would be no match for *Freyja,* and I was sure Hornigold would not be able to resist taking the prize from the smaller pirate boat. I took another deep breath and watched *Freyja* sail on.

"Yes!" He changed course, toward and just ahead of us. He'd fallen for it. He was coming.

Now that my initial rage on seeing him had fallen away, nerves fluttered at my belly. This was it. Even with two ships and surprise on our side, this would be the fight of my life. Yes, I'd managed to kill Tarr, but I'd lost too many lives in the process.

Another deep breath. This was not the time to think of the people I mourned. I had to keep my head clear and my heart closed. I looked at the men on deck and in the rigging; each of their lives rested on my shoulders. I had to get each one of them through this alive and in one piece. And kill Hornigold.

I'd hidden most of my crew below the bulwarks on the topdeck, and had my cannon hauled in where they couldn't be seen through Hornigold's telescope. On the deck below, the gunports stayed closed and sealed, and I shivered. I imagined the men crouched in the dark around their guns and powder, unable to see the enemy they knew was out there. It wasn't going to be easy to get all the guns run out and fired at the same time, but I had to wait until the last minute if I was going to fool the Englander.

Too soon, Hornigold's own ports opened, the muzzles of his own guns peeked out through the wooden planks. He fired a warning shot at my bows, just missing the sails. I held my nerve a fraction longer before giving the order to break ports. I turned *Freedom* and presented my starboard side to the buccaneer, shouting, "*Fire*", as soon as I judged my guns had a chance of hitting my target. At my mainmast, the Spanish Cross of Burgundy dropped, and my real colors, a square of plain black silk to match *Magdalena's*, flew in its place. I did offer quarter to any ship that asked for it.

We were quick, but *Freyja* was quicker and she scored a direct hit, shattering *Sound of Freedom's* hull amidships and sending lethal splinters like newly sharpened knives up to a foot long scything amongst my gunners below.

"Reload! Fire!" I shouted, hearing my commands echo down the deck and through the open scuttle to the gundeck below. *Yes! Direct hit!* We caught her stern and her aft-quarter bulwark—with any luck she'd be having difficulty steering.

Full of excitement, I screamed, "Load the chain shot! Go for her rigging!"

I flinched as my starboard side shattered not three paces away, then I heard yet more gunfire. It was too soon for *Freyja* to have reloaded after only just hitting us. *Magdalena* had joined the fight with her smaller guns and was pummeling *Freyja's* stern and rudder, trying to disable her and leave her adrift. I laughed out loud, imagining Hornigold's frustration at having to fight two vessels.

"Chain shot—aim for the masts!" I shouted again to my men, knowing full well they couldn't hear me over the combined roar of cannon, wind and flogging sail. More balls exploded from my cannon, and I saw most of them find a passage into or through *Freyja* and her canvas. We were close now, and I could see Hornigold on his quarterdeck shouting and stamping his foot. His blood-red flag dropped in defeat.

We'd done it; he was no match for the two of us. My ship was bigger than his, and so were my guns. The *Magdalena* was smaller and faster. Working together we were unbeatable, and Hornigold knew it. We'd sprung our trap and caught him; he wasn't going anywhere now. I looked across at my bo'sun, Blackman, who was ready to board, grapnel in hand, as soon as we got close enough to jump. I laughed at the grin lighting up his dark face.

"Get ready, nearly there," I called to the growing group of men at the rail. "And remember, Hornigold's mine. No one touches that murdering cabrón but me!"

The next thing I knew I was knocked to my knees by a sudden, violent heel of the deck. The wind was getting up fast, and I had far too much sail flying. I'd made a possibly fatal mistake and taken my eye off the sky.

I jumped up, saw *Freyja* bearing away and drove my fist into the rail. Hornigold had the advantage of facing upwind and I spun round myself to see what the wind gods were bringing down on us, then cursed. Targeting *Freyja's* rigging had done Hornigold a favor by downing most of his canvas, and we'd failed to destroy her rudder. He'd seen what was coming and had fooled me into thinking I'd won to give himself a chance of escape.

"Mierda! Secure the guns and lay aloft. Topgallant and fore-topsail in, now. *Now*!" I bellowed. Hornigold had a reprieve, and I had two shipfuls of men in the path of a massive towering black cloud; a great anvil larger by far than anything seen in a blacksmith's nightmare, and ready to drop its full wrath of fire and water down on us. Sheets loosed and men swarmed aloft to battle canvas for their lives in the sudden torrential rain.

I bore off to keep the wind safely behind us and looked ahead, but Hornigold was already out of sight in the stormy gloom. I looked up, anxious, and watched the topgallant sail at the top of the mainmast being slowly dragged up to its wooden yard. It was slow work at the best of times, and now the canvas had a mind of its own in the wildly shifting winds of a gathering squall. It tore at skin, whipped exposed faces and bodies with its attendant lines, and threatened the hands that attempted to tame it with a fast and lethal drop to the deck. Even as I thought the words I saw a man fall, catch a footrope below him and make his way back up the mast to re-join the fight with the heavy, lashing canvas as if nothing had happened. I looked again to windward and watched in disbelief and dread as the front of the anvil bulged, then stretched a long narrow finger down to the sea—a rare and terrifying sight at the best of times, and one I'd hoped never to see.

I did not want to be touched by that finger, but there seemed to be nothing I could do. The topgallant was only half in, and the lower courses ducked up—by hauling the foot of the sails up to the yard like that they would spill all their wind—but the fore-topsail was still full. *Freedom* had heeled so far over her decks were awash, and I had no steerage. I had to get her under control and stop her corkscrewing around into the wind or we were sunk. We were surrounded by squall clouds and lightning. We had nowhere to go.

I lashed the useless tiller and waded forward, grabbing men and putting them on the topsail braces as I went. If we could force the yards around and knock the wind out of the sails we'd have a chance. It was going to take too long to do things properly, and I was not ready for San Antonio's graveyard yet. I still had a debt to settle with both Hornigold and Blake.

I lent my weight to the forebrace, and shouted a fast heaving chant as we dragged the topyard and sail around, fighting for every inch. Then, with a tremendous boom, we fell to the flooded deck. The sail had blown out of its boltropes and was flung across the sky. I watched in disbelief as it was sucked into the waterspout and disappeared.

"On your feet! Get to the main-topbrace!"

It was a bit drastic, but to be honest we could do with losing the main-topsail as well—we could always steal another one. We were riding a little flatter, our heel not quite so dangerous with the loss of the sail, but we were still a long way from safe. I pushed my crew aft and went back to the tiller—hopefully she'd be a bit more responsive now with reduced sail. There was no way to outrun a waterspout, but maybe we could dodge it.

I thought again of Hornigold and *Freyja,* and wondered at their fate. We'd given her stern a pretty good hammering. If her steering *was* compromised in this wind she was likely to be going down. I was disappointed, and suddenly furious. No! He had to survive, I had to *see* him die, and I had to tell him why. His death had to be at *my* hand.

Chapter 17

The topgallant was finally in—although so bellied it would throw a deluge of water onto the decks when it was reset—and the maintopsail was coming round nicely. Thankfully we'd done enough and *Freedom* was responding to her helm again.

I pushed her bows to larboard, knowing I could trust my crew to adjust the sails accordingly. With a newer crew we might have gone down, but most of us had sailed together long enough now for each to know what the other would do in almost any situation.

It was difficult to see clearly; the sky was so dark it could have been night, and but for the bright, violent flashes, we may have had no vision at all. The nearest shelter was Sayba, but sheer cliffs, rocks and English buccaneers meant there was no sanctuary for us there. Although I knew that if Hornigold had survived, that was most likely where he was bound.

"Captain! Captain Santiago!" I only just heard the frightened shout and looked up to see balls of fire dancing around the masts and yards, lighting the men still hard at work up there. Knowing this was a sign the storm was abating, I looked anxiously to the finger of water still chasing us. *Is it shrinking? Or is that wishful thinking?*

The sky lit up again in a blinding flash to show, for a brief second, the spiraling sea ridged with waves around us, before plunging us back into darkness. *Is that a ship behind us near the waterspout?* I couldn't tell, but I thought I had an impression of canvas. If so, who was it? Hornigold? Or the *Magdalena*? There was nothing I could do but wait for the next flash—there! Yes, the *Magdalena*, I was sure of it. Only the one mast—although I immediately realized it could be the larger vessel partially dismasted. Whoever it was, that deadly finger was almost upon them and, even if it was our sister ship, there was nothing we could do but strain eyes and ears to learn her fate. Another flash lit the sky, smaller and yellow. A cannon.

"She's trying to break it, Capitaine! She's shooting the waterspout!" an excited Cheval shouted just behind me. "The ball should break it up, I've seen it done before!"

It was getting easier to see now, and yes, it was definitely the *Magdalena*, the waterspout almost upon her, then . . . then . . . what?

Cheval cheered, shouting out that the ball had worked. I was skeptical, but I couldn't deny it, the spout *had* broken and turned into a harmless mist. I gave the order to bear round further to larboard. The immediate danger had passed and, although still blowing hard, so had the worst of the squall. But I was concerned for the *Magdalena. Have her men survived?* I kept my eyes on the patch of water where I'd last seen her—*there! She's still there!*

Only just, though. Her mast had gone, her canvas was spread over the sea and she was low in the water. She might still be above the waves, but she wouldn't last long. We had to get to her and her men quickly.

"Duck down the main clews, get that mainsail pulling again!" I shouted. We had to get closer, and I could only hope that we'd be in time.

The curtain of rain drew back and the wind was definitely dropping off, but it still had some teeth. I could hear the roar of the mainsail as it filled and felt the deck beneath my feet surge forward. I gave the helm to Cheval and Thomas, and went forward to commend the men who had kept us afloat—especially the topmen—and got as many hands on the pumps as they would take. We had a sizable hole starboard amidships and were making water. We weren't in danger of sinking, yet, but there was far too much water coming aboard as we battled through the enormous waves the squall had stirred up. We had to get it out faster than it was coming in, or we'd be of no use to the men in the *Magdalena*; I could now see she was going down fast.

Keeping the hole in our side to leeward, we sailed in a large arc to bring us up onto the wind (or as close as we could get to it in the square-rigged *Sound of Freedom*, anyway). I had to duck up the mainsail again, but the wind was still strong enough to get us close on the smaller jibs. I hove *Freedom* to (pointed her bows into wind to hold her steady) and gave the order to fill and cast off the two boats we towed.

Magdalena was nothing but wreckage. Men clung onto her flotsam in the heaving seas, desperately trying to gulp down air rather than salted water. I could just about make out who was who through the glass by their body shape and the way they moved, and they all looked well—Phillippe, Feliciano, Rafael and George—but I couldn't see Frazer. *There.* I had him; he looked as if he was in trouble, bobbing up and sinking again. I knew he was a strong swimmer—a rarity amongst sailors too superstitious to learn—and tried to calm my heart which feared the worst. It was difficult to see through all the water in the air, both rain and spindrift, and they were only visible on the crests of the waves anyway, but I thought someone was with him; Carlos? Then I lost them again, both of them underwater. I was sure it was only Frazer who was in trouble; he must be caught up in a stray line, or injured in some way. I dropped Papá's old glass, exasperated, and cursed Blake and Hornigold that I didn't know what was happening. Whatever it was, it was their fault. We wouldn't have been anywhere near this stretch of water had it not been for them.

I held the glass up again. I had to see. I let go the breath I was holding when I saw the longboat reach the struggling man, then gasped when I saw Gibson plunge into the sea rather than pull Frazer aboard. I thought I saw a glint of metal in his teeth before he dived under, although in that weather I may well have imagined it. Then Frazer was free—properly on the surface—but he still had to get into the boat. I saw rather than heard his roar as he tried to launch himself over the stern, and my fears were confirmed when I saw the boat tip over to roll him aboard amidships, along with a heavy load of brine. Carlos and Gibson wriggled in and they pulled toward *Freedom*, leaving the pinnace to help the others.

"Gaunt! Gaunt! Where are you, amigo? Get your tools, it looks like you have a patient!"

"Who?" he asked on his way down the hatch.

"Frazer. It's his leg."

Gaunt didn't waste his words, but nodded and slid down through the scuttle to the decks below. He was not a surgeon, but as carpenter he was the closest we had. If Frazer's leg was too badly injured, it would have to come off. Gaunt was the man with the saws.

The wind had dropped a little more, but still blew a fresh gale. I had two jibs on the foremast and the reefed main-topsail was backed to hold us head to wind. We had to stay where we were, hove-to, as best we could and let the longboat come to us. It was directly upwind of us, and I had no way of moving toward it. I threw a large canvas bag over the bows as a sea anchor to minimize the amount of drift to leeward and help keep us in position. The oarsmen would have to do all the work, which was made even harder by the heavy seas. The waves were so big that the longboat disappeared entirely from view in the troughs, but at least they were rowing downwind.

Gaunt was below, readying a table with his tools and straps, and I had Cheval and Lopez prepare a carrying plank by slinging a six-foot strake of wood with line at either end. Judging by Frazer's inability to climb into the longboat, I knew he wouldn't be able to climb *Freedom's* hull; we'd have to sway him aboard.

When the longboat finally reached us, I bore off a touch to shelter the boat and make it a little easier to haul the Scot up the side. He screamed every time he bumped against the hull, which happened once or twice a wave. I'd never heard Frazer shriek or curse the way he did that day. His lower leg was a bloody mess with bone sticking out of it in at least two places. It was beyond salvage. Lopez and Cheval rushed him below decks to Gaunt.

I learned later that *Magdalena* had been knocked down, then dragged sideways into the waterspout before it broke. The wind had pulled them upright again, then knocked them over the other way. It was too much for *Magdalena's* mast which had crushed

Frazer's left leg when it fell, tangling him in its mess of rigging. They'd cut away the sail when they'd realized they were being sucked in, rather than waste time furling it, and that had probably saved his life. He'd been caught in parts of the rigging that had floated, and his duckings had simply been due to the pain of swimming. Gibson had dived in off the longboat and helped Carlos cut him free.

As soon as Frazer was on deck, I gave the order to heave-to again to wait for the other boat and the rest of my crew. I was not pleased. We'd survived the waterspout, but Hornigold had got away, *Magdalena* was in pieces, and Blake was forewarned that we were in the area. I suppose I should have been pleased there'd been no loss of life, but having my best man injured so badly destroyed any sense of relief I may have had. Instead I was angry. Enough was enough. Hornigold had got lucky, that was all. He was the weaker of the two anyway. Blake was the one I really wanted. Blake was the one we'd go after next. I did not intend to fail again.

Chapter 18

I desperately wanted to follow Frazer through the scuttle and ensure he lived. But I could not. I was the captain of this ship and Frazer wasn't the only one crippled. The ship was injured too; she had a hole in her hull and the pumps were only just keeping up with the intake of water. We needed to make repairs before I could turn downwind again. I had to see to *Freedom* first, and my carpenter was busy.

The last of *Magdalena's* men climbed aboard, and I instructed Cheval on the tiller to keep us hove-to until it was safe to set sail again. I went below to inspect the damage for myself.

The gundeck stank of brimstone, and it was hard to see and breathe—even with the extra ventilation. The gash in the side was about a foot wide and almost the same high, and the deck before it was thick with vicious splinters. The hole was not as bad as I'd feared, but was too close to the waterline to ignore in these seas; it could be enough to sink us. It was too large for a patch of lead sheeting, and Blackman and Smith struggled to cover it with tarred sailcloth, which they battened to the hull to keep the worst of the seas out. It was the best we could do until we could find a safe harbor.

"Let me know the second it's safe to bear off, Bo'sun," I said, ignoring Blackman's grumbles, and went to see the huddle of men in the bows. They were comparing wounds, each claiming to have won the pieces of eight each gunner put into the pot to go to the man with the worst injury. Despite the hammocks rolled up against the wooden hull, the splintered hull had caught three or four of them and one, Jacques, was close to serious; he would not be hauling out the heavy cannon for a while. He was enjoying the attention, though—and the twenty-odd pieces of eight he finally claimed from the others. I supposed whatever kept them shooting was fine by me. I couldn't imagine a worse place to be in a gunfight. As we'd just proved, the four-inch-thick wooden hull didn't offer much in the way of protection from cannonball. They worked with the risk of fire or cannon exploding if just one man lacked the care required. Even without accidents, gunners wore their shoulders out at about the same rate they lost their hearing.

I climbed back up the main scuttle to my upper deck, and paused for a moment in the wind to enjoy its strength on my face, then looked up at the sails. We were safe enough hove-to like this, but I didn't like being at the mercy of the wind gods. I could not steer. I could not command. We were drifting downwind, despite the sea anchor, vulnerable to the sea and anything on her, and there was nothing I could do about it.

"Keep her head to wind, Cheval," I said, looking at the sails again. "Blackman'll shout when it's safe to set a course."

I examined the decks and tried not to think about what was happening down on the dark, wet orlop deck in the bowels of the ship. I imagined Frazer screaming as Gaunt sliced and sawed; his blood streaming into the bilges. Then the smell of cooking flesh when Gaunt sealed the stump with the red-hot wide cauterizing iron.

I remembered Garcia—one of the topmen aboard Capitán Valdez's ship—when I first went to sea. He'd fallen from the mainyard and shattered his arm. I'd been one of the men tasked with holding him down for the surgeon, Don Roberto. The things I saw that day came flooding back. The way Roberto had circled Garcia's arm with his sharpest knife and peeled the skin back. Garcia's piercing screams and frantic struggles, even with copious amounts of rum and poppy, plus six sailors holding him down. Then a larger knife carving muscle as calmly as if preparing a boar for the spit; except I'd never known a boar fight back. The horrendous grating of the bone saw.

By the time Garcia had succumbed to oblivion I'd thought it a blessing, but he never woke. Despite Roberto cauterizing the stump, pulling the flap of skin back down and sewing it up, Garcia had lost too much blood. It had taken months to scrub the last of the stains from the deck.

And now Frazer was in the same position, and it was my fault. All my fault. I shook myself out of my imaginings. We were still in danger. I was still responsible for more than forty lives. I couldn't afford to dwell on Frazer's sufferings.

At last, Blackman's head appeared out of the main hatch, thumb up. The hull was seaworthy again, and we were masters of our own fates once more.

Hoping the cant of the ship as she came off the wind wouldn't affect the steadiness of Gaunt's hands, I gave the order to loose the main-topsail and set the maincourse and spanker.

"Keep the damage to leeward, Cheval. We'll have to stay on larboard and pray we find land quickly. Any ideas?"

In any other circumstances, I wouldn't take my ship even within sight of land in a blow this strong; it was usually the worst time to go ashore—there'd been many a ship wrecked whilst searching out shelter close to land. Today, we had no choice; we couldn't stay out at sea with mere canvas to keep it out.

"Well?" I barked in impatience, trying to ignore the screaming just audible from below.

"Course sou'east, Capitaine, we could probably shake the reef out of that main, but I advise on the caution with our damage."

"Muy bien, Cheval. Very well. Is there any land out there?"

"Sayba, Capitaine, right on our nose."

"Sayba!" I spluttered. "You want to take us to Sayba?"

"Oui, mon Capitaine. We can sail sou'east, maybe east with this wind and this 'ull, but there's nothing else out there. It's either Sayba or St Eustatius, another three days' sail away and with, no doubt, the even frostier welcome."

I knew he was right, but I didn't like it. Sayba was a nasty place for an injured ship in a gale. Most of her coastline was rocked and cliffed, and a lot of her rocks hid below the surface. Not to mention it being Blake and Hornigold's lair.

"Trust me, Capitaine, I know the island. I know where we'll 'ave the safety."

I paused, then nodded, I would have to trust him, I had no other choice; nowhere else to go.

* * *

The island had been settled by the Dutch until Thomas Morgan—Henry's uncle—had captured the island in 1665 and forced the Dutch settlers into servitude. Once the Anglo-Dutch war had been resolved, the Morgans recognized the mercantile potential of the Dutchmen, which was being wasted, and had allowed some of them to resettle the island. Now that Morgan had been suspended from the Council of Jamaica, Tarr, and then Blake and Hornigold, had taken over his interests here; although I was sure Morgan still took a slice of the profits.

"*Land oh.*"

Just as the call came, Gaunt appeared on deck, and I hurried over to him, desperate to hear his report.

"He's breathing, but out cold. Best thing for him, Cap."

"Will he live?"

"He likely will if he wakes. More than that I can't say. It'd help him to be up in fresher air, though."

"Yes, bring him up to the chartroom." I noticed just how drawn Gaunt looked. I grasped his shoulder and nodded. "Gracias, Robert. Thank you."

I returned to my place on the quarterdeck. If we could see the island in this weather we were close, and I did not entirely trust Cheval at the helm. The closer we got, the worse it looked—a square-rigger's nightmare. The lee shore was a jagged, confused jumble of sharp, unforgiving rock. I wanted a boat to go ahead and make sure there was a passage large enough to accommodate *Freedom,* but Cheval swore there was a way through to a hidden anchorage. I could not risk heaving-to, to get the boats manned and away anyway. With the shallowing sea, the waves were getting up higher and were messy—coming from all directions—and *Freedom* would not last long here with no way on her. I had to trust the one man aboard in whom I had the least faith.

"If you sink my ship, I'll cut your throat," I promised Cheval, just to make sure he understood my position.

"Relax, Capitaine, I know what I'm doing, let me do it—and the threats to my life are not 'elpful."

I grunted in reply. I was not happy, but could do little about it. I sent a double-lookout to the bows and aloft, and had two of my strongest men, Phillippe and Carlos, standing by with the leads. It was a beast of a job to swing the seven-pound pyramids of lead and haul them back in, but I wanted two men sounding over and over again. I needed to know exactly how deep the water was below my keel, and the soft tallow on the base of the lead would tell me whether we had sand or rock below. This would not be pleasant.

The wind was still dropping, but too slowly for *Freedom*. We approached the rocky shoreline much too quickly, and I shouted to have the smaller jib and the mainsail furled. The force of the waves and the reefed main-topsail would give us enough speed, and the last jib would help us keep the necessary course, but I was still nervous and joined Cheval on the helm once more.

"Do you see Lookout's Rock just off the starboard bow—the one with the split like a seat?"

I nodded to Cheval as Phillippe called the depth, "No bottom'. We had sixty fathoms of line attached to the lead, three hundred and sixty feet, and it did not reach the seabed. Good news.

"I'm lining that up with the clump of the trees on the cliff face behind it."

I looked carefully and could just make them out, three trees clinging on precariously and leaning over the gray teeth below.

"If I get it right we'll clear the passage through—"

"*If* you get it right?" I thundered, angry again.

He looked at me. "I haven't been here in a while," he admitted. "But with a fortuitous wave we'll clear the rocks and be well hidden while we make the repairs. There are the defensive works on the cliff, but only the one gun may give us cause for the concern 'ere, if it is manned. It isn't usually, only when they expect the trouble, and we're not showing any lights. It's the best chance we've got, Capitaine. Around that headland to the sou'west is Eckerstad, the Dutch town, and if Blake's here that's where he'll be."

"Fifty by the mark, shell and coral," Phillippe shouted. Fifty fathoms of water.

"Is that likely? How much time does he spend ashore?"

"Not a lot, he hates the landlubbers almost as much as he hates Spain, excusez-moi." I nodded to hurry him along. "I doubt 'e is 'ere or we'd likely 'ave seen him, but there's no way to be sure. 'Ornigold though, if 'e survives, 'e will be 'ere."

I nodded again, then thought of something else. "Assuming we get in safely and the wind turns fair, how's the passage out?"

"Forty, shell. Looks like conch," Phillippe called, as if he could tell.

"Tricky," Cheval answered eventually. "It's rare for the wind to be blowing like this. Sayba normally 'as the easterlies, but as you can see, the coast is 'igh and the 'eadland an odd shape—it can be unpredictable. As long as we wait for a fresh offshore breeze we'll make an offing, no problem, but it may take a little of the patience."

I kept nodding. I'd expected his answer and had only asked to calm my nerves, I hated having to rely on somebody else for the safety of my crew and ship, especially him, but he knew these waters better than I did.

"Twenty by the mark, shell." One hundred and twenty feet; there were no jokes now.

I could see the extent of the reef by this time, but was encouraged by Cheval's demeanor—he did sound as if he knew what he was talking about. But I still couldn't see the passage through the rocks myself.

"You can't see it until we're right on it, Capitaine. When you can see the beach, you'll see the gap to it. There! 'Elp me, we're a little too far to the larboard."

I grabbed the tiller and pushed it to larboard away from me as Cheval pulled, both of us muttering to *Freedom,* asking her to respond.

"Five, shell and sand."

"Loose the mainsheets! Haul the main buntlines!" Cheval shouted. The wind shook out of the mainsail, and our speed dropped.

The crew lined *Freedom's* rails, holding their breath as we slipped between the rocks. Then she shuddered as her keel scratched the reef below, but only for a moment. The next wave lifted her just enough and we carried on. Touch and go—we were through; jib flogging now as well. She beached onto the sand and I looked astern at the reef we had bested.

I shook Cheval's hand. "Your throat's safe for the time being, Second!" I laughed. "Well done. If anyone's looking for us, they'll find it difficult to spot us here. Good work, marin, I'm impressed."

I was a little taken aback by the width of his smile, but thought he was probably just as relieved as I was to get through. He wore a smug grin on his face all the way forward as the crew took their turns to clap him on the back and congratulate his navigational skills. I could almost see his vanity growing, but felt much more indulgent toward him. My opinion of him had definitely improved; maybe I'd judged him too harshly.

Chapter 19

LEO
18th March 1686
Sayba

Cheval had done well. We'd come in on the flood of the tide, and although he took the credit for this timing, it was really down to sailor's luck—and maybe a slight storm surge. Either way, the result was the same; when the tide dropped, *Sound of Freedom* was left high and dry on the sand (or if not dry, at least high and draining—she still had a tun or two of water sloshing about her guts), and ready for work to begin.

Cheval had taken a couple of men to the island's gun placement overnight—he was the only one who knew where it was, and was sure he could find it in the dark. He'd returned at first light, gun silenced. Now we had to set up our own defensive cannon before we did anything else.

"Call thysen a sailor, man? Have a care with that cannon! If she swings any harder, she'll bring the mast down!"

I jumped in surprise at the shout behind me. Gaunt was back on deck, and I walked over to him to find out how Frazer fared.

"His battle's with fever now, Cap. It's up to Providence, I can do nowt else for him." He paused. "Go and see him, Cap. I don't know if he'll know thee, but he might." He looked past me at the gun slung over the mainyard and being lowered to the beach, then shouted again, "Have a care with that cannon! What have I already told thee?"

I looked at the cabin door for a moment, then turned away, back to the deck. I wasn't ready to face Frazer yet. It was my fault he'd lost his leg, and if he died, that would be my fault too. We hadn't sunk Hornigold; it had all been for nothing. How could I look him in the eye? Besides, there was nothing I could do for him. I gave my attention back to the ship.

Freedom needed new planking which meant we needed trees, and the only ones in sight were either growing out of the cliff face or atop it. At least the problem of getting them to the beach in one piece gave me something other than Frazer to worry about. I called Cheval and Gaunt to join me. The climb itself didn't look too arduous—there was even a path—and the wind would blow us onto the cliff rather than off it, but it would still take some planning to get the wood to the beach.

Conversation was brief on the way up—all of us needed our full concentration to find safe footholds—and I for one had no breath to spare. At last, the loose dark stones of the path were behind us and the footing became surer. I stared out to sea—a view I never tired of—and studied the calm, deep blue water. It showed no trace of the storm that had pounded us more thoroughly than Hornigold's cannon the day before. It looked so beautiful and peaceful; the storm, waterspout and loss of the *Magdalena* already felt like a dream. But it was all very real, and we'd have had him if not for that squall. Instead of glory, *Freedom* lay helpless on the sand directly below me. At this height she could have been the carcass of some great stranded sea creature. She didn't belong on a beach, her body holed and her wings clipped.

I shook myself out of my reverie. We needed to get on with it and make this enforced stop as brief as possible. I turned inland to have a good look at our surroundings. The dense jungle looked just like my early home in Panama, except for the bare rock of the top half of the central volcano shrouded with gray cloud. I could see no sign of people, but Cheval assured me there was a grand estate close inland and the town of Eckerstad was three or four leagues along the coast to the south. Blake and Hornigold had close ties to that town, and we could learn something useful about them there. I resolved to visit it with my second mate once all the decisions regarding the repairs were made.

"Well, what do you think, Robert?" I asked my carpenter.

"Mahogany—it's good wood, *Freedom'll* do well with it, but it'll be a beggar to work with."

I nodded; this was going to take time then. "What do you want to do? Lower whole trees down or plank it up here?"

"Good question. I reckon it'll be easy enough to rig up a gantry to lower the smaller trees. We're not exactly short of cordage, and I can rig up a runner and tackle easy enough. I ain't dragging all the tools up here so the strakes can be damaged on the passage back down."

I nodded, that made sense.

"I'll need a dozen men up here felling and lowering, and another half dozen below," he went on. "Then it'll take time to carve and fair each strake, and there's only a handful of men who can do that work. I wouldn't count on leaving inside of two week. Mebbe three."

I nodded again. I wasn't surprised; the ball had split several strakes, and there was a lot of splintered wood to replace. It was no easy job to shape the four-inch-thick planks we needed. We'd use the time to thoroughly clean, air and scrape *Freedom's* hull to get her fighting fit and to her fastest again. I looked back down at the beach, noting the gun placements and lookout positions. I would want somebody up here as well and, once the gantry was rigged, a gun or two wouldn't be a bad idea, as long as they were the smaller ones. If we used one to signal the beach, the other would protect us from the bearing of the cliff top and the estate. We weren't quite as vulnerable as I'd feared. Nobody would find it easy to sneak up on us here, and if they did try, we were well prepared and heavily armed. The gun covering our passage out had been spiked, and if there was no perceptible threat to the island, there was no reason the sabotage would be found—and if it were, it would take time to deal with. It was a big task, but with a little thought and planning we should be able to make our repairs and put off again right under the noses of our enemies.

Chapter 20

LEO
2nd April 1686

The repairs were well under way, and Gaunt and Blackman had everything in hand. Frazer was still in his fever, and there was nothing I could do here. It was time to take the opportunity to explore Eckerstad with Cheval. He'd joined *Freedom* a couple of months before our encounter with Tarr. We'd taken his ship for a prize, and Frazer had recognized him as having sailed with Hornigold. We'd taken a chance on him as he'd fallen out with the buccaneers, and I hoped that, knowing their habits, he might prove useful. I'd put him forward for second mate as a play on his vanity, and hoped it was time to be rewarded. He knew Eckerstad and its people, and I wanted as much information as I could gather about Blake and Hornigold's pet island without drawing too much attention to myself. My mother had been English, and I'd spoken the language since I was a child, plus I was in the company of a known French buccaneer, so hopefully no one would realize I was a hated Spaniard. I put on a wide-brimmed hat to hide my face, though, just in case.

I also wanted to know more about how he'd parted company with Tarr and the others. So far he'd been tight-lipped about his past, blustering past my questions, but I was determined to get his story. I needed to know if I could trust him as a man as I now knew I could as a sailor. He'd done well after the waterspout, but I hadn't forgotten his earlier challenge. This little expedition would provide the perfect opportunity to find out more about him.

We rowed back out through the rocks in the longboat at high tide with a calm sea and sunshine. Once we were free of them, Cheval hauled up the sail and we let the wind do the work. It was only April, but already the days dawned stiflingly hot and still—apart from the odd squall. The building sea breeze and sunshine were perfect, and the little craft responded to every gust, pushing forward easily through the slight swell. Despite the recent problems and the knowledge that I was on a mission of revenge, my cares fell off my shoulders with each welcome puff of cooling wind.

"I love this," I told Cheval. "The wind at my back, the pull of the sail and the way she takes on each wave. Do you know, I've been at sea eight years now, but I can never get enough of this—there can be no better place than at the helm of a sailing boat enjoying a salted breeze."

"Oui. I first came to the sea when I was eight and could never leave 'er now."

"What took you to sea so young?"

"Mon père. It was just the two of us and Papa was one of the original boucaniers. We were amongst those invited to Port Royal by England, lured away from our life hunting on 'Ispaniola by the promise of the rich prizes."

"By Henry Morgan." It was a statement rather than a question, but he answered anyway.

"Non, 'e was just an ordinary sailor then, one of many, but we did sail with 'im, until 'e blew up 'is ship, anyway."

"Which one, the *Oxford*?" The *Oxford* had been Morgan's impressive flagship, sent west by a grateful English parliament, and had had a crew over two hundred strong. She exploded one night off Cow Island, thanks to a well-stocked powder magazine, drunken sailors and a careless candle. Only the men carousing in the great cabin had survived. She'd hardly fired a shot in anger.

"Oui. Papa was killed."

"I'm sorry. It's hard to lose a father so young."

He stayed quiet, lost in his memories. I sheeted the sail in and leaned back as I changed course to clear the headland, and waited for him to continue.

"I was alone, and didn't 'ave anywhere to go, but I was damned if I'd set foot on the same deck as 'Enry Morgan again."

"I'm not surprised."

"I ended up on Tarr's ship."

I nodded, careful not to comment. I needed him to tell his story.

"'E was more interested in the gold than claiming and protecting land for England as Morgan was, and that suited me too. I didn't give a damn for England. Nor anyplace else. Still don't. I sailed with them sixteen years and 'ave to say we were good at our trade."

"So you were at Panama with them?" I held my breath.

Cheval shuddered. "Mon Dieu, non. I stayed behind to keep the ship with three others. The men didn't want a child slowing them down in the jungle, though they took old Swan with them and 'e was eighty if 'e was a day."

I was relieved. If he'd been part of the attack on my home, I'd have had to kill him.

"Why did you leave them? What happened?"

"Look up there, that's where the gun is," he said, changing the subject.

Frustrated, I looked up, realizing I only had Cheval's word that the gun was out of action.

"Do you see those coconut trees up there? That's where van Ecken lives. He brought them over from the East Indies. Insists on making his guests eat them, hate them myself."

"Who?" I asked, wanting as much information as possible.

"Erik van Ecken. 'E's the 'Ollander who more or less owns the island. Tarr was 'is man, Blake and 'Ornigold still are. The buccaneers take the ships, then van Ecken buys them, refits them as slavers and sends them to Africa. 'E grows sugar and trades in other things too, but the slaves is where 'e makes 'is coin, and 'e makes a lot. 'Is plantation, Brisingamen, stretches the three leagues in every direction from this cliff face."

"He has a long reach."

"Oui."

"Does he live alone?" I wanted to keep Cheval talking.

"No, nothing like. 'E 'as an army of the slaves and plenty of English pirates to keep them in line. 'E never goes anywhere alone; even when 'e's stepping out on 'is wife, 'e always 'as at least two of them with 'im."

"What's the wife like?"

He paused. "Beaten."

"Beaten?"

"Oui, in every way. I 'aven't seen 'er in a long time, but I remember 'er when she arrived. Young and excited, beautiful with the laugh that could melt even Blake's 'eart. It didn't last long."

"What, the marriage?"

"No, the laugh."

I looked at him, not sure what to say.

He shrugged. "C'est vrai. It's true. I don't know what 'e did to 'er, but 'e took 'er laughter, and 'er looks. She's too thin and creeps about like a rat trying to stay out of the way of the ship's cat. A waste of a good woman if you ask me."

"It sounds it. Why does she stay? It doesn't sound as if either of them want the marriage." Not that there was much she could do about it in this day and age, divorcements were hard to come by—especially for a wife.

"She's no more wife than possession, just like the slaves. Only she lives in better quarters." He shrugged again, not that interested. "We should be able to see the town soon, the rocks become less past this last point."

I looked forward again. Eckerstad was a sizable collection of buildings nestled around a natural harbor and dwarfed by the cloud-shrouded mountain that towered over it. I wondered at the prudence of my decision to come here.

Chapter 21

LEO
Eckerstad

"*Freyja!*"

I looked around at Cheval's urgent whisper. We'd cleared the last headland, and there she was. Hornigold had survived both my attack and the waterspout.

I examined the other ships—was Blake here too? No. No *Edelweiss*, just a couple of slavers by the looks of it. I turned my attention back to *Freyja* and adjusted the tiller. Her rigging had been replaced and her hull looked sound from this distance, but I didn't want to get any closer to make sure. If I had the opportunity I'd kill him, but I didn't want to give *him* the opportunity to kill *me*. I'd stay well away from those guns. I checked her stern and rudder. Seaworthy. We had caused no lasting damage that I could see; I still had it all to do.

I scrutinized her decks as we sailed past—she seemed deserted. There must be someone on shipkeeping duty, surely, but I couldn't see any movement at all.

"'Ornigold will be ashore," Cheval said. "'E never did like staying aboard at anchor. 'e will be in one of the stews with some doxy."

"I'm not so sure." I'd watched the shore as we approached, and noticed that the men milling around the wharf were not actually milling. Nor were they drinking or sleeping in the sun. Something was going on. *Do they know we're here? But how?*

I guided the longboat to the near end of the wharf, out of the way, and Cheval jumped ashore, line in hand, to tie her off. I dropped the sail and followed, then looked up the cobbled wharf. Two heavily armed men were walking toward us, although patrolling might be a better description; they moved with purpose.

"We should go, Capitaine," Cheval whispered loudly. "They're looking for us."

"If they were looking for us, why would they be looking here? Anyway, they'd be looking for a ship, not two men in a boat."

"Well, something's wrong, I don't like it."

"Hmm, but if Hornigold is distracted, I may get my chance at him. Come on, Second."

I headed toward the nearest narrow street, and was stopped by a shout from the men walking the wharf.

"What's your business here, churl?" one of them asked.

I stared at him, but decided not to react to his insult.

"Just come ashore for a drink, mate," I said, doing my best to hide my Spanish accent, and gestured vaguely at the ships in the harbor. "We've had the devil of a day cleaning out the cable locker." The cable locker, where the enormous anchor cables were stowed when at sea, was low down in the ship, stank to high heaven, and needed heavy maintenance to keep the wood sound. It had to be scraped and tarred, and any rotten wood replaced before the anchors were weighed and the heavy, wet rope once again coiled down. The job was usually reserved as a punishment. The men laughed.

"I reckon you'll need more than a drink, mate—best alehouse is that way—the Crab and Anchor!" He laughed again. "Watch out for the crabs!" We hurried off in the direction he had indicated.

"Merde!"

I looked at Cheval. Now what? Had he been that scared by a couple of deckhands? It would have been an even fight at worst. Then I realized he was staring at one of the alleyways ahead to our left, and had his hand on his sword. We did have pistols with us, but they were unloaded and stowed in our sashes out of the way. I hadn't wanted to be quite so obvious about my intentions as to hang loaded pistols about my neck. We could load them in a minute, but by the look on his face we did not have a minute.

I followed his line of sight and saw the two men who were having such an effect on my second mate. I stiffened with surprise as I recognized the one-eyed man from Tarr's ship—the one who had called down after Magdalena.

"Who are they?"

"Sharpe, 'Ornigold's new quartermaster, and Little. We don't get on."

Something told me that was an understatement.

Sharpe spotted us and stopped in his tracks. A slow smile spread over his face, and he said something to Little, who laughed, but I did not think it was in humor. They changed direction and walked toward us.

"Well, well, well," Sharpe said as he neared us, his hand on the hilt of his cutlass. "Look at this—you never know what you'll find skulking in the backstreets of a sailortown. I've been looking forward to seeing you again, Cheval."

"I 'aven't," Cheval muttered. I glanced at him in annoyance.

Sharpe and Little both laughed. I stepped to the side. All their attention was on Cheval and, if it came to a fight, I wanted the advantage.

Sharpe glared at me. Even with a patch covering one eye, the other conveyed his message, and I stopped moving.

"You want to be careful, mate, don't turn your back to this one, he'll have a knife in it afore you even know he's there. Then he'll toss you overboard for good measure."

"That's a lie, Sharpe, and you know it," Cheval exclaimed.

"Yes, you used a mainsheet block, didn't you? But the sentiment's true enough. Don't think I don't know it was no accident. I know you tried to kill me. You're too good a steersman to be caught out by a jibe like that, just as I was standing in exactly the right place for your purposes. If I hadn't seen that boom coming, the block would have knocked me overboard, and you wouldn't have called an alarm, would you? As it was, I lost an eye and now I want restitution—I want both of yours!"

He drew his sword and lunged at Cheval. I pulled out my own blades, as did Little, and steel clashed in the narrow alley.

"*I* was quartermaster—*me*!" Cheval shouted. "You took that from me!"

"No, you lost it! You're a lazy leader of men and you were voted out. You only have yourself to blame!"

I ducked as Little swiped his cutlass where my head had been a second ago, and drove my elbow into his belly. I risked a quick look at Cheval and Sharpe. They were a good match; we weren't going to get out of here quickly.

I brought my blade up to block another of Little's hacks and pushed him back, managing to cut his swordarm. Then I heard a shout. More Freyjamen were coming, drawn by the sound of clanging steel. We had to go.

I lunged at Little, who dodged my blade and I barged into him, adding to his momentum. He hit the wall head first and slumped to the ground. I picked up a cask, threw it at Sharpe, and shouted to Cheval to run. He did not need telling twice.

Chapter 22

I doubled up, trying to catch my breath.

"I think we've lost them." I gasped.

"*Oui,*" Cheval said. "I can't 'ear them anymore."

"So that's why you left Hornigold," I said. "It's good to get the whole story at last!"

"That's *not* the whole story, Capitaine*,*" he snapped. "It *was* an accident! We caught a big windshift on a dead run. We jibed before I even knew what' ad 'appened. The boom crashed over into Sharpe and the mainsheet block caught 'im in the eye. There was nothing I could do!"

"So why jump ship?"

"He challenged me to a duel with pistols." Cheval's voice and tone were quieter now, and I realized he was ashamed. "Sharpe is the best shot I've ever seen—I didn't 'ave a chance, even with 'im losing an eye." He took a deep breath. "'Ornigold knew it was an accident. He believed me, but 'e couldn't overrule 'is new quartermaster—the crew wouldn't 'ave allowed it. 'E gave me the option of leaving unharmed rather than die on the beach at Sharpe's 'and. So I left *Freyja*—I didn't even get my share of the booty!" He sounded indignant again. "And all because of that one-eyed cochon!"

I nodded. Only Cheval knew the truth. Wrongfully accused or petty, jealous and vindictive? I took my pistols from my sash, loaded them and hung them around my neck so the shot wouldn't fall out. Cheval did the same.

"We need to get moving." It was my only comment.

Left, right, left, left, right. I could hear the sea and the shouts of men loading supply vessels, but the labyrinth of narrow alleyways did not make it easy to find, especially when having to avoid Hornigold's men. I still had my bearings—just—but was becoming frustrated. Cheval was no better.

* * *

Halfway down yet another filthy alley, we came face to face with two men who looked like they had already been in one fight today and moved as stealthily as we did. Cheval and I drew our cutlasses immediately and started our advance. We had to be aggressive to get out of here, but I did not want to waste my shot unnecessarily. They held blades of their own, but only daggers—we wouldn't have any trouble with these two. They moved and I got ready for an attack, but instead of lunging they grabbed their shirts and lifted them.

I stepped back in surprise at the sight of breasts, and just had time to note more bruises and a valuable amethyst before all thoughts of fight flew from my head. They were women! In shirt and breeches! In the back alleyways of Eckerstad's sailortown!

I turned at Cheval's snort of laughter, and when I looked back they were gone; running at full speed back the way they'd come.

"Mon Dieu! That was Gabriella van Ecken!" Cheval snorted again, hardly able to contain himself. "That was van Ecken's wife!"

So *that* was who they were looking for. I breathed a sigh of relief. Hornigold did not know we were here. Van Ecken was not hunting us. Then I remembered Sharpe; but he didn't know me, only Cheval. I still had a chance at Hornigold.

"Come on Second, vamos. We need to keep moving. And will you stop that awful noise!"

He nodded and calmed, though continued to snigger for a while longer, and we walked to the next junction. I peered around the corner, and froze.

"Silencio! It's Hornigold!"

Cheval stopped laughing.

"Who's with him?" I asked and stepped back to let Cheval look around the corner to identify the man with the English pirate.

"Van Ecken," he whispered when he drew back. I stepped forward to have another look at the man in league with my enemies. He was fairly short with a tightly-curled, overelaborate, long golden periwig and exaggerated mustaches. He was dressed expensively in a green and gold frockcoat, even in this heat. Good quality breeches, silk stockings, and shoes adorned with large gold buckles looked incongruous in the filthy alleyway.

They were coming closer, close enough to hear what they were saying. I had to do this quickly.

"—find my wife Hornigold, or I'll have your ship *and* your head." Van Ecken spoke loudly. "That bitch is going in the cage and I'll watch her thirst to death and laugh as the birds peck out her eyes!"

I thought of the women I had just seen. I could understand why they'd risked all to get away from this man. For a moment I wanted to kill him almost as much as I wanted to kill Blake and Hornigold.

"Are you ready, Second? This may be our chance."

I looked at him and realized by the look on his face that he did not have my back. His argument was with Sharpe, not Hornigold. I remembered our altercation on the beach six months ago. Sharpe was right; I may well end up with a knife in my back from my second mate.

More noise. I snapped my head back to the men in the alley. Sharpe had joined them, along with half a dozen others.

I raised my first pistol, but Cheval grabbed my arm.

"Non, Capitaine, there are too many and the sound of the shot will bring more. If you shoot, we'll never get away, and you'll not 'it 'im at this distance anyway."

I dropped my arm. He was right. Whatever his motives, he was right. A pistol ball was only likely to find its target at close-quarters, and I had but two guns—against eight heavily armed men.

"Very well, we'll get back to the wharf and *Freedom*. If Gaunt's finished we can attack from the sea."

Finally—water. We were out of the web of taverns and stews. I examined the wharf; only the same two men we saw before, the others were scattered throughout the alleyways.

"Quickly!" I hissed. "Pretend we're rumsoaked and let's get out of here."

We staggered onto the wharf, Cheval singing in French, and made our way to the longboat. The two men we'd met earlier saw us, but only laughed, and Cheval greeted them like long-lost friends. He was overdoing it.

I glanced to my left at the supply boat getting ready to cast off, and blinked. Those women were aboard. The white one—Gabriella van Ecken—was fumbling with the forward mooring line; she obviously had no idea about knots. I stepped toward her, released the line and threw it to her. I almost winked, but stopped when I saw the terror on her face and raised my hat instead. A crewman pushed off and she was on her way.

"Buena suerte," I muttered under my breath. "Good luck. You're going to need it."

A shout from Cheval brought me back to my own predicament, and I made my way toward him, bumping into him to get him moving again. The longboat was less than half a cable away and we hurried toward it.

"Avast! Stop right there!"

I glanced back to the alleyway at the far end of the wharf. Mierda! Sharpe! I followed Cheval's example and ran. We jumped in and I pushed off with the oars—we did not have time to raise the sail.

"Running again, you lily-livered cove?" Sharpe shouted. "I'll see you again, Cheval, you won't be able to run forever!" He fired his pistols, but the balls hit the water. We were already out of range, even for such a good marksman. He turned back. He didn't have time to come after us; he had other business to take care of today.

I looked at Cheval, who was hauling the mainsail slowly up the mast. I may not have reckoned my debt with Hornigold, but I did know a lot more about my second mate, and I did not want him aboard my ship. He was still loyal to my enemy.

He tied the halyard off and turned to move aft. I took my chance; I freed the leeward oar from its rowlock and swept it across the boat. It hit Cheval in the belly and he tumbled over the side.

I grabbed the tiller and hauled the sail in. I looked back once; he hung onto the oar I had dropped and screamed insults. I had another enemy, but at least he wouldn't get within a blade's-length of my back anytime soon.

Chapter 23

LEO
3rd April 1686
Sayba

Is she lifting? I held my breath and tried to translate what the wood beneath my feet was telling me. *Freedom* rolled slightly in the surf, righting herself, but was she lifting off the sand?

It had been a nervous wait for the flooding tide. Almost two weeks after the equinox, the high tide mark on the beach had retreated every day. Would we be able to get *Freedom* off this beach? My men had dug out her stern, and warps were paid out to anchors and boats standing by to pull her off the sand; but two boats and a couple of kedges would not be able to drag my 245 tun ship out to sea if the tide did not lift her first. I could not use the sails to help—the proximity of the cliff meant the wind swirled around us and was more hindrance than aid.

There! Her stern definitely lifted! We *had* to put off on this tide. We'd spent the night on high alert, watching out for *Freyja* and preparing *Sound of Freedom* for sea.

I'd realized on my solo sail back to the beach from Eckerstad that sending Cheval over the side had been a mistake. If Sharpe found him first all would be well, but what if Cheval found Hornigold before Sharpe had a chance to kill him? Cheval wouldn't hesitate to bargain his knowledge of the whereabouts of Tarr's killers for his life. How soon would they give up the search for those women and come for us? I was surprised they hadn't attacked overnight—maybe Cheval was still hiding, but he couldn't hide forever, and I couldn't wager on having any more time than this morning to get clear.

There! Lifting again! I reckoned we were free to the mainmast now, but when would the tide turn? Would we have enough brine to free our bows?

One more wave, then time to haul.

"*Stand by,*" I shouted to the men at the capstan.

"Take up the slack.

"Haul away."

I waved to Davys standing on the poopdeck, and he signaled to the boats. My men put their backs to their oars, and the capstan on the foredeck turned and wound in the anchor warps.

Nothing.

Another wave.

Nothing.

Then a larger wave lifted us further than before.

"Haul," I shouted, and we moved. Just a few inches, but we moved.

Next wave. More inches.

And again.

And again.

We crept backwards down the beach.

Now we moved feet rather than inches, and more and more of the hull was lifted with each wave.

A little more.

A little more.

Picking up speed now—almost clear. Then, with a sucking, scraping noise, the bow freed itself from its tomb of sand, and we rushed seaward, the next large wave stopping us dead when it smashed against the stern and showered us with salted rain.

I looked forward and laughed—the men at the capstan were too exhausted even to cheer their efforts and were slumped over their bars.

"Cut free the anchors!" I shouted and Gaunt took an axe to the warps stretched between anchors and capstan. We had no time to recover them; we'd replace them from our next prize. The men at the capstan stood at my shout—all except one dozy swab who collapsed to the deck as the tension on the capstan was released with Gaunt's axe.

* * *

"*Set the jib.*

"Let fall the main-topsail."

Setting those two sails should give us enough way to steer in the gentle land breeze blowing off the shore with the maximum amount of maneuverability, but I still needed the pinnace and longboat ahead on warps. Ideally I'd rely on the boats alone and not set any sail until we were through, but we'd needed the highest point of the tide to get us off the beach, and it was already falling. We had to do this quickly; we could ill afford to be stranded here, forced to wait for the next flood tide. We had to get away from Sayba. Now. Between sail and oar, we should be able to ease *Freedom* through the reef.

I took the helm myself and wished I had Frazer's company at the tiller. Gaunt and Blackman were below with a working party ready with lead sheets if we hit, and I had half a dozen pairs of the sharpest eyes at the forerails standing by with boathooks ready to fend off. They kept a close eye out for the swirling eddies of water that gave away the positions of submerged rocks, as did Juaquim from the maintop platform. A dozen of my strongest hands were in the boats, with Thomas and Phillippe as coxuns, and the rest were split between the sheets and braces for the sails and manning the pumps. I did not have a hand spare.

I looked ahead at the rock that Cheval had called Lookout's Rock, then aft at the cliff, trying to line up the two transit points. I could see the clump of trees that I had to keep dead astern above the cabins, but would need the advice of my forward lookouts to keep the rock just off the larboard bow. I did not have water to make mistakes.

I shouted forward to Alonso, one of the lookouts, who was tasked with relaying my orders to the boat crews. He signaled the boats to pull *Freedom's* bows to starboard, and I pushed the tiller over. There. We were lined up.

I shouted forward again, but Thomas and Phillippe had already straightened us up.

We sailed into the reef—Juaquim shouting out the position of the channel ahead, which only he could see. The day was bright and clear, and from forty feet up the mainmast, he could see clearly into the azure water. But I also knew the sun sparkling off that water could easily blind him, maybe only for a moment, but that could be enough for him to miss a blade of rock. If that happened, *Freedom* could be lost with all hands. I really should have been more circumspect about how I'd dealt with Cheval. He'd been here before; done this before. As it was, I was the only man aboard who had passed back out through the reef—but that had been in the small longboat.

"Larboard, Captain," Alonso shouted from the bow, and I pushed the tiller to starboard to swing the bows round—but not too much. The men forward strained over the starboard rail to fend us off from a threatening rock.

"Starboard, Captain!" Juaquim shouted from above and I reversed the tiller. There was no going back now, we had nowhere to go and the passage was tight. The tide had definitely turned and was falling quickly. I remembered scraping over the reef on the passage in and felt dread in my belly—we weren't going to make it. We'd wreck on the rocks and be an easy target for Hornigold and *Freyja's* guns.

We picked up speed with the tide, sailing faster into the gauntlet.

"How's it looking, Juaquim?" I called.

"Clear ahead, then larboard by my mark," he shouted.

I nodded and took a deep breath.

"Warps slacking, Captain!"

Mierda! We're faster than the boats!

"Tell them to put their backs into it!" I yelled, knowing that Thomas and Phillippe would have recognized the danger and would already be working the boat crews hard.

"Larboard!" Juaquim shouted, and I put the helm over.

Nothing. We didn't have enough way onto counteract the pull of the tide.

"No steerage!" I shouted. "Fend off at the starboard bow!

"Loose the topsail!"

The big sail above and forward of me cracked as it was set free and flogged loudly in the sudden silence on deck.

"Brace yourselves!" Juaquim shouted down. "Rock to starboard!"

Freedom shuddered as she hit, and I heard the nightmare sound of splintering, snapping wood; and imagined water gushing into my newly repaired ship. I could only hope the hole was small enough that Gaunt and Blackman could get a lead patch on it, and quickly.

"Stop gawping and get those pumps working!" I shouted at the men staring over the side. "And push us off that rock, we're not out of this yet!"

I stumbled as *Freedom* jerked to larboard. The boat warps had tautened and the oarsmen were dragging us off.

"Set the topsail!"

The flogging sail was hauled back into submission and sheeted home.

We were through. Holed, making water and exhausted, but away from the shore.

I turned at a thumping noise behind me and a Scottish voice. "What the bloody hell's going on?"

Frazer, on crutches, fever gone. I moved to greet him, but stopped at Juaquim's shout: 'Sail oh!"

"Where away?" I called.

"South." He pointed. "A twinmaster, by the looks."

The elation I'd felt at getting off the island and my quartermaster's recovery was crushed into despair. A twinmaster to the southward? The bearing of Eckerstad? It could only be one vessel. I trained my glass south. Yes. *Freyja*.

Chapter 24

"Get those men aboard! I need them on the guns!"

Freyja would be in range soon, and three of my best gun crews were not even aboard *Freedom*. Jean-Claude was doing his best to get all the guns ready, but the men were exhausted.

"Jimmy, break out the rum," I said to my one-legged ship's cook. "A beaker for every man, they look like they need it."

"Aye, Cap'n." He stamped off to get it, his pegleg loud on the wood of the deck.

"Alonso, go below and find out how Gaunt and Blackman are faring with that damage."

He ran below, and I finally turned to Frazer and held out my hand.

"It's good to see you on your feet, amigo."

He grinned as I cringed, and leaned on his crutch to shake my hand. "I may be short of feet, but it looks like you could use all the hands you can get."

I looked at his crutches and laughed. "Get back in the cabin, Frazer, you'll fall over at the first shot!"

He glared at me and I knew he was on the quarterdeck to stay.

"Very well, but stay out of the way."

He glared at me again, but I had no time for his pride. Alonso was back on deck and *Freyja* was drawing closer.

"Two strakes sprung, nearly patched, won't sink," he said in his broken English—the one language that everyone aboard could speak to some degree.

"Muy bien. Very well." That was something, at least. The rock had stove in the strakes—cracked them and pushed them inwards a little—not splintered them into shards as had the earlier cannonball.

I looked forward; the first boat crew was aboard and knocking back their rum, whilst the pinnace was coming alongside. To the south, *Freyja* pressed on under full canvas. We barely had minutes.

"Larboard guns, stand by."

I had eight nine-pounders to larboard, all bearing toward *Freyja*. She presented a narrow target, but I liked the odds of eight chances to hit her.

"*Fire.*"

Only two guns went off.

"What the bloody hell's going on with you, you dozy buggers!" Frazer shouted from behind me. "Fire those bloody guns!"

Three more fired, then another two. I realized the gun crew for the eighth was still climbing aboard—their task made harder by the hull rolling in response to the cannonade. I looked at *Freyja* through my glass. Her jib was shredded, and her crew busy rigging fresh canvas, but her hull looked undamaged.

"Blackman!" I shouted as my bo'sun climbed up through the mainhatch. "I need more sail—I want the outer jib, spanker and forecourse set. Quick as you can!"

He nodded and moved forward to send topmen up the masts. I watched the normally nimble men drag themselves up the ratlins. They had worked through the night to finish the repairs, reload *Freedom* and put her to rights. Then we had used every ounce of muscle aboard to get her off the beach and through the reef. My entire crew was exhausted.

A boom and splash to my left had me raise my glass again. *Freyja* had started firing on us with her smaller guns, but she wasn't yet in range and her ball had fallen short.

"Fire larboard cannon," I shouted again and waited. And waited. Frazer echoed my order just as the first gun fired, followed by a staccato of seven more. It was taking too long, and I knew my men didn't have many firings left in them. It took brute force to haul two tuns of iron inboard, load it, then haul it back out to fire. If I asked too much of them, I'd lose more men to accidents than I would to Hornigold.

Wait! We'd hit her—she bore off suddenly to westward and would soon be out of my line of fire.

"Get those sails set, Blackman. She's running!"

The forecourse was sheeted home and *Freedom* responded, surging forward as wind filled her lungs.

“Set fore-topsail as well, quick as you can.”

Once the sails were set, we could make chase and give my gunners a rest before they were called back to action.

“Sail oh,” Juaquim called down. “Dead ahead, sailing northeast. *Edelweiss*. And *Freyja’s* coming back round!”

My heart sank. I couldn’t fight both of them with my crew in such a state, I’d kill them all.

“Captain,” Frazer growled.

“I know,” I said, my teeth grinding against the words I had to shout. “Helm-a-lee, round up to starboard.” Blake and Hornigold would have to wait for another day.

“Full press aloft, Bo’sun, let’s leave them behind,” I said, then went up to the poopdeck to watch astern. I now had two buccaneer ships on my wake giving chase, but at least I was heading toward Spanish waters.

As I watched, *Freyja* jibed, Hornigold must be damaged after all if he’d given up on the chase to head back to port. It was just me and Blake now.

“He’s fastest downwind, Leo.” I turned in surprise to Frazer standing next to me. “If we keep to this course or even tighter on the wind once we’ve cleared Sayba, we’ll soon leave her in our wake.”

I nodded. Blake might be able to catch a merchantman from that distance, but not another pirate ship, and certainly not the freshly scraped *Sound of Freedom*.

Chapter 25

LEO
10th April 1686
One League South of Sankt Tomas Island

Freedom was sound again. Blake hadn't caught us, and we'd put in at the small uninhabited Danish island of Sankt Jan, about thirty leagues northwest of Sayba, to carry out new repairs after our fight with the Sayban coast. I wanted Blake and Hornigold even more badly. Van Ecken too. I wanted to destroy the whole nest of vipers—I hated that I'd been forced to run.

For now though, I needed a prize. I needed replacement anchors and lead sheeting. Not to mention gold. The nearby island of Sankt Tomas had the largest slave mart in the Caribbean. Slavers leaving here would be loaded with coin.

I climbed up to the maintop myself. Juaquim had spotted half a dozen sail, and I wanted to get a good look before deciding which one to take.

Three-masters, twinmasters. That one had an enormous copper on deck boiling away—it was still full of people. *No good. What about that one?* Twinmaster heading southeast, but a sizable hull; fire under the copper out so probably empty. *Wait a minute! I recognize that deck layout, that rigging plan—that's one of the slavers from Eckerstad!* One of van Ecken's vessels. *That's* the one I wanted. Taking one of van Ecken's ships would go a little way to make up for the frustration of my visit to Sayba, and my failure to inflict any serious harm on my foes. Losing a ship might just make Blake and Hornigold's life a little harder at the hands of their Dutch master. I caught hold of the backstay and slid down to the deck.

"Bear off a touch, Thomas. Bring that ship up." I pointed. "She should cross our bows in an hour or so—make sure we're close-to when she does.

"Prepare decks and guns for attack!" I ordered as soon as the sails had been trimmed for our new course. I wanted all the preparations made before we were in clear sight of that captain. Men ran to obey, clearing the decks of all unnecessary clutter and fetching casks of powder and buckets of water for the guns. Muskets and pistols were loaded and piled up on the maindeck; more were hauled up to the tops for Juaquim and Newton's sharpshooting. Every man loaded their own pistols and hung them around their necks; and stowed cutlasses, daggers, boarding axes, marlin spikes and various other weapons in their belts. My crew looked murderous and desperate. We were ready.

I raised my glass to my target; she was still coming on and hadn't realized who we were, and why would she? My gun ports were closed, my heavily armed men concealed behind the bulwarks and I flew a Cross of St George at the masthead. The only thing that could give us away at the moment was the rake of my masts—but that only suggested speed, not necessarily pirates—and there were a lot of vessels rigged for speed in the northern Caribbees, flying the flag of St George.

Nearly in range. Just a little more patience.

"Now!"

Jean-Claude fired a warning shot at their bows—clean through their jib—a point of pride for him, and Jimmy struck the English colors and broke out the square of black silk in their place.

The crew popped up from behind the rails as the gun ports opened in one slick move, and the quiet Caribbean afternoon was filled with the sound of blades smashed flat side down on wooden rails, and chants of "Blood!", "Death!", "Kill!". I knew from experience how intimidating the noise and spectacle we created could be, and I kept my glass trained on the other quarterdeck. Would the captain show sense and heave-to? Or run?

His colors of red, blue and white dropped, followed by his mainsail, and he turned his bows into wind to heave-to. She was ours, and we'd only fired one shot.

Thomas brought *Freedom* neatly alongside and my crew made the two ships fast, then jumped down to the prize deck. The surrender was an honorable one—no one was lying in wait with cocked flintlock to pick off my men. The crew had gathered on the maindeck and dropped what weapons they had at the first command. I had lost sight of the captain.

"Take a party below, Blackman, see what we've got," I told my bo'sun.

"Alonso, keep a guard on these men, make sure they can see Jean-Claude at the rail." Jean-Claude had remained aboard *Freedom* and manned one of the rail guns. Aimed into the heart of the group of slavecrew and loaded with small partridge shot, it would kill at least half of the two dozen men with one firing.

I took Phillippe and Rafael and dropped down to the lower deck after Blackman and his men, then quickly moved aft, holding both pistols fully-cocked and ready to fire. It worried me that the captain had not remained with his men.

Terrified faces shrank back from us. Damn it, the vessel wasn't quite empty after all, but Blackman would sort them out. There were no white faces there, so I ignored them and kept going toward the stern, my eyes streaming from the stench of the hold. That wouldn't help my aim, but I planned on getting close enough that it wouldn't matter too much.

We reached the aft bulkhead and I stood in front of the door, Phillippe and Rafael either side, then booted it open. My two crewmen wasted no time, and I followed them in as soon as I regained my balance.

There were three people in the cabin. The captain, as I'd expected, but also two women seated on chairs before him: one white, one black. The bruises had healed, but they were the same two women I'd seen in Eckerstad. The captain stood behind them and held a pistol in each hand—one to each of their heads.

Chapter 26

"Let them go and you won't be harmed," I said. "Your crew is taken, you're on your own. I have forty men, you have nowhere to go."

"*No*. Do you know who this is?" He knocked the barrel of his gun against the white woman's head. "This is Gabriella van Ecken! I couldn't believe it when I spotted her face in the women's hold. I've dined at her table many times and there she was, streaked with filth, huddled amongst the bitch slaves—I couldn't believe my luck. You can have the ship and the gold and the cargo—you'll take it all anyway—and even if you let me live, *he* won't. But he will if I return his wife and his whore to him." He knocked the other gun against the black woman's head and grinned. The women held hands and stared at the floor. They looked resigned and exhausted. I wondered what they'd been through since I'd seen them at Eckerstad.

"You're not taking them anywhere," I said, and they looked at me for the first time. My eyes met those of van Ecken's wife, then I jerked my gaze back to the captain.

"You're not taking these women. I don't care what van Ecken does to you, he's the least of your worries at the moment. If you've hurt them, you'll have to answer to me."

The man threw his head back and laughed, then stumbled backwards. The women, taking advantage of his inattention, had shoved their chairs back, knocking him off balance, before throwing themselves to the deck. His guns fired at the same time as mine and my men's. I was deafened by the noise in that confined space.

I rushed over to the man on the floor, my second pistol ready to fire, but he was dead. One lead ball had hit him in the face, obliterating his features, another had taken off his ear and part of his skull, and the third had hit him square in the throat. Blood covered the stern windows behind him, the deck and the two women. *The women! Is it all the captain's blood? Or did he shoot them when they threw themselves to the deck?*

No, Phillippe and Rafael were helping them to their feet. I looked up at two fresh scars in the deckhead; the captain had fired wildly above his head as he fell.

"Are you hurt?" I asked.

Gabriella van Ecken looked at the other, then answered. "No, we're well." They crossed to the body, and I noticed they were still holding hands. She drew her foot back and kicked his ruined head. Her friend drove her own boot into his groin.

"Ladies." I grabbed their arms, and Mrs. van Ecken screeched at my touch, ripped her arm away, and scratched my face with her nails.

"Gabby, hush," the black woman said calmly, holding onto her upper arms. "It's over, we're safe. We *are* safe, aren't we?" she added, looking at me.

"Yes." I nodded. What else could I say? But how would I keep *that* promise? Nowhere in the Caribbees would be safe for these two.

"I'm Captain Leo Santiago." I held my hand out to van Ecken's wife, and to my relief she took it. I brought her hand to my lips in greeting.

"Gabriella van Ecken," she said. "This is Klara."

I offered my hand to the other woman, who gave me her own in surprise.

"You both look like you could do with some air. Phillippe will take you topside. Wait for me there."

I wanted to ransack the cabin for riches, as well as charts and anything else of use. I could also use the time to think. The last thing I wanted was to take responsibility for those two, but to have van Ecken's wife at my disposal—*that* could be useful.

Chapter 27

Blackman and Gaunt were supervising the lading of anchors, spare rigging and other gear we were running short of by the time Rafael and I arrived on deck lugging a chest full of coin and charts. I was pleased with the haul for a twinmaster—there was definitely enough to cheer the crew after our disastrous and unprofitable stopover at Sayba. Alonso hurried to take my end of the chest, and I turned my attention to the people milling about the maindeck.

Apart from my own crew there were a couple of dozen sailors from this boat and about the same number of slaves. And the two women. I took a deep breath and walked forward. I already knew from the captain's papers that he'd sold the African women and half of the men at Sankt Tomas, and had been heading south with the strongest of the men, hoping for a higher profit.

"Do you speak English?" A couple of dark heads nodded. "I'm looking for volunteers for my decks. I can offer you a life as free men with equal shares of the plunder we take, as much meat and rum as you want—and no irons."

I waved Blackman over and pointed at the fetters binding the men. He called for his tools and started to prize open the manacles.

"And if we say no?" one of the men asked.

"You'll keep this boat and a few of her crew to sail her, and take your chances."

"Where would we go?"

"I'd advise St Vincent. There's a colony of Black Caribs settled there and no white man is welcome. It's a hard life, but you'd be your own masters." I waited whilst my words were translated for the benefit of the others.

"With a vessel you may be tempted to sail east to Africa. I wouldn't advise it. Too much can go wrong on an ocean crossing, even with an experienced crew and master, and that continent put you aboard a slaveship to begin with. Your best bet is with me. I need the hands. You'd be well treated."

I waited whilst Blackman finished releasing everyone and handed his tools to Smith, who took them back to *Freedom* for him.

"Well?"

The man who had translated my words looked at the man next to him and they both looked at Blackman, then stepped forward. Another half dozen followed their example. I looked them over and nodded. They would do. They'd soon learn to fire a gun and set a sail.

"Anyone else?" I asked. Nothing. Then a couple of the crew stepped forward. I nodded and jerked my head. They joined the others, looking nervous. The Africans glared and stepped away from them.

"Who are the ship's officers?" I asked the two ex-slavecrew, and one of them—Cartwright—pointed them out. Davys motioned with his flintlock toward the boats. I'd set them adrift and let them take their chances. Blackman led my new crew across to *Freedom* and started to get them organized. They'd need to make their mark on the ship's articles to sign onto our account.

"The rest of you are now under the command of these men. Get them to St Vincent in safety and, if you're lucky, you can go on your way. I hope you haven't mistreated them on the passage so far." I grinned.

I gave the remaining Africans the weapons the slavecrew had dropped to the deck earlier.

"There's a body in the cabin you may want to deal with fairly soon—they start to smell quickly in this heat. Good luck."

They had a lot of challenges ahead, but it would be up to them to meet them. I turned to the women. They were *my* problem.

Chapter 28

"What about us? Are we free too?" Gabriella asked. I noticed she was looking at the marks her nails had left on my jaw. I resisted the urge to put my hand to my face. I sighed. *What about them?* If I controlled her, I controlled van Ecken, and he controlled Blake and Hornigold. But the ship's articles were clear: no women aboard the *Sound of Freedom*. She'd be useful, but she'd also be trouble. I grew aware of my crew staring at the three of us.

"Please help us. If my husband finds us, he will kill us slowly and painfully."

The words were stated calmly and I had no doubt as to the truth of them, but she wasn't begging. I looked at her with more interest. She reminded me a little of Magdalena with her wild curls, and she seemed to have an inner strength to match my former sweetheart. She still stood tall, after whatever she'd endured on Sayba, her escape, and time in the hold of a blackbirder. I made my decision.

"You'll be safe enough aboard my ship," I said. "But you'll have to earn your keep."

She stiffened and scowled.

"Not like that! The only fare due aboard *Freedom* is a sailor's, and I want to know everything you can tell me about your husband—and Captains Blake and Hornigold."

"You're that Spanish pirate," she said. "The one that killed Tarr! The one that's angered Erik so much. He wants to kill you, you know, and he won't rest until he does. Neither will Blake or Hornigold."

"We'll see about that. I plan for them to feel the blade of *my* sword and the lead of *my* guns, not the other way round."

She hooked her arm through her companion's. "We'll do everything we can to help."

We? I looked at them both for a moment, then nodded. Two

couldn't be any more trouble than one.

"Very well, but time now to get aboard."

I didn't have time to prepare a cabin for them until the two ships were separated and we were underway, so they stayed close by me on the quarterdeck, watching everything with interest. They seemed particularly interested in Blackman and Jean-Claude.

I shouted at Blackman to set sail as soon as we had water between the two vessels, and he marched down the deck shouting orders, whilst Jean-Claude organized the cleaning and stowing of the guns and their dunnage. Gabriella and Klara looked at each other and I had to laugh at the expressions on their faces.

"Ashore, and in that ship, black men and women weren't even treated as human, yet here those men look to have authority over white," Gabriella said in amazement.

"Aboard pirate ships, everyone is equal. Black stands shoulder-to-shoulder with white. The color of a man's skin does not dictate his position on these decks," I said.

Gabriella looked at her friend and smiled. "So if everyone is equal, does that mean women stand shoulder-to-shoulder with men on your decks?"

I looked at her in surprise and laughed.

"I hope you know what you're doing, Leo," Frazer muttered, loud enough for the women to hear, and saving me from having to reply. "The only woman aboard ship should be half-naked, made of wood and nailed to the bow. It's bad luck to have those two aboard."

"Oh, I don't know, Frazer, our luck may have changed." I smiled.

PART TWO

Chapter 29

GABRIELLA
10th April 1686

I'd always loved the water. Virtually a prisoner on my husband's estate, I'd stare out to the horizon from the cliff tops or my secret beach, thinking of all the possibilities the sea promised; daydreaming of just sailing away, catching the wind and riding it to the ends of the earth. I imagined the distance between me and my ship and the next living person could be so vast, and so unexpected. But I'd seen enough storms to know the sea could turn in an instant. You couldn't forget her power nor her viciousness. The difference was that her brutality was avoidable; it could be harnessed and managed in a way my husband's could not. If she did hurt me, at least it wouldn't be personal, nor out of hate. A sailor's life was to live on the edge and never be fully in control, never knowing what would come next. Living at sea, I'd be living in the midst of a squall, yet free from the torturous chains of my marriage. I'd be free; both of us would. I looked at Klara and smiled. She didn't look quite so pleased at our situation.

"You have the quarterdeck, Frazer, it's time for me to show these ladies to a cabin," the Spanish pirate said.

I recoiled from the Scot's glare as we walked past him and up the steps to the structure built at the back of the boat and raised above the tiller. I passed through the door the captain held open and held my breath as I brushed past him. My heart jumped as my arm touched his, but I didn't think he noticed. Once in the cabin, I turned to look at him, but couldn't think of anything to say. My thoughts had shriveled and hidden with that touch, and I looked at him, sure that he at least would know what to do or say next.

"If you'll excuse me, my ship needs my attention. Please, make yourselves comfortable."

He was gone. I stared at the closed door then looked at Klara, and the ship picked up speed. We'd done it, we'd escaped Sayba. At last we were safe from Erik and we smiled at each other. Then I felt the knot of terror in my stomach twist tighter. What had we done? We were two women alone on a ship of pirates.

I sat on the cot heavily as the reality of our situation sank in. I'd thought that last night with Erik was the lowest point of my life; now I wasn't so sure. Was this vessel an escape or another prison? Had we swapped a life of constant fear at the hands of one man for a life of constant fear at the hands of a shipful? The captain was a pirate; a violent and brutal man who spread fear wherever he and his crew of cut-throats sailed. What did he plan to do with us? Had he rescued us from that slaveship, or taken us hostage himself? We were sailing away from Erik, true, but toward what? What did Captain Santiago want from us?

My heart had missed a beat when I'd looked into his eyes in that slaver's cabin, and I'd thought he had the same reaction to me. What if I'd been mistaken, desperate for a way out? If he'd truly taken us with him out of some deep, if brief, connection, we'd probably be safe, but what if he hadn't? What if it had just been the imaginings of a lonely, trapped woman? What if he'd taken us to use as pawns against Erik? To amuse himself, or worse, his crew? What did he expect from us?

I looked around me; at least the cabin was nice enough for a pirate's cabin, not that we had much to compare it to. It had its drawbacks, the most apparent being the very low ceiling—the deckhead—which forced us to stoop. We had to brace ourselves against it and the floor, which moved so much beneath our feet we struggled to stay upright, and were forever grabbing hold of each other to keep our balance. It had all the essentials crammed into it, though: a cot suspended from the deckhead on chains; a small chair; table; even a forbidding black iron cannon, which I viewed with mixed feelings—*is this the symbol of our new life?*

Once I could look past the great gun and its rack of iron balls, I saw a number of interesting ornaments: jewelry; a rich chalice; a carved orb of gold; a wonderful gold facemask with emeralds for eyes—stolen over the years I presumed. Klara and I amused ourselves over the coming nights by making up stories of their origin and how they came to be here, with us. I wondered if we were the same—more ornaments for his collection.

Eventually, there was a knock at the door. I jumped and looked at Klara, who came and sat next to me on the cot, but I said nothing—suddenly I wasn't so eager to know the answers to my questions. He knocked again and opened the door. He was a powerful man, and seemed taller in the small space than he had outside, but it was obvious that his bulk was muscle. He moved like a man completely at home in his own skin, with an easy yet undoubtable self-confidence.

He held up a hand, recognizing our fear, and sat on the chair opposite. "You're in no danger from me. No one will hurt you—you're guests here, not prisoners. I spoke true when I said the only fare due aboard this ship is a sailor's, and you're both free to come and go as you wish; my crew have been instructed not to harm you. That said, I advise you to be careful all the same. Don't put yourselves in a situation where you're alone with someone, other than me of course." He smiled.

"Most are good men at heart, but are inclined to be somewhat impulsive, and they haven't been this close to women for some time. Here, take these keys for the door and keep it locked.

"Now sleep, it's been a long day. Come up on deck in the morning, and I'll show you around the ship."

"What's she called?" I asked.

"Qué?"

"What's she called? The boat."

"Ship," he corrected with a smile. "*Sound of Freedom.*"

"*Sound of Freedom*?"

"Yes. Listen."

I did and could hear a gurgling swish of water somewhere

below marking our passage through the seas, and understood what he meant. The sound of freedom. My smile mirrored his.

"I need to collect some belongings," he added. "Then I'll leave you in peace. If you need me, I'll be on deck or in the chartroom." He pointed to the bulkhead and the cabin on the other side of it. "Now get some sleep, it's been a long day," he repeated.

I nodded, he was right, we were exhausted. "Some belongings, you said, is this your cabin?"

"Not anymore," he answered. "Goodnight, Gabriella van Ecken, Klara." He smiled again and left. I walked to the door and locked it, then shoved the back of the chair under the handle just to make sure. After all, I didn't know how many keys there were.

"So what now?" Klara asked.

I could see how scared she was and sat back down on the cot. I put my arm around her shoulders and hugged her.

"Now we learn to sail, and make ourselves a part of this crew. Erik will never stop looking for us—his pride won't let him—and that man hates Erik and the rest of them as much as we do. Staying aboard this ship is our best chance of freeing ourselves from my husband and his pirates. You heard the captain; he wants them to feel the blade of his sword and the lead of his guns. If we help him do that, then we can find somewhere to build a new life."

Klara smiled. "I saw the way you looked at that Spaniard, Gabby, you want *this* life!"

"I just want to be free of Erik, Klara, forever. That's all I'm thinking about at the moment."

Sleep wouldn't come thanks to the swinging of the bed on its creaking chains and the sounds of the ship. I lay for what seemed hours, envying Klara her slumber and jumping at every new noise: the wind howling through the rigging above; the water smashing against the thin wooden hull. It didn't sound like freedom now, more like threat.

If that wasn't bad enough, a bell rang out regularly, sometimes once, usually more. I counted up to eight just as I was finally dropping off.

I must have fallen asleep because I woke to the same bell being rung madly, accompanied by shouting and stamping. Even the ship's movement had become violent—doing its damnedest to throw me off the cot—although Klara still slept.

Suddenly I realized what all the fuss and noise was about, we must be sinking! I woke Klara, struggled back to my feet and immediately fell. I tried again, this time with more care. The deck beneath my feet was bucking and lurching from side to side, and I could only keep my feet by bracing my hands against the low deckhead. At this rate the ship would be on the bottom before we even got out of the cabin.

Chapter 30

A huge crash startled me, and the deck jolted under my feet as water crashed against the stern windows. We had to get out. Panicking, I knocked the chair away, wrenched the door open and staggered outside onto deck, then immediately fell. Klara crouched down beside me, still in the cabin doorway, and refused to move. All we could see was chaos. We were sailing through a tremendous storm, and I could hardly make sense of where I was. The wind, loud enough in the cabin, screamed like a banshee just over my head—its shrieks pierced my skull until I thought I must go deaf. I could see very little: a few lighter smudges in the thick black above; some white streaks in the sea; the dirty white shirts of men somehow running on that heaving, swirling deck. Another crash shuddered through the ship, and a wall of water cascaded over the rail. Thank goodness I was already sitting down; that would have taken me overboard for sure had I still been on my feet.

Soaking wet, I blinked the salt out of my stinging eyes and tried to work out what I should do. *Are we sinking? Why has nobody come to get us? Where are the boats? Are they still being towed? How will we get into one? And how will they stay afloat in the same storm that's sinking their mothership? Although, as I can't even stand up, it makes no difference, does it?*

I could see a patch of white coming toward us, which became a shirt and then the captain. He was coming to help us. I could see him talking to me, but didn't hear a word of it; the wind making him mute. But I knew we'd be safe now, he'd make sure we got to a boat. He bent and shouted directly in my ear.

"What the hell are you doing on deck? Get back to the cabin! This is no place for landswomen!"

I looked past him and pointed at the man struggling with the tiller. He turned and ran to help, caught the wooden steering bar, then put his whole weight onto it just as the helmsman was thrown to the deck. Klara and I stayed where we were. I couldn't see any way of successfully regaining my feet, and I'd rather die before I crawled across a pirate's deck—even this pirate's deck. One thing was for sure—we didn't belong here. What was also certain was that we had nowhere else to go.

I don't know how long we sat there, but it was long enough for my fear to turn to amazement. From the quarterdeck in front of the cabin I watched those men hauling on ropes, drenched by waves crashing over the bulwarks and onto the deck. How on earth did they know which rope to pull in the dark? How did they manage to stand upright? Even the man with the pegleg moved easily, and I realized this was normal. We weren't sinking; we were sailing.

I thought I was seeing things when Klara pointed upwards. My eyes had got used to the darkness, and I saw men climbing. I was grateful for my position on the deck; I could watch them, just, outlined against the sails and balanced precariously on the yards swinging wildly with the motion of the ship.

The whole ship shuddered when an enormous wave broke over her side, and I caught a glimpse of a white shirt as its wearer was swept across the deck. I was sure he must have gone over. But as soon as the force of the water eased, he picked himself up and went back to the rope he'd been heaving on as if nothing had happened. Madness.

I only looked away when I heard laughter. The captain was watching our open-mouthed amazement with great hilarity. His earlier anger appeared to be forgotten.

"This is nothing, querida, just a fresh gale—a stiff topsail breeze! He held a hand to me. "Up you get. I'm serious, you need to go back to your cabin. I haven't got eyes enough to keep you both safe out here while you find your sea legs."

I thought about refusing. I was enjoying watching these men sail the ship and, now that I knew we were safe, didn't mind the force of the wind any more—although I did have a little shelter here in front of the cabins. Now that I'd got used to it, I found its strength exhilarating, but the look in Captain Santiago's eyes told me he hadn't made a request. I took his hand and got to my wobbly feet, earning more laughter from the captain.

"Your feet are too close together, querida. If you want to walk my decks, you'll have to walk like a sailor—feet wide apart and shift your balance with the deck—use your toes. Yes, that's better."

I stumbled into him on his praise and laughed myself. "I think I'm going to need some practice!"

"Yes," he agreed. "But not now." He helped me back into the cabin, where Klara had already crawled to the cot, feeling sick with the motion of the ship.

He looked at me, and I realized my shirt was saturated and stuck to my body. I crossed my arms over my chest and glared at him. He left the cabin and returned a moment later with an armful of linen.

"Here, you both need dry clothing."

He also gave me a purple sash and a frockcoat. "I know it's not of the quality you're used to, but we don't keep any ladies' clothing in the slopchest."

I took the clothes from him, grateful that they were at least clean, if no longer quite dry, and held up the coat. "But this is yours, isn't it? I've seen you wearing it."

"It was, briefly, but it'll look better on you, you're welcome to it."

"Thank you." I was touched by his generosity, until I realized that both coat and silk sash had almost certainly been stolen. Still, he could have kept them for himself.

"Captain Santiago," I called after him.

He turned back to me. "Leo," he corrected.

"Are you Spanish or English?" I flushed and remembered my manners. "Forgive my rudeness, but I'm confused, your name sounds Spanish, but your speech is English in the main."

He smiled. "My father was Spanish and my mother English. She taught me her language as a child before she died. These days, English is the safest language on the water in a Carib Sea overrun with Jamaican privateers on the hunt for anything Spanish, even if we're not at war at present. I've spent my sailing life with Englanders, many of the crew are English or a close relation. Besides, it's the one language everyone aboard can speak to some extent."

I nodded, trying to understand, but he hadn't finished. "And you? You sound English, but the town was Dutch."

"Yes, it is. I was born in the Massachusetts Bay Colony and was married to a Dutchman." He waited for me to carry on, but I wasn't ready to discuss my life with this man, not until I'd decided whether he really was a friend. He nodded at my silence and went back to his ship. I gave one of the shirts to Klara and we both changed.

It was wonderful to be dry(ish) and warm again. I massaged my ribs, still bruised, though at least no longer bloody from the wooden stays that Erik had insisted be drawn as tight as possible under my gowns, and which I had discarded just over a week ago. I reveled in the freedom of the rough linen shirt.

I sat on the cot and wondered what to do now. Sleep was out of the question; not only did I have to hold onto the cot just to sit, I felt exhilarated and excited after experiencing the wild weather on the other side of the door and, I realized, hungry—I hadn't eaten for more than a day. We hadn't been offered anything since we came aboard. My thoughts returned to the scene outside and I couldn't stop thinking about the men up the masts. I looked around the cabin again. I'd had enough of being kept prisoner and doing what I was told. I didn't want to start a new life in the same vein. I was trapped aboard this ship, but that didn't mean I had to be trapped in this cabin; I wanted to find a place in this strange new world, somewhere I could fit in, and that meant sailing.

I put on my new coat and slipped out to Klara's admonishments, feeling very strange as I waddled along, trying to mimic Leo's walk. The result was not very ladylike, and was no doubt humorous to watch, but at least I kept my feet. More or less.

I found my way below and realized I'd picked a good time to go exploring. Everyone was above me doing things to the sails, and I followed the smell of wood smoke forward until I found a massive brick hearth, recently doused but still smoking and dimly lit by swinging lamps, right in the middle of the huge gundeck. A great copper pot of steaming water sat above the heat. I had a look around and found beakers and kye. I remembered Belinda making hot chocolate from the solid block of cocoa, and, guilty, I wondered what had become of her after our escape. I forced myself to stop worrying—there was nothing I could do for her—and I thought instead about my own situation. I was sure a hot drink would be appreciated by the men above, and I busied myself making a great pail of it, guessing at how much kye to use, and then threw some honey and peppers in for good measure. I also took some cold pork. It looked horrible and greasy, but I didn't care; I needed food. I helped myself to some fruit too—enough for both myself and Klara, then used a length of rope to tie the handles of a dozen beakers together—not enough, but all I could carry—and struggled back up to the deck. I sat down in front of the cabins where there was a little shelter from the worst of the weather, and wondered what to do next.

"Now what are you doing? I thought I told you to stay out of the way in your cabin."

"I thought you and your men would appreciate a hot drink. I'd rather be of use than hide away."

"Even in this weather?"

"Even in this weather. Besides, I owe each of them my gratitude, I thought a hot drink would be welcome."

He looked at me a moment. "It seems as if you've discarded more than just your gowns."

I grew uncomfortable under his gaze. He seemed to make his mind up and continued, pointing at the other cabin, "You stay in there, the chartroom, and let the men come to you. I don't want you stumbling about the decks, if you go overboard we'll never find you again."

"Yes."

He looked doubtful.

"I promise I'll stay put."

I wasn't sure he believed me, but he needn't have worried, wild horses wouldn't have been able to drag me along that maelstrom of wood and water again tonight.

Chapter 31

GABRIELLA
11th April 1686

I lay on the cot and listened, aware Leo slept just the other side of the thin wooden bulkhead. The shrieks, howls and crashes of last night's storm had been replaced by the relatively gentle creaking of wood along with the constant clanging of the bell, which I realized marked the half-hours in batches of eight. Sunlight streamed through the stern windows and the odd gap in the planking between me and the outside world. Everything was different; last night seemed a dream. My new clothing and the burning of the skin on my face and hands disagreed. I licked my lips and found them cracked and sore. I touched my cheeks carefully, then snatched my hand away. Salt and wind had ruined my complexion in one night—and I could not decide whether or not I minded.

Groaning at yet another ringing of the bell, each time with an added peal, I swung my feet over the edge of the cot and sat up. My whole body hurt—*and all I'd done was prepare some hot chocolate*! My legs were the worst: walking on deck had its price, and the insides of my thighs felt as though they were made of iron as heavy as the cannon invading my sleeping space. I had no idea how I was going to stand and walk, and would have preferred not to, but some things just had to be done.

There was no chamber pot in the room—I supposed they were an unfortunate and avoidable hazard on a ship in heavy weather and not to be recommended. I shuddered, remembering the state of the shittenpot aboard that slaver, then shuffled painfully to the stern windows, opened the end one and eased myself carefully onto the swaying ledge on the other side. I stopped in delight at the view and felt a big smile stretch my face. The first time I could remember smiling for a very long time.

The sea had lost all its violence of the previous night. The bright sun sparkled on the water and, as I watched, I saw a dark shadow race over the surface. The ship picked up a little more speed in the gust. We were completely alone; there wasn't another ship, and hardly even a cloud to be seen. I really had left my life behind, along with our wake, but I had to leave something else behind now. I hadn't been brave enough to do this in the dark, and was desperate. Desperate enough to squat on a few inches of wet wood and hang onto a decorative railing, all of which was moving in various directions at once. Thank goodness I wasn't still wearing a gown! It took some getting used to, but at least I had some privacy and didn't have to share the seat of easement with the men, which was hung over the bows.

I looked at Klara, still asleep, the food I'd brought for her untouched, and decided not to wake her. She was exhausted after being sick all night, and I couldn't forget that she'd lost her lover and her son through our escape. I'd leave her to her dreams for now, but for me it was time to go out on deck and face the pirates. Moving a little bit easier now that I had been up and about a while, I took a deep breath and walked out of the door onto the quarterdeck, using my new stride in spite of the pain. Erik had taught me well that it would take a lot more than that to stop me.

Leo stood right in front of me, directing the man on the tiller as to the course he should be steering. I caught my breath and paused for a moment to look at him. He'd shaved and washed, and was dressed in a clean, though damp, linen shirt and breeches to match my own. He had an indigo sash wrapped around him today, and a cutlass hung at his waist, although somehow he didn't project as much menace as Erik had with his frockcoat and cane. I caught a faint "about bloody time" telling me that Leo had been waiting for me, and I glared at the helmsman in response to his comment. I smiled and offered a "Good morning, Captain" to Leo, through a surprisingly dry mouth.

"Buenos días, Gabriella. Good morning. I trust you slept well?"

I hadn't been expecting manners, and wasn't really surprised when he carried on, laughing.

"How are your legs? Ready to try climbing up there?" He nodded up to the highest sails glistening in the sunlight at an impossible height.

"Let me find and keep my feet on deck first, then I'll tackle the masts," I said with a grin.

"You know, that wouldn't surprise me at all—the men are already laying bets on how long it'll take you, rosada. Just remember to climb up the windward side, the wind'll hold you in place, not blow you off."

"Rosada?"

"Your rosy cheeks. Don't worry, it's just a bit of windburn, once you spend a few hours in the sun, on top of the salt, you won't recognize yourself!"

"That may not be a bad thing," I muttered, thinking of my husband and not joining in with Leo's laughter. Anything that would make it harder for Erik to find me suited me well, no matter what it meant for my skin—even if that was more freckles.

He offered me his arm, and I jumped at his gesture then took it. "Would you like to meet the *Sound of Freedom*? I don't think you've been formally introduced."

"You want to introduce me to your ship?" I asked, thinking I must have misunderstood.

"She's the most important of all. If the ship doesn't take a liking to you, you're best off swimming ashore—sharks, sea serpents and all. But don't worry, I have a feeling she'll love you."

I wasn't sure whether to laugh or nod seriously. "Lead on," I instructed, and we walked the length of her decks to her bows. I was uncomfortably aware of every man stopping what he was doing to stare, but nobody said anything and Leo didn't seem to notice.

"We've been together just over a year," he said. "She was a merchant vessel when I found her, but she's taken to the piratical life as if she were born to it."

"As if she were born to it? You talk as if the ship is alive."

"She is, in her own way. She's a living being who needs constant attention. She breathes the wind in her sails and drinks the water at her bows. She can be temperamental, mixes good behavior with bad just as thoroughly as any other sailor, and makes it very clear if she's not happy. Once you know how to listen, you'll hear she talks constantly. She tells me when she needs more sail or less, whether our course suits her and when she needs some loving care. Her punishment is swift and brutal if she's mistreated. Make no mistake, Gabriella, if you want to stay at sea, you have to make her acquaintance, earn her trust and learn how to live with her as your mistress."

"If I want to stay at sea?" I asked, not sure if I was pleased or insulted at his assumption, yet excited by the invitation.

"Yes." He looked at me in surprise. "Isn't that what last night was about? In my experience, passengers don't tend to leave their warm, dry and safe cabin on their first night at sea, especially to make hot chocolate for a pirate crew they don't know and have good reason to fear—in a blow."

"Do I have good reason to fear?"

"Of course you do. Look around you."

We were on the foredeck now, the sea giving way before us with only a fine mist of spray in retaliation, and I turned to look at the ship behind me. Her well-scrubbed wooden decks were almost white in the bright sun and the men on them went about their work much more sedately than they had last night. Not such a good thing; they had plenty of time to leer, and whilst there were some smiles, there was not one I enjoyed receiving. I hung onto Leo's arm a little tighter and understood the only thing keeping me safe from these men was his word. I took a deep breath, and noticed they all turned back to their work when they realized Leo's eyes were on them.

A line of three or four men hauled together on the same rope, and I looked up to see where it led. There were more men on the highest horizontal wooden branch—yard—on the mainmast and, as I watched, the sail rolled down and reflected the sun into my eyes. I realized the rope was attached to one of the bottom corners and I watched the flogging sail come under control, making a perfect bellied square. I felt the ship beneath my feet surge forward. "She's telling you she's pleased with more sail isn't she?"

Leo nodded in approval. "You're learning her language already. That will help you with the men."

I looked at him again, remembering his warning over my safety.

"Just be careful and stay close to me. As I said when you came aboard, you are women aboard a ship of free men. Whilst I have made it clear you are not to be harmed, that you are my woman, they are still—"

"That I'm *your woman*?" I interrupted, full of outrage and, if I was honest, a small fluttering in my stomach. There was no doubt I was intrigued and yes, even fascinated by this man who'd come into my life in such dramatic fashion. But I was a married woman, however reluctantly. All I knew of being a man's woman was pain, fragility and fear. I wasn't sure I wanted to risk that again, despite the way my body betrayed me in his presence.

"Calm down." He laughed at the heat in my cheeks. "I told you before, the only fare to pay aboard this ship is a sailor's: to hand, reef and steer. Nothing else will be asked or expected of you." He laughed again at my confusion. "Don't look so worried, querida. The only way I can ensure your safety is if the men believe you're mine. If they harm you, they'd be challenging me in mutiny, which I can punish by marooning or death. Stay close to me, heed my words and you'll be fine. I won't ask anything of you that you don't want to give. Are my terms acceptable?"

"And what about Klara?"

"She's also under my protection."

I nodded. *Who knew a pirate would be honorable?* I relaxed a little, wondering what the social etiquette was for this situation. He'd been a perfect gentleman so far and had treated both myself and Klara with courtesy and respect—except for shouting at me in the storm last night. *What manner of man is he?* I watched the men set another sail and remembered what I'd seen the night before.

"How do they know which rope to pull in the dark?" I wanted to change the subject whilst I took in everything that had happened in the last couple of days.

"A lifetime of long practice and close attention. Every line has a purpose, and every man knows this ship inside and out, day and night. Any of us could board any ship and know exactly how to sail her. This is what we do. This is the world we are masters of."

I relaxed further, my attention fixed on his voice with the slight Spanish accent. He talked of his ship and men with pride, almost like a father talking about his children, and I was beginning to understand that life at sea was as much about living by your heart as it was about the skills and risks involved. I looked around me at the faces of men who had chosen this life with new insight, and realized I had a chance to be part of a family. I was seventeen years old and didn't know what that was like. I had a real chance at a real life here. It might be a short one, and it might be strange one, but that may just be outweighed by the way it was lived. I looked at my new home with hope and possibility, then grinned up at Leo.

"Hand, reef and steer, I think you said, what's first?"

Chapter 32

"First" turned out to be Jimmy, the one-legged cook. I'd spotted him on my first night aboard, somehow managing to stay upright on that heaving deck with a pegleg. He was not friendly.

"So, you're after my place are you, lovey?" he snarled after Leo had made the introductions and left us to it. "Don't think I don't know what you were trying to do the other night. Making everyone hot chocolate." He spat on the deck. "Are you trying to get me marooned or just thrown overboard? Set your sights on this ship, haven't you lovey? Aye, and the captain, I bet. Well, I ain't shifting for no one, especially not a slip of a lass like you."

"I'm not trying to steal your position," I gabbled, staring after Leo. *How can he leave me with this man?* "Only help where I can."

"Aye, well. You haven't the strength to do my job, lovey, I can tell you that right enough, but I reckon I can find some use for you." He laughed and my heart sank further as he directed me along deck.

I was glad to leave the scorching galley, although concerned about where we were going. Above decks, it was hot, below was hotter, but Jimmy's domain by the galley fire was hell. Or so I thought until we clambered down the ladder to the orlop deck, down in the bowels of the ship, and I found out where our meat lived.

There was no light down here bar the lantern that Jimmy carried with us, and as soon as we walked into the animal hold, the flame dimmed and burned blue. *Now* I understood hell. I had thought the galley scorching, but this rivaled it and the stench was unbelievable. My nose and eyes ran with the stink of excrement and brimstone, and my stomach soon followed. I ran out of there gasping for air, and clawed my way up the ladders and on up to the open deck. Jimmy's laughter followed me all the way.

"Gabriella!" Leo ran over to where I hung over the rail, still retching, although my stomach was empty. "What's wrong? What happened? Jimmy!"

I winced at his roar, but held my hand up to stay him. "Nothing, he didn't do anything, just took me to help him with the animals."

"That wasn't the idea. Jimmy, what were you thinking? She was supposed to help you with the cooking—and hopefully improve it! What did you take her down there for?"

"Well Cap'n, I've got a bit behind on clearing them out. When you said she was to help . . ."

"It's fine, Leo, if he needs help with the animals, I'll help." Now that I'd got over the initial shock of their living conditions, I couldn't stand to think of those beasts spending all their time like that, at the mercy of Jimmy's inattention. It was a wonder they lived long enough to be butchered.

"No, Gabriella, I'll not have you working down in that hold."

I could see Jimmy smirking behind Leo and knew I couldn't let Leo cosset me, not if I wanted to earn a place on this crew. My dismay turned to determination. I would do this. I *would* earn the respect of these men and I'd make life a bit more bearable for our meat while I was at it.

"Are there any spare scarves?" I asked, noticing the silk squares about the sailors' heads and necks. "And any way of getting some air down there?"

"Gabriella . . ." Leo started, then paused, assessing my new purpose. "Well, if you're sure, we'll get a windsail rigged. Jimmy, see to that will you." It wasn't a question. "Come with me," he added, and took my arm.

In the main cabin he rummaged in his seachest and pulled out a square of red silk which I tied around my hair. He looked at me a moment, then passed me another.

"You might like to tie it around your mouth and nose," he said.

Embarrassed, I took it and said nothing.

Back on deck, all the hatches stood open and canvas billowed around them, directing what little breeze there was below. I looked at Jimmy, still smirking, and tied the red silk around my face. I stared at him a moment, then went below. I would do this. Jimmy stamped along behind me and passed me a shovel.

"Buckets are over there, lovey." His smirk disappeared and we got to work.

Chapter 33

GABRIELLA
17th April 1686

Klara and I finished mucking the goats out the next day. I was getting worried about her—I'd never known her be so quiet. I realized she was taking Wilbert and Jan's deaths very hard. I didn't know what to do for her but give her time, keep her busy, and try to involve her in this new life as much as possible.

We'd delayed seeing to the sow and tried to ignore the rustling of the rats that always stayed out of sight in the dim light, but couldn't put it off any longer. I straightened up, pulled the scarf from my mouth and suggested a break and some fresh air before we took on the pigpen, when I heard laughter behind us. Expecting Jimmy, I was surprised to see three men blocking our exit. I recognized them as two of the topmen, Newton and Smith, and one of the men from the slaver—Ime—who had come aboard with us. They were not friendly. I was immediately wary.

Klara gasped in fright as they moved toward us, still laughing amongst themselves, and I realized they were drunk.

"Well, well, well, so this is where you've been hiding," Newton smirked, and he stepped forward, the other two flanking him. There was no way past them in this confined space. "How appropriate, stored with the fresh meat."

"Please, let us pass," I said as strongly as I could, but my voice betrayed my fear and cracked on the last word.

"Oh, I don't think so, darling, we've been looking everywhere for you two."

"Let us pass and we won't say a word to the captain." My voice held up better this time, but the men had not backed away and were very close. Newton drew his blade.

I stepped back, ushering Klara behind me. She coughed as the foul air from the pigpen hit us and I knew there was nowhere for us to go.

"Ahh, threatening us with the captain is it, darling? That won't wash with us. He shouldn't have brought you aboard in the first place, against articles that was, you're only making things harder for yourselves."

"Yeah," Smith added. "Be nice to us and we won't throw you overboard when we're done!"

I had started to feel safe aboard Leo's ship and part of me had actually hoped that they would let us go. I realized I was wrong. I couldn't believe this was happening to us again. I thought we'd escaped rape when we'd escaped Erik. *No! They will not do this. This can* not *happen!*

We backed away as far as we could, but ended up trapped in the corner between the wooden hull and the pigpen. We had nowhere to go and the three men kept coming. Maybe I could get one of their swords away from them? No, not a chance, they were experienced swordsmen; there was no way either of us could take one of their weapons. Newton must have seen some of my intention on my face because he laughed again and threw the large blade behind him in disdain. A small dagger, just as deadly and much easier to use in the confined space, appeared in its place, and the others followed his lead.

I edged closer to the pigpen. *Maybe we can climb over into the muck?* But we were too late. Newton's hand was on me, and with one push he pinned me to the wooden wall by my throat. The other two did the same to Klara. I jerked my bent leg, but again Newton seemed to know what I was thinking, and I only caught his thigh. We were in trouble.

He moved closer and tightened his hold on my throat, then warned, "Try that again and I'll strangle you and throw you to that pig—that way we'll all have a taste of your flesh."

I was furious! I was not going to cower in fear to this excuse for a man, not after getting away from Erik. Whatever his threats, I would fight this. Trouble was, I could hardly move my legs and my arms were no match for him—he didn't seem to feel my blows and I realized he was used to this.

My fury turned back to fear and I knew I had to stop simply reacting and think, but I was running out of time. He took the end of my struggles as defeat and moved his hand from my throat to my breast, then laughed in delight at my helplessness.

"That's it, darling, I know you want me really."

I looked at Klara from the corner of my eye and saw Smith rip open her shirt. She didn't make a sound and her eyes were closed in defeat. It was up to me. I felt Newton's leg force its way between my own and realized they meant to do this. The *Sound of Freedom* was not a safe place for us. Panic and revulsion swept through me.

I tried to jerk away and scream, but Newton was too strong. I couldn't stop him. I felt his rough face against mine, smelled breath made fetid by rotten teeth, and scythed my head from side to side, trying to keep away from that mocking mouth.

There! What's that? I'd heard something and took a moment to realize what it was; a very familiar, and now welcome, stamping.

"Jimmy!" I shouted. "In here! Jimmy!"

Newton let go of me, but didn't move away. Instead he took advantage of my sudden stillness and kissed my lips. "If you cause me trouble, I won't stop next time."

And then, bless him, my bad-tempered guardian angel arrived, along with another of the men from the slaver, Obi. For a moment I was scared they'd join in the attack, but then relief washed over me as Jimmy exclaimed, "What the devil's goin' on 'ere?"

He picked up the shovel and used it to smash Newton's head, knocking him onto the fence that trapped the pig. I quickly grabbed the bucket and bashed him over his shoulders, toppling him all the way over into the pen where he landed, cursing, head first into the muck we hadn't yet cleared. Obi launched himself with a cry at the two men who held Klara, and they joined their leader in the filth.

"Jimmy! Obi! Thank you! Your timing was perfect. I don't know what we'd have done if you hadn't turned up. Thank you." I was so relieved it was over, and Newton and the others hadn't won after all, I could feel tears force their way out of my eyes. I realized just how scared I'd been. I turned to Klara, and smiled at her in relief. She was slumped against Obi and I looked at him carefully. What were his motives? He raised his eyes to me and I saw only concern reflected in them.

"What have you brought down on us, lovey? What have you done? You can't tell the captain, that bastard Newton'll make ma life miserable—as if he don't do enough of that already. What were you two doing down here alone anyway? I told you not to mess about wiv ma animals without me. It's ridiculous having women on board, it's asking for trouble, and look at this, it's already started . . ."

He went on and on and on, the miserable old goat. As grateful as I was to him, I wished it had been somebody—anybody—else who had come to our aid, but I would do as he asked and keep it between us. We hadn't actually been hurt anyway. I glanced at Obi, but all his attention was on Klara.

"What in San Antonio's name is going on down here?" Leo had arrived, and I was sure it was obvious what was going on, especially when he kicked the discarded swords, but at least Jimmy stopped complaining.

"Nothin' Cap'n, just a misunderstanding. These men had a bit of an accident, we was just helping them up." Jimmy glared at me and I kept quiet. Newton and the others had been bested by two women, a slave and a cripple—they were not about to admit that to their captain.

I almost ran to Leo I was so pleased to see him and took his arm. Obi helped Klara away from the wall whilst covering her with the rags of her shirt as best he could. Leo frowned at me, or rather at my shaking, but I didn't think he noticed Klara's state of undress. I smiled at Obi, willing him to say nothing, but I was sure Leo knew there was something more to it.

"Excellent timing, Captain, I could do with some fresh air—and some civilized company," I said, my words gushing, and I only just resisted my urge to drag him out of there with physical force.

He looked at Newton, then back at me. "I know I warned you to take care around the crew, I didn't realize I had to warn them to beware you!"

"It was nothing, just an accident, no harm done," I replied, trying to make light of it.

"Hmm." He looked at me and I realized my breathing was so heavy from fear and relief that I was almost panting. He was not fooled and I flinched at the anger apparent in his clenched fists, jaw and eyes. He turned to Newton and his mates.

"Newton, stop playing with that sow! Get yourself on deck and do something useful! You too, Smith and Ime!" Then, quieter, "Don't think I don't know what was in your head—if any of you looks at either of them again, I'll blind you. If you touch them, I'll cut off your hand. Speak to them, I'll cut out your tongue. And if you ever try to repeat what happened here today, I'll dismember you, throw your cocks to the sharks and send the rest of you after it in pieces, do you understand me?" He turned, ignoring Newton's response and took a deep breath.

"Jimmy? Good man, I won't forget this. You too, Obi. On your way now. Shall we?" His attention turned back to me after glaring at Newton once more and, at last, we headed topside to fresh air, followed by Klara and Obi. We went up to the empty poopdeck right at the stern and sat, backs to the taffrail, and looked down at the busy, canted decks, steaming in the heat.

"What did they do to you? How far did it go?"

"Not far, Jimmy and Obi got there in time." It was not a lie, nothing did happen after all, it was only threatened, and I was furious with myself for panicking. I understood that Klara and I had to learn to fight back and protect ourselves. I did not want to be at anybody's mercy ever again.

"If they hurt you, tell me and I'll nail their guts to the mast and make them dance around them."

"No, you won't. They didn't hurt us, instead they embarrassed themselves. They won't be any more trouble. They're all talk and won't want the rest of the crew to know. We'll be more careful around them. Anyway, there's nothing they can do to us that's worse than anything that's already been done, long before. If you punish them, you'll turn the whole crew against us."

"If that's really what you want, I suppose it makes sense." He paused, watching my face. "What happened to you? What put you aboard that blackbirder?"

I shook my head, how could I explain my marriage to him? He would hate me.

Chapter 34

LEO

"There's not much to tell," she replied, looking past me to the water off our leeside. I stayed quiet, hoping she would keep talking.

"Well, not much you can't guess, anyway. My father practically sold me to my husband. Erik wasn't too bad at first, just cold and distant, but when his father died he changed, and became as cruel and ruthless as the English buccaneers he's in league with."

She paused a moment, then took a deep breath as if she'd decided she could trust me with her story.

"My married life was a hell of degradation and humiliation, and I'm not going to share that with anybody, including you. All that shame is in the past—over and done with. I want to look forward, to make a new life and forget the past."

I didn't believe her—if she was forgetting the past why did she still flinch whenever I surprised her with my approach? Why did she still expect a blow and not a helping hand? And now my own crew had threatened her. I wanted more than anything to keep her safe, but I had to know what had happened to her.

"You're not forgetting the past, though, are you?" I asked. She looked at me and I realized I had to be careful. "I hear your dreams, Gabriella."

"What do you mean?"

"I hear your cries through the cabin wall. I hear your fear, and I hear you shout for Jan."

She looked down at the deck but didn't say anything.

"What hold does your husband have over you that you still fear him?"

She did not deny it.

"Who's Jan?" I tried again.

"Jan was Klara's son. He was killed when we escaped. Because of me, my best friend's nine-year-old son is dead, is that what you want to hear? I told you I don't want to talk about it! I won't be pitied, not by you, not by anyone, now leave me alone!" she shouted, almost running forward.

I was taken aback by the force of her distress and the sudden way she'd exploded into temper, and I was consumed by hatred for her husband. But I couldn't do anything to make it better now that she'd stormed off. I would have to be patient, although all I wanted was to wear round and head straight back to Sayba, kill van Ecken and the rest of them, and take the town for our own. I wanted to keep Gabriella safe and convince her that she was completely free of her old life.

"Sail oh!"

I looked at Gabriella's back on the foredeck and the stubborn set of her shoulders, but the ship and everyone aboard was calling. I told myself it was just as well; that I should leave her alone. I would no doubt only make matters worse. I smiled to myself. She reminded me so much of Magdalena, whose temper I'd also seemed to arouse with ease.

"How does she look, Davys?" I shouted up to my lookout. Billy Davys had been with *Sound of Freedom* when I took her a couple of years ago and he'd been at sea more than half a century. I knew I could trust his instincts, and his eyes were somehow still sharp after a lifetime of working sunbaked canvas.

"A twinmaster, Cap, heavily laden," came the reply. "She's showing Dutch colors—probably on her way to St Eustatius or even Sayba."

I jumped up into the rigging to have a look myself—a Dutch prize would be perfect, it might even cheer Gabriella up, especially if there was a connection to van Ecken, although the middle of a firefight was not where I wanted to put the newest member of my crew. She needed to be safe. *I* needed her to be safe. I looked aft at the boats we were towing. Perfect! Gaunt could take both women out in the pinnace and keep them away from the guns.

* * *

"*No*. You're not sending us off out of the way. You've given us a place on your ship—let us earn it!"

"You are earning it, every day that you work aboard. This will be our first attack since you arrived—my men and ship need my full attention, I can't neglect them to make sure you're safe. Anyway, I'd have thought you'd want to stay well away from the fight, haven't you just said you've had enough of that?"

"I've had enough of being beaten. I don't mind a fight if I have the means to fight back! I won't get in your way, I know better than that, I just want to earn my place!"

"You will—the pinnace will be launched anyway and packed with water, food and gold in case we lose *Freedom*. If this goes wrong I'll need someone I can trust in her; I need someone who will come back for me."

"But why us, can't someone else go in the pinnace?"

"Everyone else can shoot." That silenced her. "Can I trust you to come back for me?"

She nodded. "On one condition."

I winced inwardly, *what's she going to demand of me?*

"I want a sailing lesson."

"A sailing lesson?"

"Yes. I want to learn to sail and it makes sense to start small."

"Gaunt?" I called, and my carpenter crossed over to us, eyebrows raised, even though he must have heard. "Is that acceptable to you? Will you teach her?"

"Aye, Cap, it'd be my pleasure." He smiled. "It'll give us summat to do whilst thee has all the fun."

I frowned; I didn't want Gabriella thinking of our way of life like that.

"Another thing." I turned back to Gabriella, wondering what she wanted of me now. "Once this is over, I want you to show me how the guns work."

"Anything else?"

"Yes, I want a glass, or telescope, or whatever you call it. I want to see what you do and make sure *you're* safe."

Pleased, in spite of myself, I handed her my father's glass. She was concerned for *my* safety.

"Whatever you do, Robert," I said, trying to cover up my

pleasure. "However much she begs, stay well back. I don't want her anywhere near the range of their guns."

"Of course, Cap, I'll keep her safe. Don't fret thysen. C'mon lassie, make thy way to the larboard bulwark and help me pull the boat alongside."

"Robert," I said, quieter, and caught Gaunt's arm. "Look after her, whether she makes it easy for you or not. If we get into trouble, don't let her see. I'm counting on you, amigo."

Robert Gaunt was nearly as old as Davys, had been at sea most of his life, and was just as reliable. I knew she would be safe in his care, and I expected him to be a patient teacher. I watched them climb into the laden pinnace, step the mast, and unfurl the sail before casting off. I raised my hand in salute rather than farewell and thought about the Dutch ship. I wondered why I felt so uneasy that Gabriella would be watching the fight, and realized I feared she might be repulsed by the way I lived.

"Sand's down on deck and guns are ready. Sharpshooters are aloft and the men on deck are ready too."

I looked at my quartermaster. "Muy bien, Frazer," I replied. Very well.

"You've never needed to be told that afore today," he pointed out.

"No." He was right, I hadn't.

"I don't like it, your attention should be on the ship, not that boat. And the carpenter should be aboard *Freedom*."

I let go of the gunwale and turned to view my decks. "It all looks shipshape, Frazer, and Gaunt's where I want him." I looked around once more to see the pinnace sailing steadily away, and tried to shake thoughts of Gabriella from my mind. I couldn't deny the fear twisting my belly. I hadn't known battle-nerves quite this strongly for some time, but then I'd thought I'd already lost everything. Now I realized I'd found something, or rather someone, I wanted to live for.

"Death or victory!" Frazer said. I looked at him and smiled. That was the same battle cry we used before every attack, the same one my father had no doubt cried before meeting Morgan in the Panamanian jungle. It didn't sound quite so noble anymore.

"Let's just make sure it's victory shall we, Frazer?"

"Always, Leo, always."

Chapter 35
GABRIELLA

"He knows what he's doing, lass, thee's no need to fret."

I looked at Mr. Gaunt, embarrassed that my thoughts were so easy to read, and ignored Klara smirking at me from her seat in the bow.

"He's done this afore, lass, relax."

"When can I steer?" I asked him, not wanting to acknowledge his amused reassurance.

"In a bit, when we're further away. Has thee sailed one of these afore?"

"No."

"Well, I'll soon have thee storming about." He lapsed into silence for a while and I watched Leo's ship grow smaller as we sailed away. My belly was full of nerves for what they were about to do, and I could see Klara felt the same. Was she concerned about the captain too? Or Obi? I smiled to myself. Obi of course, he'd made quite an impression on her.

"I reckon we're far enough away here," Mr. Gaunt said into the silence. "Why don't we swap places and see what thee's made of?"

I got to my feet—too quickly—and the boat rocked violently.

"Gabby!" Klara said in alarm. I ignored her and grabbed hold of the mast to stop myself falling overboard.

"Steady there, lass, no sudden movements, she's not ballasted like the big 'un, keep your weight to the middle and watch thy balance."

"Are you sure you know what you're doing? Why don't you sit down and let Mr. Gaunt sail the boat?" Klara said. I ignored her again, took a deep breath and moved my feet aft, more carefully this time. It was hard to find space for my feet around the stores, but even harder to let go of the mast.

When I took that risk I almost fell again; but for Mr. Gaunt's quick arm I would have done. He stood across the back of the boat with his feet wide apart, despite his instruction to me to keep to the middle, but he was balanced enough to help me find my own. I clutched at him gratefully and moved my feet exactly as he told me. He gave me the tiller and moved forward, agile and comfortable. I smiled at Klara, who looked away, but I was sure I saw a small smile on her face first. I was delighted—it was good to see her smiling.

"Sit thysen down there, lass—no not there, t'other side—and I'll balance thy weight."

I moved to where he was pointing and sat on the starboard side of the aft thwart, away from the sail and boom.

"Now, we'll find out if thee's learnt anything these past weeks," he said with a smile. "Hey! Thee has the helm, thee needs to pay attention to thy boat and sails, not them ships! Come back to me, lass!"

I turned back to face him with an apologetic smile. "Sorry, just wondering what was happening, that's all."

"We'll hear it when it starts. Leave your friend there to keep an eye on 'em, I'm going to sheet the sail in and get us moving—just keep her steady."

He hauled on the mainsheet and we started moving immediately. I heard a gurgling and leaned over the side to investigate. The boat lurched over, but thankfully I hadn't let go of the tiller; Mr. Gaunt grabbed it and used it to pull me back in to the sound of more disapproval from the bow.

"Oh! Thank you! I thought I was going to fall out!"

"And so thee should have. What were thee thinking, lass? You nearly had us over!"

Scared and confused, I could feel tears fill my eyes and I looked away from Mr. Gaunt. I'd rather be on that Dutch ship then out at sea in a twenty-foot boat that wouldn't stay upright with any kind of assurance.

"Steady now, lass, thee's all right. Even if we do fall in we'll only get wet, though I doubt the Cap would be too pleased to lose gold he's entrusted to us."

I'd forgotten about the gold and supplies. This was more than a sailing lesson, we could be the difference between life and death for Leo and the crew should the Dutch ship get in a lucky shot or two. Now I lost my battle with my tears and I thought back to how I'd almost sunk us. Twice. Already.

"Hush now, lass, thee's nowt to weep about. Look about thee; we're still upright with our cargo—and us—still safe." He gave me a moment and carried on once I nodded that I was well.

"Feel the wind, lass. Where's it coming from?"

I thought about it and replied, "Over my left shoulder."

"Aye. Now look at the sail, how's thee gonna catch it?"

I looked at the sail, only now realizing he'd let it flog again. "You need to pull it in."

"Aye. Watch it while I sheet in and see when I stop. Does thee see how she fills? The last bit to shiver is the luff, next to the mast. Remember what that looks like, and if it's flapping pull the sail in. If the sail's already in as far as it can be then it's thy steering that's at fault and you need to bear off the wind a touch."

"Bear off?"

"Aye." He looked at the confusion on my face and sighed, to more laughter from up front. I looked at Klara and smiled as our eyes met. However much of a fool I made of myself doing this, it was worth it to see her eyes sparkle once more. "Thee can sail in any direction except straight into the wind. If thee pulls the tiller toward thee, it pulls the rudder and pushes the bows away from the wind—that's bearing off. Push the tiller and you harden up to the wind, or go aloof. Push it further and you tack."

At least I knew what tack meant. "That's bad isn't it? Doesn't that mean going backwards until the wind's coming from over the other side of the boat?"

"It does on a square-rigger like *Freedom*, but it's much simpler in a little tub like this. We can sail much higher—closer to the wind direction," he added with another exasperated glance at me, "than *Freedom* can. In the ship, the yards would jam up against the stays that hold the mast up, but we ain't got that problem here."

I nodded, still a bit confused, but I wasn't scared anymore. At least Mr. Gaunt knew what I was supposed to be doing, and Klara was smiling again.

"So, if I 'harden up', like this, you need to pull the sail in and, oh!"

We picked up some speed as I tried it out, and I had wind and salt spray in my face—it felt wonderful!

"That's better, lass, blow me if you ain't a right little sea artist under them tears," said Mr. Gaunt, giving me an indulgent smile. "Hook thy feet under that loop of line down there and lean back a bit over the water. That's it, lass. That smile suits you a lot more than them tears did, shall we try a tack?"

Now that I had the feel of her and a little confidence, my first tack went well, or better than I expected anyway, which I supposed was not quite the same thing. I steered her through the wind a little too far, but I didn't tip us over and I managed to avoid the boom as it swung wildly across the boat, missing my head by only a hair.

I enjoyed myself so much that I almost forgot the reason for us to be sailing out here in the first place. It was exhilarating to be flying so close to the waves, the little boat straining her sails to go faster and faster despite her load. The first roar of cannon went straight through me; for a moment I wondered if I'd been shot. I turned to look over my shoulder (this time keeping the rudder in position) to see the puff of smoke heading our way from *Freedom*.

"What will happen now?" I asked Mr. Gaunt, my earlier joy replaced by fear. "Will they win?"

"They're sure to, lass. These things go one of three ways. The easiest and usual consequence is the prize striking her colors without firing a shot. Dropping her flag in surrender," he explained. "They know from the black flag that quarter'll be given, that means mercy, not like some of them scoundrels showing the bloody flag—a red flag promises death and destruction to the whole ship and crew whether they ask for mercy or not. I've never sailed under one meself, and never will, although I've known them that have. Turned them into devils, it did.

"Anyhow, most of them that don't strike, run, but *Freedom's* rigged for speed and she catches most of her prey."

"What's the third one? Oh, fight."

"Aye, fight. Not many do, there's too many legs and arms and other bits of men lost, including lives. Not many take the risk. Most merchants underhand their ships, and they don't pay well what crew they do take on. There ain't many who'll risk their lives for the contents of a merchant's pocket, and we've no use for a scuttled ship—can't clear her of her riches then, can we?"

"They're not striking their colors."

I saw Mr. Gaunt smile at Klara's use of his phrase. "No, they ain't, are they? There's always the stubborn ones who won't give up."

My heart sank and my breath gasped. I was grateful that Leo had ordered us off *Freedom* after all, and I turned back to Mr. Gaunt only to see him smile at my leap of fear.

"We'll swap places again, lass. I reckon thee'll be more interested in that glass than the tiller."

I nodded, moved forward toward Klara with a lot more confidence then I had aft, and took the glass from her.

"I wish I'd have been a way off when I saw my first pirate attack. It were mayhem. I didn't know what were fore and aft or larboard and starboard with all the noise and gunsmoke stinging me eyes. A good mate o' mine were killed that day, and poor Jimmy lost his leg. There's not many who'd take on a man like that—especially a man who complains as much as Jimmy does. There were a lot of us crew impressed with that, it's why most of us joined him, even if he is a Spaniard, but we don't hold that against him. Anyway, his ma were English, and that's enough for me."

"What do you mean? Joined who?"

"The Cap of course."

I was still confused.

"Leo were the pirate who attacked me ship. The one that's now called *Sound of Freedom*."

"Leo did that? Leo? And you sail with him?"

"Aye. There were nowt personal in it and a ship's a ship. He's a finer master than the last one an'all, and I'm grateful to him—well, mebbe not at first—but I've been at sea thirty year and had nowt to show for it but abuse and a body breaking down with the work. I've been with Santiago more or less a year now, and it's been the best 'un. I've more freedom, less work, and plenty of gold to show for it. I wish I'd gone pirate decades afore. Aye, he's a good man is the Cap, he never leaves a man behind, that's worth summat in this life, that is." He looked at me. "But that's the Cap all over. There might have been a few lives lost aboard *Freedom*, but not one has been thrown away as they are on a lot of ships. Life's precious to him—that's why the crew are happy to follow him on this crusade of his. That said, he brings in plenty of gold—that helps, too."

"Crusade?"

"Aye. Tarr, Blake and Hornigold. Them that killt his ma. The whole crew wants 'em dead now, not just the Cap."

We were interrupted by a massive roar and a bonfire of smoke.

"What's happened? Why's *Freedom* rolling like that? Is she hit? Is she going down? Quick, we've got to get to her!"

"Settle down, lass, she's well. He's fired all his larboard cannon together in a broadside, the roll's just *Freedom's* reaction to all that powder going off. I'm glad I ain't on that gundeck, it's a fearsome place in a fight."

"Oh." I felt a bit of a fool, but mainly relieved. Klara still looked worried though, and I remembered that Obi was on one of the gun crews.

"They must be putting up a good fight, we haven't much use for a wrecked prize; it'll take time to strip her of her treasures, and a ship's wasted on the bottom."

I fumbled the glass to my eye and tried to make sense of what I saw.

Chapter 36

"They've strung something up over the deck, I can't make out what it is—it looks like a jumble of rope," I reported.

"Ah, that explains it, lass, they've put boarding nets up—me shipmates can't get on deck—but thee can be sure that crew don't wanna stay trapped under nets on a sinking ship. As soon as she starts listing, they'll pour out of them hatches like bees out of honeycomb. Thee mark me words, there ain't nowt worse than being stuck below decks in a ship filling with water."

"Yes, here they come!" I was getting swept up in the excitement of the fight. "Oh, *Freedom's* firing at them!"

"That'll be the sharpshooters in the rigging—just a little encouragement for them to de-rig the nets. They'll only hit the ones with weapons, there's no point killing anyone we don't have to."

I shuddered at the casual way he said this, but was soon distracted again and searched through the glass for Leo. I could see ropes being flung into the rigging where their grapnel hooks caught fast; more were thrown over the rail and the two ships drew closer together whilst men swung or leapt down across the gap to the smaller vessel, but I still couldn't see him. The weight of the Freedom Fighters landing on the newly loosened netting brought it all down and they had the deck in seconds.

"There's Leo! What's he doing?" I handed the glass to Mr. Gaunt, unable to watch the captain in danger.

"He's going below to flush out the captain and the rest of the crew. There, that smoke's a grenado—a fire bomb—that's gone off down the hatch. Leo and a few others'll follow it." Then he looked at me. "Don't worry, lass, he's a master at fighting close-quarters, he won't take long."

"But why does *he* have to go below at all? Surely it's the most dangerous place. He's the captain, why isn't he safe on *Freedom* telling the others what to do?"

"*Because* he's captain, that's why. The men won't accept a leader who'll send them into dangers he wouldn't face himself, not on a fighting ship. The only place for him to be is in the thick of it, the men respect him for it."

I snatched the glass back, desperate to see him appear on deck again.

"There he is! He's done it, Mr. Gaunt, he's still alive!"

I heard Mr. Gaunt laugh at my relief and saw it anew myself. I realized I'd as good as declared love for the pirate captain, but at that moment I didn't care. I wanted to be over there with him, not stuck in this boat, an onlooker. I realized I missed the excitement of a fight, and watching wasn't enough. I wanted to be in the middle of it. I wanted to hear my blood pound through my body and I wanted to fight *with* my man—not against him.

"Ha! There! The flag's down, they've done it, they've taken her!"

I focused again on the ships and saw my new friends cheering their success—although they'd lose the prize if they didn't get on with it. She looked low in the water, and smoke poured out of more holes than just the hatches.

"Can we head back now, Mr. Gaunt? If they're on fire, they're going to need all the help they can get."

"Aye, reckon thee's right at that, lass. Does thee want to take her in? And show that captain of thine what thee can do?"

"Aye, aye, Mr. Gaunt." I smiled, and we changed places again—this time with hardly a wobble.

Chapter 37

LEO

I chased after the tarry smoke billowing through the hull. Most of the crew had escaped topside, but I knew the captain was down here somewhere; I just didn't know how many men he still had with him.

I'd been deafened by the cannon fire and could barely see in the dim light, but could tell from the stench that this was another blackbirder, a slaver, mercifully empty today, though still stinking from a recent cargo. That was good—he'd be loaded with the proceeds from the slave marts and I didn't have the problem of deciding what to do with a cargo of defeated terrified people. My stinging, streaming eyes were useless, I had to go by feel. I knew the captain would head aft to his cabin, they always did, and he had the advantage of familiarity with his ship. He was used to fumbling about below these decks in the dark. My advantage was that I'd done this before. Often. Thomas and Phillippe would go forward to find anyone else moving down here, Rafael and Smith followed me, and I fired my first gun in the general direction of the stern, knowing that none of my men were further aft than I was. I was pleased to note that I could hear it—my ears were coming back to me. I heard shouts and curses and quietly celebrated—I'd hit someone. *The captain?*

"You bloodthirsty murdering swine! You've killed one of my best men!"

Not the captain then.

"How many of my crew have you killed today? Have you no conscience?"

"That man answers to your own conscience, Captain, not mine. You chose to fight, and he chose to fight with you. And what about *your* scruples? You sail about the Caribbees with a hundred men and women shackled in your holds to sell like beasts to the highest bidder, and you challenge *my* scruples! I should put *you* in irons and to work just as brutally as the people you sold!"

I sidestepped his ball—I knew he'd aim at my voice, but did he have another gun? I coughed, although the smoke was clearing now, and fired my second gun at the flash of his, or at least I tried to—nothing happened. My powder was wet.

I saw him then, outlined in front of a splash of daylight. He'd reached his cabin. I charged forward, my blade drawn and my defective gun held by the stubbornly cold barrel. Instead of using his own weapons he tried to shut the door on my charge, and it was easy enough to club his arm with the butt of my gun. He cried out, as much in rage as pain, and drew his sword with the other. He was a foolish man and a worse captain. He'd sacrificed his crew and his ship for his pride. If he'd carried a short blade or cutlass he could have put up a fight. Instead his long rapier clattered against the deckhead before he got anywhere near me. It was simple enough to disarm him with a quick slice to his swordarm, and he was lucky that was the only injury I inflicted, although he didn't seem to appreciate it much.

"You're nothing but a yellow-livered Spanish mongrel! Anyone can make a profit with flint and steel! What went wrong? Couldn't you prosper at honorable industry?"

"Keep your mouth shut and your thoughts to yourself or you'll discover just how skilled I am at *this* industry!"

I'd had enough of him now. It had promised to be a good fight, but I'd been able to cut *and* disarm him before he'd managed to get his blade anywhere near me. I saw some line on the chart table and used it to secure his wrists, then took him back on deck to show his crew and mine the fight was won. *Freedom* had added another ship's colors to her tally. Now came the hard bit. The battle was over and the men celebrating, but all I could think of were the captain's words—how many men *had* been injured? How many had been killed today because of my decisions?

I checked the sky first, no problems there; the fresh breeze that had been blowing when I went below was still blowing, and there were no presages of storm in the bright blue above. *Freedom* looked as if she'd come off lightly. There was some work for George to do, but a bit of sail repair was no problem, we could take more sailcloth from the prize. Her hull seemed sound; the Dutch ship's captain had been no gunmaster and the only damage was high and easy to reach. I shouted over to Frazer aboard *Freedom,* and he confirmed she was still sound below the waterline.

"Very well, cast off and send the boats over," I instructed. I didn't want to take any chances now; the prize was listing and smoking, I didn't want *Freedom* made fast to her or even be close in case she blew.

I made my way aft to check on the crew. "Did we lose anybody?" I asked Blackman.

"No. One of theirs dead, but all of *Freedom's* fighters are still with us. Phillippe and Smith have nasty cuts, Jack's lost a finger, and Alonso's in danger of losing his eye, but everyone else is well. Ease yourself, enjoy your victory."

I nodded, and allowed myself a smile; I had no one else to add to my conscience, no matter what the captain had said. The man that had died was the responsibility of my opposite number, and my injured would be well compensated. However, my crew wouldn't be safe until we were off this foundering ship.

"How many to join us, Blackman?"

"Three. Butler, Thompson and Greenwoode."

"Make them welcome in the usual manner and put the rest in the smallest of the ship's boats, we'll be needing the other ones. Captain, lead the way please."

He glared at me as he held his bloodied arm where my blade had sliced through his flesh, but there was nothing he could do now, and we both knew it. He led his men to the waiting boat.

I looked around the decks whilst Blackman got rid of their remaining crew. I had to get everyone off, but I wasn't about to leave anything behind after the battle we'd fought to win it.

"Jean-Claude, get those weapons ready to ferry across to *Freedom*. And Carlos—take Rafael and Lopez and scour the holds. Gold and silver first, then sailcloth and gunpowder, we're running a bit short. Get on with it, all of you, I want us off this sinking tub and away."

I headed back to the captain's cabin; I was sure there'd be gold hidden away in there. I noticed there was less smoke than before and realized the incoming water had put the fires out—good. I knew that meant the gunpowder would most likely be wet, but I'd rather go through the laborious process of drying and remixing it than have it explode with any of my men still aboard. I rifled the cabin quickly and found the logbook. The smell hadn't lied: the *Adelheid* was a slaver and sailed under van Ecken's colors. She'd put out of Sayba three months ago with a full load of a hundred slaves, and island-hopped, visiting a string of slave-marts. We'd attacked her on her way back north with the profits. I took the logbook and charts, as well as the small seachest I found, and headed topside again.

Back atop, the decks were clearing. The boarding nets had been bundled up against the windward bulwark and there were small piles of bloody sand on the deck, but the men who had bled there were gone. Evidently the injured had elected to stay with their captain—he must have quite a hold on them, very few merchantmen gave berths to anyone not fully able. If their wounds didn't heal, I knew they'd be reduced to begging in one of the many sailortowns about the Caribbees. The other boats started back for another load, and I reminded Thomas not to forget the grapnel hooks tangled in the rigging. We were heavy in the water now—too heavy. I jumped down the after-hatch again to hurry everyone up.

"Just what you can carry, men—and fast. Vamos! Come on, get a move on! Up, up, up!"

Men rushed past, arms full; there was enough water swirling at their ankles now that they didn't need the encouragement. I checked to make sure I was alone, then headed back up to safety myself.

We were nearly there; I could see fully laden boats rowing back to *Freedom,* and only three of us were left behind. I looked at the men, then back at the boats. They'd given preference to the safe carriage of plunder over themselves. I smiled, amused, despite my frustration that they prized gold over their lives.

My smile didn't last long though, sending *Freedom* off had proved a mistake. The Dutch prize hadn't blown, and *Freedom* was too far away; the boats wouldn't make it back for us until we were up to our necks in brine. At least Thomas and Gibson could swim, although neither enjoyed it and both would rather avoid it. Truth be told, I didn't fancy being turned into flotsam myself.

"Captain! The pinnace!"

I turned from my study of *Freedom* at Thomas's shout. I'd almost forgotten about Gabriella. I'd pushed her out of mind during the fight, not wanting her involved in any way, but now she was involving herself, and I watched in amazement as she beat toward us. After only one lesson her tacks were clumsy, but they were effective and I was impressed, as were the two experienced sailors with me. I felt a grin spread over my face as I watched her sail to my rescue.

"She'll not get here in time," said Gibson. "But she'll beat the longboat at least."

I nodded, smiling. This was not a woman who wanted to be steered and cosseted through life; this was a woman who wanted to take the helm herself, to be in command of herself. A woman I could admire and who had already found a place in my heart, and I recognized that this was only the beginning. If I tried to rush her she'd run from me as she'd fled from her husband, and I resolved to give her the time she needed to throw off the shadows of her old life. She had to decide to come to me of her own accord, and I had to be patient—this was one prize that couldn't be won by force.

"What's she luffing up for?" Thomas exclaimed as she steered closer to the wind. "Can't she see we're sinking?" He waved his arms about over his head to try and signal the urgency of our situation.

I was puzzled too and went for my glass, it wasn't there. Of course—I'd left it with Gabriella. I cursed and squinted to try and see—it looked like a fourth person was climbing aboard. Fear gripped my heart. I knew that none of my men were in the water. That meant we'd missed one of the Dutchman's crew. *What would he do with Gabriella, and why had Gaunt not shown more caution?*

They sheeted the main in again and moved closer, but not as tidily as before. The sail was shivering slightly, and I didn't need to see their wake to know it was far from straight. A light flashed, and I knew my fear was justified. Their passenger had drawn a blade.

"Make your blades handy, but keep them hidden," I told my crewmen. "He probably wants to look for more survivors. Either that or he's planning to take us hostage!" I managed to laugh, but as soon as the words were out of my mouth I realized it wasn't a joke and Gabriella was already his captive. I knew I'd do whatever I needed to keep her safe.

"Does anybody have a loaded pistol or dry powder?"

They shook their heads. El infierno, I was out too.

"Do not let her get hurt." I was serious again.

"There's four of us, including Gaunt," Gibson said. "He's a fool to take us on, does he think we'll surrender for a couple of women?"

He looked at me and saw the wisdom in shutting his mouth.

"They do not get hurt," I repeated.

"What do you want us to do then?"

Chapter 38

GABRIELLA

I looked ahead at Leo and the others marooned on their sinking prize and smiled. I definitely preferred coming to the rescue to needing rescue, and I loved the fact I'd soon be out of debt to Leo. One good turn for another. Klara seemed more relaxed now that she saw Obi wasn't aboard the stricken ship and was presumably safe.

"Watch your course, lass," Mr. Gaunt warned, and my eyes snapped to the luffing sail. I pulled the tiller toward me a little and it filled properly again.

"That's it," he said, smiling. "You'll make a sailor yet."

"What's that?" I exclaimed, sheltering my eyes from the bright sun reflected on the water. "There's a man in the water!"

"Leave him, he's not one of ours."

"Leave him? *No*, I won't leave a man to drown." I was horrified and stared at Mr. Gaunt. "Pull the sail in, Mr. Gaunt, we're going to pick him up."

"Gabby, no, you don't know who he is!"

I stared at them both in turn and adjusted course. Mr. Gaunt must have seen the disgust in my face, but said, "It's too big a risk, lass. The Cap won't thank you, or me." Klara just glared at me.

"I will not leave that man to drown," I repeated. "I thought the color of *Freedom's* flag was black not red. I will not become a devil."

He looked at me, then nodded and hauled on the mainsheet despite his obvious doubts.

It didn't take us long to reach the swimmer, and he grabbed hold of the gunwale and hauled himself in. I tried to help, but only succeeded in sprawling in the bottom of the boat with my legs trapped under the man's bulk. I yelped, and he looked at me in surprise.

"Get off her," Mr. Gaunt growled, his blade drawn. "Get in the bows and don't give us any trouble. Klara, catch." He threw a knife to her, handle first.

The man laughed. "Women and an old man," he said. "Perfect. Drop your blade, old man, unless you want your lady friends as scarred as you are."

I looked down. He had a dagger in his hand, an inch from my belly. I looked at Mr. Gaunt, and he threw his blade into the bilge in disgust, then looked at me the same way. I held his gaze and heard Klara's knife clatter against wood.

"Well then." The sailor had pulled himself up and sat next to me, his blade ensuring none of us would give him any trouble. "Take me to your captain. He took my ship. I think I'll have his. Tell me, how far would he go to keep you safe, mistress? Are you worth his ship?"

I glared at him. I had no idea, although part of me wanted to find out. *Or maybe not.* I settled myself back at the helm, took hold of the tiller and got us going again. I couldn't look at Klara. *So much for coming to Leo's rescue.*

"Where are you going? I want *your* ship, mine's nearly sunk!"

"You asked for my captain, he's still aboard your ship."

"Is he now? Well, that might just work in my favor. The mothership won't fire on a boat carrying both their captain and women will they? Very well, mistress, carry on."

I glared at him again. I should have left him to drown. He didn't seem to care that he owed me his life.

"And you stay just where you are, Jack—one move and I'll give this pretty lady another smile," he continued as Mr. Gaunt shifted on the thwart. He seemed to have discounted Klara.

I glanced up at my new friend in confusion, and he wiped his forefinger across his throat. I shuddered, and concentrated on the tiller.

"Just keep her steady, lass, thee's doing fine," Mr. Gaunt encouraged me, but I didn't acknowledge him. The man I'd saved ignored me as he kept an eye on what he seemed to think was the only threat aboard the small boat, and I felt rage knot my stomach. *How dare he dismiss me and Klara? Assume we were of no consequence and that a threat was enough to subdue us?* I'd lived enough of my life like that and I determined I wasn't going to let it happen again, but what could I do?

I sat in the sternsheets and seethed, my fury growing until it matched my fear, but I didn't know how to save us, and I was running out of time.

We approached the sinking ship and I refused to look at Leo. I had to fix my mistake and quickly.

"Don't try anything," the man warned Mr. Gaunt. He stood, legs braced amongst the casks in the bottom of the boat. "My blade'll get to her before you can do anything." He looked up. "Ahoy there!" he called to Leo and the others.

I caught Mr. Gaunt's eye and noticed his hand resting on the boom. He nodded at the tiller, tapped the wooden spar and winked. My heart leapt as I understood, and I knew at once what to do. I pushed the tiller hard over, and Mr. Gaunt pulled on the sail. The heavy boom swung across the boat and crashed into the man. I launched myself at him, arms outstretched to help him overboard, and Mr. Gaunt dived into the bottom of the boat to avoid being knocked into the sea himself.

"Get the tiller, lass!" he shouted. "Get us moving again!" He straightened up, holding one of the oars that had been stored under the thwarts. He held it like a spear and jabbed at the cursing man in the water.

"Aim for the Cap, lass—get them aboard, I'll take care of this rat."

"Watch your head, Mr. Gaunt," I called and pulled the tiller toward me. He grabbed hold of the boom and hauled on it to help us turn, then ducked as it swung over and the sail filled with wind.

"Harden up, lass, quick!"

He was too late, and the boat collided with the rail of the ship with a solid thunk. Mr. Gaunt staggered with the impact and Klara screamed, but suddenly Leo was there, pulling the tiller out of my hands, and we soon left both man and ship behind.

Chapter 39

LEO

I followed Gabriella's climb up *Freedom's* hull and wondered at such a change in such a short period of time. The first time she'd come aboard, she'd been timid and frightened—lashing out at an innocent touch. Now she behaved as a sailor and a pirate. *Freedom* was working her magic on her; whether she sat on the bowsprit or just stood at the windward rail, it had become her habit to raise her face to the wind rather than shelter from it. With eyes closed and a gentle smile, her cares were brushed away from her—for a moment at least. In time, maybe they too would be left in our wake for good, along with the man who'd tried to commandeer her pinnace, and I wondered whether she realized she'd taken her first life when she threw that man back to the sea.

I wanted to hug her and hold her. I wanted to scold her recklessness and praise her courage. I wanted to put her somewhere safe and keep her there, and I wanted her by my side, even sailing into battle. I had no idea what to say to her.

She and Klara had chattered the whole passage back to *Freedom,* and Gaunt, Thomas and Gibson had joined in their excitement. She'd either missed my silence entirely or just thought the tiller had my full attention. Every time our eyes met, she pulled hers away, and I was very aware of the other men in the boat.

When I joined her on *Freedom*'s deck, she was lost in a crowd of sailors—everyone wanted to hear what had happened. I caught hold of Gaunt's arm when he tried to walk past.

"What were you thinking? You were supposed to keep her *out* of harm's way, not sail into the thick of it!"

"My apologies, Cap, that had been me intention but—"

"But what? Why did you give her the helm?" I demanded.

"I was *teaching* her the helm, Cap, not *giving* it to her. When that lass gets a thought in her head, it ain't easy to get it out again. She saw a man drowning and refused to leave him. How could I have stopped her?"

"I trusted you, Gaunt. I trusted you to keep her safe."

"Look at her, Cap, she is safe. She's probably safer now than she's ever been."

He had a point; Gabriella was enjoying telling our crewmates about her adventure. She was full of smiles and laughter, and her eyes sparkled to match the sea in her excitement. She looked up at me and smiled even wider.

Gaunt smiled too, although not quite so radiantly. "Thee should have seen her face when that man pulled his dagger. She were terrified, but there were a strength in her I don't think she knew she had—that's down to thee I reckon. She kept her head and knew exactly when her opportunity presented *and* what to do, despite it being her first time." He fell silent, lost in thought.

"What is it, Robert?" I asked, concern replacing my anger.

"Ahh, nowt . . . nowt really, it's just . . . out in that pinnace I kept thinking 'bout Lizzie—me daughter."

I raised my eyebrows. I knew Gaunt had gone to sea as a young man to earn a living to support his wife and baby after his efforts ashore had failed. He'd been away a long time, and when he returned, his family were gone. He'd never found them. He didn't talk about them often, but it was obvious when he was in his cups that he missed them desperately, and tortured himself with thoughts over his daughter, knowing he could have met her anytime over the years without recognizing her.

"I'd be a proud man if my Lizzie were as fine a lass as her."

I followed his gaze to Gabriella.

"She's a credit to thee, Cap, and she'll be good for the ship if the men accept her, but she won't make thy life any easier—I'd swear on that. Now, can I get on with looking over *Freedom*, see what her damage is?

I nodded, a little stunned by his short speech and newly brusque manner. The Robert Gaunt I knew was dour, gloomy and kept himself to himself. Gabriella seemed to have wrought quite a change in the old Yorkshireman and found herself a champion. I walked toward the huddle on the maindeck.

"The ungrateful wretch, I was trying to save his life! I couldn't believe it when he pulled that blade out! Well, the devil's welcome to him, I'll tell you that!"

"That's enough, muchachos, we've work to do—the yarning'll keep.

"Carlos, Obi, Gibson, get the courses and tops'ls set. Thomas, make a course south. I want to be well away from here in case that captain has any friends in these waters. Get us to La Isla Magdalena, I reckon it's five leagues off, then we'll sort the loot.

"Gabriella, I owe you my gratitude. If not for you, Thomas, Gibson and myself would have had a very long swim." I offered her my arm and walked her aft, enjoying the sound of her laugh.

"I thought you were angry with me, you didn't speak a word in the boat, except to take the tiller," she said, her eyes serious.

"I was. I know you thought you were doing right, but you shouldn't have taken that risk. You and Gaunt were told to stand off, out of the way of danger."

"I've had enough of doing what I'm told by my husband—I won't submit to anyone again."

"I'm well aware of that. But at sea, I'm responsible for the life of every member of the crew, and they all do the bidding of their captain. To ignore my words is to mutiny, and I won't have that on my ship. From anybody."

"What, you'd like me in a gown and a cabin, waiting to serve on you your every whim?" She was getting angry.

"No, that's not what I mean and I've told you so often enough! You've stirred this crew up. You changed the way this ship works on your first night aboard and you've shaken things up even more today. I cannot have you leading the rest of my crew astray. All our lives depend on each and every one of our shipmates. If one man hasn't completed his task, or moves from where he was put, people get hurt or killed. That's why the captain's word is law and that's why you'll do as you're told, do you understand?" I heard my voice rising and knew I was handling this badly. I didn't understand why I was berating her, and was only just beginning to realize how scared I'd been when I saw that man hold a blade to her.

“Have you finished?” Her face was expressionless, and I couldn’t hear any emotion in her voice. I nodded. What else could I do after that? She marched forward, and I watched her go and sighed. What had I been thinking bringing women aboard ship, especially *her*?

Chapter 40

We'd been sailing in a general southerly direction and were making good time with a fresh northwesterly. We'd spotted the first of the cays and another hour should see us at La Isla Magdalena. I'd used the island often since I first sailed as a pirate. It was hidden in the middle of coral reefs and cays small enough not to appear on any chart but my own. The waters seemed far too shallow for a ship of *Freedom's* size, and most stayed well away, but there was a channel if you knew where to sail and kept your wits about you, even in the dark, and I always made sure no ships were in sight before taking *Freedom* in. Finding wood, water and food here had once saved my life, and we had a safe harbor within reach of Dutch, French, English and Danish ports and, most importantly, the rich shipping between them.

Gabriella hadn't spoken to me again, but had stayed on the foredeck with Klara, listening to tall tales while she helped to spin ropeyarn, and I wouldn't approach her there. I joined Frazer on the tiller.

"She's settling in," he said, examining the compass.

"Sí, the crew's taken to her, better than I thought, or hoped."

"Ah huh."

"Maybe too quickly."

"Ah huh," Frazer repeated.

"She did well today," I carried on.

Frazer tapped the steering compass but said nothing.

"I was too hard on her," I told him.

Frazer looked at me but stayed silent.

"Yes, you're right; I'll go and talk to her."

"Ah huh."

"Gracias, Frazer, you always give good advice." I was certain I saw the beginnings of a smile touch his eyes, but it was hard to tell in the lantern light.

"Ah huh."

* * *

The two women had left the men yarning and moved to the pile of weapons we'd taken from the Dutch ship. Gabriella was admiring a rapier with a blade about the same length as her arm—wholly impractical aboard ship and I recognized it as the one I'd taken off the captain of the last prize.

"You'd find a smaller blade more to your liking. That's heavy and will be difficult to wield amongst rigging or below decks. It cost its last owner his ship."

"Is that an order?"

I stiffened but managed to catch my anger before it escaped my mouth. "No, of course not, just well-meant advice."

She nodded and pulled a falchion with a red grip out of the pile. Its foot-long blade was etched with Moorish symbols and was a beautiful weapon. As she hefted it in her hand, I realized this was it. She wasn't going to sit in the background—or in a pinnace at a safe distance from any danger. I saw that if I insisted on that I would lose her, and I couldn't lose her. I'd do whatever I needed to do to keep her with me, and if that meant she joined the fight, then I'd have to teach her how to fight.

"Can I make a suggestion?"

"A suggestion?" she asked, warily.

"A suggestion," I confirmed. "I'll save the orders for the ship." That hardly raised a smile so I quickly carried on. "You need strength in your shoulders to fight with a blade, and any sailor will beat both you and Klara on that score."

She looked thoughtful, *bien*, she was listening.

"By all means, have the blades of your choosing but concentrate on guns. If a man's close enough that you need a sword, he's too close to you. Learn to shoot, and you won't need to rely on a blade for your life."

She looked up at me, her smile was back. "You'll let us fight?"

"I'll let you fight with me."

She hugged me in her excitement, and I was acutely aware of her body pressed against mine. Klara didn't look quite so pleased.

"On one condition."

"Let me guess, I do as you tell me."

"Well, that would be nice, but it's not my condition." I paused, wondering how she was going to react.

"Well?"

"You let me teach you how to use your arms and don't join the fight until I agree your aim is true enough."

"So you'll teach us, but *not* let us fight."

"No, that's not what I said. Your lives are not the only ones that concern me. If I put you in the middle of an attack, I need to be sure you won't shoot one of this crew by mistake. They need to be sure of that too."

Silence. Then she nodded. "I'll take you at your word. Why the change of heart? You were furious with me for coming in to rescue you and the others from a sinking ship, and that was after the battle had been won."

I wanted to tell her how I'd felt when that man threatened her, but I couldn't bring myself to say it.

"You seem to have joined my crew. I was annoyed at the risk you took. I'd have reacted in the same way had it been anyone else in that boat."

She looked at me and smiled. "No, you wouldn't."

I couldn't think of a quick reply and watched her walk back to the foredeck carrying both the rapier and the smaller falchion.

Chapter 41

GABRIELLA

"*No*, what are you doing? *Leo*, we're running aground!"

I couldn't believe my eyes. After sailing around the clutch of cays for a while to wait for the tide and a clear moon, Leo had taken the tiller himself and guided us in amongst the sand and coral, then steered straight for the beach of La Isla Magdalena. Admittedly, most of the sails were stowed and we were running aground very slowly, but still, we were running aground—on purpose.

"Relax, querida." Leo laughed. "I've done this so many times now, it's normal, I forgot to warn you we're not dropping anchor, we're careening."

"Careening?"

"Yes, there's no one here and this is the only approach that isn't guarded by reefs or sand bars. Unless you know it, and know it well, this island appears unapproachable to any sizable vessel."

"So?"

"Have a look over the side."

I looked at him in amazement. My eyes were glued to the approaching shore.

"Go on, look over the side," he repeated.

I shrugged in confusion, *am I on a ship crewed by madmen?* Even a landlubber knows ships are supposed to stay in the water. I decided to humor him.

"What do you see?" he asked. *Why can't he answer a simple question?*

"Er . . . sharks." Truth be told, I couldn't see a thing, it was too dark, but I knew they were there and it seemed a good answer.

He laughed. "Look at the hull, not the beasts, do you see the color of it?"

"It's black and white."

"Yes. Weed and salt; do you see the barnacles? It's all slowing us down. We're a fighting ship—we need every knot of speed we can coax out of her, which means scraping her hull clean. We can't do that at sea, we need to beach her and tip her onto her side—careen her."

I was unconvinced. *Surely dirty and afloat's better than high and dry?*

There was a crunch and the deck shuddered hard enough to unbalance me. I stumbled against Leo and sprang back again.

"Let go the sheets! Furl those jibs!" Leo roared loudly enough to be heard at the bowsprit. I watched everyone jump into action. They hadn't needed Leo's direction, they'd let the sheets fly at the first shudder. They moved so quickly and surely, I felt useless. By the time I'd asked how Klara and I could help, the job had already been done.

Leo found it hilarious that the men, who'd been keen to ensure we pulled our weight aboard, now couldn't spare a few seconds to tell us what to do.

"There's gold to be shared, and a victory to celebrate. You'll never see them work as fast as this at any other time! Listen to the shanty." He pointed at the capstan on the foredeck where a dozen men were pushing the huge drum around to hoist one of the cannon overboard.

"*We'll measure our treasure*
and allot our loot.
We'll split the spoils
and sorty our booty.

Silver, gold and pewter too,
Rubies, emeralds and pearls.
Gather plunder from seas ayonder,
and cast it all asunder!"

"What kind of song is that? What does it mean?"

"It's a shanty—a song to set a rhythm to work to. It's a bit of nonsense really, but it serves its purpose."

"What do they mean by "cast it all asunder"? Are they going to throw it overboard or something?"

He threw back his head and laughed. "They may as well the way they spend and gamble it away! A newly rich pirate does tend to be overgenerous!"

The mood was infectious, everyone had laughter in their throats—even Frazer and Jimmy smiled—I realized there was a smile on my own face too. I looked at Klara standing at the rail with Obi, but she didn't notice me. All her attention was on the man beside her. Good, she needed to forget about Wilbert and Jan's fate, and move on. I hoped she could find happiness again.

An hour later *Freedom* was beached, a couple of cannon had been set up ashore to cover the channel we'd sailed through, and a huge fire blazed. I watched Leo organize the unloading of plunder and smiled when he turned to meet my gaze. I tried to pull my eyes away but failed, and we grinned at each other for what seemed an age over the growing pile of pirate treasure.

The mood was broken by Frazer's shout of, "Captain!" and I wrenched my eyes away, embarrassed to be staring at him. I went to join the growing crowd around the fire, helped myself to a pot of rum punch, and tried to ignore my hammering heart.

Chapter 42

I'd seen a lot of faces on Leo that day. I'd seen the general ordering his troops, and the warrior running into battle before his men. I'd seen him churlish and embarrassed after I rescued him from his sinking prize, and now I saw the proud father congratulating and rewarding his victorious sons.

He couldn't stand still but paced around his deck and men, touching each one on the shoulder or shaking his hand. I wasn't paying much attention to what he was saying, I wasn't really part of it, but I enjoyed the smile that lit up his face. His hands and arms were in constant motion, emphasizing everything he said, and I realized I was watching a man who was exactly where he was destined to be. I was watching a man who was doing exactly what he was supposed to be doing and loved it. I was watching a man who was walking toward me with a big smile, being cheered by everyone else and saying my name.

I snapped back to attention, wondering what I'd missed.

"What?"

"I was welcoming the five of you to the crew, Gabriella. Don't tell me you weren't listening."

"What?"

"Butler, Thompson, Greenwoodc, Klara and yourself. Where were you? We just voted you a full member of *Sound of Freedom's* crew!"

"Oh." Then it sank in. "Oh! Oh!"

I glanced at Klara, who looked as stunned as I felt.

"Yes, a real valuable asset. Better not put her on lookout duty, Captain!" I couldn't decide whether Newton was joking or sneering, but it didn't matter, most of them wanted me to stay.

"Thirty one to fifteen in favor."

"Oh."

"They've lost their tongues, Cap, thee'd best get on afore they finds 'em again!" I recognized Mr. Gaunt's voice and was sure *he* spoke in jest.

"Thank you, I mean, I . . ." I shut up. I knew if I said anything more I'd never hold back the tears threatening to engulf me. Against all the odds, we'd found somewhere we wanted to be and where we were wanted in return.

Leo put his arm around my shoulders and brought me into the circle of men. "Frazer, the articles, por favor."

"What's this?"

"Your agreement. Well, *our* agreement, we've all signed it. It sets out the conditions and benefits of being a full crew member of the *Sound of Freedom*. How we share our plunder, what happens if you're injured and what happens if you try to cheat your crewmates or mutiny."

"Oh, very well then." I moved to sign, then stopped. "Out of interest, what does happen if we cheat our crewmates or mutiny?" I thought it was worth knowing, just in case.

"Maybe you'd better read it."

"Maybe." I was still in shock, we'd only been aboard the ship a week, and were barely doing our share of the work. We were tolerated by the crew, most of them anyway, but I hadn't expected to be voted in so formally. We'd spent most, if not all, of our lives being treated as if we were a necessary evil—and by men who called themselves "gentle men". Now, we were wanted and welcomed by men who called themselves pirates, outlaws. We'd found a home. I signed the articles and passed them onto Klara, then the men who'd joined us from the prize for their signatures. I wouldn't cheat any of these men who had given us a new life. If I did, I'd deserve their worst punishment and accept it gladly. *Although I'll have to be careful about when and how I argue with Leo and not cross into mutiny!* I remembered something Leo had said when we first came aboard; something about marooning or death. I shivered.

"The Pirate's Salute!" cried Mr. Gaunt, and a big cheer accompanied the first beakers of rum. We all lifted our drinking arms five times to the toast of the new crew.

"Charles Butler!"

"Thomas Thompson!"

"James Greenwoode!"

"Klara!"

"Gabriella Berryngton!"

Then a final toast: 'To *Sound of Freedom* and all who sail in her! May Neptune keep us safe."

I followed the crew's—*my* crew's—example and drank it in one each time, which was the only way I could get it down my throat. It tasted disgusting and was gritty. Both Klara and I coughed and coughed, and I wondered if our first action as full members of the crew would be to vomit on the beach. Nobody seemed to mind the threat though, they roared with laughter. Even Leo.

"What the bilges was that!" I croaked out (I was picking up their turn of phrase quickly now). I'd had rum before, and, although I didn't like it much on its own (I preferred the rum punch), I'd been prepared for the fire to run down my throat, but this was something else entirely.

Still laughing, Leo said, "Black powder!"

"What?" I must have misheard.

"Gunpowder. It's the Pirate's Salute to any new crewmembers. Rum and gunpowder. What did you think would be in it?"

"Gunpowder," I repeated, aware of everyone laughing and not feeling quite so welcome anymore.

"Why would you give us gunpowder to drink, are you trying to blow us up?"

"Maybe he's trying to light you up!" I couldn't tell who'd shouted out but noticed Leo turn a touch red.

"Hush, we've all had it, not just you, and none of us will blow up—as long as we keep soaking our innards and don't get too close to the fire!"

The laughter grew even louder, and I looked hard at Leo, but couldn't find any malice in his eyes. I turned my gaze to Mr. Gaunt, who smiled and nodded.

"Does this mean you'll let me fire the cannon?" I asked, joining in the laughter.

"Not bloody likely!" a strong, sulky voice called out. I looked around, thinking it was Newton who was objecting, but it had been Jean-Claude, the master gunner. I'd said it in jest, but now I wanted more than anything to get behind a loaded cannon with a lit match.

"So when do we get the gold?" I asked.

Another cheer and rendition, now fairly drunken and extremely impolite, of the rhyme they'd chanted earlier.

"Right then, Frazer, as the lady says, when do we get the gold?"

Another cheer was silenced by Frazer when he pulled out some paper and began to read: "A dozen bags of gold dust, seventeen hundred pieces of eight."

He wasn't one to employ any unnecessary words and kept reading from his list in a dull monotone, not looking up at his crewmates as he told them their fortunes.

"A thousand English shillings, two hundred Dutch guilder, fifty gold ducats and a bag of emeralds."

He didn't join the cheer at his words but, for the first time, I saw him smile.

"Neptune bless the *Adelheid*!" shouted Blackman, holding his rumpot up for yet another toast.

"The *Adelheid?"* I asked, wondering if I'd heard right. I hadn't thought to look at the name of the Dutch ship.

"Yes," Leo confirmed.

"That's one of Erik's! Adelheid was his mother's name." I laughed. "We destroyed one of Erik's ships! I fought off one of Erik's men!" I couldn't help myself and grabbed Leo's arm in delight. He lifted me off my feet and spun me around as another toast was drunk to the destruction of that ship. I thought briefly of the three men who had joined us, and wondered what that meant for my future.

"Captain?" Frazer interrupted, and pointed at a pair of large, elaborately decorated brass scales.

Leo let go of me, looking a little embarrassed, and joined Frazer in the center of the circle. "Yes, caballeros, gentlemen. Let's get down to business before all the rum goes down the hatch."

They cheered again and I thought idly that there'd be a lot of sore throats tomorrow, with or without gunpowder in the rum.

"Battle honors go to Thomas as first aboard *Adelheid*, and he has the pick of the prize for his reward."

"Thomas!" Another beaker of rum was swallowed in a toast,

now thankfully without the earlier fiery flavoring.

"As you know, two men took injuries," Leo carried on. He'd moved around the circle and stopped by Jack. "Jack here lost a finger when a cannon crushed his hand on firing. As it was his trigger finger, he's due an extra half share, and an extra share to Alonso who took a blade to the eye."

"Never mind, Alonso, you've got another one!"

"Gracias, Newton. Frazer, do the calculations and start doling it out!"

Not surprisingly, yet another cheer and toast to the *Adelheid* rang out.

"How do you split it?" I asked Leo.

"It's all in the articles," he said, still smiling. "A full share to each man, six to the captain, four each to the quartermaster and carpenter, and two to the second mate and bo'sun. The first man to board the prize takes an item from the haul before we split it, and extra shares are given for injuries—how much depends on the injury."

"Sounds fair," I said, surprised. I couldn't imagine Erik giving any man extra money or gold because he'd been injured carrying out his orders.

"It's the only way a ship like this can sail," Leo continued. "We're all equals, or most of us are anyway."

"Except captain, quartermaster, carpenter, second mate and bo'sun," I said, laughing.

"Yes, but each of those positions carries extra responsibilities and certain skills. If I don't do my job, we don't find or win prizes and we don't make any profit. I wouldn't be captain if I couldn't fill their seachests, and we all know it. I'd be voted out or mutinied on. Same goes for Frazer and the others. Believe me, the extra shares are earned."

I nodded. However they agreed it, it seemed to work.

Mr. Gaunt interrupted us, smiling. "Here thee is, Gabriella, Klara, welcome to the crew." He held two canvas bags and when I looked inside the one he gave me, I gasped. "This is for me?"

Mr. Gaunt and Leo both laughed at my reaction.

"You mean we get full shares?"

"Yes."

"Why?"

"Don't you want it?

"Yes, why?"

"You played a full part in the attack."

"We were in the pinnace, out of the way, learning to sail."

"Yes. Somebody's always in the pinnace. You'd have been needed if *Freedom* had been damaged."

"But Mr. Gaunt was with us."

"Don't you think he deserves his share either?"

"Yes, of course he does, but if he was already in the pinnace you didn't need us there too."

"Yes we did," Leo replied. "We always have at least two in the pinnace, you took Jimmy's place today and gave him a chance at the fight."

"And I'll be in the pinnace next time an'all, lovey," he butted in. "Don't think you're taking ma place there, too."

"You'll be where I tell you to be, Jimmy, and don't you forget it."

"Aye, Cap'n," he said, still sullen.

"You also fought off an attacking sailor and saved Thomas, Gibson and myself an unwelcome swim."

"But you were angry with me for doing that."

"No, I was angry that I'd put you in danger, and relieved you weren't hurt. And, to be honest, embarrassed that you rescued me in front of my crew."

"Ahhh."

"Yes."

"So how much is a full share worth?"

"Aye, she's a pirate all right," Frazer said as he passed us.

I started counting up the mass of coins. I looked up at Mr. Gaunt.

"Thirty-odd pieces of eight, twenty shillings, a few guilder and a couple of ducats. Oh, and one or two stones," he answered.

"A good first haul," said Leo. "Piracy tends to pay better than a blackbirder." He laughed.

Chapter 43

GABRIELLA
13th April 1686
La Isla Magdalena

I woke at dawn, still on the beach; the magical green and blue driftwood fire of the night before reduced to a few glowing embers. I blinked my eyes open and tried to remember why I was lying on sand. Oh yes, treasure party. Voted onto the crew. Rich in my own right. Pirate. My eyes flew open and I sat up to look about me.

"Buenos días."

I looked down and realized I'd borrowed Leo's arm for a pillow.

"Buenos días," I replied, smiling, then winced at a pain in my head. I put my hands to my brow and groaned at its ache.

Leo laughed. "You didn't last very long. If you want to be a pirate, you'll have to learn to stay awake through the carousing!"

"No thanks, my headache's bad enough as it is." Then I remembered something. "You promised to teach me to shoot today!"

"Sí. Are you sure you want to? With a headache, I mean."

I nodded, grimacing in the early heat. Nothing was going to stop me learning how to defend myself; I was a pirate now. He stood and walked a few paces to the waterline, then stretched. I looked around for Klara and saw her curled up with Obi. I smiled, got up, and followed Leo, taking in the spectacle of the sky.

"It's beautiful," I breathed. "Like the top of a rainbow rising out of the ocean."

"Sí, beautiful it is, but don't be fooled by it. Red sky at night, sailor's delight. Red sky at morn, sailors be warned."

I looked again at the beauty of the sky—red and pink bathed

the clouds and was reflected in leagues of water. *How could something so beautiful be a warning?* Leo must have seen the doubt on my face.

"There'll be a blow afore it gets dark, and the wind's backing. We haven't got long; I'll need to get back to the ship before the storm hits. It'll have to be a short lesson, Gabriella."

Due to the threat etched in the sky, *Freedom* hadn't been laid over, so it was still possible to move about her decks. There was no time to waste and everyone was at work; whether scraping barnacles off the hull, fetching fresh water or securing anything and everything that was loose. I helped Mr. Davys coil the great anchor hawser, listening to him grumble about losing his good fishing.

"Don't listen to him, lass, he's such a poor fisherman the only way he can catch them is with the help of the barnacles to draw them in. He grumbles every time we scrape, thee's doing the rest of us no favors by giving him an ear," Mr. Gaunt said from behind me. "I'll take over here, the Cap wants thee."

I left them to it with relief.

"Is it time to go shooting?" I asked Leo when I found him on the maindeck.

"Sí, come with me." He led me to the chartroom, took a horn of powder and gave it to me with a small, heavy canvas bag. I tucked them both into my sash.

"I know I have another pair of pistols in here somewhere," he muttered, rooting about in his seachest. "I won't be a minute." I looked at the papers scattered over the table. Most looked to be charts, but there were books there too, one inscribed with a name: *Adelheid.*

"Oh, the *Adelheid,* what's this, her logbook?"

Leo left the chest, took the book out of my hands and threw it back on the table.

"Never mind that, we haven't the time. It's best you don't have your own pistols anyway until you're competent, you'll use mine for now," he said, marching back out onto deck. I looked back at the *Adelheid* logbook, wondering what was in it that he didn't want me to see.

"Don't forget that powder!"

I left the book and hurried after him. Whatever was in it could wait; I was going to learn to shoot. I caught up with Leo at the starboard rail.

"Ladies first." He smiled. I swung over the side, and started to climb down the battens fitted to the hull.

"Oh, here she goes, shirking all the hard work! I thought you wanted to be one of us, darling. You share in our plunder; you'll share in our work!"

I looked aft and saw Newton perched on a plank of wood suspended over the hull by ropes. His face was bright red as he attacked the lower hull with an iron scraper in the early morning heat. Oh, *why* had we not climbed down the larboard side?

"*I* decide who does what work on this ship, Newton. As you said, Gabriella is one of us, and you know as well as I do she needs to be competent with small arms."

"Load, point and pull the trigger, that's all she needs to know," Newton retorted.

"If you're not careful, I'll reassess and teach her on deck with you employed as the target! Get your scraper working, not your mouth!

"Never mind him, Gabriella," Leo said as we walked along the beach, my legs shaking after walking on a moving deck for so long. "He's too concerned with what everybody else is doing and not on what he's supposed to be doing himself. He complains to or about everyone—don't take it to heart."

I nodded, but stayed quiet.

"Has he tried to lay a hand on you again?"

I shook my head. "No, he's stayed away from me and I do my best to keep it that way."

"Muy bien. That's for the best. Keep your wits about you and stay out of his way, and if you can't, stick close to me."

I nodded again. I didn't need to be told to stick close to him; I already did that as much as I could.

The beach was gorgeous, a paradise, and already hot. Sand

blew about us, but we were sheltered from the worst of the rising wind as we turned north. Still reflecting pink from the sky, it glittered with coral and there was hardly a mark on it, just a few animal tracks. The heavy swell rolled in, rippling the sand as the water threw itself ashore after crossing an ocean.

"Oh, look!" There was a group of pelicans on the beach ahead of us, lumbering into the sky at our approach, bellied beaks flattened in flight. "They're beautiful."

"Ugh." Leo shuddered. "I hate those birds. I had nightmares as a boy, I kept thinking they'd eat me after my Papá told me I'd fit in one of those beaks."

I laughed. Leo afraid of birds? "And you call yourself a fearless pirate!"

"No I don't—I've never called myself fearless. A fearless man is a stupid man, especially in my line of business."

I'd put my foot in it again. It seemed Leo didn't like to be laughed at. "What's that? It looks like a chicken!"

"Oh, yes." Leo seemed as relieved as I was at the change of subject—or change of bird, at least. "We use the island often and have left stock here to breed. The chickens have struggled a bit, but there are plenty of goats and boar if you trek through the trees and have the patience to catch them. The rats have thrived as well."

"How big is the island?"

"About four leagues north to south and the same across at its widest, last time I looked."

"Last time you looked? Why do you say that?"

"It's vulnerable to the sea here, and changes shape with every storm. That's why you'll never find anyone living here, there's no real shelter—do you see the trees?"

I did, they all leaned westward, to leeward.

"Why did you become a pirate?" I asked.

Chapter 44

"Look!" Leo stopped and grabbed my arm, pointing along the beach. An enormous turtle was half-buried in the sand. "Fantástico! Turtle eggs for breakfast, they're always a treat."

I looked at him, he seemed a little too pleased at the opportunity to avoid answering my question, but then I hadn't been too forthcoming with my own life story, either. As much as I wanted to know him better, I decided to allow him his reprieve.

"What's it doing?" Sayba didn't have many turtles, it was too rocky, and I'd never been this close to one before. Her shell was as long across as my arm, and she looked heavy and tired as she worked in the morning sun.

"Look after these," Leo said and stood before taking the silk ribbon from around his neck and draping it around my own. Each end had a pistol secured to it, and was surprisingly heavy, but most of my attention was on the touch of his hands on my shoulders and my realization that we were out of sight of the ship and crew. My heart speeded up and I looked up at him, hoping he hadn't noticed. Then I thought about what this might mean.

"I'm not going to shoot the turtle!" I said, alarmed, as he stepped away.

"I'm not suggesting you do," he said, laughing. "Although if you can't shoot a turtle, how are you going to shoot a man?"

"That's different, I'd shoot a man who was trying to shoot or cut me down, but that turtle isn't threatening either of us."

"No, but she's good meat."

"What, you'd eat her?"

"Yes, of course, we all need fresh meat, and as often as possible in our way of life. It's not always so easy to come by, and turtle meat is delicious."

"How on earth would you eat something like that? How would you even cook it?"

"She's very handily carrying her cooking pot on her back."

I made no reply, it seemed cruel to just take her and eat her. She was paying us no heed at all—she had no idea of the danger she was in.

Leo laughed again. "Be calm, we'll leave her, we don't have time for a turtle hunt to feed the whole crew, but I do want her eggs."

"Is that what she's doing, laying eggs?" I asked, trying to ignore the fact that Leo was pulling his shirt over his head and off, but I found it hard to look away from the powerful shoulders and chest that marked him as a sailor. The tattoos pricked out on his skin stood out: a mermaid with an elaborate M underneath was a good likeness to the *Sound of Freedom's* figurehead, and I noticed a sandglass inside a heart as well before I realized Leo was smiling at me.

Embarrassed to be caught staring at him, I said, "She's finished." The turtle's flippers dragged her bulk slowly out of the hole in the sand, and I had to admire her determination and obstinacy as she inched up the shallow sandy incline. She flung sand about to re-cover the hole, then started her slow shuffle back toward the water. Leo dug the sand back out and placed all the eggs into his shirt, then tied it carefully into a protective packet before the oblivious shelled leviathan had made it back to sea and relative safety.

"We'll have to get a move on," Leo said, all captain again. "That sun's crept a lot further west than I thought. There—see that lump of driftwood?"

I nodded, strangely reluctant. I'd enjoyed the easy companionship we'd shared, but now he was all business. The wood was the first sizable piece I'd seen on the beach, probably due to last night's fire. Leo placed his shirt and egg parcel a few paces away, then stood to face me and lifted one of the guns still hanging from my neck. About the length of my forearm it was pretty unremarkable—except for the grinning horse's head carved into the butt. The flintlock mechanism sat atop and just afore the butt, and I wondered why Leo referred to it as a pecking bird. I thought it looked more like a man clutching the flint to his chest as if he were about to run off with his booty.

"Have you held one of these before?"

"No, Erik wouldn't let me near his guns—he kept them either locked up or on his person. I'm sure he knew who would be in my sights if he were careless."

"He didn't strike me as a careless man."

"No."

He held it out to me. "Feel the weight of it."

I took it off him and grasped the butt.

"Don't point it at *me*!"

"My apologies." Chastened, I turned and pointed the heavy gun at the lump of driftwood, then pulled the trigger. The flint struck the steel striking plate but, apart from a spark, nothing else happened.

"They don't work very well if they're not loaded," Leo said, smiling anew at my embarrassment. Then he looked serious again.

"I'll show you how to use this, but I need you to pay attention. One stray ball could kill anyone aboard, and I'm not ready to fall just yet—certainly not by your hand."

I nodded, but he hadn't finished.

"However difficult you find this on land, it will be three times as hard on the deck of a moving ship, especially charging your powder. One stray spark in the wrong place could send *Freedom* ablaze to the bottom. *Do not spill it.*

"Another thing, neither pistols nor muskets match well with water, so make sure you always keep them dry. If your powder gets wet, or the metal rusts, you may die when you could have lived.

"Next, if you have a gun in your hand you are more likely to be shot at in return." He paused. "And you'll be more likely to kill."

I looked at him, not knowing how to respond to that, but I didn't have to.

"Loading is simple." He took the horn of powder from me and poured a capful down the barrel before re-securing it and tucking it into the red sash wound around his waist. "Ball?"

"I beg your pardon?"

"You have the balls—the shot," he said, smiling.

"Oh . . . yes." I dug the small canvas bag out from the sash he'd given me when I first came aboard. My fingers were shaking slightly and I cursed them—and the fumble I made of untying the bag and extracting a lead ball about the size of my smallest fingernail.

Leo, still smiling, dropped it down the barrel, along with a greased patch of cloth which I also fumbled out of the bag. He slid out the ramrod from under the barrel, tapped down firmly and replaced the rod. Next he pulled out the pan to the right of the cock holding the flint, and poured in a little fine powder. He pulled the cock back halfway and asked, "Are you sure you want to do this? You don't have to, no one will think any the less of you."

That wasn't true—*I'd* think less of me if I didn't learn how to fight back. I nodded at him. My nerves were about being alone with a half-naked pirate captain rather than firing the gun. I held my hand out. He cocked the gun fully and gave it to me, but kept his hand on mine. He moved to my side, still facing me, put his other hand on my left shoulder and leaned against me. I was very aware that only the thin material of my shirt separated our skins, and my breathing quickened. I tried to breathe deeply, but that only made it worse. I focused on the weapon in my—our—hand.

"Hold your arm out to full stretch," Leo murmured against my ear. I did as he asked, hardly aware of anything but him.

"What are you aiming for?"

My heart pounded, then I remembered I was supposed to be shooting at driftwood. I moved my arm to the right, even closer to Leo's body, so I was pointing at my target. More or less.

"That's it, try and hold it still."

"It's heavy," I said, knowing full well that wasn't the reason for my shaking barrel.

"Take a breath." I heard Leo do the same, lips against my ear as he looked down the barrel with me. "Hold it, then breathe out as you pull the trigger. Then breathe out as you pull the trigger," he repeated. Oh yes, of course. I pulled the trigger, and banged my head against Leo's.

"Ay Caramba!" he said, laughing. "I forgot to warn you about the blowback. Well done."

"Did I hit it?"

"Well, no, try again. See if you can load it yourself, and this time keep your eyes open, it may help!"

I'd expected the gun to fire immediately the flint sparked, and I hadn't been prepared for the enormous flash as the powder in the priming pan set off the main charge a moment later. For a second I'd been blinded.

I tried again. Powder and patched shot. Ram home. Cock. Aim.

"Pan."

"What? Oh yes." I'd forgotten to fill the priming pan; my shot wouldn't fire without that. I carefully filled the small pan and pulled the flintlock to full-cock. I held it at full stretch, away from my face (my hand not trembling nearly so much now that Leo had stepped back), and fired. Sand kicked up just to the right of my target.

"Good shot!" Leo exclaimed.

"But I missed."

"Only just—they're not that accurate you know. If that log had been a man you'd have aimed for his heart and got his shoulder—that's enough to stop him. Hopefully."

"So I can join the next raid?"

"Well, if you practice, we'll see."

"What kind of answer is that?"

"A cautious one. Time for one more, then we need to get back to *Freedom*."

I turned to him, basking in his praise and attention, and he lifted his hand to my face. I jerked my head away and stepped back, then immediately realized by the look on his face that I'd misunderstood. He'd been trying to caress, not hit me. He looked shocked, then cold, and turned away from me.

"On second thoughts, we should get back to the ship, the tide's coming in and the wind's getting up. I need to make sure she's secure."

Chapter 45

GABRIELLA
20th May 1686
Three Leagues East of La Isla Magdalena

"Gabriella, I don't suppose there's any point in asking you to shelter in the cabin?" Leo asked as he passed.

"None at all," I said cheerfully. I had just come out of the cabin where Klara was suffering from seasickness. She did not like storms and had told me in no uncertain terms to get out and leave her alone. I was happy to oblige. If I stayed any longer in there with that smell, I would have been throwing up in sympathy. Anyway I *wanted* to be on deck, storm or no storm.

"Well, in that case, go forward and give them a hand hauling those clew lines, it'll free up another hand to go aloft. It looks like things are going to get interesting, I love a good storm!"

He strode down the steps to the quarterdeck, shouting orders as he went, and I stared after him in frustration. Since that day on the beach at La Isla Magdalena a month ago he had treated me as just another member of the crew. I was furious with myself, I had not really thought he would harm me, but I suppose the adage was true—old habits really did die hard. I had been thinking about the pistol and he had taken me by surprise, but surely he knew it was not him that I had shied away from? And was that really enough to put him off? I stared after him in frustration and for a moment almost hated him for turning his back on me. I had hoped he would try and kiss me again, but that seemed an impossibility now. I ran past him to help my crewmates.

My excitement grew with the increase in the wind and I caught hold of the end of the rope on the maindeck that Leo had pointed out. Jean-Claude and Jimmy were already swigging on it—grabbing hold when standing then dropping down to a crouch—

and I helped Carlos drag the slack they created through the block to make it fast around the belaying pin. They were singing their rhythm and obviously knew their shanty well. I found it strangely hypnotic and watched the sail far above me shake out its wind whilst my body did the work.

I was still trying to memorize what all the running rigging did and I watched the highest sail on the mainmast fold up on itself as we hauled. Each heave brought the bottom corners of the sail up toward the yard over which half a dozen men were lying in wait to grasp and tame it in the increasing wind. It was hard to keep my eye on them with the mast swaying around so much, but I watched open-mouthed as strong, leathery hands dragged up the center of the sail to make it fast, thinking they must have claws on those hands instead of fingers. I looked at my own ravaged hands and realized they still had a lot of hardening up to do.

"Are you helping or watching, lovey? 'Cause if it's a show you're wanting, you'd best get out of our way, we've a lot of work to do and not a lot of time to do it in!"

Jimmy had a point; if I was going to help, I had better get on with it. I ran forward to where Jean-Claude and Feliciano were now heaving on lines to knock the wind out of the fore-topsail, and I arrived just in time to grab the end of that sail's clewline and start heaving. Within minutes, all I was aware of was pain: the pain of the rope around my hand and the pain in my back and shoulders; even my legs hurt from bracing my weight on the deck.

"Let go, lovey! Let go!" I looked up at Jimmy in surprise. "Don't ever wrap the line around your hand like that! If it slips it'll haul your hand through the block and take it off. Do it like this!"

I twirled my hand to release the rope, eyeing the block in dread—would it really take my hand off? I grabbed hold again, this time clutching a single turn and kept my hand square to the line to give me some purchase. I nodded my thanks to Jimmy and hauled.

* * *

Half an hour later, sea and wind had both picked up and every third wave or so broke over the decks, leaving us waist-high in water until it drained through the scuppers and the next one thundered down on us. I felt like a pebble stuck in the rapids of a fast-flowing river as the rush of water swept my legs away again and I crashed into Jimmy, knocking him down as well.

"Get aft! Get aft!" Jimmy shouted at me. "We've one hand for the ship and one for ourselves—nobody's got none for you. You're in the way now, get yourself abaft!"

I was overwhelmed enough that I did not need telling twice and inched my way along the starboard bulwark to the aft of the ship, making sure I had something to hold onto and ducking down for shelter when the waves crashed into us. My feet were swept away again, more than once, but I fought the force of the water and hung on tight, dangling from shrouds, ratlins or anything else handy, but still with the ship. I noticed in disbelief that the men in the masts were still there; still handing sails; still being flung about left, right and center. My eyes were blinded by salt water again and I was reminded of my first night aboard—had I really thought we were sinking? That had been nothing compared to this.

I heard another voice close by and felt a strong hand grab my upper arm, but I could not see or hear who it was. I was dragged further aft where, thank God, or Neptune or whoever was in charge of the winds, I recognized my captor as Leo. I had feared it was Newton and that he would give me a helping hand overboard. I sagged in relief, but fell to the deck yet again when Leo let go of me and ran forward.

Annoyed at being abandoned so suddenly, I opened my mouth to protest, only to spit out seawater. I fumbled my way back, past the tiller with Mr. Davys and Mr. Frazer, his crutches abandoned, hanging onto it for dear life. I wondered briefly who was steering whom?

I reached the cabins and braced myself against their wall, hanging onto the steps leading up to the poopdeck. I still did not know why Leo had dropped me and was angry when I saw him emerge out of the spray. He came closer and I turned my back to the wind and the driving waves to berate him, but his expression stopped me. What would shock this man so much on his own decks?

Chapter 46

LEO

"Bear up! Get her head to wind!

"Watch those sheets, if we're caught aback in this, we'll spring the masts!"

Even as I shouted orders I knew he was gone. The waves were so big I'd lost sight of him almost immediately, but we had to try. *Freedom* was slowing, but it would take half an hour to wear her round and back to where he'd gone into the water. Jimmy's only hope was the longboat.

At least it was already in the water, being towed behind us. Thomas and a few others brought it alongside, despite the conditions, and climbed down into the tiny bucking boat.

"What happened? Did you see?" I asked Newton, who was also leaning over the rail and trying to spot our shipmate.

"I don't know. I think he was in the way of that last wave, it must have knocked the pegleg from under him and carried him over."

I nodded. The hardest thing about sailing through a storm was the enormous waves that broke over the decks. Jimmy wasn't the first sailor to be caught out, and neither would he be the last. We'd all heard the tales of ships that had lost an entire watch overboard in a heavy, gale-whipped swell.

I left Newton and went aft. Gabriella was still on deck; at least she hadn't been the one to go over. I was surprised at the stab of relief I felt and was immediately ashamed.

"What's happened? Why aren't we sailing?" she asked as soon as I got close enough to read her lips. I grabbed her arms and told her, "It's Jimmy, he's been swept overboard. He's gone."

I looked at her, her hair plastered to her face and her shirt soaked through and stuck to her skin. I was overtaken with desire and worry for her. *What had I been thinking, bringing her aboard?* She'd tried to pull away again when I'd grabbed her, and I realized she still kept her distance from the men and kept looking about her—*checking for ways of escape?* She shied away if my approach took her by surprise, and I couldn't forget the look of fear in her eyes on that beach when I'd moved to kiss her. *Do I frighten her so much?* I wanted to kill the man who'd done this to her—turned her into a frightened mouse. Although she was the most headstrong, wilful and plain disobedient mouse I'd ever met.

And now one of my crew was dead—another death that was on my hands as captain—and all I could think was how, despite my frustration, I'd never admired anyone so much for the way she held onto her strength through her fear. I was frightened by how much I wanted to hold this woman, to hang onto her and make sure she'd always be safe—yet I'd brought her to this most dangerous life. I'd most likely do worse than her husband and get her killed. I couldn't let another love die.

"You don't need to be out here, get into the cabin. I need to concentrate on finding Jimmy—I can't have you out here distracting me." I half-dragged her to the door of the chartroom despite her protests, and tried to ignore the injured look on her face before I turned away. This wasn't the time to pay attention to my heart—I needed her to be safe.

I grabbed my glass from inside and went back out. I could see the longboat, although it was obscured by the water in the troughs. I couldn't see Jimmy, and the weather was worsening. If I wasn't careful I'd lose the men in the longboat too, but could only wait for them to give up the search and return to the ship.

"He's gone, isn't he?"

I jumped. Gabriella had disobeyed me yet again, and had joined me at the rail.

"Yes. I thought I told you to stay inside."

"I decided not to."

"You realize that's mutiny?"

"Is it?"

"I could hang you from the yards for mutiny."

"But you won't."

"No."

What if it had been her? That was all I could think. *What if it had been her?*

We searched for hours, even though after only a few minutes we all knew we'd only been looking for a body. Eventually the longboat and her defeated men returned to *Freedom*, without even a pegleg to show for their labors.

We sailed on.

Chapter 47

GABRIELLA

We were back on the sands of La Isla Magdalena, but this time there was no treasure shanty. There was no singing or laughter at all. We had some damage to the rigging from the storm to repair and a shipmate to send off—his spirit, anyway. Neptune, or Leo's San Antonio, had already taken his body. I was more disturbed than I'd expected over Jimmy's death—it wasn't as if he'd been particularly welcoming or even nice to me. He'd rescued Klara and me that time from Newton and the others' attentions, but had only complained since. Now there'd be no more of his moaning, no more berating, and no more of his stamping about the decks. I realized I'd miss him.

I knew I was probably jumping to conclusions, but what if he'd been right? What if I *had* brought trouble down on him? I couldn't quite shake the suspicion that Newton, Smith or Ime had helped him overboard. But a suspicion was all it was. I was probably wrong; they were shipmates after all. I had neither proof nor certainty, and they didn't seem to be reacting to the accident any differently than the others. Yes, it was nonsense. It must be, although the smirk Newton habitually used instead of a smile kept me wondering. I knew he hadn't forgotten that day below decks, and I knew it was only Leo's threats that kept Klara and me safe from him. I shuddered. I wouldn't put it past him to have taken revenge that way.

I was more concerned about Leo. I'd thought we were getting close again and I'd enjoyed his attention the last time we were on this beach over a month ago. Since Jimmy's accident, though, we could hardly sustain a conversation, and he'd never shown any more inclination to try. He was cold, yet not rude; considerate, yet not friendly; and now he was more distant than ever. I told myself it was because of Jimmy. I knew he blamed himself, as he would for the death of anyone on his ship, and I hoped he just needed time. I tried to understand, but didn't. I was shocked at losing Jimmy so suddenly, but that shock quickly turned into a desire to live more; to make the most of each day just in case it was the last. Only the man who was the most important part of my day was staying out of my way.

I went to find the ship's sailmaker, George. We'd ripped a couple of sails when we wore round to search for Jimmy, and I knew he had a lot of repairs to get through. Despite it being very different from the embroidery I'd done before I came to sea, I found working on the sails relaxing and I took a great deal of satisfaction from forcing the big needle through canvas. I could tuck myself out of the way with the sail, needle and leather palm, and use the monotony of the task to watch my fellow crewmates at work. More than once I saw Leo start when he caught my eye and walk quickly away.

A wake for Jimmy was planned for the evening, and I hoped Leo would get back to normal afterwards. The rest of the ship too—everyone seemed quiet and irritable at this reminder of the risks we each took every day we were afloat.

Klara and I hadn't known Jimmy as well as everyone else aboard, we'd only been with them six weeks or so and, as usual, we tried to stay out of their way as they made their preparations. Another large fire took shape on the beach—there was always plenty of driftwood available in these waters—and casks were dragged out onto deck to serve as stools. The sunset behind the backdrop of large clouds was almost as spectacular as the dawn the last time we were here, and the whole world seemed bathed with fire; it was somehow very apt for a goodbye.

"Come on, lass." Mr. Gaunt had spotted me at the break of the poop, huddled against the cabin bulkhead with Klara. "He were thy crewmate an'all, and he took to thee more than he did the rest of us."

He laughed at my look of surprise. "He weren't one for showing his softer side, I knows that, but he did have a soft spot for thee, lass."

"Soft spot! He suffered me, he certainly didn't welcome me!"

"Aye. He didn't suffer anyone he didn't like."

I smiled at him, not sure if he was just trying to make me feel more included, but we walked with him to the huddle of men and rum punch on the maindeck.

"The captain has a soft spot too, he'll come round."

I looked sharply at him, but he'd moved to speak to Carlos who seemed to be guarding the rum tonight. I didn't get a chance to ask him to expand on what he'd said. He handed us beakers of rum punch, and I noticed Klara smirk, but before she could say anything, Leo stood up and everyone hushed.

"Jimmy was a hard man to get to know, and a harder one to like, but he was part of this ship and this crew and a valuable part at that."

"Aye, when he wasn't croaking about summat or other!"

I didn't see who shouted out, but I did recognize there was no malice in what was said. I was surprised at Leo's words as well, but this seemed to be the way these men grieved: with honesty.

Leo laughed. "Sí, he always told you what he thought, that's for sure!"

Then he raised his rumpot in a toast. "Jimmy. He was one of us, and he'll be missed."

"But not his cooking!"

There was more laughter and everyone drank, repeating, "Jimmy!" I did the same.

It was all very simple and somehow the laughter was appropriate—Jimmy would have had no patience with sorrow or tears. He had no tolerance in life for fuss; he wouldn't have appreciated it in death. Somehow, despite, or maybe because of the humor, this was sincere.

I lost sight of Leo for a moment while everyone was toasting and milling about, topping up their rumpots, and I stood up to look for him. He still hadn't spoken to me properly since the longboat had come back without Jimmy.

"Settle down, lass, he'll come around," Mr. Gaunt said again. I smiled, knowing I had a friend in him.

"He always takes a dying hard. Just give him time, lass."

I refilled his rumpot and gave it to him, then realized Leo was back. He and Frazer had carried a well-decorated seachest onto deck. Jimmy's seachest.

"Now where's he going?" I whispered to Mr. Gaunt as I watched Leo walk aft again. "What's he doing?"

"Cap don't do this bit," Mr. Gaunt whispered back. "He never takes none of his crew's chattels, never has. Mr. Frazer'll do the honors and Cap'll come back out when it's done."

I stayed quiet for a moment, thinking about what Mr. Gaunt had said, then asked, "He's taking this hard isn't he? I thought he was angry, but it's more than that."

"Aye, he takes loss hard does the Cap, always has for as long as I've known him. He lost his family when he were a nipper, then his childhood sweetheart were killt too. He's never forgot and he feels their loss every time he suffers a new 'un."

I looked at Mr. Gaunt again, his weather-beaten leathery face for once not stretched into a smile. He saw a lot with those sun-scorched eyes. I was saved from having to comment by Frazer's shout for attention.

"We've some business to take care of afore we drink to Jimmy proper, and I'd rather we got it over with. Jimmy didn't have no family, so there'll not be an auction, we've to share his dunnage 'tween ourselves."

"God bless him." That was Smith. I frowned. I doubted he was sincere.

"He'd not got much in the way of coin, I'll wager he'd already shared that with you through the dice."

There was laughter.

"Aye, he never had much fortune at casting the dice."

"What you left him we'll split equally with you all. Clothes and such'll go in the slopchest, I'll take his spare leg, then there's his seachest and his guns. We can't split them, so they'll go by vote or draw. Who should 'ave them?"

"He still owed me some winnings. I'll take them in lieu." That was Newton, but his words were greeted with groans.

"He couldn't stand you, Newton. He wouldn't have wanted you to have them." Frazer was nothing if not direct.

I looked at Newton. He'd turned bright red and looked like he wanted to strangle someone. I was glad I wasn't standing nearby.

"What about Gabriella?"

I looked up in surprise at the sound of Leo's voice.

"She and Klara are the only ones here without either, and she's probably the only one aboard who looked for his company, even when she wasn't hungry." More laughter. "She should take them."

I smiled at him, pleased he'd returned and was taking my part, but he didn't smile back. There was a chorus of "ayes", and more hate-filled glares from Newton and Smith, but I was getting used to those by now. I stared back until they remembered Leo's threat and dropped their eyes, and I had a pirate's chest for my riches, and the weapons to put in it.

The chest was unlike anything I'd seen before I came to sea, and was much more than a container. He'd made it himself from wood and spare canvas and had decorated it with shell and knotted line. *How many endless drifting calms had passed in this enterprise?* The handles in particular were works of art, and I couldn't work out where the complicated round knots started or ended. I loved all the intricate detailing and was proud to own it, even if I didn't have much to put in it. That would change. I wasn't going to rely on the generosity of pirates, even Leo, for my possessions and essentials. I needed to earn my own.

Whilst Mr. Gaunt and Mr. Frazer carried my new chest to my cabin for me, I went to thank Leo for his consideration.

"It was the only thing that made sense, you've nothing to thank me for."

"If you don't want my thanks can I ask for some of your time?"

"In aid of?"

"Another shooting lesson." We'd got on so well last time, I hoped it would ease whatever was wrong now, and things might even finish on a better note.

"You don't need another lesson. I've shown you how to use a gun. Take yourself off and keep practicing."

Then he looked at me for the first time since we'd dropped

anchor. He looked as if he would say something else, but instead clenched his jaw and strode from me to the flowing cask of rum punch and the rest of the crew. I went after him and grabbed his arm.

"What is it? Why are you being like this?"

Now he looked disgusted. "Jimmy's been gone less than a day and you want me to play with his guns with you? Have some respect, for the dead at least if not for the living." His voice rose until he was shouting and I watched him walk away, shocked at his outburst.

We'd spent the best part of a couple of months together, and his behavior toward me had been exemplary. Even in a place where his word was law and he could do whatever he wanted with or to me and Klara, he'd treated us with respect. Now he was angry, dismissive and rude. What was wrong with him? What was wrong with *me*? Didn't he like me after all? But if he didn't like me, why did he put up with me? Why had he spent so much time with me, patiently teaching me how to live in his world? He'd accepted me onto his crew and given me Jimmy's chest and guns, so why was he angry with me?

Chapter 48

LEO
22nd May 1686
La Isla Magdalena

I missed Jimmy. I missed his moaning and his tempers. I knew he'd done Gabriella and Klara a great service when they came aboard, even if no one would tell me exactly what that had been. If I grieved *his* loss so much, I'd break if I lost her. I couldn't risk that, not when near fifty lives besides hers depended on my decisions. I had to have her in my sight so I could protect her, and I cursed her for coming aboard in the first place. This was a dangerous life. Even disregarding the blades and guns, people died. Quickly and without warning, just like Jimmy. *What kind of life did she leave behind to feel safer at sea with me?*

"All well, Cap?"

I turned to see my carpenter, Gaunt, and I nodded in reply.

"Thee can't keep a ship at anchor forever or she'll rot away. Thee needs to let her fill her sails with wind if she's to live and love."

I knew he wasn't referring to the ship, but I pretended I'd misunderstood.

"Are we ready to weigh anchor?"

"Aye, Cap."

"Then let's be off." I didn't want his advice on anything but timber.

I looked up at the sound of the topsails filling; *Freedom's* bows swung around, and she crept closer to her anchor. The men heaved the capstan round, pulling in the anchor cable until we were up and down—right on top of it. A louder chant, followed by a sudden speeding up, marked our release from the bottom, and the jibs were sheeted in to windward. Backed against the wind like this they'd work against the topsails and hold us in position for the moment. The anchor broke the surface and was held at the bow. It would stay there until we were well away from the shallows, just in case something went wrong and we needed to drop it in a hurry.

Despite my best intentions, I sought out Gabriella. I didn't want to feast my eyes or feed my heart; I just wanted to make sure she was safe. I had a moment of panic when I couldn't find her, then spotted her when I looked up to watch the courses (the lowest and largest sails) being loosed. She was up the mainmast leaning over the yard, unfurling with the topmen. *When did she start working aloft?*

She looked down at me and, when our eyes met, she flinched backwards and caught herself on one of the hempen gaskets attached to the yard. My expression went from anger to fear and I waved at her, telling her to climb down. Instead she climbed higher, and I noticed she wasn't using the lubber's hole by the mast anymore. She got to the platform by clambering out and over the edge where the topmast shrouds anchored the topmast to the lower. This had to stop. I watched her settle herself at the maintop and realized she was staying as lookout. I tried to smile, but didn't think it was returned. She kept her gaze seaward. I didn't blame her.

Chapter 49

LEO
18th June 1686
La Isla Magdalena

"*Sail oh*, to the east."

I ran to the ratlins with my glass at Gabriella's shout. One of the benefits of this island was that it was out of the way of the more usual shipping routes—the area was littered with cays, sandbanks and reefs—and ships stayed away. A ship here could only mean trouble.

I climbed high enough to get a good look. I'd expected her to be hull down—so close to the horizon that I couldn't see her decks—but she was close, too close. She should have been spotted before this. I recognized *Edelweiss*. Blake had almost caught us unawares.

"What the devil are you doing up there, Gabriella?" I shouted. "A lookout needs to do just that, keep a sharp eye out—you could have just killed us all!"

I looked up into her shocked face and realized I'd gone too far, but if she was going to sail on my crew, she had to do the work well. This wasn't a game; there were men out there with a very real desire to kill us, and plenty more who'd happily do it for them for the contents of our seachests if they had the opportunity.

I climbed back down to the decks, shouting orders as I went, "Slip the anchor and get us underway! Gun crews, ready your pieces."

I reached Frazer on the quarterdeck and said one word, "Blake."

He nodded and looked at the approaching sail, then stood facing into wind.

"An offing will be difficult, the wind's swung southerly and we're now on a lee shore. Blake has the wind with him. Are we standing off west and running?"

"No," I replied. "East. If we can sneak between the sandbank and reef we may lure him in and wreck him."

"We might wreck ourselves," Frazer said.

"True, but I've kept charts—as you know well, Frazer. I know they're a little out of date, but I'm willing to bet the sands haven't shifted that much. We'll keep a sharp lookout."

He glanced up at Gabriella, who still looked to be sulking in the tops. "Better double it," he said.

I wanted to reprimand him, but he was right. The island was constantly exposed to the Atlantic swell and every storm could change the formation of sandbank, cay and island in hours. What I was proposing was dangerous, and I could lose *Freedom* and the lives of everyone aboard. I couldn't trust Gabriella's eyes alone. Staring into sun-sparkled water, looking for subtle changes in color to show us the sandbank, was a tall order for the experienced men; she didn't know well enough what to look for, and her eyes weren't used to the glare.

"Davys, up to the foretop. I need to know the extent of that sandbank ahead."

"Aye, Cap," he said, and leaped into the rigging, swarming up to the platform in seconds.

Frazer hauled the tiller over as the anchor warp slid into the sea, and we were free. The jibs were already backed against the wind to turn us, but we needed way on immediately to get steerage; the combination of wind and swell would have us on the beach in moments, and Blake was almost in range. Even if we executed the procedure perfectly, we had no room to maneuver. I could very well die a fool in the next few minutes, but this was an opportunity from which I could not, and would not, turn away.

We were to the southeast of La Isla Magdalena. To the north lay the headland that usually sheltered the anchorage from the prevailing northeasterly winds. To the east the sandbank lay; a hundred yards east of that, a coral reef awaited. Easterly again was Blake, coming fast with the wind. It was likely he didn't know about the reef. All I had to do was sail *Sound of Freedom* between the bank and reef to lure him in, circle around the other sandbanks to the north, then my guns could pound away at him at my leisure—but I had to get into position quickly.

"Set the main-topsail!" I shouted, and men jumped to shake out the massive sail.

"Are you sure about that?" Frazer asked, and we ducked as the first of Blake's ball hit *Freedom's* decks. "You're driving us into cannon range, *and* into treacherous waters."

"The whole of the Carib Sea is treacherous," I replied. "Easy on the helm. Fire starboard cannon!"

Chapter 50

A tremendous crunching and splitting of wood had my Freedom Fighters cheering. Blake was aground—his masts falling overboard. We had him. *I* had him and it had been easy.

A scream wiped the grin of triumph from my face, and I turned to see Smith clutch his neck as blood gushed down his shirt. A splinter from the newly shattered starboard bulwark had sliced through the side of his neck. Blake wasn't giving up without a fight, he was still firing on us. Gaunt rushed to help Smith, who had crumpled to the deck, but he soon got back to his feet and walked away. Smith was dead. He could stay where he'd fallen until we were out of this.

I shouted to my gunners to keep firing, and heard the order relayed down the decks. Frazer steered as best he could; he had no way of hearing instructions shouted down from the tops in that chaos, and was following Davys and Gabriella's hand signals from the main and foremasts.

More lead balls pummeled *Freedom* from Blake's stricken ship. I hadn't expected him to carry on firing with his ship in such dire straits, but he appeared willing to sacrifice *Edelweiss* and the safety of his men to take the opportunity to kill me. There was nothing I could do but sail on and fire back. I had the sandbank to larboard, and Blake and the reef to starboard, with no room to tack or wear round.

My guns fired again. The gunners were working quickly—they were scared.

Suddenly I fell forwards onto the deck. *Mierda!* We'd hit bottom. I shouted at Frazer, screamed at Blackman and Butler to fend us off with boat hooks, and cursed my two lookouts at the top of my voice. Jumping to my feet, I ran to the larboard rail and peered over the side. The gunners had been knocked out of their rhythm, and I could hear Blake's crew cheer in the sudden silence.

I held my breath and did my best to ignore their renewed

firing—there was nothing I could do about their guns at the moment. Our only hope was to get off this sandbank. If we were firmly aground, both crews were likely dead. I glared up at Davys and Gabriella. What had they been doing? This was *their* fault. I looked around at my decks. They were a mess. Men, lead, shards of splintered wood and rags of canvas lay in bloodied sand. My beautiful ship looked like kindling.

"She's shifting!" Blackman cried. "Ready larboard guns!"

Men ran across the decks to obey.

"Fire!"

The larboard guns fired and *Freedom* rolled to starboard, then fell free of the sandbank and we sailed on. Blake's men fell silent.

I prepared to order my men to harden up and tack so we could finish off Blake, but realized neither ship nor crew was in any state to carry on the fight. I wasn't even sure I could wear *Freedom* round safely with all the damage she'd taken. I looked across at *Edelweiss*. She was stranded and wrecked. I could leave Blake to the wind and tides; he wasn't going anywhere—the chances were good he'd die here. Yet I still found it extremely difficult to sail away and not make certain of his demise, even though I knew I had no choice. I had to repair *Freedom* and keep her men safe.

Chapter 51

GABRIELLA
25th July 1686
Two Leagues West of Gadalupe

I was the first to sight *Papillion* heading our way. It was my cry of "Sail oh," from the maintop platform that alerted Leo and the others. She was my prize, and I was determined to have a hand in taking her. Leo and I had barely spoken in the month since we'd run aground fighting Blake, but whether Leo wanted me or not, I was a member of this crew and it was time to start fighting.

My attention was divided between the growing sails ahead and the preparations being made below me, and my stomach tied up in knots as I watched them ready the ship for the fight. My shipmates tidied the rigging then cleared the deck to give themselves room to work (anything that wouldn't be needed in the next couple of hours was taken below, including the chickens and goats that I insisted got some air whenever possible), then I watched them scatter sand on the bare boards to provide grip and soak up spilled blood. The gunners got their powder up, prepared their cannon and put their rammers, spongers, ladles and other equipment within easy reach by the racks holding their shot.

Once the sharpshooters started to swarm up the rigging, I began my climb down to give my place at the maintop to Juaquim and his muskets. The best marksman aboard *Freedom*, the Portuguese would pick off the most troublesome of our adversaries should they decide to fight. It was a dangerous job, but at least he wasn't quite as exposed on the small platform as some of the others, who braced themselves in the rigging itself.

Once on deck, I headed to my cabin, now occupied by Feliciano and Juan manning the eight-pounder we shared the space with. Klara was nowhere to be seen. I grabbed Jimmy's guns, powder flask, and supply of shot and wadding—much to the amusement of the two Spaniards—glared at them, then headed back to the quarterdeck; to bump straight into Leo coming out of the chartroom, dressed up in hat, frockcoat, sash and leather boots.

"El infierno! Where do you think you're going with those?"

"I'm fighting. I'm ready."

"I don't think so—I've been watching you practice and I can't yet be sure of you hitting your mark. You're no expert with your blade either. You're staying out of this."

I stood my ground and glared at him, sick of his hostility. "I'm ready," I repeated.

He sighed; he didn't have time to argue, and I knew it. "You stay where I can see you on the maindeck. Let the men who know what they're doing take care of what they know best. You can show the colors on the first cannon shot and board with me once we're in control of her. Every one of these men, including myself, needs to concern himself with what's happening around us. We can't afford distractions or worries about your shot. See if you still think you're ready after this."

Distractions? I looked around, noting the intense expressions on every face and nodded. This wasn't the time to argue; the two ships were closing quickly, and Jean-Claude was ready on the bow cannon to give the warning shot on Leo's signal. My nerves jangled, and staying close to Leo suddenly seemed like a very good idea, despite his unfriendly manner. I nodded my acceptance of his terms.

We had the French Fleur de Lys flying to disguise us as a merchant vessel, and I moved to the foot of the mainmast, fore of Leo's position on the tiller. I watched the prize grow larger as we came together. Around me the decks were quiet; most of the men either hidden behind the bulwarks at their guns, or below and ready to open the gun ports, also on Jean-Claude's shot.

I was getting more and more excited, and more and more scared. My heartbeat thumped in my ears, my breath quickened and shallowed as I began to make out the people on the other deck—the captain strutting around his quarterdeck, shouting out orders as if it were any other day. The reality of this life sunk in then. In a few minutes a number of the human beings I could see and now hear may be dead, maybe someone from this deck, maybe even Klara or me. This was no game, and there would be no going back from this. By taking part in the attack, even if all I did was unfurl a flag to show our intention of violence, any blood spilled would be on my hands just as surely as the hand wielding the weapon that did the harm, no matter what Leo's sense of responsibility told him. In a few minutes I'd undeniably be a pirate. An outlaw and criminal who could be hung if caught, or shot at any time—and I couldn't wait to get started.

Out of the nervous stillness came a deafening roar—Jean-Claude. Stunned by the cacophony of sound in my head, I slowly grew aware of Leo shouting my name and remembered I had a job to do.

I pulled on the line in my hands and . . . nothing! I looked up and realized just how long this rope was, and how much slack I had to gather. I pulled quickly, hand-over-hand, bent my knees and fell to the deck until the knot finally pulled through way above me and the enormous square of black silk unfurled. A little late, but the order to surrender had been given. I admired it from my position supine on the deck, and thought of Leo's tattoo. It would look well picked out in white on that flag.

I stayed where I was, a heap on the wooden boards, and watched as my new friends stood over their starboard cannon with the match in their linstocks lit, ready to fire. It was an unmistakable show of force in itself. Yet more men stood at the rail, leaning forward and shouting curses and threats, blades unsheathed and waved in yet more promises of violence and murder.

Despite my bravado earlier, I didn't move even when I caught Leo laughing at me, but just watched, heart pounding with the noise and threat. I wasn't the only one. The men on the other deck looked just as scared as I was; frozen to the spot and ignoring their captain urging them to fight despite being hugely outgunned. I saw Leo look up and give a signal to Juaquim, presumably to shoot the only man prepared to stand up to us, and the opposing captain slumped to the deck, but he hadn't been shot. His own mate had beaten Juaquim to it and clubbed his captain with the butt of one of the few pistols they had. I wondered if it was carved as a horse's head like Leo's. Their flag was immediately struck.

I leaned my head back and breathed a huge sigh of relief, then heard a familiar chuckle.

"Are you ready, querida?" Leo, finally with a smile on his face, stood next to me, offering his hand. I was too shaken to be embarrassed about my earlier posturing, so took his hand and allowed him to help me up. We crossed to our prize, now secured alongside. I seemed to be in favor again.

Chapter 52

LEO

Gabriella pushed me closer to insanity every day. I knew where she was every second of every day and night. I found myself searching for her as soon as I went on deck—before I even checked the sails and compass. This was no way to command a ship. I'd given up trying to sleep in the chartroom, knowing she was the other side of a thin wooden partition. I'd taken to napping on deck with the other men, despite their smirks and laughter.

I loved her. I couldn't deny it anymore. I'd been in love with her since that day in Eckerstad and the spirit she'd shown—to have evaded van Ecken and his men—proved she was special. She'd proved it again aboard that slaver and many times since. I knew it, Frazer and Gaunt knew it, and apparently so did the rest of the crew. *Did she?* I didn't know. *Did she return my love or had I pushed her too far away?* I didn't know that either, but she had stayed aboard *Freedom* even though I'd given her an assurance I'd take her and Klara wherever they wanted to go. All she'd said was that they were happy where they were for the moment, smiled, then asked a question about the rig, or the rigging, or the wind, or anything else nautical.

Why's she making this so hard? Why's she still on my ship? She was all I could think about—even when we raided *Papillion* that morning my main concern had been to keep her safe. I'd have put her in the pinnace again, or tried to, safe with Jack and Alonso if I'd thought it would do any good, but she'd sailed *toward* the fight that first time, and I knew she'd do exactly the same again today. In the end, I let her help—to show our colors. I took the helm so she was right in front of me at the mainmast. Even though she was fully in my sight and very close (no one would be able to get to her before I could cut him down), I couldn't take my eyes off her. Her antics with the flag halyard had me laughing when I should have been concentrating on the other ship and my men.

There had been no consequences though. *Papillion* struck her colors without a fight—at least her first mate had some sense in his head. I helped Gabriella up, and we crossed to the prize together. The relief of the surrender had helped to break the tension between us, although she looked wary at my smile and seemed reluctant to take my arm. I couldn't blame her.

On the deck of *Papillion*, I shook hands with the sailor who had cold-cocked his captain. He immediately offered his ship's coin, cargo and stores in return for safe passage for the ship and crew. I agreed. We didn't need another ship of this size, and I had no intention of losing any of my men in an unnecessary fight. Besides, Gabriella was in earshot and it was suddenly important to me to appear merciful.

Papillion's crew had gathered on the foredeck and didn't appear to be armed, but Juaquim and Phillippe had formed a loose guard on them anyway. The mate joined them and I took a handful of Freedom Fighters below to have a look at what we had, then went aft, as usual, to the captain's cabin, leaving Frazer to organize the unloading of the main holds.

"You need to decide." Frazer had followed me on my search for charts and the log book. *Is everyone ignoring my orders now?* "I know you love her, it's obvious to all of us except you. You need to decide if you love her enough."

"What do you mean?"

"A mariner's life is dangerous at the best of times, a pirate's more so. The men need your attention on them. They will not trust you or fight for you when you're so distracted. There's some grumbling already and I don't blame them. Each of their lives is in your hands and I knows you well enough that you'd feel each of their deaths hard."

It was a long speech for Frazer.

"Give her up or conquer your fear and claim her," he continued.

"Are you giving me an ultimatum?"

"Aye. And if you ignore it, you'll be inviting mutiny. The men need to know where they are, or more accurately, where you and that woman are. Devil's bones, Leo! You're handing that Newton the opportunity to challenge you and he might win." He stared at me a moment, nodded, then turned and went forward to supervise the loading of the plunder.

He was right. I knew it; I'd known it a long time, but what could I do? I had to be near her, I had to have her within touching distance, but I couldn't touch her. Everyone I loved died. If I dragged her any closer to me she'd die too, and I couldn't stand to lose her. Every day I knew her that loss would be magnified. *But if she left the ship, would that not be the same loss?*

I watched her now. Excited, laughing—one of the crew enjoying our victory. I knew I'd have to take the risk—Frazer was right. I couldn't bear to lose her. I couldn't put her ashore. I had to give in to her. I had to trust her to stay alive.

Back on *Freedom's* foredeck, Gabriella looked to be overjoyed. She'd had a part in the attack (albeit a minor one), and there'd been no deaths or serious injury on either side.

"Don't speak too soon, querida, that captain would have them all hung for mutiny for the mate's actions—if they let him live. They'll have to get rid of him."

With perfect timing I saw the splash of the captain's exit overboard, but didn't draw Gabriella's attention to it.

"It's the law of the sea," I continued.

"You're not upset that another man has just died?"

So she had heard it.

"No, his blood's not on my hands."

"Well no, not directly," she agreed. "But he only died because we challenged his ship."

"He was his own man, and chose his own path—and death. I'm not held to account for another captain's decisions, only my own. He was prepared to sacrifice the lives of his crew to save his own skin from his master's anger at losing the cargo. His end was a fitting one."

"You're a difficult man to understand, Captain Santiago."

"Not really, I'm a man like any other man. I have the same desires and the same sorrows. There are rules in this life and I follow them. Well, most of them. I try to plot a navigable course through the obstacles in life and usually find passage through." I took a deep breath. "And now here you are. No matter how I try, I cannot find safe passage."

"Safe passage?"

"Sí. To keep you close is to put you in danger. To push you away is to put myself in despair. I'm sailing through a reef with submerged rocks thrown in my way just for the sheer hell of it, and I have no charts." I paused again, but I had to say it. "I don't want to lose you, Gabriella. I *can't* lose you. You have to decide whether you stay with me, but if you do, you *have* to stay. I won't survive losing you too."

"I thought you didn't want me, I thought you were pushing me away so I'd leave the ship."

"No, I was pushing you away because I thought you'd come to your senses and leave, especially after Jimmy's death. I thought you wouldn't want this life, that its price is too high. I needed to give you the opportunity to leave to see if you'd take it. I had to be sure you wanted to make your life with me before I dared offer it to you."

"Of course I want to live this life with you. Why do you think I stayed aboard, learning your trade—all your trades? Why would I have put myself through all that hard work and injury on your decks?"

"There's a difference between sharing this life and sharing this life with me. I needed to know you wanted *me*, not just *Sound of Freedom* and her adventure."

"You're a fool ever to have doubted that. I wanted to share your life when I first saw its reflection in your eyes, when you walked into that cabin and smiled instead of trembled at the threat there."

I rested my hands on her shoulders, then gently raised my right hand and slowly stroked her face. She didn't flinch.

"Gabriella." It was all I could say. El infierno, it was all I could think.

"What took you so long? You could have said all this weeks ago."

I couldn't help myself and laughed—something she made me do a lot. I could be nothing but honest, pirate or not, and the words fell out of my mouth.

"I was afraid."

"Afraid?"

"Yes."

"Why? I'm not going to hurt you, how could I?"

"It's not you."

"Then what?"

I paused, trying to find something believable to say, but I was stuck with the truth.

"I love you. Everyone I love dies. I'm afraid that if I give in to that love, I'll lose you, too."

She was silent.

I waited.

"I'll risk it," she said.

"No! I don't *want* you to take risks, I want you alive—alive and in my world." I was a little taken aback by the ferocity in my voice. She didn't blink.

"You helped me get away from Erik. He was my husband but he didn't feel that way. If not for you, he would have killed me. Possibly not by now, but if not, then soon. There's no doubt, before long he would have killed me and enjoyed doing it. You have not brought me closer to death, just the opposite, you've given me life. I told you, I'll take the risk, it's mine to take."

My heart thumped even harder with her assessment of her husband, but he could wait. I could not. I'd waited long enough. I moved my hand, which I realized was still cupping her face, around to the back of her head and pulled her toward me.

"Are you sure?" I asked, still trying to resist.

"Yes."

There was nothing left to say. I bent my neck, very slowly, and brought my lips close to hers. The moment of no return. I was lost in her eyes, her slightly salty smell, even the beating of her heart. Finally our lips touched and our faces opened to each other, drawn to each other, just as a compass needle is drawn north.

Our lips met again, this time more forcefully, and we pulled each other close. Skin and salt had never tasted so well. I felt bolts of fire connecting our bodies where we touched and could hardly breathe—not that I needed to, she was all the breath I needed. I opened my eyes (I hadn't realized I had closed them), and hers opened almost at the same moment. We stared at each other, connected by more than just sight. I was still struggling to breathe properly, but not out of fear anymore. And, even better, Gabriella's breath and heart matched my rhythm, beat for beat. It was too late for second thoughts. Wherever this took us, I was going; there was no turning back now.

Then she looked past me, over my shoulder, and I turned to see my crew standing and watching, grinning and nudging each other. I hoped Gabriella couldn't hear what they were saying, and I cursed the lack of privacy aboard a ship at sea.

I took Gabriella's arm and led her aft, shouting orders at the men as we walked past. There was still a lot of work to do to make *Freedom* shipshape again, but Frazer could handle it.

Heart hammering with anticipation I opened the door to Gabriella's cabin and followed her inside.

Chapter 53

GABRIELLA

He put his rough hands to my face, then slowly bent and kissed me again. Despite the salt, his lips tasted sweet. I knew then without doubt that I loved him, that I'd fallen in love with him almost the first time our eyes had met, back in that slaver's cabin. As I felt his tongue enter my mouth, flick over my teeth and meet my own reaching shyly toward his, I'd never felt such passion or desire. I wanted this man so badly; I hadn't known such emotion, such feeling, existed. Our lips parted and I looked into his eyes. I saw that he felt exactly the same—shocked, confused and scared. We'd both been living by our wits for so long, and been hurt so badly, albeit in very different ways, neither of us expected to want, need and trust another human being like this.

He kissed me again, and we stumbled against the bulkhead; we'd lost our sea legs, but I didn't care. Off came our coats, our breeches, our shirts. We finally stood together naked and alone in the middle of the ocean, drinking in the sight of each other. He fingered the amethyst necklace that I still wore, all he needed to do was give it one sharp tug and it would have been his, and I wouldn't have cared. Instead, he told me how beautiful it was, and that the only place he ever wanted to see it was resting on my chest.

"It belongs there," he whispered. "I want to be able to see it there against your skin, querida, always."

He kissed me again, harder this time, and pressed up against me as I leaned against the timber wall. I held him tight, enjoying the feel of his strong, well-muscled arms; his tanned back; his hard chest. His hands were all over me; touching, stroking, caressing. *Who knew that a man such as he could be so gentle?*

He pulled me away from the bulkhead and pushed me onto the cot in front of the stern windows as a large wave crashed against them; then the seas subsided again to a gentle, regular rhythm as wave after wave passed beneath *Freedom's* hull, carrying us along to who knew where.

I grew more and more excited. I couldn't believe the sensations coursing through my body. I hadn't known it was possible to feel like this, for my body to sing. Every touch from him felt like fire. I felt a tension building up in me, building and building until I screamed in frustration. I never wanted it to stop, yet I thought I'd burst from it; and then I did, and he cried out with me, both of us clinging to each other, my nails digging into the skin of his broad shoulders. Even then we couldn't pull ourselves apart, and we started to explore each other's bodies again. I had to touch every inch of him, to share every inch of myself with him. We needed to know each other physically as completely as we'd somehow known each other when we first met.

PART THREE

Chapter 54

GABRIELLA
15th January 1687
Two Leagues Southwest of St Eustatius

I sat on the forward end of the bowsprit and enjoyed the peace of a calm morning. I was happier than I'd ever known and had loved every day of my nine months at sea, despite the salt and the cuts and the bruises. In that time, I'd learnt how to sail a ship and taken part in dozens of raids. I was now truly a sailor and a pirate.

My attention was on the barely rippling deep turquoise water and the dolphins I could see playing around our stem, yet I concentrated my ears on the deck behind me, listening for Leo. It was hard to stay away from him, but the crew and ship needed his attention too, and I knew a growing number of men were grumbling about the amount of time we'd been spending together. It wouldn't be long before they made their feelings more obvious, but Leo wasn't prepared to do anything about it bar shout instructions to "¡Cállate y vela!"—Shut up and sail!—but I thought they had a point. He *was* neglecting them and *Sound of Freedom*, we both were, and whilst these past months with him had been wonderful, I wanted more. Being reliant on a man who professed to love me, a man whose crew was creeping closer to mutiny because of me, wasn't enough. I had to be in control of my own life. I hadn't escaped Erik to live looking to another as captain.

"*Sail oh*, to the sou'west."

I looked up to larboard and strained my eyes, trying to pick out the smudge of white Juaquim had seen from the maintop. I couldn't see anything but blue.

"Twinmaster, with Bermudan rig on both masts," Juaquim called down.

I squinted again, and could just make out a dirty smudge against the horizon, then lost it in the glare of sun on water and couldn't be sure I'd seen anything at all. Even so, this could be what I'd been waiting for.

I swung my legs over the bowsprit to turn myself about, stood and ran down the wooden spar to the foredeck, my feet knowing from experience where to step to avoid the knotted lines and blocks secured around it. Back on deck, I tried to contain my excitement and walked aft to the main-ratlins where Leo was entwined, glass held to his eye.

"She's flying the red, white and blue of the Netherlands, but I've not seen fore-and-afters on both masts like that afore," he called to the deck. "Heard of it though—a Dutch idea." He looked down at me, loving the thought of taking another Dutch ship, just in case it belonged to Erik. We'd been haranguing his shipping interests continually and must have put a sizable hole in his business and pocket by now. "What do you think, querida, do you fancy a little sport?"

"Aye, aye, Captain." I laughed. A Dutch vessel was indeed likely to be connected to my husband, especially in these waters. I hated that I was still married to him and was grateful for every opportunity to destroy his property and ruin his day. Leo jumped down from the rigging, his excitement clashing with concern; I'd finally managed to persuade him to allow me to lead a raid from the front. I still felt I had to prove myself to this crew, but Leo found my ambitions reckless and unnecessary.

"Are you sure you want to do this, querida? You don't have to be the first aboard."

"Yes, I do, and you know that well enough." I had other reasons for this being necessary, but this wasn't the time to confide in him. "Remember what you said to me when I first came aboard? 'There are no passengers aboard *Sound of Freedom*', you said I owed a sailor's fare."

"Yes, a sailor's fare, not a pirate's. You don't have to put yourself in danger."

"Of course I do, this is a pirate ship, I'm a member of a pirate crew and take a share in the profits. I need to do a pirate's work."

We'd been over this again and again, and he knew how determined I was—and that I was right.

"On one condition."

"You can't place conditions on me now, it's too late."

"I'm the captain of this ship, I can put whatever conditions I please on any crew member I want to. I can do what I like aboard this ship, including having you locked up in the cabin or below, out of harm's way. No, calm down, I'm not going to, but I could and you need to remember that—it's *my* word that counts on these decks."

Angry, I knew that was exactly why I needed to do what I was about to do. Whilst I loved Leo and had never been happier, it wasn't enough. He was captain and I was crew. He controlled what I did and where I did it. He decided when I slept and woke, the work I was to do and on what part of the ship, even who I spent time with. If I disobeyed he could punish me as a mutineer, and he couldn't afford to be lenient with me when the rest of the crew were watching. Erik had controlled me with violence; Leo controlled me with authority. Despite the name of the ship, I didn't feel free, rather my spirit was still chained—anchored—to a place from which I wanted to sail away.

I needed to feel *free,* to be in charge of my own fate; not to be told constantly what I was and was not supposed to do. As much as I loved Leo, I needed to make my own choices, my own decisions, but I had to be careful and keep my thoughts to myself for the time being. He must not guess my plans until I was ready to share them.

"What's the condition?" I asked, lips and voice tight.

"I'm coming with you."

I breathed a sigh of relief and nodded. That wouldn't spoil my plans, and might even show him that I was capable of looking after myself and doing this.

"Can I have a look at her?" It was my only answer—let him think he'd won something. He handed me his glass with a smile and I took a good look at my intended prize.

She was quite a bit smaller than *Freedom* and looked to have only a small crew—she wouldn't need many hands to handle that triangular rig without square sails to make it complicated. The sun lit up her canvas, which glowed with its heat, looking like something an angel would choose to take to sea, and her figurehead caught my eye. Carved in the old style, she looked to have a unicorn leaping out of her bows below her high bowsprit. Perfect.

"She's dipping her colors," I told Leo. Lowering the flag slightly and immediately re-hoisting was a customary greeting at sea, as well as a request to a ship to identify herself.

"Send up Dutch colors," he said to Gibson. "Let her think we're friendly."

I kept my eye on the prize. "She seems satisfied, she's altering course toward us—she must think we have news for her."

"Sí. Or she's playing the same game we are. Don't trust her actions, Gabriella, not until she's ours."

I nodded, unwilling to look away. The closer she got, the more beautiful she became. "She's sailing well for so little breeze," I said to Leo. "If she runs, she'll be hard to catch."

"Oh, we'll catch her all right, so long as we've got her in sight. We'll have her when the wind fills in," Gibson said from the helm. "It'll likely blow in from the nor'east'ard and she'll be downwind of us. Even with that Bermudan rig she'll not sail fast enough closehauled to get past and outrun us. Downwind we'll get her easy. It'll take time, but we'll have her in the end."

"Gracias, Gibson," Leo said. "But she's lively—you know as well as I do she'll be hard to catch unless our colors fool her long enough for us to get close-to."

"They haven't," I told them. "She's hardened up again, she's trying to sail past us to windward."

"Give me that," Leo said, his hand held out for the telescope. "Sí, nor'east, clever. If he ducks behind us, he knows we'll have no hope of tacking without more wind. It's risky, but if he pulls it off he'll have the weather gage to his advantage once the wind fills. Hard to larboard!" he shouted by my ear, taking me by surprise. "Haul those braces round, hard—we've only got the one chance to cut him off. Get the leeward bower anchor ready to loose, we'll club-haul her if we need to, to get her round! And make sure he can see you do it, I don't want him to miss our intentions."

I looked at him; his own excitement was building at the challenge of beating a captain whom he already respected. "There's no point in pretending any more, break out the black flag and give him a look at the guns, let's see if he'll scare off and run. We can't let him get past us." He'd forgotten I was to lead the raid; the challenge of the hunt had taken him over.

"If we can cut her off and force her back round to the south, we'll get behind her and have a chance, especially if we can get a touch higher," Gibson explained. "Our square sails'll take a following wind better than them she has, and if we can get and stay 'tween her sails and the wind she'll have nowhere to go. If she gets past us to windward, she's as good as gone."

She saw our intent and didn't risk sneaking past within gun range, but tacked and bore right round to the south in a bid to escape. We bore off as well and gave chase. I couldn't help but admire how easily she'd tacked in the light airs and saw she was betting on getting far enough ahead to outrun us before the wind. We were both in the hands of the same wind gods. If they sent wind, and from the usual east or northeast, we'd have our prize; if they did not, she'd get away. It was that simple.

Chapter 55

"Here, take the helm, querida. Being a pirate isn't all guns blazing and bows foaming, this is the hardest chase there is at sea—chasing your prey whilst chasing your wind. One lapse in concentration can lose both, and the whole day and effort will be for naught." I sighed in frustration at his lecturing tone, but he hadn't finished. "Keep your eye on the wind behind—what little there is—the sails, and the prize ahead. Trust Frazer on the main, Blackman at the mizzen and Newton on the foremast to trim the sails well, but it's up to you to make sure they don't work against each other on the different masts. All we need to do is keep the prize in sight until the wind fills in, and she'll do everything she can to prevent that." I nodded. "It'll be an interesting contest—what little wind we have is behind us, so we control it, at least for the moment. But that boat with that rig can maneuver quicker and easier than we can, and will gain every time she can force us to wear ship. She's smaller, lighter and faster. This will not be an easy contest. I'm going to put the boats off, maybe we can warp her to a bit more speed. Until I get back, concentrate on your helm and sing out when you change course—advance warning of a luff or loose will help the men find the set of their sails quickly."

At last he left me to it. This *was* my chase, he *had* remembered. We were barely moving, but my stomach was a nest of mosquitoes as if I were facing a battle through storm-whipped Cape Horn graybeards, not a slow drift about the Carib Sea.

The prize luffed and picked up a little more speed as she sailed closer to the wind. "Bearing up to windward!" I called and pushed the tiller over to starboard to turn *Freedom's* bows a point to larboard. I wanted to show the other vessel that we were watching and would respond to everything she did—I would not let her go.

The men grunted and chanted and forced the heavy yards round to their new positions, all of us infected with the thrill of the crawling chase. The rigging creaked and protested, the sails flapped lazily to catch what little wind there was on offer, and the bows slowly, slowly swung round.

"Bearing off!"

Everything reverted to where it had been as the prize swung back to starboard and I followed. Her rig was much easier to handle than *Freedom's*; it looked like her tactic was to tire us out.

"That's it, querida¸ let her know we can match her every course change." Leo was back, and I looked forward at the longboat and pinnace rowing out ahead of us. The warps between the boats and *Freedom* slowly tightened, and I felt a jerk shake out what little wind filled the sails as the ship responded to their oars and moved forward.

"It's times like this I think we should have sweeps after all, despite that they get in the way of the guns."

I shrugged. Sweeps were large oars fitted to the lower deck of a ship, but I wanted to sail, not row–surely warping would be enough? Anyway, every man was on a line or oar, who would man the long sweeps if *Freedom* had them?

"She's jibing. Stand by to wear ship!" Leo shouted.

Three hours, no change. Luff, bear off, wear ship. Luff, bear off, wear ship. It was exhausting work, interspersed with long periods of inactivity while we waited for the twinmaster's next move, and we didn't know what reward we would win, if any. We were dead in the water after the last wear. Again. The men in the boats had changed once more, but they were running out of strength and *Freedom* barely moved. The chanting on deck had hushed and each course change was greeted with groans. We needed wind. Leo had brought a cask of rum punch on deck after the first two hours, but that was long gone and it would be another hour before he would permit another one–it helped to keep the crew working and talking of gold aboard the prize, but it wouldn't help them shoot straight once we caught her.

Leo took a trick at the helm to give me a rest. Everyone else was on a sheet, brace or boat's oar. I was exhausted, despite not doing any of the hard work in trimming the sails. I went to the stern rail, just in case the ripples alongside our boards were lying. I wanted to see the wake we left behind us, knowing that would prove beyond doubt we were moving. I needed to know we were at least drifting in the right direction, but I got more than I bargained for. It took me a moment to realize what the shadows on the water meant, then:

"Wind! We've got wind!" I shouted, excited, and most of the crew ran aft to see for themselves.

"Get back to your braces!" Leo shouted. "This is where the real work begins!"

Teams of men ran to the larboard and starboard of all three masts, ready to haul on yards and sheets again to make the most of each new puff of air. Each extra knot of speed would be hard won, and I grabbed the Dutchman's log to record it, then dropped it. We didn't need to know how many knots we made, we only needed to sail faster than the ship ahead.

Now we were moving! Slowly, true enough, but we were moving. If I listened carefully I could just hear the gurgling of flowing water under our keel—Leo's sound of freedom, although it did not signal freedom for the sails still on our horizon. We were lucky, the wind had filled in behind us as hoped and, when it reached the prize, it would bring us with it. It was only a matter of time now, and time had just sped up with the wind. I could smile again. We would get her. *I* would get her.

Everybody came back to life: where there had been men lounging under the awning shading the maindeck from the sun, enjoying their pipes and grumbling while they waited for the next shout to man the braces, now there was organized activity and shanties. The yards were braced yet again, their gear coiled down and cleared; the guns run out once more, and their gunners ready and waiting. As usual before a fight, buckets of sand and water were positioned around the decks in case of fire; pistols and muskets were hauled to the tops. The decks were cleared for battle and black silk streamed from the masthead instead of hanging limp. We were hauling her in now. I could see her getting closer and closer.

"Frazer," Leo called. "Load grapeshot in the bow chasers, if we can shred her sails, she'll be dead in the water. And get the boats back in, the men'll be needed on deck.

"She's regretting her run downwind now," he added, almost to himself.

The sun was setting off our starboard bow by the time she was in range. We'd spent the whole day on the chase, yet had barely covered any water. No matter, she was almost done.

I could see her more clearly now. A large twinmasted sloop built of red Jamaican cedar, she didn't look like she'd been afloat long—her woodwork still gleamed and her sails were still whitish rather than dirty brown. I took my eye from the glass and handed it back to Leo with a smile.

"She's beautiful. It seems a shame to fire on her."

"That's up to her captain," Leo said. "We'll do what we have to, to take her after all the effort we've put in. There go her colors, maybe we won't have to fire, but I'll not be taking any chances."

I could see her without the glass now and gripped the tiller. We were catching her quickly; she'd put up a valiant resistance, but had dropped her colors; she seemed to know she was beaten. *Or did she?* Leo seemed fairly certain her strike was a ruse. We'd see. If it was a trick we still had our chance and it was up to me to take it. I had to keep our sails between the new wind and the sloop. As long as she was in our wind shadow, she wasn't going anywhere. It was up to me on the helm to haul her in.

Closer.

Closer.

Oh no! She's heeling! She's caught the wind. Panicking, I looked up at Leo. I'd failed. I hadn't kept the wind from her. He burst out laughing.

"Don't look so worried, Gabriella. Calm yourself, the wind was always going to get to her. We've delayed it well, as long as anyone could. She may be moving, but so are we and we still have the weather gage. We're not done yet." Then, louder: 'Prime the guns! Juaquim get aloft, we may need your sharpshooting very soon. We'll have our reward yet, men!"

A cheer went up as the crew filled with energy at the thought of the coming fight. We'd kept her in sight. Despite all her maneuvering, we'd kept her under our control. It was now time to take her for our own.

Chapter 56

I stood at the rail, screaming threats with the rest of the boarding party to intimidate the small crew. We—I—needed them to submit and be too scared to put up a fight.

I had a coil of strong line in my left hand, and the grapnel in my right would give the signal to the others to throw. Jimmy's guns were draped around my neck and my belt held my falchion and an extremely sharp dagger. I had to judge this perfectly. *Are we close enough yet?* I took a deep breath and threw. My grapnel, chased by a dozen more, hurtled into the rigging of the smaller ship, and yet more caught her bulwarks. I backed up, grabbed the line with both hands, and jumped, still screaming as I flew down to her decks. As soon as I crossed her sides I dropped to the deck and scrabbled for my guns. I needed my weapons—now.

Suddenly, cannon exploded to my right and a shot cracked out from above. Juaquim, high up in *Freedom's* rigging, had spotted the man who had fired, and killed him. He'd got his load of swan shot off, but Juaquim had spoiled his aim and it shredded our sails rather than our men.

I'd landed amidships with Leo beside me, and fired my first gun at a man who rushed me as I found my feet. At the same time, Leo discharged his. The man fell and I looked at Leo, grinning in excitement, and pulled my blades as I watched two more men fall from Juaquim's musket balls. Then another fell back down the mainhatch where he'd been hiding to fire his own muskets. So much for striking in surrender!

There was only the captain and one other left, and I pointed my second gun at him. He tried to push his man in front of him, but Leo fired and the crewman dropped to the deck. I lowered my gun and met Leo's glance, but the captain wasn't done. He saw our lack of attention and charged us, well, me. I turned back at Leo's warning shout and knocked his cutlass away to my left, brought my knee into his groin and thrust my dagger into his side. I heard Leo's grunt of rage as he knocked the man away from me. Disarmed and bleeding, he scrabbled on the deck and whimpered at our feet. Leo was disgusted.

"Get up you fool, what kind of man are you?" He turned to me. "By the smell of him he's rum-soaked himself into believing he has the courage and battle skills of a warrior." He sneered at the man on the deck again. "But look at you, swept aside by a woman and cowering on your own decks—your men dead or injured, you're a disgrace to the sea."

More Freedom Fighters swung down beside us as he spoke, shrieking and shouting every second, but there was nobody left to fight.

"We're not done yet," Leo hissed, and I ran with him to the main hatch. Thomas and Phillippe had gone below after the shooter, and we needed to know there was no more danger aboard the ship.

"Let me go first," I said, pushing at Leo. He ignored me and slid down the opening in the deck. Secretly relieved, I followed. It was over. The dead man had fallen on his two companions who hadn't had time to extricate themselves and re-join the fight. We'd won.

"Come on, querida, it's not time to celebrate yet."

I took my arms away from around Leo's neck and narrowed my eyes. I'd just taken my first prize. *My* prize—and I wanted a congratulatory kiss.

"We need to check the captain's cabin and his logbooks and see what we've won," he continued. "After you."

I led the way aft to the cabin below the quarterdeck and started to look through the papers strewn over the chart-table.

"Your shoulder!"

I hadn't noticed it until Leo exclaimed at the blood staining my shirt. The captain must have cut me when I knocked him away, and I sat on the cot to let Leo bind it, shaking after the excitement. After a slow, frustrating day, the attack had been quick, efficient and deadly. I was exhausted.

"Right then, lass, first aboard, what does thee choose for thy battle honors?" Gaunt grinned as he came in to report that mine was the only injury to our crew, and Leo paused to wait for my answer.

"I want the ship," I said. "I want my own boat."

Chapter 57

LEO
16th January 1687

I woke with the rays of the winter sun peering through the stern gallery of *Freedom's* windows. I looked at Gabriella, still fast asleep, and smiled. I thought about waking her up to enjoy the dawning of a new day with me, but decided against it and let her sleep after yesterday's excitement. Her insistence on working as hard as anyone else on the crew was exhausting her. She wasn't built for such heavy work; she needed rest—not that she'd admit it.

I loved the Carib winters; warm and dry took over from scorching and dripping, and the steady winds from the east or northeast made it a mariner's paradise, despite the occasional heavy blow from the north. I could just see the curving tip of the sun above the horizon to the east, spreading golden light north and south where sky met sea. There were no clouds to add to the beauty this morning, just blue and gold that blended and danced over the water and reached into my cabin to touch us with warmth and life. I watched the sun's rays caress Gabriella beside me, her face and arms glowing at the touch, and wondered at the last year and what it had brought. I'd thought love had died with Magdalena; I hadn't given any thought to finding it again, and certainly not aboard a slaveship!

Even then I'd held back, nearly three months. I needed to know that she'd chosen not just me, but this life. I had to be sure of what she really wanted. I'd needed to know I was more than a means of escape before I could take the risk of letting Gabriella take root in my heart, but she had taken root—there was no pulling her out now.

And now I was happy. And now I had everything to lose, again. There were so many ways for her to be killed. Just like

Magdalena; just like Mamá and Papá; just like so many members of my crew. Shot, stabbed, a fall overboard, a fall from the rigging, drowned if *Freedom* foundered, or worse: captured and hung as a pirate. Every night I lost her. Every morning my first thought was to ensure my nightmare was a dream, and now she wanted a ship of her own, where I wouldn't be able to keep her safe.

I jumped out of my thoughts at a touch to my face. Gabriella had woken and smiled at my frown. The sun had risen fully now and was a gleaming gold coin shining down on us; tempting us, promising us, with more. More riches, more love, more days. And I wanted those days with Gabriella. I wanted her at my side, all day, every day, not on another vessel, out of sight and reach.

I smiled in return and kissed her, but I hadn't succeeded in hiding my thoughts from her.

"Trust me," she said. "I don't want to leave you and I'm not going to, but I need to do this. I need to be at the helm of my own ship. I'll be with you because I want to be, not because I have to be. I've never had choice before, I've always been at the mercy of the whims of another and I can't be happy living like that anymore."

"But you do have choice," I retorted. "You're not a prisoner, you can go wherever you want, do whatever you want to do."

"On *your* ship. With *your* crew. By your *command.* I can only go where you direct the helmsman. I can only do what you allow me to do."

"Well, yes, but I'm the captain of this ship and I'm responsible for every soul aboard her. I don't want to control you. You've already seen how easy it is to die out here; I just want to keep you safe." *Did she not understand that yet?*

"But *I* want to look after *my* soul. I need to be responsible for myself, and it's just as easy to die on this ship as another. You named this ship *Sound of Freedom*, but you won't allow me the freedom to make my own choices. You keep me too close."

"How can you be too close to me? Why don't you want to be close?"

"You still don't understand! I *do* want to be close to you, I just want to be able to make decisions for myself!"

I could see her temper rising again and knew I was only barely holding onto my own. We'd get no further if we carried on like this, and in any case, a decision this big would have to be agreed by the whole crew. I knew she had little chance of captaining the prize, whatever she said. I reached for her to draw her closer.

"There's no denying you're a pirate, querida." She did not want to fight, and smiled again as she kissed me, curling her arm around my neck, the sun hot where it fell on our bodies.

I knew I should be out on deck, but my men could look after themselves for a while. *Freedom* seemed happy enough. Her motion was regular as she skipped through the waves, thrusting forward with the wind behind pushing her onward, happy to be on the move, powered up and excited, racing toward our future, exhilarated and leaving the past behind in our wake.

I hugged Gabriella tightly. A year ago I had nothing. Now I had everything, and I would do whatever was necessary to hold on to it. She would not be sailing on any vessel but this one.

A heaving shanty rang out and I looked up at the ripped fore-topsail being lowered so a new one could be bent to the yard then sent up to replace it. The best sails in a calm were the thinnest, the lightest ones, but unfortunately they tore easily, often for no apparent reason. I could feel a light breath on my left cheek; the wind was shifting already.

"Come on men, put your backs into it. I want that sail replaced before the wind picks up."

I looked back aloft at the half dozen sailors handing the sail, and realized Gabriella had taken the hardest and most dangerous position on the weather earing—right at the end of the yard—despite her wounded shoulder. I sighed when I saw her pause and look across at the prize sailing off our starboard quarter, Frazer at her helm. I realized that she wanted this badly, and there'd be no peace until she got it. *Is this what she'd wanted all along? A command rather than a captain?*

I took Papá's glass out and examined the sloop. I couldn't deny she was a good-looking boat (yes, boat, whatever Gabriella said, she didn't have enough masts to be called ship). She looked to be well-balanced with graceful lines, and I wagered she'd sail well in a breeze. She'd be easy to handle as well with those fore-and-afters; it would be like sailing an enormous pinnace and use the same boat-handling skills in the main, just doubled and enlarged.

Maybe it wouldn't be a bad idea to sail with a consort again. We'd worked well with the *Magdalena* in our lee and this one was bigger—the two vessels could work well together. She was fast and weatherly, she maneuvered well and would sail rings around a bigger, heavily laden ship. If we put topsails on her, and maybe even added a square forecourse, she'd do better in a chase, too. But was Gabriella ready? Captaining a ship, any ship, was harder than she seemed to think. Even with an experienced and willing crew that I trusted, the fact was she'd been at sea less than a year and didn't have the experience to command a pirate ship. *And* she was a woman. No.

"Watch it, I don't want to have to repair the forecourse as well!" I called as the men jerked the halyard, swinging the wooden spar around the rigging.

I thought back to Frazer's warning. The men were grumbling about the watches I spent in the cabin rather than on deck. Would this be a solution? Or would it inflame mutinous feeling? We barely had enough hands to man *Freedom* under full sail in a chase; we didn't have enough to work two vessels. Even though the sloop only needed half a dozen men to sail her, we'd need more men from somewhere to fight her, and they'd all have to be able-bodied.

The yard hit the deck and George immediately stooped to inspect the damaged sail before Gibson and the others had a chance to unbend it, whilst Blackman supervised the rigging of the replacement.

Aloft, Gabriella still stared aft. I could understand her yearning for freedom, but I still wanted to hold her close. If I allowed this, at least she wouldn't be on her own; she'd be sailing in company and would have to follow my decisions and directions. With the right first mate, preferably Frazer, the right sailing decisions would be made. If he was willing, that is, asking him to sail under the command of a woman was not a small request, especially as he knew what would happen if she came to any harm.

I realized I didn't want to let the crew vote on this. I had no idea what they would choose. *Would they be insulted? Or would the superstitious goats jump at the opportunity to get an "unlucky" woman off their decks?* But even though I was captain, I had no choice, the articles were clear. This wasn't my decision, it was the whole crew's, and I had to make the best of it.

So what do I do? Do I talk for her or against?

"Land oh!"

Cloud off our larboard bow showed the position of Saint Croix.

"Leave it to larboard, Thomas, and steer north to lay Sankt Jan Island."

Nearly there. The Danish island just off Sankt Tomas was quiet and had everything we'd need. The crew would vote as they always did, and I'd take the consequences and make them work, as I always did.

The foretop yard was back in position and, as I watched the new sail loose and set, I realized that was exactly what I needed to let Gabriella do: set her sails. She'd make her choices, but I'd be there to catch her if she made a wrong one.

Chapter 58

GABRIELLA

"Calm yourself, lass," Gaunt encouraged me. "Thee's with friends here, just talk to 'em like thee does every day. If thee's managed to talk Cap round, thee'll talk the rest of 'em round an'all."

I smiled at him and looked at the beach. A large fire had been built and the crew had ferried the few more valuable contents of the prize ashore in the remaining boats (what was left of her original crew had been set adrift in one of them, as usual). The light was almost gone and the last of the sun shone on the ships anchored in the natural bay. I admired what I hoped was my new ship off *Freedom's* starboard beam and my belly flipped again with nerves. I'd spoken to everyone together before, but this was different. I wanted this desperately and I had no idea how the men would react.

I jumped when I felt pressure on my shoulders, then relaxed against Leo's chest.

"It's time, querida."

He squeezed my uninjured shoulder, and I turned and headed to the boat where Thomas waited to take us ashore and begin the night's celebrations.

I had one chance at this. Only one chance to convince these men to trust me, and some of them to sail under me. Some would be relieved to get me off *Freedom's* decks and away from their captain, others would be insulted, but, hopefully, most would be supportive. I stood in front of the fire on the beach and took a moment to look each man in the eye.

"Klara and I owe you our lives. You saved us when you brought us aboard *Freedom* from that slaver. You've taught us a new way to live: a way of life neither of us dreamed possible. Our lives have never been so good since we came aboard *Sound of Freedom;*

until we made friends, fell in love and were loved back." I smiled at Klara and Obi. "You've become our family and I hope we've both earned your respect just as each one of you has earned ours."

"Shut up, Newton," someone said at the back, but I had missed the comment. I gulped, wondering what he had said, and turned to Leo.

"You all gave me my freedom but, ironically, my love for your captain is stopping me being free." I smiled to try and soften Leo's scowl. "You know I don't mean that I want to be free of you, but you are the captain of this ship. Your decision is final and mine doesn't count. I've lived that way all my life, controlled first by my father then my husband. I've never stood on my own. I've never been allowed to *choose* how my life unfolds.

"I've spent the past year getting to know all of you and the way you live your lives. I'm asking you for the same choices. I want to stand on my own." I turned back to Leo. "I don't want to leave you, yet I don't want to be so completely tied to you either, *Freedom's* articles notwithstanding. I want to be with you and *will* be with you, not because I'm aboard your ship on an empty sea, but because I can go where I want to, at my own helm, yet choose to sail and fight alongside you."

I tore my eyes from Leo and looked around at the men again. I couldn't tell what they were thinking, so pressed on.

"I understand you all have to agree and vote on this, and you know the tactical advantages better than I, but I hope you will see how important this is to me, and will help me prove myself to you—and that some of you will sail with me, of course." I looked at Gaunt, trying to smile. *Oh God, what if they said no?* Was I making a fool of myself? I flexed my left shoulder, my hand going to the wound I'd suffered in the fight.

"I know some of you will be angered by my presumption in asking for a command, although I'm sure most of you will be relieved to have *Freedom* free of women again." I smiled. "I'm not trying to put myself above you. I'm not trying to claim I'm a better sailor or even as good a sailor as you. I know I'm not, I'm just asking you for the chance to be." I did not know what else to say, and had a sense I was losing them. Leo came to my rescue and took my place.

"I'm not sure I'm happy about this either, but I've thought it over and I think it's a good idea to replace the *Magdalena*. As far as Gabriella as captain goes, I'm aware that I've been neglecting you and *Sound of Freedom,* and that can't go on. Neither will I go on without her. This does seem a satisfactory solution."

"It's all right, Cap, we've managed well enough without you!"

He laughed, then carried on. "I can also see that Gabriella needs to do this, and although she does lack experience, she will have experienced hands sailing with her, and my backing. If it helps, Gabriella has agreed that she will not take a share of the plunder out of this prize."

"So what? There wasn't any decent plunder in her, just cloth and sugar!"

"There's value in cloth and sugar, as you know well."

"One share, even with battle honors, doesn't pay for a boat like that."

"No, but I hadn't finished. I'll forego the captain's share too, and we've agreed that future plunder will be split as it is now. Gabriella will not be taking a captain's share of your profits. No one will lose, and we'll have more chance of taking bigger, richer prizes, just as we did with the *Magdalena*. We've seen the prize is good in light airs—and she'll be even better once we've made a few alterations. She's fast and handy and will complement *Freedom's* size and firepower well. With the right tactics, not many will escape us. Do not fear, if you allow Gabriella this chance to prove herself, she'll be earning her place on the quarterdeck, and together we'll be unbeatable."

I looked at him, *is he referring to the ships or to us?*

"We're not asking you for a decision now. Think about it, celebrate our latest victory and we'll take the vote at noon tomorrow. Gabriella will abide by your decision, as will I."

He looked at me and I nodded my agreement, albeit reluctantly. It was out of my hands now.

* * *

The next morning, I could barely look at anyone, terrified of how they would vote. My face ached from smiling, and I jumped at Leo's suggestion to go for a walk.

"Don't get upset if they say no, that'd just mean they want to keep you aboard *Freedom*. But whatever their decision, you know you'll have to abide by it, as I will."

"They won't say no. Well, yes, some will. Newton and his mates will. But most won't." I do not know who I was trying to convince, Leo or myself. It was what I had been telling myself all night.

"Even if they do agree, you'll need to find volunteers to sail with you and that won't be easy. No man wants to sail under a woman's command, it's bad enough being at the command of the seas and winds, and enough of these men came to sea to escape their women, just as you escaped a man."

"Really? The way I've seen some of those men eye that boat, I don't think it'll take much to get them working her decks."

"Maybe you have a point there, querida. We'll soon see." He looked up at the sun. Noon. It was time to go aboard the prize and learn our future.

"There's no more for us to say, but what say you? Do you vote Gabriella as captain of this vessel?"

"Aye. Nay. Aye." It was close.

"Show of hands!" A pause, I had won, I think. I had won.

"The ayes have it."

I closed my eyes in relief, I hardly dared believe it. I was a pirate captain! *Watch out Erik, I'm one step closer.*

"Thank you. You won't regret this. I won't let you down, and I won't forget the chance you've given me. Thank you."

"Very well, that's that then." Leo did not sound quite so pleased. "Bear in mind that if this doesn't work, you can be voted back to the foredeck just as easily as you were voted to the quarter. I suppose you'll need a crew. Frazer, will you sail in her?"

"Devil's bones, I will not! I'll not play nursemaid to a woman, even one of yours. I've put up with her aboard *Freedom*, but I'll not sail under her command. Dinnae ask me again."

I don't know who was more taken aback, me or Leo. I knew

Mr. Frazer didn't like me, but I had thought we were starting to understand each other. I was as shocked at his abrupt refusal as Leo.

"I'd be proud to sail with thee, lass," Gaunt called in the silence.

"Aye, me an'all."

Bless them. I soon had my crew: Klara and Obi, of course, Gaunt, Davys, Cartwright, Babawande, Butler and Greenwoode. To my surprise, even Ime volunteered, but I hadn't forgotten his early threat and didn't want him on my crew.

"Very well, we'd better get to work. I want the gundeck cleared, topmasts stepped and yards made ready." Leo said. "Gaunt, would you look to see what strengthening her lower decks will need to carry the extra canvas, and George, we'll need a couple of square topsails. Frazer, can I at least rely on you to get the work started?"

Am I not supposed to be saying all this?

"Yes! That was easy! I thought it would be a hell of a lot harder to get her and that other bitch off our decks! Now all we need to do is wait for hurricane season to sink her landlubbing arse! Who's for a drink?"

I whirled round at Newton's words, shocked, and stared at him and his mates in dismay. I knew he hated me, but I'd thought the others had voted in support of me—not to get rid of me. *Do the rest of the crew feel the same as Newton?*

"Gabriella, can I have a word in the cabin? In your cabin?" Leo corrected himself. He glanced at Newton with a frown, but said nothing.

My cabin. I smiled and led the way. Newton didn't matter. I was away from him.

"I don't know whether to be pleased or angry with them. Despite what I said, you know I'm torn over this. However, the decision has been made for me. But I want some promises from you. They are still my crew, and I make the ultimate decisions. However, you decide how you carry them out and are responsible for the men on your decks. Just keep them and yourself safe, that's all I ask. Stay close by, take the advice of your crew, and heed mine. Do not make me watch you die."

Chapter 59

I lay back on the blankets and stretched, then sat up, passed one rumpot to Leo and drank from the other. The rest of the crew were on the beach and we didn't expect to see any of them again until long after the sun had come up. My new ship was careened so the necessary work could be carried out, and Leo and I had volunteered to keep ship—stay aboard *Freedom*—in case of problem or attack. We'd brought blankets, cushions and other comforts out onto the quarterdeck where we could see most of the deck, were away from prying eyes and more comfortable than in the stuffy cabin, and had been making the most of this rare time alone aboard an otherwise empty ship.

Leo kissed me and I lay back in his arms. I couldn't have been happier.

"Salud!" He raised the rumpot in a toast. "To the most beautiful pirate in the Carib Sea!"

"Only the Carib Sea?"

"In all the seas of the world!" he amended, laughing. We'd made rather a lot of toasts throughout the evening.

I laughed with him, and touched my rumpot to his. "And the most handsome pirate captain!" I drank. "You know, I was almost born to be at sea," I said, not sure why I'd decided to tell him about my childhood.

"What do you mean?"

"My mother carried me in her belly when she sailed from England. She'd been brought to trouble by the bastard she worked for as a housemaid, and he arranged for her passage to the Americas to avoid embarrassment."

"But you've mentioned your father, I thought he lived with you in the Massachusetts Bay Colony?"

"She met the man I call my father aboard the ship. He was young, fell in love and took pity on her situation. They were married by the captain and started a home in Massachusetts as a family."

"He sounds like a good man."

"Yes, he does." I paused. "But there was no stopping the gossip, especially in a puritan colony. There were others aboard who knew the truth and disapproved, and it was soon known I was a bastard child, despite Father's efforts." I paused as the memories flooded back. I could almost see my father's face, bright red and spitting in his rage. Furious at I don't know what, the slightest thing could spark his match, a look or a simple question would be enough. He delighted in telling me that he wished I'd never been born, that his life would have been so much better if I'd never existed. On these occasions I never found out what I'd done to deserve his anger. I didn't know why he'd pinned me to the wall, all I could do was wonder how often he'd strike me this time as he screamed a torrent of hatred. When would he stop? Would he keep going until he killed me with his fists? Or would he kill my mother first?

"That can't have been easy," Leo said, and I was sorry the mood had turned somber, yet relieved to be telling him about my childhood at last.

"No," I said, then took a deep breath. "His ambitions were curtailed by the scandal and he was an ambitious man, but could not rise in business or join the congregation he coveted. It made him bitter. My parents' marriage had already dulled by the time I was born, and I'm sure Mam named me Gabriella purely to annoy my father. It was her last rebellion, and I'm grateful to her for it. Can you imagine if she'd called me by a puritan name such as Prudence or Charity or Temperance?"

He laughed and filled the rumpots again.

"He became a customs officer, having recognized that shipping was set to become a major industry, and the position gave him at least a semblance of importance and respect. But it wasn't what he'd wanted when he'd set out to the New World, and he took his frustration out on Mam and me." I took a long drink and was grateful that Leo stayed silent to wait for me to continue.

"He made private business arrangements with a number of merchants including Jan van Ecken, Erik's father. Their trade was—and is—much more than slaves. Sugar, indigo, cacao, spices, you name it, they trade it, and they need a lot of friendly customs men around the world to do it profitably. I don't know why they singled out my family, but Jan was looking for a bride for Erik and Father was happy to rid himself of me. I'm certain he benefitted in a mercantile manner from the betrothal. Maybe Jan simply wanted more control over him and thought he could get it through his daughter. If so, I doubt he succeeded."

I emptied my beaker again and Leo refilled it. "So there I was, married and banished to the Caribbees at fourteen, full of hope for my new life. But of course my husband turned out to be Erik and the rest is history."

"How bad was it, your new life?"

"Bad enough." I got up and wrapped a length of cloth around myself, then crossed to the rail and stared at the water. I didn't want to talk about my life with Erik to Leo. Ever. He pulled on his breeches and joined me.

"When you came aboard, you jumped at every creak of the timbers and every squeak of a rat. You don't have to tell me about your life with him, I think I have a pretty good idea, and I'll tell you one thing, I want to kill him for what he did to you."

"But if he hadn't been such a monster, I would not have been on that slaveship, and we would not be here today." I turned to him and smiled. I had talked enough; he wanted to kill Erik.

"That's very true, maybe we have one thing to thank him for." He bent his head to meet my lips and I shivered when he ran his hands over my skin, but pulled away.

"I can't stand being married to him, Leo. We've harassed his shipping, had run in after run in with Blake and Hornigold, but they won't die! We even heard that Blake survived Isla Magdalena's reef—built a new boat from the wreckage of *Edelweiss*!" According to the rumors, he'd sailed back to Sayba six months after we had left him and taken command of a new ship—the *Dutch Pride*. "It's time to put an end to this vendetta once and for all, and we should be the aggressors. We need to best them all."

"Kill them, you mean."

I paused. "Yes, and we need to do it soon so we can get on with our lives."

In answer, he pulled me away from the rail and any prying eyes, then pinned me against the mainmast. He kissed me and fumbled with the cloth wrapped around me, and his breeches, discarding them on the deck. He kissed me again, harder this time, and pressed up against me as I leaned against the timber and cordage of the mast. I held him tight, enjoying the feel of him and lost myself in his touch, and I forgot about the past. I was filled with now, with Leo, his touch and the sensations coursing through my body; first a gentle swell, then crashing surf.

Chapter 60

GABRIELLA
25th January 1687
10 Leagues South of Puerto Rico

Taking the helm of my ship was exhilarating. All her strength and power was in my hands, and she boasted of it with every thundering wave and every spray of spindrift. Every whistle of wind was a scream of delight, and I felt like screaming with her. I thrust the tiller to leeward, taking her upwind a fraction too far, and watched the mainsail as the leech started to tremble, then flutter until the whole sail collapsed, shaking so forcefully that the vibration was sent down the mast to the planking under my feet. We were past the point of no return now, and I gasped as the mainboom swung across, seemingly an inch from my head, and crashed loudly onto larboard, now to leeward. I brought the tiller back slowly to center as the sails settled and calmed, their bellies once again filling with wind.

Our speed, which had slowed almost to nothing, picked up until we were skipping through the white horses galloping all around us. A particularly short wave resulted in my bow diving into the next one, then we burst out the other side, spray flying, singing our way forward. I kept my hands on her reins, aware of an excitement and exhilaration that assured me I was home, and that I never wanted to leave. No other place could compare to this one.

To make it even better, I realized *Freedom's* pinnace was approaching, or trying to. Leo had tacked in my wake, and I took pity on him and shouted for the mainsail to be loosed to give him a chance to catch us. Soaked and smiling after his evening sail he finally climbed onto my decks. I gave the tiller to Greenwoode.

"*Valkyrie*?" he asked.

"Yes, *Valkyrie,*" I confirmed with a smile. Gaunt had carved the new nameboards on Sankt Jan Island, but I'd kept the new name secret from everyone else until the off. Leo wouldn't have seen them until we set sail. The name had come from Erik's books on Norse mythology, and I thought it very appropriate for a ship I wanted to use to finish him. I loved the idea of the Valkyries, Odin's shield maidens, riding into battle astride winged horses to take their pick of warriors back to Valhalla, and I'd always wished for their strength and courage.

"*Valkyrie,* as in Viking angels?" Leo asked again.

"More like Nordic demons," Greenwoode put in from the helm. He wasn't a fan of the name.

"Warriors. Female warriors who choose their heroes very carefully and well," I corrected, smiling.

"Bad luck to change a name like that," Greenwoode moaned. I ignored him and we moved further down *Valkyrie's* decks.

"How are you getting on with the new sail plan? It can take a while to get a new boat balanced, especially when you extend her masts the way we have."

"The lass is faring well, Cap," Gaunt answered for me. "There's no need to fret thysen."

"Thank you, Robert, take the decks will you," Leo replied. I bit back my objection. It was up to me who took these decks, not him, but I swallowed it, I didn't want anything to spoil this. I determined to enjoy walking my decks with my man.

Valkyrie was a lot smaller than *Freedom,* and livelier. She sailed at a more acute angle, which made her decks hard to walk with any confidence and would take some getting used to, but worse was the rope washing over her decks and getting tangled. Before I could call to Davys to sort them out, Leo beat me to it.

"Stop it. You're not taking me seriously."

"Your lines were heading overboard, querida, someone had to do something about them."

"Not someone. Not you. Me. I may not be as quick as you, but I command these decks, it's for me to tell my crew what to do, not you."

"They're still my crew, you just have command of this vessel on my behalf, but when I'm aboard, they listen to me. I do take you seriously, but you have a lot to learn and I will not stand back and say or do nothing when I see a deadly situation. If anyone caught their leg in one of those lines they'd be overboard and drowned in seconds. If you want to give the orders, spot the problems early and put them right before I do."

There was nothing I could say to that. I had to prove my worth as captain through deeds not words, so I nodded—my lips tight against my temper.

"You're doing well, querida. You looked magnificent at the helm, even if you were sailing away from me. You seemed at home there. I can understand that you wouldn't be happy for long under my command aboard *Freedom*, and I think this may actually work, but I miss you when you're not on my decks."

I smiled and leaned into him. That was better.

"I miss you too, and I do appreciate your help and advice, I just want to be good at this." I sighed. "There's a bottle of brandy in the cabin just begging for a toast, will you join me below?"

He laughed. "As if I'd refuse that offer!"

We'd been in the cabin at anchor before, but this was the first time since we'd gone to sea, and it felt different somehow. I leaned my sword against the bulkhead next to the door to warn the crew not to come in, and smiled when Leo followed suit.

"I do take you seriously as a sailor, and you've just proved you're a captain. Anybody else would have driven the tip of their blade into the wood out there. No true sailor would damage their decks in that way. Come here." He pulled me close and kissed me. He was forgiven.

"I brought you a present. Every pirate captain should have stolen gold in their cabin. Here."

He gave me a package wrapped in sailcloth. It was the facemask with emerald eyes I'd noticed when I first joined *Freedom*. I smiled. I had my answer from that day. I wasn't just an interesting ornament after all, and had started my own collection. I put it on the chart table for the moment until I could find somewhere more deserving, and kissed him before handing him a beaker of brandy, then went to sit down on the bed in front of the stern gallery of windows. I looked out to sea to watch *Freedom* following behind, suddenly serious, and considered the gentle unrelenting and never-ending power of that water. It would rear up with no warning in a fierce passion, before calming again: *a reflection and promise of the life I've chosen with Leo?* Guilt pierced me again. *How can I be so happy when I left my best friend's son dead at my husband's home?*

I woke the next morning alone, and smiled as I stretched, until I realized Leo was outside, running my decks. Again.

"Leo! Have you forgotten already? This is *my* ship; I give the orders on these decks!" Even as I spoke, I was aware that I wouldn't be on the quarterdeck without Leo. I wouldn't have authority over this crew without Leo. I still only had a semblance of independence. But I also knew that if I had more, I'd be alone and I didn't want that either.

"Well, you'd better get on with it instead of sleeping the watch away and leaving the work to everyone else!"

I glared at him—and everybody else watching and listening.

"It seems I've outstayed my welcome. I've neglected my own ship long enough anyway, it's time to go and make my presence felt aboard *Freedom*. You're welcome to come and visit when you're ready, Gabriella. Enjoy your new boat."

"Ship!" I shouted after him, furious.

I watched him spread the pinnace's sail and reach over to *Freedom*. *What have I done?* Had I got this completely wrong? Had I ruined everything by demanding this ship and leaving his decks? The last few months had been better than I ever could have dreamed, an impossibility based on my life up to a year ago, but there was no denying I'd started to resent the power Leo had over me aboard *Freedom*. If I'd let things stay as they were I'd be unhappy and weak again, and I'd had enough of that. I had to be strong; I had to prove I was strong—to myself as much as anyone else. I had to know I was worthy of this life—of *my* life—that I was worth the air I breathed, and worthy of Leo as well, although I'd never admit that to him. But it worked both ways, I had to know *he* was worthy of *me*, too. I had to know that he loved me for me and not just an idea of me, or because I happened to be married to the man he regarded an enemy. I needed him to accept me as an equal. I wanted his respect and even his admiration. I wanted to *share* this life with him, not just keep him company while *he* lived it. I wanted, no needed, to be independent, to know I could rely on myself; but I needed him too. I needed him to accept me, but to be honest; I wasn't completely sure who 'me' was. I *was* sure that I needed to find out, and I had to test Leo's love for me while I did it. *No wonder he's so confused and frustrated.*

I sighed and felt my shoulders relax and droop. Maybe I was being too hard on him. I couldn't bear it if I found myself but lost him in the process. *Then what will I do?*

"Stand by to jibe!" I called, striding amidships to take the tiller myself. My conversation with Leo was not over. I wasn't going to let him leave me in anger, not after the way we'd loved last night. Filled with resolve, I pushed the tiller hard over to windward, but immediately realized I'd been too eager. The deck canted viciously and I heard cursing from my crew. We had too much sail flying for such a violent jibe in this wind, and, after a creaking and cracking, I watched in horror as the mainmast slowly fell to the sea in a tangle of sailcloth and rigging.

Valkyrie hadn't been at sea a week and I'd broken her.

I stared at the mess that, moments before, had been my beautiful ship, my hands over my mouth in shock, and slowly raised my eyes to the men who were shouting and running toward the tangle. I suddenly realized two were missing, and put my shame aside. I ran forward and pulled out my dagger to cut away canvas and cordage. *Please let them be well. Please be well. Please don't let me have killed anyone. Please. Please. Please.*

Was wind thumping that canvas or a fist? I scrambled to the moving sail, screaming to be careful I was going to cut, when a knife blade thrust outward and ripped through the sail. Gaunt and Butler followed.

"What the hell did thee do that for, lass? This ain't a pinnace thee knows, thee needs to give us a bit of time afore thee jibes like that! We're blooming lucky not to be hurt or worse!"

"Sorry, sorry, I didn't realize, are you both well?" I paused and looked at Gaunt, ready to burst into tears. "Now what do we do?"

"Don't fret so, lass." He relented now that he was free of the shroud of mainsail. "There must've been a flaw in the mast to go like that, or a frayed stay. We'll have to cut her free and head back ashore. Just let me catch me breath and I'll check below, make sure she ain't sprung no boards an'all."

"Stay here, I'll go below," I said, suddenly desperate to get away from the glares of my crew. Bless Gaunt for his generosity, but I couldn't expect any from the others, nor did I deserve it.

It was bad news below deck, water was streaming in. The mast had pulled at the garboards next to the keel and we were filling up fast. *Am I going to lose her*? I shouted for help and all eight of my crew shot down the hatch.

"Come on, Captain," Davys said. "We'll be needed on the pumps whilst Gaunt and the others try and salve this. Hope you're feeling strong."

I nodded dumbly. I felt like I was being punished, and that I deserved it. I was not in command here: Gaunt, Cartwright, Davys, Butler and Greenwoode all knew better than me what to do in this situation. Klara, Obi, Baba and I could only follow their lead.

"Gabriella! Gabriella! Where are you? Are you hurt? Gabriella!" Leo had arrived back aboard. *Wonderful*. I took a deep breath and shouted up at him, "We're all well, but we're making a lot of water. Mr. Gaunt and the others are fitting a lead patch." I raced up through the hatch after Davys, who had already rigged the pump to the capstan, unable to look at the concern on Leo's face. I didn't deserve it.

"Can you cut away that mast? We're too unstable and need to get way on as quickly as we can." I tried to act like a captain again.

"Gabriella," Leo said, quietly, stepping toward me.

"Please, Leo. Help me save her. I can't lose her after everything, she deserves better."

He nodded and got to work, whatever he wanted to say could wait. We had a ship to save. If we could just get moving, the water would start to flow out rather than in, and *Valkyrie* would have a chance.

Chapter 61

GABRIELLA
28th January 1687
Sankt Jan Island

I took the approach to Sankt Jan Island carefully under foresails and a jury mainmast made from one of *Freedom's* spare main yards, and sounded every few feet. I wasn't taking any chances. I felt so sad running *Valkyrie* onto the beach only five days after we'd left. I'd failed her. All my posturing and my insistence that she was mine alone had nearly sunk her. *Freedom* had sailed in close company and was already at anchor. Her laden pinnace and longboats pulled toward the shore. It was time to face the rest of the men—a moment I'd dreaded all the way back.

"See, I told you, a fair weather sailor. A woman has no business being on the quarterdeck of any vessel!"

"Don't talk to her like that, Newton, whatever your thoughts on the subject, Gabriella is *Valkyrie's* captain and your talk is damn near a threat of mutiny," Leo defended me.

"I'm not on her crew. I am not mutinous."

"You are on *my* crew, and any threat to Gabriella is a threat to me. Now shut up and get to work, I'm sick of the sound of your voice."

Maybe having Leo close by on occasion wasn't such a bad thing, after all.

"Gabriella, we need to select a new mainmast for you. Gaunt will stay here to replace and seal the garboards to make the hull sound again. It won't take long, he only needs a couple of planks and we have some spare aboard *Freedom*."

I nodded and followed him inland.

"I'm sorry."

"What?"

"I'm sorry. I thought I knew it all and wanted so badly to do well and I nearly sank her."

"Oh, come here, querida, every captain is a little insufferable at first! But don't worry too much about it, your jibe was ill advised but it would not have been enough on its own to spring the mast. You saw the hull—how it hadn't been tarred properly and had rotted through at the chains. It should have been spotted before you set sail, but you won't make that mistake again."

"It's not that easy is it, commanding a vessel? Someone could have been hurt or even killed in that jibe, and it would have been my fault."

"But everyone is well. Life as a ship's master isn't an easy vocation, you can't expect to know it all straight away. He, or she, has to be master of all trades: shiphandling, war, navigation, weather, sailmaking, carpentry, gunnery, plus a competent topman, fore-the-mast hand, rigger, shipwright and expert at general maintenance. A captain does not have to be a good sailor—Henry Morgan of all people has proved that. But a captain who is not a good sailor needs a good ship's master—and to heed his advice.

"Gaunt has been at sea most of his life—and he's had a long life. He knows everything there is to know about ships and the sea—and he's a damn good carpenter too. You won't go wrong following his advice. You've only just started learning, but you have a good crew, one that encompasses all of it, and me. You'll get there, you just have to take the time to listen and learn."

He paused, his attention out to sea. "I don't like the look of that sloop. She was on the horizon last time we were here, but seems to be coming in a lot closer now. What do you think, querida, are they threatening or just watching?"

I didn't want to admit that I hadn't noticed her—today or on our last visit. "Maybe we should get *Valkyrie* off the beach quickly, just in case."

"Mmm. By the look of the rake on that mast they're pirates. There are a couple of successful crews operating out of Sankt Tomas Island, we're probably invading their territory—hopefully they're just making sure we aren't a threat to them. Anyway, it's only a small sloop and they look to be on their own, they're not likely to take on two vessels, both of them bigger than themselves."

"Even with one dismasted and high and dry?" I asked.

"We've probably taken their careenage and they're waiting for us to move on," he tried to reassure me, although I knew as well as he did there was nothing we could do at the moment, whatever their intent.

"So why haven't they hailed us?" I wondered.

"Would you approach ships this size surrounded by cannon from a boat that size? No, don't answer that, you probably would, but it's not an advisable course of action."

"No offense taken." I was just starting to realize how much I didn't know, and how much there was to think about all the time. On land as well as afloat. *Have I made a big mistake?*

"No you haven't."

"What?"

"Made a mistake."

"How did you know what I was thinking?"

"It's written all over your face. You'd better smile before we get back to *Valkyrie* and your crew realizes their captain is doubting herself—that's always something to keep hidden and closely guarded."

"What do you really think? Have I taken on too much?"

"No, I don't think you have. I was hesitant at first, but I'm coming round to the idea. Just remember to be fair, confident and honest with your crew. Their safety is your responsibility so respect that, and don't be afraid to ask for advice. You have a lot of experience and seasense on your deck—use it and learn as much as you can. You benefit and you're honoring your crew at the same time. Remember, the men who agreed to sail with you have faith in you. If you keep faith in them too, you won't go far wrong."

I nodded and sighed. "You make it sound so easy."

Leo laughed. "I assure you it isn't, especially in a heavy sea with an inconvenient island or reef to leeward. Or in the flat calms come to think of it—in a way they're worse. A bored crew can easily become a malicious one, especially if the rum's running low. But you shouldn't have too much trouble with those old salts. They've seen it all and done it all, countless times, and they chose to sail with you. Anyway, they know they'd have to answer to me if they make trouble for you. You're lucky, not many captains get such an easy passage into command. But I can assure you that despite my best efforts, it won't stay easy—as you've already discovered. Admit your mistakes, make good the damage you've done, and set your sights on your next prize."

"That's a lot to remember!"

"Not really, a bit of common sense to go with the seasense, basic human courtesy and a firm manner is all a good captain needs. Oh, and to trust his or her crew—assuming they're trustworthy—if they aren't, you've no business having them on your decks in the first place. An untrustworthy crew has been the death of many a good captain."

"There, that will serve." He leaned against the tree he had selected and ran his eye up its trunk. "It's straight and tall enough. Right, Capitana, mark it and we'll get some of the men out here, I want your new mainmast felled and hauled back to the beach before it gets dark and we don't have much time."

Night fell quickly as it always did, the sun set as if it couldn't wait to get to bed, and, instead of the brilliant golds and reds and orange and pink, we were left in near darkness. A sliver of moon and a thousand, thousand stars shone down—just as beautiful, but a poor substitute for the tropical sun, as was the fire that blazed on the beach, although at least that had some color to it: orange, yellow, green and blue flared in its depths. I sipped my rum punch, content at last. *Valkyrie* was afloat again—as she should be. Her new mast was stepped slightly further aft than the old one had been, and was raked back sharply. There was no mistaking now that she was rigged for speed. A pirate ship.

We'd spent a week stepping the new mast and everyone realized the accident hadn't been my fault. Even so, it could well have been and I'd learned a lot—and had a much better idea of the captain I wanted to be. But for now, I had the confidence of my crew back, of my man, and even of myself. I felt content and ready to take on the world, closer to confronting and divorcing Erik—although I knew a divorcement would be difficult to take from him. I'd have to force him, or trick him somehow to be free of him. Or kill him.

I shook these thoughts off, I'd deal with them another time when I was alone. For now I leaned into Leo, enjoying the weight of his arm slung around my shoulders, and laughed at the antics of our crews. After a week of hard work, we had a night of relaxation around the fire ahead of us. We'd rig the recut sails and put off again tomorrow. I looked seaward again, at my beautiful ship, and raised my rumpot in a toast to her, then squinted. *Is that vessel out there again?* I turned to Leo to point it out but he'd already seen. We had trouble.

Chapter 62

GABRIELLA
5th February 1687

"What the hell? Get off me!" I shouted. Something had landed in the fire with a bang, shooting flame high into the air, and Leo had shoved me down. I had a mouthful of sand and no idea what was going on.

"Arrows," he hissed in my ear. "Stay down, we need to find some cover."

Another explosion from the fire; they must be tipped with powder. Then more, this time alight, and fire rained down on us. The campsite was chaos: drunken men ran shouting for cover, their superstitious souls sent into blind panic, guns firing wastefully at I didn't know what. I stayed down, trying to think.

"Over there, get behind the boats," Leo instructed and shifted his weight off me. "Don't waste your ball, find someone to shoot at afore you fire." Then, louder, "Feliciano! Phillippe! Can you see anyone? Get to the cannon!" We had readied both vessels for sea and only had one cannon still ashore. The other guns were aboard *Freedom* and *Valkyrie*, but the gun crews were all on the beach. That boat had chosen her moment well. "Mierda, what's that?"

I stared open-mouthed at the sea: it had erupted into flame. I could just make out bundles in the waves and as I watched, another was hit by a flaming arrow and spilled more fire.

I looked at Leo, who waved at me to stay down. He'd managed to calm the men after the initial surprise, but we all had the same problem. With a lake of fire at our backs and flaming arrows firing down on us from inshore we were trapped, we had no night-sight, and no one to shoot back at. We were easy targets. Then a louder boom, and I followed Leo's jerk of the head seaward: the boat offshore had opened fire.

Leo shouted at Phillippe and Feliciano again to fire to seaward.

All was utter confusion, and I was more scared than I had been since I'd first come to sea. It was the first time I'd seen Leo at a loss. I didn't like it.

Another boom from the water grabbed my attention, and I watched the flickering shadow of another mast come down in horror. This time *Freedom's* foremast toppled overboard, lit up by flames, accompanied by a roar of rage from Leo. They meant to trap us ashore—they wanted *Valkyrie* and had just made sure we couldn't pursue when they took her.

Leo was furious. "They are *not* going to steal the new boat, especially after all the hard work we've put into her. I've not been through everything the last few weeks have brought just to lose her now!"

He wasn't the only one who thought that way. Sense and well-honed fighting instincts had quelled most of the confusion and rampant superstition, and the men had taken what little cover there was behind the boats and faced inland, recognizing they could do nothing at the moment for *Freedom* or *Valkyrie* on the other side of that wall of fire.

"They can't find anyone to shoot at," I hissed at Leo. As I spoke, a couple of shots from the shore cannon blasted out to sea, and Leo shouted to take care. Thanks to some clever positioning by the attacker's helmsman, we were in danger of hitting *Valkyrie*, but Feliciano on the cannon couldn't hear.

"Look! Someone's boarding *Valkyrie*!" I watched the boarding of my ship in horror, my eyes now used to the flaring light as the flames subsided.

Leo laughed. "They're in for a surprise then!"

"Why? What do you mean?" I asked.

"Frazer's aboard, and Jean-Claude. Half a dozen others too. That boat's been standing off and on for far too long, I thought they might be up to something. I wasn't quite expecting this, though!"

A big cheer went up around the beach. Feliciano had succeeded in hitting the pirate boat just as she tacked round to get behind *Valkyrie* again, and it had been a good shot. By the looks of it, it wouldn't be long before she went down. Then I realized they would only want *Valkyrie* more.

"Newton, take Thomas and Juaquim, get into those trees and see if you can find whoever's shooting those arrows, but take care—they seem to know the island well."

A noise to seaward grabbed our attention again—shots sounded from *Valkyrie*. They had boarded her. Men from the beach started running to the boats to row out, despite the flaming sea. They were angry now, and a little embarrassed that we'd been taken by surprise, despite our numbers and preparations—and of the way they had panicked. Leo and I jumped into the first boat to hit the surf.

"Only a small crew," Leo mused, "but a good plan. I liked the powder arrows in the fire, we should remember that one. I'm looking forward to meeting the man behind their tactics." I looked at Leo in surprise: he sounded nervous, but of course if Frazer wasn't in control of *Valkyrie*, we had no defense from her guns. "Come on, Capitana, let's go and see who dared to attack your new boat."

"Ship." I repeated the joke dryly, my mind on what would happen next. *What's happening on my decks?*

So far so good. *Valkyrie's* new gunports remained closed, and as we approached I saw that Frazer and the others held two people on deck at gunpoint. *Valkyrie* was safe. We climbed aboard and Frazer reported directly to Leo.

"We had ourselves some visitors, Captain. What do you think, throw them to the sharks? Or maybe we could find some crocs. Shooting at all our hard work, I reckon they deserve a wee bitty torturing afore they die."

The tall pirate spoke with a Danish accent: 'There's no need for that, gentlemen. You should take our attack as a compliment, she's a beautiful boat."

I stared—she was a woman! I had found another woman pirate captain, and she'd attacked my ship! Tall, blonde and muscular, probably in her mid-twenties, and dressed in the usual sailor's short-clothes of shirt and breeches, she also wore a bright emerald-green sash wound around her middle. I didn't know whether to laugh or cry. I wanted to hug her: there was someone else out there like me; but I also wanted to push her overboard for trying to steal my ship—the ship I'd been through so much to take for myself and keep. I smiled to myself; whatever else she was, she was proof that women could not only live, but command at sea. I straightened my face before she saw my smile.

Frazer was disgusted. "Another bloody woman. I'm plagued by deviling skirts."

Leo laughed at his quartermaster's discomfort. "Nobody's dying tonight—at least I hope not, but if any of my men have perished there'll be a score to reckon."

The other pirate spoke: 'If they have, it'll be as a result of their own poor shooting." He didn't sound quite so friendly. "We don't kill unless we have to."

"Introductions seem like a good idea, if not overdue. I'm Leo Santiago, Captain and Master of *Sound of Freedom* yonder. The one that seems to be trailing her fore-topmast overboard." He smiled tightly, enjoying his little performance and victory, but I could see he was hurting to see his ship injured.

The woman turned back to Frazer. "So that makes you captain of this little beauty, I suppose?"

"No, that would be me. Gabriella Berryngton. You'd better not have hurt my ship!"

"Not a splinter. As I said, she's a beauty, we were careful with her. It's good to meet another lady captain at last."

Leo and Frazer looked at each other and laughed. "I don't know about 'lady', not many ladies find employment as pirates."

Ignoring them, I carried on. "It's your turn for introductions."

"Ah yes. Carmen Elvström. Captain and Master of *Awilda*, or I was until you sank her. This is my quartermaster, Andy Fowler—she's the expert with fire and powder."

Another woman. I wouldn't have known if I hadn't been told. She was shorter and stockier than her captain, with dark hair and eyes, and an even darker scowl, which I suspected may be a permanent feature.

"Impressive. Very impressive. It would be a shame to waste that skill and ingenuity, I'm surprised to find it in a woman. How many more of you are there out there?" Leo said, looking at me.

"Another four," Carmen said, misunderstanding. "All women, and a successful crew at that. Or at least we were when we had a boat. I really had my heart set on this one." She perked up. "Maybe the night doesn't have to be a total loss after all, do you need any more hands? As you're aware, we find ourselves free of a deck at present."

I ignored Frazer's grumbling and thought. We did need more crew, especially aboard *Valkyrie*, but I was not ready to make a decision yet, even if signing on a bested crew was a tradition of the Carib Sea. How could I possibly live and sail with any of the women who had attacked *Valkyrie*?

"There's no denying your experience and ingenuity would be useful, but would I be able to trust you on my decks?" I asked.

"You can trust our work. We'll sign your articles and abide by them. We've never mutinied yet, and don't intend to. We'll sail with you, assuming the others agree."

"Let me think on it," I said, and looked at Leo when he put his hand on my arm.

"Load them in the boat, Frazer, we'll all go ashore; there won't be any more trouble tonight."

We stayed where we were as everyone else crowded around the gate in the bulwark and he added, "Be careful, querida."

"What do you mean?"

"Signing them onto your crew. That was a daring attack, six women against near on fifty men, and they nearly pulled it off. They'd have succeeded if we hadn't spotted their boat so often and left such a large and alert shipkeeping party.

"They'd be useful to have fighting alongside us, there's no doubt about that, but I don't think you can trust them, whatever she says. There's more than one way to take a prize, you know, and it's always easier from the deck. If you do decide to sign them up, at least promise me that we'll split them between both vessels to lessen the threat of mutiny. But they would be useful," he mused, "assuming you can keep your authority over those on your decks."

"That wouldn't be a problem, they know they're beaten, and

they'd be outnumbered by the existing crew." Truth be told, I quite liked the idea of more women aboard my ship, despite the way we met. There was also the fact that they'd be *my* crew—not Leo's. I led the way to the rail and climbed down to take my place in the longboat. I had a lot to think about.

"Would you mind pulling to *Awilda* before we go ashore?" Carmen asked. "Two of my crew are clinging to her masthead."

Chapter 63

"Devil's bones!"

"More bloody women!"

"What the Devil?"

I couldn't tell whether the men were more surprised or embarrassed to see who had instilled so much panic in them earlier, and I couldn't help but smile.

Leo motioned Carmen, Andy, Carrie and Jayde to the fire where they were most visible, and the men crowded around, still grumbling and cursing.

I looked up as Newton, Thomas and Juaquim approached from the treeline, unaccompanied and shrugging their shoulders. They hadn't been able to find the other Awildas. I looked at Carmen and raised my eyebrows. She grinned—no doubt proud of her crew for evading capture—then raised one hand to her mouth and gave a piercing, complicated whistle. Everybody stopped talking, startled at the noise, and Carmen smiled. Five minutes later, two women, heavily armed with blade, gun and bow, walked onto the beach and stood staring at the Freedom Fighters.

"I'm pleased to introduce the rest of my crew," Carmen said. "Bess and Annika."

The women didn't react, and the Freedom Fighters glared at them. They were no doubt shocked at how few there were.

"Awildas, we're with friends here. *Awilda* has foundered, and, with any luck, we'll be signing onto Captain Santiago and Captain Berryngton's accounts."

The beach erupted in fury as the men realized what she'd said.

"No! No, no, no, no, no!" Newton's was the loudest voice.

"Aye, for once I'm with Newton," Frazer's Scottish brogue cut through the babble. "Ye'll have to take a vote on this one, Captain."

"Very well." Leo sighed, and I looked at him in disappointment, wondering why he didn't stand up for his decision as captain. Then I realized that with the crew, and most especially the quartermaster, asking for a vote, he had no choice; *Freedom's* articles were clear. I'd used the same circumstance against him to win command of *Valkyrie.*

"By a show of hands," he shouted, quieting the throng. "Votes to allow the Awildas to sign onto *Freedom's* account?"

I raised my hand and looked around me—only about a dozen hands were held high.

"Votes against?"

A wave of hands reached for the lightening sky.

"There you are then, sorry ladies, it looks like Sankt Jan Island will be your home for the foreseeable future."

I had kept my eyes on Carmen's all through the vote and her expression hadn't changed.

"Just a moment," I said. "*Freedom* has voted—*Valkyrie* hasn't."

"There's only one vote, Gabriella, and I seem to remember your hand being counted. The women stay here."

"We've only voted for *Freedom's* account, we should also vote on whether they join *Valkyrie.* I could use some more hands, and we've all seen how skilled these women are."

"Aye, she's right," someone called, and more voices murmured an assent.

I stared at Leo and he narrowed his eyes. I was doing exactly what he'd cautioned me against. "Very well," he said. "All those in favor of the Awildas joining *Valkyrie*?"

Almost every hand was raised.

Leo nodded, but didn't look pleased. Carmen nodded to me, and I held her gaze.

"Be very careful, Gabriella," Leo said quietly. "There are too many of them, they could still take *Valkyrie* from you and I may not be able to stop them—especially after you've challenged me and my authority in front of them."

I glanced up at him and saw he was extremely angry and only just managing to contain it. I wondered if I would regret this.

Chapter 64

GABRIELLA
6th February 1687

I had hardly slept after all the excitement of the night before, and left the group slumbering around the fire at dawn to wander down to the water's edge. That was twice I'd almost lost *Valkyrie* already. I knew I couldn't tolerate another threat, and now I'd agreed to sign all her attackers onto my crew, against Leo's advice.

I looked at the carnage in the bay. *Freedom's* fore-topmast hung overboard and *Awilda's* single mast just topped the sparkling pink-tinged turquoise waves off her lee. *Valkyrie*, despite everything, was the only vessel undamaged off Sankt Jan Island.

I brought my attention back to the stinking beach, littered with charred turtle shell from last night's feast and thought back. What had they used to set the sea afire? I poked at some of the sludge washed up on shore with a stick.

"Pig bladders and whale oil."

I looked up, startled, at Carmen who had walked up behind me, lighting her pipe.

"Effective, wasn't it?" She grinned.

I relaxed. "You're not joking, you had those pirates running round the beach screaming like frightened babes!"

"A particular talent of Andy's." As she spoke, Andy joined us carrying beakers of hot chocolate. I took one and received a nod in response to my thank you. Andy did not seem to talk much. "She doesn't hear so well," Carmen explained around her pipe, "because of all the powder. She finds it easier to stay silent." She smiled at her friend and held her hand a moment after taking her drink, then they sat down to face the sea and enjoy the dawn. I watched them for a moment: one tall and friendly, with hair scorched white from the relentless sun, the other dark, strong and silent. The sun's pink light touched their left cheeks and I wondered what had brought them both to the sea.

"My mother was Spanish—I was named for her—but she died young and my Danish father had been a seaman all his life, there was nowhere else for us to go. For Andy, the sea was the lesser of two evils and it turns out she's happy wherever there are guns. Why *Valkyrie?"* Carmen changed tack. "I couldn't believe it when I saw the name, she almost called to me. I'm from an old Viking family." She laughed at my unspoken question. "Hence *Awilda*—a Viking pirate princess."

I laughed, liking her in spite of my misgivings, and told her about my life on Sayba and how I'd escaped. "*Valkyrie* was the only name for her, nothing else would be good enough."

"Sayba?" Carmen asked, her laughter gone now, and she puffed furiously on her long, white clay pipe. "You introduced yourself as Berryngton, not van Ecken."

"Berryngton's my maiden name. Would you use van Ecken's name if you didn't have to?"

"Bastard!" I looked at Andy in surprise. Her scowling face was red with fury and Carmen put her hand on her arm to calm her.

"The Dutchman and his pirates killed my father," she explained. "I met Andy soon after it happened, and she's very protective." She paused, drew on her pipe, then used it to point southeast.

"We swore revenge on them and have sunk a few of their ships, but the place is a fortress and we haven't found a way in yet." She stopped, wary of saying too much.

"I can get in," I said, "and I think I can get out again too, with help. I may still have friends there," I added.

"It's not a place to leave friends," Andy observed. She obviously heard more than she wanted people to realize.

"No, it's not," I agreed.

"Any plans?"

"I'm working on it, and I think they may have just got a little stronger."

"Does Captain Santiago share your ambitions?" Carmen asked.

"He does—he has his own scores to settle."

"Not to mention having his eye on Dutch gold." Carmen laughed.

"There'll be enough to keep the men happy, that's for sure," I agreed.

Carmen nodded. Andy had lapsed back into silence.

"Do I take it *Valkyrie* hasn't been in your possession long?" Carmen asked with a smile.

I looked at her and smiled back. "Don't get any ideas, she's mine and she's staying that way."

"I told you last night, we don't mutiny. But we have experience, a lot of it. It appears we have the same aims."

"It does, doesn't it?" I mused.

"You'll find a loyal crew in my girls if you're going after van Ecken, and we'd enjoy sailing alongside the larger ship and her firepower," Carmen said. "Are you sure about your decision to take us? Your man didn't look too happy about it."

I looked at her; enemy of mine enemy and all that. "Yes, I'll take a chance on you, I'm short on both sailors and gunners, and female ones would be all the better, you're welcome aboard my ship." She nodded. "And Andy?" I prompted. "Your firesense will be essential."

Andy nodded. I gathered she'd follow wherever Carmen led. Pleased, we shook hands, just as Leo joined us.

"Buenos días, ladies, I hope you slept well, there's a lot of work to be done on my ship."

"Morning. We're just discussing Erik and Sayba—Carmen and Andy have their own history with him," I said in greeting, then turned back to Carmen. "I'm pleased to have you aboard *Valkyrie*, but do not forget for a moment that she is my ship and I her captain. I will not put up with any nonsense. We sail in company with *Sound of Freedom*, and if you try and take my ship away from me again I'll heave you overboard, throats cut, without a second thought—and there are fifty men on this beach who'll help me do it. Do you understand me?"

"Ja, reckon we do."

"That's settled then," Leo said. "And take note of what

Gabriella said. She sails with me and is under my protection, I will not stand any threat to her or to *Valkyrie*. We'll sort the articles out after breaking our fast, and then we'll see how well you work. There's a mast needs replacing and a tangle of rigging to sort out on my ship. You felled it, you fix it. Your woodwork and rigging skills had best be up to the same standard as your fireworks."

Freedom's fore-topmast had been felled by chainshot from *Awilda's* cannon and hadn't damaged any of the planking of the ship herself. Carmen and Andy helped Carrie, Annika, Jayde and Bess to clear the rigging, but *Freedom's* crew stepped the new mast and handled the re-rigging themselves. It would be their lives that depended on it, after all, not those of the women. I spent the afternoon in *Valkyrie's* longboat directing the salving of *Awilda*. Andy had more whale oil and other materials which *Valkyrie* might find useful, and wanted all her guns up before the salt silenced them forever. We also wanted Carmen's navigational instruments and some other bits and pieces. I was surprised at the lack of gold and other plunder being brought up and wondered where they'd hidden it.

Whilst they dived, I stared at the water and the black silk that swamped *Awilda's* masthead. I wanted that too, *Valkyrie* didn't have any pirate colors yet.

"You *haven't* had her long, have you?" Carmen laughed as we hauled the sodden material aboard.

"A month or so." I laughed back. "But she's a beautiful ship!" She deserved more than an anonymous, plain black flag as well and I remembered Leo's tattoo. *Maybe we should have a symbol?* It would set *Valkyrie* apart from the other pirates in these waters, and might help to band the new crew together. We were a bit of a motley mix, and I recognized I had a challenge ahead to bring together the women from *Awilda* and the old tars from *Freedom,* Gaunt and Davys, who had seen and done it all before. I knew they'd be instrumental in keeping order and my authority over an experienced captain and her crew, and I recognized that I'd be walking a tightrope between my old friends and my new. Then there was Butler and Greenwoode from the *Adelheid,* and Cartwright and the others from my slaver. If I was to command this crew effectively, I knew I had to prove myself in battle and profit, as well as seamanship, and I'd done neither yet. I was determined to do everything I could, and not make any more blunders.

Finally, we were ready for the off, again. My new crew started to haul up the anchor and the backed jibs swung *Valkyrie's* stem toward the open sea. The anchor broke out and Andy and Greenwoode catted it whilst Carmen and Davys supervised the set of the sails. The jib was pulled through to leeward and we were free of the land, new colors at the mainmasthead. I stared up at the flag crowning my sails and grinned at the heart and cutlasses suspended over angel wings.

It struck home just how much my life had changed in the past year. I hadn't been born to this way of life, far from it, and I hadn't chosen it, it had chosen me. It was a far cry from my upbringing and previous existence of cruel men in nice houses. Was I really the same woman who had turned in disgust at the sight of a brawl spilling out of a drinking hole, whilst enduring worse at home?

I grew aware of *Freedom's* crew looking and pointing at the new mast and colors, and my smile widened. I straightened up the helm, set my course by the wind for the moment rather than our destination—just for the joy of feeling it across our weather bow—and the deck canted with the increased speed and power. This was what she was made for, where she should be; where all of us should be. At sea flying with the wind, not beached or lashed to the shore, trapped by anchor or mooring warps. Out here we were free just to be.

I looked across at *Freedom*'s quarterdeck and waved at Leo, whose grin matched mine. This is where he needed to be too. I had a pang of regret. I wanted to embrace him, to share his joy as well as my own, but was unable to from this deck and missed him already. We wouldn't have been in each other's arms when working the ship away from shore anyway, but on separate decks it would be too long before we could come together as we wanted. I smelled smoke and turned to see Carmen lighting her pipe—a gesture I soon came to know as an indication all was well on deck. I remembered Leo's advice to trust her sailing instincts and knowledge, but to keep her close and avoid giving her too much leeway. She was used to being in command and had coveted this ship, I had to make sure she got used to *me* being *her* captain.

"How does she feel?" I asked her.

"The foremast needs a little adjustment," she replied. "She's not quite balancing the raked main. It won't take long, but we'll need a calmer day to snug up the shrouds. Other than that she's as fine a sailer as she looks."

She took the pipe out of her mouth and whistled toward the bows, raised her right hand and clenched her fist twice in a signal to Annika to sheet in the outer jib to starboard. *Valkyrie* responded immediately and skipped a little higher over the waves. I knew she was in good hands.

Chapter 65

GABRIELLA
13th February 1687
Four Leagues off Gadalupe

It was frustrating to sail in the opposite direction to Sayba, but even I knew that I, not to mention *Valkyrie*, was not ready yet, and an attack on Brisingamen now could be suicide. I wanted it so badly though, I was desperate to cut Erik out of my life.

We headed south toward Martinico, east of La Isla Magdalena and where Leo had long-standing arrangements with a couple of merchants in Saint Pierre. They were keen to buy his goods and not too particular about where they'd come from, as long as they hadn't come out of the holds of any of their own ships—Leo had long ago agreed to leave their trade alone. With a fair wind we could be back in the Northern Caribbees in a week, but at this time of year, northing could be hard to come by, no matter how much I yearned to be back, and the return passage could take much longer. On top of that, Leo had promised the men time to enjoy the entertainments of Saint Pierre's sailortown; we'd been at sea or on deserted beaches too long for their continued compliance, and they missed their women—any women.

"*Sail oh.*"

We were a week out and I grabbed Carmen's glass to see for myself. Brand new and made with mirrors it put Leo's to shame, although he wouldn't hear a word said against his old one. I examined the sail off our port bow. A French merchantman—a large round-hulled ship, slow and heavy. Perfect. *Valkyrie* bristled with a variety of guns, thanks to Andy, and you'd never have known that they'd spent a night on the bottom. I also had two of *Freedom's* small, two-pound cannon with their plum-sized shot installed at the bows either side of the figurehead, and we got ready to give chase. As the faster boat upwind, we would leave Leo and *Freedom* off astern; I wanted *Valkyrie* to do this alone, without him.

We had a strong breeze, the waves breaking with white, and I ordered the topsails down to avoid the merchantman spotting us too soon. With main- and foresails flying we had the speed we needed, and both Gaunt and Carmen nodded when I turned for their opinions. The wind was close-to this morning, so coming over our larboard foredeck, and we headed toward our prey and the Gadalupe coast. Whilst the wind was likely to swing round in the afternoon, we were early enough that it came off the island to the east, essentially trapping the vessel. Her only chance was to get close to shore somewhere with decent defenses, but she had big problems. She was slow, having been designed to carry as much cargo as conceivable with the smallest possible crew, and her square-rigged sails couldn't sail into the wind. She had to take a much shallower angle than *Valkyrie,* giving us plenty of opportunity to intercept her before she reached her safe harbor.

I hoisted our new colors once it was obvious she'd realized we were a threat to her, and set a collision course. When she was in range of the bow cannon, Andy fired at the rigging of the fleeing ship. Her second shot was right on target, and I gasped as I watched their mainmast shudder and slowly fall, bringing a tangle of canvas and rigging down with it.

"Don't celebrate too soon, we've still got to get aboard. I hope you're ready to fight because I can't see them asking quarter of women."

Davys was right, of course, we had only just started, we hadn't won our prize yet. Looking around the decks at my crew, I saw them how the mariners across the water would see them, and I ordered the Awildas to hide their hair and loosen their shirts to hide their shape—hopefully this would be enough until it was too late for the other crew to do anything foolish. They'd be expecting men, and something so simple may just delay their realization of our sex until our swords and muskets were on them, and they were at our mercy.

Unwilling to risk their lives, they didn't try to protect their ship, and we herded them into the forecastle and had a good look around. She had six cannon aboard, but all broadside—if she'd had even one mounted at her stern, this might have been a very different story. I left it to Andy as to how to utilize this extra firepower for the best now that I could return the rest of the guns *Freedom* had provided when we first took *Valkyrie,* and she immediately headed abaft to install a new gun at our own stern.

Below decks was a disappointment, they were still laden with goods, not silver, but at least we could stock up our food and drink supplies, and there were anchors and other gear that would come in useful, including all their spare cordage and spars. The spices and cloth could be traded at Martinico, but I'd really wanted to prove myself to Leo with a big haul of gold or silver. Not this time.

Now I had to face Leo. I knew he'd be angry that I'd done this myself without warning or agreeing it with him, but he *had* to see me as a pirate captain in my own right, and this was the only way I could think of to prove it to him.

He laid us aboard and crossed to the prize. I stood my ground and used all my determination not to flinch at the expression on his face—it was one I'd been much more used to seeing on Erik. I squared my shoulders, set my jaw and waited for him, ignoring both crews who had stopped what they were doing to watch us. He grabbed my arm and pulled me aft in a vain attempt at privacy.

"What the hell did you think you were doing?" he hissed through clenched teeth. "We work together, as a team, what were you trying to prove?"

"I can do this, Leo, I needed to show that to my crew and yours, and yes, you as well."

"And make me look a fool in the bargain?"

"No! Why do you look a fool? The only one risking looking a fool was me if I failed, but I didn't. My crew worked together, and we took our prize. I needed to show everyone that *Valkyrie* is not a weak link, and we just proved that."

Leo blew out a breath in frustration. "Next time, do you think you could give me a bit of warning? I didn't get you this boat for you to risk your life in an unnecessary and solitary fight. We work together, you and I, and you still answer to me. Don't sail off on your own again."

"You didn't 'get' me this boat, I won it, and if you think I'm going to be your little consort, your pirate concubine, you can think again! You freed me from one life, I won't be shackled to another. I will always be grateful to you for bringing me to the sea, and it's where I want to stay—with you. I had to do this. I had to prove to myself, to my crew and to you too, that I am a worthy captain of *Valkyrie*, and that I deserve to be on her quarterdeck. I cannot ask any of my crew to risk their lives if I'm not prepared to risk mine along with them, and I'm surprised you have a problem with that."

"You're damn right I have a problem with that!" Leo shouted, and I took a step backwards at the force of his temper.

"I thought I'd made it clear—whilst you command that vessel, you are still a member of *my* crew, and you do what *I* say! You are my proxy on that quarterdeck, nothing more. You follow *my* instructions! You attack only the ships I tell you to attack and you do it in the way I describe! Do you understand?"

"How *dare* you speak to me like this? And in front of everybody!" I was furious and knew I had lost control, but could not stop. "How am I supposed to command the respect and authority of my crew if they only see me as your . . . proxy?" I spat the word. "I will not be treated like this, you're no better than Erik!"

He slapped me. Shocked, I could think only one word. *No.* My hand went to my belt and the hilt of the blade stowed there. God help me, I think I was prepared to use it.

He swallowed his own shock, moved his hand to his own blade, and hissed, "Take care, Gabriella, your words and actions are close to mutiny. If you continue, I'll put you in irons and lock you below deck. Do not push me further."

Put me in irons and lock me away? My heart chilled. I looked at him and saw another man trying to force me to his will. I pushed aside all the feeling I had for him.

"Mutiny? I'll give you bloody mutiny!" I snarled, then turned and strode down the deck, shouting to my Valkyries to return to our ship. He could keep the bloody prize, I just had to get away from him.

We cast off and set sail as quickly as we could. I looked back once and wept when I saw his flag break in the breeze. He had sewn on his tattoo—a heart and sandglass—and added a pair of blades in parody of mine.

PART FOUR

Chapter 66

LEO

I watched her go in disbelief. Everything she had said had been a lie. She hadn't wanted me; she'd only wanted a boat—a command of her own. But I didn't really believe it. I knew she loved me, I *knew* it. I'd pushed too hard, that was all, but it had to be said. I was captain. She had to do as she was told. She'd be back.

"Break out the colors," I ordered.

The flag George had put together to complement Gabriella's flew proudly at the masthead.

She didn't come back.

"You have the deck," I muttered to Frazer and went aft, shutting myself into what had been our cabin, a bottle of rum in each hand. I locked the door.

I walked back on deck to utter silence from my crew. I had only left the cabin in the last few days to collect more rum. They no doubt expected the same today.

"Back to work! What are you all looking at?" I shouted. One by one they turned from me, back to their tasks.

I stayed where I was for the moment, glaring at my crew, the sails, then the horizon. Nothing was in sight but sea, and I realized I had no idea where we were. There was no sign of *Valkyrie*.

"She can take the fore-topsail as well, Blackman. See to it!"

"Aye, Capt'n," he muttered, looking less than convinced, but immediately sent topmen up the foremast to unfurl the huge sail. Good. At least someone was obeying my orders.

I couldn't see Frazer, so turned and entered the chartroom next to my cabin. He was there, hunched over charts with backstaff, traverse board and writing stick, plotting our position. I stood behind him and stared at the chart. We were south of Hispaniola and heading east.

"What are you doing? Why are we headed for Jamaica?" I demanded, stumbling a little as the deck heeled.

Frazer made to get up. "We're carrying too much sail—what's Blackman thinking?"

"Leave him be. And leave the canvas, it's about time we drove her a bit harder—give those lazy goats something to do instead of lounging about on deck all day with their pipes and rum punch."

Frazer stared at me, but I couldn't read any expression on his face. He pulled his stool close to the table again and resumed his inspection of the chart.

"Why Jamaica?" I asked again in the silence.

"We're not bound for Jamaica, we're bound for Tortuga. The men need some recreation, then we can get back to taking plunder instead of pandering to bloody women."

"Watch your tongue, Frazer, no one pandered to Gabriella, she's a full member of this crew and earned it."

"Was."

"Qué?"

"*Was* a full member of this crew."

"Is. She'll come back."

"You really think so? After you hit her? Threatened her?" I glared at him. "What were you thinking, Leo? You know, and we can all guess, what van Ecken did to her, why would she come back to you when you've shown the same colors as he?"

I stared at him in silence, turned and left the chartroom. Van Ecken. It was his fault. I had to do something. I had to show Gabriella that I was not van Ecken. I had to free her. I had to kill him for her. If only to stop her attacking Sayba herself.

"Shake that reef out of the fore-topsail, Blackman! Let's sail!"

"But Captain, it's too much, the rigging'll part!"

"Not if it's been properly kept! And it had better be sound, or the man responsible will be up there making repairs under full sail!"

Blackman stared a moment, then relayed my order. He knew the dangers of working on the rigging under full canvas. Many men had died in falls as a result of a fiercely whipping line, but an order from the captain was an order from the captain, and he obeyed, just as the topmen obeyed him. That did not stop Newton glaring at me as he climbed. I stared back. The sooner we got to Tortuga, the sooner we could leave and attack Sayba.

Chapter 67

LEO
20th April 1687
Sayba

Raid Eckerstad; kill van Ecken; appropriate Brisingamen's gold; free Gabriella—it had been all I'd thought about whilst impatiently watching my crew carouse themselves senseless over the past two months. She'd come back to me as soon as she heard about this. This is what I needed to do to make amends. I had to succeed here or my life was lost—again. Everything that had gone wrong in my life was down to this one man and his cohorts. It was van Ecken who had terrorized Gabriella and made her scared of a shadow, who had sent her running at the feel of my palm. It was van Ecken who supported Blake and Hornigold. If not for van Ecken, I'd have sunk both buccaneers years ago, but van Ecken kept giving them safe haven to repair their ships, and when their ships were unseaworthy, he gave them new ones. It had to stop. I had to stop him, and I would soon have my chance—Sayba was just visible off my bow, darkness still shrouding her volatile peak.

"Bear off a touch," I muttered. We had no lanterns lit in the early dawn light and navigated by the phosphorescence of sea meeting rock. I didn't want to get too close, we had to stay invisible until our guns opened fire. I had remembered the intelligence I'd received from Cheval, and we approached from the northwest, past the beach where we'd made repairs almost a year before, past Brisingamen—van Ecken's estate, past the gun placement that Cheval had assured me was rarely manned—he'd insisted an alert crew was only present when they expected trouble. Arrogant foolishness, if you ask me—when did trouble arrive only when it was expected?

On we crept in the gentle dawn breeze, my men silent. Only the creak of rigging and the swish of our passage through the waves belied our presence.

Boom!

A flare of black powder startled everyone aboard—the gun placement atop the cliff was not only manned, but primed by alert gunners. I cursed myself. Cheval! Of course he'd have apprised Hornigold of our layover here. He'd have known, given my animosity to both Blake and Hornigold, and now van Ecken, that I'd attack. It was reasonable to expect I would take the passage I knew, along the one stretch of coastline I'd already explored, and where I knew I'd be hidden from Eckerstad until the last minute by the headland.

Only moments ago it had seemed a risk worth taking. I now saw it for arrogant foolishness of my own. *Mierda!*

Boom!

I ducked. Not that it did any good. The first shot had allowed the gunners to judge their range. They were good and their second shot was a direct hit, shattering the aft larboard quarter. I didn't need to enter my and Gabriella's old cabin to know it had been destroyed.

"Return fire!" I yelled.

"Blackman—patch that hole, quick as you can!"

With the aft cabin open to the sea, I could not maneuver off this course. Wearing round meant turning and presenting my stern to the wind and oncoming waves. When the wind was dead astern, the Carib Sea would surge in. Nor could I tack—Sayba's shoreline was in the way. I couldn't steer off the course I was on. Badly damaged, all I could do was sail onward. Our—my—destiny was fated until my bo'sun could patch up my ship. I had to fight, not only my mortal enemies, but to keep ship and crew afloat.

"Fire!" I shouted—it was my only option.

Chapter 68

The next ball splashed into our wake. I breathed a sigh of relief. We were out of range. I turned my attention from the cliff above and astern, and looked forward once again. Eckerstad would have heard the guns. We were no longer attacking a sleeping port. The men at the fort to the south of the town would be at the ready with primed guns. Any ships in the harbor would be ready to fire. The people of the town would be running to safety. I had no doubt van Ecken would be the first to hide. Still I could not wear round. Blackman was working as fast as he could, I could hear him cursing his assistants clearly—I couldn't rest until the sound of his voice had been muffled by lead.

"Ready bow and larboard guns," I shouted, trying to sound sure of myself to instill some confidence in my men; already knowing my plans were doomed.

"Bow cannon find your targets!" I wanted the six-pounders in the bow to target the biggest ships in the roads—the ones most likely to be carrying armaments.

"Bows—fire!"

The largest ship in the harbor was hit by both ball. She fired back, but her crew were no master gunners. She missed.

"Bow—fire again!"

No return fire—her crew were busy trying to save their ship, and themselves, from foundering. I didn't think any of the other smaller vessels posed a threat to us, so concentrated on the town itself.

"Larboard guns, fire!"

Shorefront buildings crumbled.

Boom!

The fort had opened fire. I had thought we'd be well out of range here in the northern reaches of the bay, but they had big guns, maybe even a thirty-two-pounder. Their first ball hit the water to starboard and a cable length ahead. Too close. My own guns kept up the bombardment on the town, my six-pounders wouldn't trouble the fort from here, and I shouted at my crew to harden up—to sail as close as possible to the wind—to delay entering the range of those guns for as long as possible.

"Blackman! What's taking you so long? Get that patch fixed pronto!"

"Nearly there, Capt'n!"

His voice was not nearly muffled enough, and in the meantime, we were sailing closer to the fort and her guns. We'd soon be within their range.

"Fire larboard guns!"

There was nothing else I could do but cause as much mayhem as possible. I listened to the screams just audible from the shore. *Is van Ecken's amongst them?*

Then a scream from my decks, a cry I realized had originated in many throats—including my own. A ball from the fort had found our main-topsail—the biggest and most powerful sail of our rig. Not only had it shredded the sail, it had knocked Thompson off his perch on the maintop—I'd find out later if he was dead—and destroyed the rigging holding the topmast aloft.

A tangle of wood, hemp and canvas descended on our heads. Frazer shouted at men to get aloft and cut away the topmast and attendant rigging—shrouds, ratlins, braces, sheets and the like—but I knew *Sound of Freedom* had never been more vulnerable.

Chapter 69

"Twin sail to the west!"

My heart lurched at Juaquim's shout, but I spun to starboard and brought my glass up. I would not have believed things could get worse: holed, maintop sprung, mainmast itself in danger of following, fired on by Eckerstad's fort. The only course *Freedom* was able to lay was dead ahead toward Eckerstad itself, and now two ships were approaching. Both flew blood-red flags: Blake and Hornigold.

I recognized *Freyja*, Hornigold's boat, easily enough, but this was the first time I'd seen Blake's new vessel, the *Dutch Pride*. My heart sank. Although I'd heard the Carib sailortown gossip of Blake's survival, part of me hadn't believed it. I hadn't *wanted* to believe it, but I couldn't deny it now. My glass picked out the familiar, heavily bearded figure on the quarterdeck of the three-masted ship. A little smaller than *Edelweiss*, the *Dutch Pride* was just as heavily armed. Both vessels headed our way.

"Blackman!" I roared, by way of encouragement.

"Nearly there, Captain!" came the muffled reply.

I looked up at the mess atop my mainmast and winced.

I looked to starboard at the fort—we couldn't bear off in that direction. There were too many big guns.

I looked ahead—the shore was coming up fast, too fast, even with the loss of the main-topsail.

Now that we were past the headland and had water, my only option was to tack soon, and pray my hull and rigging would stand up to the strain.

Tacking was the hardest, and—in this situation at least—the riskiest maneuver a square-rigged ship could undertake. She had to turn through at least ninety degrees, with her bows passing through the wind. For a time we'd be going backwards. Away from the waiting shore, yes, but straight toward Blake and Hornigold, and we only had two-pounders mounted on the sternrail. The manoeuvre would put a great deal of strain on

Blackman's patch, and I had no way of knowing just how securely he'd been able to fix it. He was the bo'sun, not carpenter, the sails and rigging were his area of expertise, and I had no time to check his work myself. If only Gaunt . . . No, I could not think like that, could not get distracted. I had to focus on the moment, on this situation, and try and get us all out of it.

I looked up at the rigging again. If I tacked too soon, I could lose the mainmast—we'd be at Blake and Hornigold's mercy.

"Mierda!"

Even if we made it, we'd still have to run the gauntlet of Brisingamen's headland gun, this time with *Freyja* and *Dutch Pride* in hot pursuit.

Mierda!

"All clear for going about!" I gave the first command to prepare the crew for the tack. I noticed a number of wild glances aft, but they all ran to sheets and braces, ready to haul the sails round. They all knew the stakes, especially as ball now hit the water both astern and close to starboard. Hardening up earlier had kept us at the limit of the fort's range, although the current was slowly and inevitably dragging us into it. At least Blake and Hornigold were not quite near enough—yet.

I had no hands spare for the guns now, I needed all hands to trim the sails and do it perfectly. Our bombardment of Eckerstad stopped.

"Helm a'lee!" Thomas thrust the tiller to leeward to push the bows into wind.

"Mainsail haul!"

Men shouted heaving chants as they hauled on mainsail sheets. I watched the rigging, trying not to show my crew my tension. The yards swung round. We all held our breath as we drifted backwards. If we were going to get stuck, this was when. If we were going to lose the mainmast, this was when.

"Let go and haul!"

We made it. All we had to do now was set the sails on the new tack. I heaved a sigh of relief, we were round and the mainmast had held. Now I only had Blake and Hornigold to worry about—and the gun on the cliff top, of course. I pointed my glass toward my enemies and prepared my gunners to fight.

Chapter 70

GABRIELLA
13th February 1687
Seven Leagues West of Dominico

I woke to find Klara in the cabin with hot chocolate, fresh bread and meat.

"You don't have to do that, I'm not your mistress."

"No, you're my captain," she replied, smiling. "And you need to eat."

I sighed and heaved myself out of the cot. Yes, I was a pirate captain, but at what price? *Why did I have to lose Leo? What else would I have to lose to be free in this world?*

"Drink, you'll feel better." Klara shoved the beaker of hot chocolate at me. "You have a boatful of confused people out there; they need to know what your plans are."

I nodded, and made a huge effort to suppress my desolation and fear. I was the captain of this vessel, that had been my choice, and it was time to act the part. I had a quick wash, gulped my breakfast down, used the privy ledge and went topside just as the bell rang five times. It was midway through the morning watch, about six of the clock. The sun was climbing rapidly, we had a gentle breeze and *Valkyrie* was sailing well. I went aft to Carmen, who was standing her trick at the tiller, to check the course, then walked down the deck to hear Mr. Gaunt's report. He was at the mainsheets instructing the crew on the set of the sails.

"Morning, Mr. Gaunt," I interrupted. "Is all well?"

"As well as can be, I reckon," he grumbled. "I hope thee knows what thee's doing. Thee should never have left the Cap, lassie, never. Who knows what'll happen now. I don't like it. I tells thee, I don't like it."

"Neither do I, Mr. Gaunt, but I had no choice, I couldn't stay, not after what he did. I couldn't stay, so let's just make the best of it shall we?"

"Aye, lassie," he muttered.

"Aye what?" I asked sharply. He looked at me. "Captain. Aye, Captain."

"Thank you, Mr. Gaunt. I'm relying on you, you know. I'm going to need your help to get *Valkyrie* through this. I'm sure Leo would expect it."

He looked at me and I wondered if I'd gone too far, but if my quartermaster wouldn't respect me as captain and show it, why would the rest of the crew?

"Aye, Captain," he said with a hint of a smile. "That's more like it, but thee'll have to do this without calling on the cap's name, thee knows. But I'll help thee, don't fret about that."

I touched his arm. "Thank you, Mr. Gaunt," I almost whispered. "You don't know how glad I am to hear that."

I looked around and my eyes met Carmen's at the helm. She couldn't possibly have heard us, but I didn't like the small smile I could see around her pipe.

I went back to the quarterdeck and looked over my boat again. The enormity of what I'd done had hit me whilst I had been talking to Gaunt. I had seven men I thought I could rely on, although I was only sure of two of them, and they were all annoyed at my leaving the man they still thought of as their captain. Added to that, five women looked to a sixth and still thought of her as their captain. *What had I been thinking?* The only person aboard I knew I could trust fully was Klara. She'd never taken to sails or gun and seemed to have taken over the galley, but, thanks to her, I was sure Obi was my ally. And Gaunt, of course. I knew he wasn't happy and was still loyal to Leo, but I also knew he looked on me as a daughter and I trusted him completely. I realized he'd be the key to my captaincy—if he showed support, then Davys, Butler, Cartwright and Greenwoode would most likely fall into line. I had no idea where Baba's loyalty lay.

Carmen and the Awildas, however, were my biggest problem, and by the looks of it, the problem was growing. I noticed the men each had an Awilda working closely beside him. Was that coincidence, or was Carmen preparing the way to make a challenge against me? Or did the women just want some male company after sailing together for so long? *Bloody hell.*

Carmen smiled at me. “A motley crew,” she said.

I looked at her, not sure of her motives, and realized I didn’t like them, whatever they were. I knew she was unhappy at leaving *Freedom’s* firepower behind, and the tentative friendship we’d enjoyed at first was gone.

“Umm,” I replied. “What’s Andy doing?” She was heading forward with a bag of tools, chased by Gaunt.

“Oh, she’s sorting your guns out for you,” Carmen explained. “It looks like she wants a gunport in the bows. I think your carpenter is going to help her. Now that we’re on our own, we need to be better prepared.”

“Nobody cuts holes in my ship without my say so,” I stormed. “And I doubt very much Mr. Gaunt wants to help.”

I left her smirking at the tiller and headed forward once again.

“Put down the saws,” I ordered, in my best commanding voice. “How dare you cut into *Valkyrie* without my knowledge or agreement!”

“You told me I was Master of Arms. I cannot be a master gunner without gunports. We’ll be chasing a multitude of ships and need a bigger gun here now that we’re on our own.” Andy turned to continue what she was doing, and the similarity of her words to Carmen’s was not lost on me.

“You still need to report to me before you make any structural changes on this boat, and Mr. Gaunt needs to agree the change.”

“Will a gunport here cause any weakness to *Valkyrie*?” Andy asked Gaunt.

He examined her marks, then said, “Well, no, but that’s not the point, lass.”

Andy glowered at the epithet. “I am used to being trusted and allowed to get on with my duties,” she stated. “Is that not the case aboard *Valkyrie*?”

I could feel myself losing this one. “Of course it’s the case, but please let me know before you cut into my ship!”

She nodded and turned back to her work.

"What gun do you want to place here?" I asked.

"I'll bring up a six-pounder from the waist. We're hunters—chasers, we need more range forward."

"But they're iron guns, there's too much spray forward—the salt will rot them!"

"I'm a master gunner, Captain, and excel at my craft. I will take care that it does not," she replied stiffly. I could not think of another reason to stop her and looked at Gaunt helplessly. He shrugged.

"I'm changing the other guns too," Andy said, her back still to us.

"What?"

She stood and turned. "I'm changing the other guns too. They're all different sizes and take different balls and powder. I want you to target ships with six-pounders to match those I brought from *Awilda*. If all our cannon are the same, we'll be more efficient, and there'll be fewer mistakes with shot and powder."

She turned back to her saws without waiting for an answer, and I realized she hadn't actually asked a question. I stared at her back in frustration and clenched my fists. I knew I was in grave danger of losing my temper which would only make things worse. I forced myself to turn and walk away. I'd have to find a way of controlling the pair of them, but at the moment I didn't have a clue how to go about it.

"Thee'll have to keep an eye on that 'un, Captain," Gaunt said. "She's a law unto hersen, and won't do a damn thing she's told. Be careful with the both of 'em. There'll be trouble there, thee mark ma words. Aye, they's trouble, them two."

"Yes, I know, but we're stuck with them, Mr. Gaunt, so we'll have to make the best of it," I managed to say quite calmly. I looked up at the sky. "Nearly noon, time to take a sight, will you accompany me?"

He smiled. "Aye, 'course I will, lass."

He was teaching me how to carry out the day's work by dead reckoning, but was kind enough to let me pretend he was keeping me company. I went below to the cabin to get the backstaff, then joined him on the foredeck where we'd get the best view of the sun on this course, Klara's words ringing in my ears—another warning to beware Carmen. She'd noticed Carmen smiling at my altercation with Andy, and thought she'd set it up in the first place. I was to keep a close eye on her. At least that wouldn't be a problem on a boat this size, but it didn't help me to know what to do with either her or Andy. They'd both been at sea a lot longer than I, Carmen on the quarterdeck of her own pirate vessel. She was a more experienced sailor and leader, and was already making trouble. Although without directly threatening my position, I couldn't accuse her of mutiny. *Does she still want* Valkyrie *for her own? And with a ragtag crew at best, how will I stop the Awildas taking her?*

Chapter 71

"We'd do better tacking round and finding *Sound of Freedom* again, lassie, thee knows that don't thee?" Gaunt reiterated. He was not going to leave it alone.

I studied the shadow cast onto the unwieldy backstaff by the noon sun behind me, and said nothing. The length of my arm, it had a large arc at one end through which I sighted and used to obtain one reading, and a smaller arc at the other end with a shadow vane which I adjusted to the sun to give a second reading. Our line of parallel, or latitude, was the sum of these two angles, but it wasn't easy to decide on the right numbers when I was constantly heaved about on deck.

"Whatever went on 'tween thee and Cap, thee can mend it. The both of thee have been through so much and come out the other side, thee can get through this an'all."

"No we can't, Gaunt. You don't know."

"I knows enough."

"No you don't!" I shouted, unable to keep hold of the temper that had been threatening to engulf me since I'd last seen Leo. "He hit me! He threatened to put me in irons! He's just like my father, just like my husband! I won't have it! Not from him, not from anyone!"

Gaunt stepped back as I shook the two-foot-long backstaff at him.

"I don't think it were that simple, lassie," Gaunt said.

"Gabriella? What's wrong?" Klara had arrived.

"Of course it was that simple," I shouted, shaking Klara's hand off my arm.

"You defied him in front of the whole crew. That were mutiny. He had to show his authority—to thee and to everyone else. Does thee not think that might have summat to do with it?"

"Damn him and his authority!" I screamed. "He knows about Erik and he knows about my father, and he threatened me anyway!"

Memories of my father flooded back and I shook them off. I'd been free of him for years and done so much, why was he in my thoughts now? Erik had been little better. Well, he'd been worse really. He'd looked remarkably similar to my father when his temper was ignited—even though they'd never met. Erik *had* been worse. He'd used a weapon as well as fists—his cane—although he'd usually been careful enough not to leave any visible bruises larger than the width of his thumb. The times he broke this rule of thumb, I'd been so incapacitated that I couldn't have shown anyone the evidence of his brutality anyway. Except for Klara of course, and she and the other slaves didn't count. I should be grateful, he hadn't really had to take the care, as nobody on Sayba would have done anything about it. He could have killed me at any time, at his leisure. Then Leo had turned on me, and threatened me, and Gaunt was telling me to go back!

"Gabriella, please," Klara said quietly, still trying to keep the peace. "This is not helping you—everyone's watching."

I looked around, shaken by my memories, and realized I was behaving in the same manner as the men I was railing against. I was alone with a hostile crew, I needed to keep control—I was hardly filling them with confidence in their captain.

"I can't go back," I repeated, my voice almost normal again, although I was still shaking. "He threatened me. I won't go back. I have to make the best of this."

Gaunt nodded, too wise to say anything more, and pointed up to larboard. "Thee sees them birds, lassie?" he asked. "Thee has to choose which of them thee's gonna be: man-o-war or booby. Just watch 'em a minute."

I'd seen them before. The white boobys were excellent fishers, and hardly ever returned home without a prize—unless they became prey to the black men-o-war. Rather than catch their own, the larger birds ganged up on a laden booby and forced it to give up its treasure.

He saw I understood and handed me the backstaff I'd dropped in my rage. "The sun'll be past its zenith soon, and thee hasn't a parallel yet," was all he said.

Once again, I turned my back to the sun and balanced myself

as well as I could on the heaving deck to hold up the instrument to read its shadowfall. "It's right between fifteen and sixteen."

"Right then, we'll check the traverse board so thee knows the course and speed over the whole watch, then thee can make our position." Gaunt was all business again.

"Very well." I smiled, trying to repair some of the damage my tantrum had caused, and led the way back to the quarterdeck.

Down in the cabin I looked in despair at the mess on the chart table, and cursed myself that I hadn't worked at this harder before striking out on my own. Charts, log book, dividers, compass, traverse board, slate, paper, and sharpened, string-bound sticks of plumbago for writing covered the wood. At least I could put the backstaff away for another day; the nocturnal, or star clock, wasn't needed; nor was the astrolabe. What I needed now was my head—and Mr. Gaunt's guidance. The line of parallel was easy enough, I'd just read it off the backstaff, and I drew a faint horizontal line on the relevant chart to represent it.

I studied the traverse board next, a wooden roundel laid out like a compass with a length of wood above, all drilled with rows of small holes. The pegs stuck into it translated to how fast we'd travelled and in which direction since the last time I'd fixed our position. I added the details to my slate, tallying the previous watches' information so the traverse board itself could be cleared ready for the next pegs to be inserted on the half hour. At least heading south with a fair wind our course had been fairly steady, with no constant tacking, so this dead reckoning would be easier than most to plot.

"Thee'd be better leaving that traverse board in place on the taffrail by the tiller," Gaunt advised. "Just make a note of its reading and them on the slate, then wipe it clean for the next watch. Then thee can take as long as thee likes in the cabin over thy positioning."

I nodded and scratched my calculations with my writing stick. I underlined my answer and did it again, and again, until I got the same result three times. I crossed the line of parallel where I reckoned our position to be, and raised my eyebrows at Gaunt.

"Hmm, I'd have put us a bit more to the west," he said. "The current from the Atlantic swell will have pushed us sideways no matter how much southing we've made, but not bad, lassie, not bad."

I threw the writing stick down in exasperation. "How can I work out where I'm going if I can't work out where I am?" I exclaimed. "And I've told you to call me Captain, not lassie!"

"Settle down lassie—Captain. Thee's doing right enough. It takes time and practice, and even then thee can't be sure—every navigator at sea has the same problems. Make a good guess, keep an eye out for land and do thy best, that's all thee can do. It'll get easier, thee's not far off. Thee'll do better fretting about that lot out there than the charts, anyhow. That Dane and her saw-happy mate's the biggest problem on the boat if thee asks me."

I nodded; he was right. I finished off the log, determined to get back out on deck and keep a closer eye on Carmen. I couldn't bear to lose *Valkyrie* to her—but I had a lot of work to do if I were to avoid the booby's fate.

Chapter 72

GABRIELLA
21st February 1687
Four Leagues East of St Vincent

I grabbed for the backstaff, which had been about to fly off the chart table, and cursed. *Valkyrie's* motion had been getting wilder all day; the waves were too violent for the wind strength and now, as they'd promised, the wind was getting up. I put the navigational gear away with relief—at least that was done for another day—and headed back up onto deck.

Davys had the tiller with Gaunt standing by, and I looked up at the sails and sky, then checked the swinging needle of the compass.

"What are we in for, Mr. Gaunt? It smells like a hurricane to me."

He smiled at my choice of words, knowing full well I had yet to experience a full-blown hurricane. "Nay, it's February lass, wrong time of year for hurricanes, but we're in for a blow all right."

With his words the big mainsail shivered and the canvas by the mast lost its wind and flapped.

"Aye, pay her off, Mr. Davys, keep her sailing with the wind abeam."

I nodded my agreement and moved forward. I'd loved the strong wind ever since that first night—once I'd got over the conviction we were sinking. I ducked down below the windward bulwark as another wave broke over the side, and held onto the mainshrouds whilst water swirled around my legs, trying to pull them from under me. It cleared through the scuppers and I started moving again, gasping with the exhilaration of our speed through the waves and keeping an eye out for the next big sea. I checked the sails; the wind was definitely fouling—backing to the north and forcing us to bear away westerly as we had the square topsails flying. So be it, I couldn't risk them being caught aback, and possibly springing a mast or two. I reached the soaking wet foredeck. Every wave cascaded over the bows and windward rail as the crests broke over us with a face full of spray before we plunged down the back into the trough, then started the rolling climb up the next one.

Despite my excitement, I reminded myself that we were on our own out here, and I was responsible for every life on this deck. If something—anything—went wrong, *Valkyrie* could be knocked down and sunk, and we'd all die. I'd have killed my entire crew. I had to curb in my instinct to revel in the storm and concentrate on keeping everyone safe.

"Carmen!" I shouted. She was directing the activity on the foredeck. "Get the tops'ls and forecourse in!"

"What?" She looked at me as if I'd lost my sanity. "Why? She can take it, she's loving this."

"Shorten sail, Carmen! Annika, Bess, Baba! Lay aloft and get that forecourse in, then the tops'l!" I shouted.

Babawande went straight to the ratlins, but Annika and Bess looked at Carmen.

"*I'm* your captain, not her! Do *not* look to her for instruction! I told you to lay aloft! Move! Now!"

They went. Carmen glowered. This could not go on.

"Will you take over here, or do I have to do it all?"

Still glowering, Carmen nodded, then turned her back.

I turned my own back to the wind and spray, and scanned my decks. I realized the water level was never below my knees and we were taking on more water than the scuppers could clear. As the crew got to work, the square sails quickly lost the wind, and we sailed on a more even keel, but I didn't think we were out of danger yet.

"Douse the galley fire, then get below," I told Klara, knowing she still was not comfortable on deck in a storm. Then I noticed Carmen glance to windward, looking worried, and I turned to face the cascade of wind and water myself. This was going to get worse before it got any better; I should have shortened sail before this.

Sky and water darkened rapidly except for the white horses and streaks of foam, and I didn't think it would be long before spindrift was whipped off the crests of the waves. I turned back to Carmen.

"Reef the fores'l."

She nodded. No arguments now, the wind was getting up quicker than even she had realized; now she was pure sailor. I left her to it, sure her complaints had been purely for the sake of argument, and headed aft to supervise the reefing of the main. Gaunt had already followed my example with the fore-topsail, and the maintop was coming in. Everything was under control. I was far enough aft now to be able to breathe through the spray, and I faced the wind, enjoying the feel of raw power and speed on my face. I almost felt like I was flying. I was strong, invincible.

"Captain, look out, lassie!" I barely heard the cry against the wind, even though Gaunt was just behind me, and was aware of his grip on my arm only when he pulled me violently backwards and something landed heavily on the deck where I'd been standing. Not something, someone: Cartwright.

Blood spread round a body obviously broken—even if he somehow lived I couldn't imagine that body talking, walking, sailing. Arms and legs pointed in directions arms and legs shouldn't point. Head faced . . . head faced . . . well, not ahead.

I looked up, but Jayde and Greenwoode didn't have a moment to spare to look down after their fallen comrade, they had their hands full with the wildly flapping topsail that had blown free and knocked Cartwright from the yard. If they weren't careful, they'd soon join him on deck.

Gaunt rushed to him, but shook his head. There was nothing he could do for him, poor devil. I was shocked. *One of my crewmen is dead. Would he be alive if I'd shortened sail earlier? Is this my fault?*

I realized Jayde and Greenwoode still needed help to bring in the sail and looked about me. Everyone was busy fighting tiller or cordage. I made my decision quickly and jumped for the ratlins, climbing with the wind at my back. Higher and higher. Forty feet, fifty feet. I clambered up to the maintop platform and hung on for my life as I waited to go over the edge, wind howling and trying to whip me off and away.

Then up the next set of smaller ratlins to the topyard seventy feet above the dark-gray and white maelstrom that, hours before, had been the placid sparkling blue Carib Sea. I clung to the mast, my eyes streaming from the wind and salt spray—even up here. My heart thumped in fear and I tried to judge the moment I would leave the mast's solidity and step out onto the footrope. Upright, roll to leeward, pitch forward, upright, over to windward, pitch, upright, back to leeward—an impossible arc. I wanted to go on the lesser roll to windward and had to will myself to do it. Now. I took a deep breath and stretched my bare foot forward onto the thin line tied at intervals the length of the yard—all that would prevent me from plummeting to the deck below.

I threw myself forward and put all my trust into the wind blowing me onto the yard that moved toward me. My breath was punched out of me as my belly hit solid wood and I hung on desperately, hoping I hadn't hurt the life I was almost sure was growing inside. That was the worst bit over.

I gave myself a minute to get my breath and nerves back, then inched my way windward toward Jayde and Greenwoode, who were still doing battle. I wrapped my right arm around one of the hempen gaskets, and hoped my shoulders would prove strong enough for this. I braced my weight between the footrope and yard, and leaned forward over the wooden spar, hands outstretched to begin to force the wet, heavy canvas into submission, knowing that Cartwright had died falling from this spot.

My legs and arms were agony and I forced myself to ignore them, concentrating instead on turning my fingers into claws to drag the sail up, tuck it under my slightly swollen stomach, and pull up more in a fight for every inch. Jayde and Greenwoode disappeared. The deck below disappeared. Even the sea disappeared into the thundering of the canvas and the shrieking of the wind in the rigging. All that existed for me was the wood beneath my belly and the yard of canvas before my face. Time reduced to seconds; there was no past, no future, only now, this instant, this sail—and the knowledge that if I couldn't do this, I would lose my ship and every soul aboard her, and all their deaths would be my fault. Just like Cartwright's.

I gave another almighty heave to trap yet another fold of canvas beneath me as a gust hit. The footrope slackened, and suddenly I was leaning too far over, only balanced rather than braced. I gripped the wood between my belly and thighs, terrified, and braced my arms against the sail, pushing the canvas away from me. The line I'd wound round my right arm cut into my skin, and both my shoulders burned in agony. I didn't dare breathe in case that was enough to tip me over. I hung there for what seemed an age, sobbing in terror as I balanced precariously over the yard of my ship. *I can't do this, I've already killed one man, am I now going to kill myself and my unborn child? And everyone else aboard* Valkyrie, *both friend and crew, while I'm at it?* The gust passed and I rocked backwards into the lull, my feet scrabbling for the footrope. I took a moment to rest and let the blood flow back into my right arm, wanting to hug my stomach but unable to do so. I looked across at the other two and saw that Jayde, furthest out on the earing, was nearly done and stowing the sail. She'd managed to fold the canvas into itself and was now fighting whipping cordage to secure it. I winced as I saw the thin line of gasket catch her face, but she didn't let go and I was filled with respect for her determination and courage. *I have to do this. Have to do this. Have to.* I took a deep breath and leaned over the yard again, flexing my fingers before curling them back into claws. I grabbed a fistful of canvas and hauled, then grabbed another, and another. It would get easier now there wasn't so much canvas exposed for the wind to catch, and both Greenwoode and Jayde moved closer to me, tying gaskets as they went, taming the sail.

There. Done. A quick breather and scan of the furious cloud and water, then across to leeward to do it all over again.

Chapter 73

"What the hell were you thinking? You're carrying a child, Gabriella! What the hell were you doing up there!"

"Klara, hush, I'm well, calm yourself." There was no point denying it. If Klara had seen the signs, I could be sure I was with child. I sighed; *maybe it would be better if the child isn't born—what kind of life is this for a child? Or for a mother?* But I wasn't going to say that out loud, not even to Klara.

"What if you'd fallen, too? What then? All this would have been for naught and you'd be dead!"

I ignored Klara's temper and sat down in relief, my arms and legs shaking from my climb and exertions in the tops. I didn't want to think about what had happened to Cartwright.

"Here," Klara said, shoving a steaming beaker of chocolate at me. I would have preferred rum. "Not that you deserve it, but you're soaked through and shaking. You'd best not succumb to fever." As if that would be by choice.

"Thank you, Klara." I ignored her rebuke and reached out to take the beaker with both hands. I didn't trust my fingers and had been flexing them whenever I could—both they and my feet cramped painfully. On top of that, the shaking in my legs was getting worse, not better, now that I'd sat down.

I put the beaker down before my arms followed suit and I dropped it. I wasn't used to lying over a yard and fighting canvas in this weather, and I hugged my belly, hoping after all that I hadn't hurt the life growing in there.

"Thee knows thee threatened thy babby just as much, if not more, than the Cap did you, lassie," Gaunt pointed out. "Is thee gonna run from theesen now?"

I looked at him, angry. "You know as well as I do I had no choice but to go aloft, we could have lost the ship and then we'd all be dead, 'babby' included. You're no topman, and *Valkyrie* did not have time for me to wade along deck to find someone else, and neither did Jayde or Greenwoode—you know that as well as I do, Mr. Gaunt. I'm the captain of this vessel and everyone aboard is my responsibility, not just my belly, so why don't you stop fussing and get out on deck!"

"Aye, Captain," he replied, stony-faced, and I wondered if I'd once again gone too far, but I wasn't having him berate me in front of others, and I *knew* I'd done the right thing—the only thing I could have done in the circumstances.

"Drink your chocolate!" Klara instructed. "And put this on." She'd found a dry shirt in my seachest. I flexed my fingers a few times, then obeyed, reflecting how quickly I'd grown used to the lack of privacy at sea. The shirt was immediately damp, but I had to confess it was better than the sodden rag the last one had become. I flexed my fingers again, the feeling in them was coming back, and I risked picking up the beaker to drink. I couldn't remember the last time I had felt so tired; even drinking was an effort.

"Thee's got more trouble, lass." Gaunt was back and continued, "Both tops'ls are in, the mains'l's reefed, fores'l and course both stowed, and both jibs are flying. *Valkyrie's* sailing well, but that Dane's on the warpath."

Carmen burst into the cabin.

"You're a damned fool to sail like this; that crew's not up to it, there's not enough of us and it's not safe out there for my Awildas!" she stormed. "A captain needs to be on deck, not aloft or hiding in the cabin! Do you even care what's happening on your decks?"

I drained the chocolate then stood up with a sigh. "There are no Awildas anymore, Carmen. *Awilda* is wrecked off Sankt Jan Island. There are only Valkyries aboard this ship and you need to get used to that. Make your report and be quick about it." I was fast running out of patience with this woman, no matter how good a sailor she was.

"Your crew doesn't know what it's doing, and my girls are having to do all the work! Those slaves still don't know the difference between a sheet and a brace, and your husband's men are hiding in here with you." She glared at Gaunt.

"Now 'ang on a minute, lass . . ." Gaunt said.

"There are no slaves aboard *Valkyrie,* and Leo is not my husband," I started, but she hadn't finished.

"We've no business being out here with this crew, you should've run for shelter as soon as the wind started getting up." This from the woman who hadn't wanted me to take in the topsails.

"If you carry on like this you'll kill us all! You've already killed one man, who's next? If it's one of mine I promise you there'll be trouble. You've no business being out here!"

"Are you challenging me?" I was cold. I had suspected this was coming, I'd have had to be blind and simple not to, but I'd been hoping for a bit more time.

"Lass . . . Captain . . ." Gaunt cautioned us.

"Damn right I am!" Carmen ignored him. "This boat deserves a better captain—so far you've left her sister ship and the strength and opportunity *Sound of Freedom* lent us, you've killed Cartwright, risked all our lives, and we've not taken an ounce of gold or a single coin. This is not what I signed on account to! I call for a vote. *I'd* make sure the crew worked together and pulled their weight out there!"

"Stop this now, the pair o' you! Leo Santiago's captain, whether he's 'ere or not! This boat is still under his command! Thee can't change his crew without his say so! Settle down!" Gaunt tried again.

"How can the crew work together if we can't?" I retorted, ignoring him myself now. "If *you're* arguing with your captain, how can there be any discipline or unity out there?"

"Then put it to a vote. As he said, Santiago isn't here." She glanced at Gaunt, then glared at me again, "You've left him and his protection—and his command. You've mutinied. You're on your own, so let the crew vote. If you're voted captain, you'll have no more trouble from me, and if *I* am, we'll all live longer and get rich in the process!"

"And what would you have done differently? We haven't spotted a prize to take, and you'd have kept the tops'ls flying out there—how would that have kept us alive and rich? You know what? Yes," I said. "Make course for the lee of St Vincent, let the wind drop and everyone rest. We'll hold a crew council, make a decision and get on with it." I realized the first step for the crew to come together was to elect their leaders in the tradition of the Carib Sea, and I had to accept whatever and whomever they chose. Listening to Carmen rant and abuse her crewmates, I thought I had a good chance of winning and would take that whilst I could, and before she and the men realized I was with child. With any luck, Carmen had played her hand too soon. "In the meantime, get back out there and sail my ship."

Her lips pursed in a tight smile and she left the cabin. I looked at Gaunt in dismay as he shook his head in silent yet obvious disapproval.

Chapter 74

We spent the best part of three watches drifting to leeward under small canvas until we were in a good position to seek shelter in St Vincent's lee, and the storm still raged. It had been an exciting sail, but we were all relieved to be at anchor and nursing our aches and pains, out of danger. Cartwright's death had shocked us all, and I knew Carmen was right. As captain, his death was on my hands.

The sails were furled, those that hadn't been struck for patching, anyway, and *Valkyrie* was pumped nearly dry. My crew were hard at work repairing the rigging. The new topyards had chafed against the shrouds, and some seams had worked loose in the hull as she'd ridden the waves, but all in all *Valkyrie* had weathered the storm well. All my own pains were in my arms and legs, not my belly, thank Neptune, although that didn't keep Klara from fussing. There was no sun and the charts gave me my parallel, so I made up the log early, then went up to the damp, windy and fresh deck to face my challenger.

All looked snug aloft, and the gray cloud raced above my mastheads. I looked with pride at my colors whipping overhead, and which let the inhabitants of this island know we were as much outcasts as they were. I hoped they'd stay exactly where they were—I had no fight with them, and didn't want to take up arms against the Black Caribs. A community of Carib Indians and escaped Africans, they were known to guard their island fiercely—especially against Europeans.

I looked at my crew gathered on the maindeck under the awning rigged against the rain. Klara doled out chunks of roast goat, calming the grumbling about being called out on deck as everyone gorged on the delicious meat and drank their rum. It was too cramped below for this, and anyway, I wanted to enjoy the freshness before the sun baked us again. I looked around at my motley crew.

Carmen stood in the middle of the maindeck surrounded by her Awildas and smoking her pipe, looking confident. Gaunt, Davys and Obi were on the quarterdeck, and Butler and Greenwoode flanked the rum cask, all sucking hard on their own pipes. Baba had joined Carmen's group. I sighed; it was only to be expected, and I understood the women had been working toward this since we had left Leo. The captaincy probably rested in the hands of that one man.

I took a beaker of rum from Klara and held it up in a salute. "To Cartwright," I toasted. "He was a brave man and will be much missed."

I drank and the crew followed my example. "Cartwright," they all murmured.

"We'll say goodbye when we head out to sea again, he would not want to be buried so close to shore." Everyone nodded and drank again, then looked at me expectantly. I took a deep breath. There was only one way to do this and that was to dive straight in.

"As you all know, a challenge has been made for captain. Everyone on this vessel has chosen to be here, and it's time to decide how we sail forward. At the moment we're strangers, but we need to start living and working together as shipmates. We'll vote on captain and ship's officers, agree and sign new articles and make plans to take some gold!"

A muted cheer went up and I smiled. I didn't know if I'd be addressing them like this again, and I determined to make the most of it.

"*Valkyrie* is my ship and she always will be, but I am only her captain with your blessing, and I hope you will continue to trust me with that responsibility today. It's time we stopped being Awildas and Freedom Fighters. From this day on we will *all* be Valkyries, we will *all* have our place on the crew and will be shipmates—family." I paused and looked around again at the men and women on deck.

"Nowhere else in the world can we live like this. Women, maroons, outlaws. Nowhere else do we have so much choice, so much power over our own lives and decisions. Today we will all exercise that power of choice."

I walked forward and jumped onto the rum cask on the maindeck.

"I am asking you to elect me your captain today. I know I haven't been at sea long, but in my short time in this life I have taken this beautiful, handy ship and not only led a successful raid on a French merchantman, but defended this very vessel against surprise attack." Laughter rippled around the deck, the Awildas laughing hardest of all. Even Carmen smiled around her pipe.

"I promise you I will fill this boat with gold and coin, and I'll do my utmost to keep you in one piece while we do it. Everything I've learned about captaining a pirate ship, I've learned from Captain Leo Santiago, and I won't forget what he has taught me. But if you think I'm soft—a lily-livered landlubber." I looked at Carmen. "I remind you that I've also learned at the hands of Erik van Ecken. Do not doubt that I *am* a pirate captain." I pointed to the masthead and my flag whipping in the wind, and met every eye in turn.

"Those colors threaten broken hearts and death by our blades. But look at the wings supporting them—they symbolize *me* through the angel I'm named for. Those colors will be feared the length and breadth of the Carib Sea by the time I'm done."

"I'm sure they will, but you're not the *only* pirate captain aboard this boat." Carmen stepped forward to stand next to me, but I didn't relinquish my higher position. "And *I've* been proving it for years. I know better how to win gold, and a lot more than the measly shares we took from that French ship and left behind!" She glared at me. "I know better how to keep a boat above the waves, and I know better how to fight. And the only way you defended this boat against surprise attack was with the help of the *Sound of Freedom*, whom you mutinied against. You cannot do this on your own. You don't know how.

"Oh, and I don't have the distraction of an expanding belly," she added and looked at me in triumph. I met her eyes and kept my face impassive.

"I'm not one for long speeches," she continued, looking back at the crew and meeting every eye. "There's only one thing I have to say—you *will* live longer *and* richer if you choose me as your captain."

I was surprised at her brevity until I remembered that she'd been preparing for this, probably since she first came aboard, certainly since we'd parted ways with Leo. She'd already done all her talking, every day, and her Awildas had helped. I remembered again how they'd been paying attention to the men.

"Are there any more contenders?" I asked.

"Aye," Butler shouted. "Mr. Gaunt for captain!"

"Nay, nay. I've nay ambitions there, Butler. I'm happy as quartermaster. We shouldn't be voting on captaincy anyhow, not without Santiago 'ere."

"You've hit the nail on the head, Mr. Gaunt, Leo isn't here—we have to do what's right for *Valkyrie* in our present circumstances."

I beckoned to Klara, jumped down and took two sheets of paper and writing sticks from her, then spiked both of them to the cask. I wrote Carmen's name on one, and my own on the other.

"Make your marks and drink your rum. Then we'll talk ship's officers!"

Chapter 75

It was close. Baba voted for Carmen and everyone else voted as expected. We had seven votes each—I'd only won by my own, casting, vote. If Cartwright had lived, Carmen may have won.

It wasn't all bad news for Carmen though. She was elected quartermaster, much to Gaunt's shock. It seemed the crew wanted a second-in-command who would challenge their captain, rather than encourage and protect me. We'd have to make it work, I could not afford any more mistakes.

We divided the crew into two watches run by Carmen (starboard) and my new second mate Davys (larboard). Jayde was elected bo'sun, Mr. Gaunt ship's carpenter, and Klara was now officially in charge of the galley she'd more or less taken over anyway. Then we agreed on articles. They were unsurprisingly similar to *Freedom's,* but not quite as generous to the captain and officers. I could live with that, *Valkyrie* was still mine.

So I had my ship's officers and crew. I wrote out the names as carefully as I could on the swaying deck, with space for each crewmember to sign their name, or make their mark if they didn't know their letters, and passed the sheet around along with my falchion to swear on.

"Sail oh! Sail to west'ard, twinmaster, no colors!"

I gave the articles and writing implements to Klara to put away and jumped into the rigging to see for myself, just as a plain red flag broke out at her masthead: *Freyja*. She was making her way round the headland, probably looking for shelter to ride out what was left of the storm. *Damn*, we weren't ready to take her on. Bess struck three bells for five of the clock, and I grabbed the bell rope from her grasp and rang it wildly for attention.

"All hands! All hands! Starboard Watch, man the halyards—jibs and mains'l! Larboard Watch, make ready to weigh anchor!

"Andy, not you—stick to the guns."

I had to laugh at the look on her face—as if she'd be anywhere else with an enemy ship heading toward us. She took Baba and Butler astern and starboard and got ready to fight.

I took a deep breath in an attempt to calm my excitement, but couldn't help grinning when I caught Carmen's eye as she knocked out her pipe, and I saw the same exhilaration reflected on her face. I turned aft again to check on *Freyja*. She had tacked inshore, was laid over and gaining on our position fast. We didn't have time to weigh anchor after all, we had to leave it.

"Mr. Gaunt, go forward with an axe and stand by to slip the cable as soon as the jib's set. Send the larboards aft to the guns."

"Tell them to run out the larboard guns first," Carmen interrupted.

"What good will that do?" I demanded. As we came round off the wind, *Freyja* would be to starboard not larboard.

"The weight will lay *Valkyrie* over and help the rudder," she explained, impatient. "It'll help us get underway."

Gaunt nodded agreement.

"Very well," I agreed, not sure I entirely understood, but realizing I had to start to trust my new quartermaster. "Go ahead, Andy, run out the larboard guns." I was too late; she was already running across the deck with the larboard watch in tow.

I looked again at *Freyja*. "Put your backs into it!" The sails were creeping up the masts, but it was a hard job at the best of times. Soaking wet canvas and a new crew did not combine well. A splash nearby told me *Freyja* was getting too close. Her cannonball would soon do damage, and there was nothing I could do about it trapped and tethered between her and the shore. We needed to get way on, and quickly.

"Mr. Gaunt, stand by!" I shouted into the wind, knowing it was unlikely he'd be able to hear me. Mind you, he knew better than I what was needed. As carpenter he was the most skilled with the axe and would be the one to repair any damage if he missed his target. I could be sure he'd split the cable first time and at the right instant.

Finally the head of the first jib reached its mark and was made fast. Carrie and the others ran to starboard to start hauling the sail in on the wrong side to pull the bows around, and Gaunt raised his axe ready to cut us free.

Carmen shouted something to Andy, and I joined Davys on the tiller, all of us ready for the first bite of wind. There! Davys and I shoved the tiller hard over to larboard, the jib filled, and Gaunt's axe fell. We were adrift and our bows slowly turned to starboard.

I felt a sharp pain in my right arm and was surprised to see blood. *Freyja* had hit us at last and the starboard quarter-rail was in splinters. I flexed my arm. Not a serious problem, just a scratch. She was only at the limit of her range; it had been a lucky shot.

"Haul away on that main halyard! Carrie, I want it reefed, then get ready at the mainsheets!"

There was no time for anyone to rest; the boom swung over as the bows turned, and the mainsail flogged madly as it climbed the mast. The deck heeled and I heard a rumble; the guns were run out and now I understood why Carmen had suggested it. The shape of *Valkyrie's* hull at this angle helped to push her bows off the wind, quicker than if we'd had to rely on the rudder and jib alone.

The main was up and being hauled in. I risked another look to leeward and *Freyja,* and couldn't help but admire her. She'd be in more sheltered water soon, but at the moment she was full and by (full of wind and by the wind) and there was no better sight at sea, no matter who stood on the quarterdeck. Sails full and bellied, her hull was laid over and water sluiced her windward rail. She was a little bigger than *Valkyrie*, also with two masts, but was square-rigged on the fore and had a large gaff on her main. That gave her an advantage over us with the wind dead fair, but we had the advantage here; as long as we could get moving, that is. She ignored the two-pound shot Baba and Butler fired at her from the stern gun—she was still too far away for that to be a problem—and I shouted at them to hold their fire until they could make it count.

"Let go the jib and set her to starboard!" I shouted, and immediately the small triangular sail set between mast and bowsprit flogged and filled to leeward, then the mainsail filled and we straightened up on the tiller.

"Haul in larboard guns!" I shouted, and Carmen echoed my words down the deck.

"Ready the starboard guns!" Again, Carmen relayed the order.

We slowly picked up speed, Davys watching the water carefully to make the most of the wind swirling around this sheltered bay. *Freyja* tacked and was now headed straight for us. It was a straight race, and *Freyja* was gaining. At least she was heading into the same windshadow that held us, and which would soon slow her down.

"Stand by to fire," I screamed, echoed once again by Carmen to the men and women at the guns.

"*Fire*."

"Let go the mains'l," Carmen shouted, then: "*Fire*," she repeated. As we lost the wind and the deck leveled off, the guns boomed, their ball traveling much further than they otherwise would have, thanks to *Valkyrie's* flatter angle.

"Haul in the mainsheet!" Carmen shouted, and ran to lend her own muscle to hemp, whilst cannon were hauled in, sponged out and reloaded.

I looked back at *Freyja*. She headed straight for us, presenting a much smaller target bows-on than we did broadside-on, but she only had small guns in her bows, and I laughed out loud remembering the frustration I'd felt when Andy had cut the gunport in *Valkyrie's* bow. If Hornigold had done the same, he'd have had us; as it was, we had a good chance of getting away.

I could see him now on his quarterdeck through my glass: a tall, thin bald man, with a long goatee and the usual broad shoulders and bandy legs of a sailor, and I remembered his dark eyes and the thick black eyebrows that I found so startling.

I dropped the glass and glanced at Klara, remembering it had been Hornigold who had hurt her that last night at Brisingamen—and many times before. He wouldn't hurt her again—ever. She stared at *Freyja*, her face set, looking more ready for a fight than I'd ever seen her.

"Fire when ready, Carmen," I shouted forward, knowing she was better placed to decide when to adjust the sails to give the guns their best chance of hitting Hornigold, and happy now to trust her judgement.

We'd almost reached the eastern headland as the mainsail

shivered again, *Valkyrie* flattened and another broadside flew *Freyja's* way. *Yes, a hit to her bows!* Too high above the waterline to cause her much consternation at the moment, but he wouldn't be able to take her out past the lee of the island in that state. Not in those seas. I looked forward again at what awaited us. The wind might be dropping, but the sea was still high—those waves were twenty-footers at least, and they'd be confused. The waves kicked up by the storm and interrupted by the island would combine with the easterly Atlantic swell in unpredictable and dangerous ways, and it was getting dark, but we had no choice, we had to go.

We cleared the headland and immediately *Valkyrie* jumped forward and lay over so her starboard rail was underwater. I grabbed hold of the larboard rail to stop myself falling and screamed, "Let go the main," just as Carmen shouted the same. The reefed mainsail shivered and flogged and *Valkyrie* righted again. "Bear off, Mr. Davys," I instructed. "Find your safest course."

I thought hardening up into the wind in this would be more dangerous than running free with it, but it would take experience and skill to stay ahead of the waves and keep them from swamping us. I recognized that Davys had more of both than I did.

"Well done, Captain." I felt a hand on my shoulder and turned to see Gaunt, face creased into a wide grin, whether from the excitement of the fight or the weather, I didn't know.

"Thank you, Mr. Gaunt. Please stay with Mr. Davys and help him with the tiller."

Keeping a course in this wind and sea was too much for one man alone. If Davys was thrown to the deck, *Valkyrie* would screw up into wind, then founder and sink once broadside-on to those waves.

Carmen joined me on the quarterdeck, her hand held out, and I grasped it, both of us grinning madly. Although a little extreme, *Freyja's* arrival had pulled this crew together in a matter of minutes.

"He'll know the colors now," she shouted over the roar of wind and water. I repositioned myself so the spray hit my back before replying.

"Yes, and when he sees them again, we'll be ready for him."

She nodded. "I do not want to run from that skraeling again."

"Nor me, next time we see him it'll be on our terms," I promised. "I've had just about enough of Edward Hornigold." And I meant it. I'd run from Erik over a year ago, I'd run from Leo, and now I'd been forced to run from Hornigold and that galled me, this had to stop. No more running.

We both looked astern in the gathering gloom. As I'd hoped, *Freyja* hadn't risked the open sea with that hole in her bows and had slunk back into the lee of St Vincent.

"*No*. No lights, Klara, not until we're well away from here, just in case any of Hornigold's friends are nearby," I called. I wanted to keep *Valkyrie* invisible until we could be sure we were safe. She nodded and blew out the stern lantern.

I grabbed hold of Carmen as the stern rose on a wave and I slid forward, much to her amusement.

"Another half hour," she suggested. "We should be safe enough on this course, the islands are further south, then we can bear north and heave-to until this calms down."

I agreed.

Chapter 76

I had stayed up all night until I was sure *Valkyrie* was out of danger, and I'd been treated to a fabulous display at sunrise. The departing clouds had created a vista worthy of van Goyen himself, using a full palette of oranges, yellows and pinks.

The wind had dropped off with the dawn, and I'd slept the four-hour forenoon watch through. Carib life was back to normal: beating sun, steaming decks (at least they were not sticky yet), and uncomfortable, salty clothes. Even the supposedly dry clothes in the cabin had acquired a stiffening layer of salt, and the rigging looked like a washerwoman's line as everybody took advantage of the casks brimming with fresh rainwater.

Valkyrie had ridden out the last vestiges of the storm well, and the crew looked and acted like a crew. Thanks to a Carib storm and Ed Hornigold, *Valkyrie* was a different vessel. Leo would be impressed.

Once the day's work was done and I had a vague idea of where we were, I was presented with a steaming plateful of roast pork—Klara had decided we needed to replenish our strength and had butchered one of the pigs as soon as it had been safe to relight the galley hearth on the maindeck. I hadn't realized how hungry I was until I started eating, and I didn't want to stop. Coupled with pint after pint of cool fresh water to wash away the salt, it was a meal fit for Neptune himself.

Halfway through, Carmen joined me in the cabin with a heaped plateful of her own.

"What news?" I asked her.

"The usual chafing," she replied. "And the forestay needs to be re-rove." If that line between foremast and bow snapped, we would lose the foremast. "I've got Butler and Bess on that as a priority. The damage to the timber is only superficial, Mr. Gaunt can take his time. One of the gun truckles is damaged, which Andy can sort out, but there's nothing to trouble *Valkyrie* unduly."

"Very well," I said, relieved.

"St Vincent is still in sight, although only just. We must have been blown a fair fetch south overnight, but we can get the fores'ls flying as soon as Butler and Bess are done with the stay, and we'll soon leave it in our wake," she continued. "The crew are full of blisters and bruises, but they're used to that—there's no serious injury."

I nodded. I was tormented by aches and pains myself.

It was not good that the island was still in sight, I could only hope *Freyja* was busy making her own repairs, and that the St Vincentians would not be too accommodating to their visitors.

Carmen finished her meat and sat back, taking out her pipe and tobacco.

"What happened to your pipe?" I asked—it was much shorter than the last time I'd seen it. "Did you sit on it or something?"

"No." She laughed in return. "The long stems don't do so well in a blow—they don't last long."

I laughed along with her but wondered if it had really broken in the weather and fight, or had it broken when she lost the captain's vote? I wasn't going to risk our newfound camaraderie by pressing the matter though, and the laughter died away.

"I want to get the crew working better." I turned to more serious matters. "I want them drilled on the guns and sailhandling, and I want Andy to find the best sharpshooters, too."

"Ja, everybody knows their trade, but they're not working well together yet. We were lucky yesterday, but I'll admit they're all keen enough now, it won't be difficult to arrange. We should plan and rehearse some set maneuvers too—that's how we were so successful with *Awilda* with such a small crew. We did the unexpected and took advantage of the confusion."

"You certainly did!" I laughed. "That's a good idea, *Valkyrie's* strength is her handiness. You're right, we should make the most of that, what do you propose?"

***

An hour later, we had a page of ideas and Gaunt stuck his head through the door. He nodded.

"Good to see you two lasses working together," he commented. "The new forestay's rove and holding if one of thee wants to come up on deck."

"Very good, Mr. Gaunt, thank you." I noticed his smile didn't quite reach his eyes and realized he was still wary of my Danish quartermaster.

"Will you make a start with that, Carmen, while I get us underway? I want to be ready to attack the next likely prize we spot. I promised everyone gold!"

"They'll be ready; they're halfway there now, just choose your prize wisely."

Chapter 77

GABRIELLA
2nd March 1687
Seven Leagues Southwest of Martinico

I have to admit, I was impressed with Carmen and Andy. The crew was working together well on both guns and sails, and we'd figured out a number of set maneuvers and signals. Baba, in particular, had proved to be a crack shot and would join Annika in the rigging with the muskets when we came to attack. Now all we needed was a suitable prize.

I leaned over the starboard forerail and stared out to sea, then down at *Valkyrie's* stem cutting through the waves, and enjoyed the feel of spray on my face. The white water flung aside to swirl and torment in our wake mirrored exactly how I felt. Leo had done the same thing to me.

When Leo had turned on me, my heart had broken and so had, briefly, my spirit. I hadn't seen Leo threaten me, I'd seen Erik, and I was not having it. I would not live with him again, not in any guise. I told myself that Leo would snap out of it and come chasing after me, and I couldn't help but take a good look at the horizon in all directions every time I came on deck, even climbing into the tops—just in case. But of course there was no *Freedom*, and I'd sit up there for hours at a time, legs and arms gripping the trunk of the mainmast with the wind screeching in my face, reminding me there were many more reasons to live than Leo, and after a while it worked. I convinced myself I didn't care, that I didn't need him or want him by my side. I was terrified of living with another Erik. I was starting to believe that I preferred being alone than risk being hurt again, than risk trusting a man I loved.

The baby was a reminder of all that, a reminder of all, of *whom*, I loved, but I didn't know if it would ever meet its father. I couldn't go back because I'd be showing him his behavior was acceptable, yet the further we sailed, the further away he was and, despite everything, that still mattered. Alone in my cabin, feeling the tiny movements inside me, in spite of my crew who were now my family, in spite of Klara, the one person who'd always been true to me, I knew I'd always be lonely if Leo wasn't with me, and I was slowly admitting this to myself, if not to anyone else.

Even if, somehow, Leo found me and still wanted me, how could I trust him again? My heart and body ached for him, but at the same time I dreaded the thought of seeing him.

At the moment I could deny these feelings. I could wear my cloak of anger and pain, and insist I was better off without him, but what about when the baby came? What if it was a boy and had his eyes, his face? How could I love a child that reminded me of so much pain? Of betrayal and violence—his father?

Yet I'd never wanted to do this without him. If I was honest, I hadn't wanted to become a mother at all.

"Damn you, Leo, damn you to Hell!" I turned back to the decks before the tears threatening my eyes overwhelmed me, just as a cry came from the tops.

"*Sail oh*, off the starboard bow, heading east. Two leagues off."

My heart leaped. *Freedom*? Angry at the hope I felt, I studied the horizon with my glass and could just make out topsails. Big. A three-master then, but not *Freedom*.

"Bring in the tops'ls and harden up, Mr. Davys," I called, walking aft. "Let's take a closer look."

The bell clanged again, a double ring. Two bells, a half hour past noon. The ship was a league and a half off now—we were catching, despite having had to tack—and I could just make out her topsails from the deck.

"Spanish built, you see that narrow stern?" Carmen observed from my left shoulder. "But she could be a prize, especially in these waters, and she's not showing any colors."

"Yes," I agreed. "Or she could be exactly what she looks like: a rich Spanish merchantman running to the home country. Let's find out.

"Break out the Burgundy Cross," I shouted at Bess who was already at the mainmast having anticipated my order. "If she's Spanish, she'll heave-to for the Garda Costa. If not, she'll run for one of the islands. Either way, we'll have our answer," I added to Carmen.

Four bells, an hour and a half into the afternoon watch, one league off, still running for the open sea.

"What do you think?" I asked Carmen and Gaunt, both of whom had joined me on the quarterdeck and all of us on tenterhooks.

"I must admit, I'd expected a reaction to the Spanish colors," said Carmen, thoughtfully.

"Aye, she must be pirate—or freebooter," Gaunt added.

"Umm," I mused. "Well, I suppose if she's pirate, she'll turn and fight at some point. We'd best be ready."

"And if she's a smuggler?" Klara had joined us. "What would she do then?"

"Then she'll run, lass," Gaunt answered. "And hope some ill befalls us or that she can stay ahead until nightfall and give us the slip in the dark."

Six bells. We were steadily overhauling her, and it was clear we would weather her in time. If she was going to do something, it was time to try it, but she carried on heading east. She didn't have a choice. If she bore off, we would follow, get the weather gage and catch her. If she tacked, we'd tack after her and do it faster with our fore-and-aft sails. All she could do was coax as much speed as she could from her square sails and hope. We were faster and more weatherly, and, in Gaunt's words, if no ill befell us such as a sudden squall or a rigging failure, we'd catch her to windward in another couple of hours, well before dark.

Eight bells, half an hour before the start of the first dog watch at four of the clock. Half a league off, just one and a half knots away.

* * *

One bell. One knot. I could see her clearly from the deck, but still had no idea who she was. She was of a similar size to *Freedom*, but with less sail. She carried square course and topsails on the main and foremasts, and a lateen-rigged spanker on the mizzen. She was fairly long and low in the water for a Spanish ship, and had a well-decorated stern with an overabundance of carvings and gilt, and still she flew no colors.

"Andy, ready the starboard guns," I called to her, to be greeted by the black look I had expected. The guns had been readied hours ago, and I nodded my acknowledgement. She had her six-pounder as well as a couple of two-pound rail guns in the bows, two more swivel two-pounders on each rail and another five guns on each side of the gundeck.

"I hope she has six-pounders aboard her," she said and I jumped. She rarely made any spontaneous comment, and I remembered she wanted all the guns to be of the same caliber.

"Let's hope," I replied. "You can have the pick of her guns once we've taken her."

Another look. She wouldn't have accepted anything less.

"It concerns me that we've seen no reaction," Carmen said. "They must be planning something. It's clear we're faster, and we've been weathering her for hours. He must have something in mind."

"Aye lass, but don't bend theesen in knots over it. Thee keep thy mind on thy own plans, and don't give him a chance to carry his out. Thee has to have faith in theesen and thy crew, we'll deal with whatever that captain heaves our way."

"Thank you, Mr. Gaunt." I smiled. I trusted his advice and didn't know how I'd have coped without him. I wished my father had been more like him.

"Annika, prepare your muskets. Baba, it's nearly time to show us what you can do." I raised my voice to address the whole crew.

"You've all worked hard the past few weeks, and it's time to put it into practice. You can do this; *we* can do this. When you voted me your captain, I promised you I'd fill this boat with gold and coin—well this is where it starts! We'll catch her in another hour and shortly after that we'll be rich. This is why we're out here. This is what we've been working for, practicing for. We are Valkyries, every single one of us! Now let's introduce ourselves to that ship!"

This was the worst part of being captain for me, addressing the crew before a battle, desperately hoping I chose the right words, and that they wouldn't be the last any of my crew would hear. But my words, thank goodness, were greeted with cheers. We'd been on the chase for over four hours and their blood was up. My Valkyries were ready for a fight.

Chapter 78

Three bells. Almost in range. Just a little closer, a little nearer.

"Fire warning shot!

"Break out the true colors!"

Andy's big bow cannon fired at the same instant my flag broke out proudly at the masthead in place of the Burgundian Cross. I watched Andy reload and wondered that there was still no response from the Spanish ship.

"Harden up!" Carmen shouted.

"No!" I suddenly realized something. "Bear off, we're doing exactly what he expects. He's waiting for us to come to windward of him! Tell Andy to ready the larboard guns!"

Klara ran forward whilst Carmen protested, "We'll lose the wind! We'll struggle to get alongside!"

"We've enough way on and firepower in the bows. Don't you see? He's ready for us to lay his larboard side—that's why he's not reacting. He's waiting to get us in the way of his guns. If we move quickly, we'll rake his starboard side before he knows what's happening! It's our best chance!"

"Andy wishes you to understand that all guns are ready to fire at all times when we sail into battle," Klara reported very carefully, having rushed back from the bows, and I laughed, imagining how Andy would have actually phrased it.

"Bear off, Mr. Davys, bring her alongside to windward with as much speed as you can. Tell the gundeck to stand by to fire to larboard." Klara ran off again. She would stay at the waist now to relay my orders forward.

"Bow! Target the rudder! Fire when ready! Keep firing!"

Butler and Bess manned both two-pounder bow chasers and fired at the Spanish stern, working hard to sponge and reload despite the new cant of the deck as *Valkyrie* swung downwind, whilst Andy supervised the gun crew on the bow six-pounder.

I trained my glass on the decks of the ship ahead. I couldn't see much beyond the high stern, but as we came closer I grew aware of frenetic activity. I'd been right, they'd been waiting for us to windward.

"Fire as soon as they can be sure of a hit!" I shouted to Klara, and the most forward guns boomed, ejecting clouds of putrid smoke which blew aft to envelop the whole crew before clearing.

"Larboard rail, fire when ready!"

The smaller swivel gun was loaded with swan shot—a canister filled with musket balls—and targeted the sails. The bow cannon fired again—chain shot now. Two small cannonballs linked by a foot of chain would do a lot of damage to wood, and I cheered as the Spanish ship lurched at the hit to her rudder. Her bows began to swing off the wind.

"Bear off! Bear off!" I screamed at Davys, full of visions of the larger ship crashing into us.

"No, belay that! Harden up!" Carmen bellowed. "Let's not give him a chance to organize himself or his guns," she said more quietly. I looked at her then repeated her order.

"Are you sure we'll make it?" I asked as Davys put the tiller over and our bowsprit closed on the slim and elegant stern. I stared up at her nameboard, *Santa Anna Maria*.

The two ships were close, and I held my breath as they lined up. If the bowsprit caught what was left of her rudder, we'd lose it, the foremast too, and be at the mercy of the Spaniard, instead of the other way round.

"Steady, steady," Carmen chanted, and silence fell on *Valkyrie's* deck as all eyes were drawn to the tiny gap between the two vessels.

I held my breath, and I expect Carmen and everyone else did as well. The bowsprit connected with the Spanish rudder. Then it was free, and still in one piece.

"Fire bow cannon. *No*, not you, Bess!" I shouted as Bess picked up the lit linstock and Klara repeated my order at the top of her lungs. If Bess fired, she could well take out our forestay and accomplish what the Spanish stern had not. She heard, and only the six-pounder fired. Their rudder was in splinters; they were dead in the water.

"Starboard gundeck, ready to fire!" Klara echoed again, and Andy and her forward gun crew moved to starboard.

"Sharpshooters get ready!" I bellowed up into the rigging.

I took a moment to look at my decks. Greenwoode, Obi and Jayde worked the sails, trying to keep up with the course changes, knowing we couldn't afford to lose any speed. The whole deck was misted with smoke, and the air stung with the hellish stink of black powder.

The Spanish ship towered above us and we crept around her.

"Fire starboard guns!"

Another broadside rocked *Valkyrie* and splinters flew from the other ship. Andy had aimed for her waterline, knowing she didn't have a hope of taking out any Spanish guns, and had scored four out of five direct hits. Our aftermost gun had just missed her stern.

Without steerage and taking on water, still unable to get us into her cannon's sights, surely she'd surrender?

Maybe, but not yet. Men lined her rails and sent down a hail of pistol and musket shot. The message was clear; they weren't giving up easily. That meant she was likely a rich prize. Whatever she was carrying, I meant to have it. She *would* be mine. And I must admit—I did enjoy attacking a Spanish ship. *Take that, Leo!*

Andy fired again—more hits on stern and rudder. Surely she'd strike soon—she had no steerage, was starting to settle by the stern and had no big guns far enough aft to return fire. The best they could do was musketfire, but their musketeers now had to lean around the high stern or fire at too steep a downward angle from their rigging, where sail was now being taken in.

"What was that?" Carmen exclaimed and ran forward. I ran after her. "She's stopped drifting to leeward, look, she's dropped her windward anchor, she's club-hauled!"

Dropping anchor would stop her bows swinging round, and I was sure the Spanish captain hoped it would be enough to keep her head-to-wind. Whether it did or no, we had a problem.

"Davys," I shouted, running aft again. "Harden up, she's club-hauled!

"Gunners, keep pounding the stern!" I screamed.

"Starboard rail, aim for their cannon! Try and knock them off their truckles, they'll soon have a bearing on us!"

As I shouted, the Spanish aftermost cannon fired and her shot went high, decimating our fore-topmast. Then Carrie fired her rail gun—direct hit! The next cannon skewed up at an angle, we were safe from that one.

"Good shot, Carrie. Reload!"

The bow cannon fired, Butler had waited until the sea helped his aim—his timing was perfect and a six-pound ball splintered the Spanish bulwark, sending iron and fragmented wood into the gundeck.

"She's dragging her anchor!" Gaunt shouted in my ear. "Her stern's too heavy, she can't hold it!"

"She's hoisting colors—finally! The Cross of Burgundy!" Carmen laughed. "And striking!" She cheered loudly and everyone joined in, myself included. *We've done it!*

Chapter 79

I pushed my hat firmly onto my head—it made much more of an impression on defeated captains than the cotton headscarf I customarily wore at sea—then checked the pistols draped around my neck and blades stuffed into my sash. The rail guns were still manned, but Andy and the other gunners had joined me and were making their own preparations to board our first prize.

The *Santa Anna Maria* was made fast alongside, but was larger than *Valkyrie* and I couldn't see her decks. I looked up into *Valkyrie's* rigging. Annika and Baba had muskets trained on the Spaniards from their positions in the tops, and I trusted the captain was covered. This was where I would be most vulnerable, but, as ever, there was only one way to do this and find out if the strike was genuine—get on with it.

I threw up a grapnel hook and line, and led the swarm up the five feet of freeboard that separated the two decks, then strode toward the man I assumed was captain, my hands now bearing my pistols. He stood on the maindeck alone, slightly apart from the huddles of seamen around the decks, legs akimbo and wearing a fierce frown.

"Call all hands on deck please, Capitán," I said.

He visibly started. "You're a woman!"

"Well spotted. All hands please," I prompted, realizing I was going to have to get used to this reaction. He nodded at one of his men who shouted the order down the main hatch.

"Mr. Gaunt, would you do the honors?" He stepped forward with a coil of rope to restrain the Spaniards.

"Carmen, take three and check below." Andy, Greenwoode and Obi joined her and disappeared down the main hatch to search out any hidden men and take a first look at her cargo.

"Capitana." I turned to my Spanish counterpart, my eyebrows raised. "I surrendered to your attack in the hope you'd allow me to begin repairs to my ship immediately. You're welcome to my cargo of coffee and cacao, but I beg you to allow me to save my ship."

I thought for a moment. *Coffee and cacao?* I didn't think so.

"And what about the gold you're carrying? Tell me where you've hidden it, and I'll allow your carpenter and a working party down to your bilges."

"Gold? We aren't carrying gold, Capitana, we're only merchants carrying New Spain's crops home."

"I don't believe you. A merchant wouldn't have run from an apparent Garda Costa."

"I didn't believe your colors."

"*I* don't believe *you*—you didn't show caution, you completely ignored the colors. Nor did you show colors of your own, but ran for open water. Why?"

His face fell. "Very well, we do not have the, er, requisite paperwork for our cargo."

"Ahh, freebooters."

"I wouldn't use so coarse a word."

"I would. And I don't believe a smuggler would take the risk you ran for coffee and cacao alone. Where have you hidden your gold?"

"Coffee and cacao fetch high prices in Spain," was his only reply.

"Tell me where your gold is, and I will let you save your ship," I reiterated, the pistol in my hand underlining my point. We stared at each other, then he dropped his eyes.

"The deckhead in the gundeck is false. There's a cavity up there filled with coin."

I nodded. "Thank you. Please show Mr. Gaunt here exactly where to look, then I'll arrange an escort for your carpenter."

Three bells in the last dog watch, about seven of the clock. Night had fallen and we were nearly ready to cast off.

"Get us away from here, as fast as you can, Mr. Davys," I ordered. "Set the main-tops'l.

"Mr. Butler, see what you can do about the ruin of the foretop."

There'd be no celebrating yet, not until we were well away from the prize and there could be no threat of retaliation. I watched the Spanish ship recede into the night, her jib and topsails flying to hold her in position close to the wind until they could jury-rig a new rudder. They had worked hard on their hull and it looked like the ship would be saved. The worst holes were patched with lead, and we'd left their carpenter working on the smaller ones, whilst the majority of the crew worked the pumps. Water spewed from her scuppers and she would soon be seaworthy, if without any helm, but that was their problem.

It was getting hard to make her out now, only her lanterns were visible, and then they disappeared from view and I told Davys to tack so she wouldn't know in what direction we lay.

Now that we were out of sight of our prize, we could light our own lanterns and crack open a cask of fine stolen Spanish brandy. This was our first haul and nobody wanted to wait to count it.

"Valkyries!" I shouted, beaker of brandy held high and the chattering deck fell silent. "Congratulations! *Valkyrie* has made her first conquest!" Carmen led the cheer. "Now I suppose you want to know what we've taken!"

Another cheer greeted Gaunt and Klara, who had been below decks where the loot had been loaded out of the way. They carried small but heavy canvas bags. I thought the occasion demanded a longer speech, but I no longer held anyone's attention and, not a little relieved, walked over to them, grabbed a couple of bags and held them up to more cheers.

Each full share amounted to half a bag of golden doubloons and a full one of silver eight-reales coins, or Spanish dollars, and I got four shares. Not a bad day's work.

"Gabriella! Captain!" Klara called and beckoned me over to the nearly empty brandy cask. I heaved myself to my feet and, rather unsteadily, walked over to her. At least the wind had dropped with the sun and *Valkyrie* was sailing on a pretty even keel.

"What-is-it?" I mumbled.

"Look." She handed a sopping canvas bag to me. "I wondered

why they were taking Spanish brandy to Spain, look what I found in the cask."

She emptied the bag into my hands. Emeralds. Enough for two or three each. I laughed, and laughed. This just kept getting better. Soon the whole deck rolled with delight. "Salud!" I mumbled, holding my beaker up in what might have been the direction of our crippled Spanish prize. "You should have stuck with me, Leo," I added to myself. "Look what I've done."

Then my laughter died in my throat. That captain had hidden the coins we'd stolen, and I realized now he'd given them up too easily. We'd only found the emeralds by chance—what else had we overlooked? Had I missed an even larger haul aboard the Spanish freebooter?

Chapter 80

GABRIELLA
3rd May 1687
St Pierre, Martinico

The Spanish smuggler had been the first of many conquests, and *Valkyrie's* holds were full to bursting. It was time to convert goods into metal. Saint Pierre, Martinico's main port, was sighted and we headed into the mouth of the Roxelane River.

I rubbed my left forearm absently and looked again at the pattern pricked out and stained with gunpowder. We'd all woken with Andy's reproductions of the symbols on *Valkyrie's* colors after taking the Spanish smuggler, but I was the only one who had the wings included and it still smarted a bit. We were all truly Valkyries now, although I have to admit I'd been a little nervous when she advised us to take care around naked flames for the time being, at least until the skin grew back.

We tacked again in the river mouth, and I couldn't help but reflect that if *Freedom* had been with us she would have had to stand out to sea to wait for a fair wind. I grinned as *Valkyrie* worked her way in. Damn Leo, I didn't need him, we were fine on our own and had filling treasure chests to prove it. I looked up at the sails and held on. We had both jibs flying, plus fore- and mainsails, and *Valkyrie* flew into harbor with a bone in her teeth—white water flung from her bows in a graceful arc. I knew we made an impressive sight.

I wanted to anchor a little apart from the other shipping and directed Carrie on the tiller, then shouted, "Helm-a-lee!"

She pushed the tiller across, forcing *Valkyrie's* bows into wind, and she lost her way. The big sails above my head deafened as they thundered, starved of wind, and Gaunt struck the pin to let go the anchor we'd commandeered from the *Santa Anna Maria* to replace the bower we had left behind at St Vincent. As soon as it hit bottom, Jayde shouted for the jibs to be backed to hold us head-to-wind and slowly push us backwards until the anchor bedded in.

I'd wanted to make an impression and so we had: a beautiful boat brought to anchor perfectly. *Take that Leo!* But I'd already checked. *Sound of Freedom* wasn't here.

I left Carmen to supervise stowing the sails, and sailed ashore with Gaunt and Obi in the pinnace. We had hardly put off before *Valkyrie* was surrounded by bumboats selling everything from potatoes and fresh fruit to women. Whatever they were offering, they'd likely do a good trade aboard *Valkyrie*. We'd not had a chance to spend our winnings, and I knew Klara was relishing the opportunity to stock up with fresh food; she was starting to despair of a diet of meat and rum punch.

I'd only been to Saint Pierre once before, and that had been with Leo before I'd taken *Valkyrie*. We'd spent a fair amount of time here though, and I felt quite familiar with the port. I thought wistfully of the nights we'd spent alone aboard *Freedom*.

I searched for Monsieur Blanchard's warehouse, hoping he'd trade with me after having been introduced by Leo—*was it only six months ago? How things change*. My holds were full of all manner of cargoes, including cacao, coffee beans, indigo, cloth, cochineal, tobacco, and molasses. We stowed what we wanted for our own use, and selling off the excess would add a sizable sum to the pot and pay for fresh provisions.

The fact that I'd be dealing with a man who may conceivably have news of Leo and *Sound of Freedom* was purely incidental.

"Monsieur Blanchard," I greeted as we tied up outside his warehouse.

"Madame van Ecken," he replied, holding my hands and kissing them.

I started in surprise, I hadn't been introduced as Erik's wife—but that was sailortown gossip for you, nothing stayed private for long.

"Please, call me Gabriella," was all I said.

Blanchard smiled.

"We're here on business, Mewseur Blanchar." Gaunt came to my rescue. "Coffee and cacao, same terms as Captain Santiago, is thee innerested?"

"Ah, will Capitaine Santiago be joining us?" Blanchard smiled.

"No doubt he won't be far behind," Gaunt replied with a straight face. He probably believed it.

"Well, I'm sure you know better than I. Last I heard he was drowning off Sayba, having crossed swords with Blake and Hornigold—for the last time. But you know how sailors exaggerate. I'm sure he'll catch up with you soon." He smiled at me again. "Now, café and cacao you say, how much do you have to sell?"

We came to an agreement but my heart wasn't in it. I kept thinking of Leo. *Drowning off Sayba? Crossed swords for the last time? Is he really dead?* I suspected M. Blanchard got the better of the deal, but truth be told I was glad to get the damned casks offloaded so I could head back out to sea. *Can it be true? Has Leo's vendetta with the buccaneers killed him?*

Back aboard *Valkyrie*, I came out of my daze far enough to appreciate the good harbor stow Carmen and my crew had managed on the sails. I knew it was time to let everyone go ashore and enjoy their spoils, but I had no stomach for it. I'd stay aboard to keep ship.

"Have you heard?" Carmen greeted me.

"What, Leo and *Freedom*?" I asked, weary.

"No, not that—that's just sailortown gossip, don't set any store by that. No, Hornigold. He's been here and he's looking for us. He knows who we are and apparently he's got his sails in a right twist over us. He wants us dead and *Valkyrie* scuttled. We need to get out of here before he puts back in."

I nodded. "Very well, make sure the repairs are done. Give the crew a night ashore, and we'll make sail in the morning."

"Gabriella, did you hear me? Hornigold has sworn to sink us."

"I heard. Don't worry, we're very nearly ready for him, and he isn't here now. We'll put out tomorrow."

I knew I should be reacting with more urgency, but all I could think, despite Carmen's easy dismissal, was that whatever, or whomever the cause, Leo was dead.

Chapter 81

GABRIELLA
10th May 1687
Ten Leagues Southeast of Barbados

Almost three months and six prizes. My Valkyries were forging one hell of a reputation for themselves, and my flag of falchions, heart and wings was feared all around the southerly Caribbees. I should have been satisfied, but there was something missing. Well, someone. But there was nothing I could do about that, it was too late. He was dead. I would never see him again. Unless . . . unless Blanchard was wrong and he still lived. But no, it wasn't just Blanchard, Carmen had heard the tale too, although wasn't treating it seriously, but then she didn't care one way or the other, did she? I put my hands to my head and grabbed fistfuls of my hair. I couldn't stand not knowing. I wanted to scream—in both frustration and terror. I felt tears threaten. *What if he's really dead?*

"I don't like it."

I turned to Carmen. "What?" I snapped.

"Hornigold," she elaborated. "The skraeling's been looking for us for all this time, telling every ship and port he wants us, but we've not seen even a flash of his sails, and I don't like it. He's got something planned."

"Whatever he's planning, we're ready. The Valkyries are working well together. Andy has the gunners drilled to perfection and we're more than a match for him now."

"I know that, but I still don't like it. He's been at this game a long time and I don't trust him; he'll turn up when we least expect it and when we're not ready. We should search out *Freyja*, and take *him* by surprise."

I looked at her. I knew her well enough now not to disregard her advice out of hand, but where would we start? The Carib Sea was big and he had friends—many more than we had.

"What do you suggest?" I asked.

Her eyes narrowed and she squinted to windward. "Sail," she said, then shouted up to Annika in the tops. "Sail to windward! What do you see?"

"Twinmaster, topsail on the fore. Main gaff-rigged!" Annika shouted back. "Hull down!"

I looked at Carmen with new respect. She had good eyes.

"You don't think," I said. "*Freyja*?"

She shrugged. "Hard to say, we'll know soon enough. Andy?" She raised her voice. "Ready your guns!" Then, quieter, to me. "It won't hurt us to be prepared." She knocked the contents of her pipe overboard and I nodded. In these waters it was more likely a slaver or merchantman, but Carmen was right, we'd find out soon enough.

"Break out the Cross of Saint George," I ordered. If it was *Freyja*, we may as well pretend to be friendly and give ourselves some time.

"Annika!" I called up the mast. "Steady reports please! Identify her as soon as you can!" I didn't want to shout *Freyja's* name across the decks yet, just in case it was a false alarm.

Butler hoisted the white flag with its vertical red cross and pulled on the line to free the silk. If the other vessel was English, she may well decide to intercept us for gossip or trade.

"She's changing course!" Annika shouted down. "And she's flying a George Cross of her own!" Whoever she was, pirate or prize, she was coming. "It's *Freyja*! I'm sure of it!"

I moved to the ratlins to go up and have a look for myself, but stopped before I started to climb and smiled ruefully at Klara's worried look at my belly. I couldn't risk my child's life. *Leo's child.* I took a deep breath and squared my shoulders.

"Out of the way, Captain." Carmen laughed, took the glass from my hand, and reached the tops in record time. "Ja, that's *Freyja*!" She slid down the shroud and landed next to me, still laughing. "Great! A fight with the skraelings!" She rubbed her hands together. "Time to show him exactly what we think of him."

"Let's just concentrate on surviving this," I tempered, not quite as excited at the prospect. Our usual targets were merchants, not warriors. This would be different. "They're still over a league off, any ideas?"

We knew *Freyja* was fast downwind—she carried a lot of canvas for her size, just like *Valkyrie*—but she wouldn't maneuver quite as well, and needed more hands to work those square sails on her foremast. For the moment, we needed to get her off the wind. Not only was she running on her fastest point of sailing, she was to windward of us, giving her too much of an advantage and, if I could get her working her sails, we might get a better idea of the size of her crew and even pull some of them away from her guns.

"Let him come to us," was Carmen's advice. "He thinks he's stronger than we are and we ran last time we met, he'll remember that."

I agreed and shouted, "Get in the tops'l! Stow the forecourse!" I turned back to her as the quiet deck erupted into action and thumping feet. "Just in case he hasn't recognized us, we don't have to make it obvious who we are. What would a merchantman trying to get away do?"

Carmen smiled. "Harden up and try to sneak past."

"You heard the lady," I said to Carrie on the helm. "Harden up as soon as the square sails are in."

"You know she won't let us get to windward," Carmen added.

"Of course she won't, but with the gaff sails on both masts we'll have the advantage over her, and force her to act. Will you let Andy know the plan?"

"Already done," said a voice behind me, and Carmen laughed.

"She has a sixth sense about upcoming battle, you should know that by now!"

"Get me in range and we'll take her," Andy said, a rare smile on her face. "We're ready, we've been waiting for a proper fight."

"Well, you might get one," I said, the familiar nerves jumping in my belly. I rubbed my hands over it. I didn't relish the fight quite as much these days. "Launch the longboat, fill it with gold and put two oarsmen in it, but don't let *Freyja* see. We may need it today."

Chapter 82

"Fire bow cannon!"

As we expected, *Freyja* hardened up to keep the advantage of the weather gage and we fired at her larboard side from two hundred yards. I realized we were re-enacting our last meeting, only we'd swapped places. And *Valkyrie* had a six-pounder mounted in her bows with a longer range than the two-pound swivel chasers *Freyja* had attacked us with at St Vincent.

"*Yes*, hit!" Andy screamed from the bows. "Got her amidships."

"Stand by to jibe," I shouted, and helped Carrie push the tiller over to windward.

"Let go the sheets.

"Break out the true colors."

Valkyrie circled away from *Freyja* in the breeze—fresh enough to give us speed, yet not too strong to swamp us as we spun away. *Valkyrie* lay over as the main- and foresails slammed across and refilled with wind at the same time as my flag cracked open in celebration. Once again, Andy's firesense triumphed. *Freyja* was holed. She was still to windward of us, but she couldn't tack or jibe without taking on water. She had to keep her damaged board to leeward and that meant *we* now had the advantage. We'd need it—though it was unlikely to be enough.

Cannonball hit the water around us as we kept turning. The gunners were all at their pieces, which made it hard work for Carmen and the other three sailors who were working the sheets, but that couldn't be helped. The sails needed hauling in as we hardened up and we had to do it as quickly as possible. I wanted to keep Hornigold guessing and reacting to us. I knew I couldn't let him take the lead—*Valkyrie* had to be the aggressor if we were going to live through this.

"Ready about!"

We came up behind *Freyja* and into the wind. We had to tack, and tack quickly so our bow cannon could fire on her stern. She was already firing her stern chasers (more two-pounders) at us, and there was nothing I could do about that yet. I noticed her own colors were flying now—blood red, la jolie rouge. No quarter.

"Haul in! Haul in!"

We needed to be quicker, the sails were taking too long to come in; we needed to be faster!

Freyja fired again and my outer jib shredded; he was using swan shot—canisters of musket balls—and had targeted our sails. We still had the inner jib, which was essential to maneuvering quickly, but we'd be in big trouble if we lost that one too.

"Bow—fire!"

Butler and Andy both hit *Freyja's* stern, but not her rudder.

"Reload, fire again!"

I heard Klara echo my shouts forward and hoped both gunners could hear, but they knew what to do and fired again within two minutes.

A scream chilled me and I looked up to see Annika crashing down off the maintop and into the sea, she had fallen on *Valkyrie's* roll to leeward, and missed the deck. *Freyja* had targeted our sails and my sharpshooters. I realized I didn't know if she could swim. I doubted it.

"Klara, no! Stay where you are!" She'd run toward the larboard rail, but Jayde was already there with a line to throw. *Freyja's* next shot sounded across the deck and knocked Klara off her feet.

"Klara!" I screamed again, but could do nothing for her. I had to leave her where she lay. I pushed the tiller to leeward to try and get to windward of *Freyja*, but the other vessel wasn't having any of it and luffed up herself. I reached for the ship's bell and clanged it six times. The gunners fired a broadside, then everyone held onto shroud, mast or stay.

"Ready?" I asked Carrie. She nodded, we had to time this just right, we wouldn't get a second chance. "Now!" We heaved the tiller to starboard.

Chapter 83

Cannonball bullied their way through the air around us as *Freyja* fired a broadside, but we were soon bow-on again and most splashed either side of us. The ones that did find us missed our rig and inflicted only nominal damage to our woodwork.

Butler and Andy worked hard at the bow cannon, and Bess and Greenwoode fired a medley of musket balls and sharp shards of metal through their sails from the swivels, then quickly sheltered behind the bulwarks. I prayed we had enough speed to ram them before they got in a lucky shot. It was a risky maneuver, and one Leo had cautioned me never to take, but he wasn't here, and I thought it was our only chance of besting Hornigold. *Freyja* was bigger, more heavily armed, and had a larger and more experienced crew; we had to risk it all for this slim chance to come out on top.

"Brace yourselves!" I shouted to my crew as *Valkyrie's* figurehead made contact with *Freyja* midway between fore- and mainmasts. The way the bow had been carved, with the unicorn in a solid beam of wood, gave the structure a great deal of strength.

As the boats collided, the bowsprit shattered and the remaining jib blew free. The larger sails were left to flog and the Valkyries charged—running full pelt and unimpeded as *Freyja's* crew were still trying to work out what was happening.

We'd hit them amidships where *Freyja's* mainmast was secured and it had fallen, bringing down a tangle of rigging and sail across her decks and crew, who were scattered and down, having to disentangle themselves and get into better positions before they could fight back. A few had gone overboard at the moment of impact and more were dispatched as they tried to struggle free.

My eyes met Obi's. We both wanted to go to Klara, but neither of us could leave our posts. The best thing we could do for her now was win this fight, but I could tell his attention was split. I hoped it wouldn't kill him. Or me.

We'd gathered and loaded all our pistols and muskets, storing some at the bow with Butler and Andy, and the others on the foretop platform with Annika and Baba, ready to pick off as many of our rivals as we could. I took Butler's place at the bow, freeing him to join the rest of the Valkyries aboard *Freyja*. It would be up to me and Baba to make sure the fight did not stray to *Valkyrie's* decks, and up to Carmen and the rest of the Valkyries to claim *Freyja* for our own.

Frustrated that I had to stay behind, I watched the two crews fight until I couldn't make out who was who. I heard only howls of excitement and pain, the clashing of metal blades coming together with full force, the odd pistol shot and the noise of my small cannon as I targeted with grape shot—a canister of small ball—any man who tried to mount the unicorn. This fight had to stay aboard *Freyja*. If I allowed even one buccaneer aboard *Valkyrie,* we were done for.

At last, I saw *Freyja's* crew pushed back into the tangle of their own dismantled rigging, and suddenly Hornigold was there, right in front me, pulling himself up the hooves of my unicorn. I grabbed a pistol, aimed and fired, hitting him in the face. He fell, and I thought gleefully of telling Leo I'd hit the man I was aiming for, smiling until I remembered he was dead. At least I'd killed one of the men who had taken his life.

I fired another, but not quickly enough. The man who had gone for Butler cut him before he fell. I watched in horror as Butler slowly sank to his knees, his bloodied hand grasping at his belly. I got a glimpse of something gray and slimy, which he caught and pushed back inside. He looked up at me with a look of surprise on his face, then crumpled to the deck.

"Butler!" I jumped up to go to him, but realized we had to finish the fight first, and fired again to send a hail of ball and shot over the heads of the writhing mass below me.

The Freyjamen backed up in a huddled group surrounded by Valkyries, with nowhere to go and no captain to lead them. Almost as one, they dropped their weapons in surrender, with Andy the only one left still trying to fight.

* * *

We'd done it, it had been no easy contest, but we'd bested the bigger, better armed boat and more experienced crew against the odds. Yet it seemed a hollow victory—we'd taken heavy losses and didn't have *Freedom* to celebrate with. I shook those thoughts off, time enough for that later—there was much to do before we counted the cost of this battle.

I rushed to where Klara lay in a pool of blood, and stroked her face. "Klara?" I whispered.

She moaned, but didn't open her eyes. I sat back on my heels and let the tears fall. She was still alive. I looked up and shouted for Bess. I only left Klara's side once Bess had taken my place and I could be sure she would be cared for. Walking away from her when she was so badly hurt was the hardest thing I'd ever done, but I knew I had to check on the rest of the crew.

I carefully lowered myself down to *Freyja's* deck to walk my latest conquest. Andy was herding the men that were left to the foredeck, and Carmen and Greenwoode checked our wounded and made stretchers from *Freyja's* downed canvas to get them back to *Valkyrie*. Obi looked at me, but I couldn't meet his eyes. He rushed back to *Valkyrie*.

I moved to join them, wanting to find out how badly my crew was hurt and if anyone else had died, but a shout rose up.

"Sail oh!"

I was torn, I wanted to go to Klara and the others, but the whole crew was my responsibility, and I needed to find out what was happening, prepare for what came next. Were they friendly, or more pirates?

They turned out to be both.

"It's *Sound of Freedom!*" Baba cried.

Chapter 84

My heart stopped—*Freedom? She still sails? And Leo? What of Leo?* I looked at the sails in dread. I desperately wanted to find out if he lived, but what if he didn't? I could live without *that* knowledge. It was bad enough as a mere fear. At least at the moment I had hope. *Is that hope about to die?*

I had to pull myself together, and quickly. My heart pounded from all the excitement and concern for Klara and the others, never mind the possibility of having Leo's death confirmed. I also needed to check on the rest of my crew, find out who else was hurt, who we'd lost, and assess the damage to *Valkyrie*. I had no idea how badly my ship was damaged.

I looked again at the still distant sails, made my decision and went to have a look at the damage.

The whole of *Valkyrie's* bow below the unicorn was cracked and we were taking on water. Luckily, *Freyja* held us in such a way that we weren't sinking, but I couldn't see how we were going to separate them and get *Valkyrie* to land for repair, without sinking both vessels on the way.

The good news was that the worst of *Freyja's* damage was above her waterline, so we had time to figure it out. I looked up again and gasped. *Freedom* would be alongside in a few minutes. I'd soon know. *Alive or dead?* I put my arms around my belly, trying to hug the child inside.

"Let's give them the welcome they deserve," I said, just in case he was on that quarterdeck. I couldn't act as if he wasn't there. I wouldn't.

My crew lined up on *Freyja's* larboard side, blades in hand, jeering and laughing, whilst I stood on the remains of the bowsprit above the unicorn's back, where I'd previously sat as she leapt over the waves, tears running down my face, hair flying, trying to ease the pain in my heart with the thrill of the ride. Now, though, it gave me a good vantage point above the chaos on deck, and I waited to see if the cause of that pain was drawing closer. I aimed for dramatic effect: standing above the wreckage, firm, in control and victorious over my prize.

He *was* there. He lived! I recognized the familiar walk on the quarterdeck as he took over the tiller. *He lived*—the gossips had been wrong. My whole body sagged in relief, yet my emotions were so confused I was fighting tears.

I wanted to fling a grapnel into their rigging and quickly swing aboard, take him into my arms and never let go. Yet I was furious. Because of his recklessness I'd believed him dead. Even though I hadn't wanted to, a large part of me had believed him dead, and I'd grieved. For nothing. And all because he'd taken exception to me behaving as the pirate captain I was!

But I'd proved myself beyond any doubt now, however much I wanted him, I knew I didn't *need* him as a sailor or a pirate, and I'd managed perfectly well without him as a lover—or so I told myself. It only remained to be seen whether I needed, or wanted, him as the father of my child.

He drew closer and the two crews shouted good-natured insults at each other across the water.

I watched Leo bring *Freedom* in; a tricky maneuver needing perfect timing if he wasn't going to add to the carnage. The wind was off his larboard bow and, as he grew close, he thrust the tiller over and brought his bows round to luff up into wind. The momentum he'd built up brought him sideways the final few yards to bump gently alongside *Freyja's* larboard rail. Perfect.

Mr. Frazer supervised making *Freedom* fast and Leo moved quickly to board. My Valkyries parted to let him through, quiet now, and waited to see my reaction.

I watched him coming and couldn't understand the expression on his face. He looked relieved, even pleased to see me, as if nothing had happened and I'd welcome him with open arms. Well, *that* wasn't going to happen, but I resolved to give myself time to decide what I wanted and not put on a show for the reuniting crews. He climbed up the wreckage to the unicorn and looked around at the two ships joined together.

"¡Hola, querida! You don't do things by halves do you?"

I don't believe it, after all that's happened, that's *what he chooses to say? Laughing at me, mocking me?* I saw my fist connecting with his jaw before I was even aware my arm was moving. He wasn't well balanced and he crashed down to *Freyja's* deck below. I watched him fall, furious. It all seemed unreal, too much to cope with.

He was fine, waving Andy away when she tried to help him up. He stayed on his back, propped himself up on his elbows and watched me. *He doesn't look so pleased to see me now!* Rather, he looked scared and bewildered. Whatever. I had a good friend to check on. I turned my back on him and made my way to *Valkyrie's* infirmary.

The extent of my anger had shocked me; I was storming. *How dare he turn up and mock me after the way he'd behaved? How dare he take so long to come and find me?*

The anger I had for Erik came flooding back and, for a moment, Leo and Erik once more became one: a man I'd trusted who'd betrayed that trust. I was angry with Leo for behaving like Erik and angry with him for leaving me—even though I'd sailed away from him. I was even angry at the hands who'd been injured, and especially at the ones who had died—they'd also let me down and left me. I was especially angry with Klara, and all thoughts of Leo flew from me as I realized how badly she'd been hurt.

They'd taken her to my cabin and she lay face down on my cot while Bess bent over her, removing lead musket balls from her back with a pair of forceps from the physick chest. Klara had fainted from the pain long ago. It was a mercy.

"How bad?" I asked, all thoughts of Leo gone as I looked at the bloody pulp that was Klara's back.

"It could be worse, but not much," Bess replied. "She's taken almost a dozen balls, and I don't know if I can get them all out. It'll be a miracle if none of the wounds rot. She'll have to battle fever to live, that I *am* sure of."

I nodded my understanding, knelt in the blood next to the cot and stroked Klara's hair as Bess pulled another ball out of her flesh. Klara moaned then sank back into oblivion. I bowed my head, resting it on my arm.

"We were supposed to escape—to be safe! I wanted her to be free and I've killed her," I moaned.

"She *was* free, Captain. She was on this deck of her own free will. She chose to be here and face sea and gun. You know as well as I do that if you'd stayed on Sayba, the Hollander would have killed her eventually. You too, and made every day a living hell until he did.

"You've not failed her, Captain," she added.

"No?" I didn't agree.

Klara was the only person in the world I trusted, the only person I knew for sure would be there for me, as I would be for her. The only one I loved, and I did love her, of course I did. She was my one true friend, my sister. She shared my secrets, my deepest shames.

Now I had to prepare for her death, knowing she was dying because I'd put her on this boat and into that battle. I had brought her to this life, and her death was on my head, her blood on my hands.

"Captain!" Greenwoode appeared at the door. "You're needed on deck."

"What is it?"

"They need to know what to do with the Freyjamen. And we're still jammed tight."

I groaned, kissed Klara's ruined face and rose. I turned to tell Bess to do everything she could but realized they'd be wasted words. She would do nothing less. I gripped her shoulder instead, then headed topside to face the other problems needing my attention.

PART FIVE

Chapter 85

LEO

I was too late to do anything to help. I could only watch, helpless and useless, convinced I'd found Gabriella only to see her die. How could I have let Hornigold get away from me at Sayba? Twice? Now I'd have to pay for my failures. Or rather, Gabriella and the Valkyries would. It would be my punishment, my reckoning, to watch.

She at least put up a good fight and used *Valkyrie's* advantages well, tacking and jibing around *Freyja,* who kept her course and fired continuously. Then they came together, and my heart sank. It was a brave move, but even if Gabriella did by some miracle win this fight, she'd just lost her own vessel *and* her prize.

I looked up at *Freedom's* sails. "Haul those mainsheets!" I shouted. "Blackman, what's wrong with your eyes? Don't let me see any more sails ashiver!"

I knew I wasn't being fair. We were sailing close-hauled, and a little more weatherly than *Freedom*'s square sails could reasonably cope with. The sails were bound to shiver on this course, no matter how hard the men sweated the sheets and braces, which were already chock-a-block.

I turned my attention back to the two pirate vessels and the thickening pall of gun smoke drifting toward us like a hellish sea mist. The noise of the guns sounded like the barking of Hell's hounds. Getting closer.

Closer. Still only able to watch. Helpless.

The smoke cleared to silence. The battle was over, but whose battle was it? Who lived? Was I sailing toward friends in need or mortal enemies?

Closer.

* * *

There! There she is! Is that really her? But she's so big! Then I realized, and my breath caught in my heart. *She's carrying my child!*

"Loose sail.

"Helm to leeward.

"Stand by to fend off."

I guided *Freedom* to lay the tangle of hull and rigging alongside, and neatly avoided *Freyja*'s mast hanging over her larboard quarter. That would need to be cut away before it could damage *Freedom's* hull.

Laughing at the cheering and celebrating crew, I boarded and headed amidships where Gabriella waited for me. My heart swelled with pride, and I couldn't wait to take her into my arms and tell her what a magnificent woman she was.

Just look at her! High on her bowsprit, overlooking her victory—a victory she'll soon be famous for across the Caribbees. She's humbled the mighty Hornigold! And with a child in her belly! What a child that will be!

Moments later, I lay on my back in the wreckage of her victory, looking up at her. I realized it wasn't going to be that simple.

She turned and left me there, staring up at the unicorn pawing the gray air above me. If the boats shifted, those hooves could well stove in my head. I realized I'd been so set on finding Gabriella; I hadn't put any thought into how I would win her back. *What did I say to her? Why?*

Jayde, *Valkyrie's* bo'sun, was organizing Valkyries and Freedom Fighters alike in cutting away *Freyja's* fallen mast. There was splintered wood and tangled rigging everywhere, and *Valkyrie's* figurehead and shattered bowsprit loomed over it all—the conqueror of Hornigold.

Against a background of flogging sails, creaking wood, and water splashing against the wooden hulls came the moans of the injured, complaints of the vanquished, and orders of the captain. No, not the captain, the quartermaster. Gabriella was nowhere to be seen. Carmen was directing the victory dance around her short-stemmed pipe. *Where's Gabriella?* She *should be directing these decks, not leaving the work to the Dane.*

The felled mast had gone, left to drift downwind and sink—a little bit of carnage cast off—but I noticed the huddle of men and women didn't disperse. *Valkyrie's* longboat was pulled up alongside, presumably after being put off full of plunder and supplies until the fight was over, and Valkyries were gathered around something on the deck.

"What are you doing?"

"Annika was shot out of the rigging," Jayde replied, her arm bandaged and in a sling. "Gaunt and Davys found her, but they were too late, she's dead."

I left them to it.

"Who's that?" I asked Carrie. She was sewing another body into a shroud of sailcloth.

"Butler."

I nodded. A pity.

I looked up at the sky again as rain started to fall. I was drenched in seconds—a welcome respite from the heat for the moment, it would soon seem worse. I had to find Gabriella, and headed starboard to climb up onto *Valkyrie's* decks, but Gaunt stopped me.

"Leave her, Cap. It's Klara, I don't think she'll make it, thee'll only make things worse than they already are if thee goes now. The lass'll come round, she's not lost if thee plays it right, I'd swear to it."

I hoped he was right. I looked after her again, then the news about Klara sank in. I rubbed my jaw and understood why she'd reacted that way. Maybe she had enough to cope with for the moment. I shook Gaunt's hand. "Gracias, Robert. It's good to see you again, old friend. What do you make of the damage? I'm surprised you let her do it."

"Not much choice, Cap, I were in the longboat. Most of us

seem to have lived through it, though. I were glad to see thy sails, I don't mind telling thee. Give me half an hour to have a good look below, then I'll tells thee what needs to be done. But I reckon we'll be lucky to save 'em both."

"Pity. It'd be something to have *Freyja* sailing under my flag. Or *Valkyrie's."* I corrected myself hastily. "Very well, I'll let you get on with your work. Maybe I'll pay our old friends a visit." I shook his hand again, then headed forward to gloat over the Freyjamen huddled in the rain.

Chapter 86

Carmen had taken no chances. She had the thirty surviving Freyjamen shackled and roped together by the half dozen so no one would be looking for escape overboard, and they were guarded by eight men and women. I noticed she had commandeered some of my own men to help, and smiled in spite of myself. I looked over the huddle, enjoying the embarrassed look on Sharpe's face and the sullen look on Cheval and the others. *He* had wasted no time joining his old enemy against me. I was not surprised.

"What will you do with them?" I asked Carmen, wanting to tease the Freyjamen whose fate now rested with my women.

"Turn them out in the longboat, most likely, and get their ugly mugs off our decks," Carmen snapped back, obviously not too pleased at my presence.

"Really? Is that what Gabriella ordered?"

She glared at me. "I'm sure she will."

I was surprised. "You'd send them off knowing where you are and how badly damaged? The state you're in, they could launch an attack from a longboat! And they'd have had a chance at success too, if *Freedom* weren't alongside."

She glared at me again. "An attack? What with? We wouldn't put them off with any weapons aboard!"

"No of course not, but if they're picked up by another privateer, or even if they aren't, they'd soon take any ship careless enough to offer them aid, and they'd head straight back. And where's their ship's boat? He'll have put one off just as we do, and they'll be armed. No, you'd do better keeping hold of them and marooning them where they can't cause you any more trouble. Besides, you may need extra hands to get the boats ashore."

Another glare, then she stomped off to the maindeck, shouting instructions to Valkyries as she went.

"Clear that canvas!

"You, start work on the outer jib, I want *Valkyrie* shipshape again, even if she has mated with *Freyja*!

"Gather those weapons off this deck—I want them on *Valkyrie*!

"Jayde, get a lookout posted up every mast still standing, I want to know if any more sail approaches!"

I hadn't expected a welcome from Carmen, but this was a bit over the top. Had I foiled some design of hers? Did she want *Freyja*? Or *Valkyrie*? Or maybe it was just the after effect of battle. I resolved to keep a close eye on her, but she could wait.

I walked over to where Hornigold's bloody corpse lay unattended on the deck and stared at the man—one of the men—I'd hated for so long. I felt nothing. No joy, no pain, no relief. His death had changed nothing. Mamá and Magdalena were still dead. Hornigold had joined Tarr in Hell. Blake was still to join them; van Ecken too. I turned away and smiled when I saw Gabriella climb, with difficulty, down to *Freya's* deck. I followed, and walked toward the mainhatch.

"What do you suggest we do with *Freyja*?"

I looked at her—her tone wasn't friendly, but she *was* talking to me—a definite improvement—although the question was most likely a test.

"Keep her," I replied. "Having her in our fleet would be the talk of the Carib Sea and do our reputations no end of good."

"*Our* fleet? *Our* reputations?" Her voice was cold. "*Valkyrie* took her. *Freedom* didn't have a hand in it."

I was tempted to point out that she'd most likely lose both *Valkyrie* and *Freyja* without *Freedom* to help her ashore, but thought better of it, this was not the time. "You're quite right," I said, instead.

"So who'd sail her?" Gabriella mused.

"She has a crew. They can be forced if necessary, but I don't think so. They don't really care who they sail under as long as they win enough coin. Their letter of marque is no more than convenience to most."

"What, even Sharpe? You'd sail with him after . . . after Magdalena?"

I shrugged. "It's all passed. It doesn't matter anymore."

Gabriella and the child were all that were important to me now, and I'd even put up with Sharpe on my decks if that would prove it to her.

"You don't think he'd cause too much trouble?" The smile, if it had been there at all, was gone.

"No, if I read him right, he doesn't bother about who he sails with as long as he has a plentiful supply of rum, and coin enough to wager at the dice, but time will tell." I paused. "Gabriella," I said, serious again, and reached out to stroke her face.

Was she softening? Maybe, then her face tightened and she pulled away. "Not now," she said, "I need to think about *Valkyrie*."

We'd gone through *Freyja's* mainhatch and had reached Gaunt for our first look below decks. Gabriella went pale as she took a good look at the damage she had wrought. Frazer, Blackman, Carrie and Jayde didn't look much happier.

"Mr. Gaunt, report if you will," she said, her voice strained.

Chapter 87

"Right then, lass," Gaunt said. "For a start, they're both taking on water, though they ain't in danger of foundering just yet—I've put teams on the pumps and they'll need relieving every hour.

"We've two options. Either split them at sea and make the best of it, or tow them ashore and do the job proper. Me biggest concern is what happens if a blow hits. Even if we get *Valkyrie* separated at sea and patched, her bow's weak and her forward strakes need replacing. Hell, her stem might even be cracked and then there'll be no salving her; but even if stem's sound, I don't think she'll stand up to heavy seas, especially wi' that bowsprit, and we'll lose *Freyja* o'course.

"The only other thing to do is for *Freedom* to tow them ashore as they are, then I have a chance at salving both of them. They'll be awkward to tow and if we do get a blow, we risk losing them both."

"At least it isn't hurricane season, and we'll plot a course carefully and head for the nearest safe island or cay," I said. "I don't think we should worry overmuch. Would you have a chance at salving *Freyja* if we split them at sea?"

"Nay," Gaunt replied. "Does thee see how *Freyja's* laid over? If we warped *Valkyrie* out of her, she'd flatten out again and sea'd flood in. We'd have no chance at patching her and she'd go down for sure. It's up to Gabriella; we've a better chance of salving *Valkyrie* if we warp her out now, but we'd lose *Freyja* for sure and could end up losing both anyway."

"I want *Valkyrie* free and floating. I don't care what happens to *Freyja*, she's already beaten," Gabriella replied.

"Yes, but think what it would tell the rest of the Caribbees if you had command of Hornigold's boat," I reasoned. "Reputation counts for a lot in our trade, and more ships would call for quarter without a shot being fired. She's well known and we would be too. *You* would be."

"I agree with Leo," Carmen said, surprising me. "We'll take more prizes with less risk with three vessels."

So at least *she* included *Freedom*—that had to be a good sign.

"Aye," agreed Jayde.

"Frazer? Blackman?" I asked.

"Aye, salve them both," Frazer said and Blackman nodded.

"Oh, very well," Gabriella snapped. "But if we lose *Valkyrie* there'll be the devil to pay—and you'll be the one to do it, Leo. We'll try to salve them both, but if needs be, we warp *Valkyrie* free at sea and cast *Freyja* loose."

"Agreed," I said, and the others nodded.

"Right then, Mr. Gaunt." Gabriella sighed. "What needs doing to keep *Freykarie* afloat?"

He smiled at the name, then said, "I want to patch *Valkyrie* up as well as I can to give her the best chance. Both boats will want lightening too to keep them high in the water."

"Very well, we can get on with that. Is there room on *Freedom* for our plunder and stores, Leo?"

"Sí, no problem, we'll stow as much as we can, anything else will have to go overboard."

"No, the ballast can go overboard. Guns and spare rigging will go in its place."

That was a good idea. The boats still needed some weight to keep them stable and stop them rolling, especially as we wouldn't be able to rig them. We'd only have to worry about reballasting if we managed to salvage both vessels.

"But I'm warning you, Leo, if *Freedom* sails off with our gold, I won't rest until I take it back."

"Don't worry, querida, I'm not going anywhere without you."

"Captain!" Jayde called down the hatch. "Bess is calling for you, it's Klara."

I went after Gabriella and gave her a leg up to *Valkyrie's* deck—she wasn't quite so agile now—then climbed up to follow her, but she stopped me.

"Stay here Leo, I don't need you."

"I know, querida, but I'm coming with you anyway."

She looked at me for a moment and decided not to argue. She nodded and hurried toward the cabin.

"Frazer, Carmen, will you check the charts and find us a likely island while we wait for a fair wind?" I called down through the unrelenting rain.

"Aye, Captain." He nodded from the hatch whilst Carmen glowered, and I hurried after Gabriella.

Chapter 88

GABRIELLA

My heart felt as if pounded by a tempest. I'd bested Hornigold, but lost two of my own crew and may well be losing Klara too. I'd won *Freyja*, but if I'd cracked *Valkyrie's* stem post, she'd never sail again. And that was when Leo had decided to show his face.

For months, I hadn't known whether he lived or had been killed, and now he was here I didn't know what to do, or what I truly wanted to do with him. I wanted to grab him and hold him tight. I wanted to clear the cabin, rid him of his clothing and mine, and lock the door. I also wanted to shoot him.

But I couldn't think about him now. I hurried down the hatch and to the cabin and Klara as best I could. She lay on her side, very still, and her dark skin looked gray. My heart jumped in fear. "Klara!"

Nothing. No reaction at all. Obi looked up at me in despair.

"She's very weak," Bess said. "There was just too much lead in her back and she's lost a lot of blood. I think she's only hung on this long to say goodbye."

I looked at Klara again, stricken. *No! She can't be dying! Not Klara! Not after we risked everything to escape Erik. No!*

I slumped to the deck next to Obi, took a rag of cloth and wet it in the bucket near the cot then dabbed Klara's brow. She opened her eyes and smiled at me. *How can I lose her? I can't say goodbye to Klara.* She could not only be a part of my past; I couldn't bear the thought that my child wouldn't know her.

"Gabriella."

I grabbed her hands and rested my head on her shoulder with a sob.

"Klara, I'm so sorry. I promised to keep you safe, and now, and now . . ." I couldn't continue. Leo rested his hand on my shoulder and I shrugged him off.

"You've nothing to be sorry for Gabriella, you freed me." She paused, her breathing shallow. "This year of freedom, of Obi." She smiled weakly at him. "It's been worth so much more than any number of years of slavery, of Erik, even if he'd have allowed me to live them. Thank you." She quietened again, exhausted. Bess passed me a beaker of water and I encouraged Klara to drink. She started to talk again, her voice a little stronger now.

"I'll be sorry to leave you, Gabriella, and the other friends I've found on the water—especially you, Obi. I'll miss the wind and the laughter, but I'll be with my son soon and I want so much to see him again.

"Let your child bring her parents together again. Whether you admit it or not, you're lost without Leo, you need him as much as he needs you. If you don't forgive him, your heart will never mend and you'll become all the things we escaped from. Promise me you'll let him back into your heart. Promise?"

"Yes, yes, anything, just don't leave me. I don't want to be on my own."

"You won't be." She looked at Leo. "Your man is here and your daughter will join you both shortly. I'll be with you in spirit, but it's time for me to go to my own child now."

Obi bowed his head, unable to speak. I leaned my head against his shoulder, wanting to comfort him, but unwilling to let go of Klara's hand. I didn't want to let her go, no matter how resigned to death she seemed to be.

"There's something I never told you, but I have to before I leave. I've never known how to and I'm nearly out of time. Erik was my brother. My mother was only thirteen—a child—when Jan Senior, Erik's father, forced her."

"The bastard!" I was shocked, remembering the way Erik had offered her to his dinner guests. "But, but I thought he was Jan's father?"

She nodded, tears running down her face. "He is. You know Jan Senior gave me to Erik as a child; he didn't recognize me as his daughter. I don't think he even recognized me as a person. Erik certainly didn't recognize me as a sister. I named my son Jan to try and make them realize what they had done, but it only made them hate me more.

"Kill him, Gabriella, please. I only wish I'd had the courage to do it myself. He's an animal, just like his father, kill him for me."

She took a few labored breaths. Obi hadn't moved.

"Do you hate me?" she asked, after a long silence.

"Hate you, no of course not, why would I? I'm sickened by him—if not for him, how many lives would have been lived instead of cut short? I can't believe you'd think I could hate you, why?"

"I have van Ecken blood running though my veins," she said simply.

"Yes, but your mother's too, his blood was diluted by hers," I encouraged. "And I've never seen any evidence of van Ecken in you."

"I suppose." She fell quiet.

"I hated that house; I was so happy when you arrived, I thought Erik would be happy, and life would get better. Are you sure you don't hate me?"

"Of course I don't hate you, you're my sister, I love you. Why didn't you tell me before? All that time, everything he did, and he was your half-brother." I wanted to cry, but couldn't let her see I was upset.

The effort of talking had visibly weakened her again. She tried to smile, to reassure me, but it was clear she was going. Obi put his own hands around mine, still cupping Klara's. He stayed silent. I moved my hands away.

"Make me another promise," she whispered, and I leaned closer to her so she could place her hand on my belly. "Call her Raphaella—let her heal you both. Don't waste any more time."

"I can't believe she won't know her aunt," I sobbed.

"Promise." She was extremely weak.

I nodded, tears running down my face. We stayed like that for what seemed hours, but was only minutes, until she found enough strength to speak once more.

"Thank you. Free." Followed by a silence that was total.

"Klara? *Klara*? No. Don't leave me, come back!" Louder and louder until I was aware of Leo dragging me away.

"Gabriella." He spoke gently and grasped my shoulders. I let him. He hugged me. I stayed in his arms for a while then pulled away. I couldn't do this; whatever she'd said, Klara still needed me.

"Bess, would you fetch her hammock please? I'll prepare her myself." I had no idea how I kept my voice so level and in command.

"No, Captun. Me." Obi spoke as he stroked her immobile face. I was about to argue, but stopped, touched by his tenderness.

"Gabriella," Leo said. "Come back out on deck. Your crew needs you now."

"Klara needs me."

"No, she needs Obi. Your crew have lost her too, as well as two others. You're their captain. You need to be out on deck with them."

I looked at Obi. He was still stroking Klara's face.

"Come on, Gabriella, she's gone," Leo urged. "There's nothing more you can do, it's time to let her go. Let Obi take care of her."

Chapter 89

LEO
13th May 1687

Gabriella was badly affected by Klara's death. I knew it, her crew knew it, but Gabriella would not acknowledge it. She'd been distressed in the cabin, but once I'd taken her away from Klara's body, she acted as if nothing had happened. She offered no tears, no laments, she simply got on with the business of sailing.

She hadn't thrown any recriminations or accusations at me. It was as if nothing had happened. Nothing. No love, no hate, just blank. Like the still sea in the dead calm that we drifted in, we were wallowing in place, going nowhere, and it was time to bury our dead.

Klara, Annika and Butler, shrouded in canvas, lay on a pile of splintered wood, ripped canvas and a scattering of black powder inside one of *Freyja's* longboats.

"Cast off," Gabriella said quietly, and Jayde untied the boat's tether, tossed the line on top of the corpses and pushed the boat off.

"Stand by, Andy," Gabriella instructed. "Carmen, carry on please."

I was surprised. I'd expected Gabriella to say the service, not Carmen. She intoned the usual service of the dead, but finished a little differently.

"We now commend the bodies of the Valkyries, Charles Butler, Annika Svennson and Klara, to Valhalla. Courageous warriors all, we thank them for their sacrifice, and honor their deeds in our service."

She stepped back and Andy touched an arrow to a lantern sitting on the deck beside her, notched it to her bow string and fired it at the boat grave.

The Valkyries cheered as flames leapt up and called out the names of their dead. I noticed some of my Freedom Fighters were moved, but not Gabriella. She stood still and silent at the bulwark, grasped the rail of her prize and stared at the burning boat grave drifting westward on the swell. Nothing showed on her face at all, only in the whites of her knuckles. I wished I knew how to help her.

Obi watched the flames take hold, then turned and walked away.

I thought back to the first deaths I'd borne as captain, and knew Gabriella's impassivity was a lie. I knew she felt responsible. Whatever was happening inside her, she had to let it out sooner or later, and the longer she let it brew, the more violent would be its release.

Hornigold and the other dead Freyjamen went overboard in weighted canvas shrouds with no ceremony, then Gaunt thrust a couple of brimming rumpots at us. Gabriella emptied hers in one. I took a smaller drink, then urged her to leave the rail and join the others. She shook her head and headed awkwardly down *Valkyrie*'s mainhatch. I followed her to the cabin.

"Gabriella, don't." She'd downed another full rumpot.

"Gabriella don't? Gabriella don't?" she repeated. She didn't look adrift in a calm now, quite the opposite. Her cheeks flushed red and her eyes flashed as her voice rose. I dodged the empty beaker she threw at me and she drank from the bottle instead.

"Gabriella, please, the child!"

"The child? The child? You didn't care about the *child* when you hit me or threatened to lock us up!" she screamed at me. "How dare *you* remonstrate with *me*, now? How dare you!"

"Gabriella . . ." She wasn't being fair; I'd known nothing about the child. I moved toward her, then stopped at her glare.

"Don't you come near me. Don't you touch me! What are you even doing here? You made it damned clear you didn't want me—you're only here for Hornigold. Tell me, how does it feel that I succeeded where you failed?"

"I'm not here for Hornigold, Gabriella. I'm here for you. Whatever you believe, I'm here for you," I repeated.

She threw the bottle at the bulkhead and opened another as rum and broken glass pooled on the deck.

"Gabriella."

Nothing. I carried on regardless. "I know I let you down and I promise I will never threaten you again. You *are* a captain in your own right. You *have* succeeded where I failed, *and* bested Hornigold. You are my equal, and my future." I paused. "A future, *our* future, that is right here in this cabin, and I will do anything in my power to keep that safe. To keep you and our child safe and together."

I moved toward her again, she was crying now, hopefully her rage was spent. I put my arms around her, but she pushed me away and slapped my face, hard. I stared at her. I could not let her provoke me. She had to know she could trust me again. I kept my eyes on hers and made no effort to control my breathing, which was as heavy as hers. My hands had clenched into fists, but stayed at my sides.

Her eyes changed and she reached for me. I stiffened to take the blow, but she grabbed my shirt, hauled me toward her, and kissed me roughly. My shirt tore and she yanked it off me. I reached around and took hold of her own shirt and tore it from her body. Our lips parted and we pressed our foreheads together, panting heavily. I waited to see what her next move would be, and caressed her back, hoping it wouldn't be violent.

I waited.

She pulled the dagger from my belt and I caught her eyes again. I couldn't hide my nerves. She looked at me, and I didn't care for the smile that flickered across her lips. Then she made her mind up, and, obviously amused, stabbed the blade into the wood of the chart table. Quickly followed by my cutlass. I breathed a sigh of relief and she pushed me hard toward the bed. With her belly bulging with life, I did as I was bid, and she stood over me, her eyes wild.

"Care," I whispered, stroking her stomach. She slapped my hand away, pulled her own dagger out of her belt and cut the ties that bound my breeches, then lightly traced the blade over my chest. I held my breath. Enough was enough. She lifted the dagger and I grabbed her wrist and pushed it away from me. We stared at each other, chests heaving and she smiled, then let the blade drop to the deck. Her breeches followed and I wriggled out of what was left of mine so that she could climb on top of me.

Gabriella was back.

Chapter 90

GABRIELLA
14th May 1687

My eyes fluttered open though it was still dark and very quiet. *Why is it so quiet? Why are we not under sail? Something's wrong*. Then I remembered: *Freyja,* Klara, Leo. I startled wide awake, and realized Leo's arm was slung over my belly. I was lying on my side, with Leo nestled behind me. I could smell him: sweat, salt and something else, something indefinable, something that was just . . . Leo. I couldn't decide if I felt protected—or trapped.

I slowed my breathing and stayed still. Judging by Leo's snores he still slept, and I didn't want to wake him. I didn't want to talk to him, or even look at him. But I didn't want to move away from him either. I squeezed my eyes shut and felt tears trickle down my face and into my ear. I didn't dare move to wipe them away and had to put up with the tickling.

What am I going to do now? What do I want *to do?* My best friend was dead, my ship stove into another, and my child would be coming soon.

It was all too much. Leo might have come back to me, but I'd never felt so alone. I sighed and moved my arm to grasp his strong forearm resting on my belly. I loved him. Despite everything, I knew I loved him, and my belly clenched as I remembered our passion of the night before. I wanted him and I'd missed him. But he'd threatened me, betrayed me, and I thought I hated him a little as well.

I let my hand drop back down to the bed. *What do I do?* I couldn't lose command of myself now, I'd worked too hard to let go of the ropes, to let Leo take over and make my decisions for me, but what did I really want?

This was getting me nowhere and I tried to think like a captain, like the captain I was. First the boats, *Valkyrie* and *Freyja*. I'd lose them both without *Freedom* and Leo, I knew that. Without him, my best chance at saving my crew would be to stow them into the longboat and limp ashore. But none of them would choose that, they'd all elect to sail with *Freedom*. No one else had wanted to leave *Freedom* in the first place. I'd be left with nothing and no one and would likely die alone at sea; and what about the child? What if she came when I was adrift in a longboat? She'd die too. And she wasn't mine alone, didn't she have a right to know her father? He hadn't harmed her, how could I take him away from her?

I blinked more tears away and froze as Leo's fingers stroked my skin. He was waking. I wasn't ready to speak to him yet. I concentrated on keeping my breathing steady, trying to fool him into thinking I was still asleep. His fingers stilled and he moved his head on the cushions, burrowing a more comfortable nest. His breathing grew louder again. He wasn't snoring, but I relaxed, he was still more in sleep than out of it.

My hand stroked the fabric I lay on, feeling the soft nap of the velvet. This was where Klara had died, and all the old bedclothes had been burnt in her boat grave with her. I'd got a bit carried away in replacing them, finding the richest brocades and softest cottons. The crew had been happy to indulge their pregnant captain after our victory, and had raided *Freyja's* and *Freedom's* holds as well as our own to collect the richest cloth taken as plunder all over the Carib Sea.

Klara. She'd known me better than anyone, yet had begged me to forgive Leo, almost with her dying breath. But *could* I forgive him? I could honor her by taking him back, yes, but could I forgive him? And the child. Of course, the child. *His* child.

I sighed. The ships, the crew, Klara and the child. I needed to accept Leo again for all of them. But what about me? What did *I* want? What would win? Love? Or hate? But was it really hate, or was it fear? Fear that living with Leo would end up like living with Erik? I'd had enough of living in fear, *and* enough of living in hate. How could I be sure that living with Leo, that loving Leo, would be different?

"Buenos días, querida." Leo stroked my belly again. He knew I was awake. I didn't trust my voice, and stroked his arm in greeting. My breath hitched in my throat, and I clamped my lips shut, hoping he hadn't heard.

His hand moved higher, cupping my breast and his thumb circled my nipple. It betrayed me and hardened and my breath caught in my throat again. Part of me wanted to stop him, but I made no move.

His hand moved lower, back over the swell of my body, then lower still. I stiffened, then relaxed. I was glad he was behind me. I couldn't see him, or touch him. I didn't have to take any part in this. I could feel tears flowing freely down my face, but I made no sound. I didn't want to do this. I didn't want to stop this.

He moved and I felt him behind me. I gasped. That wasn't distress. I didn't want him to stop. Whatever happened, I did not want him to stop. I moved against him, made it easier for him, yet my tears still flowed, silent.

He kissed my shoulder and neck and held me to him tightly, moving against me and groaning. He was gentle, tender, and we rocked together. My breathing quickened and grew heavier, but I was still aware of my tears. I gripped his arm, wanting him to hold me tighter, tighter, and I knew I loved him. I knew I needed him. I was crying as much for missing him as for what had been lost, and I didn't want this to stop. I didn't want to have to look at him, to talk to him, I just wanted to love him.

His movements grew more urgent, and I went with him, pitching through the stormy sea, then, with another groan, it was all over and he was just holding me.

He sighed and pulled me onto my back, propping himself up next to me and we finally looked at each other. He wiped the salt water from my face and smiled. Despite myself, I smiled back.

"I keep thinking of Klara and Obi. How their time together ended too quickly, and kept thinking, *what if it had been you?* I missed you so much, Gabriella, I couldn't stand it if I lost you. We have to make the most of all the time we have. Marry me."

My smile shrank and I stared at him in horror.

"What?"

"Marry me."

"I'm still married to Erik," I pointed out, staring at the deckhead. I wasn't ready for this. I couldn't answer this. *What is he doing*?

"I hadn't forgotten," he said. "Nor have I forgotten Klara's request. We can honor her, free you and rid the Carib Sea of one of its devils—two if we get Blake as well."

"I'm not sure I want to be legally tied to a man again; any man, even you," I carried on. "I don't want to be viewed as property, or servant, or slave."

"¡El infierno! I will never view you as property, woman," he retorted. "Or servant or slave! I love you. I want you by my side, I've tried living without you and it's no life. I live for freedom, and have shown you how to be free.

"Marrying me won't be a shackle but a declaration. A declaration to each other, to the world, the sea, and to everyone on it. As my wife, you'll have the protection of my name. As your husband, I'll have the protection of yours, as well as the promise of many adventures to come. I want us to be together, forever. I want us to live together, sail together and fight together. Even die together—eventually. I want to tell the world we belong together. I want a place in history as the richest husband and wife pirate team on the seas. I want to be with you in every way I can.

"We've already lived as husband and wife, let us seal it, on board. A pirate wedding, at sea, aboard *Freedom*, let's start a new life together—now."

I thought back to all my doubts, all the reasoning I'd done in the dark, to my last conversation with Klara, and held my hands to my belly. I'd recently sworn I wasn't going to run again, and I'd faced Hornigold and won. I looked up at Leo's worried frown and hesitated again. *Can I really do this?*

"Isn't it only the captain who can perform a wedding?"

"Yes, so? There are two of us you know, it shouldn't be a problem."

"But if we're doing the marrying, how can we perform the service?"

He laughed. "We're captains of pirate ships, querida. We can do what we like. If the ceremony doesn't work for us, we change it until it does! We'll even do it before we head to Sayba, it doesn't really matter to me whether Erik dies before our wedding or after. What do you say?"

I relaxed. That was more like it. A marriage where we set the rules, that was tailor-made for us. No interference from anybody else. No judgments, no arbitrary rules pushed onto us. This would be a marriage I could live with, be proud of and feel loved and safe in. A marriage I could bring our child into.

I reached for him again, pushing away the doubts. I didn't have the strength to fight him anymore. I didn't have to do everything on my own anymore. I wasn't sure I could do this, but I'd try. For Klara, for Raphaella, even for myself. I'd try.

"Yes."

Chapter 91

LEO
21st May 1687
Forty Two Leagues East of the Grenadine Islands

"Do you take me for your lawful wedded husband?"

"Aye. Do you take me for your lawful wedded wife?"

"Sí. As Captain of *Sound of Freedom,* I pronounce us husband and wife."

"As Captain of *Valkyrie, I* pronounce us husband and wife!"

Our crews cheered and I kissed my wife and held her. We'd done it. Against the odds and in spite of everything, I'd done it. I'd won her back.

It had been a simple service and Gabriella had looked more pirate than bride. I didn't know if she had any gowns aboard *Valkyrie,* but she certainly didn't have one to fit her that day. I realized I'd never seen her in a gown, but even if she had worn one, it wouldn't have suited her new tattoo. She wore her usual breeches, shirt and colorful sash—but they were clean and her hair was dressed with jewels and pearls. My beautiful pirate bride. Nobody mentioned that her first husband still lived. Nobody cared—they knew it wouldn't be for long.

"Now things had better bloody well get back to normal," a Scottish voice grumbled behind us. I turned to berate Frazer, but stopped when I realized he was grinning. Gabriella looked shocked. I think it was the first time she'd seen him smile. He shook both our hands. "Congratulations and felicitations to the pair of you," he added.

"Thank you, Mr. Frazer."

"Wind!"

I looked up at Juaquim perched in *Freedom's* maintop and

who pointed northeast. Typical! We'd been becalmed a week and now we were about to celebrate our marrying, we all had to go to work. Gabriella smiled up at me.

"We've been waiting for wind for long enough, we can't waste it. I need to get *Valkyrie* ashore."

I nodded. Every day we spent out here increased the risk of storm, and whilst I quite liked the idea of Gabriella returning to *Freedom*, I knew she wouldn't be able to bear another loss.

We had gathered on *Freedom* in the end, simply because her decks were bigger, and now men and women ran about them. All *Freedom's* sails needed setting, *Freykarie* had to be cast off and towing warps rigged to her instead. Neither *Freyja* nor *Valkyrie* would set any sail—*Freedom* would do all the work.

"Valkyries to the starboard rail!" Gabriella roared, and the shout was carried forward until her crew had assembled to windward. I looked around *Freedom's* decks and rigging—the yards were littered with men and I couldn't spot a single idle hand. I walked over to the Valkyries to hear what Gabriella had in mind.

"Starboard Watch aboard *Freyja,* Carmen in command. I want hands on the pumps, watch and watch about, and Jayde? You'll need to keep her patched and prevent her from making water as best you can. Andy, I want you aboard *Freyja* too, the Freyjamen are bound below decks and shouldn't be any trouble—they'll be under your charge. Any questions?" There were none.

"Larboard watch, you're with me and *Valkyrie*. Keep her dry and afloat. Make haste!" she added, getting everyone moving. She looked at me, brow raised in question and I nodded. *Freedom* would be safe enough in Frazer's hands, I'd join Gabriella on *Valkyrie*, but I'd have a longboat on hand to ferry me between the vessels as I needed.

Aboard *Valkyrie,* I lifted my chin to windward. It was only faint, but the slight movement of air felt wonderful. We'd drifted long enough, the water around us was littered with the flotsam and jetsam of near a hundred men and women, and stank of rotten meat and shit in the hot sun; it was good to have the promise of movement again. The breeze strengthened slowly, and although *Freedom's* sails were full and the towing warps taut, we had no way on yet. All the crew, except those on the pumps, craned over the side, looking for the tell-tale ripples that would attest to our passage, all of us eager to find a safe harbor for our crippled fleet.

Gabriella had her glass trained to windward and a gust ruffled her hair, still garnished with jewels. I felt the timbers move beneath my feet. We were off. Finally. Now we'd see how *Freykarie* moved through the water.

I went forward, Gabriella close behind, to get a better look. All was well, so far at least. Gabriella waved to her quartermaster and bo'sun who both hung over *Freyja's* rail with the same intent, but there didn't appear to be any problems—Gaunt and Jayde had made *Valkyrie* fast with plenty of line to prevent the timbers working loose. *Freykarie* was towing well enough. Slowly, true, very slowly, but well enough.

Chapter 92

We limped along behind *Freedom* at maybe one knot. Slow progress, but steady, and we should get there without much risk to *Valkyrie* and her prize—assuming we kept a fair wind. I carried a beaker of ale to Gabriella, who leaned on the larboard rail and stared out to sea. She'd been very quiet since we'd got underway.

Despite the light breeze it was hot, and most of the crew sprawled on the maindeck under the awning. With no sails set and no duty at the tiller, there was nothing to do but man the pumps in short, regular tricks and keep a sharp lookout for squalls and other pirates. We sounded below regularly, and the pumps were keeping on top of the water in the bilges. All was well, for the moment at least. Just hot, humid and uncomfortable.

When I reached Gabriella she didn't turn, but kept staring at the same spot to leeward. I realized we'd drawn level with what was left of the boat grave—just a few charred strakes of wood.

"What kind of world are we bringing a child into? What kind of life are we offering her, Leo?"

"The only kind of life either of us wish to live," I replied. "Yes, there are dangers, but we'll do everything in our power to keep him safe, and there's danger enough ashore, don't forget."

She shuddered. "I couldn't consider living ashore again," she said. "Babe-in-arms or no."

"Don't worry overmuch." I put my arm around her shoulders. "We'll teach our son to swim as soon as he can walk, despite the superstition of the sea. We'll tie a safety line to him on deck and keep him out of harm's way during raids. Look around you, look how big a family he'll have; he'll be safe aboard our ships."

"And our daughter?"

"Our daughter?"

"If our son is a daughter as Klara foretold, do you promise the same?" She looked up at me. "Erik always told me if I bore him a girl, he'd throw her from the cliff top so she couldn't grow to be like me."

I pulled her close and held her as tightly as I dared. "Van Ecken will be dead soon," I growled. "I promise you, I will keep our child safe no matter whether son or daughter. It makes no difference to me whether I sire a pirate prince *or* princess. And I couldn't be happier with a daughter just like her mother—the fear of the Carib Sea!"

A cry from above interrupted us, and Gabriella quickly wiped her eyes and ran to windward as best she could, glass already in hand, although she didn't need it to see the black clouds gathering to the northeast.

"Squall!"

Everyone jumped to their feet, but there was nothing to do—no sails to trim, no course to adjust—so we lined the rails.

"Mr. Gaunt, stand by below with your tools and plenty of oakum. Take Carrie and Obi to help. This will be *Valkyrie's* biggest test yet."

"Aye, aye, lass."

I smiled at her glare. Gaunt found it difficult to call her Captain when I was aboard.

"Slip the towing warp!" Gabriella shouted, waddling forward to shout down to *Freyja*, knowing Carmen probably wouldn't have heard her. I approved, both wind and sea would get up quickly, and I didn't want to be tied to *Freedom*. If anything happened to the crippled boats, I wanted *Freedom* free and clear to come to our aid. Carmen clearly did too, the towing warp splashed into the sea before Gabriella reached the foredeck, and we were on our own.

"Leo, I want *Freyja's* starboard anchor dropped and her jibs hoisted. Tell Carmen to protect *Valkyrie* and *Freyja's* damage as much as she can."

"Aye, aye, lass," I joked, and Gabriella glared at me in turn. I was sure she hated not being able to run forward and take care of it herself. Seconds later, I was up on the remains of *Valkyrie's* bowsprit bellowing Gabriella's orders to *Freyja's* decks below, which were already a frenzy of activity. A large splash announced that the starboard anchor had been let go to spin *Freykarie* around into wind, and half a dozen Valkyries ran aft along the deck with a jib halyard. The small sails at the bow would help to push *Freyja's* bow around further and keep *Valkyrie* in her lee, protected from the sea.

All we could do now was sit it out.

"Where's *Freedom* going?" Gabriella had caught up and stood in the bows at the foot of the bowsprit—there'd be no more climbing for her until our child was born, and I could see the frustration on her face. I looked downwind to see my ship bearing away, and immediately realized what Frazer was up to.

"He's wearing round. He'll sail around us and back up to windward—he'll put himself between us and the weather, and use *Freedom* to shelter us from the worst of it."

A cheer rang out from the Valkyries at this. Being adrift at sea in a crippled vessel was one of a sailor's worst nightmares. Not as bad as adrift afire, but not far off. Seeing another vessel prepared to put themselves into our service wouldn't be forgotten. Frazer had just won himself, and *Freedom,* a great deal of goodwill.

I couldn't help but admire my ship as she sailed to larboard. We were still on the edge of the squall, but the sea had whipped up whitecaps, and *Freedom* wallowed for a moment before her yards swung around and caught the wind on the other board, then she was under full sail with a bone in her teeth—that white water at her bow one of my favorite sights. The other—white sails bellied with wind and laying the ship over—filled my heart with pride at my ship and crew. With two triangular jibs spanning bowsprit to mast, two square sails lending power to her foremast, three to her main and the triangular spanker to her mizzen, she looked heaven-sent—her crew of angels harnessing the clouds and skipping effortlessly through the seas.

I waved my greeting to my quartermaster and crew as they prepared to shorten sail and heave-to to windward of us. The square sails were loosed, the jibs backed to work against the spanker, and her bows swung obediently to the northeast. *Freykarie* settled in the calm water of the windshadow cast by her towering hull. Frazer had judged it perfectly, and *Freedom* now protected us from the worst of the wind and waves.

Lightning flashed above us, and I clambered back down onto deck to stand with my wife. "You should go below, shelter in the cabin," I told her as the heavens opened.

"Why? I'm already drenched," she retorted. "I'm not about to cower below while my boat and crew are in danger. My place is on deck, child or no child—you know that as well as I do."

I laughed, not having expected anything less—at least she hadn't cursed me. Then she softened and took my face in her hands. "I'll head down to the cabin once the danger has passed, and you can join me, but not before." She kissed me and turned away with a smile.

I stood behind her, wrapped my arms around her and tried to protect her from the worst of the weather whilst the heavens flashed and thundered, but she shook me off to put more crew on the capstan working the pumps. The message was clear—*Valkyrie* came first. Despite all our precautions, some of this water would undoubtedly be finding its way below; and she was right, as captain her place was on deck. I shook my head in resignation and turned to windward to watch the progress of the squall, and I remembered the one I'd encountered when I tangled with *Freyja* just over a year ago. I knew waterspouts were rare enough and wasn't too worried, but I was also aware that if we were unlucky enough to encounter one in our current condition, it would sink us for certain.

Chapter 93

LEO
4th June 1687
The Grenadine Islands

The squall blew for an hour and proved our greatest peril, but we didn't have to contend with a waterspout. Once the worst of it had passed, we slipped *Freyja's* anchor, re-rigged the towing warp and recommenced our slow, clumsy progress west until the sun dawned this morning with a cry of, "Land oh!"

I was back aboard *Freedom*, my honeymoon over, but I still counted my blessings, although part of me wondered if I would be married now if Klara hadn't died or *Valkyrie* been crippled. I shook the thoughts off—the answers didn't matter. I *was* married to Gabriella, back in command of my ship and soon to be a father. That was all that mattered, and if Gabriella had changed—hardened—that was my fault and I'd have to bear it. Hopefully it wouldn't last long.

I looked again at our options through the glass. My father's Spanish forebears had slaughtered most of the Arawak and Carib Indians here long ago, and now these islands were mainly used by pirates for watering, wooding and careening. But they weren't the greatest danger; the waters teemed with sharks thanks to the large number of turtles who bred here, and whose young provided many an easy meal. Nobody liked to linger here. We should be safe.

Of the three closest islands, the middle one was the smallest and so less likely to be visited by other pirates, who tended to take the easier option as a rule. There looked to be a clear sizable passage through the reef, the island itself was well-wooded—which boded well for water and meat—and there was no obvious sign of permanent human habitation.

We had only one chance of beaching the boats in their condition without making our situation worse, and no choice but to go at high tide, which gave us little time to make our preparations.

I stood at the bow and stared at the horizon and the lumpy island that rose out of the early morning gray water into an even grayer sky. Surrounded by thin cloud, I felt a sense of foreboding that only grew the closer we got, and which wasn't helped by the knowledge of all those sharks between us and the distant land.

I gave the order to Frazer to bear away, and we headed for the channel between two large mounds of rock rising from the sea, keeping guard. I half imagined them moving toward us as we passed. The sun was stronger now, and the gray of the sea became a vibrant and beautiful blue, the greenery of the island the color of malachite, and what had earlier looked a place of doom now seemed a paradise.

Leaving the safety of the ship for the vulnerability of the pinnace, I remembered again the tales I'd heard of these waters. How one unwary sailor sat with his feet overboard to cool them, instead losing them in a flash of a gaping mouth filled with blades of teeth; of a wager where the loser was to swim ashore and only lost his already wooden leg; and others I couldn't, or wouldn't, believe.

At the flood of the tide, Gabriella had *Freyja's* foremast rigged, and the conjoined vessels launched their largest boats. My pinnace took the existing towing warp, the women each had another, and the three boats steadily warped *Freykarie* to the beach across that River Styx of teeth. Another boat stood by to help *Freyja's* rudder by hauling her round so that she'd be left high and dry with *Valkyrie's* stern fair to the sea.

Now we had time to rest before the work started all over again at the next high tide, but these crews had been idle too long during our slow westward passage and, after a swift fortification of rum, they set about exploring the island.

I looked around at what would be our new home for the foreseeable future and smiled. It would do. White sand, dotted with the green and brown shells of turtles, was lapped by the gentle swell of the sparkling sea. Shoreward, the beach was lined by palm and lush greenery, so there must be plenty of fresh water. The casks were rancid after so long adrift—I'd put a water party together straight away.

Further inland, a rocky outcrop towered over jungle, and I racked my brains trying to remember which island this was. It didn't look very long, maybe only a league across, but I'd have to verify that. I looked back to the beach and my exploring crew, wondering if some of them had had the same idea, then I realized they weren't exploring at all. They were simply charging down the beach after the turtles and flipping them onto their backs. Unlike the sharks, we could eat the fully grown despite their armor. There were hundreds, if not thousands of them, and it promised to be quite a feast. There was still work to be done today, but I decided to leave them to their fun for now. It had been a tense and frustrating few weeks, if not months, which had affected everyone. The work could wait a day.

"What do you think we should do with the Freyjamen?" Gabriella joined me.

"They're your prisoners, what do you want to do with them?" I hoped that was the right answer.

"Get them out of that stinking hold for a start, any that want to join us, that is. Do you really think they'll sign our articles?"

"Sí. You bested Hornigold and have a hold full of plunder, why wouldn't they want to join a successful pirate crew?

"Talking of articles, you realize you broke them?" I added.

She stared at me. "Is that really the way you want to start married life?" she asked.

I sighed, we would have to start again. "Will your Valkyries sign articles with *Freedom* again?"

She didn't answer for a while, then laughed. "I'll have to take a vote, but I doubt it unless you agree to better terms—we've proved ourselves now."

I nodded, that would have to be thrashed out in a crew council and could wait. Gabriella was negotiating, not arguing. Not only did I have my woman back, even if she did seem a little distant, but I had my fleet back too, and it was growing.

"We'll split the boats at the morning's high tide," I said. "Assuming we can save them both, what are your plans for *Freyja?"*

"She's *Valkyrie's* prize and Carmen's my quartermaster, so she has first refusal as *Freyja's* captain and I'm sure she'll take it."

"Mmm, you're probably right. Will she be trouble?"

"I expect so, but that would be true whatever deck she sailed on!" She laughed, then grew serious again. "If she agrees and signs the articles, she shouldn't be too much of a problem, not with her own command again. She wasn't happy about leaving *Freedom's* firepower behind, she'll behave well enough."

I laughed with her. That was probably the best we could hope for, whoever captained her. If Carmen did take *Freyja*, I decided to make sure I had some of *Freedom's* best men aboard her, just in case. Not that it had done me much good with Gabriella and *Valkyrie*.

Chapter 94

GABRIELLA
Freykarie Island

Whilst *Freedom's* crew found and fetched water, and gathered driftwood for tonight's feast—our wedding feast I realized, even if it was a week or two belated—my Valkyries organized the warps and kedges that would be needed tomorrow to haul *Freykarie* apart, and I admit I was nervous. We'd only be sure of *Valkyrie's* stem once she was free, and if it was cracked, she'd rot here. I wanted to know now, but I also wanted to put the knowing off for as long as possible. In the meantime, I had thirty-odd men captive in my prize, and it was high time I sorted them out.

Andy supervised bringing them topside, still bound, and they emerged onto decks that had so recently been theirs: blinking, stinking and beaten. They gathered on the maindeck in full view of the activity on the beach and the Valkyries patrolled around them. I could almost see them salivating at the growing pile of keel-up turtle and the trench of driftwood. I decided to keep this short.

"I'll not mess about with any fancy speech, you've done this enough yourselves to know what's coming," I started. "You've a choice to make. Your captain's dead, I suppose the most senior Freyjaman left is Sharpe and you can join him, although I have to say his prospects are not looking too bright at the moment. Or you can sign onto our account and sail under myself or Leo. But don't think you'll have it easy under a woman captain—and never forget it was me and my crew that beat you in a fight where you had all the advantages.

"I will not tolerate any disrespect on my ship, whether it's aimed at me or a member of my crew—male or female. I will not hesitate to maroon any one of you who steps over the line or makes a nuisance of himself. Do I make myself clear?

"Do not forget who I am or what I've done." I glared at each of them in turn to make sure they understood my sincerity.

"You, what do you say?" I pointed at the man closest to me. Dirty, scrawny and unshaven, he croaked. "With you, ma'am."

"Very well, untie him and give him some water and a writing stick to make his mark."

They would have to sign *Valkyrie's* existing articles until we agreed new terms with Leo and the Freedom Fighters.

"Oh, and if you call me ma'am again I'll cut out your tongue. You'll address me as Captain. Who's next?"

One by one, they joined us. Leo was right, they didn't care who they sailed with now that Hornigold had been routed. Meat, rum and gold would be enough to keep them loyal to the articles. Cheval was next.

"I'm with you, Capitaine."

"No you're not, Cheval." I turned at Leo's interruption and raised my eyebrows in question. "We go back a while, Gabriella, I've given Cheval a chance once before, he is not to join us again."

I stared at him, annoyed that he was telling me what to do in front of my crew and captives, then nodded my agreement—I knew Cheval of old. "Very well, he's yours to do with as you will."

Leo smiled and hauled Cheval off the deck.

"Sharpe?" I'd left him until last. I'd once counted him a friend, and knew I owed him my life, but he'd killed Jan and Wilbert. He was also one of the men who had taken Leo's first love, Magdalena, and I didn't know how to react to his presence aboard my ship.

"Yes, Captain. It will be a pleasure to serve under you." He smiled. I nodded, still unsure of him.

"Very well. That's it. Everyone ashore and get to work, we have my wedding feast to prepare!"

I watched Jack grab another turtle from the dwindling pile and slit its neck. He slid his knife between belly and shell and worked it all the way round, then gutted it, cut away the ill-tasting dark meat from the shoulders, and threw the body on the fire to cook. I tore another mouthful of flesh from the one in front of me and chewed slowly. It was delicious—by far the sweetest delight in the sea.

"Mr.-and-Mrs.-Captain!" I turned to Greenwoode, who had proffered the slurred and annoying toast yet again, smiled and drank. Again. The wedding toasts had got overly numerous by now and I was getting a bit tired of raising my rumpot to them.

Leo leaned closer and put his hand on my belly. "Any regrets?" he asked me—he must have sensed my irritation and the rum had made him bold enough to risk my answer. I smiled and shook my head, resting it on his shoulder for a moment. I couldn't bring forth any more enthusiasm, even if I had only been married a week.

Truth be told I had plenty of regrets, and they started with my belly. I was sick of being fat and lumbering around deck. I wanted the child out, but, just like separating the boats, I also wanted her to stay exactly where she was for as long as possible. I was a sailor, a pirate, not a mother, how could I rear a child at sea? I thought back to Klara's last words. *I did as you asked, Klara. I've married him and I'll call her Raphaella. I'm keeping my promises to you, and we'll attack Brisingamen and kill Erik—I hope you knew what you were saying. I hope I'm doing right by my child. I wish you were here, Klara, I wish you were still with me.*

"What is it, Gabriella? Why are you crying?"

"I-miss-Klara," I mumbled, then sat up and wiped my face. I didn't want my crew—especially the new members—to see my tears.

"We have to decide what to do with the Freyjamen," I added, all business again.

"Sí, we should spread them round all three of the ships."

"Yes. I want a handful on *Valkyrie* to replace those who'll sail with Carmen aboard *Freyja*, and she'll need more men too. But I'm worried there'll be trouble, Leo. I'm nervous about having so many Freyjamen on our decks."

"Hmm, let's put most aboard *Freedom* where there's a bigger crew to keep an eye on them. Both *Valkyrie* and *Freyja* are light and maneuverable, *Sound of Freedom* is by far the bigger ship and the better fighting platform—I can use plenty of hands on guns." He paused. "What do you want to do with Sharpe? I know he helped you in the past, but you can't trust his obedience, especially now that he's the most senior Freyjamen. We need to take care with him."

I smiled. "Put him aboard *Freyja*. Let Carmen deal with him."

Chapter 95

GABRIELLA
5th June 1687

Despite the previous night's festivities, the crews were up at dawn to secure warps from *Freyja*—bow, amidships and stern—to the sturdiest trees. The bitter ends of the kedges had all been made fast to *Valkyrie,* and the iron anchors were in the boats waiting for the high tide.

"You may as well put the boats off, querida. High tide's only a couple of hours away."

"You heard him! Launch the boats!" I called, too nervous to mind Leo giving me advice. I had thought about trundling them down the beach on gun carriages at low tide, but the anchors were too heavy for wet sand, the boats would manage them better. The two that had been towed were pushed down the beach and the others joined them, until I had six boat crews braving the shark-infested waters to drop the kedges a musket-shot offshore. I stood at *Valkyrie's* stern to watch and could see it was damned hard work to row out against the surf, but eventually the first anchor was dropped and soon there was a fan of half a dozen kedges spread off the stern, their positions marked by empty barrels.

"Take up the slack and bed them in!" I shouted forward, and the Freyjamen at each of *Valkyrie's* capstan and windlasses started to heave. The real work would begin when there was enough water around *Valkyrie's* hull to float her. I grasped *Valkyrie's* rail so tightly my knuckles showed white.

One by one, the anchor warps tautened and held. "Very well, leave it there, make it fast!" I shouted and walked slowly forward past the teams of sweating men all downing the clear fresh water from the spring we'd found ashore. When I eventually reached the bow, I leaned over the rail as best I could. Leo had joined Gaunt once the boats had been put off and I ahoyed below.

"How does she look?" I asked.

Gaunt had cleared away the lines we'd used to secure the two ships to avoid them working loose when under tow, cut away some of *Freyja's* timber and was rubbing tallow on *Valkyrie's* bow to ease her passage as much as possible.

"We're making good progress, querida. We'll be ready in half an hour."

"Very well. The rudder's awash already, we don't have much longer than that."

"Don't fret, querida, we have to wait until there's enough depth under her bows."

I knew that, but was still nervous. I'd soon know if I had killed my boat as well as my best friend and three others of a crew that had trusted me. I gripped the rail again.

"Haul away!"

High tide had come at last and teams of Freyjamen, Valkyries and Freedom Fighters hauled on capstan and windlass bars, as well as bare hawser. Even the bowers had been deployed, although they hadn't been taken very far out. By working directly on *Valkyrie's* bows, they gave that bit more leverage.

A heaving chant rang out from the main capstan and was taken up by the whole crew. I smiled at Leo—everyone was working together.

"Heave away, my hearties, Haul away!"

I grabbed Leo's arm in excitement. I'd felt a shudder beneath my feet.

"She's coming, querida, she's coming."

Another verse of the shanty and another shudder, then another. All at once *Valkyrie* shot backwards and men tumbled to the deck, cheering. I kept my feet thanks to my grip on Leo, and his on the bowrail, but I was holding on too tightly.

"What's wrong?" Leo asked.

"Nothing. Look!" I could clearly see the hole stove into *Freyja's* board. *Valkyrie* was free, but we had no time to rest and I shouted for the anchor cables to be loosed. *Valkyrie* would be taking on water, and I didn't have time to haul them all aboard.

"Set the jibs and mainsail!" I shouted. The sails were unfurled and sheets hauled in. *Valkyrie* sailed again, but not for long. I'd headed aft as soon as I'd seen *Freyja* clear, and now grabbed the tiller.

"Back the jibs!" I screamed, and pushed the tiller to windward. *Valkyrie's* nose swung downwind and we started to move. I hauled the tiller back amidships and she responded. We had steerage. "Let go the jibs!

"Haul leeward jib sheets!"

The two triangular sails filled to leeward—larboard in this case—and we sailed back ashore, just downwind of *Freyja.*

"Let go all sheets!"

The surf took us, lifted us, and deposited *Valkyrie* onto the beach.

"Well done everyone! Rum all round! But keep a clear enough head to recover the anchors!"

Everyone cheered again and swarmed down the lines thrown over the hull to the sand. I followed a little more slowly in a bo'sun's chair, cursing with impatience at my careful descent at Baba and Greenwoode's hands. It was time to find out *Valkyrie's* fate, and I was stuck on a plank of wood being lowered to the sand as if I were made of fine porcelain.

"Querida." Leo grabbed me as soon as my feet looked like touching the beach, and Bess hovered nearby. I stumbled slightly, cursing at my lack of balance.

"Well, Mr. Gaunt?" I huffed. He had dashed down the beach and was busy making his inspection as I reached him.

Valkyrie's prow loomed above us like a towering wooden wave, freshly scarred from her recent battle. The pale wooden splits and cuts in her dark tarred wood seemed shocking, and I felt guilty knowing that I was the cause of them. I'd almost come to think of her as a living, breathing being, and I had to remind myself she was wood, she didn't feel pain or injury. Just as well, Gaunt was repeatedly sticking an awl into her beams, tutting or umming and ahhing at the results of his prodding, more for the benefit of the crew ringed around us than anything else, I was sure.

I looked around, everyone was tense and silent. It was unnerving. These men and women were never quiet, they constantly argued or laughed or sang, and I turned my attention back to Gaunt, who took a step back.

"Well?" I demanded, ready to hit him if he did not stop stroking his chin and start speaking.

He sighed and looked around him at the crew, then focused his gaze on me.

"Her stem's sound, lassie, she's sound. Most of her forward strakes'll need replacing, but I'll have her shipshape again, lass, with time."

"Thank God for that," I gasped, but my relief was short-lived.

"*Sail oh!*"

I spun seaward as best I could, then looked at Leo—I didn't recognize the ship bearing down on the island.

"It's Blake," he said, then shouted, "All hands to *Freedom*!

"Sorry, querida," he added. "We'll have to leave *Valkyrie* where she is for now. We'll come back for her soon."

"We'd better," I muttered, and followed him to the ship's boats. I knew *Valkyrie* wasn't fit for another fight, but I hated abandoning her and *Freyja* on this beach. However much I didn't want to admit it, our best chance was *Sound of Freedom*.

I looked seaward again. Blake's sails were growing, we didn't have much time.

Chapter 96

The first cannonball hit just offshore long before we reached *Freedom's* boats, and panic spread along the beach faster than plague. We had two guns on the beach a cable away, but no one was there to man them: we'd all been involved in separating *Valkyrie* and *Freyja*. Our only other working guns were aboard *Freedom*, anchored offshore, but the closest men were still too far away from the boats.

Leo pulled ahead of me and grabbed my arm. "Come on, Gabriella, come on!"

"I can't," I gasped, *how the hell does he think I can run like this?*

Jean-Claude and Feliciano reached the defensive guns on the beach. They were tackled by three Freyjamen. The Carib creed of offering quarter and a place to a bested crew was backfiring on us badly. With Blake's arrival, their old loyalties shone through, stronger than their new oaths. We were doomed. The enemy was amongst us, and we were poorly armed and outmanned.

Blake's cannon were almost within range of *Freedom*. Of course she'd be his target, I could almost feel Leo's anguish at his helplessness. He loved that ship as he would a lover. He mastered her, fed her, clothed and maintained her. But today he couldn't protect her.

I turned at the sound of laughter. Cheval was free of his hempen bonds and, amongst all the panic on the beach, had made us his target.

"We're not finished yet, Santiago—I have a score to settle with you, and I will not rest until you're either crawling at my feet begging for mercy, or dead. I do not forget wrongs done against me, and you have wronged me, you Spanish dog, you have wronged me!"

He stepped toward us and Leo squared his shoulders ready for attack, but Cheval fell to the sand, tackled from behind by Carmen and Baba.

"Not today, viejo amigo." Leo laughed. "Not today, old friend." Then he whipped around, along with the rest of us to stare out to sea.

I followed his gaze, horror-struck. The *Sound of Freedom* was ablaze. Whether the ship had been hit by a lucky ball from Blake, striking metal with a spark close enough to set black powder on fire, or whether it had been a Freyjaman who'd sized up the situation quickly and destroyed our only means of fighting back, we'd never know. I put my bet on a Freyjaman. It made no difference.

More Freyjamen ringed us. Even though they weren't armed, there were too many of them for my and Leo's cutlasses. And Blake's men were coming in boats. They had us. We were beaten with most of our crews now fleeing into the interior of the island to hide in the trees.

Only Carmen, Baba and Greenwoode were close and I allowed myself a moment's gratification that it was my Valkyries who had stayed to fight. Carmen and Baba stepped away from Cheval, who got back to his feet, grinned and said, "Not only are you mine, you're his." He nodded toward the *Dutch Pride* and her boats. They bristled with sailors and muskets, and were well within range.

One by one, we dropped our blades. God alone knew what our fate would be.

Chapter 97

GABRIELLA
13th June 1687
Sayba

I couldn't believe my eyes. Sayba. Eckerstad. Brisingamen was just over that cliff. Had I really been through all this just to be subjected once again to *his* mercy? It wasn't fair. I'd been through so much. *We'd* been through so much. Me, Klara, Leo and everyone on my crew, and of course Wilbert and Jan who'd died to give Klara and me a chance. And now look, Klara was dead too, and I was back here a prisoner, a helpless slave. My new husband, however strong he'd seemed, was just as powerless. We were amongst the many lost in this New World.

The shore grew larger. Our future inevitable. Erik van Ecken would be waiting there for us both. Despite everything, Erik had won. I looked at Leo, shackled and beaten, as I was myself, and recognized the despair in his eyes. He'd promised me protection and freedom. I was big with his child and he'd failed to keep us safe. My past was about to claim us all.

Time stretched out, but not long enough. Soon the familiar shouts and sounds of a ship brought to anchor announced we'd run out of time. Sayba. Eckerstad. Erik. Like it or not, I was home.

Thrown into boats, shoved into the bilges, rowed ashore. Blake's men laughing and gloating—speculating on their reward. *What on earth awaits us? What kind of hell awaits me?*

Drawing closer to the wharf, I recognized a familiar stance, a familiar green frockcoat—Erik was here to welcome us. I hugged my belly, more fearful for my child than for myself or for Leo. What would Erik do to my unborn child that was not his? I remembered all those taunts I'd suffered about being a "barren English whore". My belly proved that a lie. I knew him well enough to know he would not take my pregnancy well.

Closer.

Close enough for me to see his features, and him to see mine.

I longed to grab Leo's hand, his arm, his leg, anything, just to have that contact, but my arms were bound, my wrists and ankles tied. I couldn't reach out to him. Our eyes met. I had to be content with that.

Erik grew closer. I didn't look at him. I kept my eyes on Leo, my lion. My strength grew, knowing I had his love, knowing I loved him, that whatever happened now, the last year had been worth the pain to come. Leo smiled. I smiled back. He knew. He understood.

The boat drew up against the wharf and Cheval threw a line to Erik. I didn't look up. I didn't move my eyes from Leo's. Sharpe grabbed me and hauled me to my feet. "So help me God, I'd not wish this on you or anyone—give me a chance to help you."

I turned to look at him, but was thrown onto the cobbled wharf before I could complete the move. I lay on my side, hands roped behind my back, unable to see Leo, hoping my baby was unhurt.

"Hello, wife!" Erik crouched in front of my face and spat. I looked away, refusing to show him any emotion, any fear. I should have known better. He grasped my chin and dragged my face to his. I heard Leo protest, but at his treatment or mine I didn't know.

"Look at me," Erik said. "Look. At. Me."

I closed my eyes.

"Whore!" He slapped me.

I smiled. I stayed on the cobbles, bruised, pregnant and bleeding, and smiled. Whatever he did to me, I had known freedom. I loved and was loved back. I'd fought battles and won. That in itself was worth it. And now I had Leo's cub in my belly. I would give our baby a life, a free life, or die trying. Erik would not beat me now.

I looked at him.

He stepped back.

He knew.

"Strap her to the cart, I want her at Brisingamen, the rest of them can go to the dungeons in the fort."

My smiled broadened.

"No, on second thoughts, I want her nowhere near me—she can go to the fort too."

He leaned down. "I won't send you to the gallows, not in your state, whore that you are." He glanced at my belly, then grinned. "You can hang your pirate lover, and your friends. And if you don't do as I say, I'll cut that whoreson out of you and let you both drown in your blood."

Chapter 98

GABRIELLA
15th July 1687
Sayba

The dungeon door opened at dawn. I could tell it was daybreak by the faint light coming through the iron grille on the wall above my head. I had counted every dawn since I'd been thrown in here with Carmen—there had been thirty two of them.

I had no idea where Leo and the others were. The walls were so thick, they could even have been in the next cell and we wouldn't have been able to hear them.

I put my hands on my belly. I was getting near my time—I reckoned I had another month at most before I gave birth. The child inside moved, and I could only hope her father was still alive, that we would all be alive tomorrow.

Four men entered—all sailors—and dragged us outside. I blinked at the sudden bright light, almost blinded, and was told to climb. I looked up at the cart, and held my belly. A hand was held out to me and hauled me up, hands behind pushing my bulk upwards. I blinked at Sharpe, whose hand I still held, and he moved aside.

"Gabriella! Thank God!"

"Leo!" I sobbed, fear and emotion getting the better of me. He was dirty, ragged and too thin, but he was alive. I went to him and hugged him. He couldn't hold me, his hands were bound behind him with rope. I moved to untie him but one of Blake's men saw me and shouted. My arms were pulled behind me and tied together.

"Watch it!" I heard Carmen threaten as she received similar treatment.

"Are you well? The child?" Leo asked.

"Yes, yes, we're well." I sobbed. "You?"

"Sí, for what it's worth," he replied.

"Baba! Greenwoode! Jean-Claude! Feliciano!" I'd only just noticed them standing with Leo.

"Captain," they replied. Carmen joined them.

"Shut up the lot of you! No talking!" Blake's man shouted. The cart jerked into motion as the mule started its trudge toward Eckerstad's square, and I wondered if Erik was sticking to his word and would really try to make me hang Leo.

Ten minutes later, I knew for sure that he intended a hanging at least. We arrived in the crowded square, the centerpiece of which was a simple wooden frame, wide enough to straddle the cart, with a noose hanging from the center of the crossbar.

The mule was directed through the frame, leaving the noose hanging down over the bed of the cart. All seven of us shrank away from it, desperate not to touch it.

"Down!" Erik had arrived. Carmen and the others jumped down, leaving Leo and myself on the cart. I was relieved to see none of them stumbled when they hit the ground. I wondered how I'd get down with my bulk and my hands tied—I certainly wouldn't be able to jump. I moved to the edge.

"Not you. Turn around." Erik clambered onto the cart and cut my hands free. "Now, *wife*," he spat. "I've given you long enough to think about it—you know what to do."

I turned back and stared at him.

"Put the noose around his neck."

I neither moved nor looked away.

"I said, put the noose around his neck!" Erik shouted. He barely had himself under control and I shuddered. I still didn't move though. He drew his dagger and pressed it to my belly. Hard. I flinched, the blade was sharp and cut my skin. I gritted my teeth, determined not to give him the satisfaction of crying out or shying away, but couldn't help my tears which had started to flow again.

The whole town had turned out, dressed in their finest, to

watch the spectacle, but everyone was silent.

"Querida."

I turned to look at Leo. Tears ran down his cheeks, although he sounded calm.

"Do it, don't let him kill our child. Just do it."

"Leo, no!" I sobbed.

"You have no choice," he said.

"That's right, whore," Erik spat. "You have no choice. You'll pay for embarrassing me and running away. Put the noose around his neck or I'll cut this child out of you and he can watch you both bleed to death right here. Then I'll hang your lover myself—and with great pleasure." He laughed, although there was no mirth in the sound.

"Gabriella, please," Leo said. "It's the child that matters now. You and the child. If I have to die so the two of you can live, then so be it."

Erik pulled the knife across my belly, and I screamed in pain, my resolve completely gone in the terror of what I had to do. I jerked back from the knife, closer to Leo and clutched my hands to my stomach. My shirt was red with blood, but it wasn't a mortal wound, and my baby still moved inside me as she had before. Erik hadn't hurt her. Yet.

I looked around at the crowd, desperate for help, but there was none. Carmen and the others looked horrified, but bound and under guard there was nothing they could do to help me. My eyes met Sharpe's, but he looked away. Nobody would meet my eyes.

"Get on with it," Erik said, under control again. "Do it."

I turned and faced Leo, who now stood by the noose. I could barely meet his look, but when I did I couldn't look away, despite the tears that flooded my eyes. I didn't think I'd ever stop crying again.

I took a step toward him, put my hands to his face and held him. I kissed him. We both knew it would be for the last time.

"Stop that! Get on with it!" Erik shouted.

"I'm sorry, I'm so sorry, I'm so sorry," I whispered over and over. "I love you."

"I love you too, and this isn't your doing. I forgive you. Promise me you'll forgive yourself."

I didn't answer. What could I say? Sobbing, my heart breaking, I put the noose around his neck.

"Gabriella?"

I looked at him.

"Make it quick—pull on my legs. Please. Make it quick?"

I remembered previous hangings I'd witnessed—the condemned man swinging for what seemed an age, slowly strangling to death, his friends and family putting all their weight into pulling on his legs to quicken his death and lessen his suffering. I nodded, but didn't know if I'd be able to do it.

Chapter 99

"Move away from him."

I ignored Erik, and he grabbed my arm and dragged me away from Leo. I fell off the back of the cart, and landed on him, winding him. I struggled up and rushed to the mule tethered between the shafts. If I prevented the animal from moving, Leo would still be safe, despite the noose. He'd only die if the cart moved away from under his feet.

I wrapped my arms around the animal's neck, begging it to stay still, while my eyes stayed fixed on Leo. He had turned so his last sight would be me. He hadn't been offered a blindfold.

His eyes flicked up, over my head, and hope shone on his face. I turned.

"Yes!" It was *Valkyrie* and *Freyja*. After Blake had left the island, the crews had salvaged the ships. But my delight turned to dismay when they opened fire on the square. The mule, so far placid, jumped in its traces, and I couldn't blame it. Cannon fire and screams did not help to keep an animal calm. I whispered soothing words into its ear, and hung onto its neck with all my strength, willing it to stay still and keep Leo alive.

I was barely aware of the destruction in the square, or of Blake's men running to the fort and other gun positions to return fire on my ships. All I could think about was getting that bloody animal to stand still to keep the cart in place.

"Mistress Gabriella?"

I turned in surprise to see a dark face almost hidden by a hat and curled wig. He held a knife out to me by the blade. I grabbed it and peered at him.

"Hendrik!" He was one of Erik's slaves who had escaped the night Klara and I left Brisingamen. "Thank you."

"No, thank *you,*" he said, and melted back into the crowd. I was staggered at the risk he'd taken, not only to help me, but just by being here. As an escaped slave—a maroon—any townsman could shoot him on sight, and would be celebrated and well rewarded for it. His life was worth nothing in this town—especially with Erik only feet away.

I turned back to the mule. I didn't have time to think about Hendrik, not at the moment.

I slashed the knife across the traces that harnessed the animal to Leo's cart, and thanked God it was sharp. The leather parted and the mule bolted. I breathed a sigh of relief until the cart tipped onto its shafts. It only had two wheels and needed the bulk of the animal to keep it level.

"*No*!"

Leo couldn't brace his feet on the sharp incline and I panicked as I heard his gurgle. His fall tightened the noose around his neck, strangling him. *No! Oh no! Have I killed him after all?* He kicked hard but found nowhere to take his weight.

I put the blade between my teeth as if I were boarding a prize ship, grabbed the rail and tried to haul myself up. If I could cut the rope, he could still live.

"Out of the way!"

I was pushed from behind and fell to the ground, stunned. I rolled over and looked at the gallows. Sharpe jumped past me and up onto the cart's rail. I'd never have been able to do that with my belly, no matter how long I kept trying.

A moment later he was out of sight, and Leo . . . thank God . . . Leo slid down the wooden slope and landed in a heap next to me.

"Leo!"

He couldn't talk. Although the rope had been cut, the noose was still tight around his neck. He was still being strangled—his face bright red. I forced the fingers of both my hands into the noose by the knot and pulled it through. A harmless length of rope with a complicated knot at one end, landed by our heads.

"Leo!"

"Urgh!" he said. I supposed that meant he was still breathing.

I realized I had dropped the knife when I fell, scrambled for it, and cut his hands free.

"Urgh!"

His hands flew to his throat, massaging the skin there.

"Leo! *Leo*, can you talk?"

"Sí." At least I think that's what he said. I hoped it was. I kissed him, crying again, he was alive!

"No time for that," Sharpe said and hauled Leo to his feet. "Here—I hope you can fight!" He thrust a cutlass, hilt first, at Leo and turned to face the crowd, his own blade held at the ready, searching out the familiar faces of his former crewmates.

"Why?" I gasped at him, my own knife held ready to fight.

"I never did take to van Ecken," he said. "And besides, I gave you my oath of loyalty—that means something to me, even if it doesn't to those reprobates." He nodded at the mix of Freyjamen and Blake's crew heading toward us, as more cannonball hit the square from *Valkyrie* and *Freyja*. "Watch out!" he shouted.

I spun round to see Erik back on his feet and charging toward us, his face red with anger. I stepped forward to meet his attack, raising my knife. He dodged and I caught his shoulder. He stared at me in shock. Then he looked to either side of me and I realized Leo and Sharpe stood with me.

"Kill them," Erik said to three slaves who stood nearby. They looked at us. They were unarmed; we were pirates with swords. They didn't move, despite Erik's curses. They backed away. Erik might kill them for it, but only if he survived the day. My first husband screamed curses at their backs, then looked back at me. I smiled when I saw him realize his predicament. He was one man standing against three experienced fighters. It was too much for him.

"Whore!" he spat, turned, and ran.

Chapter 100

LEO

I watched van Ecken run from us and would have laughed—if I hadn't wanted him so badly. I looked at Gabriella, and we both moved to go after him, but Sharpe's shout stopped us. I looked round. Blake's men were advancing. There were too many of them. Van Ecken would have to wait. But I promised myself I would not leave this island until I'd found him. I readied myself.

More broadsides from *Valkyrie* and *Freyja* hit the square, and it was too much for the townspeople who remained. They'd come to witness a hanging, not become targets for cannon. The square emptied, leaving the eight of us to face Blake's men. At least they were well dispersed and most of them were more concerned with our ships than with us. I wondered why the two vessels hadn't come under attack from the cliff top gun in the way *Freedom* had when we'd last attacked, but didn't have time to think about it.

The first man reached us and raised his sword. I lifted my own to meet it and was aware of Gabriella freeing the still-bound crew. I thrust at the man and kicked his kneecap at the same time. He went down. I finished him off quickly and looked up at Carmen, who hadn't waited for his grip to slacken before she wrenched his cutlass away from him. She looked at my neck, then nodded at me.

"Where's Gabriella?" she asked.

Confused, I looked up and saw her hurrying out of the square in the same direction as van Ecken.

"Van Ecken," I whispered, my voice still not working. She didn't hear. I pointed and tried again a little louder. "Van Ecken. Help her." She understood and ran, and I stood to meet the next man.

When he was down, Greenwoode bent and took his sword. I turned to meet the next attack, and saw Cheval and Sharpe.

Sharpe may have been an expert marksman, but as a swordsman he looked to be evenly matched with Cheval—their fight could take some time. But it was an old score they had to settle, I wouldn't interfere unless I had to. Not that I had any opportunity.

Another man attacked and I parried his first thrust with ease, though I was getting tired and every breath hurt enough that I was struggling to find the strength to keep fighting. The man saw my difficulty and grinned. He launched a vicious attack, slashing first left, then right, then stabbing at me.

I jumped backwards, but was in an incredible amount of pain. Just when I wondered how I could defeat him, Jean-Claude charged at us and booted my attacker in the kidneys. I saw my opportunity and stabbed. He fell and Baba bent down to take his sword. I doubled up trying to get my breath.

Before I could thank him, Baba fell too, blood streaming from his neck. I looked at the man who had felled the man who had just saved my life, then threw my sword. Direct hit. He fell to the ground and I bent to pick up the cutlass Baba had tried for. Feliciano took the cutlass I'd thrown, and Jean-Claude grabbed another.

I looked about me—no more danger yet—although Sharpe and Cheval were still locked in battle. Cheval looked to be getting the upper hand. They moved closer to me, and Sharpe took a nasty cut to his temple and stumbled backwards. Cheval moved to strike the killing blow, and I slashed out at him. I would not allow Cheval to kill the man who had saved my, and probably Gabriella's, life.

Cheval screamed as my blade sliced his swordarm and he dropped his weapon.

"You bastard! I should have killed you when I had the chance!"

I laughed as best I could to give Sharpe time to get to his feet. Even to my own ears it was a chilling sound, and I rubbed my throat again. Cheval looked at the two of us and at the cutlass at his feet, then turned and ran, shouting abuse all the way.

"He might baulk at fighting both of you, but I won't."

I spun round to see Blake's sneering face, and Sharpe and Jean-Claude both stepped to my side. The man standing with

Blake beckoned to Jean-Claude and raised his sword, Jean-Claude grinned and lunged. The man dodged, but I didn't take my eyes off Blake. Sharpe raised his sword.

"No, Sharpe, he's mine, we have an old score to reckon."

"And what would that be? The only score to settle is mine." Blake looked confused.

"Panama City."

Blake raised an eyebrow in question. "What about it?"

"You killed my mother. I saw you. After you . . . after you . . ." I couldn't speak the words.

Blake shrugged. "I killed a lot of women that day—bedded them too. Which one was yours?" He laughed. "Ah, I have you now, you're that boy—the boy who watched!"

I couldn't stand it and charged him. It was too rash, that was what he'd wanted. Blake struck out, and I felt a tremendous white-hot pain across my chest. My left hand flew to the wound and came away bloodied. I forced a deep breath down my ravaged throat. This man knew how to fight—he couldn't have survived as a pirate, never mind a pirate captain, for so long if he did not. I'd have to take more care and use more wit to defeat him. I circled to give myself a little time to catch my breath.

Blake lunged at me and I jumped back, but hadn't realized how close I was to the cart that had nearly become my hearse. I had nowhere to go.

Blake lunged again and I rolled to the side, hacking at him blindly. He missed and his blade drove into the wood. My cutlass caught his side. It was a lucky blow, I hadn't had time to aim it, but it wasn't deep enough to decide the fight. Blake wrenched his sword free of the cart with a roar and turned to parry my next attack.

Now he was backed up against the cart and I booted him in the groin, feeling the savage satisfaction of a blow well landed. He wouldn't be raping anyone else for quite some time—never, if I could finish him off. He doubled up and I hit him—hard. Suddenly swords weren't enough. I wanted to feel Blake's bones crunch under my fists. I wanted Blake's blood running over my hands.

Blake had other ideas though, and kicked out, catching my shin, and followed up with a fist of his own. I was driven backwards, losing my advantage, and Blake slashed out with his cutlass again. Hacking away at me he looked like a madman, blood pouring down his face from a cut above his eye. He slashed at me again, missed, and I realized he was blinded by the blood. I took the opportunity and struck, driving the tip of my cutlass into his heart.

Blake fell, dead, and I stared down at him, my chest heaving, my breath rasping in a throat that felt on fire. That was it, all three were dead. I looked up and met Sharpe's eye. He'd killed another of Blake's men, and Greenwoode's was also dead. Jean-Claude and Feliciano were finishing off one other. No one else challenged us with Blake dead in the dirt. I bent double and tried to catch my breath.

Gabriella! How had she fared? It didn't matter anymore that Blake was beaten, what had become of my wife?

I looked in the direction she and Carmen had taken and took a step to follow, but I couldn't get enough breath down my bruised throat to make any speed.

Chapter 101

GABRIELLA

I followed Erik as fast as I could. He'd taken the road that led to Brisingamen, and I knew I'd catch him there. What I would do then, I didn't know, but I had a sizable walk ahead of me to think of something.

"Where are we going?"

I turned in surprise at Carmen's voice and was very glad to see her. "Erik's running. I won't let him escape."

"Which way?"

"There." I pointed at the path that led to my former home. "Hurry."

She snorted with laughter, and I couldn't help my smile. I was the slow one. But we made as much progress as we could and walked the next quarter of a league in silence, both conserving our breath—we'd not had much exercise locked up for a month, and whilst both of us appreciated being outside again, we found the going hard.

"Mistress Gabriella, stop." Two dark figures stepped out onto the path in front of us. "Go back."

"No, Hendrik, I won't. Please don't try to stop us."

"Leave him to us," the other man said.

"No, Hans, I need to do this. Please—let us pass."

"We're not Hans and Hendrik. We left those Dutch names behind us when we left Brisingamen, and you no longer own us. You cannot tell us what to do."

"I'm not telling you, I'm asking you. And I know I don't own you. Who gave you the chance to be free? Or have you forgotten?" I was angry. I would not be prevented from reaching Erik.

They stared at me, not saying anything, their loyalties conflicting.

"What are your new names?"

"They're not our new names; they're the ones our mothers gave us," Hans spat. "I'm Kofi, he's Ndidi."

I nodded. "Kofi, Ndidi, Erik caused us all injury and pain. We can do this together."

"We're not alone. The others will not want two white women interfering."

"We're more than women, we're pirates, with weapons and the ability to use them. And I *will* reckon my score with Erik van Ecken." I spoke slowly and clearly. There could be no doubt I meant what I said, and both men recognized the unspoken threat. They looked at each other and stood aside.

"We'll come with you."

I nodded. They could do what they liked as long as they didn't prevent me from killing Erik.

"How far ahead is he? Why did you let him through? Surely you left the square before he did."

"Mmm," Hendrik—Ndidi—said. "There are more of us up ahead. Many want their revenge on van Ecken. Over a dozen of us got away that night, but he caught four and killed them all—right in that square."

"So you want your vengeance too." I nodded.

"Mm. We all do. We've taken the big gun on the cliff and we've released everyone from the estate. Rensink tried to stop us, but we dealt with him." He spat in the dirt. "We knew today would be our best chance—all the attention would be on you and your Spanish pirate. We knew you wouldn't give in without a fight."

I smiled at him, but my mind was still on Erik.

"Where are the others?"

"About a quarter of a league up the road, lying in wait. Even Jan." Hans/Kofi glared at me.

"Jan? Klara's boy? He lives?"

"Mm. No thanks to you and his mother. How could you leave him like that?" Ndidi sounded just as disgusted.

"We thought he was dead . . . we thought Sharpe had shot him . . . we'd never have run had we thought there was a chance he lived."

"He was only wounded. At least he'll get to see his mother

again. Where is she? On one of those ships out there?"

My hands flew to my mouth in shock. I didn't need to tell them. The two men looked at each other in distress. I could only imagine what my news would do to Jan. Thanks to me, his mother had left him twice, and there was no way of reckoning that.

"Wilbert?" I hardly dared asked.

"No. He *was* killed," Kofi said.

We walked on in silence.

The awkward silence grew more uncomfortable with every step, and I was relieved when I heard shouts up ahead. I recognized Erik's voice—I didn't need to hear the Dutch accent, the disdain in his words marked him just as surely.

"Get out of my way! Who do you think you are? You'll be flogged in that square before the day's out, now get out of my way! Get off me, you hond!"

We walked around the bend and he silenced when he saw me, then: 'You! *Whore.*"

I smiled. I had my cutlass in my hand, Carmen was armed and ready to kill at my side, and a dozen of his ex-slaves encircled him, all holding pistols. I knew Jan would be in the circle of men, but couldn't look for him. I wouldn't be able to meet his eyes anyway. I kept my attention on Erik.

"And you! Another whore!" He recognized Carmen.

"Hej, van Ecken. Told you we'd meet again."

He went pale and looked about him. I enjoyed the look that came over his face and the slump of his shoulders as he realized he was alone and surrounded.

"Someone help me. I have gold. I'll reward you well," he pleaded.

Someone laughed. "We'll have all the reward we want very soon, van Ecken. Then we'll take your gold too."

Erik stayed silent, his eyes darting about looking for a way out. There was none. His gaze settled on me.

"Gabriella, wife, help me. I'm your husband, it's your duty," he commanded.

I laughed. "Fire!" I said, calmly. I didn't have a gun, but I could at least decide the moment of his death, and it could not come soon enough. The pistols fired. Erik dropped. I walked to his body prone in the mud and stared down at him. I felt only contempt.

"What are you planning to do with him?" I asked the men.

"Leave him—the animals can have him."

I smiled and looked around the circle. I gasped. Jan. I walked toward him; he looked at the floor.

"I'm so sorry, Jan, we didn't know. We heard the shots, we thought you were dead. We'd never have left if we'd known. Klara would never have left you."

"Where . . .? Where . . .?"

"I'm sorry, Jan, she was killed fighting Hornigold." I stepped closer and hugged him. He pulled away and turned to Ndidi. He buried his face in the man's chest and sobbed. I'd never felt so guilty and helpless.

"Jan?" He ignored me. I didn't blame him. "Jan?" I tried again, tears pouring down my own face, and very close to losing control to sobs. He turned his head and wiped his face.

"She was very brave. Brave like you were that night and like you've been today. She fought back and she was free. She never stopped thinking of you. Even when she died, she was talking about you and about seeing you again."

"Well, she won't will she? I'm here—where she left me."

"I know, I can't think of anything that would make her happier, knowing that you're alive and free."

He looked around him. "Free?" He laughed. "Living in the jungle with the whole island wanting to kill us? I'd hardly call that free!"

I looked at Carmen, she saw what was in my mind and nodded. Not that I needed her agreement, but being locked up together for the past month had finally settled our differences.

"If you want to be free, there are two ships in that harbor that need sailors and gunners." I raised my voice. "All of you are welcome to join our crews—as free men. Earning equal shares in the profits we make! It's safer and easier to hide at sea than in the jungles of this godforsaken island, even if Erik is dead. What do you say? Will you join us?"

Chapter 102

Most of them agreed. I was pleased—a year and a half ago these men had been my slaves, but they recognized my position had been just as horrific. I was touched that so many of them—including Jan—wanted to sail under my command.

But it would be different to before, very different. They would be there by choice and they'd be paid. If they weren't happy with my command, they could leave at any time, or, if enough crew agreed, they could depose me by a simple vote and elect a new captain. I was honored that they chose to sail with me. No, I was humbled.

Some of the men went to the house to ferret out Erik's gold and riches. That would be split amongst the current and ex-Brisingameners alone—they'd earned it. The other men joined Carmen and me in returning to the square. We wanted to make sure all Erik's men—including Blake's and the ex-Freyjamen—were defeated, and that Erik's slave sheds were liberated.

I realized *Valkyrie* and *Freyja* may have much larger crews than they could cope with—I'd have to give everyone the option of settling on St Vincent with the existing community of maroons. I hoped most would stay though, we could do no better than these men and women from Brisingamen.

We reached the square, and I looked around. I breathed a sigh of relief when I saw Leo stride toward me, Sharpe still at his side. I sank into his arms, close to tears.

"Van Ecken?" he asked.

"Dead," I said.

"So we're truly man and wife?"

I laughed. "Leo, we always were, you know that!" He grinned and hugged me, and I belatedly realized I could hear him. He had a voice. It was raspy, but it was louder than a whisper. I leaned against him in relief and looked around. The square and buildings nearby had been decimated by our cannon—Eckerstad was hardly recognizable. I looked at the dead and injured lying in the square, then at the men still standing.

"Where's Baba?" I demanded. Leo shook his head. I'd lost another life. "We have to find him, give him a proper *Valkyrie* burial," I said.

"Of course. He's over there." Leo nodded to his left. "Greenwoode's with him—he's taken a blade to the arm, but it should heal. It could have been a lot worse."

I nodded, the day's events only now hitting me. I'd almost killed Leo, then participated in Erik's killing instead. I thought of something else. "Blake?"

"Dead."

"By whose hand?"

"Mine."

"So that's it then, they're all dead, we're free?"

"Sí, we're free, querida." Still in his arms, I leaned into him. Free at last. Our pasts dead, our future ahead.

"Andy!" Carmen and the gunner embraced hard, and I smiled at the depth of their friendship. I looked up—the square now swarmed with Valkyries and Freedom Fighters. We had the town, and man after man after woman greeted us, smiling, celebrating our win.

I was overjoyed to see Belinda, the housekeeper from Brisingamen, and hugged her in tears. She was barely able to speak—anger, worry and delight all warring inside her. When she finally let me go, I knew I was forgiven for leaving her.

Once the reunions were done, our crews raided what was left of Eckerstad. Gold, silver, jewels and anything else of value was carried to the shore and *Valkyrie's* boats. The slave sheds were opened, and a hundred men, women and children ventured into the sunlight; blinking, confused, overwhelmed, free. I determined to give every one of them the chance to live with us at sea or safe on land with the St Vincentians. I would do what little I could to undo the harm my husband's cruelty and arrogance had caused them.

I introduced Kofi and Ndidi to Leo and the others, and they took charge of the Africans and guided them to the boats. I was horrified at some of the reactions, and remembered my own terrible experience as a stowaway on a slaveship. I'd spent a week in a slaver's hold cruising around the Carib Sea. What had they endured on the ocean crossing from Africa? I could only imagine the horrors etched into their memories, and wasn't surprised to see a large group running away inland.

We eventually managed to load the boats—crew, passengers and plunder—and Leo and I climbed into the last one. I could hardly believe that, after everything, we were pulling out to *Valkyrie*. Had I really come so close to killing Leo today? Had our child really been in so much danger? How would he ever forgive me?

I looked at Jan, sitting in the bows, and smiled. He looked away and my smile faltered. I determined that I would do right by him. It was my fault he'd been left behind that day. It was my fault Klara had been killed. I would do what I could to be mother to him. I owed it to both him and Klara. I would repent and repair my mistakes as best I could.

"Leo. Gabriella." Frazer, understated as always, nodded to us as we climbed aboard.

"It's good to see you, Frazer," Leo said warmly, extending his hand. Frazer shook it. "Excellent timing once again."

"You too, Captain."

I noticed he didn't take his eyes off Leo's throat and the bruises blooming there. I couldn't blame him, it was quite a sight, and I winced at the memory of his kicking legs.

The conversation, such as it was, was interrupted by *Valkyrie's* gunners firing another broadside on Eckerstad in farewell, followed by *Freyja*, although resistance had ceased some time ago. It was just a little reminder—we were in charge now.

Frazer kept the helm—I was too exhausted to assert command over this melee—I was just relieved to be back aboard. I looked over the decks, crammed full of people, and sighed. I had no idea what to do with everyone. I simply could not think.

"What's our heading, Captain?" Frazer asked as we prepared to get under way.

"There." Leo pointed. "The *Dutch Pride*. Blake may be dead, but he still owes us a ship.

The Scot smiled.

Chapter 103

LEO

We wasted no time, and headed straight for the *Dutch Pride*, *Valkyrie's* bow cannon firing effectively under Jean-Claude's direction. Carmen and Andy aboard *Freyja* followed suit. Blake's ship—or what had been Blake's ship at least, she had no master now—got off a shot at us. It missed. It seemed she had men enough for only one gun, everyone else was ashore. They were hopelessly outnumbered.

As we drew up alongside, four men appeared on deck, their hands raised above their heads. They were realists, they knew they had no chance, and if they resisted further they would die.

We boarded, put them into the smallest boat and sent them shoreward. I had a ship again.

"What now?" Sharpe asked.

"Now we weigh anchor, put off from this godforsaken island, and Gaunt gets to work on the new nameboards."

"What new nameboards?" Gabriella asked.

"*Sound of Freedom*. I will not sail about the Carib Sea in a ship called the *Dutch Pride*. Blake took *Freedom* from me, now I'm claiming her back." I hugged her, thrilled at her smile. I'd feared I would never see it again. "Are you staying aboard or returning to *Valkyrie*?"

"I'm staying with you," she said, smiling. "I nearly killed you today, I'm not going to abandon you too—*Valkyrie's* in safe hands with Frazer and Gaunt, and *Freyja* will do well with Carmen and Andy."

"Do you trust them?"

"I do now. Carmen and I spent a month alone in a cell together. Things were a bit fraught at first, but we came to an understanding."

I hugged her. Truth be told, I didn't care at the moment if the Dane sailed *Freyja* away and we never saw her again. I had all I wanted on this deck.

"Slip the anchor!" Davys shouted from the quarterdeck, and Jean-Claude brought a boarding axe down on the anchor warp. We'd had our fill of Sayba, we wouldn't spend another hour here hauling up an anchor—they were easy enough to come by for a pirate ship in the Caribbees.

We started to drift and Davys shouted for the sheets to be hauled in. The sails filled and we were underway, finally heading to our future, the past avenged. The only thing to spoil our victory was the knowledge that Cheval had got away, and if any man had murder in his heart, it was he. He'd voiced such intentions on the last two occasions we'd met, I would be prudent to beware him.

And what about Sharpe? He'd betrayed van Ecken when he helped Gabriella to escape, and he'd fought against Blake. Could we trust him now? Then there was Magdalena—he'd shared a ship with her, had he mistreated her? I hadn't forgotten it was he who had appeared at the stern gallery after she'd jumped. I shrugged the thoughts off as Gabriella moved closer to me, hands on her enormous belly, and I embraced her as best I could.

"Where to, querida? The whole Carib Sea is at our bows, and we have no ties left."

"Not quite true, I want to give the Africans the option of settling on St Vincent—not all of them are happy to be at sea again." She smiled. "And then . . . hmm, when does the Flôta sail?"

"The Flôta?" I laughed. "You want to attack Spain's treasure fleet?"

She shrugged, then gasped in pain. "Aye, but it might have to wait a while."

I raised my eyes in question, then realized. "The child? It's coming now?"

"Soon."

"Davys, set a course for La Isla Magdalena, a new Freedom Fighter's on his way!" I shouted in glee, then panicked. It was too soon. How many knocks had she taken in that square? She could die.

"Hurry!" Gabriella gasped, bending and grasping the rail. "For pity's sake, hurry!"

"Full canvas aloft!" I shouted. I guided Gabriella to our cabin. We were followed by a couple of the women from Brisingamen. I left her in their hands and went back out on deck to see about sailing my new ship as fast as I could to La Isla Magdalena.

Two days later, I stood on my decks, *Freedom* anchored off La Isla Magdalena, Gabriella standing by my side and our daughter cradled in my arms. I smiled down at Raphaella, and Gabriella leaned against me. I had never been so happy.

THE END

* * *

Want more? Look out for the free Valkyrie short story *Where Away*—read on for more details.

* * *

If you enjoyed *The First Fleet*, please consider leaving a few words in review. Reviews are very important to an author and do help me understand what you enjoy, as well as guide other readers to books they would like to read.

Thank you – Karen Perkins

Why not try a ghost story by the same author?
Karen Perkins has published four **Yorkshire Ghost Stories** with more coming, all of which are available individually or as a box set.

For more information on Karen Perkins' fiction, including links for the main retailer sites and details of her current writing projects, please go to Karen's website:
www.karenperkinsauthor.com/

Fiction by Karen Perkins

Yorkshire Ghost Stories

Parliament of Rooks: Haunting Brontë Country
Knight of Betrayal: A Medieval Haunting
The Haunting of Thores-Cross – Read on for short excerpt
Cursed (Short Story)

The Yorkshire Ghost Stories are also available in a box set at a reduced price:
Ghosts of Yorkshire

To find out more about the full range of Yorkshire Ghost Stories, including upcoming titles, please visit: www.karenperkinsauthor.com/yorkshire-ghosts

Coming 2018
Jennet (Ghosts of Thores-Cross #3)

Valkyrie Series

Look Sharpe! (Book 1)
Ill Wind (Book 2)
Dead Reckoning (Book 3)
Where Away – Free Short Story – Read on to get your copy

To find out more about the full range of books in the Valkyrie Series, including upcoming titles, please visit: www.karenperkinsauthor.com/valkyrie

Where Away—A Valkyrie Short Story

A Caribbean Pirate Adventure

Magdalena Ortega is bored. She hates her life in Porto Belo—a town that comes alive every year with the arrival of the Spanish Treasure Fleet, then dies once more until the next visit. The thought of marrying, raising children, and spending the rest of her life here terrifies Magdalena and she is determined to escape.

Can she sneak aboard a galleon of the treasure fleet to stowaway? Will a pirate raid prove to be her making or her undoing?

Where Away is being offered FREE for readers of the Valkyrie Series and will not be released separately—if you would like to read it, please visit Karen's website:

www.karenperkinsauthor.com/valkyrie

About the Author – Karen Perkins

Karen Perkins is the author of seven fiction titles: the Yorkshire Ghost Stories and the Valkyrie Series of Caribbean pirate adventures. All of her fiction has appeared at the top of bestseller lists on both sides of the Atlantic, including the top 25 in the UK Kindle Store in 2018.

Her first Yorkshire Ghosts novel – THE HAUNTING OF THORES-CROSS – won the silver medal for European fiction in the prestigious 2015 Independent Publisher Book Awards in New York, whilst her Valkyrie novel, DEAD RECKONING, was long-listed in the 2011 MSLEXIA novel competition.

Originally a financial advisor, a sailing injury left Karen with a chronic pain condition which she has been battling for over twenty-five years (although she did take the European ladies title despite the injury!). Writing has given her a new lease of – and purpose to – life, and she is currently working on *Jennet*, a sequel to *The Haunting of Thores-Cross* and *Cursed*, which will be followed by a return to Haworth and The Rookery.

When not writing, she helps other authors prepare their books for publishing and has edited over 150 titles, including the 2017 Kindle UK Storyteller Award winner, *The Relic Hunters* by David Leadbeater, and has also published a series of publishing guides to help aspiring authors realise their dreams.

See more about Karen Perkins, including contact details, on her website:
www.karenperkinsauthor.com

Karen is on Social Media:

Facebook:
www.facebook.com/karenperkinsauthor
www.facebook.com/Yorkshireghosts
www.facebook.com/ValkyrieSeries

Twitter:
@LionheartG

Instagram
@YorkshireGhosts

Read on for an excerpt from ***The Haunting of Thores-Cross*** by Karen Perkins:

Prologue

26th April 1988

'I dare you to go up to the haunted house.'

I glared at my sister in annoyance, then up at the house. I'd been there plenty of times with Alice and my friends, but never on my own. I did not want to go on my own now.

'Double dare you.'

'You little—!' I lunged at her, but she danced out of my way. She might have been small, but she was quick.

She laughed. 'Scaredy-cat, scaredy-cat, Emma's a scaredy-cat!'

I eyed the house again, then frowned at Alice. But a double dare was a double dare. And I was not a scaredy-cat. At ten years old, I could do this. I took a deep breath, ignored the butterflies in my stomach and started walking up the hill. I didn't rush.

I scrambled through the gap in the crumbling dry stone wall that separated the house from the field, using both hands to steady myself. Something caught my eye and I stopped to have a closer look. Curious, I reached into the jumble of stones, and pulled it from the dark recess in the wall.

A little pot. Made of stone, it was rich brown in colour, roughly an inch high and two inches round with a small neck and lip. An old inkpot. I shook my head. How did I know that?

'My story.'

I froze, then spun round to check behind me. *Who said that?* I looked back at the house. There was nobody here. Although the stone walls still stood, there were no doors, windows, nor roof. Dark holes gaped in the walls and, I knew from earlier visits, it was knee deep in sheepshit inside. I must have imagined the voice. I glanced back at Alice, braced my shoulders and took a step towards the house.

'Write my story.'

My breath caught in my throat, then I sucked in a great lungful of air, turned and ran. Dashing past Alice, I didn't care that she was laughing at me, that I'd lost the dare. I was terrified, desperate to get away from that house, that voice. It was only when I'd stopped running that I realised I still clutched the inkpot.

The Haunting of Thores-Cross is available now

www.ingramcontent.com/pod-product-compliance
Lightning Source LLC
Chambersburg PA
CBHW020948310726
48980CB00001B/100

* 9 7 8 1 9 1 2 8 4 2 0 3 2 *